STORIES TO REMEMBER

VOLUME II

STORIES TO REMEMBER

SELECTED BY

Thomas B. Costain and John Beecroft

ILLUSTRATED BY MARTHA SAWYERS AND WILLIAM REUSSWIG

Doubleday & Company, Inc., Garden City, New York, 1956

CONTENTS

VOLUME ONE

A Novel

THE BRIDGE OF SAN LUIS REY

THORNTON WILDER

THE BRIDGE OF SAN LUIS REY

THORNTON WILDER

PART ONE: PERHAPS AN ACCIDENT

On Friday noon, July the twentieth, 1714, the finest bridge in all Peru broke and precipitated five travellers into the gulf below. This bridge was on the highroad between Lima and Cuzco and hundreds of persons passed over it every day. It had been woven of osier by the Incas more than a century before and visitors to the city were always led out to see it. It was a mere ladder of thin slats swung out over the gorge, with handrails of dried vine. Horses and coaches and chairs had to go down hundreds of feet below and pass over the narrow torrent on rafts, but no one, not even the Viceroy, not even the Archbishop of Lima, had descended with the baggage rather than cross by the famous bridge of San Luis Rey. St. Louis of France himself protected it, by his name and by the little mud church on the further side. The bridge seemed to be among the things that last forever; it was unthinkable that it should break. The moment a Peruvian heard of the accident he signed himself and made a mental calculation as to how recently he had crossed by it and how soon he had intended crossing by it again. People wandered about in a trance-like state, muttering; they had the hallucination of seeing themselves falling into a gulf.

There was a great service in the Cathedral. The bodies of the victims were approximately collected and approximately separated from one another, and there was great searching of hearts in the beautiful city of Lima. Servant girls returned bracelets which they had stolen from their mistresses, and usurers harangued their wives angrily, in defense of usury. Yet it was rather strange that this event should have so impressed the Limeans, for in that country those catastrophes which lawyers shockingly call the "acts of God" were more than usually frequent. Tidal waves were continually washing away cities; earthquakes arrived every week and towers fell upon good men and women all the time. Diseases were forever flitting in and out of the provinces and old age carried away some of the most admirable citizens. That is why it was so surprising that the Peruvians should have been especially touched by the rent in the bridge of San Luis Rey.

Everyone was very deeply impressed, but only one person did any-

thing about it, and that was Brother Juniper. By a series of coincidences so extraordinary that one almost suspects the presence of some Intention, this little red-haired Franciscan from Northern Italy happened to be in Peru converting the Indians and happened to witness the accident.

It was a very hot noon, that fatal noon, and coming around the shoulder of a hill Brother Juniper stopped to wipe his forehead and to gaze upon the screen of snowy peaks in the distance, then into the gorge below him filled with the dark plumage of green trees and green birds and traversed by its ladder of osier. Joy was in him; things were not going badly. He had opened several little abandoned churches and the Indians were crawling in to early Mass and groaning at the moment of miracle as though their hearts would break. Perhaps it was the pure air from the snows before him; perhaps it was the memory that brushed him for a moment of the poem that bade him raise his eyes to the helpful hills. At all events he felt at peace. Then his glance fell upon the bridge, and at that moment a twanging noise filled the air, as when the string of some musical instrument snaps in a disused room, and he saw the bridge divide and fling five gesticulating ants into the valley below.

Anyone else would have said to himself with secret joy: "Within ten minutes myself . . . !" But it was another thought that visited Brother Juniper: "Why did this happen to *those* five?" If there were any plan in the universe at all, if there were any pattern in a human life, surely it could be discovered mysteriously latent in those lives so suddenly cut off. Either we live by accident and die by accident, or we live by plan and die by plan. And on that instant Brother Juniper made the resolve to inquire into the secret lives of those five persons, that moment falling through the air, and to surprise the reason of their taking off.

* * *

It seemed to Brother Juniper that it was high time for theology to take its place among the exact sciences and he had long intended putting it there. What he had lacked hitherto was a laboratory. Oh, there had never been any lack of specimens; any number of his charges had met calamity,—spiders had stung them; their lungs had been touched; their houses had burned down and things had happened to their children from which one averts the mind. But these occasions of human woe had never been quite fit for scientific examination. They had lacked what our good savants were later to call *proper control*. The accident had been dependent upon human error, for example, or had contained elements of probability. But this collapse of the bridge of San Luis Rey was a sheer Act of God. It afforded a perfect laboratory. Here at last one could surprise His intentions in a pure state.

You and I can see that coming from anyone but Brother Juniper this plan would be the flower of a perfect skepticism. It resembled the effort of those presumptuous souls who wanted to walk on the pavements of Heaven and built the Tower of Babel to get there. But to our Franciscan there was no element of doubt in the experiment. He knew the answer. He merely wanted to prove it, historically, mathematically, to his converts,—poor obstinate converts, so slow to believe that their pains were inserted into their lives for their own good. People were always asking for good sound proofs; doubt springs eternal in the

human breast, even in countries where the Inquisition can read your very thoughts in your eyes.

This was not the first time that Brother Juniper had tried to resort to such methods. Often on the long trips he had to make (scurrying from parish to parish, his robe tucked up about his knees, for haste) he would fall to dreaming of experiments that justify the ways of God to man. For instance, a complete record of the Prayers for Rain and their results. Often he had stood on the steps of one of his little churches, his flock kneeling before him on the baked street. Often he had stretched his arms to the sky and declaimed the splendid ritual. Not often, but several times, he had felt the virtue enter him and seen the little cloud forming on the horizon. But there were many times when weeks went by . . . but why think of them? It was not himself he was trying to convince that rain and drought were wisely apportioned.

Thus it was that the determination rose within him at the moment of the accident. It prompted him to busy himself for six years, knocking at all the doors in Lima, asking thousands of questions, filling scores of notebooks, in his effort at establishing the fact that each of the five lost lives was a perfect whole. Everyone knew that he was working on some sort of memorial of the accident and everyone was very helpful and misleading. A few even knew the principal aim of his activity and there were patrons in high places.

The result of all this diligence was an enormous book, which as we shall see later, was publicly burned on a beautiful Spring morning in the great square. But there was a secret copy and after a great many years and without much notice it found its way to the library of the University of San Marco. There it lies between two great wooden covers collecting dust in a cupboard. It deals with one after another of the victims of the accident, cataloguing thousands of little facts and anecdotes and testimonies, and

concluding with a dignified passage describing why God had settled upon that person and upon that day for His demonstration of wisdom. Yet for all his diligence Brother Juniper never knew the central passion of Doña María's life; nor of Uncle Pio's, not even of Esteban's. And I, who claim to know so much more, isn't it possible that even I have missed the very spring within the spring?

Some say that we shall never know and that to the gods we are like the flies that the boys kill on a summer day, and some say, on the contrary, that the very sparrows do not lose a feather that has not been brushed away by the finger of God.

PART TWO: THE MARQUESA DE MONTEMAYOR

Any Spanish schoolboy is required to know today more about Doña María, Marquesa de Montemayor, than Brother Juniper was to discover in years of research. Within a century of her death her letters had become one of the monuments of Spanish literature and her life and times have ever since been the object of long studies. But her biographers have erred in one direction as greatly as the Franciscan did in another; they have tried to invest her with a host of graces, to read back into her life and person some of the beauties that abound in her letters, whereas all real knowledge of this wonderful woman must proceed from the act of humiliating her and of divesting her of all beauties save one.

She was the daughter of a cloth-merchant who had acquired the money and the hatred of the Limeans within a stone's-throw of the Plaza. Her childhood was unhappy: she was ugly; she stuttered; her mother persecuted her with sarcasms in an effort to arouse some social charms and forced her to go about the town in a veritable harness of jewels. She lived

alone and she thought alone. Many suitors presented themselves, but as long as she could she fought against the convention of her time and was determined to remain single. There were hysterical scenes with her mother, recriminations, screams and slamming of doors. At last at twenty-six she found herself penned into marriage with a supercilious and ruined nobleman and the Cathedral of Lima fairly buzzed with the sneers of her guests. Still she lived alone and thought alone, and when an exquisite daughter was born to her she fastened upon her an idolatrous love. But little Clara took after her father; she was cold and intellectual. At the age of eight she was calmly correcting her mother's speech and presently regarding her with astonishment and repulsion. The frightened mother became meek and obsequious but she could not prevent herself from persecuting Doña Clara with nervous attention and a fatiguing love. Again there were hysterical recriminations, screams and slamming of doors. From the offers of marriage that fell to her, Doña Clara deliberately chose the one that required her removal to Spain. So to Spain she went, to that land from which it takes six months to receive an answer to one's letter. The leave-taking before so long a voyage became in Peru one of the formal services of the Church. The ship was blessed and as the space widened between the vessel and the beach both companies knelt and sang a hymn that never failed to sound weak and timid in all that open air. Doña Clara sailed with most admirable composure, leaving her mother to gaze after the bright ship, her hand pressing now her heart and now her mouth. Blurred and streaked became her view of the serene Pacific and the enormous clouds of pearl that hang forever motionless above it.

Left alone in Lima the Marquesa's life grew more and more inward. She became increasingly negligent in her dress and like all lonely people she talked to herself audibly. All her existence lay in the burning center of her mind. On that stage were performed endless dialogues with her daughter, impossible reconciliations, scenes eternally recommenced of remorse and forgiveness. On the street you beheld an old woman her red wig fallen a little over one ear, her left cheek angry with a leprous affection, her right with a complementary adjustment of rouge. Her chin was never dry; her lips were never still. Lima was a city of eccentrics, but even there she became its jest as she drove through the streets or shuffled up the steps of its churches. She was thought to be continuously drunk. Worse things were said of her and petitions were afloat that she be locked up. She had been denounced three times before the Inquisition. It is not impossible that she might have been burned had her son-in-law been less influential in Spain and had she not somehow collected a few friends about the viceregal court who suffered her for her oddity and her wide reading.

The distressing character of the relations between mother and daughter were further embittered by misunderstandings over money. The Condesa received a handsome allowance from her mother and frequent gifts. Doña Clara soon became the outstanding woman of intelligence at the Spanish court. All the wealth of Peru would have been insufficient to maintain her in the grandiose style she fancied for herself. Strangely enough her extravagance proceeded from one of the best traits in her nature: she regarded her friends, her servants and

all the interesting people in the capital, as her children. In fact there seemed only one person in the world towards whom she did not expend herself in kind offices. Among her *protégés* was the cartographer De Blasiis (whose *Maps of the New World* was dedicated to the Marquesa de Montemayor amid the roars of the courtiers at Lima who read that she was the *"admiration of her city and a rising sun in the West"*); another was the scientist Azuarius whose treatise on the laws of hydraulics was suppressed by the Inquisition as being too exciting. For a decade the Condesa literally sustained all the arts and sciences of Spain; it was not her fault that nothing memorable was produced in that time.

About four years after Doña Clara's departure Doña María received her permission to visit Europe. On both sides the visit was anticipated with resolutions well nourished on self-reproach: the one to be patient, the other to be undemonstrative. Both failed. Each tortured the other and was on the point of losing her mind under the alternations of self-rebuke and the outbursts of passion. At length one day Doña María rose before dawn, daring no more than to kiss the door behind which her daughter was sleeping, took ship and returned to America. Henceforth letter-writing had to take the place of all the affection that could not be lived.

Hers were the letters that in an astonishing world have become the text-book of schoolboys and the ant-hill of the grammarians. Doña María would have invented her genius had she not been born with it, so necessary was it to her love that she attract the attention, perhaps the admiration, of her distant child. She forced herself to go out into society in order to cull its ridicules; she taught her eye to observe; she read the masterpieces of her language to discover its effects; she insinuated herself into the company of those who were celebrated for their conversation. Night after night in her baroque palace she wrote and rewrote the incredible pages, forcing from her despairing mind those miracles of wit and grace, those distilled chronicles of the viceregal court. We know now that her daughter barely glanced at the letters and that it is to the son-in-law that we owe their preservation.

The Marquesa would have been astonished to learn that her letters were immortal. Yet many critics have accused her of keeping one eye on posterity and point to a number of letters that have all the air of being bravura pieces. To them it seems impossible that Doña María should have put herself to the same pains to dazzle her daughter that most artists expend on dazzling the public. Like her son-in-law they misunderstood her: the Conde delighted in her letters, but he thought that when he had enjoyed the style he had extracted all their richness and intention, missing (as most readers do) the whole purport of literature, which is the notation of the heart. Style is but the faintly contemptible vessel in which the bitter liquid is recommended to the world. The Marquesa would even have been astonished to learn that her letters were very good, for such authors live always in the noble weather of their own minds and those productions which seem remarkable to us are little better than a day's routine to them.

This was the old woman who hour by hour would sit upon her balcony, her odd straw hat casting a purple shadow across her lined and yellow face. How often as she turned her pages with her gemmed hands, she would ask herself, almost with amuse-

ment, whether the constant pain at her heart had an organic seat. She wondered whether a subtle doctor cutting through to that battered throne could at last discover a sign and lifting his face to the amphitheatre cry out to his students: "This woman has suffered, and her suffering has left its mark upon the structure of her heart." This idea had so often visited her that one day she wrote it into a letter and her daughter scolded her for an introspective and for making a cult of sorrow.

The knowledge that she would never be loved in return acted upon her ideas as a tide acts upon cliffs. Her religious beliefs went first, for all she could ask of a god, or of immortality, was the gift of a place where daughters love their mothers; the other attributes of Heaven you could have for a song. Next she lost her belief in the sincerity of those about her. She secretly refused to believe that anyone (herself excepted) loved anyone. All families lived in a wasteful atmosphere of custom and kissed one another with secret indifference. She saw that the people of this world moved about in an armour of egotism, drunk with self-gazing, athirst for compliments, hearing little of what was said to them, unmoved by the accidents that befell their closest friends, in dread of all appeals that might interrupt their long communion with their own desires. These were the sons and daughters of Adam from Cathay to Peru. And when on the balcony her thoughts reached this turn, her mouth would contract with shame for she knew that she too sinned and that though her love for her daughter was vast enough to include all the colours of love, it was not without a shade of tyranny: she loved her daughter not for her daughter's sake, but for her own. She longed to free herself from this ignoble bond; but the passion was too fierce to cope with. And then on that green balcony a strange warfare would shake the hideous old lady, a singularly futile struggle against a temptation to which she would never have the opportunity of succumbing. How could she rule her daughter when her daughter saw to it that four thousand miles lay between them? Nevertheless Doña María wrestled with the ghost of her temptation and was worsted on every occasion. She wanted her daughter for herself; she wanted to hear her say: "You are the best of all possible mothers"; she longed to hear her whisper: "Forgive me."

About two years after her return from Spain there took place a series of inconspicuous events that had a great deal to tell about the inner life of the Marquesa. Only the faintest allusion to them occurs in the Correspondence, but as that is found in Letter XXII which contains other signs I shall do my best to give a translation and commentary of the first part of the letter:

"*Are there no doctors in Spain? Where are those good men from Flanders that used to help you so? Oh, my treasure, how can we punish you enough for letting your cold endure so many weeks? Don Vicente, I implore you to make my child see reason. Angels of Heaven, I implore you to make my child see reason. Now that you are better, I beg of you, resolve that when the first warning of a cold comes you will steam yourself well and go to bed. Here in Peru I am helpless; I can do nothing. Do not be self-willed, my beloved. God bless you. I am enclosing in today's packet the gum of some tree which the sisters of San Tomás peddle from door to door. Whether it be of much use I know not. It can do no harm.*

I am told that in the convent the silly sisters inhale it so diligently that one cannot smell the incense at Mass. Whether it be worth anything I know not; try it.

"Rest easy, my love, I am sending His Most Catholic Majesty the perfect gold chain." (Her daughter had written her: *"The chain arrived in good condition and I wore it at the christening of the Infante. His Most Catholic Majesty was gracious enough to admire it and when I told Him that you had given it me He sent you His compliments upon your taste. Do not fail to send Him one as like it as possible; send it at once, by way of the Chamberlain."*) *"He need never know that in order to obtain it I had to walk into a picture. Do you remember that in the sacristy of San Martín there is a portrait by Velasquez of the Viceroy who founded the monastery and of his wife and brat? and that his wife is wearing a gold chain? I resolved that only that chain would do. So one midnight I slipped into the sacristy, climbed upon the robing-table like a girl of twelve and walked in. The canvas resisted for a moment, but the painter himself came forward to lift me through the pigment. I told him that the most beautiful girl in Spain wished to present the finest gold chain that could be found to the most gracious king in the world. It was as simple as that, and there we stood talking, we four, in the gray and silvery air that makes a Velasquez. Now I keep thinking about a more golden light; I keep looking at the Palace: I must pass the evening in a Titian. Would the Viceroy let me?*

"But His Excellency has the gout again. I say 'again' because the flattery of the court insists that there are times when he is free of it. This being Saint Mark's day His Excellency started out to visit the University where twenty-two new doctors were being brought into the world. He had hardly been carried from his divan to his coach when he screamed and refused to go any farther. He was carried back to his bed where he broke a most delicious cigar and sent for the Perichole. And while we listened to long doctrinal addresses, more or less in Latin, he heard all about us, more or less in Spanish, from the ruddiest and cruellest lips in town." (Doña María permitted herself this passage, although she had just read in her daughter's last letter: *"How many times must I tell you to be more cautious in the things you say in your letters? They often show signs of having been opened on the journey. Nothing could be more ill-judged than your remarks on the you-know-what-I-mean at Cuzco. Such remarks are not funny, even though Vicente did compliment you upon them in his postscript, and they might get us into a great deal of trouble with Certain Persons here in Spain. I continue to be astonished that your indiscretions have not long since led to your being ordered to retire to your farm."*)

"There was a great press at the Exercises and two women fell from the balcony, but God in His goodness saw that they fell on Doña Merced. All three are badly hurt, but will be thinking of other things within a year. The President was speaking at the moment of the accident and being shortsighted could not imagine what the disturbance of cries and talk and falling bodies could be about. It was very pleasant to see him bowing, under the impression that he was being applauded.

"Speaking of the Perichole, and of applause, you should know that Pepita and I decided to go to the Comedia this evening. The public still idolizes its Perichole; it even forgives her her

years. We are told that she saves what she can, every morning, by passing alternate pencils of ice and fire across her cheeks." (Translation falls especially short of this conceit which carries the whole flamboyance of the Spanish language. It was intended as an obsequious flattery of the Condesa, and was untrue. The great actress was twenty-eight at this time; her cheeks had the smoothness and polish of dark yellow marble and would certainly have retained that quality for many years. Apart from the cosmetics required by her performances the only treatment Camila Perichole afforded her face was to throw cold water at it twice a day, like a peasant woman at a horse trough.) *"That curious man they call Uncle Pio is by her all the time. Don Rubio says that he cannot make out whether Uncle Pio is her father, her lover, or her son. The Perichole gave a wonderful performance. Scold me all you like for a provincial ninny, you have no such actresses in Spain."* And so on.

It is on this visit to the theatre that further matter hangs. She decided to go to the Comedia where the Perichole was playing Doña Leonor in Moreto's *Trampa Adelante;* perhaps some material could be derived from the visit for her daughter's next letter. She took with her Pepita, a little girl about whom later we shall learn much. Doña María had borrowed her from the orphanage connected with the Convent of Santa María Rosa de las Rosas to be her companion. The Marquesa sat in her box gazing with flagging attention at the brilliant stage. Between the acts it was the Perichole's custom to lay aside the courtly rôle and appear before the curtain to sing a few topical songs. The malicious actress had seen the Marquesa arrive and presently began improvising couplets alluding to her appearance, her avarice, her drunkenness, and even to her daughter's flight from her. The attention of the house was subtly directed to the old woman and a rising murmur of contempt accompanied the laughter of the audience. But the Marquesa, deeply moved by the first two acts of the comedy, scarcely saw the singer and sat staring before her, thinking about Spain. Camila Perichole became bolder and the air was electric with the hatred and glee of the crowd. At last Pepita plucked the Marquesa's sleeve and whispered to her that they should go. As they left the box the house arose and burst into a roar of triumph; the Perichole flung herself into a frenzied dance, for she saw the manager at the back of the hall and knew that her salary had been increased. But the Marquesa remained unaware of what had taken place; in fact she was quite pleased, for during the visit she had contrived a few felicitous phrases, phrases (who knows) that might bring a smile to her daughter's face and might make her murmur: "Really, my mother is charming."

In due time the report reached the Viceroy's ears that one of his aristocrats had been openly baited in the theatre. He summoned the Perichole to the Palace and ordered her to call upon the Marquesa and to apologize. The trip was to be made barefoot and in a black dress. Camila argued and fought, but all she gained was a pair of shoes.

The Viceroy had three reasons for insisting. In the first place the singer had taken liberties with his court. Don Andrés had contrived to make exile endurable by building up a ceremonial so complicated that it could be remembered only by a society that had nothing else to think about. He nursed his little aristocracy and its minute distinctions and any insult

paid to a Marquesa was an insult to His Person. In the second place, Doña María's son-in-law was an increasingly important personage in Spain, laden with possibilities of injury to the Viceroy, nay with the possibility of supplanting him. The Conde Vicente d'Abuirre must not be vexed, even through his half-wit mother-in-law. Finally, the Viceroy was delighted to humble the actress. He suspected that she was deceiving him with a matador, perhaps with an actor,—between the flattery of the court and the inertia of gout he could not quite make out who it was; at all events, it was clear that the singer was beginning to forget that he was one of the first men in the world.

The Marquesa, beside not having heard the scurrilous songs, was in other ways unprepared for the actress's visit. You should know that after the departure of her daughter, Doña María had lighted upon a certain consolation: she had taken to drinking. Everyone drank *chicha* in Peru and there was no particular disgrace in being found unconscious on a feast day. Doña María had begun to discover that her feverish monologues had a way of keeping her awake all night. Once she took a delicate fluted glassful of *chicha* on retiring. Oblivion was so sweet that presently she stole larger amounts and tried dissimulating their effects from Pepita; she hinted that she was not well, and represented herself as going into a decline. At last she resigned all pretense. The boats that carried her letter to Spain did not leave oftener than once a month. During the week that preceded the making of the packet she observed a strict regimen and cultivated the city assiduously for material. At last on the eve of the post she wrote the letter, making up the bundle towards dawn and leaving it for Pepita to deliver to the agent. Then as the sun rose she would shut herself up in her room with some flagons and drift through the next few weeks without the burden of consciousness. Finally she would emerge from her happiness and prepare to go into a state of "training" in preparation for the writing of another letter.

Thus on the night following the scandal in the theatre she wrote Letter XXII and retired to bed with a carafe. All next day Pepita moved about the room, glancing anxiously at the figure on the bed. The next afternoon Pepita brought her needlework into the room. The Marquesa lay staring at the ceiling with wide-open eyes, talking to herself. Towards dusk Pepita was called to the door and informed that the Perichole had come to see the mistress. Pepita remembered the theatre very well and sent back word angrily that the mistress refused to see her. The man carried the message to the street door, but returned awestruck with the news that the Señora Perichole was armed with a letter from the Viceroy presenting her to the lady. Pepita tiptoed to the bed and started talking to the Marquesa. The glazed eyes moved to the girl's face. Pepita shook her gently. With great effort Doña María tried to fix her mind on what was being said to her. Twice she lay back, refusing to seize the meaning, but at last, like a general calling together in a rain and by night the dispersed division of his army she assembled memory and attention and a few other faculties and painfully pressing her hand to her forehead she asked for a bowl of snow. When it was brought her, she long and drowsily pressed handfuls of it against her temples and cheeks; then rising she stood for a long time leaning against the bed and looking at her shoes. At last she raised her head with decision,

she called for her fur-trimmed cloak and a veil. She put them on and tottered into her handsomest reception room where the actress stood waiting for her.

Camila had intended to be perfunctory and if possible impudent, but now she was struck for the first time with the dignity of the old woman. The mercer's daughter could carry herself at times with all the distinction of the Montemayors and when she was drunk she wore the grandeur of Hecuba. For Camila the half-closed eyes had the air of weary authority and she began almost timidly:

"I come, señora, to make sure that you could not have misunderstood anything I said on the evening that Your Grace did me the honour to visit my theatre."

"Misunderstood? Misunderstood?" said the Marquesa.

"Your Grace might have misunderstood and thought that my words were intended to be disrespectful to Your Grace."

"To me?"

"Your Grace is not offended at her humble servant? Your Grace is aware that a poor actress in my position may be carried beyond her intentions . . . that it is very difficult . . . that everything. . . ."

"How can I be offended, señora? All that I can remember is that you gave a beautiful performance. You are a great artist. You should be happy, happy. My handkerchief, Pepita. . . ."

The Marquesa brought out these words very rapidly and vaguely, but the Perichole was confounded. A piercing sense of shame filled her. She turned crimson. At last she was able to murmur:

"It was in the songs between the acts of the comedy. I was afraid Your Grace . . ."

"Yes, yes. I remember now. I left early. Pepita, we left early, did we not? But, señora, you are good enough to forgive my leaving early, yes, even in the middle of your admirable performance. I forget why we left. Pepita . . . oh, some indisposition. . . ."

It was impossible that anyone in the theatre could have missed the intention of the songs. Camila could only assume that the Marquesa, out of a sort of fantastic magnanimity, was playing the farce of not having noticed it. She was almost in tears: "But you are so good to overlook my childishness, señora,—I mean Your Grace. I did not know. I did not know your goodness. Señora, permit me to kiss your hand."

Doña María held out her hand astonished. She had not for a long time been addressed with such consideration. Her neighbors, her tradespeople, her servants—for even Pepita lived in awe of her,—her very daughter had never approached her thus. It induced a new mood in her; one that must very likely be called maudlin. She became loquacious:

"Offended, offended at you, my beautiful, . . . my gifted child? Who am I, a . . . an unwise and unloved old woman, to be offended at you? I felt, my daughter, as though I were—what says the poet?—*surprising through a cloud the conversation of the angels.* Your voice kept finding new wonders in our Moreto. When you said:

'Don Juan, si mi amor estimas,
Y la fe segura es necia,
Enojarte mis temores
Es no quererme discreta.
¿Tan Seguros. . . .'

and so on,—that was true! And what a gesture you made at the close of the First Day. There, with your hand *so.* Such a gesture as the Virgin made,

saying to Gabriel: *How is it possible that I shall have a child?* No, no, you will begin to have resentment at me, for I am going to tell you about a gesture that you may remember to use some day. Yes, it would fit well into that scene where you forgive your Don Juan de Lara. Perhaps I should tell you that I saw it made one day by my daughter. My daughter is a very beautiful woman . . . everyone thinks. Did . . . did you know my Doña Clara, señora?"

"Her Grace often did me the honour of visiting my theatre. I knew the Condesa well by sight."

"Do not remain so, on one knee, my child.—Pepita, tell Jenarito to bring this lady some sweet-cakes at once. Think, one day we fell out, I forget over what. Oh, there is nothing strange in that; all we mothers from time to time. . . . Look, can you come a little closer? You must not believe the town that says she was unkind to me. You are a great woman with a beautiful nature and you can see further than the crowd sees in these matters.—It is a pleasure to talk to you. What beautiful hair you have! What beautiful hair!—She had not a warm impulsive nature, I know that. But, oh, my child, she has such a store of intelligence and graciousness. Any misunderstandings between us are so plainly my fault; is it not wonderful that she is so quick to forgive me? This day there fell one of those little moments. We both said hasty things and went off to our rooms. Then each turned back to be forgiven. Finally only a door separated us and there we were pulling it in contrary ways. But at last she . . . took my . . . face . . . thus, in her two white hands. So! Look!"

The Marquesa almost fell out of her chair as she leaned forward, her face streaming with happy tears, and made the beatific gesture. I should say the mythical gesture, for the incident was but a recurring dream.

"I am glad you are here," she continued, "for now you have heard from my own lips that she is not unkind to me, as some people say. Listen, señora, the fault was mine. Look at me. Look at me. There was some mistake that made me the mother of so beautiful a girl. I am difficult. I am trying. You and she are great women. No, do not stop me: you are rare women, and I am only a nervous . . . a foolish . . . a stupid woman. Let me kiss your feet. I am impossible. I am impossible. I am impossible."

Here indeed the old woman did fall out of her chair and was gathered up by Pepita and led back to her bed. The Perichole walked home in consternation and sat for a long time gazing into her eyes in the mirror, her palms pressed against her cheeks.

But the person who saw most of the difficult hours of the Marquesa was her little companion, Pepita. Pepita was an orphan and had been brought up by that strange genius of Lima, the Abbess Madre María del Pilar. The only occasion upon which the two great women of Peru (as the perspective of history was to reveal them) met face to face was on the day when Doña María called upon the directress of the Convent of Santa María Rosa de las Rosas and asked if she might borrow some bright girl from the orphanage to be her companion. The Abbess gazed hard at the grotesque old woman. Even the wisest people in the world are not perfectly wise and Madre María del Pilar who was able to divine the poor human heart behind all the masks of folly and defiance, had always refused to concede one to the Marquesa de Montemayor. She asked her a great many questions and then paused to

think. She wanted to give Pepita the worldly experience of living in the palace. She also wanted to bend the old woman to her own interests. And she was filled with a sombre indignation, for she knew she was gazing at one of the richest women in Peru, and the blindest.

She was one of those persons who have allowed their lives to be gnawed away because they have fallen in love with an idea several centuries before its appointed appearance in the history of civilization. She hurled herself against the obstinacy of her time in her desire to attach a little dignity to women. At midnight when she had finished adding up the accounts of the House she would fall into insane vision of an age when women could be organized to protect women, women travelling, women as servants, women when they are old or ill, the women she had discovered in the mines of Potosi, or in the work-rooms of the cloth-merchants, the girls she had collected out of doorways on rainy nights. But always the next morning she had to face the fact that the women in Peru, even her nuns, went through life with two notions: one, that all the misfortunes that might befall them were merely due to the fact that they were not sufficiently attractive to bind some man to their maintenance and, two, that all the misery in the world was worth his caress. She had never known any country but the environs of Lima and she assumed that all its corruption was the normal state of mankind. Looking back from our century we can see the whole folly of her hope. Twenty such women would have failed to make any impression on that age. Yet she continued diligently in her task. She resembled the swallow in the fable who once every thousand years transferred a grain of wheat, in the hope of rearing a mountain to reach the moon. Such persons are raised up in every age; they obstinately insist on transporting their grains of wheat and they derive a certain exhilaration from the sneers of the bystanders. "How queerly they dress!" we cry. "How queerly they dress!"

Her plain red face had great kindliness, and more idealism than kindliness, and more generalship than idealism. All her work, her hospitals, her orphanage, her convent, her sudden journeys of rescue, depended upon money. No one harbored a fairer admiration for mere goodness, but she had been obliged to watch herself sacrificing her kindliness, almost her idealism, to generalship, so dreadful were the struggles to obtain her subsidies from her superiors in the church. The Archbishop of Lima, whom we shall know later in a more graceful connection, hated her with what he called a Vatinian hate and counted the cessation of her visits among the compensations for dying.

Lately she had felt not only the breath of old age against her cheek, but a graver warning. A chill of terror went through her, not for herself, but for her work. Who was there in Peru to value the things she had valued? And rising one day at dawn she had made a rapid journey through her hospital and convent and orphanage, looking for a soul she might train to be her successor. She hurried from empty face to empty face, occasionally pausing more from hope than conviction. In the courtyard she came upon a company of girls at work over the linen and her eyes fell at once upon a girl of twelve who was directing the others at the trough and at the same time recounting to them with great dramatic fire the less probable miracles in the life of Saint Rose of Lima. So it was that the search ended

with Pepita. The education for greatness is difficult enough at any time, but amid the sensibilities and jealousies of a convent it must be conducted with fantastic indirection. Pepita was assigned to the most disliked tasks in the House, but she came to understand all the aspects of its administration. She accompanied the Abbess on her journeys, even though it was in the capacity of custodian of the eggs and vegetables. And everywhere, by surprise, hours would open up in which the Directress suddenly appeared and talked to her at great length, not only on religious experience, but on how to manage women and how to plan contagious wards and how to beg for money. It was a step in this education for greatness that led to Pepita's arriving one day and entering upon the crazy duties of being Doña María's companion. For the first two years she merely came for occasional afternoons, but finally she came to the palace to live. She never had been taught to expect happiness, and the inconveniences, not to say terrors, of her new position did not seem to her excessive for a girl of fourteen. She did not suspect that the Abbess, even there, was hovering above the house, herself estimating the stresses and watching for the moment when a burden harms and not strengthens.

A few of Pepita's trials were physical: for example, the servants in the house took advantage of Doña María's indisposition; they opened up the bedrooms of the palace to their relatives; they stole freely. Alone Pepita stood out against them and suffered a persecution of small discomforts and practical jokes. Her mind, similarly, had its distresses: when she accompanied Doña María on her errands in the city, the older woman would be seized with the desire to dash into a church, for what she had lost of religion as faith she had replaced with religion as magic. "Stay here in the sunlight, my dear child; I shall not be long," she would say. Doña María would then forget herself in a reverie before the altar and leave the church by another door. Pepita had been brought up by Madre María del Pilar to an almost morbid obedience and when after many hours she ventured into the church and made sure that her mistress was no longer there, still she returned to the street-corner and waited while the shadows fell gradually across the square. Thus waiting in public she suffered all the torture of a little girl's self-consciousness. She still wore the uniform of the orphanage (which a minute's thoughtfulness on the part of Doña María could have altered) and she suffered hallucinations wherein men seemed to be staring at her and whispering—nor were these always hallucinations. No less her heart suffered, for on some days Doña María would suddenly become aware of her and would talk to her cordially and humorously, would let appear for a few hours all the exquisite sensibility of the Letters; then, on the morrow she would withdraw into herself again and, while never harsh, would become impersonal and unseeing. The beginnings of hope and affection that Pepita had such need to expend would be wounded. She tiptoed about the palace, silent, bewildered, clinging only to her sense of duty and her loyalty to her "mother in the Lord," Madre María del Pilar, who had sent her there.

* * *

Finally a new fact appeared that was to have considerable effect on the lives of both the Marquesa and her companion: *"My dear mother,"* wrote the Condesa, *"the weather has been most exhausting and the fact that the*

*orchards and gardens are in bloom
only makes it the more trying. I could
endure flowers if only they had no
perfume. I shall therefore ask your
permission to write you at less length
than usual. If Vicente returns before
the post leaves he will be delighted
to finish out the leaf and supply you
with those tiresome details about my-
self which you seem to enjoy so. I
shall not go to Grignan in Provence
as I expected this Fall, as my child
will be born in early October."*

What child? The Marquesa leaned
against the wall. Doña Clara had fore-
seen the exhausting importunities that
this news would waken in her mother
and had sought to mitigate them by
the casualness of her announcement.
The ruse did not succeed. The famous
Letter XLII was the answer.

Now at length the Marquesa had
something to be anxious about: her
daughter was to become a mother.
This event, which merely bored Doña
Clara, discovered a whole new scale of
emotions in the Marquesa. She became
a mine of medical knowledge and sug-
gestion. She combed the city for wise
old women and poured into her let-
ters the whole folk-wisdom of the New
World. She fell into the most abomi-
nable superstition. She practiced a de-
grading system of taboos for her
child's protection. She refused to allow
a knot in the house. The maids were
forbidden to tie up their hair and she
concealed upon her person ridiculous
symbols of a happy delivery. On the
stairs the even steps were marked with
red chalk and a maid who accidentally
stepped upon an even step was driven
from the house with tears and screams.
Doña Clara was in the hands of malig-
nant Nature who reserves the right to
inflict upon her children the most
terrifying jests. There was an etiquette
of propitiation which generations of
peasant women had found comforting.

So vast an army of witnesses surely
implied that there was some truth in
it. At least it could do no harm, and
Perhaps it did good. But the Marquesa
did not only satisfy the rites of pagan-
ism; she studied the prescriptions of
Christianity as well. She arose in the
dark and stumbled through the streets
to the earliest Masses. She hysterically
hugged the altar-rails trying to rend
from the gaudy statuettes a sign, only
a sign, the ghost of a smile, the furtive
nod of a waxen head. Would all be
well? Sweet, sweet Mother, would all
be well?

At times, after a day's frantic resort
to such invocations, a revulsion would
sweep over her. Nature is deaf. God
is indifferent. Nothing in man's power
can alter the course of law. Then on
some street-corner she would stop,
dizzy with despair, and leaning against
a wall would long to be taken from
a world that had no plan in it. But
soon a belief in the great Perhaps
would surge up from the depths of
her nature and she would fairly run
home to renew the candles above her
daughter's bed.

At last the time came to satisfy the
supreme rite of Peruvian households
looking forward to this event: she
made the pilgrimage to the shrine of
Santa María de Cluxambuqua. If
there resided any efficacy in devotion
at all, surely it lay in a visit to this
great shrine. The ground had been
holy through three religions; even be-
fore the Incan civilization distraught
human beings had hugged the rocks
and lashed themselves with whips to
wring their will from the skies.
Thither the Marquesa was carried in
her chair, crossing the bridge of San
Luis Rey and ascending up into the
hills toward that city of large-girdled
women, a tranquil town, slow-moving
and slow-smiling; a city of crystal air,
cold as the springs that fed its many

fountains; a city of bells, soft and musical, and tuned to carry on with one another the happiest quarrels. If anything turned out for disappointment in the town of Cluxambuqua the grief was somehow assimilated by the overwhelming immanence of the Andes and by the weather of quiet joy that flowed in and about the side-streets. No sooner did the Marquesa see from a distance the white walls of this town perched on the knees of the highest peaks than her fingers ceased turning the beads and the busy prayers of her fright were cut short on her lips.

She did not even alight at the inn, but leaving Pepita to arrange for their stay she went on to the church and knelt for a long time patting her hands softly together. She was listening to the new tide of resignation that was rising within her. Perhaps she would learn in time to permit both her daughter and her gods to govern their own affairs. She was not annoyed by the whispering of the old women in padded garments who sold candles and medals and talked about money from dawn to dark. She was not even distracted by an officious sacristan who tried to collect a fee for something or other and who, from spite, made her change her place under the pretext of repairing a tile on the floor. Presently she went out into the sunshine and sat on the steps of the fountain. She watched the little processions of invalids slowly revolving about the gardens. She watched three hawks plunging about the sky. The children who had been playing by the fountain stared at her for a moment, and went away alarmed, but a llama (a lady with a long neck and sweet shallow eyes, burdened down by a fur cape too heavy for her and picking her way delicately down an interminable staircase) came over and offered her a vel-

vet cleft nose to stroke. The llama is deeply interested in the men about her, is even fond of pretending that she too is one of them and of inserting her head into their conversations as though in a moment she would lift her voice and contribute a wan and helpful comment. Soon Doña María was surrounded by a number of these sisters who seemed on the point of asking her why she slapped her hands so and how much her veiling cost a yard.

Doña María had arranged that any letters arriving from Spain should be brought to her at once by a special messenger. She had travelled slowly from Lima and even now as she sat in the square a boy from her farm ran up and put into her hand a large packet wrapped in parchment and dangling some nuggets of sealing-wax. Slowly she undid the wrappings. With measured stoic gestures she read first an affectionate and jocose note from her son-in-law; then her daughter's letter. It was full of wounding remarks rather brilliantly said, perhaps said for the sheer virtuosity of giving pain neatly. Each of its phrases found its way through the eyes of the Marquesa, then, carefully wrapped in understanding and forgiveness it sank into her heart. At last she arose, gently dispersed the sympathetic llamas, and with a grave face returned to the shrine.

While Doña María was passing the late afternoon in the Church and in the Square, Pepita was left to prepare their lodging. She showed the porters where to lay down the great wicker hampers and set about unpacking the altar, the brazier, the tapestries and the portraits of Doña Clara. She descended into the kitchen and gave the cook exact instructions as to the preparations of a certain porridge upon which the Marquesa principally sub-

sisted. Then she returned to the rooms and waited. She resolved to write a letter to the Abbess. She hung for a long time over the quill, staring into the distance with trembling lip. She saw the face of Madre María del Pilar, so red and scrubbed, and the wonderful black eyes. She heard her voice as at the close of supper (the orphans sitting with lowered eyes and folded hands) she commented on the events of the day, or as, by candlelight, she stood among the beds of the hospital and announced the theme for meditation during the night. But most clearly of all Pepita remembered the sudden interviews when the Abbess (not daring to wait until the girl was older) had discussed with her the duties of her office. She had talked to Pepita as to an equal. Such speech is troubling and wonderful to an intelligent child and Madre María del Pilar had abused it. She had expanded Pepita's vision of how she should feel and act beyond the measure of her years. And she had unthinkingly turned upon Pepita the full blaze of her personality, as Jupiter had turned his upon Semele. Pepita was frightened by her sense of insufficiency; she hid it and wept. And then the Abbess had cast the child into the discipline of this long solitude, where Pepita struggled, refusing to let herself believe that she had been abandoned. And now from this strange inn in these strange mountains, where the altitude was making her lightheaded, Pepita longed for the dear presence, the only real thing in her life.

She wrote a letter, all inkstains and incoherence. Then she went downstairs to see about fresh charcoal and to taste the porridge.

The Marquesa came in and sat down at the table. "I can do no more. What will be, will be," she whispered. She unbound from her neck the amulets of her superstition and dropped them into the glowing brazier. She had a strange sense of having antagonized God by too much prayer and so addressed Him now obliquely. "After all it is in the hands of another. I no longer claim the least influence. What will be, will be." She sat for a long time, her palms against her cheeks, making a blank of her mind. Her eyes fell on Pepita's letter. She opened it mechanically and started to read. She had read a full half of it before her attention was aware of the meaning of the words: *". . . but all this is nothing if you like me and wish me to stay with her. I oughtn't to tell you but every now and then the bad chambermaids lock me up in rooms and steal things and perhaps My Lady will think that I steal them. I hope not. I hope you are well and not having any trouble in the hospital or anywhere. Though I never see you I think of you all the time and I remember what you told me, my dear mother in God. I want to do only what you want, but if you could let me come back for a few days to the convent, but not if you do not wish it. But I am so much alone and not talking to anyone, and everything. Sometimes I do not know whether you have forgotten me and if you could find a minute to write me a little letter or something, I could keep it, but I know how busy you are. . . ."*

Doña María read no further. She folded the letter and put it aside. For a moment she was filled with envy: she longed to command another's soul as completely as this nun was able to do. Most of all she longed to be back in this simplicity of love, to throw off the burden of pride and vanity that hers had always carried. To quiet the tumult in her mind she picked up a book of devotion and tried to fix her

attention upon the words. But after a moment she suddenly felt the need to reread the whole letter, to surprise, if possible, the secret of so much felicity.

Pepita returned bringing the supper in her hands, followed by a maid. Doña María watched her over the top of her book as she would have watched a visitor from Heaven. Pepita tiptoed about the room laying the table and whispering directions to her assistant. "Your supper is ready, My Lady," she said at last.

"But, my child, you are going to eat with me?" In Lima Pepita generally sat down at the table with her mistress.

"I thought you would be tired, My Lady. I had my supper downstairs."

"She does not wish to eat with me," thought the Marquesa. "She knows me and has rejected me."

"Would you like me to read aloud to you while you are eating, My Lady?" asked Pepita, who felt that she had made a mistake.

"No. You may go to bed, if you choose."

"Thank you, My Lady."

Doña María had risen and approached the table. With one hand on the back of the chair she said haltingly: "My dear child, I am sending off a letter to Lima in the morning. If you have one you can enclose it with mine."

"No, I have none," said Pepita. She added hastily: "I must go downstairs and get you the new charcoal."

"But, my dear, you have one for . . . Madre María del Pilar. Wouldn't you . . . ?"

Pepita pretended to be busy over the brazier. "No, I'm not going to send it," she said. She was aware during the long pause that followed that the Marquesa was staring at her in stupefaction. "I've changed my mind."

"I know she would like a letter from you, Pepita. It would make her very happy. I know."

Pepita was reddening. She said loudly: "The innkeeper said that there would be some new charcoal ready for you at dark. I'll tell them to bring it up now." She glanced hastily at the old woman and saw that she had not ceased from staring at her with great sad inquiring eyes. Pepita felt that these were not things one talked about, but the strange woman seemed to be feeling the matter so strongly that Pepita was willing to concede one more answer: "No, it was a bad letter. It wasn't a good letter."

Doña María fairly gasped. "Why, my dear Pepita, I think it was very beautiful. Believe me, I know. No, no; what could have made it a bad letter?"

Pepita frowned, hunting for a word that would close the matter. "It wasn't . . . it wasn't . . . brave," she said. And then she would say no more. She carried the letter off into her own room and could be heard tearing it up. Then she got into bed and lay staring into the darkness, still uncomfortable at having talked in such a fashion. And Doña María sat down to her dish amazed.

She had never brought courage to either life or love. Her eyes ransacked her heart. She thought of the amulets and of her beads, her drunkenness . . . she thought of her daughter. She remembered the long relationship, crowded with the wreckage of exhumed conversations, of fancied slights, of inopportune confidences, of charges of neglect and exclusion (but she must have been mad that day; she remembered beating upon the table). "But it's not my fault," she cried. "It's not my fault that I was so. It was circumstance. It was the way I was brought up. Tomorrow I begin a new

life. Wait and see, oh my child." At last she cleared away the table and sitting down wrote what she called her first letter, her first stumbling misspelled letter in courage. She remembered with shame that in the previous one she had piteously asked her daughter how much she loved her, and had greedily quoted the few and hesitant endearments that Doña Clara had lately ventured to her. Doña María could not recall those pages, but she could write some new ones, free and generous. No one else has regarded them as stumbling. It is the famous Letter LVI, known to the Encyclopedists as her Second Corinthians because of its immortal paragraph about love: "Of the thousands of persons we meet in a lifetime, my child . . ." and so on. It was almost dawn when she finished the letter. She opened the door upon her balcony and looked at the great tiers of stars that glittered above the Andes. Throughout the hours of the night, though there had been few to hear it, the whole sky had been loud with the singing of these constellations. Then she took a candle into the next room and looked at Pepita as she slept, and pushed back the damp hair from the girl's face. "Let me live now," she whispered. "Let me begin again."

Two days later they started back to Lima, and while crossing the bridge of San Luis Rey the accident which we know befell them.

PART THREE: ESTEBAN

One morning twin boys were discovered in the foundlings' basket before the door of the Convent of Santa María Rosa de las Rosas. Names were found for them almost before the arrival of the wet-nurse, but the names were not as useful to them as our names are to most of us, for no one ever succeeded in telling the boys apart. There was no way of knowing who their parents were, but Limean gossips, noticing as the boys grew older how straight they held themselves and how silent and sombre they were, declared them to be Castilian and laid them in turn at all sorts of crested doorways. The person in the world who came nearest to being their guardian was the Abbess of the Convent. Madre María del Pilar had come to hate all men, but she grew fond of Manuel and Esteban. In the late afternoon she would call them into her office, send for some cakes from the kitchen, and tell them stories about the Cid and Judas Maccabeus and the thirty-six misfortunes of Harlequin. She grew to love them so, that she would catch herself gazing deep into their black and frowning eyes, looking for those traits that would appear when they grew to be men, all that ugliness, all that soullessness that made hideous the world she worked in. They grew up about the convent until they were a little past the age when their presence began to be a slight distraction to the dedicated sisters. From thence they became vaguely attached to all the sacristies in town: they trimmed all the cloister hedges; they polished every possible crucifix; they passed a damp cloth once a year over most of the ecclesiastical ceilings. All Lima knew them well. When the priest rushed through the streets carrying his precious burden into a sickroom either Esteban or Manuel was to be seen striding behind him, swinging a censer. As they grew older, however, they showed no desire for the clerical life. They gradually assumed the profession of the scribe. There were few print-

ing presses in the New World and the boys soon made a fair living transcribing comedies for the theatre, ballads for the crowds, and advertisements for the merchants. Above all they were the copyists of the choirmasters and made endless parts of the motets of Morales and Vittoria.

Because they had no family, because they were twins, and because they were brought up by women, they were silent. There was in them a curious shame in regard to their resemblance. They had to live in a world where it was the subject of continual comment and joking. It was never funny to them and they suffered the eternal pleasantries with stolid patience. From the years when they first learned to speak they invented a secret language for themselves, one that was scarcely dependent on the Spanish for its vocabulary, or even for its syntax. They resorted to it only when they were alone, or at great intervals in moments of stress whispered it in the presence of others. The Archbishop of Lima was something of a philologist; he dabbled in dialects; he had even evolved quite a brilliant table for the vowel and consonant changes from Latin into Spanish and from Spanish into Indian-Spanish. He was storing up notebooks of quaint lore against an amusing old age he planned to offer himself back on his estates outside Segovia. So when he heard one day about the secret language of the twin brothers, he trimmed some quills and sent for them. The boys stood humiliated upon the rich carpets of his study while he tried to extract from them their *bread* and *tree* and their *I see* and *I saw*. They did not know why the experience was so horrible to them. They bled. Long shocked silences followed each of the Archbishop's questions, until finally one or the other mumbled an answer. The priest thought for a while that they were

merely in awe before his rank and before the luxury of his apartment, but at last, much perplexed, he divined the presence of some deeper reluctance and sadly let them go.

This language was the symbol of their profound identity with one another, for just as resignation was a word insufficient to describe the spiritual change that came over the Marquesa de Montemayor on that night in the inn at Cluxambuqua, so *love* is inadequate to describe the tacit almost ashamed oneness of these brothers. What relationship is it in which few words are exchanged, and those only about the details of food, clothing and occupation; in which the two persons have a curious reluctance even to glance at one another; and in which there is a tacit arrangement not to appear together in the city and to go on the same errand by different streets? And yet side by side with this there existed a need of one another so terrible that it produced miracles as naturally as the charged air of a sultry day produces lightning. The brothers were scarcely aware of it themselves, but telepathy was a common occurrence in their lives, and when one returned home the other was always aware of it when his brother was still several streets away.

Suddenly they discovered that they were tired of writing. They went down to the sea and found an occupation in loading and unloading vessels, not ashamed of working side by side with Indians. They drove teams across the provinces. They picked fruit. They were ferrymen. And always they were silent. Their sombre faces took on from these labors a male and gypsy cast. Their hair was seldom cut and under the dark mat their eyes looked up suddenly surprised and a little sullen. All the world was remote and strange and hostile except one's brother.

But at last the first shadow fell across this unity and the shadow was cast by the love of women. They had returned to the city and resumed the copying of parts for the theatre. One night the manager, foreseeing a thinning house, gave them a free admission. The boys did not like what they found there. Even speech was for them a debased form of silence; how much more futile is poetry which is a debased form of speech. All those allusions to honour, reputation, and the flame of love, all the metaphors about birds, Achilles and the jewels of Ceylon were fatiguing. In the presence of literature they had the same darkling intelligence that stirs for a time behind the eyes of a dog, but they sat on patiently, gazing at the bright candles and the rich clothes. Between the acts of the comedy the Perichole stepped out of her rôle, put on twelve petticoats and danced before the curtain. Esteban had some copying still to do, or pretended so, and went home early; but Manuel stayed on. The red stockings and shoes of the Perichole had made their impression.

Both brothers had fetched and carried their manuscripts up and down the dusty stairs behind the stage. There they had seen an irritable girl in a soiled bodice mending her stockings before a mirror while her stage director read aloud her lines for memorization. She had let fall upon the boys for a moment the detonation of her amazing eyes, immediately dissipated in her amused recognition that they were twins. Forthwith she had dragged them into the room and placed them side by side. Carefully, amusedly and remorselessly she had peered into every square inch of their faces, until finally laying one hand on Esteban's shoulder she had cried out: "This one is the younger!" That had

been several years before and neither brother had thought of the episode again.

Henceforth all Manuel's errands seemed to lead him past the theatre. Late at night he would drift about among the trees beneath her dressing-room window. It was not the first time that Manuel had been fascinated by a woman (both brothers had possessed women, and often, especially during their years at the waterfront; but simply, latinly), but it was the first time that his will and imagination had been thus overwhelmed. He had lost that privilege of simple nature, the dissociation of love and pleasure. Pleasure was no longer as simple as eating; it was being complicated by love. Now was beginning that crazy loss of one's self, that neglect of everything but one's dramatic thoughts about the beloved, that feverish inner life all turning upon the Perichole and which would so have astonished and disgusted her had she been permitted to divine it. This Manuel had not fallen in love through any imitation of literature. It was not of him, at all events, that the bitterest tongue in France had remarked only fifty years before: that many people would never have fallen in love if they had not heard about it. Manuel read little; he had only been once to the theatre (where above all there reigns the legend that love is a devotion) and the Peruvian tavern-songs that he might have heard, unlike those of Spain, reflected very little of the romantic cult of an idealized woman. When he said over to himself that she was beautiful and rich and fatiguingly witty and the Viceroy's mistress, none of these attributes that made her less obtainable had the power to quench his curious and tender excitement. So he leaned against the trees in the dark, his knuckles be-

tween his teeth, and listened to his loud heart-beats.

But the life that Esteban was leading had been full enough for him. There was no room in his imagination for a new loyalty, not because his heart was less large than Manuel's, but because it was of a simpler texture. Now he discovered that secret from which one never quite recovers, that even in the most perfect love one person loves less profoundly than the other. There may be two equally good, equally gifted, equally beautiful, but there may never be two that love one another equally well. So Esteban sat up in their room by a guttering candle, his knuckles between his teeth, and wondered why Manuel was so changed and why the whole meaning had gone out of their life.

One evening Manuel was stopped on the street by a small boy who announced to him that the Perichole wished him to call upon her at once. Manuel turned in his path and went to the theatre. Straight, sombre and impersonal, he entered the actress's room and stood waiting. Camila had a service to ask of Manuel and she thought a few preliminary blandishments were necessary, but she scarcely paused in combing a blond wig that was dressed upon the table before her.

"You write letters for people, don't you? I want you to write a letter for me, please. Please come in."

He came forward two steps.

"You never pay me the least visit either of you. That's not Spanish of you."—meaning 'courteous.'—"Which are you, Manuel or Esteban?"

"Manuel."

"It doesn't matter. You are both unfriendly. Neither of you ever comes to see me. Here I sit learning stupid lines all day and no one ever comes to see me but a lot of peddlers. It is because I am an actress, no?"

This was not very artful, but for Manuel it was unspeakably complicated. He merely stared at her from the shadows of his long hair and left her to improvise.

"I am going to engage you to write a letter for me, a very secret letter. But now I can see that you don't like me and that to ask you to write a letter would be as good as reading it aloud in all the wine-shops. What does that look mean, Manuel? Are you my friend?"

"Yes, señora."

"Go away. Send me Esteban. You do not even say Yes, señora as a friend would say it."

Long pause. Presently she raised her head: "Are you still there, Unfriendly?"

"Yes, señora . . . you can trust me to do anything for you . . . you can trust . . ."

"If I ask you to write one letter for me, or two letters, you promise never to mention to a human being what is in them, or even that you wrote them?"

"Yes, señora."

"What do you promise by?—by the Virgin Mary?"

"Yes, señora."

"And by the heart of St. Rose of Lima?"

"Yes, señora."

"Name of the Name, Manuel, anyone would think you were as stupid as an ox. Manuel, I am very angry with you. You are not stupid. You don't look stupid. Please don't say just Yes, señora again. Don't be stupid or I'll send for Esteban. Is anything the matter with you?"

Here Manuel cast himself upon the Spanish language and exclaimed with unnecessary vigor: "I swear by the Virgin Mary and the heart of St. Rose of Lima that all that has to do with the letter will be secret."

"Even from Esteban," prompted the Perichole.

"Even from Esteban."

"Well, that's better." She motioned him to sit down at a table where writing materials were already laid out. As she dictated she strode about the room, frowning, swinging her hips. With her arms akimbo, she hugged her shawl about her shoulders defiantly.

"Camila Perichole kisses the hands of Your Excellency and says—No, take another piece of paper and begin again. *The señora Micaela Villegas, artist, kisses the hands of Your Excellency and says that, being the victim of the envious and lying friends that Y. E.'s goodness permits about Him, she can no longer endure Y. E.'s suspicions and jealousy. Y. E.'s servant has always valued Y. E.'s friendship and has never committed, nor even thought, an offense against it, but she can no longer fight against the calumnies that Y. E. believes so readily. Señora Villegas, artist, called the Perichole, therefore returns herewith such of Y. E.'s gifts as have not been placed beyond recall, since without Y. E.'s confidence, Y. E.'s servant can take no pleasure in them."*

Camila continued walking about the room for several minutes, consumed by her thoughts. Presently without so much as glancing at her secretary, she commanded: "Take another leaf. Have you gone mad? Do not ever think of dedicating another bull to me again. It has caused a frightful war. Heaven protect you, my colt. Friday night, the same place, the same time.

I may be a little late, for the fox is wide-awake. That will be all."

Manuel rose.

"You swear that you have made no errors?"

"Yes, I swear."

"There is your money."

Manuel took the money.

"I shall want you to write me more letters from time to time. My uncle Pio generally writes my letters; these I do not wish him to know about. Good night. Go with God."

"Go with God."

Manuel descended the stairs and stood for a long time among the trees, not thinking, not moving.

Esteban knew that his brother was continually brooding over the Perichole, but he never suspected that he saw her. From time to time during the next two months a small boy would approach him in great haste and ask whether he were Manuel or Esteban, and being informed that he was only Esteban, the boy would add that Manuel was wanted at the theatre. Esteban assumed that the call was for copyist's work and was therefore utterly unprepared for a visit that they received one night in their room.

It was almost midnight. Esteban had gone to bed, and lay gazing out from under the blanket at the candle beside which his brother was working. There was a light tap at the door and Manuel opened to admit a lady heavily veiled, out of breath and nervous. She threw back the scarf from her face and said hurriedly:

"Quick, ink and paper. You are Manuel, yes? You must do a letter for me at once."

For a moment her glance fell on the two bright eyes that glared at her from the edge of the cot. She murmured: "Eu . . . you must excuse me. I know it is late. It was necessary . . . I must come." Then turning to Manuel, she whispered into his ear: "Write this: *I, the Perichole, am not accustomed to wait at a rendez-vous. Have you finished that? You are only a cholo, and there are better matadors than you, even in Lima. I am half Castilian and there are no better actresses in the world. You shall not have the opportunity*—Have you got that? *to keep me waiting again, cholo, and I shall laugh the last, for even an actress does not grow old as fast as a bullfighter."*

To Esteban in the shadows the picture of Camila leaning over his brother's hand and whispering into his ear was complete evidence that a new congeniality had formed such as he would never know. He seemed to shrink away into space, infinitely tiny, infinitely unwanted. He took one more glance at the tableau of love, all the paradise from which he was shut out, and turned his face to the wall.

Camila seized the note the moment it was done, pushed a coin along the table and in a last flurry of black lace, scarlet beads and excited whispers left the room. Manuel turned from the door with his candle. He sat down, put his hands over his ears, his elbows on his knees. He worshipped her. He murmured to himself over and over again that he worshipped her, making of the sound a sort of incantation and an obstacle to thought.

He emptied his mind of everything but a singsong, and it was this vacancy that permitted him to become aware of Esteban's mood. He seemed to hear a voice that proceeded from the shadows saying: "Go and follow her, Manuel. Don't stay here. You'll be happy. There's room for us all in the world." Then the realization became even more intense and he received a mental image of Esteban going a long way off and saying good-

bye many times as he went. He was
filled with terror; by the light of it he
saw that all the other attachments in
the world were shadows, or the il-
lusions of fever, even Madre María
del Pilar, even the Perichole. He could
not understand why Esteban's misery
should present itself as demanding a
choice between him and the Perichole,
but he could understand Esteban's mis-
ery, as misery. And at once he sacri-
ficed everything to it, if it can be said
we ever sacrifice anything save what
we know we can never attain, or what
some secret wisdom tells us it would
be uncomfortable or saddening to pos-
sess. To be sure there was nothing on
which Esteban could base a complaint.
It was not jealousy, for in their earlier
affairs it had never occurred to either
of them that their loyalty to one an-
other had been diminished. It was
merely that in the heart of one of
them there was left room for an elabo-
rate imaginative attachment and in the
heart of the other there was not.
Manuel could not quite understand
this and, as we shall see, he nourished
a dim sense of being accused unjustly.
But he did understand that Esteban
was suffering. In his excitement he
groped for a means of holding this
brother who seemed to be receding
into the distance. And at once, in one
unhesitating stroke of the will, he re-
moved the Perichole from his heart.

He blew out the candle and lay
down on his bed. He was trembling.
He said aloud with exaggerated casual-
ness: "Well, that's the last letter I
write for that woman. She can go and
find a pander somewhere else. If ever
she calls here or sends for me when
I'm out, tell her so. Make it plain.
That's the last I have to do with her,"
and with that he began reciting his
evening psalm aloud. But he had
hardly reached *A sagitta volante in die*
when he became aware that Esteban

had risen and was lighting the candle.
"What's the matter?" he asked.
"I'm going out for a walk," replied
Esteban sombrely, fastening his belt.
After a moment, he broke out with an
assumption of anger: "You don't have
to say . . . what you just said, for me.
I don't care whether you write her
letters or not. You don't have to
change for me. I haven't anything to
do with that."
"Go to bed, you fool. God, you're
a fool, Esteban. What made you think
I said that, for you? Don't you be-
lieve I mean it when I say I'm through
with her? Do you think I want to
write any more of her dirty letters
and get paid for them like that?"
"It's all right. You love her. You
don't have to change because of me."
" '*Love* her?' *Love* her? You're crazy,
Esteban. How could I love her? What
chance would there be for me? Do
you suppose she'd give me those let-
ters to write if there were any chance?
Do you suppose she'd push a piece
of money across the table every time.
. . . You're crazy, Esteban, that's all."
There was a long pause. Esteban
would not go to bed. He sat by the
candle in the middle of the room, tap-
ping with his hand on the edge of the
table.
"Go to bed, you fool," shouted
Manuel, rising on one elbow under
the blanket. He was talking in their
secret language and the new pain at
his heart gave a greater ring of reality
to his assumption of rage. "I'm all
right."
"I won't. I'm going out for a walk,"
replied Esteban picking up his coat.
"You can't go out for a walk. It's
two o'clock. It's raining. You can't go
and walk about for hours like that.
Look, Esteban, I swear to you there's
nothing left to all that. I don't love
her. I only did for a time."
By now Esteban stood in the dark

of the open door. In the unnatural voice with which we make the greatest declarations of our lives, he muttered: "I'm in your way," and turned to go.

Manuel leapt out of his bed. His head seemed to be full of a great din, a voice crying out that Esteban was going away forever, was leaving him alone forever. "In the name of God, in the name of God, Esteban, come back here."

Esteban came back and went to bed and the matter was not mentioned again for many weeks. The very next evening Manuel had an opportunity of declaring his position. A messenger arrived from the Perichole and was told harshly to inform the actress that Manuel would write no more letters for her.

One evening Manuel tore open the flesh on his knee against a piece of metal.

Neither brother had ever been ill for as much as a day in his life, and now Manuel, utterly bewildered, watched his leg swell and felt the waves of pain rise and fall in his body. Esteban sat by and stared at his face trying to imagine what great pain was. At last one midnight Manuel remembered that the signboard of a certain hairdresser in the city described the proprietor as an experienced barber and surgeon. Esteban ran through the streets to fetch him. He pounded on the door. Presently a woman leaned out of a window and announced that her husband would be back in the morning. During the fearful hours that followed, they told one another that when the doctor had seen the leg all would be well. He would do something about it, and Manuel would be out around the town in a day or two, even in a day perhaps, even less than a day.

The barber arrived and prescribed various draughts and ointments. Esteban was instructed to lay cold cloths on his brother's leg every hour. The barber withdrew and the brothers sat down to wait for the pain to subside. But while they continued staring into one another's face waiting for the miracle of science the pain grew worse. Hour after hour Esteban approached with his dripping towel and they discovered that the moment of its application was the worst of all. With all the fortitude in the world Manuel could not prevent himself from shouting and from flinging himself about upon the bed. Night came on and still Esteban stolidly waited and watched and worked. Nine, ten, eleven. Now when the time drew near to apply the cloths (the hour struck so musically from all those towers) Manuel would plead with Esteban not to do his work. He would resort to guile and declare that he scarcely felt it. But Esteban, his heart bursting with pain and his lips a line of iron, would roll back the blanket and bind the towel fiercely in its place. Manuel gradually became delirious and under this application all the thoughts he did not permit himself in his right mind would burst magnified from his mouth.

Finally at two o'clock, out of his mind with rage and pain, and flinging himself half out of the bed until his head struck the floor, Manuel cried: "God condemn your soul to the hottest hell there is. A thousand devils torture you forever, Esteban. God condemn your soul, do you hear?" At first, the air gone out of his body, Esteban went out into the hall and leaned against the door, his mouth and eyes wide open. Still he heard from within: "Yes, Esteban, may God damn your beastly soul forever, do you hear that? For coming between me and what was mine by right. She

was mine, do you hear, and what right had you. . . ." And he would go off into an elaborate description of the Perichole.

These outbursts recurred hourly. It was some time before Esteban was able to realize that his brother's mind was not then clear. After some moments of horror, in which his being a devout believer had its part, he would return to the room and go about his duties with bent head.

Towards dawn his brother became serener. (For what human ill does not dawn seem to be an alleviation?) It was in one of these intervals that Manuel said quite calmly: "God's son! I feel better, Esteban. Those cloths must be good after all. You'll see. I'll be up and around to-morrow. You haven't slept for days. You'll see I won't cause you any more trouble, Esteban."

"It's no trouble, you fool."

"You mustn't take me seriously when I try and stop you putting on the old cloths, Esteban."

A long pause. At last Esteban brought out, barely audible: "I think . . . don't you think it would be fine if I sent for the Perichole? She could just come and see you for a few minutes, I mean. . . ."

"Her? You still thinking about her? I wouldn't have her here for anything. No."

But Esteban was not content yet. He dragged up a few more phrases from the very centre of his being: "Manuel, you still feel, don't you, that I came between you and the Perichole and you don't remember that I told you it was all right with me. I swear to you I'd have been glad if you'd gone away with her, or any-thing."

"What are you bringing that up for, Esteban? I tell you, in God's own name, I never think of that. She's nothing to me. When are you going to forget that, Esteban? I tell you I'm glad things are as they are. Look, I got to get angry when you keep go-ing back to that."

"Manuel, I wouldn't speak of it again, only when you get angry at me about the cloths . . . you, you get angry at me about that, too. And you talk about it and you . . ."

"Look, I'm not responsible what I say. My old leg hurts then, see."

"Then you don't damn me to hell because . . . it looks like I came be-tween you and the Perichole?"

"Damn you to . . . ? What makes you say that? You're going crazy, Esteban; you're imagining things. You haven't had any sleep, Esteban. I been a curse to you and you're losing your health because of me. But you'll see, I won't trouble you much more. How could I damn you to hell, Esteban, when you're all I've got? Understand, see, that when the cold cloths go on, I just lose myself, see. You know. Don't think about it twice. It's time to put them on now. I won't say a word."

"No, Manuel, I'll skip this time. It won't do you any harm, I'll just skip this time."

"I've got to get well, Esteban. I've got to get up soon, you know. Put them on. But one minute—give me the crucifix. I swear by the blood and body of Christ that if I say anything against Esteban, I don't mean it and it's just the foolish words when I'm dreaming because of the pain in my leg. God make me well again soon, amen. Put it back. There. Now I'm ready."

"Look, Manuel, it won't hurt if I skip just this once, see. It'll be good for you, sure, to not get it all stirred up just this once."

"No, I've got to get well. The doc-tor said it had to be done. I won't say a word, Esteban."

And it would begin all over again. During the second night a prostitute in the next room started beating on the wall, outraged at such language. A priest in the room on the other side would come out into the hall and beat on the door. The whole floor would gather before the room in exasperation. The innkeeper came up the stairs loudly promising his guests that the brothers would be dumped into the street the very next morning. Esteban, holding his candle, would go into the hall and permit them to rage at him for as long as they pleased; but after that he took to pressing his hand firmly over his brother's mouth during the moments of greatest stress. This increased Manuel's personal rage at him and he would babble all through the night.

On the third night, Esteban sent for the priest and amidst the enormous shadows Manuel received the sacrament, and died.

Thereafter Esteban refused to come near the building. He would start off upon long walks, but presently drifting back, would hang about, staring at passers-by, within two streets of where his brother lay. The innkeeper failing to make any impression upon him and remembering that the boys were brought up at the Convent of Santa María Rosa de las Rosas, sent for the Abbess. Simply and soundly she directed all that was to be done. At last she went down to the street corner and spoke to Esteban. He watched her approach him, a glance mixed of longing and distrust. But when she stood near him he turned sideways and looked away.

"I want you to help me. Won't you come in and see your brother? Won't you come in and help me?"

"No."

"You won't help me!" A long pause. Suddenly as she stood there full of her helplessness there flashed through her mind an incident of many years before: the twin brothers about fifteen years old were sitting at her knee and she was telling them the story of the crucifixion. Their large grave eyes were fixed upon her lips. Suddenly Manuel had cried out loudly: "If Esteban and I had been there we would have prevented it."

"Well, then, if you won't help me, will you tell me which you are?"

"Manuel," said Esteban.

"Manuel, won't you come and sit with me up there for just a short time?"

After a long pause: "No."

"But Manuel, dear Manuel, can't you remember as children how you did so many things for me? You were willing to go across the town on some little errand. When I was ill you made the cook let you bring me my soup?" Another woman would have said: "Do you remember how much I did for you?"

"Yes."

"I, too, Manuel have lost. I too . . . once. We know that God has taken them into His hands. . . ." But this did not do at all. Esteban turned vaguely and walked away from her. When he had gone about twenty paces he stopped and stared down a side-street, like a dog who wants to go away, but is reluctant to offend the master who calls him back.

That was all they could get out of him. When the fearful procession passed through the city, with its black hoods and masks, its candles in broad daylight, its display of heaped-up skulls, its terrifying psalms, Esteban followed it in the parallel streets, catching glimpses of it from a distance, like a savage.

All Lima was interested in this separation of the brothers. Housewives whispered together sympathetically

about it as they unfurled their carpets from the balconies. The men in the wine-shops, alluding to it, shook their heads and smoked in silence for a while. Travellers from the interior told of seeing Esteban as he strayed with eyes like coals along the dried-up beds of rivers or through the great ruins of the old race. A herder of llamas had come upon him standing upon a hilltop, asleep or dazed, wet with dew under the stars. Some fishermen surprised him swimming far out from shore. From time to time he would find work to do, he would become a shepherd or a carter, but after a few months he would disappear and stride from province to province. But he always returned to Lima. One day he appeared at the door of the Perichole's dressing-room; he made as though to speak, gazed earnestly at her and vanished. One day a sister came running into the office of Madre María del Pilar with the news that Esteban (whom the world called Manuel) was lingering about the door of the convent. The Abbess hurried out into the street. For months she had been asking herself what strategy could reconcile this half-demented boy to living among them again. She assembled as grave and calm a manner as she was able and appearing at the street door murmured "My friend" and looked at him. He gazed back at her with the same glance of longing and distrust that he had shown her before, and stood trembling. Again she whispered "My friend" and moved a step forward. Suddenly Esteban turned and breaking into a run disappeared. Madre María del Pilar rushed stumbling back to her desk and fell upon her knees, exclaiming angrily: "I have prayed for wisdom and You have given me none. You have not chosen to give me the least grace. I am a mere scrubber of floors. . . ."

But during the penance she set herself for this impudence the thought came to her to send for Captain Alvarado. Three weeks later she had a ten-minute conversation with him. And the next day he started for Cuzco where, it was said, Esteban was doing some copying for the University.

There was this strange and noble figure in Peru during these years, the Captain Alvarado, the traveller. He was blackened and cured by all weathers. He stood in the Square with feet apart as though they were planted on a shifting deck. His eyes were strange, unaccustomed to the shorter range, too used to seizing the appearances of a constellation between a cloud and a cloud, and the outline of a cape in rain. His reticence was sufficiently explained for most of us by his voyages, but the Marquesa de Montemayor had other light on the matter. "*Captain Alvarado is bringing you this letter in person,*" she wrote to her daughter. "*Introduce him to some of your geographers, my treasure, though it may make them a little uncomfortable, for he is the diamond of sincerity. They will never see anyone who has travelled so far. Last night he described to me some of his voyages. Imagine him pushing his prow through a sea of weeds, stirring up a cloud of fish like grasshoppers in June; or sailing between islands of ice. Oh, he has been to China and up the rivers of Africa. But he is not merely an adventurer and he seems to take no pride in discovering new places; nor is he a mere merchant. One day I asked him narrowly why he lived so, and he avoided my question. I found out from my laundress what I think is the reason of his wandering: My child, he had a child; my daughter, he had a daughter. She was just old enough to cook a holiday meal, and do a little sewing for him. In those days*

he merely sailed between Mexico and Peru and hundreds of times she waved him farewell or welcome. We have no way of knowing whether she was more beautiful or intelligent than the thousands of other girls that lived about him, but she was his. I suppose it seems ignoble to you that a great oak of a man should go about the world like a blind man about an empty house merely because a chit of a girl has been withdrawn from it. No, no, you cannot understand this, my adored one, but I understand and grow pale. Last night he sat with me and talked of her. He laid his cheek against his hand and looking into the fire, he said: 'It sometimes seems to me that she is away upon a voyage and that I shall see her again. It seems to me that she is in England.' You will laugh at me, but I think he goes about the hemispheres to pass the time between now and his old age."

The brothers had always entertained a great respect for Captain Alvarado. They had worked for him a short time and the silence of the three of them had made a little kernel of sense in a world of boasting, self-excuse and rhetoric. So now when the great traveller came into the dark kitchen where Esteban was eating, the boy drew his chair farther into the shadow, but at a distance, he was glad. The Captain gave no sign of recognizing or even of seeing him until he had finished his meal. Esteban had finished long before, but not wishing to be spoken to, waited until the Captain should have left the cave. At last the Captain walked over to him and said:

"You are Esteban or Manuel. You helped me once with some unloading. I am Captain Alvarado."

"Yes," said Esteban.

"How are you?"

Esteban muttered something.

"I am looking for some strong fellows to go on my next trip with me." Pause. "Would you like to come?" Longer pause. "England. And Russia. . . . Hard work. Good wages. . . . A long way from Peru.—Well?"

Apparently Esteban had not been listening. He sat with his eyes on the table. At last the Captain raised his voice, as to a deaf person:

"I said: Do you want to go on my next trip with me. . . ."

"Yes, I'll go," answered Esteban suddenly.

"Fine. That's fine. I want your brother, too, of course."

"No."

"What's the matter? Wouldn't he want to come?"

Esteban mumbled something, looking away. Then half rising, he said: "I got to go now. I've got to see somebody about something."

"Let me see your brother myself. Where is he?"

". . . dead," said Esteban.

"Oh, I didn't know. I didn't know. I'm sorry."

"Yes," said Esteban. "I got to go."

"Hmm.—Which are you? What's your name?"

"Esteban."

"When did Manuel die?"

"Oh, just a . . . just a few weeks. He hit his knee against something and . . . just a few weeks ago."

They both kept their eyes on the floor.

"How old are you, Esteban?"

"Twenty-two."

"Well, that's settled then, you're coming with me?"

"Yes."

"You may not be used to the cold."

"Yes, I'm used to it.—I've got to go now. I got to go in the city and see somebody about something."

"Well, Esteban. Come back here for supper and we'll talk about the trip.

Come back and have some wine with me, see. Will you?"

"Yes, I will."

"Go with God."

"Go with God."

They had supper together and it was arranged that they were to start for Lima the next morning. The Captain got him very drunk. At first they poured and drank and poured and drank in silence. Then the Captain began to talk about ships and their courses. He asked Esteban questions about tackle and about the guide-stars. Then Esteban began to talk about other things, and to talk very loudly:

"On the ship you must give me something to do all the time. I'll do anything, anything. I'll climb up high and fix ropes; and I'll watch all night, —because, you know, I don't sleep well anyway. And, Captain Alvarado, on the ship you must pretend that you don't know me. Pretend that you hate me the most. So that you'll always give me things to do. I can't sit still and write at a table any more. —And don't tell the other men about me . . . that is, about . . ."

"I hear you went into a burning house, Esteban, and pulled someone out."

"Yes. I didn't get burned or anything. You know," cried Esteban, leaning across the table, "you're not allowed to kill yourself; you know you're not allowed. Everybody knows that. But if you jump into a burning house to save somebody, that wouldn't be killing yourself. And if you became a matador and the bull caught you that wouldn't be killing yourself. Only you mustn't put yourself in the bull's way on purpose. Did you ever notice that animals never kill themselves, even when they're sure to lose? They never jump into a river or anything, even when they're sure to lose. Some people say that horses run into bonfires. Is that true?"

"No, I don't think that's true."

"I don't think it's true. We had a dog once. Well, I mustn't think of that.—Captain Alvarado, do you know Madre María del Pilar?"

"Yes."

"I want to give her a present before I go away. Captain Alvarado, I want you to give me all my wages before I start—I won't need any money anywhere—and I want to buy her a present now. The present isn't from me only. She was . . . was . . ." Here Esteban wished to say his brother's name, but was unable to. Instead he continued in a lower voice: "She had a kind of a . . . she had a serious loss, once. She said so. I don't know who it was, and I want to give her a present. Women can't bear that kind of a thing like we can."

The Captain promised him that they would choose something in the morning. Esteban talked about it at great length. At last the Captain saw him slip under the table, and himself, rising up, went out into the square before the inn. He looked at the line of the Andes and at the streams of stars crowding forever across the sky. And there was that wraith hanging in mid-air and smiling at him, the wraith with the silvery voice that said for the thousandth time: "Don't be gone long. But I'll be a big girl when you get back." Then he went within and carried Esteban to his room and sat looking at him for a long while.

The next morning he was waiting at the bottom of the stairs when Esteban appeared:

"We're starting when you're ready," said the Captain.

The strange glitter had returned to the boy's eyes. He blurted out: "No, I'm not coming. I'm not coming after all."

"Aïe! Esteban! But you have promised me that you would come."

"It's impossible. I can't come with you," and he turned back up the stairs. "Come here a moment, Esteban, just a moment."

"I can't come with you. I can't leave Peru."

"I want to tell you something." Esteban came down to the foot of the stairs.

"How about that present for Madre Maria del Pilar?" asked the Captain in a low voice. Esteban was silent, looking over the mountains. "You aren't going to take that present away from her? It might mean a lot to her . . . you know."

"All right," murmured Esteban, as though much impressed.

"Yes. Besides the ocean's better than Peru. You know Lima and Cuzco and the road. You have nothing more to know about them. You see it's the ocean you want. Besides on the boat you'll have something to do every minute. I'll see to that. Go and get your things and we'll start."

Esteban was trying to make a decision. It had always been Manuel who had made the decisions and even Manuel had never been forced to make as great a one as this. Esteban went slowly upstairs. The Captain waited for him and waited so long that presently he ventured half the way up the stairs and listened. At first there was silence; then a series of noises that

his imagination was able to identify at once. Esteban had scraped away the plaster about a beam and was adjusting a rope about it. The Captain stood on the stairs trembling: "Perhaps it's best," he said to himself. "Perhaps I should leave him alone. Perhaps it's the only thing possible for him." Then on hearing another sound he flung himself against the door, fell into the room and caught the boy. "Go away," cried Esteban. "Let me be. Don't come in now."

Esteban fell face downward upon the floor. "I am alone, alone, alone," he cried. The Captain stood above him, his great plain face ridged and gray with pain; it was his own old hours he was reliving. He was the awkwardest speaker in the world apart from the lore of the sea, but there are times when it requires a high courage to speak the banal. He could not be sure the figure on the floor was listening, but he said, "We do what we can. We push on, Esteban, as best we can. It isn't for long, you know. Time keeps going by. You'll be surprised at the way time passes."

They started for Lima. When they reached the bridge of San Luis Rey, the Captain descended to the stream below in order to supervise the passage of some merchandise, but Esteban crossed by the bridge and fell with it.

PART FOUR: UNCLE PIO

In one of her letters (the XXIXth) the Marquesa de Montemayor tries to describe the impression that Uncle Pio "our aged Harlequin" made upon her: "I have been sitting all morning on the green balcony making you a pair of slippers, my soul," she tells her daughter. "As the golden wire did not take up my whole attention I was able to follow the activity of a coterie of

ants in the wall beside me. Somewhere behind the partition they were patiently destroying my house. Every three minutes a little workman would appear between two boards and drop a grain of wood upon the floor below. Then he would wave his antennae at me and back busily into his mysterious corridor. In the meantime various brothers and sisters of his were

trotting back and forth on a certain
highway, stopping to massage one an-
other's heads, or if the messages they
bore were of first importance, refusing
angrily to massage or to be massaged.
And at once I thought of Uncle Pio.
Why? Where else but with him had
I seen that very gesture with which
he arrests a passing abbé or a courti-
er's valet, and whispers, his lips
laid against his victim's ear? And
surely enough, before noon I saw him
hurry by on one of those mysterious
errands of his. As I am the idlest and
silliest of women I sent Pepita to get
me a piece of nougat which I placed
on the ant's highway. Similarly I sent
word to the Café Pizarro asking them
to send Uncle Pio to see me if he
dropped in before sunset. I shall give
him that old bent salad fork with the
turquoise in it, and he will bring me
a copy of the new ballad that every-
one is singing about the d—q—a of
Ol—v—s. My child, you shall have the
best of everything, and you shall have
it first."

And in the next letter: "My dear,
Uncle Pio is the most delightful man
in the world, your husband excepted.
He is the second most delightful man
in the world. His conversation is en-
chanting. If he weren't so disreputa-
ble I should make him my secretary.
He could write all my letters for me
and generations would rise up and call
me witty. Alas, however, he is so moth-
eaten by disease and bad company,
that I shall have to leave him to his
underworld. He is not only like an
ant, he is like a soiled pack of cards.
And I doubt whether the whole Pa-
cific could wash him sweet and fra-
grant again. But what divine Spanish
he speaks and what exquisite things
he says in it! That's what one gets by
hanging around a theatre and hearing
nothing but the conversation of Cal-
derón. Alas, what is the matter with

this world, my soul, that it should
treat such a being so ill! His eyes are
as sad as those of a cow that has been
separated from its tenth calf."

You should know first that this Un-
cle Pio was Camila Perichole's maid.
He was also her singing-master, her
coiffeur, her masseur, her reader, her
errand-boy, her banker; rumor added:
her father. For example, he taught her
her parts. There was a whisper around
town that Camila could read and
write. The compliment was un-
founded; Uncle Pio did her reading
and writing for her. At the height of
the season the company put on two or
three new plays a week, and as each
one contained a long and flowery part
for the Perichole the mere task of
memorization was not a trifle.

Peru had passed within fifty years
from a frontier state to a state in ren-
aissance. Its interest in music and the
theatre was intense. Lima celebrated
its feast days by hearing a Mass of
Tomás Luis de Victoria in the morn-
ing and the glittering poetry of Cal-
derón in the evening. It is true that
the Limeans were given to interpolat-
ing trivial songs into the most exquisite
comedies and some lachrymose effects
into the austerest music; but at least
they never submitted to the boredom
of a misplaced veneration. If they had
disliked heroic comedy the Limeans
would not have hesitated to remain at
home; and if they had been deaf to
polyphony nothing would have pre-
vented their going to an earlier service.
When the Archbishop returned from
a short trip to Spain, all Lima kept
asking: "What has he brought?" The
news finally spread abroad that he had
returned with tomes of masses and
motets by Palestrina, Morales and Vit-
toria, as well as thirty-five plays by
Tirso de Molina and Ruiz de Alarçon

and Moreto. There was a civic fête in his honor. The choirboys' school and the green room of the Comedia were swamped with the gifts of vegetables and wheat. All the world was eager to nourish the interpreters of so much beauty.

This was the theatre in which Camila Perichole gradually made her reputation. So rich was the repertory and so dependable the prompter's box that few plays were given more than four times a season. The manager had the whole flowering of the 17th Century Spanish drama to draw upon, including many that are now lost to us. The Perichole had appeared in a hundred plays of Lope de Vega alone. There were many admirable actresses in Lima during these years, but none better. The citizens were too far away from the theatres of Spain to realize that she was the best in the Spanish world. They kept sighing for a glimpse of the stars of Madrid whom they had never seen and to whom they assigned vague new excellences. Only one person knew for certain that the Perichole was a great performer and that was her tutor Uncle Pio.

Uncle Pio came of a good Castilian house, illegitimately. At the age of ten he ran away to Madrid from his father's hacienda and was pursued without diligence. He lived ever after by his wits. He possessed the six attributes of the adventurer—a memory for names and faces, with the aptitude for altering his own; the gift of tongues; inexhaustible invention; secrecy; the talent for falling into conversation with strangers; and that freedom from conscience that springs from a contempt for the dozing rich he preyed upon. From ten to fifteen he distributed handbills for merchants, held horses, and ran confidential errands. From fifteen to twenty he trained bears and snakes for travelling circuses; he cooked, and mixed punches; he hung about the entries of the more expensive taverns and whispered information into the travellers' ears—sometimes nothing more dubious than that a certain noble house was reduced to selling its plate and could thus dispense with the commission of a silversmith. He was attached to all the theatres in town and could applaud like ten. He spread slanders at so much a slander. He sold rumors about crops and about the value of land. From twenty to thirty his services came to be recognized in very high circles—he was sent out by the government to inspirit some half-hearted rebellions in the mountains, so that the government could presently arrive and whole-heartedly crush them. His discretion was so profound that the French party used him even when they knew that the Austrian party used him also. He had long interviews with the Princesse des Ursins, but he came and went by the back stairs. During this phase he was no longer obliged to arrange gentlemen's pleasures, nor to plant little harvests of calumny.

He never did one thing for more than two weeks at a time even when enormous gains seemed likely to follow upon it. He could have become a circus manager, a theatrical director, a dealer in antiquities, an importer of Italian silks, a secretary in the Palace or the Cathedral, a dealer in provisions for the army, a speculator in houses and farms, a merchant in dissipations and pleasures. But there seemed to have been written into his personality, through some accident or early admiration of his childhood, a reluctance to own anything, to be tied down, to be held to a long engagement. It was this that prevented his thieving, for example. He had stolen several times, but the gains had not been sufficient to

offset his dread of being locked up; he had sufficient ingenuity to escape on the field itself all the police in the world, but nothing could protect him against the talebearing of his enemies. Similarly he had been reduced for a time to making investigations for the Inquisition, but when he had seen several of his victims led off in hoods he felt that he might be involving himself in an institution whose movements were not evenly predictable.

As he approached twenty, Uncle Pio came to see quite clearly that his life had three aims. There was first this need of independence, cast into a curious pattern, namely: the desire to be varied, secret and omniscient. He was willing to renounce the dignities of public life, if in secret he might feel that he looked down upon men from a great distance, knowing more about them than they knew themselves; and with a knowledge which occasionally passed into action and rendered him an agent in the affairs of states and persons. In the second place he wanted to be always near beautiful women, of whom he was always in the best and worst sense the worshipper. To be near them was as necessary to him as breathing. His reverence for beauty and charm was there for anyone to see and to laugh at, and the ladies of the theatre and the court and the houses of pleasure loved his connoisseurship. They tormented him and insulted him and asked his advice and were singularly comforted by his absurd devotion. He suffered greatly their rages and their meannesses and their confiding tears; all he asked was to be accepted casually, to be trusted, to be allowed like a friendly and slightly foolish dog to come and go in their rooms and to write their letters for them. He was insatiably curious about their minds and their hearts. He never expected

to be loved by them (borrowing for a moment another sense of that word); for that, he carried his money to the obscurer parts of the city; he was always desperately unprepossessing, with his whisp of a moustache and his whisp of a beard and his big ridiculous sad eyes. They constituted his parish; it was from them that he acquired the name of Uncle Pio and it was when they were in trouble that he most revealed himself; when they fell from favour he lent them money, when they were ill he outlasted the flagging devotion of their lovers and the exasperation of their maids; when time or disease robbed them of their beauty, he served them still for their beauty's memory; and when they died his was the honest grief that saw them as far as possible on their journey.

In the third place he wanted to be near those that loved Spanish literature and its masterpieces, especially in the theatre. He had discovered all that treasure for himself, borrowing or stealing from the libraries of his patrons, feeding himself upon it in secrecy,—behind the scenes, as it were, of his mad life. He was contemptuous of the great persons who for all their education and usage, exhibited no care nor astonishment before the miracles of word order in Calderón and Cervantes. He longed himself to make verses. He never realized that many of the satirical songs he had written for the vaudevilles passed into folk-music and have been borne everywhere along the highroads.

As the result of one of those quarrels that arise so naturally in brothels his life became too complicated and he removed to Peru. Uncle Pio in Peru was even more versatile than Uncle Pio in Europe. Here too he touched upon real-estate, circuses, pleasures, insurrections and antiques. A Chinese junk had been blown from

Canton to America; he dragged up the beach the bales of deep-red porcelain and sold the bowls to the collectors of virtú. He traced down the sovereign remedies of the Incas and started a smart trade in pills. Within four months he knew practically everyone in Lima. He presently added to this acquaintance the inhabitants of scores of seacoast towns, mining camps and settlements in the interior. His pretensions to omniscience became more and more plausible. The Viceroy discovered Uncle Pio and all this richness of reference; he engaged his services in many affairs. In the decay of his judgment Don Andrés had retained one talent, he was a master of the technique of handling confidential servants. He treated Uncle Pio with great tact and some deference; he understood which errands the other should not be asked to undertake and he understood his need for variety and intermission. Uncle Pio in turn was perpetually astonished that a prince should make so little use of his position, for power, or for fantasy, or for sheer delight in the manipulation of other men's destinies; but the servant loved the master because he could quote from any of Cervantes' prefaces and because his tongue had a little Castilian salt about it still. Many a morning Uncle Pio entered the Palace through corridors where there was no one to cross but a confessor or a confidential bully and sat with the Viceroy over his morning chocolate.

But for all his activity nothing made Uncle Pio rich. One would have said that he abandoned a venture when it threatened to prosper. Although no one knew it, he owned a house. It was full of dogs that could add and multiply and the top floor was reserved for birds. But even in this kingdom he was lonely, and proud in his loneliness, as though there resided a certain superiority in such a solitude. Finally he stumbled upon an adventure that came like some strange gift from the skies and that combined the three great aims of his life: his passion for overseeing the lives of others, his worship of beautiful women, and his admiration for the treasures of Spanish literature. He discovered Camila Perichole. Her real name was Micaela Villegas. She was singing in cafés at the age of twelve and Uncle Pio had always been the very soul of cafés. Now as he sat among the guitarists and watched this awkward girl singing ballads, imitating every inflection of the more experienced singers who had preceded her, the determination entered his mind to play Pygmalion. He bought her. Instead of sleeping locked up in the wine bin, she inherited a cot in his house. He wrote songs for her, he taught her how to listen to the quality of her tone, and bought her a new dress. At first all she noticed was that it was wonderful not to be whipped, to be offered hot soups, and to be taught something. But it was Uncle Pio who was really dazzled. His rash experiment flourished beyond all prophecy. The little twelve-year-old, silent and always a little sullen, devoured work. He set her endless exercises in acting and mimicry; he set her problems in conveying the atmosphere of a song; he took her to the theatres and made her notice all the details of a performance. But it was from Camila as a woman that he was to receive his greatest shock. The long arms and legs were finally harmonized into a body of perfect grace. The almost grotesque and hungry face became beautiful. Her whole nature became gentle and mysterious and oddly wise; and it all turned to him. She could find no fault in him and she was sturdily loyal. They loved one another deeply but without passion.

He respected the slight nervous shadow that crossed her face when he came too near her. But there arose out of this denial itself the perfume of a tenderness, that ghost of passion which, in the most unexpected relationship, can make even a whole lifetime devoted to irksome duty pass like a gracious dream.

They travelled a great deal, seeking new taverns, for the highest attribute of a café singer will always be her novelty. They went to Mexico, their odd clothes wrapped up in the selfsame shawl. They slept on beaches, they were whipped at Panama and shipwrecked on some tiny Pacific islands plastered with the droppings of birds. They tramped through jungles delicately picking their way among snakes and beetles. They sold themselves out as harvesters in a hard season. Nothing in the world was very surprising to them.

Then began an even harder course of training for the girl, a regimen that resembled more the preparation for an acrobat. The instruction was a little complicated by the fact that her rise to favor was very rapid; and there was some danger that the applause she received would make her content with her work too soon. Uncle Pio never exactly beat her, but he resorted to a sarcasm that had terrors of its own.

At the close of a performance Camila would return to her dressing-room to find Uncle Pio whistling nonchalantly in one corner. She would divine his attitude at once and cry angrily:

"Now what is it? Mother of God, Mother of God, what is it now?"

"Nothing, little pearl. My little Camila of Camilas, nothing."

"There was something you didn't like. Ugly fault-finding thing that you are. Come on now, what was it? Look, I'm ready."

"No, little fish. Adorable morning star, I suppose you did as well as you could."

The suggestion that she was a limited artist and that certain felicities would be forever closed to her never failed to make Camila frantic. She would burst into tears: "I wish I had never known you. You poison my whole life. You just think I did badly. It pleases you to pretend that I was bad. All right then, be quiet."

Uncle Pio went on whistling.

"The fact is I know I was weak tonight, and don't need you to tell me so. So there. Now go away. I don't want to see you around. It's hard enough to play that part without coming back and finding you this way."

Suddenly Uncle Pio would lean forward and ask with angry intensity: "Why did you take that speech to the prisoner so fast?"

More tears from the Perichole: "Oh God, let me die in peace! One day you tell me to go faster and another to go slower. Anyway I shall be crazy in a year or two and then it won't matter."

More whistling.

"Besides the audience applauded as never before. Do you hear me? As never before. There! Too fast or too slow is nothing to them. They wept. I was divine. That's all I care for. Now be silent. Be silent."

He was absolutely silent.

"You may comb my hair, but if you say another word I shall never play again. You can find some other girl, that's all."

Thereupon he would comb her hair soothingly for ten minutes, pretending not to notice the sobs that were shaking her exhausted body. At last she would turn quickly and catching one of his hands would kiss it frantically: "Uncle Pio, was I so bad? Was I a

disgrace to you? Was it so awful *that you left the theatre?*"

After a long pause Uncle Pio would admit judiciously: "You were good in the scene on the ship."

"But I've been better, Uncle Pio. You remember the night you came back from Cuzco——?"

"You were pretty good at the close."

"Was I?"

"But my flower, my pearl, what was the matter in the speech to the prisoner?"

Here the Perichole would fling her face and arms upon the table amid the pomades, caught up into a tremendous fit of weeping. Only perfection would do, only perfection. And that had never come.

Then beginning in a low voice Uncle Pio would talk for an hour, analyzing the play, entering into a world of finesse in matters of voice and gesture and tempo, and often until dawn they would remain there declaiming to one another the lordly conversation of Calderón.

Whom were these two seeking to please? Not the audiences of Lima. They had long since been satisfied. We come from a world where we have known incredible standards of excellence, and we dimly remember beauties which we have not seized again; and we go back to that world. Uncle Pio and Camila Perichole were tormenting themselves in an effort to establish in Peru the standards of the theatres in some Heaven whither Calderón had preceded them. The public for which masterpieces are intended is not on this earth.

With the passing of time Camila lost some of this absorption in her art. A certain intermittent contempt for acting made her negligent. It was due to the poverty of interest in women's rôles throughout Spanish classical drama. At a time when the play-wrights grouped about the courts of England and France (a little later, of Venice) were enriching the parts of women with studies in wit, charm, passion and hysteria, the dramatists of Spain kept their eyes on their heroes, on gentlemen torn between the conflicting claims of honour, or, as sinners, returning at the last moment to the cross. For a number of years Uncle Pio spent himself in discovering ways to interest the Perichole in the rôles that fell to her. Upon one occasion he was able to announce to Camila that a granddaughter of Vico de Barrera had arrived in Peru. Uncle Pio had long since communicated to Camila his veneration for great poets and Camila never questioned the view that they were a little above the kings and not below the saints. So it was in great excitement that the two of them chose one of the master's plays to perform before his granddaughter. They rehearsed the poem a hundred times, now in the great joy of invention, now in dejection. On the night of the performance. Camila peering out between the folds of the curtain had Uncle Pio point out to her the little middle-aged woman worn with the cares of penury and a large family; but it seemed to Camila that she was looking at all the beauty and dignity in the world. As she waited for the lines that preceded her entrance she clung to Uncle Pio in reverent silence, her heart beating loudly. Between the acts she retired to the dusty corner of the warehouse where no one would find her and sat staring into the corners. At the close of the performance Uncle Pio brought the granddaughter of Vico de Barrera into Camila's room. Camila stood among the clothes that hung upon the wall, weeping with happiness and shame. Finally she flung herself on her knees and kissed the older woman's hands,

and the older woman kissed hers, and while the audience went home and went to bed the visitor remained telling Camila the little stories that had remained in the family, of Vico's work and of his habits.

Uncle Pio was at his happiest when a new actress entered the company, for the discovery of a new talent at her side never failed to bestir the Perichole. To Uncle Pio (standing at the back of the auditorium, bent double with joy and malice) it seemed that the body of the Perichole had become an alabaster lamp in which a strong light had been placed. Without any resort to tricks or to false emphasis, she set herself to efface the newcomer. If the play were a comedy she became the very abstraction of wit, and (as was more likely) it was a drama of wronged ladies and implacable hates, the stage fairly smouldered with her emotion. Her personality became so electric that if she so much as laid her hand upon that of a fellow actor a sympathetic shudder ran through the audience. But such occasions of excellence became less and less frequent. As her technique became sounder, Camila's sincerity became less necessary. Even when she was absent-minded the audience did not notice the difference and only Uncle Pio grieved.

Camila had a very beautiful face, or rather a face beautiful save in repose. In repose one was startled to discover that the nose was long and thin, the mouth tired and a little childish, the eyes unsatisfied—a rather pinched peasant girl, dragged from the cafés-chantants and quite incapable of establishing any harmony between the claims of her art, of her appetites, of her dreams, and of her crowded daily routine. Each of these was a world in itself, and the warfare between them would soon have reduced to idiocy (or triviality) a less tenacious physique. We have seen that in spite of her discontent with her parts, the Perichole knew very well the joy that might reside in acting and warmed herself from time to time at that flame. But that of love attracted her more often, though with no greater assurance of happiness, until Jupiter himself sent her some pearls.

Don Andrés de Ribera, the Viceroy of Peru, was the remnant of a delightful man, broken by the table, the alcove, a grandeeship and ten years of exile. As a youth he had accompanied embassies to Versailles and Rome; he had fought in the wars in Austria; he had been in Jerusalem. He was a widower and childless of an enormous and wealthy woman; he had collected coins a little, wines, actresses, orders and maps. From the table he had received the gout; from the alcove a tendency to convulsions; from the grandeeship a pride so vast and puerile that he seldom heard anything that was said to him and talked to the ceiling in a perpetual monologue; from the exile, oceans of boredom, a boredom so persuasive that it was like pain,—he woke up with it and spent the day with it, and it sat by his bed all night watching his sleep. Camila was passing the years in the hardworking routine of the theatre, savoured by a few untidy love-affairs, when this Olympian personage (for he had a face and port fit to play gods and heroes on the scene) suddenly transported her to the most delicious midnight suppers at the Palace. Contrary to all the traditions of the stage and state she adored her elderly admirer; she thought she was going to be happy forever. Don Andrés taught the Perichole a great many things and to her bright eager mind that was one of the sweetest ingredients of love. He

taught her a little French; to be neat and clean; the modes of address. Uncle Pio had taught her how great ladies carry themselves on great occasions; he taught her how they relax. Uncle Pio and Calderón had trained her in beautiful Spanish; Don Andrés furnished her with the smart slang of *El Buen Retiro*.

Uncle Pio was made anxious by Camila's invitation from the Palace. He would have much preferred that she continue with her little vulgarian love-affairs in the theatrical warehouse. But when he saw that her art was gaining a new finish he was well content. He would sit in the back of the theatre, rolling about in his seat for sheer joy and amusement, watching the Perichole intimate to the audience that she frequented the great world about whom the dramatists wrote. She had a new way of fingering a wine-glass, of exchanging an adieu, a new way of entering a door that told everything. To Uncle Pio nothing else mattered. What was there in the world more lovely than a beautiful woman doing justice to a Spanish masterpiece?—a performance (he asks you), packed with observation, in which the very spacing of the words revealed a comment on life and on the text—delivered by a beautiful voice—illustrated by a faultless carriage, considerable personal beauty and irresistible charm. "We are almost ready to take this marvel to Spain," he would murmur to himself. After the performance he would go around to her dressing-room and say "Very good!" But before taking his leave he would manage to ask her where, in the name of the eleven thousand virgins of Cologne, she had acquired that affected way of saying *Excelencia*.

After a time the Viceroy asked the Perichole whether it would amuse her to invite a few discreet guests to their midnight suppers, and he asked her whether she would like to meet the Archbishop. Camila was delighted. The Archbishop was delighted. On the eve of their first meeting he sent the actress an emerald pendant as big as a playing-card.

There was something in Lima that was wrapped up in yards of violet satin from which protruded a great dropsical head and two fat pearly hands; and that was its archbishop. Between the rolls of flesh that surrounded them looked out two black eyes speaking discomfort, kindliness and wit. A curious and eager soul was imprisoned in all this lard, but by dint of never refusing himself a pheasant or a goose or his daily procession of Roman wines, he was his own bitter jailer. He loved his cathedral; he loved his duties; he was very devout. Some days he regarded his bulk ruefully; but the distress of remorse was less poignant than the distress of fasting and he was presently found deliberating over the secret messages that a certain roast sends to the certain salad that will follow it. And to punish himself he led an exemplary life in every other respect.

He had read all the literature of antiquity and forgotten all about it except a general aroma of charm and disillusion. He had been learned in the Fathers and the Councils and forgotten all about them save a floating impression of dissensions that had no application to Peru. He had read all the libertine masterpieces of Italy and France and reread them annually; even in the torments of the stone (happily dissolved by drinking the water from the springs of Santa María de Cluxambuqua), he could find nothing more nourishing than the anecdotes of Brantôme and the divine Aretino.

The Archbishop knew that most of the priests of Peru were scoundrels. It required all his delicate Epicurean education to prevent his doing something about it; he had to repeat over to himself his favourite notions: that the injustice and unhappiness in the world is a constant; that the theory of progress is a delusion; that the poor, never having known happiness, are insensible to misfortune. Like all the rich he could not bring himself to believe that the poor (look at their houses, look at their clothes) could really suffer. Like all the cultivated he believed that only the widely-read could be said to *know* that they were unhappy. On one occasion, the iniquities in his see having been called to his notice, he almost did something about it. He had just heard that it was becoming a rule in Peru for priests to exact two measures of meal for a fairly good absolution, and five measures, for a really effective one. He trembled with indignation; he roared to his secretary and bidding him bring up his writing materials, announced that he was going to dictate an overwhelming message to his shepherds. But there was no ink left in the inkwell; there was no ink left in the next room; there was no ink to be found in the whole palace. This state of things in his household so upset the good man that he fell ill of the combined rages and learned to guard himself against indignations.

The addition of the Archbishop to the suppers was so successful that Don Andrés began to think of new names. He had grown increasingly dependent upon Uncle Pio, but waited until Camila should propose his inclusion of her own accord. And in due time Uncle Pio brought with him that courser of the seas, the Captain Alvarado. Generally the reunion had been several hours under way before Camila was able to join them after her performance at the theatre. She would arrive towards one o'clock, radiant and bejewelled and very tired. The four men received her as they would a great queen. For an hour or so she would carry the conversation, but gradually reclining more and more against Don Andrés' shoulder she would follow the talk as it flitted from one humorous lined face to the other. All night they talked, secretly comforting their hearts that longed always for Spain and telling themselves that such a symposium was after the manner of the high Spanish soul. They talked about ghosts and second-sight, and about the earth before man appeared upon it and about the possibility of the planets striking against one another; about whether the soul can be seen, like a dove, fluttering away at the moment of death; they wondered whether at the second coming of Christ to Jerusalem, Peru would be long in receiving the news. They talked until the sun rose, about wars and kings, about poets and scholars, and about strange countries. Each one poured into the conversation his store of wise sad anecdotes and his dry regret about the race of men. The flood of golden light struck across the Andes and entering the great window fell upon the piles of fruit, the stained brocade upon the table, and the sweet thoughtful forehead of the Perichole as she lay sleeping against the sleeve of her protector. There would ensue a long pause, no one wishing to make the first move to go, and the glances of them all would rest upon this strange beautiful bird who lived among them. But Uncle Pio's glance had been upon her all night, a quick glance from his black eyes, full of tenderness and anxiety, resting on the great secret and reason of his life.

But Uncle Pio never ceased watching Camila. He divided the inhabitants of this world into two groups, into those who had loved and those who had not. It was a horrible aristocracy, apparently, for those who had no capacity for love (or rather for suffering in love) could not be said to be alive and certainly would not live again after their death. They were a kind of straw population, filling the world with their meaningless laughter and tears and chatter and disappearing still lovable and vain into thin air. For this distinction he cultivated his own definition of love that was like no other and that had gathered all its bitterness and pride from his odd life. He regarded love as a sort of cruel malady through which the elect are required to pass in their late youth and from which they emerge, pale and wrung, but ready for the business of living. There was (he believed) a great repertory of errors mercifully impossible to human beings who had recovered from this illness. Unfortunately there remained to them a host of failings, but at least (from among many illustrations) they never mistook a protracted amiability for the whole conduct of life, they never again regarded any human being, from a prince to a servant, as a mechanical object. Uncle Pio never ceased watching Camila because it seemed to him that she had never undergone this initiation. In the months that followed her introduction to the Viceroy he held his breath and waited. He held his breath for years. Camila bore the Viceroy three children, yet remained the same. He knew that the first sign of her entrance into the true possession of the world would be the mastery of certain effects in her acting. There were certain passages in the plays that she would compass some day, simply, easily, and with secret joy, because they alluded to the new rich wisdom of her heart; but her treatment of such passages became more and more cursory, not to say embarrassed. He presently saw that she had tired of Don Andrés and had returned to a series of furtive love-affairs with the actors and matadors and merchants of the town.

She became more and more impatient of acting and another parasite found its way into her mind. She wanted to be a lady. She slowly contracted a greed for respectability and began to refer to her acting as a pastime. She acquired a duenna and some footmen and went to church at the fashionable hours. She attended the prize days at the University and appeared among the donors of the great charities. She even learned to read and write a little. Any faint discrimination against her as a bohemian she challenged with fury. She led the Viceroy a horrible life with her passion for concessions and her gradual usurpation of privileges. The new vice displaced the old and she became noisily virtuous. She invented some parents and produced some cousins. She obtained an undocumented legitimatization of her children. In society she cultivated a delicate and languid magdelinism, as a great lady might, and she carried a candle in the penitential parades, side by side with ladies who had nothing to regret but an outburst of temper and a furtive glance into Descartes. Her sin had been acting and everyone knows that there were even saints who had been actors,—there was Saint Gelasius and Saint Genesius and Saint Margaret of Antioch and Saint Pelagia.

There was a fashionable watering place in the hills not far from Santa María de Cluxambuqua. Don Andrés had travelled in France and had thought to build himself a little mock

Vichy; there was a pogoda, some drawing-rooms, a theatre, a little arena for bull-fights and some French gardens. Camila's health had never known a shadow, but she built herself a villa in the vicinity and sipped the hateful waters at eleven o'clock. The Marquesa de Montemayor has left a brilliant picture of this *opéra bouffe* paradise with the reigning divinity parading her fierce sensitiveness along the avenues of powdered shell and receiving the homage of all those who could not afford to offend the Viceroy. Doña María draws a portrait of this ruler, stately and weary, gambling all through the night in sums that would have raised another Escurial. And beside him she sets the portrait of his son, Camila's little Don Jaime. Don Jaime, at seven years, was a rachitic little body who seemed to have inherited not only his mother's forehead and eyes, but his father's liability to convulsions. He bore his pain with the silent bewilderment of an animal, and like an animal he was mortally ashamed when any evidences of it occurred in public. He was so beautiful that the more trivial forms of pity were hushed in his presence and his long thoughts about his difficulties had given his face a patient and startling dignity. His mother dressed him in garnet velvet, and when he was able he followed her about at a distance of several yards, extricating himself gravely from the ladies who tried to detain him in conversation. Camila was never cross to Don Jaime and she was never demonstrative. When the sun was shining the two could be seen walking along those artificial terraces in silence, Camila wondering when the felicity would begin that she had always associated with social position, Don Jaime rejoicing merely in the sunlight and anxiously estimating the approach of a cloud. They

looked like figures that had strayed there from some remote country, or out of an old ballad, that had not yet learned the new language and had not yet found any friends.

Camila was about thirty when she left the stage and it required five years for her to achieve her place in society. She gradually became almost stout, though her head seemed to grow more beautiful every year. She took to overdressing and the floors of the drawing-rooms reflected a veritable tower of jewels and scarves and plumes. Her face and hands were covered with a bluish powder against which she drew an irritable mouth in scarlet and orange. The almost distraught fury of her temper was varied by the unnatural sweetness of her address in the company of the dowagers. In the earliest stages of her progress upward she had intimated to Uncle Pio that he was not to be seen with her in public, but finally she became impatient even of his discreeter visits. She conducted the interviews with formality and evasion. Her eyes never crossed his and she angled for pretexts to quarrel with him. Still he ventured out once a month to try her patience and when the call had become impossible he would climb the stairs and finish the hour among her children.

One day he arrived at her villa in the hills and, through her maid, begged for an opportunity to talk with her. He was told that she would see him in the French gardens a little before sunset. He had come up from Lima on a strange sentimental impulse. Like all solitary persons he had invested friendship with a divine glamour: he imagined that the people he passed on the street, laughing together and embracing when they parted, the people who dined together with so many smiles,—you will

scarcely believe me, but he imagined that they were extracting from all that congeniality great store of satisfaction. So that suddenly he was filled with the excitement of seeing her again, of being called "Uncle Pio," and of reviving for a moment the trust and humour of their long vagabondage.

The French gardens were at the southern end of the town. Behind them rose the higher Andes and before them there was a parapet overlooking a deep valley and overlooking wave after wave of hills that stretched toward the Pacific. It was the hour when bats fly low and the smaller animals play recklessly underfoot. A few solitaries lingered about the gardens, gazing dreamily into the sky that was being gradually emptied of its colour, or leaned upon the balustrade and looked down into the valley, noting in which village a dog was barking. It was the hour when the father returns home from the fields and plays for a moment in the yard with the dog that jumps upon him, holding his muzzle closed or throwing him upon his back. The young girls look about for the first star to fix a wish upon it, and the boys grow restless for supper. Even the busiest mother stands for a moment idle-handed, smiling at her dear and exasperating family.

Uncle Pio stood against one of the chipped marble benches and watched Camila coming towards him:

"I am late," she said. "I am sorry. What is it you wish to say to me?"

"Camila,—" he began.

"My name is Doña Micaela."

"I do not wish to offend you, Doña Micaela, but when you let me call you Camila for twenty years, I should think——"

"Oh, do as you like. Do as you like."

"Camila, promise me that you will listen to me. Promise me that you will not run away at my first sentence."

At once she burst out with unexpected passion: "Uncle Pio, listen to me. You are mad if you think you can make me return to the theatre. I look back at the theatre with horror. Understand that. The theatre! The theatre, indeed! The daily payment of insults in that filthy place. Understand that you are wasting your time."

He answered gently: "I would not have you come back if you are happy with these new friends."

"You don't like my new friends, then?" she answered quickly. "Whom do you offer me in their stead?"

"Camila, I only remember . . ."

"I will not be criticized. I don't want any advice. It will be cold in a moment, I must go back to my house. Just give me up, that's all. Just put me out of your mind."

"Dear Camila, don't be angry. Let me talk to you. Just suffer me for ten minutes."

He did not understand why she was weeping. He did not know what to say. He talked at random: "You never even come to see the theatre, and they all notice it. The audiences are falling away now, too. They only put on the Old Comedy twice a week; all the other nights there are these new farces in prose. All is dull and childish and indecent. No one can speak Spanish any more. No one can even walk correctly any more. On Corpus Christi Day they gave *Belshazzar's Feast* where you were so wonderful. Now it was shameful."

There was a pause. A beautiful procession of clouds, like a flock of sheep, was straying up from the sea, slipping up the valleys between the hills. Camila suddenly touched his knee, and her face was like her face twenty years before: "Forgive me,

Uncle Pio, for being so bad. Jaime was ill this afternoon. There's nothing one can do. He lies there, so white and . . . so surprised. One must just think of other things. Uncle Pio, it would be no good if I went back to the theatre. The audiences come for the prose farces. We were foolish to try and keep alive the Old Comedy. Let people read the old plays in books if they choose to. It is not worth while fighting with the crowd."

"Wonderful Camila, I was not just to you when you were on the stage. It was some foolish pride in me. I grudged you the praise that you deserved. Forgive me. You have always been a very great artist. If you come to see that you are not happy among these people you might think about going to Madrid. You would have a great triumph there. You are still young and beautiful. There will be time later to be called Doña Micaela. We shall be old soon. We shall be dead soon."

"No, I shall never see Spain. All the world is alike, Madrid or Lima."

"Oh, if we could go away to some island where the people would know you for yourself. And love you."

"You are fifty years old and you are still dreaming of such islands, Uncle Pio."

He bent his head and mumbled: "Of course I love you, Camila, as I always must and more than I can say. To have known you is enough for my whole life. You are a great lady now. And you are rich. There is no longer any way that I can help you. But I am always ready."

"How absurd you are," she said smiling. "You said that as boys say it. You don't seem to learn as you grow older, Uncle Pio. There is no such thing as that kind of love and that kind of island. It's in the theatre you find such things."

He looked shamefaced, but unconvinced.

At last she rose and said sadly: "What are we talking about! It is growing cold. I must be going in. You must be resigned. I have no heart for the theatre." There was a pause. "And for the rest? . . . Oh, I do not understand. It is just circumstance. I must be what I must. Do not try to understand either. Don't think about me, Uncle Pio. Just forgive, that's all. Just try to forgive."

She stood still a moment, searching for something deeply felt to say to him. The first cloud reached the terrace; it was dark; the last stragglers were leaving the gardens. She was thinking of Don Jaime, and of Don Andrés and of himself. She could not find the words. Suddenly she bent down and kissed his fingers and went quickly away. But he sat for a long time in the gathering clouds trembling with happiness and trying to penetrate into the meaning of these things.

Suddenly the news was all over Lima. Doña Micaela Villegas, the lady that used to be Camila the Perichole, had the small-pox. Several hundred other persons had the small-pox also, but popular interest and malignity were concentrated upon the actress. A wild hope ran about the town that the beauty would be impaired that had enabled her to despise the class from which she sprang. The news escaped from the sick-room that Camila had become ludicrous in homeliness and the cup of the envious overflowed. As soon as she was able she had herself carried from the city to her villa in the hills; she ordered the sale of her elegant little palace. She returned her jewels to their givers and she sold her fine clothes. The Viceroy, the Archbishop, and the few men at court who had been her sincerest admirers besieged her door still with

messages and gifts; the messages were ignored and the gifts were returned without comment. No one but her nurse and maids had been permitted to see her since the commencement of her illness. As an answer to his repeated attempts Don Andrés received a large sum of money from her with a letter compounded of all that is possible in bitterness and pride.

Like all beautiful women who have been brought up amid continual tributes to their beauty she assumed without cynicism that it must necessarily be the basis of anyone's attachment to herself; henceforth any attention paid to her must spring from a pity full of condescension and faintly perfumed with satisfaction at so complete a reversal. This assumption that she need look for no more devotion now that her beauty had passed proceeded from the fact that she had never realized any love save love as passion. Such love, though it expends itself in generosity and thoughtfulness, though it give birth to visions and to great poetry, remains among the sharpest expressions of self-interest. Not until it has passed through a long servitude, through its own self-hatred, through mockery, through great doubts, can it take its place among the loyalties. Many who have spent a lifetime in it can tell us less of love than the child that lost a dog yesterday. As her friends continued in their efforts to draw her again into society she grew more and more angry and dispatched insulting messages to the city. It was said for a time that she was retiring into religion. But new rumours that all was fury and despair on the little farm, contradicted the old. For those near to her the despair was fearful to behold. She was convinced that her life was over, her life and her children's. In her hysterical pride she had given back more than she owed and the approach of poverty was added to the loneliness and the gloom of her future. There was nothing left for her to do but to draw out her days in jealous solitude in the center of the little farm that was falling into decay. She brooded for hours upon the joy of her enemies and could be heard striding about her room with strange cries.

Uncle Pio did not allow himself to be discouraged. By dint of making himself useful to the children, by taking a hand in the management of the farm and by discreetly lending her some money he obtained his entrance into the house and even into the presence of its veiled mistress. But even then Camila, convinced in her pride that he *pitied* her, lashed him with the blade of her tongue and derived some strange comfort from heaping him with sneers. He loved her the more, understanding better than she did herself all the stages in the convalescence of her humiliated spirit. But one day an accident befell that lost him his share in her progress. He pushed open a door.

She thought she had locked it. For just one hour a foolish secret hope had come to her; she wondered whether she could make a paste of chalk and cream to spread upon her face. She who had sneered so often at the befloured grandmothers of the court wondered for a few moments whether she had learned anything on the stage that would aid her now. She thought she had locked the door and with hurried hands and beating heart she laid on the coat, the grotesque pallor, and as she gazed into the mirror and recognized the futility of her attempt she caught the image of Uncle Pio standing in the door amazed. She rose from the chair with a cry and covered her face with her hands.

"Go away. Go away out of my house forever," she screamed. "I never want to see you again." In her shame

she drove him out with blasphemy and hatred, she pursued him down the corridor and hurled objects down the stairs. She gave her farmer orders that Uncle Pio was forbidden to come into the grounds. But he continued for a week trying to see her again. At last he went back to Lima; he filled in the time as best he could, but he longed to be by her as a boy of eighteen would long. At last he devised a stratagem and returned up into the hills to put it into effect.

One morning before dawn he arose and lay on the ground below her window. He imitated in the darkness the sound of weeping, and, as nearly as he could, of a young girl's weeping. He continued in this for the whole quarter of an hour. He did not let his voice rise above that degree of loudness which Italian musicians would represent by the direction *piano,* but he frequently intermitted the sound trusting that if she were asleep it would insinuate itself into her mind as well by duration as by degree. The air was cool and agreeable. The first faint streak of sapphire was appearing behind the peaks and in the east the star of morning was pulsating every moment with a more tender intention. A profound silence wrapped all the farm buildings, only an occasional breeze set all the grasses sighing. Suddenly a lamp was lit in her room and a moment later the shutter was thrown back and a head wrapped in veils leaned far out.

"Who is there?" asked the beautiful voice.

Uncle Pio remained silent.

Camila said again in a tone edged with impatience:

"Who is there? Who is there weeping?"

"Doña Micaela, my lady, I beg of you to come here to me."

"Who are you and what do you want?"

"I am a poor girl. I am Estrella. I beg of you to come and help me. Do not call your maid. I pray you, Doña Micaela, to come yourself."

Camila was silent a moment, then said abruptly: "Very well," and closed the shutter. Presently she appeared around the corner of the house. She wore a thick cloak that dragged in the dew. She stood at a distance and said: "Come over here to where I am standing,—Who are you?"

Uncle Pio rose up. "Camila, it is I,—Uncle Pio. Forgive me, but I must speak to you."

"Mother of God, when shall I be free of this dreadful person! Understand: I want to see no one. I don't want to speak to a soul. My life is over. That is all."

"Camila, by our long life together, I beg of you to grant me one thing. I shall go away and never trouble you again."

"I grant you nothing, nothing. Stay away from me."

"I promise you I shall never trouble you again if you listen to me this once." She was hurrying around to the door on the other side of the house and Uncle Pio was obliged to run beside her to make sure that she heard what he was saying. She stopped:

"What is it then? Hurry. It is cold. I am not well. I must go back to my room."

"Camila, let me take Don Jaime for a year to live with me in Lima. Let me be his teacher. Let me teach him the Castilian. Here he is left among the servants. He is learning nothing."

"No."

"Camila, what will become of him? He has a good mind and he wants to learn."

"He is sick. He is delicate. Your house is a sty. Only the country is good for him."

"But he has been much better these last few months. I promise you I shall

clean out my house. I shall apply to Madre María del Pilar for a house-keeper. Here he is in your stables all day. I shall teach him all that a gentleman should know,—fencing and Latin and music. We shall read all. . . ."

"A mother cannot be separated from her child like that. It is impossible. You are crazy to have thought of it. Give up thinking of me and of everything about me. I no longer exist. I and my children will get on as best we can. Do not try to disturb me again. I do not want to see any human being."

Now it was that Uncle Pio felt obliged to use a hard measure. "Then pay me the money that you owe me," he said.

Camila stood still, confounded. To herself she said: "Life is too fearful to bear. When may I die?" After a moment she answered him, in a hoarse voice: "I have very little money. I will pay you what I can. I will pay you now. I have a few jewels here. Then we need never see one another again." She was ashamed of her poverty. She took a few steps, then turned and said: "Now I see that you are a very hard man. But it is right that I pay you what I owe you."

"No, Camila, I only said that to enforce my request. I shall take no money from you. But lend me Don Jaime for one year. I shall love him and take every care of him. Did I harm you? Was I a bad teacher to you in those other years?"

"It is cruel of you to keep urging gratitude, gratitude, gratitude. I was grateful,—good, good! but now that I am no longer the same woman there remains nothing to be grateful for." There was a silence. Her eyes were resting on the star that seemed to be leading forth the whole sky in its wonder. A great pain lay at her heart, the pain of a world that was meaningless. Then she said: "If Jaime wishes to go with you, very well. I shall talk to him in the morning. If he wishes to go with you, you will find him at the Inn about noon. Good night. Go with God."

"Go with God."

She returned to the house. The next day the grave little boy appeared at the Inn. His fine clothes were torn and stained now and he carried a small bundle for change. His mother had given him a gold piece for spending-money and a little stone that shone in the dark to look at in his sleepless nights. They set off together in a cart, but soon Uncle Pio became aware that the jolting was not good for the boy. He carried him on his shoulder. As they drew near to the bridge of San Luis Rey, Jaime tried to conceal his shame for he knew that one of those moments was coming that separated him from other people. He was especially ashamed because Uncle Pio had just overtaken a friend of his, a sea-captain. And just as they got to the bridge he spoke to an old lady who was travelling with a little girl. Uncle Pio said that when they had crossed the bridge they would sit down and rest, but it turned out not to be necessary.

PART FIVE: PERHAPS AN INTENTION

A new bridge of stone has been built in the place of the old, but the event has not been forgotten. It has passed into proverbial expressions. "I

may see you Tuesday," says a Limean, "unless the bridge falls." "My cousin lives by the bridge of San Luis Rey," says another, and a smile goes around the company, for that also means: under the sword of Damocles. There are some poems about the accident, classics to be found in every Peruvian anthology, but the real literary monument is Brother Juniper's book.

There are a hundred ways of wondering at circumstance. Brother Juniper would never have arrived at his method had it not been for his friendship with a certain master in the University of San Martín. This student's wife had stolen away one morning on a boat for Spain, following a soldier, and had left him the care of two daughters in their cradle. He was possessed of all the bitterness that Brother Juniper lacked and de-

but ineffectual. Now she lies in the splendor of Monreale, and a few inches above her heart may be read the words: *I shall fear no evil.*

It was by dint of hearing a great many such sneers at faith that Brother Juniper became convinced that the world's time had come for proof, tabulated proof, of the conviction that was so bright and exciting within him. When the pestilence visited his dear village of Puerto and carried off a large number of peasants, he secretly drew up a diagram of the characteristics of fifteen victims and fifteen survivors, the statistics of their value *sub specie aeternitatis.* Each soul was rated upon a basis of ten as regards its goodness, its diligence in religious observance, and its importance to its family group. Here is a fragment of this ambitious chart:

	Goodness	Piety	Usefulness
Alfonso G.	4	4	10
Nina	2	5	10
Manuel B.	10	10	0
Alfonso V.	−8	−10	10
Vera N.	0	10	10

rived a sort of joy from the conviction that all was wrong in the world. He whispered into the Franciscan's ear such thoughts and anecdotes as belied the notion of a guided world. For a moment a look of distress, almost of defeat, would come into the Brother's eyes; then he would begin patiently explaining why such stories held no difficulty for a believer. "There was a queen of Naples and Sicily," the student would say, "who discovered that she was carrying an angry tumor in her side. In great dismay she commanded her subjects to fall to their prayers and ordered that all the garments in Sicily and Naples be sewn with votive crosses. She was well loved by her people and all their prayers and embroideries were sincere,

The thing was more difficult than he had foreseen. Almost every soul in a difficult frontier community turned out to be indispensable economically, and the third column was all but useless. The examiner was driven to the use of minus terms when he confronted the personal character of Alfonso V., who was not, like Vera N., merely bad: he was a propagandist for badness and not merely avoided church but led others to avoid it. Vera N. was indeed bad, but she was a model worshipper and the mainstay of a full hut. From all this saddening data Brother Juniper contrived an index for each peasant. He added up the total for victims and compared it with the total for survivors, to discover that the dead were

five times more worth saving. It almost looked as though the pestilence had been directed against the really valuable people in the village of Puerto. And on that afternoon Brother Juniper took a walk along the edge of the Pacific. He tore up his findings and cast them into the waves; he gazed for an hour upon the great clouds of pearl that hang forever upon the horizon of that sea, and extracted from their beauty a resignation that he did not permit his reason to examine. The discrepancy between faith and the facts is greater than is generally assumed.

But there was another story of the master of San Martín (not so subversive, this one) that probably gave to Brother Juniper the hint for his procedure after the fall of the bridge of San Luis Rey.

This master was one day walking through the Cathedral of Lima and stopped to read the epitaph of a lady. He read with an increasingly prominent lower lip that she had been for twenty years the centre and joy of her home, that she had been the delight of her friends, that all who met her went away in astonishment at her goodness and beauty, and that there she lay awaiting the return of her Lord. Now on the day that he read these words, the master of San Martín had had much to fret him, and raising his eyes from the tablet he spoke aloud in his rage: "The shame of it, the persecution of it! Everyone knows that in the world we do nothing but feed our wills. Why perpetuate this legend of selflessness? Why keep this thing alive, this rumour of disinterestedness?"

And so saying he resolved to expose this conspiracy of the stone-cutters. The lady had been dead only twelve years. He sought out her servants, her children and her friends.

And everywhere he went, like a perfume, her dear traits had survived her and wherever she was mentioned there arose a suffering smile and the protest that words could not describe the gracious ways of her. Even the eager youth of her grandchildren, who had never seen her, was made more difficult by the news that it was possible to be as good as that. And the man stood amazed; only at last he muttered: "Nevertheless, what I said was true. This woman was an exception, perhaps an exception."

In compiling his book about these people Brother Juniper seemed to be pursued by the fear that in omitting the slightest detail he might lose some guiding hint. The longer he worked the more he felt that he was stumbling about among great dim intimations. He was forever being cheated by details that looked as though they were significant if only he could find their setting. So he put everything down on the notion perhaps that if he (or a keener head) reread the book twenty times, the countless facts would suddenly start to move, to assemble, and to betray their secret. The Marquesa de Montemayor's cook told him that she lived almost entirely on rice, fish and a little fruit and Brother Juniper put it down on the chance that it would some day reveal a spiritual trait. Don Rubío said of her that she used to appear at his receptions without invitation in order to steal the spoons. A midwife on the edge of the town declared that Doña María called upon her with morbid questions until she had been obliged to order her away from the door like a beggar. The bookseller of the town reported that she was one of the three most cultivated persons in Lima. Her farmer's wife declared that she was absent-minded, but compact of goodness. The art of biography

is more difficult than is generally supposed.

Brother Juniper found that there was least to be learned from those who had been most closely associated with the subjects of his inquiry. Madre María del Pilar talked to him at length about Pepita, but she did not tell him of her own ambitions for her. The Perichole was at first difficult of approach, but presently even liked the Franciscan. Her characterization of Uncle Pio flatly contradicted the stores of unsavory testimonies that he had acquired elsewhere. Her allusions to her son were few and conceded with pain. They closed the interview abruptly. The Captain Alvarado told what he could of Esteban and of Uncle Pio. Those who know most in this realm, venture least.

I shall spare you Brother Juniper's generalizations. They are always with us. He thought he saw in the same accident, the wicked visited by destruction and the good called early to Heaven. He thought he saw pride and wealth confounded as an object lesson to the world, and he thought he saw humility crowned and rewarded for the edification of the city. But Brother Juniper was not satisfied with his reasons. It was just possible that the Marquesa de Montemayor was not a monster of avarice, and Uncle Pio of self-indulgence.

The book being done fell under the eyes of some judges and was suddenly pronounced heretical. It was ordered to be burned in the Square with its author. Brother Juniper submitted to the decision that the devil had made use of him to effect a brilliant campaign in Peru. He sat in his cell that last night trying to seek in his own life the pattern that had escaped him in five others. He was not rebellious. He was willing to lay down his life

for the purity of the church, but he longed for one voice somewhere to testify for him that his intention, at least, had been for faith; he thought there was no one in the world who believed him. But the next morning in all that crowd and sunlight there were many who believed, for he was much loved.

There was a little delegation from the village of Puerto, and Nina (Goodness 2, Piety 5, Usefulness 10) and others stood with drawn puzzled faces while their little friar was given to the congenial flames. Even then, even then, there remained in his heart an obstinate nerve insisting that at least St. Francis would not utterly have condemned him, and (not daring to call upon a greater name, since he seemed so open to error in these matters) he called twice upon St. Francis and leaning upon a flame he smiled and died.

* * *

The day of the service was clear and warm. The Limeans, their black eyes wide with awe, poured through the streets into their Cathedral and stood gazing at the mound of black velvet and silver. The Archbishop enclosed in his wonderful and almost wooden vestments perspired upon his throne, lending from time to time a connoisseur's ear to the felicities of Vittoria's counterpoint. The choir had restudied the pages that, as his farewell to music, Tomás Luis had composed for his friend and patron, the Empress of Austria, and all that grief and sweetness, all that Spanish realism filtering through an Italian mode, rose and fell above the sea of mantillas. Don Andrés, under the colours and feathered hangings of his office, knelt, ill and troubled. He knew that the crowd was furtively glancing at him, expecting him to play the father

who has lost his only son. He wondered whether the Perichole was present. He had never been obliged to go so long without smoking. The Captain Alvarado pushed in from the sunny square for a moment. He looked across the fields of black hair and lace at the trooping of the candles and the ropes of incense. "How false, how unreal," he said and pushed his way out. He descended to the sea and sat on the edge of his boat, gazing down into the clear water. "Happy are the drowned, Esteban," he said.

Behind the screen the Abbess sat among her girls. The night before she had torn an idol from her heart and the experience had left her pale but firm. She had accepted the fact that it was of no importance whether her work went on or not; it was enough to work. She was the nurse who tends the sick who never recover; she was the priest who perpetually renews the office before an altar to which no worshippers come. There would be no Pepita to enlarge her work; it would relapse into the indolence and the indifference of her colleagues. It seemed to be sufficient for Heaven that for a while in Peru a disinterested love had flowered and faded. She leaned her forehead upon her hand, following the long tender curve that the soprano lifts in the Kyrie. "My affection should have had more of that colour, Pepita. My whole life should have had more of that quality. I have been too busy," she added ruefully and her mind drifted into prayer.

Camila had started from the farm to attend the service. Her heart was filled with consternation and amazement. Here was another comment from the skies; that was the third time she had been spoken to. Her small-pox, Jaime's illness, and now the fall of the bridge,—oh, these were not accidents. She was as ashamed as though letters had appeared on her forehead. An order from the Palace announced that the Viceroy was sending her two daughters to a convent-school in Spain. That was right. She was alone. She gathered a few things together mechanically and started to the city for the Service. But she fell to thinking of the crowds gaping over her Uncle Pio and over her son; she thought of the vast ritual of the church, like a chasm into which the beloved falls, and of the storm of the *dies irae* where the individual is lost among the millions of the dead, features grow dim and traits fade. At a little more than half the journey, at the mud church of San Luis Rey she slipped in and knelt against a pillar to rest. She wandered through her memory, searching for the faces of her two. She waited for some emotion to appear. "But I feel nothing," she whispered to herself. "I have no heart. I am a poor meaningless woman, that's all. I am shut out. I have no heart. Look, I won't try and think of anything; let me just rest here." And scarcely had she paused when again that terrible incommunicable pain swept through her, the pain that could not speak once to Uncle Pio and tell him of her love and just once offer her courage to Jaime in his sufferings. She started up wildly: "I fail everybody," she cried. "They love me and I fail them." She returned to the farm and carried for a year the mood of her self-despair. One day she heard by accident that the wonderful Abbess had lost two persons whom she loved in the same accident. Her sewing fell from her hand: then *she* would know, she would explain. "But no, what would she say to me! She would not even believe that such a person as I could love or could lose." Camila decided to go to Lima and

look at the Abbess from a distance. "If her face tells me that she would not despise me, I will speak to her," she said.

Camila lurked about the convent church and fell humbly in love with the homely old face, though it frightened her a little. At last she called upon her.

"Mother," she said, "I . . . I . . ."

"Do I know you, my daughter?"

"I was the actress, I was the Perichole."

"Oh, yes. Oh, I have wished to know you for a long while, but they told me you did not wish to be seen. You too, I know, lost in the fall of the bridge of San. . . ."

Camila rose and swayed. There! again that access of pain, the hands of the dead she could not reach. Her lips were white. Her head brushed the Abbess's knee: "Mother, what shall I do? I am all alone. I have nothing in the world. I love them. What shall I do?"

The Abbess looked at her closely. "My daughter, it is warm here. Let us go into the garden. You can rest there." She made a sign to a girl in the cloister to bring some water. She continued talking mechanically to Camila. "I have wished to know you for a long while, señora. Even before the accident I had wished much to know you. They told me that in the *autos sacramentales* you were a very great and beautiful actress, in *Belshazzar's Feast*."

"Oh, Mother, you must not say that. I am a sinner. You must not say that."

"Here, drink this, my child. We have a beautiful garden, do you not think so? You will come and see us often and some day you will meet Sister Juana who is our gardener-in-chief. Before she entered religion she had almost never seen a garden, for

she worked in the mines high up in the mountains. Now everything grows under her hand.—A year has gone by, señora, since our accident. I lost two who had been children in my orphanage, but you lost a real child of your own?"

"Yes, Mother."

"And a great friend?"

"Yes, Mother."

"Tell me. . . ."

And then the whole tide of Camila's long despair, her lonely obstinate despair since her girlhood, found its rest on that dusty friendly lap among Sister Juana's fountains and roses.

* * *

But where are sufficient books to contain the events that would not have been the same without the fall of the bridge? From such a number I choose one more.

"The Condesa d'Abuirre wishes to see you," said a lay-sister at the door of the Abbess's office.

"Well," said the Abbess, laying down her pen, "who is she?"

"She has just come from Spain. I don't know."

"Oh, it is some money, Inez, some money for my house for the blind. Quick, bid her come in."

The tall, rather languorous beauty entered the room. Doña Clara, who was generally so adequate, seemed constrained for once. "Are you busy, dear Mother, may I talk to you for a while?"

"I am quite free, my daughter. You will excuse an old woman's memory; have I known you before?"

"My mother was the Marquesa de Montemayor. . . ." Doña Clara suspected that the Abbess had not admired her mother and would not let the older woman speak until she herself had made a long passionate de-

fense of Doña María. The languor fell away in her self-reproach. At last the Abbess told her of Pepita and Esteban, and of Camila's visit. "All, all of us have failed. One wishes to be punished. One is willing to assume all kinds of penance, but do you know, my daughter, that in love—I scarcely dare say it—but in love our very mistakes don't seem to be able to last long?"

The Condesa showed the Abbess Doña María's last letter. Madre María dared not say aloud how great her astonishment was that such words (words that since then the whole world has murmured over with joy) could spring in the heart of Pepita's mistress. "Now learn," she commanded herself, "learn at last that anywhere you may expect grace." And she was filled with happiness like a girl at this new proof that the traits she lived for were everywhere, that the world was ready. "Will you do me a kindness, my daughter? Will you let me show you my work?"

The sun had gone down, but the Abbess led the way with a lantern down corridor after corridor. Doña Clara saw the old and the young, the sick and the blind, but most of all she saw the tired, bright old woman who was leading her. The Abbess would stop in a passageway and say suddenly: "I can't help thinking that something could be done for the deaf-and-dumb. It seems to me that some patient person could, . . . could study out a language for them. You know there are hundreds and hundreds in Peru. Do you remember whether anyone in Spain has found a way for them? Well, some day they will." Or a little later: "Do you know, I keep thinking that something can be done for the insane. I am old, you know, and I cannot go where these things are talked about, but I watch

them sometimes and it seems to me . . . In Spain, now, they are gentle with them? It seems to me that there is a secret about it, just hidden from us, just around the corner. Some day back in Spain, if you hear of anything that would help us, you will write me a letter . . . if you are not too busy?"

At last after Doña Clara had seen even the kitchens, the Abbess said: "Now will you excuse me, for I must go into the room of the very sick and say a few words for them to think about when they cannot sleep. I will not ask you to come with me there, for you are not accustomed to such . . . such sounds and things. And besides I only talk to them as one talks to children." She looked up at her with her modest rueful smile. Suddenly she disappeared a moment to return with one of her helpers, one who had likewise been involved in the affair of the bridge and who had formerly been an actress. "She is leaving me," said the Abbess, "for some work across the city and when I have spoken here I must leave you both, for the flour-broker will not wait for me any longer, and our argument will take a long time."

But Doña Clara stood in the door as the Abbess talked to them, the lamp placed on the floor beside her. Madre María stood with her back against a post; the sick lay in rows gazing at the ceiling and trying to hold their breaths. She talked that night of all those out in the dark (she was thinking of Esteban alone, she was thinking of Pepita alone) who had no one to turn to, for whom the world perhaps was more than difficult, without meaning. And those who lay in their beds there felt that they were within a wall that the Abbess had built for them; within all was light and warmth, and without was the

darkness they would not exchange even for a relief from pain and from dying. But even while she was talking, other thoughts were passing in the back of her mind. "Even now," she thought, "almost no one remembers Esteban and Pepita, but myself. Camila alone remembers her Uncle Pio and her son; this woman, her mother. But soon we shall die and all memory of those five will have left the earth, and we ourselves shall be loved for a while and forgotten. But the love will have been enough; all those impulses of love return to the love that made them. Even memory is not necessary for love. There is a land of the living and a land of the dead and the bridge is love, the only survival, the only meaning."

BASQUERIE

ELEANOR MERCEIN KELLY

I

Emily found Biarritz, now that the season was over, something of a bore; but they lingered on, partly because the rates were so much lower, and partly because her stepmother, Suzanne, seemed to be finishing up a little affair with the director. Emily shrugged at the thought. Duval was presentable enough, thanks to his opportunities; and of course Suzanne at her age had to take her men as she could get them; but really, a hotel director— Surely one might fly one's kite a little higher than that.

Some weeks earlier the beach, even at this early hour—that charming intimate curve of beach, like the dress circle of a theater—would have been brilliant with striped bathing tents, vivid great parasols, gayly dressed and undressed ladies of the three worlds: great, lesser, and half. Emily wondered in which of these she and Suzanne were usually classed by the onlookers. But what did they matter, the onlookers? There was still a yacht or two about. Emily had noticed a very nice one, Spanish probably, docked in the lower town, but the owners did not come to the casino, or Emily would have met them. Duval was very useful in that way. Nobody of any importance was stopping at the hotel, merely a few domestic parties, of the onlooker class.

Emily yawned. She seemed, in her shapeless little-girl frock, with the pale waves of hair cropped close to her pretty head, very young and frail, her skin of that delicate magnolia pallor which is thick enough never to burn or freckle. . . .

Flowerlike every feature
As if one's breath would fray the lily
of a creature.

And, indeed, a good deal of breath had been wasted in the effort here and there. Emily owed her unfrayed lilyhood, and also the fact that her exquisite, fragile little body was as muscular and active as that of a cat, to the dying counsels of her father— his best and practically his only legacy to her.

"The contours, my pet, are essential," Mr. Weldon had adjured her. "To keep really fit, exercise is advisable—swimming, riding, skiing, tennis, whatever is the *jeu* of the place, that you must do well; but not too well. Sports are as helpful in making ac-

quaintance as a good dog, or going to the English church. Bridge, too, but in moderation, my pet; otherwise it is bad for the expression. And, of course, you will not be seen at the tables"—he meant the sort in casinos—"until after you are thirty. By that time you will have married, so it will not matter what you do. But it is wretched form to appear sporting before thirty.

"With regard to marriage," went on this very experienced gentleman, "my advice to you is the same as in golf: Keep your eye on the ball. Remember that a prince, Oriental or Slavic, is the equivalent of a duke, Continental; of a baronet, English; and of a millionaire, American. No matter what distractions offer, no matter what temptations arise—and there will be temptations, or you are not my daughter—keep your eye on the ball."

She was his daughter, and she had done so. Poor dear papa! He, too, had known the difficulties which beset the path of a wandering beauty in Europe, none better; and he had done his best for her. Since he found himself unable to leave his daughter a suitable income, he had made what amend was possible; he had left her a stepmother who had one, and who could furnish as well the necessary background of chaperonage. Not that Suzanne as a background was all that could be desired, perhaps; but one did what one could. She was at least of an amiable and generous nature.

"I think," said the girl to herself, "that I shall go out into the Bay of Biscay and think things over." She always did her best thinking in the bathtub.

Since nobody was about to stare except a few natives, she did not bother to shroud her slim loveliness in a beach wrap, but ran out on to the nearer of the two little pine-clad promontories which jut out into the water

and took a neat header. Then she turned over on her back and let the Atlantic playfully slap at her face and tug at her with its undertow, while she thought.

There was a good deal to think about; for example, young Prince Abdul—only an Egyptian, to be sure, and almost dark enough to be doubtful; it was hard to shed one's American prejudices. But she loved his yacht and his string of polo ponies, and he adored her silvery blondness; and the dot was certainly no object. What had happened to put him off? Had she seemed too cool? And old Sir Harry Congers, correct, substantial as his appearance; he had been on the very point of speaking to mamma—as Suzanne became on occasion—when something had called him away from Biarritz. He had left a bushel or so of roses and a very pretty bracelet, but he had not returned. Why? Had she been too approachable?

There were moments when Emily confessed to a slight inward panic. Nearing thirty and nothing in sight! Was she never to have done with this roving from pillar to post, this robbing Peter, as it were, to keep from paying Paul? Could the trouble be Suzanne?

Poor dear papa, she had to admit, had rather overreached himself when he married that lady. If he could only have postponed his demise a little longer, until his child was safely settled in a suitable walk of life! An unattached father can do so much more for a girl than she can do for herself.

A wave slapped her suddenly too hard to be pleasant, and she saw that she was in danger of being swept against the boiling rocks, where a man had recently, at a high tide like this, been pounded to a jelly. She exerted

herself and got out of the caldron, but the effort left her tired. She thought she would land on the farther rocks, where the slope was gradual. But after a few moments she saw that she could not make it, and glanced over her shoulder to call the coast-guard boat which usually waited near that dangerous point. But the season was over; a frugal municipal government had withdrawn the boat.

"Well, well!" said Emily aloud. "Here I am in the Bay of Biscay with nobody to rely on but myself." Not, however, an unusual situation for her.

She struggled a little and swallowed water. "If I don't make it," she thought, "they'll find me in the surf in a very messy condition, and the newspapers will have headlines—The Beautiful Miss Weldon of Kentucky Drowned at Fashionable Biarritz— why must beauties always be from Kentucky or from Baltimore?—and Suzanne will have a chance to wear mourning again; which would suit her very well; so why struggle?"

She was roused from these macabre reflections by a voice which spoke to her out of the deep: "If mademoiselle will put her hand on my shoulder, please—" So a coast guard had been watching after all.

She lay in a cove on the rock island, resting, a little sick from the salt water she had swallowed, glad of the sun that beat down upon her in that sheltered place. She wished she had more clothes on; the tide breeze was chilly, and after all, coast guards are men. But this one stood with his back to her, as far away as he could get; if the rock had been larger he would have been farther. It got smaller as the tide rose. She smiled to realize that. He was a handsome fellow, young, with straight black hair, high cheek bones, deep-set eyes; not a Spanish type, nor yet quite

French. Emily looked him over appreciatively before she spoke.

"Thank you so much for saving me from a watery grave."

"It is nothing—mademoiselle, I mean, was still swimming quite strongly. I was not necessary."

"Oh, but you were! I was about to give up swimming. I wonder," she murmured idly, "if your name happens to be Neptune?"

"No, mademoiselle. My name is Esteban."

Still he would not look at her. She saw with amusement that he was embarrassed rather than intrigued by her appearance. Evidently this was no Frenchman.

"Neptune and siren alone on rock," she murmured, imagining the picture; and saw his cheek twitch a little as if he understood. "You need not wait, thank you," she added pleasantly.

"Mademoiselle has been good enough to say I was necessary—"

"Not now," she replied. "I shall not commit suicide today. You must remember your duties. There may be other discouraged swimmers about."

He hesitated, and then said quietly, "Mademoiselle is mistaken in thinking me a coast guard. I was watching —only for mademoiselle."

"Oh!" It was her turn to be embarrassed. She looked at him more closely. There was something vaguely familiar in his appearance. The smooth skin, brown as an Indian's, tattoo marks on the chest like a sailor's, a fine athlete's figure—also, despite the shyness, his air of quiet confidence. It was difficult, she reflected, to be sure of a gentleman without his clothes on. Her rescuer wore only a scant swimming suit.

"I beg your pardon," she murmured. "You say you were watching for me?"

He replied surprisingly, with a sort

of controlled fervor, "I have been watching for mademoiselle ever since the first moment I saw her."

She bit her lip. "Really? You are not stopping at our hotel, I think?"

He shook his head. There were other hotels near by, of course; there was that yacht in the lower town. "I am native here," he said.

Emily regretted her apology. Her hand lifted haughtily. For a native he had been impertinent. But for all she knew there might be native gentlemen.

"You mean you are Basque?"

"Yes, mademoiselle, Basque."

"But you speak English remarkably well."

He said quietly, "To one who speaks the Euskara, no language is impossible; in that we are like Russians. But I have been in England; also in America."

"In the United States?"

"In both Americas. Basques are a seafaring people."

"You are a sailor, you mean? A fisherman, perhaps?" She had heard of Basque whalers off Newfoundland.

"Both, mademoiselle; and other things."

Suddenly she knew where she had seen him; down in the lower town, working over a boat on the stocks, barefoot, his trousers rolled to the knee. She had realized for the first time how becoming the Basque costume was to a handsome man, the close-fitting béret worn over one ear, the wide red sash. She remembered, too, that the man had looked at her as he was doing now, with grave shy glances which turned away when they met hers. Emily was expert in such matters; she knew there was nothing to resent or fear in admiration such as this, no matter from whom it came. She decided to play Cophetua, as it were, to his beggar maid.

"Sit down here beside me," she said kindly—"you will have to soon, anyway, if this rock gets any smaller—and tell me about Basques. It is so strange to be living among a people of whom one knows nothing, whose life goes on independently of us, as if we were not here."

"It has been going on independently of you for thirty centuries," he remarked quietly. "You find it strange to see a people deeply rooted as a forest; while we find it strange to see a people who wander about in families, like the Arabs, but without the Arab's tents, living in hotels, railway cars, other people's houses—"

Emily found herself somewhat on the defensive. "But the Basques are wanderers too; you said so yourself. Sailors and fishermen—"

"—and smugglers and at one time pirates," he finished for her. "Yes, mademoiselle; but with this difference: Basques return. The *etcheonda* is our home, our abiding place, no matter from how far we come to it."

"The *etcheonda?*"

"In Germany it is called the *Stammhaus;* in America—it is not called at all." He smiled gravely. "The *etcheonda* is the home to which one of our families belongs from generation to generation; where all the sons may bring their wives to live when they are done with roving; to whose shelter every member of the family has his right, and to which all pay tribute."

"No," said Emily thoughtfully, "in America it is not 'called at all,' because it does not exist. With most of us the nearest approach to an *etcheonda* would be an apartment building, changed every few years. Which is perhaps why we do so much family wandering."

"Doubtless, mademoiselle," he agreed.

Emily found the fellow oddly

stimulating, intelligent; even humorous in a grave, simple way. And he was right. Roots—was not that what they needed, people like her and her father; what they desperately wanted and somehow could never find? They had torn themselves loose from their own foothold, the place where they belonged; yet where was that place? Certainly not an ugly prairie town near Chicago, where she had happened to be born! Again the slight panic came over her. Nearing thirty and no haven in sight; youth gone, beauty going, her charm acquiring a rather professional edge. She pulled herself together with a shiver. What nonsense! Her beauty going, when she could see the reflection of it in the eyes of every man she met—even this enamored native?

"I wonder why you have been watching for me," she murmured. It was playing with fire, of course, but Emily wanted to play with fire just then; it gave her a fictitious sense of warmth.

"Because I could not help myself," he muttered. "On the beach, at the casino windows, beneath your terrace —I could not keep away." Still he did not look at her.

She shook her head gently. "I am afraid you have been falling a little in love with me, Esteban. You must not do that."

"Why?" he demanded abruptly.

She laughed a little. Why, indeed, when his respect was so extreme that he could not make up his mind to sit beside her? She shivered again, this time not from cold. The game was beginning—the old exciting game. "Mademoiselle is chilled!" he exclaimed, noticing the shiver out of the back of his head, apparently. "It would be best to run about a little."

It would be best, thought Emily dryly, to swim straight back to shore; but aloud she said, "In bare feet, on these rocks? No, thank you." She looked up at him from under plaintive lashes. "If you want to go on saving my life, I really think you will have to come and—keep me warm yourself." Her tone was quite matter-of-fact.

The temptation had come upon her too suddenly to resist; the need of strong arms about her, the touch of that powerful shoulder on which she had rested as they swam. It was not the first time she had been aware of primitive emotions, but as a rule she did not yield to them; she merely used them. Nobody had warned her that emotions, like muscles, strengthen with use.

He was no longer glancing at her with swift, shy looks like caresses; he had turned to stare at her in startled questioning.

"Don't be afraid of me, Esteban," she smiled encouragingly. "I'm not afraid of you. See how I trust you?"

With a muttered exclamation he did as he was bid. His arm, stiff as a ramrod, encircled her coldly, but she could feel him trembling. Certainly this was no Frenchman! Even one of her own compatriots might have felt the national chivalry strained by such circumstances. She laughed a little, but she was trembling, too.

"You are trustworthy, aren't you?" she teased him. "Perhaps you'd better go then, or you might be tempted to kiss me. Just as you like, of course!"

"Madre de Dios!" he exclaimed, and made his choice.

The tide had turned when they swam slowly and easily back together; easily, because the tide went out more calmly than it had come in, slowly because below the point of pines they were to separate forever. Esteban did not know this, but Emily did.

"Look here! I don't want you to

think American girls are all like this," she said suddenly, and rather oddly, considering that she rarely had anything to do with her compatriots. "We're not so bad as our bark—fortunately. We're rather decent as a rule. I hardly know what came over me—a touch of sun, perhaps."

He turned toward her a look of grave and happy understanding. "We Basques are called the children of the sun, mademoiselle. You are not accustomed to it. Do not fear! Love comes so, without warning, if the heart is ready. It was so that it came to me."

"You think this has been love, then?" she asked with some irony.

His answer shamed and touched her: "Have I not proof?"

She wondered about it as they breasted the long waves together, side by side, gazing at each other. She wanted to remember how he looked, always. Was he right, this stranger whom she had kissed and would never see again? Love—the meaning of things, the reason for them? No wonder, she thought rather piteously, that people were always trying to find it.

Emily had matched her skill with famous amorists more than once, and had not lost. True, she had not won, either, but there are contests in which not to lose is sufficient victory. Despite a somewhat intensive experience, she had remained not so much skeptical of love as entirely ignorant of it. She believed it, indeed, one of those picturesque myths in which people conspire to pretend credence for some reason; like the pretty idea that to be good is to be happy. She, for example, was quite good, technically speaking; but she had never been at all happy. Whereas Suzanne was always happy, and yet— The girl shrugged a cynical shoulder, and gave her stepmother the benefit of the doubt.

Thrills of the sort women discuss so freely nowadays she was quite familiar with; the thrill of the chase, of being chased; the thrill of uncertainty, not quite sure whether you could handle your man or not—far more exciting than, though on the same order as, the thrill of handling a lively horse. But this queer weakness, the melting sensation behind the eyeballs when you looked at each other, this absurd feeling that somebody was of more importance to you than yourself—an hour or two since, Emily could not have conceived the sensation of finding anybody more important to her than herself. Yet here she was dreading her final parting with this new lover, not so much for her sake as for his; she feared to hurt him. Curious!

She let Esteban down easily when the time came, promising to meet him on the point of pines as soon as it was dark enough.

Her stepmother did not appear to have missed her particularly. "You've been gone ages, dear," she said, glancing up from her novel. "Swimming again? Such a blessing to have skin that doesn't burn! I should have worried about you horribly, except that Duval fortunately discovered you through his field glass, out on the rocks with a strange young man. Quite a beauty, too, he said. Who was it, darling?"

"Really, I don't know," replied Emily indifferently; but her face flushed.

"Eh? You don't know?" Suzanne put down her book, interested more in the blush than in the stranger; she had not often seen Emily blush. "Yet Duval reported that you seemed to be on very friendly terms with him. What chances girls do take nowadays! Before I was married, I wouldn't have dreamed of going swimming with a man I did not know, especially in a one-piece bathing suit without stockings!" She added a bit of maternal counsel: "Always remember to sit on the far side of the rocks, darling. This place simply bristles with field glasses."

Emily, of course, had no intention of going to the point of pines as soon as it was dark. That episode was over. She was not so much ashamed of it as alarmed by it. Was her little brainstorm a symptom? Could it be possible that she was getting susceptible as age crept up on her, like Suzanne? Inclined to what she called sloppiness? A Basque fisherman! Why, it was worse than a hotel director!

She invited herself to spend the night with an English spinster she knew, living over in Saint-Jean-de-Luz, who had fallen in love, as plain old women often did, with Emily's cool young beauty. Miss Dibbs should be an antidote for Esteban.

But she was not. Miss Dibbs was specializing, in her mild artist fashion, on things Basque, collecting *cruches, ferratas, makhilas,* gay Basque linens. She talked constantly of her hobby. Emily, all night long, could not lose the thought of Esteban—Esteban taking her in his arms, Esteban waiting for her under the dark pines. She tossed about feverishly in Miss Dibbs' spinsterly verbena-scented sheets and listened to a *basauflûte* played by some native lover down among the mimosas. "Cool young beauty," indeed!

Her hostess was delighted with Emily's new interest in what she called "Basquerie"; took her to see an ancient church with its little ancient ship suspended from the roof in memory of some sea disaster; its triple galleries, where the men sat in tiers so as not to distract the attention of their women, who knelt below on the

black praying rugs—seafaring folk having special need of the prayers of their women. She drove Emily to a graveyard to see certain inscriptions she had found on the discoid crosses there; sun symbols, moon and stars, jagged streaks to represent lightning.

"You see, they've not been Christians long, poor dears. Only a matter of a few centuries," she explained. But they could not, after all, inspect the gravestones, because some men were playing *pelota* there.

"Isn't it quaint of them to use their church wall as a *frontón* to bounce the eternal ball against?" smiled Miss Dibbs indulgently.

Emily's attention was caught by one player, a splendidly built young man in white flannels confined by the usual broad red sash, whose muscles rippled under the skin like those of a young tiger, and who caught and returned the ball from the scoop-shaped wicker *chistera* on his arm with the speed and precision of a machine. Did all Basques, she wondered, look alike, or was it that she could not get Esteban out of her mind? As if drawn by her gaze, he turned toward her.

"Why," exclaimed Miss Dibbs, who had her British interest in all manly sports, "if it isn't the champion, the man who has been winning all the *pelota* tournaments this summer! Yes, yes, it's Urruty himself!"

It was also Esteban; and after a long unsmiling gaze at Emily, he turned quietly back to his game.

That made it a little better, she told herself ironically; he was an athlete then, as well as a sailor, carpenter, what not. It was almost like one's schooldays—being smitten with the charms of a baseball hero, who delivered the groceries in odd moments. Her lip curled in self-scorn. After it was dark that night, she

went out alone onto the point of pines. Not that she expected to find Esteban; doubtless he had learned his lesson. The moon had not yet risen; it was dark under the trees, and quite deserted. Emily wondered where the natives did their courting out of season. She was, nevertheless, not surprised to hear his voice from the near darkness: "I have been waiting, mademoiselle."

"Waiting? When I failed you before?" she rallied him.

"I knew that you would fail the first time. Love is terrifying when it comes like this."

"You speak," she said lightly, "as if you have had a good deal of experience, my friend."

"I am a man," was the simple reply. "But to a young girl it is even more terrifying, naturally. I was well content. All night I played to you, there under the mimosa. You heard my *basauflûte?*"

"Unfortunately, no!" Emily laughed a little. "I was not at home, Esteban. I had run away."

"Nevertheless, you heard me," he said mysteriously, and smiled. "Ah, mademoiselle, do you not know that if you do not come to me, I must come to you, always?"

It was a curious thing to have happened to Emily Weldon, of all people; Emily, who prided herself on a steady head; who knew to a hairbreadth the limit of the danger line; who had an instinct for the moment a look must be turned into a laugh, the moment champagne ceases to exhilarate and begins to relax. She had never been of those who are more kissed against than kissing, as the phrase goes; an untrammeled young modernist, she would have been ashamed not to bear her full share of anything that happened to be going. But her kisses had been experimental

rather than symptomatic; she employed them as scientists employ their test tubes, very accurately.

Now her hand seemed to have lost its cunning. She, the manipulator of emotions, was being manipulated by them; she abandoned herself to this impossible affair with a native *pelota* player as if her father had never given her the benefit of dying counsels. True, there was no ball about at the moment to keep an eye upon.

She was with Esteban at all hours of the day and night; swam with him at dawn, spent hours out on the rocks with him—on the far side—watched the moon rise and set with him down on the beach of the lower town, where there were only native eyes to see. What, she thought sometimes angrily, was her stepmother thinking about to ask no questions? But Suzanne was probably grateful enough for liberty of her own; the girl had not the heart just then to be too severe with her in the matter of Monsieur Duval. Emily had, as usual, nobody to take care of her but herself.

And Esteban. The simple fellow's passion for her amounted to adoration; never in her experience had she been wooed with such intensity of fervor—the "fiery Basque," indeed! Yet no discreet man of the world could have shown more restraint, more delicacy in his wooing. It baffled and rather annoyed her. Since she had chosen thus to fling her slipper over the hedge, who was he to decline to pick it up?

"Esteban"—she was lying in his arms out on the rocks, with only the wide Atlantic before them—"why is it you are always so—so careful of me, as if I were something fragile? I'm not! Why do you never kiss me—enough?"

"It would not be possible to kiss you enough," he said under his breath,

in a tone that thrilled her. "But do you not know," he added more calmly, "that with Basques, as with Americans, women are sacred?"

"You flatter my countrymen," she murmured. "Even if they'd rather not be sacred, Esteban? If they'd rather just be loved?"

"With us, it is the same thing." He repeated a legend current among his people: The Romans, in pagan days, had twitted the Basques with having only one god to worship. "It is true we have but one god," they admitted, "but we have many goddesses."

"Who are they?" asked the Romans.

"Our wives," replied the Basques.

For the first time Emily realized—realized with a pang that was part anger and part pain—that this absurd, adorable creature expected to marry her. Marry "the beautiful Miss Weldon," as the fashion sheets called her; she who had almost been the Princess Abdul, who might yet become, with luck, the second Lady Congers.

She urged her stepmother that night to come away from Biarritz; but Suzanne, usually of so yielding a nature, was quite firm. "You see," she explained, "it really is a matter of economy, darling. The *moustiques* aren't too bad yet, and we're practically guests of the house. Now don't get on your high horse about it! Why shouldn't we be? We've been good patrons, the hotel is practically empty, and they like to have people of our sort about; it gives tone. Besides," she added innocently, "it isn't as if we were any personal expense to Monsieur Duval, you know."

Suzanne really was a remarkable manager; what she accomplished in the way of concessions, commissions from tradespeople and the like, was quite miraculous; also mysterious.

Emily gave her little mental shrug. After all, this was Suzanne's affair; she could hardly be expected to look a gift horse in the mouth.

In the end it was Esteban who decided to leave Biarritz; announced his intention quite suddenly, as they sat together in their favorite trysting place. "Tomorrow, my heart, I must go home," he said.

"Home! But I thought you lived here?"

"In the town? Ah, no, I shall never live in a town. My home is not far away, in the hills. My grandmother wants me now."

"Your grandmother!" She laughed and drew his lips down to hers. "Does your grandmother want you, do you think, as much as I do?"

"It is for the haying," he explained. "And after that comes the irrigation of the fields. Then there are some young mares to be taken at this season to the haras. Yes, I am needed. Also" —he exploded his bomb quietly—"my grandmother wishes to see you."

"Me?" She sat upright in his arms.

"Yes. I have written to her and to my father that I have found you at last. They are glad. It is time I should have sons. I am, since my brother's death, the heir of our etcheonda."

"You mean," gasped Emily, "that you are expecting to take me with you as your wife?"

"Oh, no. First they must see you; I must have my grandmother's consent. She is the head of our house." He spoke as if it were the house of princes.

The girl crowed with laughter. "This is delicious! You want to take me home with you on approval?"

"Yes," he said simply, and kissed her.

She sobered; an idea had come to her. Why not go with him, add a few days more to the idyl, away from prying eyes, away from the world— her world, with its artificial restraints? She had given him so much; if she could give him more, a little time of happiness to remember always, it might lessen the hurt, afterward. It was not of herself she thought now, only of him; it had come to that. Marriage between them was, of course, not possible; but there was one sacrifice she could make on the altar of this her only love—herself; if necessary, her good name. She felt for the first time her woman's need of giving, and she had nothing else to give.

She thought rapidly. She could pretend she was going over to stay with her friend Miss Dibbs. She would see his home, his people—they had become of peculiar interest to her. She would be very sweet to them, and to Esteban. Then, having made him quite happy, she would go quietly away to her own life, as he was now going back to his. Happiness, observation had taught her, was not a thing that lasts in any case. Theirs would be shorter than most, perhaps, but at least they would have had something. She put her hand in his.

"How do we get there, Esteban? By train? By diligence?" she asked.

No, no, such ways were good enough for Basquaises. "When an American lady travels," he cried, "she travels in style!" His eyes sparkled with triumph; he was happy as a child over her consent. His plans, he confessed, were already laid. They would travel by automobile.

"But," demurred Emily with unwonted consideration—she was not accustomed to poor lovers—"I'm afraid you will find it very expensive to take an automobile, dear."

He smiled tenderly. What a good little housewife it would be! But for once they could afford to be expensive, he said. "We are not too poor, we

Urruty." She had been tactless; she should have remembered his good peasant pride.

"And your grandmother—she will not be shocked by my making this journey with you, alone?"

"Shocked?" He stared a little, then smiled, again. "It is not a long journey by automobile—barely a day. And my grandmother is not so easily shocked; she is not *mondaine*."

Emily felt rather foolish. Naturally, in this class there would be few conventions.

That night she asked some casual questions of Monsieur Duval, whose business it was to know as much as possible about everybody. Could he tell her something of a family named Urruty, in that neighborhood? What sort of people they were? How they lived?

The director gave her a shrewd little glance, which she noticed. Doubtless he had seen her with Esteban; but what of that?

"Urruty? It is a Basque name, not uncommon hereabouts. Living in the *Basses-Pyrénées*, you say? In that case they would be farmers, herdsmen. All Basques are farmers, mademoiselle; unless they are fishermen, sailors, smugglers; or shopkeepers, perhaps, or laborers—"

"That is to say that they are working people," she interrupted impatiently—she never troubled herself to be too polite to this gentleman, which was a mistake. "There is no sort of aristocracy among them?"

He shrugged ironically. "In the American sense, no. All Basques are noble. They were ennobled as a nation some centuries ago, for services against the Saracens in the battle of Las Navas de Tolosa. But," he murmured, slightly smiling, "it is not an effete nobility. As mademoiselle suggests, it is not too proud to sweat."

II

As their panting car wound up and up the Route des Pyrénées, leaving behind the blue curve of the Atlantic, edged with its dazzling red-roofed houses, Emily began to feel the dreamy exhilaration which comes so often in high places. It was as if the day, all gold and green and fragrant with sea and snow, had just been washed for them and hung out to dry in the sun.

"Like the clothes of the Infant Jesus," Esteban assented to her fancy, "which the Virgin Mary washes always on Saturday. That is why there is always sun on Saturday—or so say our Catholic neighbors, the Catalans."

"Basques are not Catholic then?" she asked.

"Not always. Some of us have been Huguenot. Basques are adaptable; or I should not dare be taking to my home a wife who is—of what faith, mademoiselle?"

Emily shrugged. "Beauty worship, I think. In cities I go to the handsomest cathedral. I, too, am adaptable, you see."

He turned a serious, questioning look upon her. "Do you mean that, if I were to ask, you would be willing to become Catholic?"

"Perhaps," she said, "if you were to ask— Anything, Esteban!"

He was deeply moved; his hand closed over hers. "Ah, mademoiselle, you make me proud, and humble."

"Too humble," she exclaimed impatiently. "Why do you still call me mademoiselle? Surely you are no longer afraid of me?"

He did not answer for a moment. Then he said very low, "Of you, no. It is for our happiness I have fear. It is too much."

The girl thrilled. This man, she realized, would be hard to get away from.

Their progress was impeded sometimes by odd vehicles: a two-wheel cart like an ancient Roman chariot, drawn by white oxen with pads of fleece on their heads and fringe across their eyes; heavy-laden *carros* with five or six mules driven tandem; a top-heavy three-storied diligence, women seated below, behind curtains of red-checked calico, men on the banquette above, without curtains, and a curious assortment of luggage on top. The horses shied from their noisy engine to the very edge of a precipice. There was a moment of great danger; but the women did not scream, the men were silent. Only the driver muttered to his leaping horses, "Hari, Pompon! Grisette!" and went stolidly on.

Sometimes they passed men on foot, moving along easily mile after mile in their light canvas *espadrilles,* wearing hooded capes, carrying over the shoulder a two-ended bag, or *bursac,* sometimes with a big blue cotton umbrella, and always the *makhila,* a sort of alpenstock with a knife screwed inside for defense against the fierce dogs and the fiercer wild pigs of the Pyrenees.

Now and again their laboring engine had to be refreshed with water; an easy matter, since every few yards a cataract came tumbling down the mountain and added itself to the stream that flowed beside the road. Emily was reminded that they were crossing one of the world's great watersheds.

Esteban's naïve pride in his rented car's performance amused the girl, accustomed, in lack of other evidence, to select her admirers according to the make of automobile they drove. "It is no longer young," he commented, "but vigorous, like my father, who, with but one arm, has managed to marry himself a plump young wife and can still plow his field in a day."

Emily frivolously suggested that their engine sounded as if it, too, could plow its field in a day.

"Yes, it is a fine car," he assented in all seriousness. "Mademoiselle, I suppose, has not often driven in such a car as this?"

"Indeed, no," she confessed with truth, careful not to smile at his simplicity. But stealing a glance at him, she saw that he himself was smiling quietly. They laughed together. Perhaps he was not so simple as she thought.

Presently they came to higher, lonelier places, where they passed no vehicles at all, only now and then great pink-white cattle that lumbered across the road under the clever, anxious direction of shaggy dogs of the same color. There was everywhere a faint, blowing sound of bells and of rushing water. Far below, the little fields made a patchwork quilt of the valley, with here and there a village flatly embroidered, or a church steeple. A tiny wisp of fleece detached itself from the nearest peak and drifted toward them. The sun disappeared; a curious opaque light was around them, as if they had penetrated the heart of a moonstone. Looking down, Emily saw that the valley was no longer visible. They were above a cloud.

She shivered a little. "No, I am not cold," she told Esteban. "But I feel as if that cloud had come between me and any world I know—blotted it out completely. It is my turn," she said a little wanly, "to feel rather frightened."

He stopped the car and got out for her a hooded cape such as the peasants they passed had worn. It was so heavy she could hardly lift it.

"My grandmother had it made on the place out of the wool of our own black sheep, and sent it to me in your New York for fear I should be cold there."

New York—the name seemed strange to her. She had a momentary vision of Esteban stalking along Fifth Avenue with his shepherd's cape and *bursac* and *makhila,* attracting from the crowds as they passed no more attention than they gave the great blond Swede who used to exercise along Fifth Avenue on winter days in white flannels, hatless, his blouse open at the throat. The memory of those hurrying, indifferent crowds frightened her far more than the realization that she was alone, high above civilization, lost in the mountain peaks with a man who loved her. It would take more than a shepherd's cape to keep one warm in New York.

"Will mademoiselle have a bouquet?" Esteban suggested, smiling.

She saw that though they had passed the timber line, the bleak slope was covered with millions of little flowers—bluebells, buttercups, gentians, exquisite rare ferns.

"They say it is the blood of Roland that brings so many flowers here," he told her.

"What—our Roland? 'Childe Roland to the Dark Tower came—' "

"Our Roland, too," he reminded her. "It was here at Roncesvalles that he blew upon the great horn and died. Our children know him well—my little stepbrother had once a tin sword and a hobbyhorse, called Durandel and Veillantif, after the sword and horse of Roland; and even now his sheep dog is named Olivier for Roland's friend. We do not forget easily, we Basques! They call our country 'the land where time delays.' "

She repeated it after him rather wistfully—"The land where time delays."

"And it was here also," he added, "that my brother died."

"You mean during the war?"

"No, he was caught smuggling. Our grandmother was so angry with him that she would not look upon his dead face."

Emily asked sympathetically, "Because she felt the—disgrace of it?"

His eyebrows lifted. "There was no disgrace. With us, smuggling is a matter of principle—there should be no tax on necessities between Basques of Spain and Basques of France. It is not a just tax; therefore we ignore it. We would never, of course, bribe a guard, nor attack him; and my brother, who was of a very sensitive honor, felt that he should not even defend himself from a guard, since the man was but doing his duty. So it was that he happened to be killed. But our grandmother was very angry. She felt that he should first have remembered his duty to the *etcheonda,* as oldest son of an oldest son; he who had been trained for the land, as I was not."

"But why is your father not the heir himself, then?"

"His second marriage has displeased my grandmother," said Esteban. "He took a wife from Béarn, where the women are fat and lazy—lowland folk. She is not fitted to succeed my grandmother. The head of a house, with us, appoints the heir," he explained, "and his wife becomes in time the head of the house. You," he added softly, "will, if I outlive my grandmother, become in time the head of our house." His eyes shone at the thought.

A qualm of compunction touched Emily; also a growing dread of the old Spartan matriarch who took her family inheritance so seriously.

"How do you know that I shall please your grandmother any better

than the lazy Béarnaise?" she mur-
mured.

"It is not possible," he said with
quiet conviction, "that you could fail
to please her."

She kissed him for that. He put
her away suddenly, however, as if he
were listening. "There—do you hear?"

It was a faint little airy music com-
ing down from above them, together
with a tinkle of sheep bells; a thin
elfin sound, infinitely lonely, breath-
ing of sun and wind and peace. It
seemed the very voice of the Pyrenees.

"A bird?" she whispered.

He shook his head. "It is my little
brother, who plays the *chirilion* to
amuse his sheep and to keep himself
from fear of spirits." He smiled. "Our
high pastures are near La Rhune"—he
indicated the tallest of the black peaks
—"which is the abode of the devil, and
Ignacio is timid for his years. My fa-
ther's wife spoils him; she did not
even wish that he should take his year
with the sheep."

He explained their custom of send-
ing a boy, when he was twelve, to
guard the flocks in the high pastures
for a season, quite alone, in order to
make of him a man.

"A man at twelve years!" exclaimed
Emily pityingly.

"A man at birth, if he is Basque,"
was the calm reply. "But he must
learn to know it."

After all, it was no worse than the
English custom of sending even
younger lads away to the brutality of
the public schools.

"I don't blame your father's wife,"
said Emily. "Did you too have your
time alone with the sheep, poor little
Esteban?"

"Naturally. It was a very good time.
That was when I came to enjoy books.
I have brought some books to Ignacio."

He cupped his hands about his
mouth and shouted, "Nacio! Nacio!"

The echoes came back to them, re-
bounding from cliff to cliff, faintly
and more faint—Nacio-o-o, Nacio-o-o.
He put two fingers into his mouth and
whistled, sharp and shrill.

Presently they saw movement far
above, near the snow line. Sheep ap-
peared; then a dog, bounding eagerly;
then a boy's thin little figure descend-
ing toward them in great leaps, using
his *makhila* as a vaulting pole, hurling
himself recklessly down the rock-
strewn slope.

"Hi, Olivier—*sois sage, mon cher!*"
laughed Esteban, putting down the
great dog that leaped upon him, whin-
ing with joy; while the grinning, eager
lad, seeing Emily, stopped short, shy
as one of his own sheep, ready to run
away.

Esteban caught him in both arms
and they kissed on either cheek. It
touched Emily to see such obviously
male creatures so unashamed of their
affection. Then he led the boy to her,
murmuring something in Basque.

"*B'jou', madame,*" Nacio muttered,
in an agony of bashfulness. Esteban,
laughing, whispered again. "I mean
—ma'm'selle!" groaned the boy; and
then Emily, to put him out of his
misery, bent and kissed him herself.

"I—give you welcome—*belle-sœur!*"
he gasped unprompted, and turned
and fled. Esteban had to run after
him to give him the books and a box
of sweets he had brought.

They left him halfway up the
mountain, near his sheep, staring after
them wistfully, the dog beside him
staring, too, waving a bushy tail in
farewell.

"Nacio will not have to play his
chirilion tonight," said his brother.
"He will be too happy."

"With that great box of chocolates?"

"With the memory of his kiss," said
Esteban. "We Basques know how to
remember. Ah, Emilie—Emilie!" He

did not call her mademoiselle again.

They lunched deliciously, upon the terrace of a crude little inn down the next valley, on trout caught before their eyes, wild mountain strawberries and soured cream; with the golden wine of Jurançon, in which they had bathed the little Henry of Navarre at birth to make him strong. He, too, seemed a familiar hero of the day.

Afterward, to make more palatable the thick Spanish coffee, Esteban ordered her a little glass of that liqueur compounded of flowers and fire which Basques called Yzarra. The patronne of the inn, a thickset peasant woman, shared this with them, speaking to Esteban by name, staring anxiously and inimically at Emily.

"She doesn't seem to like me," murmured Emily in English.

"She is not accustomed to Americans of your sort," he explained. "Only to the kind who rush past in motor lorries, staring and laughing and pointing with the finger as if one were not there. My people love their privacy. That is why strangers are never able to learn the Euskara."

She began to dread the meeting with Esteban's family. It would have been pleasant to linger at this humble, clean little place; to go no farther. Why should they hurry? After all, it was not to see his grandmother that she had come with Esteban.

She caught at his hand, as he was rising to get the car. "Must we?" she whispered. "Can't we stay here awhile?"

"There is still a long way to go over these winding roads, and the night comes early here in the valleys."

"What of that? What," she murmured, "if it should overtake us here?" Languor was gaining upon her, a dreamy content. Nothing mattered but to be with him, away from yesterdays and tomorrows. It was so, she thought,

that a happy bride must feel—a bride who had married for love.

But he rallied her in great amusement. "Who is the shy one now? You do not wish to see my home, then? You would like to turn and run away, like Nacio?"

She pulled him down to murmur against his lips, "I want nothing but you—you! To have you hold me in your arms, keep me—"

He laughed tenderly. "I should not have given you the Yzarra," he observed. "It is a man's drink, too fiery for little unaccustomed heads of girls."

She pushed him away and jumped to her feet, very angry. Was he too simple to understand—or did he prefer not to understand? Had he the impertinence to try to teach her, Emily Weldon, a lesson?

She did not speak to him again for some time; but apparently he failed to notice her silence. As they neared his home his spirits soared higher and higher; he began to sing, half under his breath, those melancholy little songs with which primitive peoples express joy. Sometimes the words were unintelligible, but when they were in French, Emily was constrained to listen. One was about a bird which pined in the cage until it was released, and then pined for the cage again. Another was about a valley, such as the deep and narrow gave they were traversing, down which stream and road hurried together toward the distant plains and the cities:

"The valley of Andoce, oh, the long valley,
Three times it has broken my heart—"

sang Esteban; and added soberly, "That is a song for my grandmother. Three times it has broken her heart, indeed, this valley—once when all her sons and grandsons together marched

down it to the war, from which only three returned; once when they brought her the body of my brother, which she was too angry to look at—but she has never laughed since; and once when they carried down to the churchyard my own little mother, whom she loved better than any child of her own, because she was small and delicate and true, like you. But now," he said—"now joy is coming to her up 'the long valley'!"

Again compunction smote the girl. They were going too fast for her, these few hours together. She forgot to be angry with him, made him stop the car now and again so that they might listen awhile to the cow bells and sheep bells, to the Angelus from a steeple far below. How simple life was for these people, how pure and clean! A song of her own land ran through her head, in fragments:

"Watching the white mist stealing
O'er valley and mead and town, . . .
Like children with violets playing—"

Had she ever been a child playing with violets? She began to weep a little—why, she did not know. It could hardly be an exciting pastime, playing with violets.

Esteban kissed the tears away as they fell, asking no questions. Perhaps he attributed them to the Yzarra.

The shadows were purpling when they came in sight of Esteban's home, from below—a large timbered farmhouse of orange-toned plaster, stained with great age, a queer little turret at one corner, the inevitable high balcony facing the east—a remnant of the old sun worship. Above the arched doorway she made out a sort of defaced escutcheon.

"Why, Esteban, is it a coat of arms?"

He explained that every family which had provided an alcalde was entitled to such an escutcheon over the doorway; but that the alcalde might be the village blacksmith, the tailor, any man whom his neighbors elected at the yearly *junta* as suitable to fill the position.

"We have had several alcaldes from our house—my father is alcalde now." He added carelessly, "It is a nuisance for a busy man, but one does not refuse."

There was a woman's figure visible in the arch of the doorway.

"That will be Stancia, my brother's widow," remarked Esteban. "She always watches for me. I should tell you that there has been thought among the elders of our marrying. She is good with the ménage, a great help to my grandmother. It would be a pity for her to marry away from our family. But that, I believe, she will never do."

"Why not?" demanded Emily with a sudden stab of jealousy. "Because she is in love with you?"

"I think so," he replied simply. "And she has tempted me—it is always tempting to be loved. But it seems more suitable that she remain true to my brother's memory."

The sentiment, thought Emily, was creditable, but a little hard on Stancia. Was the suttee idea a remnant of their Eastern origin?

"Esteban," she asked suddenly, "have many women—tempted you?"

He shrugged. "Oh, yes; there are many strong, handsome girls here in our valleys. The Spanish are very beautiful, as you know; and in France —what a look they have out of the eye! Up alone with the sheep or out on the ocean, a man has time to think of women. But—you take them in your arms, and what is there but the dream? You kiss them on the painted red lips, and even the dream is gone. One like another."

"But me, my dear? What did you

find in me?" This was a new Esteban, here against his own background—rather a startling one.

He turned and looked at her tenderly. "A need," he said; "a need of help—little white butterfly buffeting the wind with its wings."

His insight chagrined her—she who had thought herself condescending to his simplicity! She caught at his arm. "It's true, Esteban. I do need help. I'm so tired of—buffeting the wind. Oh, hold me! Try to hold me if you can."

His hand closed over hers. "I shall hold you," he promised.

As they neared the house, he in turn asked a question—his first, yet it showed her that he knew far more of her affairs than she of his.

"That lady whom you sometimes call 'mamma' was the *wife* of your father?"

"Of course!" Emily flushed a little. He had put it oddly.

"And before that she was married to another man—who still lives?"

"Yes"—fortunately enough, Emily thought, since that gentleman's generous alimony formed a large part of their income.

"We shall not speak of this to my grandmother," he suggested quietly. "In all respects, Basques are not adaptable. There is no word in our language," he added with his terrible simplicity, "for adultery."

They had reached the doorway, from which a young woman in a black mantilla stepped out to them. "You are late, Esteban. *La madre* has been long expecting you," she said in a tone of reproof; but how her eyes smoldered as she looked at him! She turned to Emily with the light dying out, and said politely, "Enter, mademoiselle. You are welcome."

That night, alone in an enormous room with a high square bed in each of the four corners—fortunately there happened to be no other guests to share the Urruty hospitality at the moment—Emily tried to fix the impressions of the day on her memory. There was a curious mixture in her mind of peace with perturbation, strangeness with a blessed familiarity, as if she had come home—she who knew no home; as if this ancient hacienda in the hills, shelter to many generations of a people utterly foreign to her, were her shelter too, her stem house. Perhaps—and the thought thrilled while it startled her—it meant that this home of Esteban's was to be the home of Urruty yet to come who would be her children, her children's children.

She shook the thought away, tried to wake from it as from a nightmare. What was she dreaming of?—she, Emily Weldon, marrying into a family of peasants! Even Esteban, with his promise to hold her—or was it a threat?—could not make her commit such a folly as that.

The *etcheonda* in which he took such pride had been disappointing on closer inspection. Picturesque, yes; but primitive to an appalling degree. The fine arch of the entrance led into nothing more than a cobbled runway to the stable yard beyond, where manure was more than evident. There were horses stabled in the house itself, beneath the room where she lay. Opposite the stalls, they had entered a sort of hall or entrance chamber of great size, but without furniture. Farm implements and harness seemed to be stored there. Inside the door she had noticed a long row of high-peaked wooden sabots, like those worn by Stancia, who added her own to the rest.

"Here our people thresh grain and hold the harvest feasts," Esteban told her. "A fine floor for the dance, eh,

Stancia?" He put an affectionate arm about his sister-in-law, from which the young widow visibly shrank. "You should see this Stancia in the *farandole!* She used to be the prettiest dancer in the valleys. Ah, but you shall see her—at our wedding." He seemed unconscious of cruelty, in his boyish happiness to have brought the woman he loved into the home he loved.

From this bleak hall a flight of worn stone stairs led to chambers above, where Emily glimpsed something of the treasures often hidden in these old hill homes of a seafaring, pirate people. Tall *armoires,* rich with dim gold and red and blue; great carved chests, chairs of stamped Spanish leather, faded arras and soft-toned thread-bare velvets against the plastered wall; intermingled with highly colored modern lithographs of saints and martyrs.

But Stancia, giving her barely time to make herself neat, hurried her down to the supper table.

"*La madre* is waiting," she said, as if it were sufficient explanation of any haste.

The room into which Emily was led appeared to be a kitchen, a stone-flagged chamber of great size, with two large chimneys, in one of which she noted the anachronism of a modern iron cookstove. Vessels of brass and copper gleamed fitfully, festoons of dried peppers and garlic hung from the beams, a long narrow table was covered at one end with a red damask cloth, and about it people sat eating. But to Emily everything in the room was dwarfed in interest by the woman at the head of the table—not a large figure, but one of great dignity: white hair brushed straight up from a dark wrinkled face more Oriental than Spanish in type, with the flat features, high cheek bones and

serene immobility of an ancient Buddha. Only the eyes were not old. They flashed with interest, vitality, surprising youth. Without rising, she motioned Emily courteously to a seat at her right hand, beside Esteban, who stood awaiting her.

Opposite, his father also stood waiting, a soldierly looking man with an empty sleeve pinned across his blouse, who bowed stiffly but with a shy quick smile for her, like Esteban's. This was Pedro Urruty, who bore apparently no ill will to the mother who had deposed him in favor of his son as heir. Beside him sat the fat young wife from Béarn; and there were several children, all girls. At the far end of the table, beyond the damask cloth, were other men and women, who made no attempt to rise or to greet her, merely stared and swallowed and stared again. These were evidently farm laborers. There was no service of any sort. People helped themselves at will out of dishes on the table. Now and then the daughter-in-law, Stancia, apparently the cook, replenished these with food hot from the stove.

It was a strangely patriarchal scene, impressive in its simplicity. Emily felt as if she had stepped into the pages of the Old Testament. They spoke little to one another, and to her not at all; yet she felt no embarrassment, since they seemed to feel none. The business of the moment was obviously to eat. At the end of the meal, Stancia handed the matriarch a large vessel of pewter shaped like the pottery water *cruches* to be found anywhere in the South of France, with a handle and a spout.

"It is the *pourru.* They drink the *régalade* in our honor!" whispered Esteban to Emily, evidently much pleased. It passed from hand to hand down the table. Each drinker lifted

the vessel above his head and inclined it so that the liquid streamed into his mouth, without touching the spout with the lips. Emily gathered that this was a point of etiquette rather than of sanitation, and was able by the time the *pourru* came to her hands to drink in the same manner, without spilling a drop. For the first time the old woman smiled.

"This girl is quick. We shall make of her a good little Basquaise!" she remarked to Esteban; but she spoke in French, and Emily was evidently expected to hear.

Then Pedro Urruty made a sign, and suddenly every man at the table sprang to his feet with a high wild shout, as startling as the Confederate rebel yell or a Highland clan call.

"It is the *irrezina*, our battle cry," explained Esteban, his eyes shining. "These men have fought with us." He put his hand up in a brief military salute of acknowledgment.

Emily was oddly moved by the little ceremony. So might a young lord of feudal days have been greeted by his vassals. She did not mind the frank category of questioning that followed; it seemed quite in keeping.

What, inquired the old woman briefly, was the amount of her dot? Mr. Weldon, who knew his Europe, had fortunately been able to lay aside a modest sum for this purpose, which the amiable generosity of Suzanne had left so far unimpaired. Emily mentioned it.

"It should buy you those meadows from the Etcheverray," remarked the old woman casually to her grandson. And mademoiselle was orphaned? In that case, who was empowered to arrange her marriage?

Emily explained that in America young women sometimes performed this service for themselves. The matriarch glanced at Esteban for corroboration. He nodded. "C'est l'habitude, ma mère."

The Americans, remarked Madame Urruty, were still *un peu sauvage,* then? However, one had heard they were a virtuous people. And mademoiselle's religious faith?

She seemed very little disturbed when Emily admitted that she had none in particular.

"Eh, well, these things arrange themselves," she commented indifferently. "That is an affair of the priests. A loving and obedient young wife—there should be little difficulty." She shrugged. Perhaps Esteban had already hinted that his fiancée might prove adaptable.

Then, somewhat to Emily's dismay, the old woman had come to her and kissed her, ceremoniously but very kindly, on each cheek. Pedro Urruty did likewise, followed by everyone at the table except the farm servants, who continued to stare and masticate. And so Emily, the beautiful Miss Weldon of the fashion sheets, found herself accepted as the affianced bride of a Basque hill farmer, shut off behind the Pyrenees from the far-away, vague, unreal world she had left only that morning.

She lay there listening, quivering to the thought that she was at last under the same roof with her lover. Through open windows, a breath of the near-by snow fields stirred the heavy woolen curtains of the bed, mingled with a delicious fragrance from the beehives in the courtyard. Esteban had shown them to her, gay little houses painted in colors like flowers, his grandmother's pride.

"There are no such bees as the bees of our valley," he said. "*La madre's* hydromel is famous throughout the Basses-Pyrénées. You do not know hydromel? It is the honey wine; in England they call it mead."

She was aware, lying there, of many unaccustomed sounds; always the faint, far tinkle of herd bells, the whisper of rushing water; below her, in their stalls, the munching and moving of drowsy beasts. Presently voices from the next room became audible in the stillness—high voices of little girls, with now and then a deeper note. Apparently the family of Pedro Urruty were talking her over from their beds, chiefly in French for the benefit of the Béarnaise mother, though there were phrases of Spanish and Basque also—the household seemed to be trilingual.

"But how white, *maman*, how white her skin! And such little, little feet, like a princess. Silk stockings on them—"

"And silk lingerie also; I have seen it when she crossed the knees."

"But certainly, that was easy," mocked an older voice. "Crossing the knees! Fine behavior for your princess, hein? Such a useful wife she will make in the house! Not only the feet are ridiculous but the whole person. What breasts, what hips! *Il n'y a rien du tout.* Esteban would have done better to take Stancia, who is mad for him. Do you notice, my Pedro, how she could not keep from touching him at the table, the poor girl? What sort of children will this one bear him, I ask you—pygmies?"

"Would you have her bear him—pigs?" It was the masculine murmur of Esteban's father to the rescue. "True, there is less of her than of yourself, my angel, which is to be regretted; but, in the end, it is livestock we select for the weight, rather than wives."

Emily smiled into her pillow. Evidently she had a strong ally in the elder Urruty. But, of course, the woman was right. What was she doing in such a place? There must be only another day of it.

She sighed, and fell asleep at last; to be startled half awake by a hand trying her door, softly opening it. So her lover had been dreaming of her then, as she of him—needing her!

"Esteban! You have come?" she whispered into the darkness.

A woman's voice replied dryly, "No, it is not Esteban. I bring the little *déjeuner*. *La madre* suggests that if mademoiselle would dress quickly— We go to the mass early, since there is still hay to be stacked."

III

Chagrined and resentful, Emily sipped the thick hot chocolate Stancia had brought her, spiced with cinnamon, and nibbled at a sweet cake which she wished had been a roll. Mass, at such an hour—or at any hour, for that matter!

It was broad daylight when she was wakened at last by four eyes gazing fixedly at her, two belonging to a large dog and two to a very small girl.

"Myself, I am Bette," said the little girl, when she was sure of complete attention, "and this one is Nagarro. We have been left to guard you. We are doing so."

The rest of the household, it appeared, had gone to mass. She, being of a responsible nature, had been given the position of trust.

"But Esteban?" asked Emily. "Where is he?"

"Also at mass. *La madre* wished for his company."

Emily began to be thoroughly out of patience with this matriarchate. To be left, on her last day with Esteban, to the company of a child!

The glamour of her adventure sud-

denly palled. An idea came to her of getting away without the necessity of farewells. She would take the automobile that had brought them, and leave before the household returned—unless Esteban had already taken it.

But no, the responsible Bette assured her, it waited under a shed, hidden away from the brood mares, which must not be frightened at this season. She, Bette, had no such matronly fears; in fact, Esteban had promised to drive her in the automobile, if she succeeded in keeping mademoiselle well amused during his absence. Therefore she had prepared quite a program of entertainment. First, they would inspect the poultry yard, her especial charge; then by natural progression the pigsties and the dovecot; next the dairy, and the looms where the winter's cloth was weaving. Was mademoiselle a friend of bees? Otherwise they might resent intrusion. Mademoiselle was not? A pity! But at least she should see the children who had been born to Gathid recently under the brew house.

"Who," asked Emily, "is Gathid?"

"Gathid? But she is as always the house cat, mademoiselle! And surely of an age to know better. However, if they were kept a secret, la madre would not be able to have her children drowned as usual in the water butt. Cats were, of course, creatures of the devil; and la madre felt that one Gathid was sufficient to represent the devil in any household.

Here, thought Emily, was a people who took no chances—they went to mass, but they managed to keep also on neighborly terms with the devil. On further consideration she decided to remain and see what Bette had to offer. She had never known any children except of the unnatural hotel variety; and there was something about this little future matriarch that caught her fancy, reminded her disarmingly of Esteban, in a smaller and fatter manifestation.

She was almost sorry when they saw the household returning from mass; quite a cavalcade, the men riding mule or horses, the women in a large white-hooded *tartane*, all except the matriarch, a stately old figure in her voluminous black cape and thimble-shaped hat, who rode a tall, spirited horse, mounted sidewise on a Spanish saddle with a shelf for the feet. The other women had black scarfs over their heads, and Stancia carried a tall brass candlestick tied in crêpe.

"See, she has burned another candle for her husband, who is dead," commented the informative Bette. "Tante Stancia is very devout! She will enter religion if Esteban does not marry her, perhaps."

Emily felt sudden pity for the woman Esteban did not love.

He came to her, running like a boy. "To see you waiting so at the door of my house—what happiness! And you have made friends with the little sister? You have not been bored?"

"Not for a moment," she said with truth. "But she has made me feel ignorant, Esteban, and singularly useless."

He smiled tenderly. "Ah, you will not feel useless long, my Emilie! *La madre* will soon find something for you to do—there! You see?"

"Esteban! My son!" It was the matriarch's stern voice calling. "Why do you two idle there? Do you forget the hay?"

He smote himself reproachfully on the brow and hurried away, calling out orders.

This was rather more than Emily had bargained for. "Surely, madame," she protested, "you do not work in your fields on Sunday?"

"Why not?" The old woman's eyes twinkled. "They are good Catholic fields, blessed yearly with the embers of Saint Jean. And the rain, my child, is no respecter of holidays—look where clouds gather about La Rhune." She pointed toward the somber peak that broods over the range to the west, and raised her voice: "*Vite, vite*, Pedro, Bette, all of you! The rakes, and make haste! We eat no more today until the hay is up."

There seemed nothing for Emily to do but to follow down to the fields. The children made a great business of finding her sabots small enough, a wide hat to protect her beautiful whiteness. She asked for a rake as well.

"But you, mademoiselle, who are still a guest? *La madre* will not expect it of you," they protested; delighted nevertheless. They led her in triumph to the meadows, where the entire household was at work, Esteban leading the others, directing, helping, everywhere at once, in a short peasant smock and a scarlet handkerchief tied over his head to keep the sweat out of his eyes. He stared with pleasure at Emily's appearance, but did not pause.

"So you have learned already that in a Basque family every member is useful?" he cried as he passed.

The matriarch, pitchfork in hand, was giving orders like a general on a battlefield; encouraging, speeding up her forces, herself setting a stout example, gray head bare to the sun, full black Sunday skirts turned up over a white starched petticoat. Everybody was at it, women and children raking, piling up the carts, men staggering about like miniature haystacks, invisible beneath the loads piled high on their shoulders, on forklike *porte-foins*. In the west new clouds rode the wind like great white galleons.

"*Vite, vite*, my little ones!" came now and again the high carrying call of the matriarch.

Emily had caught the contagion and worked with the rest, worked till blisters broke on her hands, and her back ached furiously, and her breath came hard. It was partly anger that spurred her; this old woman and the others, they should see that she was not so useless as she looked; that there was plenty of strength in her "ridiculous" body; that the sword, when it chooses, makes as good a bread knife as another. Meanwhile she found this mad race with the elements more exciting than any sport she had tried. She heard herself singing. When she paused once to put the hair out of her eyes, she caught the matriarch's amused glance.

"*Ça va*," said the old woman briefly. "We shall win."

Suddenly it was upon them, not with a few first drops of warning, but like a cloudburst, a deluge: one of the terrible rainstorms of the Pyrenees.

"We have done!" came a ringing shout from Esteban, and laughing joyously, he swung Emily up into his arms and ran with her to shelter under the pelting torrent.

A fine fire roared in the kitchen, where Stancia, who alone had not gone to the haying, was putting food on the table: a soup savory with herbs, fowls stuffed with *choucroute*, a salad of crisp cresses, omelets blazing with rum.

"And because you have been such good children—" The matriarch smiled mysteriously, rising herself to fetch a large brass-bound *ferrata* of wood, beaded with cool moisture, from which she filled mugs for everyone at the table, children included.

"Hydromel!" cried Esteban. "There is no better in the *Pays Basque*, in the

world. Drink, my Emilie! It is safer for woman heads than the *Yzarra.*"

The girl thought she had never tasted food or drink so exquisite. What an art, if an unconscious art, they made of living! The cup in her hand was crude, but beaten out of silver so pure she could almost have bent it with her fingers. The great stone-flagged room shone with cleanliness, danced with firelight that turned brasses and coppers into molten gold. Outside, the rain thundered down the steep slates of the roof, poured across the windows in cataracts. At this meal everybody talked and laughed together with new freedom, even the laborers, relaxed by the consciousness of work well shared. Under the table, Esteban's hand found hers.

"You are content?" he whispered.

She replied simply, "I have never been so happy in my life!" She spoke in English, but the old woman smiled at her as if she understood.

"Certainly she understands—my grandmother understands any language she chooses! She was educated at the best convent in Spain. And to-day, my Emilie, you have won her heart—you will see!"

The matriarch beckoned Emily and the other women, later, to follow her upstairs; men were evidently not expected. She led them into a room furnished with one bed, a *prie-Dieu,* a single chair—evidently her own Spartan chamber; but there were several *armoires* and chests against the walls, before one of which she stopped. She handed Stancia a key. "Open," she said.

The young widow did so with evident reluctance. The contents made Emily catch her breath—linens like yellowed silk, laced and embroidered; lengths of uncut brocade and velvet, rolls of cobweb filet.

"You like these things?" said the matriarch carelessly. "They are for you."

"For me?"

At the girl's flush of embarrassed surprise, the other put a kindly hand on her shoulder. "For little orphans who are poor and have, perhaps, no trousseau, the good God sometimes provides. Lift out the rest, Stancia."

There were dresses made of beautiful materials in the elegance of many years past; décolleté, with court trains. "As you see, this is not the trousseau of a Basquaise," remarked the matriarch. "It belonged to my first *belle-fille*—petite like you, and also of the world. Men of this house," she added, "do not necessarily take wives out of their own valley. The Urruty range far afield."

Stancia continued stoically to lift treasures out of the chest for Emily's inspection—small square-toed slippers, jewel boxes, fans, plumes. At the bottom was a tray of little filmy garments, stiff with needlework—tiny dresses, jackets, petticoats, bibs. The little girls clapped ecstatic hands.

"For the *bébé!* Oh, see, mademoiselle! For the first *bébé!*"

Emily had gone quite pale and silent. She began to realize what she had done in deceiving Esteban, in deceiving this old woman who so trusted and honored her. For the first time in her life, perhaps, she was ashamed. "Madame is too kind!" she muttered with stiff lips. "I can't—it is not possible—"

The matriarch took her hand reassuringly. "Your hesitation does you credit, my child. But remember the gift is not from Esteban, your fiancé; nor from myself, a stranger, since these things are not mine to give. They come to you from Esteban's mother, now with God, who thus provides for her little *belle-fille* a suitable trousseau."

There were rare tears in her eyes, tears suddenly in Emily's throat. She remembered that the stern old Spartan had loved this daughter-in-law better than her own children, because she was small and delicate and rare, Esteban had said, like herself.

Small and delicate and rare! Then what had she done in such a place, such a life as this? The answer was obvious: She had died of it! Died very young, at the birth of her second child, who was Esteban.

Unreasoning panic overtook Emily, a reaction from the emotions of the day. She must get away at once, instantly, before it was too late. . . . Too late? They could hardly force her to marry against her will—the matriarch, Esteban who had sworn to hold her? Nonsense!

But she must make them angry enough not to want to keep her; so angry that Esteban would not be hurt. Despite her panic, it was still of importance that Esteban should not be hurt. She had meant to go quietly away without undeceiving them, so that they should know the truth gradually; but this trust, this generosity, had made such a course impossible. There was more decency in the girl than she knew.

She must give them a reason for not marrying Esteban; a reason that they could understand and accept. She could hardly say to the man in his own house, "My dear fellow, I'd no more think of marrying a picturesque Basque peasant than I'd think of marrying a prosperous Greek bootblack!"

For a moment the fact that she was not Catholic suggested a loophole of escape; but they had accepted this already without demur, expecting her to be adaptable. Suddenly the idea came. Divorce! That was the thing these people would not tolerate; laxity of the marriage laws.

She said, not very steadily, "Perhaps, madame, I should not accept your kindness, your hospitality, without making a confession. I am not altogether what you think; not—a young girl."

Madame Urruty drew back. "You mean you have been married? You are a widow?"

Emily's hand went to her throat. It was harder than she had thought. "Not—exactly. My husband and I—are not together. In America"—she smiled rather desperately—"we have, as you perhaps know, the custom of divorce."

The old woman's face stiffened. With a stern gesture she dismissed the others from the room. "Send me Esteban," she said.

They went reluctantly, Stancia with a queer backward look of triumph.

"She will get him now," flashed miserably across Emily's mind. She heard him running up the stairs. He paused on the threshold, then came to her and took her hand in a strong clasp.

"What is this, *ma mère?*" His eyes were as stern as the old woman's. "What are you saying to trouble our guest?"

"How does it happen that we have such a guest?" demanded the old woman in measured tones. "How does it happen that my son's son brings into our house a woman who is wife to another man?"

"Divorced wife," corrected Emily faintly.

"How have you dared?" said the old woman, as if she had not spoken.

Emily made a final effort. "He did not know—he never asked. Oh, let me go!" she sobbed, and jerked her hand from Esteban's.

She heard him following as she ran along the corridor. He overtook her, seized her shoulder roughly, jerked her about to face him. "This—this is not true?" She could not speak for sobbing, but she saw the blazing anger die gradually out of his face. "No, it is not true," he answered himself. "It is to my grandmother you have lied. But why? Because you do not wish to marry me?" Emily nodded helplessly. "So, the test was too great," he muttered, still to himself. "Or perhaps you never wished to marry me?"

Emily could only shake her head.

"But why?" he repeated again. "Why have you done this to me? You love me?"

She found her voice at last. "Oh, my dear, can't you see—can't you see how absurd it was to expect a woman like me to live such a life as this— a life that killed your own mother?" Esteban winced. "Oh, I did not wish to say that! But think of me, me, Emily Weldon, living among the cattle, hoeing the fields, handling—handling manure, for all I know! There's enough of it about." She laughed hysterically. "I'm not a woman like your grandmother or Stancia—I'm a lady!"

"What," he asked oddly, "is a lady?"

She laughed again. "You see? You don't even know the difference! Should I have to cook meals for the farm hands? Why, I've never done a useful thing in my life, and never shall. It's impossible, ridiculous! Girls like me are brought up to be useless. We must marry rich men, my dear— rich, can you understand? As my world counts riches, not as a peasant does, who prides himself on how many cows he keeps, or pigs! Motor cars, country houses, yachts—my own or other people's—those things are necessities to me—"

"More than love?" he interrupted.

"I'm not fool enough to expect everything at once— But love is so cheap! You can find that as you need it, Esteban. . . . Oh, don't! You're hurting me!"

He thought she meant the hand on her shoulder, and took it away; but she meant his eyes. "Yes"—he had to moisten his lips to speak—"I suppose I have been—ridiculous."

"No, no, not you!" She had been crueler in her hysteria than necessary. "I don't mean that our love is cheap! Listen, my dearest; I came away with you as the price of it—that's not cheap! I wanted to make some little sacrifice to it, to give—what I could. Oh, don't you see, to give you something you might keep always, that has nothing to do with marriage? You would not understand, you were too simple. This patriarchal, pastoral, humble sort of life—I am not fitted for that sort of thing. It—it is too real for me! I am not good enough, perhaps—"

Her voice trailed away before the weariness in his eyes, the sudden disillusionment. She had accomplished her purpose only too well.

"No," he said after a moment, "I see you are not good enough." And he went heavily away.

Presently, lying face downward on her bed, she ceased to sob and began to listen for him. He would return, of course; they could not part like this! The rain had passed as suddenly as it came, and released fragrance from the contented earth blew in across her fevered thoughts, soothing, suggesting. The light that presaged dusk was mystically clear and serene. From without came homely sounds which are the same in any language— lowing of cows, the call of the child Bette to her chickens.

Emily's own words were in her ears. Yes, this life was real; the life of human beings on the earth since Adam.

All that had gone before was empty, anxious dreaming. Why go back to it? There was nothing worth going back to. Something had happened to Emily. She was no longer a lady; only a woman, waiting—Esteban's woman. When he returned to her, she would know better how to make her little sacrifice to love. But he did not return.

"Then I must go to him," she said aloud. Had she been mad—was she mad now? Who cared? She knew suddenly that no price was too high to pay for this sense of belonging to life, this hold on reality; even the price of marriage, of personal extinction.

She dried her eyes and dabbed powder over her face. With a little laugh, in a magnificent gesture of renunciation she flung her powder puff out to the birds and bees.

It was then that she saw Esteban going down towards the woods, still moving heavily, with bowed head; but not alone. His arm was about the waist of the sister-in-law, who no longer shrank from it. She leaned against him as they walked, turning up to his a face eager with tenderness. Stancia, whose love had tempted him; Stancia the comforter—

"So be it," said the girl; and something within her, some larger thing that had come into her heart with Esteban, was glad.

The details of her return to Biarritz were always vague to Emily. At the village where she had lunched with Esteban a motor lorry of tourists had paused for refreshment. She left the rented automobile—her rather odd education had included the driving of other people's cars—for Esteban to find when he followed her, and went on with the tourists.

"Sure, lady—always room for a pretty girl!" This friendly gallantry, in the accents of her native land,

stayed in her mind, together with the steady pounding of the lorry, mile after mile, as she listened backward, listened despairingly, for Esteban to follow.

It was late at night when she reached the hotel and found in the drawing-room of the suite she shared with her stepmother a little entertainment going on, over a bottle of champagne. Monsieur Duval, Suzanne explained in some embarrassment, had stopped for a moment, merely, to discuss certain plans for the next day.

"Plans," suggested Emily grimly, "for our departure tomorrow?" And Suzanne, with a scared glance at her stepdaughter's face, had agreed that this was so.

The departure had been less immediate, of course; there were boxes to pack, arrangements to effect; but on an evening some days later Emily stood alone on the terrace, looking for the last time over the Bay of Biscay, exquisite under the moon she had shared with Esteban—"the light of the dead," as Basques call it.

It was all to begin over again, the old aimless wandering, the search for something which perhaps did not exist: her place in life, something to take the place of love.

As she gazed, a boat as graceful as a cat slipped out into the moon mist toward the open sea. It was a boat she had noted once in the lower town, the last of the smart steam yachts to leave after the Biarritz season.

"Ah!" murmured the voice of the director at her elbow. "Mademoiselle is admiring the *Gathid*, off for America again? One heard that she had been put into commission for a honeymoon. Romantic, *n'est-ce pas*? Mademoiselle would perhaps like to be on that pretty boat?"

"Not," she replied listlessly, "if it is

going to America." Then the name struck her, brought a sharp picture of a little fat girl with kittens in her arms. "The *Gathid*—but that is a Basque name!"

"Assuredly. And a Basque boat," assented the director pleasantly. "Built for a man who knows boats—the young Urruty."

"Urruty—" Emily put a hand to her throat.

"But yes, the *pelota* player, a great sportsman—you have doubtless heard of him? Ah, I recall that mademoiselle was asking me about a family of that name some time since. I should have remembered to tell you of Esteban. But he is so rarely here. Often one finds surprising wealth among these people; but this one appears to have outdone himself—a gold mine, I think, or perhaps an oil well. Something fabulous of the sort, in the Americas.

And how unspoiled, how filial! Always returning at this season because of the haying, to help with the work of the farm! A charming gesture, is it not? No wonder our young ladies and their mammas excite themselves over his visits. And now it is too late; there has been a marriage, one hears —a family marriage. Such a pity," he murmured gently, "that mademoiselle herself could not have made the acquaintance of this delightful fellow. But what have you? What is the matter here?"

For Emily had begun to laugh; laughed and laughed and could not stop, though she dug her nails into her palms, stuck a handkerchief into her mouth and bit it; laughed until Monsieur Duval in some alarm ran to get her a glass of *eau-de-vie*—which appeared in due time upon the bill, with a franc charged extra for service.

JUDITH

A. E. COPPARD

I

This is the story of a great lady who did a great wrong to a mere man, a man so nearly insignificant and uncouth as to be almost unworthy of the honour. He was—may Heaven determine his rewards—a village schoolmaster, she the great dame of their part of the Suffolk county, and her name was Judith. Of high but untitled birth, she had been married young to a baronet of greater age, whose family distinction was as high, and whose life was devoted to the timely destruction of ferocious things in field and flood and air, by gun or hound or angle. Master of hounds and owner of choice coverts, he was a Nimrod; when birds were coming freely over, his loader had more than once seen—left, right; left, right—the four birds falling in the air at the one time. Often! Duffy Dallow tell you the same. Sir Gulistan Leeward was a tall thin man with a seared and apparently vexed face; though his chest was not broad, his lungs were powerful, for he spent a great part of each hunting day around the coppices yodelling a piercing tenor cry: "Barley! Barley! Barley! Barley!" in a voice whose demoniacal lustre must have added a mile a minute to the pace of absconding foxes. "Flew wind him in there!" he would cry with passion, "flew wind him, my beauties!" and if some silly Cressid or Rampart ambled from the thicket to wag a tail at him, the thong of his whip would crack at their misguided behinds.

For ten years Judith shared in his sport and enjoyed his company "reverently, discreetly, advisedly and soberly, duly considering the causes for which Matrimony was ordained," but by the time she was thirty there was an ache in her bosom—she had no child. Sir Gulistan Leeward may have regretted this, but whether the omission was hers (as he had no doubt), or the lapse his (as Judith believed), he was not profoundly concerned, and being by this time fifty years old, he declared that his burning desire to shoot hippopotami—and possibly anthropophagi—in the swamps of Africa must be immediately realized or for ever relinquished, heaven itself being no place for hippo. Judith did not accompany him upon that happy business, and it was during his twelve-

month's absence that this little episode of the schoolmaster occurred.

Early one hunting morn, a crisp morn full of hoar-frost and slanting sunlight that laid shadows of trees halfway across fields, the bay she was riding had refused a hedge that everything else took easily, and she was left alone. Judith coaxed and scolded and clouted her timid gelding, but he was feckless—perhaps he was not properly awake. Blast the wretch! they had only just cast off. The lady realized soon that she was entirely alone, the hunt had swept on, there was not a sight or sound of it; she was inimitably, almost terribly, alone. So they went at it again, but the devil took the hedge so timorously that he only landed halfway across it and stuck there like a fool with his forelegs on one side and his hind legs on the other, while Judith had flown haplessly over his head into a lane. She dropped on some boggy turf, still clutching the bridle, but she had wrenched her stirrup foot. Very ruffled and shaken, she adjusted her hat and then sat huddled up, clutching her knee, although it was her foot that tortured her. The horse soon wriggled himself free from the hedge and stood before her, snuffing the rank herbage, until Judith terribly told him the unmentionable truth about his behaviour. He tossed his head, champed, and briskly flourished his cropped tail. The lady pulled herself up by the bridle and stood on her sound foot, but as soon as she began to hop towards the saddle, the beast sidled away from her.

"Ach, cantankerous offal!" she sighed.

Then, startled by her strange approaches, the bay wrenched itself away from her altogether and galloped down the lane.

A little way off it passed a cottage with a smoking chimney, standing back a little from the road, and Judith saw a man run out from the cottage and stare after the flying horse. Then the man turned and looked in Judith's direction. She had sunk down on the grass again. She waved her crop at him. The man stared doubtfully for a while, with one hand upon his hip, but when Judith gave a faint shout he ran down the road towards her. He was only half-dressed, in grey trousers and white shirt, he had no coat or waistcoat on, there was a brown belt round his waist. He did not run strenuously or excitedly, but with a long casual lope that brought him quickly.

"What's the matter?"

He was tall and lean, fair and shaven, with mild eyes and a blunt nose; perhaps thirty years old; his face had a country tan. Judith could not quite tell if he were a gentleman, but he was very friendly and sympathetic.

"My horse threw me, I've hurt my foot, I can only stand on one leg. . . ."

"Like a heron," he grinned.

Certainly no gentleman.

"You can't walk, then?" he asked.

"No. I want you to send for my car."

He stared down at her, she up at him. The man apparently did not know her!

"I'm Lady Leeward," she said, a shade too casually perhaps.

"Leeward? Oh—from the park! Dear—that's two miles away. You'd better come along to my cottage."

"But I can't walk, you see," explained the lady. "If you'll send to the park and tell them to bring the car—"

"I've no one to send."

"Haven't you a bicycle?"

"No, I think bicycles are such—"

"If you aren't gone too long I can

stop here. Would it be putting you to—" Her head began to sag and her mind to grow hazy; "—if you aren't gone long."

"I think I'd better not leave you," interrupted the man, quickly bending. "Not like this. I can see you are sweating with pain. I must carry you, it's just along there, two minutes, you can see it. Let me help you to get up."

"I wish you wouldn't," she muttered pettishly, but somehow she was tilted up on to her sound foot. Then she swooned away and was remotely aware that he was carrying her huddled across his shoulders, like a sick sheep, for hours and hours. When she revived she could hear a loud steady noise—boom, boom, boom— and she was lying on a couch in his cottage. The man was sitting beside her, his left arm was around her, her head was against his breast, and she was sipping from a cup of water in his right hand. She did not want to move, she was aware of a fine log fire on the open hearth, and a kettle boiling. There was her hunting hat lying upside down under the table. Boom, boom, boom. The door was open, she could see the sunlight blazing on the asters in the garden. It was blazing, too, diagonally across the white cloth on the table, on the teapot and mug and jug and loaf and plate of red apples. Such yellow butter, too! Boom, boom . . . why, yes, that was his heart beating.

"How did I get here?" she murmured, and stirred; she took the cup from him.

"Pulling round now?" asked the man.

"How did I get here?"

He told her he had carried her. She sipped the water, then gave him the cup again. He reached down and put it on the floor beside him.

"A weight," sighed Judith.

"Pooh! a feather," he laughed. "But it was lucky you had stood up. You fainted, you know, and I had to carry you like—like a sack of corn."

She sat up, away from him now. She had beautiful hair, a dark gold, and there was a perfume in it. Her hat lay under the table.

"Yes," the man nodded briskly, "I was the lost shepherd—no, I was the shepherd and you the lost lamb, on my shoulders. Really! But there was nobody passing. If your foot is swelling, I'd better take your riding-boot off at once, or it may be difficult."

"I can do it." Judith took off her gloves, still with a good deal of languor, but tugging at the boot made her giddy and he had to kneel down and assist her. Then he drew off her stocking and looked at the swollen ankle.

"I've got some liniment, what about that?" he suggested.

"My—car—" suggested she.

"Ah, yes." But he got up from his knees, went to a shelf, and brought a bottle of oil. The man hovered over the naked foot and rubbed oil upon the swelling. His fingers were long and thin, their touch was soothing. Occasionally he hurt her, but she was stoical and leaned back on the couch watching his bent head. The fair hair was thick and tousled, his features brown and pleasant, a nice creature.

"It feels much better now," said Judith. "Do you live here? But of course you do."

"Yes," said he.

"Always?"

"Always."

"Alone?"

"Alone."

He was laconic. Judith sighed. "I wonder where my beast of a horse is?"

"Oh, he's galloped right out of the story," said the man. After a moment

or two he continued: "Yes, alone. It is my habit to do so, it suits me."

Judith meditated. "Well, you have friends to visit you. It would be lonely otherwise."

"I have no friends." He gave the foot its final massage.

"Is that because you don't want them?" Judith was staring interestedly at her foot. "I'm sure that must be the reason."

He was picking up the cork and replacing it in the liniment bottle.

"Oh no, no," he said. "I do, I do."

Then he glanced at the clock on the shelf, it was nearly nine o'clock.

"I must go now, I am the schoolmaster," he explained, rising to his feet. "Directly I get to school I'll send a boy over to the park and your car ought to be here in half an hour. You'll be quite all right here until then."

"I am very much obliged to you," said Lady Leeward.

He put on a coat and a hat, and took a stick from the corner.

"Shall I leave the door open?" He paused.

"Please," the lady answered.

"You might shut it when you go," he added.

"I will, yes," Judith nodded brightly.

"Good-bye. You'll be all right. Half an hour."

"Thank you so very much," said Judith.

She lay on the couch for a while, then she sat up. There were no pictures on the walls, but there was a shelf of books close at hand. Astronomy he appeared to like, and moths. A lot of books about philosophy and history, and, yes, Socialism—dozens. Judith drew on her stockings. There was a horrid bulge at the ankle but it was much easier now. And the horse had galloped out of the story! No friends: *My mind to me a kingdom is.* What story? The lost lamb—over nine stone, too! Must be strong, never turned a hair.

The car came with her maid and a footman, they had come instantly without hats or coats. Her ladyship explained her accident and then with their aid limped out to the car. The maid took the riding-boot, the footman the hat from under the table.

"Wait a minute," cried Lady Leeward. "There's a bottle of liniment on the table. Just fetch it, Maude, will you?"

When the liniment was safely stored the car turned and took them all away.

Had they telephoned for a doctor? "No, my lady."

"Why not!" What fools servants were! "Well, it doesn't matter, don't." A hundred of them were not worth one sensible friend; they were willing but stupid, it was all a question of love. Oh dear, I did not even ask his name.

No, Maude did not know his name, but the footman said the schoolmaster's name was Jones. Judith sighed. How awful! It must be terrible for him. It would be impossible, utterly impossible to like a person with the name of Jones. Bones, groans, moans.

"Jones," she echoed.

"Yes, m'lady." The footman enlarged: "Christopher Jones."

"Oh," the lady mused, "Christopher. Yes." The car entered the lodge gates and soon drew up at the Hall. Oh, there was a thing she had forgotten! And the chauffeur was sent flying back to close the door of Mr. Jones's cottage.

II

A few days later a letter was posted and delivered.

Old Hall, Leeward Park
Thursday, Nov. 1

Lady Leeward presents her compliments to Mr. Jones and desires to thank him for his recent great kindness. Her foot is almost well, but the injury still prevents her calling to thank Mr. Jones personally. If Mr. Jones could find it convenient to take tea with her on Saturday afternoon Lady Leeward would esteem it a very great pleasure.

The reply was as follows:

Rose Cottage, Frogmoor Lane

Mr. Jones begs to acknowledge Lady Leeward's letter of the 1st, but regrets he is unable to accept her kind invitation. Mr. Jones is glad to hear of Lady Leeward's recovery from her mishap.

"Heavens above!" gasped Judith. And there the matter might very well have rested. But Fate himself would have a meagre business if human nature did not probe and prove him. The pitcher may go once too often to the well, but until that date there are no other such delightful journeys. What is a pitcher for—if not to fill? Or a well—but for the use we may make of what lies in the bottom of it?

Old Hall, Leeward Park
Nov. 6

Dear Mr. Jones,
I am sorry that I chose an unsuitable date. I am the most unlucky person in the world. May I try again? Will you come over at any time con-

venient to yourself? I should be so pleased.
Yours sincerely,
Judith Leeward

The answer ran:

Dear Lady Leeward,
It is very kind of you, but I feel sure that there are (if I could only think of them!) many reasons why I am unable to come to tea at Old Hall. Please excuse me. Good luck to your foot.
Sincerely,
Christopher Jones

"What the—the deuce does that mean! Many reasons—unable—luck to your foot. Why foot! It's an extraordinary Jonesy letter, complete Jones—bones, moans, groans—Christopher, friendless man. Oh well, thank you, Jones, thank you very much."

So the next evening Lady Leeward drove herself over in the small car to Rose Cottage, Frogmoor Lane. It was some distance away from the village; why did the man poke himself away in such an absurd place, all by itself? It was as much as she could do to find it in the dark. She stopped the engine at his gate and hooted. There was a light from the window, but nobody answered her call. She had to get out of the car and walk up the black path, slipping off her gloves as she did it, and knock the door smartly with her knuckles.

"Come in," his voice cried, and she opened the door. There was a splendid fire on the hearth, a green silk shade on the lamp, it was cosy. And he—he was sewing! Sewing a piece of yellow stuff. With cotton and a needle.

"Do excuse me bursting in on you like this," began Lady Leeward, half in and half out of the doorway.

He quickly stood up, dropped the sewing on the chair behind him, and

went towards her with a smiling "Good evening." She found herself shaking hands with him as he said: "Come in" again.

"No no, I only came to—"

"There's a draught," he said, glancing at his lamp flickering on the table. And so Lady Leeward walked in.

"What am I doing with this thimble?" she asked brightly. "I found it in my hand." She set a thimble on the table.

"It slipped off my finger," he explained, shutting the door. "Won't you sit down?"

"And it slipped into my hand!" She laughed again. "How funny!"

"Well, you write with a pen, you know, instead of your finger—won't you sit down?—and you sew with a thimble for the same reason."

"But it's funny to see a man sewing at all!"

"I don't do it often," he replied, "but I believe I follow all the rules. I can hemstitch, herring-bone, and make a seam." He picked up the yellow stuff and showed her what he had been doing.

"It's quite good," said Lady Leeward. "What is this you are making—curtains!"

"For my window," he added.

Said the lady, bending over the sewing: "You must let me give you some."

"Oh no, no, no." So decidedly, she might have been offering him some infectious fabric. "Thank you, no, I prefer these homemade things."

"But I mean I will make them for you myself."

"Thank you," he smiled, "but these will be all I want. Yes, thank you."

The lady looked astoundingly handsome, though exceedingly berobed in a heavy grey corduroy cloak with dark fur at the neck and wrists. A perfume seemed to float from her copper-coloured hair, and her fine features had a rosy glow. She was not wearing a hat.

"Ah, yes." With a mock sigh she shrugged her shoulders. "You are a self-sufficient man. That's why you have no friends."

"No friends!"

"You told me you had none."

"Oh, that was just bunkum." He moved a chair for her to use, as she still stood, rich and gracious, in the low-ceilinged room. She seemed to tower in and pervade his home.

"No, thank you," said Lady Leeward. "I've only just run over to bring you this. I stole all your liniment, it was so good, and I've brought you another bottle. Thank you, so much."

"Oh," he murmured, with a deprecating gesture.

"My foot is quite well now—"

"Good," he said.

"—and that is entirely due to your treatment. I did not even call our doctor in."

"Risky, wasn't it?" suggested the schoolmaster.

"Was it? Well, I didn't want to," she said, "I was in your good hands, and the lost lamb is very grateful to you." She moved to the door. "Good evening," she said, smiling and very handsome. He held her proffered hand for a moment and then unlatched the door for her. The asters down the pathway glared lividly in the sudden light thrown upon them; her heavy cloak brushed them as she walked by. Outside his gate she stopped and glanced up and down the road, then at the sky. Miles away, a cloud hanging low over a lighted town shone like a cushion of luminous wool. He had followed her quietly down the path. It was a cold clear night, the stars rippled in the sky like diamonds on a bed of dark velvet. A wind threshed gently in the trees, and

dry leaves ticked along the road, running across the path of the headlights like little brisk tumbling gnomes. Lady Leeward squeezed herself into the little car and the schoolmaster fastened the door for her. Then she leaned towards him from under the hood, and it seemed as if all her imperious beauty had become tender in that close secrecy of the dark vehicle. He heard her whisper: "Come for a ride."

Instantly he said: "Yes," ran back to the cottage, put on an overcoat, turned down the lamplight, pulled to the door, and so back to her and away.

He could not tell whether they rode for an hour or for five minutes. They were fleeing from darkness, with a light under their feet—and they talked of the price and condition of hay. They discoursed of hay, sanfoin, clover, and old meadow, but they never chopped it into chaff. They were too absorbed for that. Of the price of hay, this year's, last year's, next year's hay, they speculated and prophesied; the time to mow it, and the way to make it. They found themselves hopelessly enmeshed, buried and swaddled in a great cock of hay. Like the ass-headed weaver they had a great desire, it seemed, to a bottle of it. So at last the lady stopped the car by the roadside, and turning to the man, she said:

"Don't you think Mahomet might come to the mountain now?"

Mahomet prevaricated: "What do you mean?"

"I mean you did me a great kindness. I want to show that I'm not ungrateful."

"It isn't worth," he wavered, "not worth a cup of tea."

"No? Not to you. But I have my own sense of it."

He was silent, she was silent. Both stared ahead along the road where the farther trees seemed to cringe from their light.

"Are you hungry?"

He was, yes, a little bit hungry; rushing through the air gave you an appetite.

"Good," she cried. "So am I. Now I'll take you to the Hall and we'll have a meal straight away."

"My—excuse—no, no," he ejaculated, stirring as if about to leap out of the car.

"Why not?"

He did not answer.

"Do come."

"You see," he said, fumbling for words, "I'm not used to such things. You must let me off. I'm not dressed. I'm plebeian. You must excuse me. Some other time. I'm not used to such things."

"What things!" she cried. "There's nobody to meet, not a single visitor." She brushed a strand of hair back from her cheek. "I'll get them to scrape up a meal for just you and me. We'll have something up on a tray, in my own room. Yes, yes, that's quite settled."

She edged in the clutch, and the car ran on again, turned into the great park at the lodge gates, and drew up at Lady Leeward's home. A shaft of light gleamed from the hall. A footman ran down the steps and stood by the car while they alighted.

"How bright the stars are!" Lady Leeward said. Jones did not answer, although he too looked up into the sky. The footman looked up into the sky and smiled. He followed them up into the huge hall that seemed all grey and white tiles, barometers, long clocks, shining brass and mahogany. The bewildered schoolmaster was bereft of his coat and hat by the footman, and then Lady Leeward ushered him along to the library, a room

furnished in dark heavy sumptuous-
ness, leather and black oak, with sere
busts on the tops of the bookcases,
glasses of stuffed fish hanging in re-
cesses, and family portraits huge and
gloomy. A bright fire was there.

"What will you drink?" she asked,
opening a cupboard where there were
decanters.

"I—no, thank you."

"A cigarette?" There was a silver
box.

"No, thank you."

"There are a few books." She
nodded towards the cases as she lit a
cigarette for herself. "Can you amuse
yourself with them for ten minutes—
there are lots of astronomy and history
—until supper is ready? I don't know
about philosophy, but I'm sure there's
no Socialism."

"Yes, I will—see what I can see,"
he grinned.

"I must go and change," said Lady
Leeward. "Excuse me for ten min-
utes."

The schoolmaster sat down and for
a while pored mindlessly over an old
volume of Punch. There was not a
sound to be heard anywhere save the
faint ticking of a china clock in a
glass cover. He wondered if he might
get up and steal away. The box of
cigarettes was still open on the table
beside him. He began to count them,
but there were too many. His watch
was three minutes ahead of that clock.
He leaned forward and sat holding
his head in his hands.

"Supper is ready, sir." The footman
stood in the doorway. Jones got up
and followed him along a corridor,
with the incomparable and tragic ti-
midity of a nervous cricketer walking
out from the pavilion to take his
innings. In the midst of that green
desert lurk eleven white sardonic
harpies, and he walks as a man into
the trap of death, one against many,

but he dare not hurry and he may
not lag.

At the end of another corridor
across the hall he was shown into a
room furnished with a heavy but
bright sumptuousness. It was oblong,
with huge white chimneypiece, pink
silk lights, a smallish table laid with
silver dishes, and wine. And Lady
Leeward was standing by the fire
dressed in a gown of black silk, pale
stockings, black shoes with high red
heels. He hovered vaguely in the
room. The footman pulled out a chair
at the table, and the lady came half-
way across the room.

"Well," she asked, "did you find any
disgraceful books?"

"I looked at Punch," he replied,
sitting down as she indicated.

"I like Punch," remarked his
hostess.

"Enthralling," the schoolmaster ex-
claimed.

There was a plate of cold pheasant
and tongue before him. The servant
helped him to salad.

"Claret, sir?" murmured the foot-
man, and Jones nodded.

After putting another log of wood
on the fire the footman went away,
and the schoolmaster by constant
sipping drank up his glass of claret.

"I am so glad you came."

"I did not come," he ventured, "I
was abducted."

"Oh no, you were not!" She pushed
the wine towards him and he refilled
his glass. "Besides, what was I to do!
You don't mind now?"

He laughed. "No, I am quite, quite
happy."

"Glad I am not so terrifying, after
all."

He had begun to look about the
room, at the couch of green velvet, the
little black piano, the water-colours
on the wall. But his glance came back
to her and her sweetly innocent eyes.

The red-gold hair that slightly curled was bunched in a thick casual roll on her neck. The black dress gave a lustre to the pale moulding of her shoulders and the graceful arms. There were a few jewels on her fingers, and from each ear hung a tiny chain of gold ending in a golden hollow ball; he could hear the tinkle of the pellets in them when she sharply moved her head.

"It was not you, no, no," he began to explain, "it was myself, my plebeian self. I never go out anywhere. I do not even know how to address you."

Lady Leeward fumbled with her bread; it seemed to amuse her.

"Formally?" she asked, then looking at him keenly with her marvellous eyes. "But what is it you want to say?"

"I mean your title, yes, and that sort of thing," he added, lamely.

She was really amused. "Oh, but my dear man! The servants say 'M' lady.' My friends call me what they like." She pushed her empty wineglass towards him. "I've a dozen nicknames —give me a new one. Have some trifle?"

"Please," said he. He filled her glass and his own and took the plate of trifle she handed him.

"Well?" She took up her dessert-spoon. "What is my name to be?" Her elbows rested on the table, she was smoothing the spoon with her finger and thumb. "Do you know, I don't care very much for your name."

The schoolmaster swallowed a portion of his trifle and laid the spoon carefully back on his plate.

"Which one?" he inquired.

Lady Leeward said: "Jones."

"That is not really my name," the schoolmaster replied.

She looked at him inquiringly: "Not!" And then eagerly: "You are going to tell me you are a prince in disguise! I guessed it!"

"Ha, ha, no. My real name is a hideous one. So I changed it many years ago."

"But 'Jones!' Why did you change to Jones? It's so—so—I mean it's like jumping out of the frying-pan into the stove."

And Mr. Jones mused: "Humph, perhaps so. But it was a question of good taste, I did not want to make spurious capital out of that opportunity. I chose the commonest name I could think of."

"What is your dreadful name?"

"My name?" He paused to drink again, then with burlesque solemnity he said: "My name is Death."

Her vivacity was a little quenched. "Really?" She peered earnestly at him, spinning the stem of her glass between finger and thumb, and he bowed assent. "How lugubrious! Yes, you were right to change it—for anything."

They had finished with the trifle and were bedevilling the oranges and nuts. The perfume she exhaled came, he thought, from her splendid hair—may-blossom after warm showers.

"My maiden name was Catterick."

"Scotch?" he inquired.

"No. Suffolk," said the lady.

"Well," he was picking a stubborn nut from its shell. "I can't call you that."

"No." She was parting an orange in her plate; her gaze was concentrated upon that object.

"I can't stand calling you Lady Leeward. I hate titles."

"Socialist! But yes, they are a great bore. Don't you like my Christian name?"

"No."

"Why not?" asked Judith, still intent upon her orange.

"She cut off the head of her lover."

Lady Leeward stared up uncomprehendingly for some moments. "Oh —you mean that Judith—in the Bible

—and that Holofernes man. Ah, I promise not to do that."

In the tingling silence that followed she began to blush, and to cover her confusion she raised her glass towards him.

"Here's to you—Christopher!"

He raised his until it clinked with hers, and he murmured: "To you, Judy." She sought his hand across the table.

And then the footman arrived with the coffee, and a maid to clear the table.

Coffee was served to them on the green velvet couch, and while the servants were clearing the table the lady chatted to Mr. Jones of those interesting things in her house which she desired to show him on some other occasion. It was an old house, an admiral had built it after the naval victory at La Hogue. William and Mary's reign. Sixteen ninety something. "You like old furniture?"

"No," said the schoolmaster. The servants withdrew so quietly that he did not perceive their going.

"Are there any legends about the place?" he asked.

"No, there are none that I know of."

"Or ghosts?"

"No. No legends or ghosts. The Leewards have always, as they say, feared God and honoured the King. Always. Doing nothing magnificent and no wrong thing."

Jones put his coffee cup carefully aside and said:

"Your neighbours, you know, do just the opposite." He leaned back into a corner of the couch, crossed his legs, and clasped his hands across one high knee. A sort of wry grin appeared upon his face. Lady Leeward had already noticed that his features seldom presented anything so soft, so tender, as a smile. Yes, he was a satirical

creature, downright and indubitable; and there was a lack of breeding even in the expression of his sympathies, they did not flow in a gentle crystal spring, but in a fountain of brine. And yet. . . . When she asked him who, precisely, he meant by her neighbours, he retorted:

"The country folk, the poor, Hodge, the cowman, the ploughman. They do everything magnificently, but they do nothing right—the poor preposterous poor!"

Lady Leeward took a cigarette, the guest refused one. "Oh, the villagers! You are unjust to them, aren't you?" She waited for Jones to offer her a light, but he did not notice this. "What have they done wrong? On the whole I find them charming, yes, very industrious. Oh no, oh no. What do you find wrong about my neighbours?"

Jones said: "They've kept the cuckoo in their nest."

She struck a match and puffed meditatively at the cigarette. "Cuckoo!" It puzzled her; there were one or two cases of infidelity in the village, it was true, but . . . "What on earth do you mean?"

"I mean that the village pipits have maintained and cherished the Leeward cuckoo for—so you tell me—over two hundred years."

She blew out a long puff of smoke. "Oh, I get your meaning. Humph, you *are* a Socialist! I'm the wicked cuckoo, then. That is not very complimentary to me."

"Neither is it," he said grimly, "complimentary to them."

"And you think it is all wrong?"

"Both grand and wrong," said Jones.

"Nature," continued Lady Leeward, "created the real cuckoos, that's a natural precedent."

"Ah," he sighed, "you're still in a state of nature rather than of grace."

"It is no bad thing if you are born

to be a Leeward. I prefer it. One might have been a Jones—or a Brown or Robinson. There had to be a cuckoo."

"Yes, that's the grandeur of it," murmured he.

"You see," she went on eagerly, "you can't all be leaders, some must be servants in a world like ours. And as the Bible says, *They also serve who only stand and wait.*"

"Bible! Bah! They always wait who only stand and serve!"

"You're an atheist, too, then?"

"No, I'm not," the schoolmaster's tone was gruff. "It isn't in the Bible, it's Milton."

"I must own that I prefer a gentleman to a peasant. In the long run you'll find he is the better. Breeding counts. The important thing in life is to be well-bred."

"Ah! Take care of the parents and the offspring will pay for itself."

Nothing could be more charming than her patience. "These village people are nice things to have in a landscape, or to read about in books, but what is there inside them? They have mean souls, mean minds, they are musty in body and brain. They lie and shuffle, steal, scandalize, flatter, and deceive. And that is because their souls are mean."

"Or how else," he blandly inquired, "could you have deceived them for so long? Whether the pipit was made for the cuckoo, or the cuckoo for the pipit, cuckoos there are and they thrive on the blood of the poor. Hasn't the cuckoo a mean soul? Does it not live meanly?"

"Do you really think that's the sort of person I am?" Her voice was soft, velvety.

He replied, with the nearest thing to a smile that he ever achieved: "I assure you I am speaking quite impersonally."

Judith shook her head distrustfully. "No, you are not. But what do you take us for? We have the best of things because we are the better people. We have the advantage because we have developed the finer type; it's like the flower of a tree, what comes to the top after centuries, the seed of culture, courage, integrity, all the higher things the race is capable of. I don't mean that we alone possess them, but that we have promoted and conserved them. And that would only be possible in a leisured class, the possibility of it even would be gone without us. . . ."

He intervened: "In one word you mean the gentry are a national profit?"

She hesitated. "I don't like that one word, but in general we haven't mean souls, we can be trusted, we are staunch, our word is a pledge to death. Esprit de corps, and so on. But I suppose you would deny that?"

He would: "To add my weak word to the verdict of history, justice, and common sense," he said, "would be superfluous."

Was he angry? She could not tell. She felt angry, but she was sure it was not with him. Yet you could scarcely be angry with yourself.

"Oh, stop this, please!" she suddenly cried. "Why, what are we arguing about? Why have we drifted into such a discussion? It's snobbish of me."

Judith went over to the little black piano and let her fingers ripple over the keys. Without turning round she called to him:

"I did not mean one word of what I said about them."

As he made no answer she played a pretty phrase or two over and over again, then stopped and facing him said:

"Neither did you."

Ah, but he did! And there was no

doubt that he meant it. Again primping on the piano, she exclaimed: "I wish you did not think such things, you are wrong about us, you know. I wonder when I shall see you again. You look on me as 'the enemy,' I suppose. I am going away soon." At last he stood at her side, saying he must go, yes, really he must go. Bannerman shall take you in the car," said Lady Leeward.

"No, no," protested Christopher Jones. He preferred to walk, much, yes, truly.

Lady Leeward then put on a cloak of yellow velvet trimmed with white fur and went along to the hall with the schoolmaster. He put on his coat and then the lady said she would walk with him to the lodge gates for a breath of air if the night were fine. The night was fine. The lodge gates were a quarter of a mile away, and the road dark though the sky was sparkling. It lay between trees and he walked slowly, warily, as if at any moment he might put his foot through the crust of the earth into the next world. The lady slipped her arm into the schoolmaster's and immediately they began to hurry. They walked quickly, step to step.

"Why are you going so fast?" whispered Judith.

Then they stopped, quite still, and without a word the schoolmaster pulled her quickly to him with both his arms.

"Oh, be careful, Jones! Chris, be careful," murmured the lady, returning his kisses. "Why—you have gone mad, anyone could see me in this cloak."

The madman only pressed her lips more fondly, with little moans of tenderness.

"Listen," she breathlessly gasped. "I'll write to you. Will you write to me? Chris, Chris! I must go. Oh, be careful, I must. Good-bye, I will write."

She swung out of his arms and began to walk steadily back to the Hall, while he stood watching her, mumbling: "Lovely she is. I am a boor, she is a queen."

For ten days he hungered, in fevers of anticipation, for that something which hung in the air between them. As to what it was, Jones would not permit himself to gaze too deeply: was it a flame too bright for his eyes, or a mere mist of ecstasy? Jones only knew that his mind and emotions, thought, desire, and fear were charged with an image of her splendour, her friendliness and frankness. Of course she had been right to defend her class from his trite gibes, she herself was the living proof against him. No pharisee, no, she was no pharisee, though she was surely "not as these others are." The poor were mean, and the high-born were fine, though the claim of the under-class was age-old and unconfutable. But she did not write to him, why did she not write to him? And he could not see her again, she was beyond his reach; he did not even hear of her, she was beyond his range. Yes, and beyond him in everything—beauty, position, pride, and beyond him—oh, unalterably!—beyond him in love. How had it come about that he, a son of the people—yes, that was his own grandiloquent appellation—should have leaned to take one step in an intrigue, a dishonourable intrigue, with one of the class he had been born to despise? As the days slunk by, his fervour, unabated, swerved to meet his own cynical challenge; she had been only too right about social quality and tone, it was he who had been the offensive snob, he had begun it, he had scoffed at the "honour" of her class and he had paraded the "honour" of his own.

And then he had tempted her! What a lesson! You could not trust a boor with an agreeable lady. Judith had dropped him like a hot coal. And how that coal still flamed! *My name is Death!* Bah, you fine phrasing fellow, now you have caught a tartar. What a lesson, oh, what a lesson!

And then there came a letter. From abroad. From the south of France. She did not explain that annihilating transit, but she called him her dear Chris. He was, she wrote, so wise, so experienced, so sympathetic about the poor, it had moved her very deeply, and she longed to know more, and much more about himself. He was to tell her all about himself. And she signed: *Yours, Judy.*

In his quick reply he threw serenity to the dogs, gave pride, gave scruple, the discard—his bubbling, baffled blood told him he was lost—he wanted passionately to know why she had gone, and when she was coming back.

Lady Leeward moved serenely eastwards in the south of France, and at Christmas she had gone into Switzerland for the winter sports. She was travelling with friends. Many letters passed between them; hers were tender, his were ardent. It was unwise, she wrote, for him to keep her letters. She entreated him to burn hers as soon as read, just as she was doing. He obeyed, with the feeling of a devout man forced to commit a violent sacrilege. Then she went on to Italy, and the despairing schoolmaster feared that she would not come back again until Sir Gulistan was home from his hunting in Africa. But he did not ask her about that; he dared not ask himself why he feared Sir Gulistan's return. February went, March went, April came. At last she was coming home! By then the treetops in the lane were just heaps of waving buds, petulant when the skies were grey or white, but when the sun shone and the breezes blew them in that bold cerulean air they were angelic, unearthly; the twirl of the universe was in their movement. And they would ripen, when she came, as if their whole body was one enchanting fruit. The schoolmaster set his small house in order, day by day, with marvellous care. When he laid his white sheets on the grass to air they had an immensity that surprised him. And when May was near, Judith came home once more to the Hall in the park.

III

The western bounds of Leeward Park were determined by a wide dense wood, and from the wood stretched a heathery moor wherein lay many dells of greensward and dens of furze. In the middle of the moor, at a distance of nearly a mile from Old Hall rose a small grassy hill crowned with a dozen dark pines. Whatever its geological significance might have been, Black Knoll had no known historical or legendary affiliations; its contour was comely, its situation singular, and its loneliness endowed it with charm or the reverse according to the mood of the passer-by. It was this remote spot that Judith indicated for their place of meeting, enjoining the utmost secrecy and caution upon the schoolmaster. He was to be there at eight o'clock, there would be a moon, and she would come to him by the pathway through Leeward Wood that led from the park to the moor. On the appointed evening he stole there by uncustomary paths, avoiding the village. The evening air was so mild that it quivered when the evening bells of St. Nicholas shook their melancholy note into it, and a long shroud of white fume from the allotment fires

dispersed laterally without movement, meditating. After a while the schoolmaster came to a road leading from the village. A young bedraggled woman was sitting on a bank there as if waiting for someone. At Jones's approach she got up and walked a few yards behind him.

"Mister!" she whined, "will you give me something for a night's lodging?"

He stopped and gave her a shilling. Then they walked on together for a few moments in the dusk until someone advanced along the road towards them. The woman stopped and turned fearfully. "Christ, is that Jimmy?" she whispered. The schoolmaster looked ahead. "That's the shoemaker," said he. "Oh," sighed the woman, relieved, "is it?" Jones laughed and the woman laughed and they moved on again.

"Good night, George," said Jones in reply to the passing shoemaker, and the beggar-woman commented:

"Shoemaker! Well, it don't much matter what it is, to get a living is all a worry."

"Ah," agreed the schoolmaster. "But I turn off here, good night."

"God bless you," said the woman, and he left her in the road and took a footpath beside a hedge. He did not hear her footsteps resume their march along the road; perhaps she was watching him, but he could not tell if this was so because of a bend in the hedge path. By and by he came to another road, and beyond it Leeward Great Wood began, shaped in a half-circle curling round the park. Jones did not enter the wood, but advanced along its outside contour until he came to the moor, and there, suddenly closer, loomed Black Knoll. He climbed its easy slope and reached the pines, and there he waited. The moon was high aloft in the windless air. Passionate moon! The man waited

and the lady came wrapped in a dark cloak.

Oh, for weeks this promised assignation had been their fiery secret, and now the encounter was cool—How d'ye do?—almost polite, but once they moved into the shadow of the grove they seemed to leap and melt into a wordless unity, a thing of lips but no tongue. But what is this? He swung her back to the light again to behold her beautiful hair cropped in a new foreign fashion. At the edge of the trees they sat side by side on a thick mat of pine needles, conversing about her travels, but in a little while, when they had fallen to whispering, they lay down together. Her arms stole round his neck, and his hands went rudely, caressingly, about her until Judy threw off her cloak and they took the ultimate embrace.

At a later moment the lady sat up and uttered a sound of dismay. "Somebody has been watching us!" A dark figure was running from the shadows of Leeward Wood towards them. Twice it stopped and looked, its face a pallid spot before the moonlight, and then ran stumbling on, skirting the knoll until it passed out of their sight, lost among the bushes.

"Who is it?" asked the startled Judith.

"He saw nothing," her lover assured her, "he was too far away. He was unaware of us, a poacher, I fancy. Something in the wood alarmed him, perhaps. He could not see us."

"I hope not; it must never be known, Chris. Let us go now."

Jones lifted her to her feet with tender joy, she put on her cloak again, and they descended the hill and crossed over the moor to Leeward Wood. He was to go with her as far as the wall on the other side. They entered the dark glades, away from

that passionate moonlight, and walked in the paths steadily, never speaking, but only clasping each other. In a quarter of an hour they came to the wall and the private door into the park. Judith took a key from a pocket in her cloak and unlocked the door, and the holy radiance of the moon burst on them again. There lay the smooth choice park with its flint wall stretching right and left of them and trees curving benignantly over it, and across the grass, a quarter of a mile away, was her home, the great Hall. There were lights shining in a few of the windows in the wing that was in shadow.

"I do not want to go there," Judith murmured. "I could stay here for ever with you," and she pulled him back behind the dark secrecy of the wall and hung silently against his breast.

"You will never speak of this, dear Chris, not to a living soul. You'll swear it."

"How could you imagine it of me!" he asked reproachfully.

"I know, I know; but men do love to boast of their conquests."

"Not I."

"I trust you, beloved. Think of my reputation. Are you—aren't you hungry?"

He laughingly reminded her that she had asked him the same question on their first night together in the car. But he had eaten little today.

"Nor I. I was too excited. I knew," she whispered, "I knew we were going to love." She peeped into the park again. "It isn't far. Wait. Will you wait? I will go and fetch something to eat and we will have a moonlight picnic, eh? You must be starved, poor dear. What is the time?"

It was ten o'clock.

"Keep the door shut while I am gone," said she, "and wait only a tiny time."

She stepped boldly and quickly across the park. Carefully Jones closed the door and waited behind it in the shadow thrown by the wall, listening to little scratching movements in the undergrowth. The moonlight glared above the wall and there was a sort of terror in the unshaking shadows of some of those skeleton trees; that radiance from aloft lay upon their trunks like scrofula. But there was a wild cherry tree blooming alone there; the moonbeams caressed its bosomed whiteness with a lustre infinitely precious and pure. To the waiting anxious lover it seemed that his lady had gone out of this fantasy of time and the miracle of space; it was not possible that she would return, but he would wait and wait, under the wild white cherry tree. It had the gleam of her breasts and her smooth tremulous limbs. And though all her beauty and richness had been crumpled in passionate disarray, she had been strangely triumphant. How nonchalant that witnessing moon!

Across the park she came flitting back to him. Under her cloak Judith had brought a bag with slices of plum cake.

"Look!" she whispered gaily; there was a bottle.

"What is it?" he asked.

"Hock," said she breathlessly. "Isn't it a lark! I couldn't get anything else without making a fuss. We'll go just inside the park, it's lighter, and we can sit under a yew tree; the grass is dry. Chris, break the neck off the bottle in here, quietly, and then come over to the yew tree."

Judith darted off into the park. "And, Chris, shut the door after you," she cautiously called. Having done these things, he joined her under the

tree and they quaffed the wine from her collapsible drinking-cup. For an hour they lay and lingered there, and before parting, there had been a repetition of that flaring passion of the pine knoll.

"Chris, have I given myself too easily—will you despise me?"

Her melting tenderness exalted him. "Judy, Judy!"

"Oh, take care!"

"I'll be mum as the grave."

"My dear secret lover!"

Jones drew off her shoe and stocking and kissed the foot he had once comforted.

"Take," she whispered at last, "that empty bottle with you and heave it somewhere into the wood; mustn't leave it here. And, Chris, remember: be discreet, I am far too fond of you."

As she stole away from him he stood in the shadow of the tree, with the bottle clutched in his hands, watching her all the way until she was lost in the gloomy angle of the Hall. What was the curious fear in his heart as he turned away? That this was the end of it, that she would never, never come again, and he was lost, lost, lost for evermore! By the time he had got safely into the wood again he was happy, and in his exhilaration he flung the bottle with all his might among the trees. Stupid ass! He flung it carelessly and gashed the palm of his hand on its splintered neck. The blood streamed. Wrapping his handkerchief against his palm, he hurried on. There was no pain, nothing could pain him now, with all that fostering bliss in the heaven of a world. Sometimes he broke into a run, so exhilarated was he. When he reached home it was midnight and, going at once to bed, he fell into a dreamless sleep.

Three days later he was arrested for murder.

IV

In Leeward Great Wood the body of an unknown woman of the tramping class had been found; she had been violated and then murdered by a cruel blow from a stake on the back of her skull. It would be tedious to follow in detail the process by which suspicion fell upon the schoolmaster, but it will be seen that he was himself largely to blame for the position he was in when the local court committed him. Briefly, the woman was the beggar-woman to whom he had given a shilling, and she was killed on the night he and Judith had met on Black Knoll. Absolutely nothing was known of the woman; it was as if she had just sauntered into the world of Christopher Jones for a few moments and blasted it. The salient pieces of incriminating evidence were these. A shoemaker, as we know, had seen Jones walking with the woman on the fatal evening. Jones explained that matter. He had gone out for a stroll and the woman, a complete stranger, had accosted him and begged a shilling from him. He had given her a shilling and left her standing in the road. He did *not* know that she had, as the shoemaker declared, followed him down the hedge path to Leeward Great Wood. The accused man declared that he had walked past Leeward Wood, quite alone, and gone to the Black Knoll. While resting there, he had seen a man run out of Leeward Wood in a suspicious way, but had not passed close enough for Jones to recognize him or describe him; then he had returned home. Another witness had seen Jones enter the wood with a woman between nine and nine thirty on that night. Jones emphatically denied that. It was certainly him-

self and Judith who had been seen, but he dared not implicate her. Witness was certain it was Jones he saw, but the woman was a stranger; it was full moonlight and he had been sitting on a stile not twenty yards from the entrance to the wood. Another person had seen Jones near his home just before midnight. He was running. It seemed to Jones that the world that night had been crowded with spying eyes. He swore that he had reached his home at nine o'clock. Then a handkerchief of his, soaked with blood, had been found in the path not very far from the body. Jones could not deny that the handkerchief was his, but he could not explain that he must have dropped it while running, or that it was his own blood.

Jones was bewildered by the astounding circumstances that implicated him. It was unthinkable that an innocent man could be convicted of this crime, but it looked as though Judith might be drawn into it if he was not very careful. Otherwise he was not unduly alarmed. He was, indeed, more deeply moved because he was hurried into prison just as he had attained a topmost peak of joy. Until the trial was over, the intolerable separation must be endured. Pending any move from Judith—and he could not know what course she would be desirous of pursuing—he maintained this untrue version of his movements. There was time enough, if the worst incredibly came to the worst—well . . . of course . . . then . . . well, they would have to see. . . .

So Christopher Jones endured the ordeal of his trial with stoicism, if not with a quite clear conscience. None knew of his secret meeting with Judith on Black Knoll, and not all the King's horses nor all the King's

men should drag that knowledge from him until she signified her submission to his supreme need. And he had never a doubt of her, only a vague wonder, until he was condemned to be hanged by the neck until he was dead. The crashing doom, the appalling certainty, moved him only to a grinding silent ironic commination of the great lady who feared God and honoured the King. The queenly thing was a carcass stuffed with rags. It was not God alone, then, whom she so falsely feared, and if she honoured the King she could yet shame the King's justice! This was what *her* breeding, culture, courage, integrity came to when encountering a terrific fact that could not veil their shame. As for *his*, he would have to teach her a lesson, a great lesson. Horrible! Her infatuation with her "good name" had doomed him to death. Ancient Judith cut off her lover's head! Her pride of caste was a tyrannous fiction, a foible, without ultimate quality. Honour, fine thinking, fine doing, were in the blood of those she despised. His pride should triumph. Perhaps, in the end, it was less pride than pity, and more love than either. He had but to lift a finger, a little tiny finger—but let her be comforted! For her to have declared the truth would have been a glory indeed. For him to declare it would be infamy. That was how it worked. Poor, poor Judith, she had failed. Poor heroic dunce, need he fail too?

The whole village was saddened by his fate; even those villagers who had betrayed him believed in him, somehow, against all reason. All remembered his kindness, his honesty, his queerness. Pots of paint! Every month he had given the best boy in his classes a pot of paint. "If you have no other use for it," he would say to the boy, "you could paint your front door

with it." Each month the paint was of a different colour, and that was how the cottage doors had come to have the bright hues that so surprised casual visitors. He had painted the village not red, but green and purple, blue and orange. Butterflies! At the summer fete a year or two ago Lady Leeward had presented the prizes, and at the close of that function half a dozen of Jones's boys had come forward, each bearing a cardboard box. As they came up to her ladyship the boys had opened the boxes—they were full of living butterflies. The boys had cast the butterflies into the air above the great lady, and while they hovered, fluttered, and wandered about her the people had cheered. But pots of paint and butterflies are no defences against the assaults of misfortune.

Meanwhile Judith had lived in such anguish of love and shame, and agony of fear so great, that her beauty melted from her like a white cloud in the blaze of noon. With a thousand equivocations she cajoled her conscience. Perhaps, after all, he *had* committed the foul crime. She did not, could not, know, no one would ever know. The evidence was overwhelming, and he had not communicated with her, he had lied and lied and lied. To save such a man she would have to betray her husband and their kindred—far-reaching subtle ruin. Why need she reveal anything yet? Not yet, all might yet be cleared up and he would be saved without her sacrifice. He would be sure to disclose the truth sooner or later, and when *he* did so she would accept it, confirm it, she would not deny it. But one white fact shone through all her sophistries with blinding ray—he had not betrayed her. Perhaps her one sincere but deeply hidden wish was that he *would* tell;

beyond that one possibility of escape for him her mind could not dare to grope. When she learned the dreadful issue of the trial she determined to flee away, she could not rest, neither night nor day, with such a sword plunging into her heart, but after making preparations flesh and blood failed her, her spirit was wrecked, and she was carried to her bed, and her physician summoned from London. He was an old bachelor, a friend of Sir Gulistan's, and he slept at the Hall for a while. On the day before Jones was to die Judith gulped down a dose of poison—veronal or some such drug to which high-born women seem to have easy access. On the table by her bedside she had left a sealed letter addressed to the doctor marked: *"Open immediately."* When it was discovered what Judith had done, Dr. Paton Cope, an exceedingly capable man despite the fact that he had himself suffered from hernia for twenty years, plunged after the poisoned woman as Orpheus plunged after Eurydice. He saw the letter and he scrambled it into his pocket. She lay in a state of coma for three days, and if the spirit really goes awandering at such times, Heaven knows what frightful visitation the soul of Judith made. This was her letter: the doctor read it when he was quite alone, in Sir Gulistan's study.

"Dear Paton:

"I am going to poison myself. There is no way out, a horrible thing is killing me, so horrible that it is only a question of a few hours one way or the other. I shall die in any case. There is nothing more for me to do except write this letter and confess everything. That is so difficult. I made the acquaintance of Christopher Jones some months ago; he did me a great

kindness when I was thrown once at hunting. I liked him at once, he was curiously *good*, a high-minded though low-spirited man. And he was friendless, and I was lonely. Now he has been convicted of the murder of a wretched tramp-woman. Well, he had nothing whatever to do with that, but I am the only person who knows it. He has been wrongly condemned. He is *innocent*. He knows that I know it, but he will not call me because my own evidence would involve me so seriously. It would be so easy for him. When I was abroad we wrote long loving letters, we were in love, and when I came back I was mad to see him again. I do not love him now, I hate him. I hate his fearful generosity. I am in a trap. I am angry, not sorry at all, angry that I have got to die, more angry that I have got to die because of some stupid mistake, and most angry of all because it is no use dying unless I tell you why. It is impossible to tell a thing like this and go on living. And I can't live any longer. There are times when that hysterical statement is true. On the night of this horrible murder we had arranged to meet at Black Knoll at eight o'clock. We had not seen each other for months and we had been writing—oh, the things men and women do write! We met there, the most beautiful evening in all time. Moonlight and spring. It was wonderful. Kisses and caresses were not enough, it was all wild and impetuous, and there we were lovers. You *understand*, real lovers. I gave everything, willingly. It was no time to think of honour. After all, my honour is my own, to do what I like with. That is why I throw it away now, for *nothing*. I loved him passionately then. I do not love him now. I hate him as I hate myself. Afterwards we saw a man break out from the wood

and run away as if he were afraid of something. It must have been *that* man who killed the woman. She was killed while we were loving. We walked back together in the lovely moonlight, through Leeward Park to the gate in the park wall, and then we did not want to leave each other. Even then. He said he was hungry, so I went across to fetch something from the house. I could only get a bottle of wine and some cake. We sat under a yew tree just inside the park, and after we had drunk the wine it was all so magical and still, the grass cold and soft. A long way off, a bird was making a long frantic purring noise. Again there was kissing and embracing, and once again we were lovers. So you see it was impossible for him to have done this thing to that woman, for twice that night he had been my lover. He was with me. She was already dead. She was lying in the wood beyond the wall, dead, as I shall be dead in an hour. It was past eleven o'clock when I left him. I told him to take the empty bottle away and throw it in the wood, and I see it must have been that bottle which gashed his hand so dreadfully. I have not seen him since. I dared not go to the trial, I dared not, I dared not, you must realize that. There is another thing besides. I know now that I am with child. If I lived I should have *his* child. Gulistan has been away for months. I am in a trap whichever way I turn. What mad, mad irony! Do you see, that child itself is the proof of its father's innocence.

"This is all true, quite true, the whole truth, so help me God. I am not mad, I am quite calm, I do not love him now. I have no feeling but rage, rage against these evil circumstances, everything is so stupid, stupid, stupid. I can only free him by doing

what I am going to do. You must
take all the necessary steps, old friend,
at once. He has risked everything to
keep my name out of this affair, but
that must not matter now. As I said,
my honour is my own. I did what I
liked with it. This is all I can do now.
Tell him from me that he was right
after all, he will remember and un-
derstand.

"Good-bye, Paton.

"Good-bye, Gulistan.

"These are the last words of Judith
Leeward.

"Good-bye, Chris.

"P.S.—I *did* love him, and O my God
I love him *now*."

The doctor was confounded. He
was a tall, slightly stooping, rather
ascetic man, with high, bare brow
and pince-nez. Sour though his fea-
tures looked, he had a pleasant voice
and pleasant manner. He was highly
esteemed.

"It's preposterous," he murmured,
"of course, it's preposterous."

Again he read the letter, and again
certain passages.

"Pooh, impossible, my dear Judith,
impossible. Sheer neurotic dementia.
If ever there was a woman free from
erotomania I should have said it was

Judith, you know. It's this long sepa-
ration from Gulistan, ought to have
gone with him. Highly strung, nerv-
ous state, sex hallucinations playing
the devil. They play the devil with
you."

Once more he read the letter.

"By Jove, yes, it *is* impossible.
Never was a clearer case against a
scoundrel. I'll get rid of this."

Paton Cope stooped over the fire
and dropped the letter in. It burnt to
a grey trembling ash.

"Neurotic dementia," repeated the
doctor. "Must get Gulistan back at
once. Neurotic dementia."

The following day he began efforts
to get into touch with Judith's hus-
band, but they proved to be all in
vain, for poor Sir Gulistan had been
stung by a poisonous insect in East
African territory and suffered a most
unhappy end. The great lady was ill
for a week or two longer, then she
recovered. At a safe interval, much
later, Paton Cope questioned her
about the letter. What letter? She did
not understand, did not quiver an
eyelid. He dropped the subject and
congratulated himself. Paton Cope
was fond of her. Certainly she never
had a child. Perhaps some day she
will marry him.

A MOTHER IN MANNVILLE

MARJORIE KINNAN RAWLINGS

The orphanage is high in the Carolina mountains. Sometimes in winter the snowdrifts are so deep that the institution is cut off from the village below, from all the world. Fog hides the mountain peaks, the snow swirls down the valleys, and a wind blows so bitterly that the orphanage boys who take the milk twice daily to the baby cottage reach the door with fingers stiff in an agony of numbness.

"Or when we carry trays from the cookhouse for the ones that are sick," Jerry said, "we get our faces frostbit, because we can't put our hands over them. I have gloves," he added. "Some of the boys don't have any."

He liked the late spring, he said. The rhododendron was in bloom, a carpet of color, across the mountainsides, soft as the May winds that stirred the hemlocks. He called it laurel.

"It's pretty when the laurel blooms," he said. "Some of it's pink and some of it's white."

I was there in the autumn. I wanted quiet, isolation, to do some troublesome writing. I wanted mountain air to blow out the malaria from too long a time in the subtropics. I was homesick, too, for the flaming of maples in October, and for corn shocks and pumpkins and black-walnut trees and the lift of hills. I found them all, living in a cabin that belonged to the orphanage, half a mile beyond the orphanage farm. When I took the cabin, I asked for a boy or man to come and chop wood for the fireplace. The first few days were warm, I found what wood I needed about the cabin, no one came, and I forgot the order.

I looked up from my typewriter one late afternoon, a little startled. A boy stood at the door, and my pointer dog, my companion, was at his side and had not barked to warn me. The boy was probably twelve years old, but undersized. He wore overalls and a torn shirt, and was barefooted.

He said, "I can chop some wood today."

I said, "But I have a boy coming from the orphanage."

"I'm the boy."

"You? But you're small."

"Size don't matter, chopping wood," he said. "Some of the big boys don't chop good. I've been chopping wood at the orphanage a long time."

I visualized mangled and inade-

Copyright 1936 by The Curtis Publishing Company; from *When the Whippoorwill*, by Marjorie Kinnan Rawlings. Reprinted by permission of the publishers, Charles Scribner's Sons.

quate branches for my fires. I was well into my work and not inclined to conversation. I was a little blunt. "Very well. There's the ax. Go ahead and see what you can do."

I went back to work, closing the door. At first the sound of the boy dragging brush annoyed me. Then he began to chop. The blows were rhythmic and steady, and shortly I had forgotten him, the sound no more of an interruption than a consistent rain. I suppose an hour and a half passed, for when I stopped and stretched, and heard the boy's steps on the cabin stoop, the sun was dropping behind the farthest mountain, and the valleys were purple with something deeper than the asters.

The boy said, "I have to go to supper now. I can come again tomorrow evening."

I said, "I'll pay you now for what you've done," thinking I should probably have to insist on an older boy. "Ten cents an hour?"

"Anything is all right."

We went together back of the cabin. An astonishing amount of solid wood had been cut. There were cherry logs and heavy roots of rhododendron, and blocks from the waste pine and oak left from the building of the cabin.

"But you've done as much as a man," I said. "This is a splendid pile."

I looked at him, actually, for the first time. His hair was the color of the corn shocks and his eyes, very direct, were like the mountain sky when rain is pending—gray, with a shadowing of that miraculous blue. As I spoke, a light came over him, as though the setting sun had touched him with the same suffused glory with which it touched the mountains. I gave him a quarter.

"You may come tomorrow," I said, "and thank you very much."

He looked at me, and at the coin, and seemed to want to speak, but could not, and turned away.

"I'll split kindling tomorrow," he said over his thin ragged shoulder. "You'll need kindling and medium wood and logs and backlogs."

At daylight I was half wakened by the sound of chopping. Again it was so even in texture that I went back to sleep. When I left my bed in the cool morning, the boy had come and gone, and a stack of kindling was neat against the cabin wall. He came again after school in the afternoon and worked until time to return to the orphanage. His name was Jerry; he was twelve years old, and he had been at the orphanage since he was four. I could picture him at four, with the same grave gray-blue eyes and the same—independence? No, the word that comes to me is "integrity."

The word means something very special to me, and the quality for which I use it is a rare one. My father had it—there is another of whom I am almost sure—but almost no man of my acquaintance possesses it with the clarity, the purity, the simplicity of a mountain stream. But the boy Jerry had it. It is bedded on courage, but it is more than brave. It is honest, but it is more than honesty. The ax handle broke one day. Jerry said the woodshop at the orphanage would repair it. I brought money to pay for the job and he refused it.

"I'll pay for it," he said. "I broke it. I brought the ax down careless."

"But no one hits accurately every time," I told him. "The fault was in the wood of the handle. I'll see the man from whom I bought it."

It was only then that he would take the money. He was standing back of his own carelessness. He was a free-will agent and he chose to do careful work, and if he failed, he took

the responsibility without subterfuge.

And he did for me the unnecessary thing, the gracious thing, that we find done only by the great of heart. Things no training can teach, for they are done on the instant, with no predicated experience. He found a cubbyhole beside the fireplace that I had not noticed. There, of his own accord, he put kindling and "medium" wood, so that I might always have dry fire material ready in case of sudden wet weather. A stone was loose in the rough walk to the cabin. He dug a deeper hole and steadied it, although he came, himself, by a short cut over the bank. I found that when I tried to return his thoughtfulness with such things as candy and apples, he was wordless. "Thank you" was, perhaps, an expression for which he had had no use, for his courtesy was instinctive. He only looked at the gift and at me, and a curtain lifted, so that I saw deep into the clear well of his eyes, and gratitude was there, and affection, soft over the firm granite of his character.

He made simple excuses to come and sit with me. I could no more have turned him away than if he had been physically hungry. I suggested once that the best time for us to visit was just before supper, when I left off my writing. After that, he waited always until my typewriter had been some time quiet. One day I worked until nearly dark. I went outside the cabin, having forgotten him. I saw him going up over the hill in the twilight toward the orphanage. When I sat down on my stoop, a place was warm from his body where he had been sitting.

He became intimate, of course, with my pointer, Pat. There is a strange communion between a boy and a dog. Perhaps they possess the same singleness of spirit, the same

kind of wisdom. It is difficult to explain, but it exists. When I went across the state for a week end, I left the dog in Jerry's charge. I gave him the dog whistle and the key to the cabin, and left sufficient food. He was to come two or three times a day and let out the dog, and feed and exercise him. I should return Sunday night, and Jerry would take out the dog for the last time Sunday afternoon and then leave the key under an agreed hiding place.

My return was belated and fog filled the mountain passes so treacherously that I dared not drive at night. The fog held the next morning, and it was Monday noon before I reached the cabin. The dog had been fed and cared for that morning. Jerry came early in the afternoon, anxious.

"The superintendent said nobody would drive in the fog," he said. "I came just before bedtime last night and you hadn't come. So I brought Pat some of my breakfast this morning. I wouldn't have let anything happen to him."

"I was sure of that. I didn't worry."

"When I heard about the fog, I thought you'd know."

He was needed for work at the orphanage and he had to return at once. I gave him a dollar in payment, and he looked at it and went away. But that night he came in the darkness and knocked at the door.

"Come in, Jerry," I said, "if you're allowed to be away this late."

"I told maybe a story," he said. "I told them I thought you would want to see me."

"That's true," I assured him, and I saw his relief. "I want to hear about how you managed with the dog."

He sat by the fire with me, with no other light, and told me of their two days together. The dog lay close to him, and found a comfort there

that I did not have for him. And it seemed to me that being with my dog, and caring for him, had brought the boy and me, too, together, so that he felt that he belonged to me as well as to the animal.

"He stayed right with me," he told me, "except when he ran in the laurel. He likes the laurel. I took him up over the hill and we both ran fast. There was a place where the grass was high and I lay down in it and hid. I could hear Pat hunting for me. He found my trail and he barked. When he found me, he acted crazy, and he ran around and around me, in circles."

We watched the flames.

"That's an apple log," he said. "It burns the prettiest of any wood."

We were very close.

He was suddenly impelled to speak of things he had not spoken of before, nor had I cared to ask him.

"You look a little bit like my mother," he said. "Especially in the dark, by the fire."

"But you were only four, Jerry, when you came here. You have remembered how she looked, all these years?"

"My mother lives in Mannville," he said.

For a moment, finding that he had a mother shocked me as greatly as anything in my life has ever done, and I did not know why it disturbed me. Then I understood my distress. I was filled with a passionate resentment that any woman should go away and leave her son. A fresh anger added itself. A son like this one— The orphanage was a wholesome place, the executives were kind, good people, the food was more than adequate, the boys were healthy, a ragged shirt was no hardship, nor the doing of clean labor. Granted, perhaps, that the boy felt no lack, what blood fed the bowels of a woman who did not yearn over this child's lean body that had come in parturition out of her own? At four he would have looked the same as now. Nothing, I thought, nothing in life could change those eyes. His quality must be apparent

to an idiot, a fool. I burned with questions I could not ask. In any, I was afraid, there would be pain.

"Have you seen her, Jerry—lately?"

"I see her every summer. She sends for me."

I wanted to cry out, "Why are you not with her? How can she let you go away again?"

He said, "She comes up here from Mannville whenever she can. She doesn't have a job now."

His face shone in the firelight.

"She wanted to give me a puppy, but they can't let any one boy keep a puppy. You remember the suit I had on last Sunday?" He was plainly proud. "She sent me that for Christmas. The Christmas before that"—he drew a long breath, savoring the memory—"she sent me a pair of skates."

"Roller skates?"

My mind was busy, making pictures of her, trying to understand her. She had not, then, entirely deserted or forgotten him. But why, then— I thought, "I must not condemn her without knowing."

"Roller skates. I let the other boys use them. They're always borrowing them. But they're careful of them."

What circumstance other than poverty——

"I'm going to take the dollar you gave me for taking care of Pat," he said, "and buy her a pair of gloves."

I could only say, "That will be nice. Do you know her size?"

"I think it's 8½," he said.

He looked at my hands.

"Do you wear 8½?" he asked.

"No. I wear a smaller size, a 6."

"Oh! Then I guess her hands are bigger than yours."

I hated her. Poverty or no, there was other food than bread, and the soul could starve as quickly as the body. He was taking his dollar to buy gloves for her big stupid hands, and

she lived away from him, in Mannville, and contented herself with sending him skates.

"She likes white gloves," he said. "Do you think I can get them for a dollar?"

"I think so," I said.

I decided that I should not leave the mountains without seeing her and knowing for myself why she had done this thing.

The human mind scatters its interests as though made of thistledown, and every wind stirs and moves it. I finished my work. It did not please me, and I gave my thoughts to another field. I should need some Mexican material.

I made arrangements to close my Florida place. Mexico immediately, and doing the writing there, if conditions were favorable. Then, Alaska with my brother. After that, heaven knew what or where.

I did not take time to go to Mannville to see Jerry's mother, nor even to talk with the orphanage officials about her. I was a trifle abstracted about the boy, because of my work and plans. And after my first fury at her—we did not speak of her again—his having a mother, any sort at all, not far away, in Mannville, relieved me of the ache I had had about him. He did not question the anomalous relation. He was not lonely. It was none of my concern.

He came every day and cut my wood and did small helpful favors and stayed to talk. The days had become cold, and often I let him come inside the cabin. He would lie on the floor in front of the fire, with one arm across the pointer, and they would both doze and wait quietly for me. Other days they ran with a common ecstasy through the laurel, and

since the asters were now gone, he brought me back vermilion maple leaves, and chestnut boughs dripping with imperial yellow. I was ready to go.

I said to him, "You have been my good friend, Jerry. I shall often think of you and miss you. Pat will miss you too. I am leaving tomorrow."

He did not answer. When he went away, I remember that a new moon hung over the mountains, and I watched him go in silence up the hill. I expected him the next day, but he did not come. The details of packing my personal belongings, loading my car, arranging the bed over the seat, where the dog would ride, occupied me until late in the day. I closed the cabin and started the car, noticing that the sun was in the west and I should do well to be out of the mountains by nightfall. I stopped by the orphanage and left the cabin key and money for my light bill with Miss Clark.

"And will you call Jerry for me to say good-by to him?"

"I don't know where he is," she said. "I'm afraid he's not well. He didn't eat his dinner this noon. One of the other boys saw him going over the hill into the laurel. He was supposed to fire the boiler this afternoon. It's not like him; he's unusually reliable."

I was almost relieved, for I knew I should never see him again, and it would be easier not to say good-by to him.

I said, "I wanted to talk with you about his mother—why he's here—but I'm in more of a hurry than I expected to be. It's out of the question for me to see her now too. But here's some money I'd like to leave with you to buy things for him at Christmas and on his birthday. It will be better than for me to try to send him things. I could so easily duplicate—skates, for instance."

She blinked her honest spinster's eyes.

"There's not much use for skates here," she said.

Her stupidity annoyed me.

"What I mean," I said, "is that I don't want to duplicate things his mother sends him. I might have chosen skates if I didn't know she had already given them to him."

She stared at me.

"I don't understand," she said. "He has no mother. He has no skates."

KERFOL

I

"You ought to buy it," said my host; "it's just the place for a solitary-minded devil like you. And it would be rather worth while to own the most romantic house in Brittany. The present people are dead broke, and it's going for a song—you ought to buy it."

It was not with the least idea of living up to the character my friend Lanrivain ascribed to me (as a matter of fact, under my unsociable exterior I have always had secret yearnings for domesticity) that I took his hint one autumn afternoon and went to Kerfol. My friend was motoring over to Quimper on business: he dropped me on the way, at a cross-road on a heath, and said: "First turn to the right and second to the left. Then straight ahead till you see an avenue. If you meet any peasants, don't ask your way. They don't understand French, and they would pretend they did and mix you up. I'll be back for you here by sunset—and don't forget the tombs in the chapel."

I followed Lanrivain's directions with the hesitation occasioned by the usual difficulty of remembering whether he had said the first turn to

the right and second to the left, or the contrary. If I had met a peasant I should certainly have asked, and probably been sent astray; but I had the desert landscape to myself and so stumbled on the right turn and walked across the heath till I came to an avenue. It was so unlike any other avenue I have ever seen that I instantly knew it must be *the* avenue. The gray-trunked trees sprang up straight to a great height and then interwove their pale-gray branches in a long tunnel through which the autumn light fell faintly. I know most trees by name, but I haven't to this day been able to decide what those trees were. They had the tall curve of elms, the tenuity of poplars, the ashen colour of olives under a rainy sky; and they stretched ahead of me for half a mile or more without a break in their arch. If ever I saw an avenue that unmistakably led to something, it was the avenue at Kerfol. My heart beat a little as I began to walk down it.

Presently the trees ended and I came to a fortified gate in a long wall. Between me and the wall was an open space of grass, with other gray

From *Xingu*, by Edith Wharton. Copyright 1916 by Charles Scribner's Sons, 1944 by Elisina Tyler, reprinted by permission of the publishers.

avenues radiating from it. Behind the wall were tall slate roofs mossed with silver, a chapel belfry, the top of a keep. A moat filled with wild shrubs and brambles surrounded the place; the draw-bridge had been replaced by a stone arch, and the portcullis by an iron gate. I stood for a long time on the hither side of the moat, gazing about me, and letting the influence of the place sink in. I said to myself: "If I wait long enough, the guardian will turn up and show me the tombs——" and I rather hoped he wouldn't turn up too soon.

I sat down on a stone and lit a cigarette. As soon as I had done it, it struck me as a puerile and portentous thing to do, with that great blind house looking down at me, and all the empty avenues converging on me. It may have been the depth of the silence that made me so conscious of my gesture. The squeak of my match sounded as loud as the scraping of a brake, and I almost fancied I heard it fall when I tossed it onto the grass. But there was more than that: a sense of irrelevance, of littleness, of futile bravado, in sitting there puffing my cigarette-smoke into the face of such a past.

I knew nothing of the history of Kerfol—I was new to Brittany, and Lanrivain had never mentioned the name to me till the day before—but one couldn't as much as glance at that pile without feeling in it a long accumulation of history. What kind of history I was not prepared to guess: perhaps only that sheer weight of many associated lives and deaths which gives a majesty to all old houses. But the aspect of Kerfol suggested something more—a perspective of stern and cruel memories stretching away, like its own gray avenues, into a blur of darkness.

Certainly no house had ever more completely and finally broken with the present. As it stood there, lifting its proud roofs and gables to the sky, it might have been its own funeral monument. "Tombs in the chapel? The whole place is a tomb!" I reflected. I hoped more and more that the guardian would not come. The details of the place, however striking, would seem trivial compared with its collective impressiveness; and I wanted only to sit there and be penetrated by the weight of its silence. "It's the very place for you!" Lanrivain had said; and I was overcome by the almost blasphemous frivolity of suggesting to any living being that Kerfol was the place for him. "Is it possible that any one could not see——?" I wondered. I did not finish the thought: what I meant was undefinable. I stood up and wandered toward the gate. I was beginning to want to know more; not to see more —I was by now so sure it was not a question of seeing—but to feel more: feel all the place had to communicate. "But to get in one will have to rout out the keeper," I thought reluctantly, and hesitated. Finally I crossed the bridge and tried the iron gate. It yielded, and I walked through the tunnel formed by the thickness of the *chemin de ronde.* At the farther end, a wooden barricade had been laid across the entrance, and beyond it was a court enclosed in noble architecture. The main building faced me; and I now saw that one half was a mere ruined front, with gaping windows through which the wild growths of the moat and the trees of the park were visible. The rest of the house was still in its robust beauty. One end abutted on the round tower, the other on the small traceried chapel, and in an angle of the building stood a graceful well-head crowned with mossy

urns. A few roses grew against the walls, and on an upper window-sill I remember noticing a pot of fuchsias.

My sense of the pressure of the invisible began to yield to my architectural interest. The building was so fine that I felt a desire to explore it for its own sake. I looked about the court, wondering in which corner the guardian lodged. Then I pushed open the barrier and went in. As I did so, a dog barred my way. He was such a remarkably beautiful little dog that for a moment he made me forget the splendid place he was defending. I was not sure of his breed at the time, but have since learned that it was Chinese, and that he was of a rare variety called the 'Sleeve-dog.' He was very small and golden brown, with large brown eyes and a ruffled throat: he looked like a large tawny chrysanthemum. I said to myself: "These little beasts always snap and scream,

and somebody will be out in a minute."

The little animal stood before me, forbidding, almost menacing: there was anger in his large brown eyes. But he made no sound, he came no nearer. Instead, as I advanced, he gradually fell back, and I noticed that another dog, a vague rough brindled thing, had limped up on a lame leg. "There'll be a hubbub now," I thought; for at the same moment a third dog, a longhaired white mongrel, slipped out of a doorway and joined the others. All three stood looking at me with grave eyes; but not a sound came from them. As I advanced they continued to fall back on muffled paws, still watching me. "At a given point, they'll all charge at my ankles: it's one of the jokes that dogs who live together put up on one," I thought. I was not alarmed, for they were neither large nor formidable. But they 'let me

wander about the court as I pleased, following me at a little distance—always the same distance—and always keeping their eyes on me. Presently I looked across at the ruined façade, and saw that in one of its empty window-frames another dog stood: a white pointer with one brown ear. He was an old grave dog, much more experienced than the others; and he seemed to be observing me with a deeper intentness.

"I'll hear from him," I said to myself; but he stood in the window-frame, against the trees of the park, and continued to watch me without moving. I stared back at him for a time, to see if the sense that he was being watched would not rouse him. Half the width of the court lay between us, and we gazed at each other silently across it. But he did not stir, and at last I turned away. Behind me I found the rest of the pack, with a newcomer added: a small black grey-hound with pale agate-coloured eyes. He was shivering a little, and his expression was more timid than that of the others. I noticed that he kept a little behind them. And still there was not a sound.

I stood there for fully five minutes, the circle about me—waiting, as they seemed to be waiting. At last I went up to the little golden-brown and stooped to pat him. As I did so, I heard myself give a nervous laugh. The little dog did not start, or growl, or take his eyes from me—he simply slipped back about a yard, and then paused and continued to look at me. "Oh, hang it!" I exclaimed, and walked across the court toward the well.

As I advanced, the dogs separated and slid away into different corners of the court. I examined the urns on the well, tried a locked door or two, and looked up and down the dumb façade; then I faced about toward the chapel.

When I turned I perceived that all the dogs had disappeared except the old pointer, who still watched me from the window. It was rather a relief to be rid of that cloud of witnesses; and I began to look about me for a way to the back of the house. "Perhaps there'll be somebody in the garden," I thought. I found a way across the moat, scrambled over a wall smothered in brambles, and got into the garden. A few lean hydrangeas and geraniums pined in the flower-beds, and the ancient house looked down on them indifferently. Its garden side was plainer and severer than the other: the long granite front, with its few windows and steep roof, looked like a fortress-prison. I walked around the farther wing, went up some disjointed steps, and entered the deep twilight of a narrow and incredibly old box-walk. The walk was just wide enough for one person to slip through, and its branches met overhead. It was like the ghost of a box-walk, its lustrous green all turning to the shadowy grayness of the avenues. I walked on and on, the branches hitting me in the face and springing back with a dry rattle; and at length I came out on the grassy top of the *chemin de ronde*. I walked along it to the gate-tower, looking down into the court, which was just below me. Not a human being was in sight; and neither were the dogs. I found a flight of steps in the thickness of the wall and went down them; and when I emerged again into the court, there stood the circle of dogs, the golden-brown one a little ahead of the others, the black greyhound shivering in the rear.

"Oh, hang it—you uncomfortable beasts, you!" I exclaimed, my voice startling me with a sudden echo. The dogs stood motionless, watching me. I knew by this time that they would not try to prevent my approaching the

house, and the knowledge left me free to examine them. I had a feeling that they must be horribly cowed to be so silent and inert. Yet they did not look hungry or ill-treated. Their coats were smooth and they were not thin, except the shivering greyhound. It was more as if they had lived a long time with people who never spoke to them: as though the silence of the place had gradually benumbed their busy inquisitive natures. And this strange passivity, this almost human lassitude, seemed to me sadder than the misery of starved and beaten animals. I should have liked to rouse them for a minute, to coax them into a game or a scamper; but the longer I looked into their fixed and weary eyes the more preposterous the idea became. With the windows of that house looking down on us, how could I have imagined such a thing? The dogs knew better: *they* knew what the house would tolerate and what it would not. I even fancied that they knew what was passing through my mind, and pitied me for my frivolity. But even that feeling probably reached them through a thick fog of listlessness. I had an idea that their distance from me was as nothing to my remoteness from them. The impression they produced was that of having in common one memory so deep and dark that nothing that had happened since was worth either a growl or a wag.

"I say," I broke out abruptly, addressing myself to the dumb circle, "do you know what you look like, the whole lot of you? You look as if you'd seen a ghost—that's how you look! I wonder if there *is* a ghost here, and nobody but you left for it to appear to?" The dogs continued to gaze at me without moving . . .

It was dark when I saw Lanrivain's motor lamps at the cross-roads—and I

wasn't exactly sorry to see them. I had the sense of having escaped from the loneliest place in the whole world, and of not liking loneliness—to that degree—as much as I had imagined I should. My friend had brought his solicitor back from Quimper for the night, and seated beside a fat and affable stranger I felt no inclination to talk of Kerfol . . .

But that evening, when Lanrivain and the solicitor were closeted in the study, Madame de Lanrivain began to question me in the drawing-room. "Well—are you going to buy Kerfol?" she asked, tilting up her gay chin from her embroidery.

"I haven't decided yet. The fact is, I couldn't get into the house," I said, as if I had simply postponed my decision, and meant to go back for another look.

"You couldn't get in? Why, what happened? The family are mad to sell the place, and the old guardian has orders——"

"Very likely. But the old guardian wasn't there."

"What a pity! He must have gone to market. But his daughter——?"

"There was nobody about. At least I saw no one."

"How extraordinary! Literally nobody?"

"Nobody but a lot of dogs—a whole pack of them—who seemed to have the place to themselves."

Madame de Lanrivain let the embroidery slip to her knee and folded her hands on it. For several minutes she looked at me thoughtfully.

"A pack of dogs—you *saw* them?"

"Saw them? I saw nothing else!"

"How many?" She dropped her voice a little. "I've always wondered——"

I looked at her with surprise: I had supposed the place to be familiar to

her. "Have you never been to Kerfol?" I asked.

"Oh, yes: often. But never on that day."

"What day?"

"I'd quite forgotten—and so had Hervé, I'm sure. If we'd remembered, we never should have sent you today —but then, after all, one doesn't half believe that sort of thing, does one?"

"What sort of thing?" I asked, involuntarily sinking my voice to the level of hers. Inwardly I was thinking: "I *knew* there was something . . ."

Madame de Lanrivain cleared her throat and produced a reassuring smile. "Didn't Hervé tell you the story of Kerfol? An ancestor of his was mixed up in it. You know every Breton house has its ghost-story; and some of them are rather unpleasant."

"Yes—but those dogs?"

"Well, those dogs are the ghosts of Kerfol. At least, the peasants say there's one day in the year when a lot of dogs appear there; and that day the keeper and his daughter go off to Morlaix and get drunk. The women in Brittany drink dreadfully." She stooped to match a silk; then she lifted her charming inquisitive Parisian face. "Did you *really* see a lot of dogs? There isn't one at Kerfol," she said.

II

Lanrivain, the next day, hunted out a shabby calf volume from the back of an upper shelf of his library.

"Yes—here it is. What does it call itself? *A History of the Assizes of the Duchy of Brittany. Quimper*, 1702. The book was written about a hundred years later than the Kerfol affair; but I believe the account is transcribed pretty literally from the judicial records. Anyhow, it's queer reading. And there's a Hervé de Lanrivain mixed

up in it—not exactly *my* style, as you'll see. But then he's only a collateral. Here, take the book up to bed with you. I don't exactly remember the details; but after you've read it I'll bet anything you'll leave your light burning all night!"

I left my light burning all night, as he had predicted; but it was chiefly because, till near dawn, I was absorbed in my reading. The account of the trial of Anne de Cornault, wife of the lord of Kerfol, was long and closely printed. It was, as my friend had said, probably an almost literal transcription of what took place in the courtroom; and the trial lasted nearly a month. Besides, the type of the book was very bad . . .

At first I thought of translating the old record. But it is full of wearisome repetitions, and the main lines of the story are forever straying off into side issues. So I have tried to disentangle it, and give it here in simpler form. At times, however, I have reverted to the text because no other words could have conveyed so exactly the sense of what I felt at Kerfol; and nowhere have I added anything of my own.

III

It was in the year 16— that Yves de Cornault, lord of the domain of Kerfol, went to the *pardon* of Locronan to perform his religious duties. He was a rich and powerful noble, then in his sixty-second year, but hale and sturdy, a great horseman and hunter and a pious man. So all his neighbours attested. In appearance he was short and broad, with a swarthy face, legs slightly bowed from the saddle, a hanging nose and broad hands with black hairs on them. He had married young and lost his wife and son soon after, and since then had

lived alone at Kerfol. Twice a year he went to Morlaix, where he had a handsome house by the river, and spent a week or ten days there; and occasionally he rode to Rennes on business. Witnesses were found to declare that during these absences he led a life different from the one he was known to lead at Kerfol, where he busied himself with his estate, attended mass daily, and found his only amusement in hunting the wild boar and water-fowl. But these rumours are not particularly relevant, and it is certain that among people of his own class in the neighbourhood he passed for a stern and even austere man, observant of his religious obligations, and keeping strictly to himself. There was no talk of any familiarity with the women on his estate, though at that time the nobility were very free with their peasants. Some people said he had never looked at a woman since his wife's death; but such things are hard to prove, and the evidence on this point was not worth much.

Well, in his sixty-second year, Yves de Cornault went to the *pardon* at Locronan, and saw there a young lady of Douarnenez, who had ridden over pillion behind her father to do her duty to the saint. Her name was Anne de Barrigan, and she came of good old Breton stock, but much less great and powerful than that of Yves de Cornault; and her father had squandered his fortune at cards, and lived almost like a peasant in his little granite manor on the moors . . . I have said I would add nothing of my own to this bald statement of a strange case; but I must interrupt myself here to describe the young lady who rode up to the lych-gate of Locronan at the very moment when the Baron de Cornault was also dismounting there. I take my description from a faded drawing in red crayon, sober and

truthful enough to be by a late pupil of the Clouets, which hangs in Lanrivain's study, and is said to be a portrait of Anne de Barrigan. It is unsigned and has no mark of identity but the initials A.B., and the date 16—, the year after her marriage. It represents a young woman with a small oval face, almost pointed, yet wide enough for a full mouth with a tender depression at the corners. The nose is small, and the eyebrows are set rather high, far apart, and as lightly pencilled as the eyebrows in a Chinese painting. The forehead is high and serious, and the hair, which one feels to be fine and thick and fair, is drawn off it and lies close like a cap. The eyes are neither large nor small, hazel probably, with a look at once shy and steady. A pair of beautiful long hands are crossed below the lady's breast . . .

The chaplain of Kerfol, and other witnesses, averred that when the Baron came back from Locronan he jumped from his horse, ordered another to be instantly saddled, called to a young page to come with him, and rode away that same evening to the south. His steward followed the next morning with coffers laden on a pair of pack mules. The following week Yves de Cornault rode back to Kerfol, sent for his vassals and tenants, and told them he was to be married at All Saints to Anne de Barrigan of Douarnenez. And on All Saints' Day the marriage took place.

As to the next few years, the evidence on both sides seems to show that they passed happily for the couple. No one was found to say that Yves de Cornault had been unkind to his wife, and it was plain to all that he was content with his bargain. Indeed, it was admitted by the chaplain and other witnesses for the prosecution that the young lady had a softening influence on her husband, and

that he became less exacting with his tenants, less harsh to peasants and dependents, and less subject to the fits of gloomy silence which had darkened his widowhood. As to his wife, the only grievance her champions could call up in her behalf was that Kerfol was a lonely place, and that when her husband was away on business at Rennes or Morlaix—whither she was never taken—she was not allowed so much as to walk in the park unaccompanied. But no one asserted that she was unhappy, though one servant-woman said she had surprised her crying, and had heard her say that she was a woman accursed to have no child, and nothing in life to call her own. But that was a natural enough feeling in a wife attached to her husband; and certainly it must have been a great grief to Yves de Cornault that she bore no son. Yet he never made her feel her childlessness as a reproach —she admits this in her evidence— but seemed to try to make her forget it by showering gifts and favours on her. Rich though he was, he had never been openhanded; but nothing was too fine for his wife, in the way of silks or gems or linen, or whatever else she fancied. Every wandering merchant was welcome at Kerfol, and when the master was called away he never came back without bringing his wife a handsome present—something curious and particular—from Morlaix or Rennes or Quimper. One of the waiting-women gave, in cross-examination, an interesting list of one year's gifts, which I copy. From Morlaix, a carved ivory junk, with Chinamen at the oars, that a strange sailor had brought back as a votive offering for Notre Dame de la Clarté above Ploumanac'h; from Quimper, an embroidered gown, worked by the nuns of the Assumption; from Rennes, a silver rose that opened and showed an amber Virgin with a crown of garnets; from Morlaix, again, a length of Damascus velvet shot with gold, bought of a Jew from Syria; and for Michaelmas that year, from Rennes, a necklet or bracelet of round stones— emeralds and pearls and rubies—strung like beads on a fine gold chain. This was the present that pleased the lady best, the waiting-maid deposed; and, as it happened, it was produced at the trial, and appears to have struck the Judges and the public as a curious and valuable jewel.

The very same winter, the Baron absented himself again, this time as far as Bordeaux, and on his return he brought his wife something even odder and prettier than the bracelet. It was a winter evening when he rode up to Kerfol and, walking into the hall, found her sitting by the hearth, her chin on her hand, looking into the fire. He carried a velvet box in his hand and, setting it down, lifted the lid and let out a little golden-brown dog.

Anne de Cornault exclaimed with pleasure as the little creature bounded toward her. "Oh, it looks like a bird or a butterfly!" she cried as she picked it up; and the dog put its paws on her shoulders and looked at her with eyes "like a Christian's." After that she would never have it out of her sight, and petted and talked to it as if it had been a child—as indeed it was the nearest thing to a child she was to know. Yves de Cornault was much pleased with his purchase. The dog had been brought to him by a sailor from an East India merchantman, and the sailor had bought it of a pilgrim in a bazaar at Jaffa, who had stolen it from a nobleman's wife in China: a perfectly permissible thing to do, since the pilgrim was a Christian and the nobleman a heathen doomed to hellfire. Yves de Cornault had paid a

long price for the dog, for they were beginning to be in demand at the French court, and the sailor knew he had got hold of a good thing; but Anne's pleasure was so great that, to see her laugh and play with the little animal, her husband would doubtless have given twice the sum.

So far, all the evidence is at one, and the narrative plain sailing; but now the steering becomes difficult. I will try to keep as nearly as possible to Anne's own statements; though toward the end, poor thing . . .

Well, to go back. The very year after the little brown dog was brought to Kerfol, Yves de Cornault, one winter night, was found dead at the head of a narrow flight of stairs leading down from his wife's rooms to a door opening on the court. It was his wife who found him and gave the alarm, so distracted, poor wretch, with fear and horror—for his blood was all over her—that at first the roused household could not make out what she was saying, and thought she had suddenly gone mad. But there, sure enough, at the top of the stairs lay her husband, stone dead, and head foremost, the blood from his wounds dripping down to the steps below him. He had been dreadfully scratched and gashed about the face and throat, as if with curious pointed weapons; and one of his legs had a deep tear in it which had cut an artery, and probably caused his death. But how did he come there, and who had murdered him?

His wife declared that she had been asleep in her bed, and hearing his cry had rushed out to find him lying on the stairs; but this was immediately questioned. In the first place, it was proved that from her room she could not have heard the struggle on the stairs, owing to the thickness of the walls and the length of the intervening passage; then it was evident that she had not been in bed and asleep, since she was dressed when she roused the house, and her bed had not been slept in. Moreover, the door at the bottom of the stairs was ajar, and it was noticed by the chaplain (an observant man) that the dress she wore was stained with blood about the knees, and that there were traces of small blood-stained hands low down on the staircase walls, so that it was conjectured that she had really been at the postern-door when her husband fell and, feeling her way up to him in the darkness on her hands and knees, had been stained by his blood dripping down on her. Of course it was argued on the other side that the blood-marks on her dress might have been caused by her kneeling down by her husband when she rushed out of her room; but there was the open door below, and the fact that the finger-marks in the staircase all pointed upward.

The accused held to her statement for the first two days, in spite of its improbability; but on the third day word was brought to her that Hervé de Lanrivain, a young nobleman of the neighbourhood, had been arrested for complicity in the crime. Two or three witnesses thereupon came forward to say that it was known throughout the country that Lanrivain had formerly been on good terms with the lady of Cornault; but that he had been absent from Brittany for over a year, and people had ceased to associate their names. The witnesses who made this statement were not of a very reputable sort. One was an old herb-gatherer suspected of witchcraft, another a drunken clerk from a neighbouring parish, the third a half-witted shepherd who could be made to say anything; and it was clear that the

prosecution was not satisfied with its case, and would have liked to find more definite proof of Lanrivain's complicity than the statement of the herb-gatherer, who swore to having seen him climbing the wall of the park on the night of the murder. One way of patching out incomplete proofs in those days was to put some sort of pressure, moral or physical, on the accused person. It is not clear what pressure was put on Anne de Cornault; but on the third day, when she was brought in court, she "appeared weak and wandering," and after being encouraged to collect herself and speak the truth, on her honour and the wounds of her Blessed Redeemer, she confessed that she had in fact gone down the stairs to speak with Hervé de Lanrivain (who denied everything), and had been surprised there by the sound of her husband's fall. That was better; and the prosecution rubbed its hands with satisfaction. The satisfaction increased when various dependents living at Kerfol were induced to say—with apparent sincerity—that during the year or two preceding his death their master had once more grown uncertain and irascible, and subject to the fits of brooding silence which his household had learned to dread before his second marriage. This seemed to show that things had not been going well at Kerfol; though no one could be found to say that there had been any signs of open disagreement between husband and wife.

Anne de Cornault, when questioned as to her reason for going down at night to open the door to Hervé de Lanrivain, made an answer which must have sent a smile around the court. She said it was because she was lonely and wanted to talk with the young man. Was this the only reason? she was asked; and she replied: "Yes,

by the Cross over your Lordships' heads." "But why at midnight?" the court asked. "Because I could see him in no other way." I can see the exchange of glances across the ermine collars under the Crucifix.

Anne de Cornault, further questioned, said that her married life had been extremely lonely: "desolate" was the word she used. It was true that her husband seldom spoke harshly to her; but there were days when he did not speak at all. It was true that he had never struck or threatened her; but he kept her like a prisoner at Kerfol, and when he rode away to Morlaix or Quimper or Rennes he set so close a watch on her that she could not pick a flower in the garden without having a waiting-woman at her heels. "I am no Queen, to need such honours," she once said to him; and he had answered that a man who has a treasure does not leave the key in the lock when he goes out. "Then take me with you," she urged; but to this he said that towns were pernicious places, and young wives better off at their own firesides.

"But what did you want to say to Hervé de Lanrivain?" the court asked; and she answered: "To ask him to take me away."

"Ah—you confess that you went down to him with adulterous thoughts?"

"No."

"Then why did you want him to take you away?"

"Because I was afraid for my life."

"Of whom were you afraid?"

"Of my husband."

"Why were you afraid of your husband?"

"Because he had strangled my little dog."

Another smile must have passed around the court-room: in days when any nobleman had a right to hang his

peasants—and most of them exercised it—pinching a pet animal's wind-pipe was nothing to make a fuss about. At this point one of the Judges, who appears to have had a certain sympathy for the accused, suggested that she should be allowed to explain herself in her own way; and she thereupon made the following statement.

The first years of her marriage had been lonely; but her husband had not been unkind to her. If she had had a child she would not have been unhappy; but the days were long, and it rained too much.

It was true that her husband, whenever he went away and left her, brought her a handsome present on his return; but this did not make up for the loneliness. At least nothing had, till he brought her the little brown dog from the East: after that she was much less unhappy. Her husband seemed pleased that she was so fond of the dog; he gave her leave to put her jewelled bracelet around its neck, and to keep it always with her.

One day she had fallen asleep in her room, with the dog at her feet, as his habit was. Her feet were bare and resting on his back. Suddenly she was waked by her husband: he stood beside her, smiling not unkindly.

"You look like my great-grandmother, Juliane de Cornault, lying in the chapel with her feet on a little dog," he said.

The analogy sent a chill through her, but she laughed and answered: "Well, when I am dead you must put me beside her, carved in marble, with my dog at my feet."

"Oho—we'll wait and see," he said, laughing also, but with his black brows close together. "The dog is the emblem of fidelity."

"And do you doubt my right to lie with mine at my feet?"

"When I'm in doubt I find out," he answered. "I am an old man," he added, "and people say I make you lead a lonely life. But I swear you shall have your monument if you earn it."

"And I swear to be faithful," she returned, "if only for the sake of having my little dog at my feet."

Not long afterward he went on business to the Quimper Assizes; and while he was away his aunt, the widow of a great nobleman of the duchy, came to spend a night at Kerfol on her way to the *pardon* of Ste. Barbe. She was a woman of piety and consequence, and much respected by Yves de Cornault, and when she proposed to Anne to go with her to Ste. Barbe no one could object, and even the chaplain declared himself in favour of the pilgrimage. So Anne set out for Ste. Barbe, and there for the first time she talked with Hervé de Lanrivain. He had come once or twice to Kerfol with his father, but she had never before exchanged a dozen words with him. They did not talk for more than five minutes now: it was under the chestnuts, as the procession was coming out of the chapel. He said: "I pity you," and she was surprised, for she had not supposed that any one thought her an object of pity. He added: "Call for me when you need me," and she smiled a little, but was glad afterward, and thought often of the meeting.

She confessed to having seen him three times afterward: not more. How or where she would not say—one had the impression that she feared to implicate some one. Their meetings had been rare and brief; and at the last he had told her that he was starting the next day for a foreign country, on a mission which was not without peril and might keep him for many months absent. He asked her for a

remembrance, and she had none to give him but the collar about the little dog's neck. She was sorry afterward that she had given it, but he was so unhappy at going that she had not had the courage to refuse. Her husband was away at the time. When he returned a few days later he picked up the animal to pet it, and noticed that its collar was missing His wife told him that the dog had lost it in the undergrowth of the park, and that she and her maids had hunted a whole day for it. It was true, she explained to the court, that she had made the maids search for the necklet —they all believed the dog had lost it in the park . . .

Her husband made no comment, and that evening at supper he was in his usual mood, between good and bad: you could never tell which. He talked a good deal, describing what he had seen and done at Rennes; but now and then he stopped and looked hard at her, and when she went to bed she found her little dog strangled on her pillow. The little thing was dead, but still warm; she stooped to lift it, and her distress turned to horror when she discovered that it had been strangled by twisting twice round its throat the necklet she had given to Lanrivain.

The next morning at dawn she buried the dog in the garden, and hid the necklet in her breast. She said nothing to her husband, then or later, and he said nothing to her; but that day he had a peasant hanged for stealing a faggot in the park, and the next day he nearly beat to death a young horse he was breaking.

Winter set in, and the short days passed, and the long nights, one by one; and she heard nothing of Hervé de Lanrivain. It might be that her husband had killed him; or merely that he had been robbed of the neck-

let. Day after day by the hearth among the spinning maids, night after night alone on her bed, she wondered and trembled. Sometimes at table her husband looked across at her and smiled; and then she felt sure that Lanrivain was dead. She dared not try to get news of him, for she was sure her husband would find out if she did: she had an idea that he could find out anything. Even when a witch-woman who was a noted seer, and could show you the whole world in her crystal, came to the castle for a night's shelter, and the maids flocked to her, Anne held back.

The winter was long and black and rainy. One day, in Yves de Cornault's absence, some gypsies came to Kerfol with a troop of performing dogs. Anne bought the smallest and cleverest, a white dog with a feathery coat and one blue and one brown eye. It seemed to have been ill-treated by the gypsies, and clung to her plaintively when she took it from them. That evening her husband came back, and when she went to bed she found the dog strangled on her pillow.

After that she said to herself that she would never have another dog; but one bitter cold evening a poor lean greyhound was found whining at the castle-gate, and she took him in and forbade the maids to speak of him to her husband. She hid him in a room that no one went to, smuggled food to him from her own plate, made him a warm bed to lie on and petted him like a child.

Yves de Cornault came home, and the next day she found the greyhound strangled on her pillow. She wept in secret, but said nothing, and resolved that even if she met a dog dying of hunger she would never bring him into the castle; but one day she found a young sheep-dog, a brindled puppy with good blue eyes,

lying with a broken leg in the snow of the park. Yves de Cornault was at Rennes, and she brought the dog in, warmed and fed it, tied up its leg and hid it in the castle till her husband's return. The day before, she gave it to a peasant woman who lived a long way off, and paid her handsomely to care for it and say nothing; but that night she heard a whining and scratching at her door, and when she opened it the lame puppy, drenched and shivering, jumped up on her with little sobbing barks. She hid him in her bed, and the next morning was about to have him taken back to the peasant woman when she heard her husband ride into the court. She shut the dog in a chest, and went down to receive him. An hour or two later, when she returned to her room, the puppy lay strangled on her pillow . . .

After that she dared not make a pet of any other dog; and her loneliness became almost unendurable. Sometimes, when she crossed the court of the castle, and thought no one was looking, she stopped to pat the old pointer at the gate. But one day as she was caressing him her husband came out of the chapel; and the next day the old dog was gone . . .

This curious narrative was not told in one sitting of the court, or received without impatience and incredulous comment. It was plain that the Judges were surprised by its puerility, and that it did not help the accused in the eyes of the public. It was an odd tale, certainly; but what did it prove? That Yves de Cornault disliked dogs, and that his wife, to gratify her own fancy, persistently ignored this dislike. As for pleading this trivial disagreement as an excuse for her relations—whatever their nature—with her supposed accomplice, the argument was so absurd that her own lawyer mani-

festly regretted having let her make use of it, and tried several times to cut short her story. But she went on to the end, with a kind of hypnotized insistence, as though the scenes she evoked were so real to her that she had forgotten where she was and imagined herself to be re-living them.

At length the Judge who had previously shown a certain kindness to her said (leaning forward a little, one may suppose, from his row of dozing colleagues): "Then you would have us believe that you murdered your husband because he would not let you keep a pet dog?"

"I did not murder my husband."

"Who did, then? Hervé de Lanrivain?"

"No."

"Who then? Can you tell us?"

"Yes, I can tell you. The dogs——"

At that point she was carried out of the court in a swoon.

It was evident that her lawyer tried to get her to abandon this line of defence. Possibly her explanation, whatever it was, had seemed convincing when she poured it out to him in the heat of their first private colloquy; but now that it was exposed to the cold daylight of judicial scrutiny, and the banter of the town, he was thoroughly ashamed of it, and would have sacrificed her without a scruple to save his professional reputation. But the obstinate Judge—who perhaps, after all, was more inquisitive than kindly—evidently wanted to hear the story out, and she was ordered, the next day, to continue her deposition.

She said that after the disappearance of the old watch-dog nothing particular happened for a month or two. Her husband was much as usual: she did not remember any special incident. But one evening a pedlar woman came to the castle and was selling trinkets to the maids. She had no

heart for trinkets, but she stood looking on while the women made their choice. And then, she did not know how, but the pedlar coaxed her into buying for herself a pear-shaped pomander with a strong scent in it—she had once seen something of the kind on a gypsy woman. She had no desire for the pomander, and did not know why she had bought it. The pedlar said that whoever wore it had the power to read the future; but she did not really believe that, or care much either. However, she bought the thing and took it up to her room, where she sat turning it about in her hand. Then the strange scent attracted her and she began to wonder what kind of spice was in the box. She opened it and found a gray bean rolled in a strip of paper; and on the paper she saw a sign she knew and a message from Hervé de Lanrivain, saying that he was at home again and would be at the door in the court that night after the moon had set . . .

She burned the paper and sat down to think. It was nightfall, and her husband was at home . . . She had no way of warning Lanrivain, and there was nothing to do but to wait . . .

At this point I fancy the drowsy court-room beginning to wake up. Even to the oldest hand on the bench there must have been a certain relish in picturing the feelings of a woman on receiving such a message at nightfall from a man living twenty miles away, to whom she had no means of sending a warning . . .

She was not a clever woman, I imagine; and as the first result of her cogitation she appears to have made the mistake of being, that evening, too kind to her husband. She could not ply him with wine, according to the traditional expedient, for though he drank heavily at times he had a strong head; and when he drank beyond its strength it was because he chose to, and not because a woman coaxed him. Not his wife, at any rate—she was an old story by now. As I read the case, I fancy there was no feeling for her left in him but the hatred occasioned by his supposed dishonour.

At any rate, she tried to call up her old graces; but early in the evening he complained of pains and fever, and left the hall to go up to the closet where he sometimes slept. His servant carried him a cup of hot wine, and brought back word that he was sleeping and not to be disturbed; and an hour later, when Anne lifted the tapestry and listened at his door, she heard his loud regular breathing. She thought it might be a feint, and stayed a long time barefooted in the passage, her ear to the crack; but the breathing went on too steadily and naturally to be other than that of a man in a sound sleep. She crept back to her room reassured, and stood in the window watching the moon set through the trees of the park. The sky was misty and starless, and after the moon went down the night was black as pitch. She knew the time had come, and stole along the passage, past her husband's door—where she stopped again to listen to his breathing—to the top of the stairs. There she paused a moment, and assured herself that no one was following her; then she began to go down the stairs in the darkness. They were so steep and winding that she had to go very slowly, for fear of stumbling. Her one thought was to get the door unbolted, tell Lanrivain to make his escape, and hasten back to her room. She had tried the bolt earlier in the evening, and managed to put a little grease on it; but nevertheless, when she drew it, it gave a squeak . . . not loud, but it made her heart stop; and

the next minute, overhead, she heard a noise . . .

"What noise?" the prosecution interposed.

"My husband's voice calling out my name and cursing me."

"What did you hear after that?"

"A terrible scream and a fall."

"Where was Hervé de Lanrivain at this time?"

"He was standing outside in the court. I just made him out in the darkness. I told him for God's sake to go, and then I pushed the door shut."

"What did you do next?"

"I stood at the foot of the stairs and listened."

"What did you hear?"

"I heard dogs snarling and panting." (Visible discouragement of the bench, boredom of the public, and exasperation of the lawyer for the defence. Dogs again! But the inquisitive Judge insisted.)

"What dogs?"

She bent her head and spoke so low that she had to be told to repeat her answer: "I don't know."

"How do you mean—you don't know?"

"I don't know what dogs . . ."

The Judge again intervened: "Try to tell us exactly what happened. How long did you remain at the foot of the stairs?"

"Only a few minutes."

"And what was going on meanwhile overhead?"

"The dogs kept on snarling and panting. Once or twice he cried out. I think he moaned once. Then he was quiet."

"Then what happened?"

"Then I heard a sound like the noise of a pack when the wolf is thrown to them—gulping and lapping."

(There was a groan of disgust and repulsion through the court, and an-

other attempted intervention by the distracted lawyer. But the inquisitive Judge was still inquisitive.)

"And all the while you did not go up?"

"Yes—I went up then—to drive them off."

"The dogs?"

"Yes."

"Well——?"

"When I got there it was quite dark. I found my husband's flint and steel and struck a spark. I saw him lying there. He was dead."

"And the dogs?"

"The dogs were gone."

"Gone—where to?"

"I don't know. There was no way out—and there were no dogs at Kerfol."

She straightened herself to her full height, threw her arms above her head, and fell down on the stone floor with a long scream. There was a moment of confusion in the court-room. Someone on the bench was heard to say: "This is clearly a case for the ecclesiastical authorities"—and the prisoner's lawyer doubtless jumped at the suggestion.

After this, the trial loses itself in a maze of cross-questioning and squabbling. Every witness who was called corroborated Anne de Cornault's statement that there were no dogs at Kerfol: had been none for several months. The master of the house had taken a dislike to dogs, there was no denying it. But, on the other hand, at the inquest, there had been long and bitter discussions as to the nature of the dead man's wounds. One of the surgeons called in had spoken of marks that looked like bites. The suggestion of witchcraft was revived, and the opposing lawyers hurled tomes of necromancy at each other.

At last Anne de Cornault was

brought back into court—at the instance of the same Judge—and asked if she knew where the dogs she spoke of could have come from. On the body of her Redeemer she swore that she did not. Then the Judge put his final question: "If the dogs you think you heard had been known to you, do you think you would have recognized them by their barking?"

"Yes."

"What dogs do you take them to have been?"

"My dead dogs," she said in a whisper . . . She was taken out of court, not to reappear there again. There was some kind of ecclesiastical investigation, and the end of the business was that the Judges disagreed with each other, and with the ecclesiastical committee, and that Anne de Cornault was finally handed over to the keeping of her husband's family, who shut her up in the keep of Kerfol, where she is said to have died many years later, a harmless mad-woman.

So ends her story. As for that of Hervé de Lanrivain, I had only to apply to his collateral descendant for its subsequent details. The evidence against the young man being insufficient, and his family influence in the duchy considerable, he was set free, and left soon afterward for Paris. He was probably in no mood for a worldly life, and he appears to have come almost immediately under the influence of the famous M. Arnauld d'Andilly and the gentlemen of Port Royal. A year or two later he was received into their Order, and without achieving any particular distinction he followed its good and evil fortunes till his death some twenty years later. Lanrivain showed me a portrait of him by a pupil of Philippe de Champaigne: sad eyes, an impulsive mouth and a narrow brow. Poor Hervé de Lanrivain: it was a gray ending. Yet as I looked at his stiff and sallow effigy, in the dark dress of the Jansenists, I almost found myself envying his fate. After all, in the course of his life two great things had happened to him: he had loved romantically, and he must have talked with Pascal . . .

THE LAST LEAF

O. HENRY

In a little district west of Washington Square the streets have run crazy and broken themselves into small strips called "places." These "places" make strange angles and curves. One street crosses itself a time or two. An artist once discovered a valuable possibility in this street. Suppose a collector with a bill for paints, paper and canvas should, in traversing this route, suddenly meet himself coming back, without a cent having been paid on account!

So, to quaint old Greenwich Village the art people soon came prowling, hunting for north windows and eighteenth-century gables and Dutch attics and low rent. Then they imported some pewter mugs and a chafing dish or two from Sixth Avenue, and became a "colony."

At the top of a squatty, three-story brick Sue and Johnsy had their studio. "Johnsy" was familiar for Joanna. One was from Maine; the other from California. They had met at the *table d'hôte* of an Eighth Street "Delmonico's," and found their tastes in art, chicory salad and bishop sleeves so congenial that the joint studio resulted.

That was in May. In November a cold, unseen stranger, whom the doctors called Pneumonia, stalked about the colony, touching one here and there with his icy fingers. Over on the east side this ravager strode boldly, smiting his victims by scores, but his feet trod slowly through the maze of the narrow and moss-grown "places."

Mr. Pneumonia was not what you would call a chivalric old gentleman. A mite of a little woman with blood thinned by California zephyrs was hardly fair game for the red-fisted, short-breathed old duffer. But Johnsy he smote; and she lay, scarcely moving, on her painted iron bedstead, looking through the small Dutch window-panes at the blank side of the next brick house.

One morning the busy doctor invited Sue into the hallway with a shaggy, gray eyebrow.

"She has one chance in—let us say, ten," he said, as he shook down the mercury in his clinical thermometer. "And that chance is for her to want to live. This way people have of lining-up on the side of the undertaker makes the entire pharmacopœia look silly. Your little lady has made up her mind that she's not going to get well. Has she anything on her mind?"

"She—she wanted to paint the Bay of Naples some day," said Sue.

"Paint?—bosh! Has she anything on her mind worth thinking about twice —a man for instance?"

"A man?" said Sue, with a jew's-harp twang in her voice. "Is a man worth—but, no, doctor; there is nothing of the kind."

"Well, it is the weakness, then," said the doctor. "I will do all that science, so far as it may filter through my efforts, can accomplish. But whenever my patient begins to count the carriages in her funeral procession I subtract 50 per cent from the curative power of medicines. If you will get her to ask one question about the new winter styles in cloak sleeves I will promise you a one-in-five chance for her, instead of one in ten."

After the doctor had gone Sue went into the workroom and cried a Japanese napkin to a pulp. Then she swaggered into Johnsy's room with her drawing board, whistling ragtime.

Johnsy lay, scarcely making a ripple under the bedclothes, with her face toward the window. Sue stopped whistling, thinking she was asleep.

She arranged her board and began a pen-and-ink drawing to illustrate a magazine story. Young artists must pave their way to Art by drawing pictures for magazine stories that young authors write to pave their way to Literature.

As Sue was sketching a pair of elegant horseshow riding trousers and a monocle on the figure of the hero, an Idaho cowboy, she heard a low sound, several times repeated. She went quickly to the bedside.

Johnsy's eyes were open wide. She was looking out the window and counting—counting backward.

"Twelve," she said, and a little later "eleven"; and then "ten," and "nine"; and then "eight" and "seven," almost together.

Sue looked solicitously out of the window. What was there to count? There was only a bare, dreary yard to be seen, and the blank side of the brick house twenty feet away. An old, old ivy vine, gnarled and decayed at the roots, climbed half way up the brick wall. The cold breath of autumn had stricken its leaves from the vine until its skeleton branches clung, almost bare, to the crumbling bricks.

"What is it, dear?" asked Sue.

"Six," said Johnsy, in almost a whisper. "They're falling faster now. Three days ago there were almost a hundred. It made my head ache to count them. But now it's easy. There goes another one. There are only five left now."

"Five what, dear? Tell your Sudie."

"Leaves. On the ivy vine. When the last one falls I must go, too. I've known that for three days. Didn't the doctor tell you?"

"Oh, I never heard of such nonsense," complained Sue, with magnificent scorn. "What have old ivy leaves to do with your getting well? And you used to love that vine so, you naughty girl. Don't be a goosey. Why, the doctor told me this morning that your chances for getting well real soon were—let's see exactly what he said—he said the chances were ten to one! Why, that's almost as good a chance as we have in New York when we ride on the street cars or walk past a new building. Try to take some broth now, and let Sudie go back to her drawing, so she can sell the editor man with it, and buy port wine for her sick child, and pork chops for her greedy self."

"You needn't get any more wine," said Johnsy, keeping her eyes fixed out the window. "There goes another. No, I don't want any broth.

That leaves just four. I want to see the last one fall before it gets dark. Then I'll go, too."

"Johnsy, dear," said Sue, bending over her, "will you promise me to keep your eyes closed, and not look out the window until I am done working? I must hand those drawings in by to-morrow. I need the light, or I would draw the shade down."

"Couldn't you draw in the other room?" asked Johnsy, coldly.

"I'd rather be here by you," said Sue. "Besides, I don't want you to keep looking at those silly ivy leaves."

"Tell me as soon as you have finished," said Johnsy, closing her eyes, and lying white and still as a fallen statue, "because I want to see the last one fall. I'm tired of waiting. I'm tired of thinking. I want to turn loose my hold on everything, and go sailing down, down, just like one of those poor, tired leaves."

"Try to sleep," said Sue. "I must call Behrman up to be my model for the old hermit miner. I'll not be gone a minute. Don't try to move 'til I come back."

Old Behrman was a painter who lived on the ground floor beneath them. He was past sixty and had a Michael Angelo's Moses beard curling down from the head of a satyr along the body of an imp. Behrman was a failure in art. Forty years he had wielded the brush without getting near enough to touch the hem of his Mistress's robe. He had been always about to paint a masterpiece, but had never yet begun it. For several years he had painted nothing except now and then a daub in the line of commerce or advertising. He earned a little by serving as a model to those young artists in the colony who could not pay the price of a professional. He drank gin to excess, and still talked of his coming masterpiece. For

the rest he was a fierce little old man, who scoffed terribly at softness in any one, and who regarded himself as especial mastiff-in-waiting to protect the two young artists in the studio above.

Sue found Behrman smelling strongly of juniper berries in his dimly lighted den below. In one corner was a blank canvas on an easel that had been waiting there for twenty-five years to receive the first line of the masterpiece. She told him of Johnsy's fancy, and how she feared she would, indeed, light and fragile as a leaf herself, float away, when her slight hold upon the world grew weaker.

Old Behrman, with his red eyes plainly streaming, shouted his contempt and derision for such idiotic imaginings.

"Vass!" he cried. "Is dere people in de world mit der foolishness to die because leafs dey drop off from a confounded vine? I haf not heard of such a thing. No, I will not bose as a model for your fool hermit-dunderhead. Vy do you allow dot silly pusiness to come in der brain of her? Ach, dot poor leetle Miss Yohnsy."

"She is very ill and weak," said Sue, "and the fever has left her mind morbid and full of strange fancies. Very well, Mr. Behrman, if you do not care to pose for me, you needn't. But I think you are a horrid old—old flibbertigibbet."

"You are just like a woman!" yelled Behrman. "Who said I will not bose? Go on. I come mit you. For half an hour I haf peen trying to say dot I am ready to bose. Gott! dis is not any blace in which one so goot as Miss Yohnsy shall lie sick. Some day I vill baint a masterpiece, and ve shall all go away. Gott! yes."

Johnsy was sleeping when they went upstairs. Sue pulled the shade

down to the window-sill, and motioned Behrman into the other room. In there they peered out the window fearfully at the ivy vine. Then they looked at each other for a moment without speaking. A persistent, cold rain was falling, mingled with snow. Behrman, in his old blue shirt, took his seat as the hermit miner on an up-turned kettle for a rock.

When Sue awoke from an hour's sleep the next morning she found Johnsy with dull, wide-open eyes staring at the drawn green shade.

"Pull it up; I want to see," she ordered, in a whisper.

Wearily Sue obeyed.

But, lo! after the beating rain and fierce gusts of wind that had endured through the livelong night, there yet stood out against the brick wall one ivy leaf. It was the last on the vine. Still dark green near its stem, but with its serrated edges tinted with the yellow of dissolution and decay, it hung bravely from a branch some twenty feet above the ground.

"It is the last one," said Johnsy. "I thought it would surely fall during the night. I heard the wind. It will fall today, and I shall die at the same time."

"Dear, dear!" said Sue, leaning her worn face down to the pillow, "think of me, if you won't think of yourself. What would I do?"

But Johnsy did not answer. The lonesomest thing in all the world is a soul when it is making ready to go on its mysterious, far journey. The fancy seemed to possess her more strongly as one by one the ties that bound her to friendship and to earth were loosed.

The day wore away, and even through the twilight they could see the lone ivy leaf clinging to its stem against the wall. And then, with the coming of the night, the north wind was again loosed, while the rain still beat against the windows and pattered down from the low Dutch eaves.

When it was light enough Johnsy, the merciless, commanded that the shade be raised.

The ivy leaf was still there.

Johnsy lay for a long time looking at it. And then she called to Sue, who was stirring her chicken broth over the gas stove.

"I've been a bad girl, Sudie," said Johnsy. "Something has made that last leaf stay there to show me how wicked I was. It is a sin to want to die. You may bring me a little broth now, and some milk with a little port in it, and—no; bring me a hand-mirror first, and then pack some pillows about me, and I will sit up and watch you cook."

An hour later she said:

"Sudie, some day I hope to paint the Bay of Naples."

The doctor came in the afternoon, and Sue had an excuse to go into the hallway as he left.

"Even chances," said the doctor, taking Sue's thin, shaking hand in his. "With good nursing you'll win. And now I must see another case I have downstairs. Behrman, his name is—some kind of an artist, I believe. Pneumonia, too. He is an old, weak man, and the attack is acute. There is no hope for him; but he goes to the hospital to-day to be made more comfortable."

The next day the doctor said to Sue: "She's out of danger. You've won. Nutrition and care now—that's all."

And that afternoon Sue came to the bed where Johnsy lay, contentedly knitting a very blue and very useless woollen shoulder scarf, and put one arm around her, pillows and all.

"I have something to tell you, white mouse," she said. "Mr. Behrman died of pneumonia to-day in the hospital. He was ill only two days. The janitor found him on the morning of the first day in his room downstairs helpless with pain. His shoes and clothing were wet through and icy cold. They couldn't imagine where he had been on such a dreadful night. And then they found a lantern, still lighted, and a ladder that had been dragged from its place, and some scattered brushes, and a palette with green and yellow colors mixed on it, and—look out the window, dear, at the last ivy leaf on the wall. Didn't you wonder why it never fluttered or moved when the wind blew? Ah, darling, it's Behrman's masterpiece—he painted it there the night that the last leaf fell."

THE BLOODHOUND

ARTHUR TRAIN

I

"Next!" The dejected file of prisoners beneath the glaring windows stiffened and limped forward. There were twelve of them—the same number as the minor prophets, the apostles, the tribes of Israel and the officers of King Solomon—a bullet-headed negro in a red sweater, charged with vivisection during a crap game, bringing up the rear. The line humped along beside the iron grating like a caterpillar, those behind butting forward those in front, turned the corner by the jury box and disgorged two prisoners before the bar of judgment. It was the first Monday in January—pleading day.

"Next!" repeated Phelan, the court captain, standing inside the rail, to McNamara, his whipper-in. "Lively now!"

McNamara turned to the head of the line.

"You two there! Step up here!"

Mr. Dougherty, the tiny, bald-headed clerk with the big mustaches that made him look like an animated mushroom, picked up the indictments on the top of the blue pile in front of him.

"Patrick Mooney and Daniel Mulligan," he intoned as if officiating at the high altar of the cathedral, "you are jointly indicted for the crime of burglary in the third degree, grand larceny in the first degree, assault in the first degree, receiving stolen goods and carrying concealed weapons. How say you? Do you plead guilty or not guilty?"

Neither of the two made reply.

"Have you counsel?" sang Dougherty.

"Got a lawyer?" interpreted Captain Phelan.

There was a slight bustle on one of the nearer benches as a heavily built man with sideburns came forward.

"I appear for both defendants, Your Honor," said he. "They plead not guilty. Will Your Honor set the case down for the twenty-first for trial?"

The judge nodded and made a note, and the stout lawyer turned away, about to resume his seat.

"Next!" shouted Phelan to the world at large. "Next!"

The taller of the two prisoners—a plug-ugly—wheeled from the rail and started on the return trip. The other did not stir. He was a much smaller man, hardly five feet six, and of a different make altogether. He might have been your plumber, or electri-

cian, or the grocer's clerk who takes your order at the side door; and though his demeanor was more timid than any of these it was, nevertheless, defiant—some spark of courage, or at least resolution, still surviving after his year in Sing Sing.

"Judge—Your Honor," he said huskily, twisting his cap in his hands— "this man don't represent me. I haven't got any lawyer."

Old Judge Watkins peered down from the dais at him over his reading glasses. He then looked after the retreating attorney.

"How's this, Mr. Hogan?" he asked. "I thought you said that you appeared for both defendants."

The attorney paused with a half smile.

"So I did, judge."

"The prisoner Mooney says you do not represent him."

"They're indicted together—for the same offense, committed at the same time. The defendant Mulligan's sister came to my office yesterday and retained me for both of 'em."

"Judge—Your Honor," repeated the man at the bar of justice stubbornly, "I don't know this lawyer and I don't know this man I'm indicted with. I never saw him before that night. I'm innocent, and I want a separate trial with my own lawyer."

Captain Phelan hoisted a blue shoulder and grinned at Mr. Dougherty. It was the old game—the ancient grandstand play—of seizing this opportunity to make a vigorous denial of guilt in the presence of the panel of jurors newly assembled in court for a month's service, in the hope that by so doing one might avoid going on the stand later at one's trial, and so escape the disagreeable necessity of submitting to cross-examination upon one's record and earlier history.

"I only got out of prison Saturday, Your Honor," continued the prisoner Mooney, "after serving fourteen months—with an allowance off for good behavior. I'm in no hurry to get back either, believe me! Sunday night I was walking home, and this here defendant, Mulligan, came along with a bag and began talking to me. Just then a bull jumped out and drew his gun on us. He rapped for his side partner and they yanked us up to headquarters, and when they found out I'd been in stir they said I was due for another bit. Clubbed me, into the bargain! See that lump on my forehead? Then the first cop said he found a gun on me. It's a plant, judge, I didn't have one. What would I want with a gun, judge? What I want is a chance to earn an honest living!"

He made his plea doggedly, yet with obvious hopelessness, for he no longer had any faith in "the course of justice."

Judge Watkins, sent down from Utica by his friend the governor to hold a special criminal trial term and so relieve the congestion in the Tombs Prison, beckoned to Mr. Dougherty, who elevated himself upon his glossy little tiptoes and held a whispered colloquy with His Honor across the edge of the dais. Behind the prisoner on the first row of benches a homely girl in a gray shawl, her broad honest face covered with a screen of freckles, leaned forward hungrily. She had waited for Mooney over a year; she would wait ten more if need be, or until they carried her out in a box feet first. She also had lost all faith in the supposed equality of the law. For Paddy had been railroaded because he had swatted Micky Morrison over in Fagan's saloon, Micky being heir apparent of the lower East Side, a friend of Bloodhound O'Brien, the assistant district attorney, and honor-

ary colonel of the Pearl Button Kids; while Paddy Mooney was a stationary fireman in an office building, without political affiliations, and not even a member of the union. This he now perceived to have been a grievous lapse, due, however, only to the reason that they had sought to bully him into it, and he wouldn't be bullied.

Judge Watkins saw the tense look on the girl's face, and guessed its significance. For an upstate judge he knew a great deal about the Big Burg. There are some people who suppose that after Jerome cleaned up the Red Light District and jailed a few policemen New York became whiter than snow, and has stayed so every since! Yet wasn't Boss Tweed nearly sent up after the greatest political housecleaning ever staged by old Father Knickerbocker? Weren't the Tammany Tiger's ribs clearly visible for years? And would it not have died of starvation had it not been for the defeat of John Purroy Mitchel as recently as 1917? Has it changed its stripes? And after all, is a Republican cop—if there be such a thing—any different from a Tammany cop? Is not the nature of cops generic? Just as the nature of prosecutors is generic?

It is said somewhere by Frazer, in "The Golden Bough," that mankind as a whole resembles the ocean, and that civilization, like the wind of heaven, merely ruffles the surface, leaving the depths untouched. So it is with municipal reforms. You can have torchlight processions galore and political-fusion love feasts and spasms of civic virtue, but cops will remain cops, and crooks will remain crooks, and out of the enmity between their respective seeds will spring all the evils of any sort of warfare—brutality and malign trickery and *schrecklichkeit*. This hateful contest between human rats and human ferrets rarely fails to contaminate or at any rate to harden most of those who take part in it. For the rat is fighting for life and the ferret is fighting for his living.

The danger to the young lawyer who out of a desire for public service seeks an appointment as an assistant district attorney, is that in the passion of the chase the conviction and punishment of some—to him—obviously guilty criminal may seem more important at the moment than the strict preservation of his own integrity or the unwavering maintenance of the principles of justice. Shall the murderer go free simply because some foolish law prohibits hearsay evidence or the proving of more than one offense at the same time? Should we not praise, rather than condemn, the young enthusiast who is willing to sacrifice his virtue, his ideals, his very soul in order that some ruffian may hang? Should we not pay tribute to one who is willing to be damned for the glory of God?

Judge Watkins looked searchingly around the court-room until his eye came to rest in a far corner.

"I will assign Mr. Ephraim Tutt to the case," said he, and at the summons the old lawyer arose from his seat and, stovepipe hat in hand, approached the bar.

At that moment the door was pushed violently open and Billy the Bloodhound, surrounded by his minions, entered. Ancient enemy faced ancient enemy.

II

It must not be presumed from the foregoing philosophic disquisition that we intend to lay any floral offering upon the bier of William Francis O'Brien's moral reputation. Far from it! We desire to provide for him no

apology, extenuation or excuse; and the reader may perhaps recall that he has hitherto at sundry times been described and figured in other pages as "the yellow dog of the district attorney's office," for that was exactly what he was—a legal bulldog or human bloodhound, as you may prefer. One who viewed it as his duty to his God, his country, and himself to convict by any means at his command every hapless defendant brought to the bar of justice.

Through his pertinacity, his resourcefulness, and his lack of scruple he had achieved great notoriety as a prosecutor. Lawyers feared him, defendants shuddered at the mere thought of facing his merciless cross-examination; for he was without consideration to the former or sympathy for the latter. He had no bowels or mercies. To achieve his end he astutely made use of a veneer of apparent honesty, of naïve enthusiasm, that often made him seem to juries merely a blunt, well-meaning blunderer. Yet there was no guile of serpent he did not possess, no venom not in his teeth.

Billy the Bloodhound, as he was called, was a more prominent figure in the Criminal Courts Building than District Attorney John Henry Peckham himself, who was content to have it so, since he shared the widespread belief that there had to be a crook in every law office, whether public or private. In fact, he found O'Brien more than a mere convenience, particularly because he could always count upon him for a conviction in any difficult case. As he used to say to his confidential friends: "If the Bloodhound hasn't got the necessary evidence—he goes and gets it!"

Hence, because O'Brien was not only an asset but a valuable political go-between, the Honorable John Henry Peckham smothered his personal dislike for the dog and encouraged it to lick his hand. He also was forced to put up with his noise, and his overbearing and swashbuckling ways. For outside the court-room —as well also, to be accurate, sometimes inside it—Billy the Bloodhound was a swaggering, blustering sort of legal bravo—wherever he went preceded, surrounded, and followed by a cohort of sycophants, clerks, process servers, and police officers on special detail, who ran his errands, carried his books, bags, and papers, bought his theatre tickets, did his telephoning, acclaimed his coming and did him lip service—much as we may imagine some Roman senator of the same type to have been accompanied by his bodyguard of lictors who shoved the crowd aside at his approach. All this to Billy the Bloodhound was as the breath of his life, and he played the part, bellowing down the corridors, shouting from the elevators, kicking his slaves in the shins and then handing them out cigars, whispering out of the corner of his mouth about "the big fellow" and "the one next," with so effective an air of mystery that he had everybody buffaloed; and the crowd all swore among themselves and to him that he was the greatest little man on earth.

He was thickset, bullet-headed, with closely cropped reddish hair and freckly sandy skin, and his short aquiline nose and square chin would have made the features of a cigar-store Indian—alas, poor redskin, he deserves an apology!—seem filled with the milk of human kindness.

Everybody feared and kowtowed to him. People who wanted favors of Peckham went first to placate O'Brien, who was supposed to have the boss in his pocket; cops and detectives sought

to have him handle their cases; judges were apt to try to conciliate him as a coming man politically, and as possibly the next district attorney. Whenever a "star case," a *cause célèbre,* or any matter attracting public attention came into the office, O'Brien sent to the chief clerk for the papers and grabbed it. He had even been known to send for the papers in a case already assigned to another assistant and grab that too. He gave out interviews to the papers, assumed the office of "acting district attorney" whenever Peckham absented himself, and likewise frequently when the latter was there, and constituted himself pretty much the whole show.

If one stood for him he wasn't so bad, and if he hadn't been a crook he might easily have been a power for good instead of a power for evil. It is not easy to overestimate that power, for he was the grand vizier of the most powerful public office-holder in the United States, not even excepting the President himself. He could make or break a cop or blast the reputation of any man in the community at will. This the Honorable William Francis O'Brien!

Alas "the law's delay, the insolence of office, and the spurns that patient merit of the unworthy takes"! What price beside him, poor old Ephraim Tutt?

But wait! There is life in the old dog yet—old Tutt, we mean! So far Billy the Bloodhound has but opened the door and entered the court-room, and Mr. Tutt has but turned to gaze at him. Let us reserve our lamentations until we see what will happen when they meet. Will not the gods lend courage and strength to the kindly old lawyer, who never yet did aught but good, although mayhap he may have done it in queer ways? And who never retired wholly van-

quished from the field of honorable battle?

So, heralds, your fanfares! And summon all to the lists to behold the contest between the Bloodhound and the Knight of the Stovepipe Hat. Blow, bugles, blow! Set the echoes of the forum ringing for the legal joust! Court officers, bawl your best, with "Oyez! Oyez!" and "Hear ye! Hear ye!" Pound the railings and shout the honest burghers out of their hats and into their seats, make them move up and on, close the windows, lock the door so that none may escape, and let all who have business in our Honorable Court now with due deference draw near, give your attention, and let Mr. Tutt be heard!

III

Billy the Bloodhound strutted into the inclosure in front of the dais, bowed to the judge and preened himself before the gaping crowd—the little czar, the Pooh-Bah, the high-cockalorum of the Sessions—as the old lawyer was in the act of consulting his new client. Something about Mr. Tutt inspired Paddy Mooney with instant confidence, and while the court waited he hastily explained to him the circumstances surrounding his arrest. He had no witnesses, he said; he was being framed and he wanted to be tried at once. O'Brien swaggered to the bar.

"Well," he inquired roughly, "how do you plead? What are you going to do? You can't talk there forever."

Mr. Tutt smiled with the old-time courtesy he invoked when in his most dangerous mood.

"I am sorry to have unduly delayed the proceedings, Mr. O'Brien. We plead not guilty, and we ask an immediate trial."

It was at this moment that the
Devil, in the shape of Delaney the
cop, leaned over the rail and plucked
the Bloodhound's sleeve.
"S-st, Mr. O'Brien! Put the screws
on him and he'll plead guilty. We've
got him cold. Here's the gun I took
off him—loaded."
He shoved the revolver into
O'Brien's hand, and the latter, always
willing to oblige, slipped it into his
pocket.
"Has he got a record?" he asked
sideways.
"Sure! Just out of stir. Caught him
with a valise full of stuff he took
out of a cigar store. He's an old-timer
—Gas House Gang. If he won't plead,
stick him right on trial. It's a pipe! A
conviction sure!"
The Bloodhound nodded.
"Leave him to me! Here, you!"—
addressing Mooney and Mr. Tutt to-
gether and as one—"plead guilty and
I'll give you attempted grand in the
second."
Mr. Tutt gravely shook his head.
"No," he replied. "I cannot let an
innocent man falsely admit under any
conditions that he is guilty."
O'Brien's face hardened.
"Suit yourself!" he snapped back.
"If he doesn't he'll get the limit."
"Not unless he's convicted!" mur-
mured Mr. Tutt.
"Oh!" sneered his adversary. "You
think you can get him off, do you?
Don't fool yourself! It's a dead open-
and-shut case. Will you or won't you?
If you won't he'll be on his way up
the river by two o'clock."
Mr. Tutt's blood boiled and tingled.
"Mister District Attorney," he said
sternly, "may I ask if you have ex-
amined into the merits of this case?"
"I've seen the only witness there
is!" retorted O'Brien. "This man is an
ex-convict. His picture is in the gal-
lery. So are his thumb tracks. He's

guilty all right, all right! He's got no
more chance than an icicle in Hades."
"Have you talked to him? Have
you heard his story? Have you ques-
tioned the officer who arrested him?"
went on the old lawyer.
"I have not! And I don't intend
to!" answered O'Brien shortly. "He
can tell his story on the stand—and
if there's anything to it the jury can
acquit him."
"What chance has he got to have
the jury believe him if you bring out
the fact that he has been in prison?"
asked Mr. Tutt. "It will hopelessly
prejudice them against him."
"That's why he'd better plead
guilty!" grinned the Bloodhound.
"And you call that justice!" cried
Mr. Tutt, his lips quivering. "Well,
put him on trial—and be damned to
you!"
"I will!" laughed O'Brien. "I'll put
him on trial in ten minutes—as soon
as the pleas are over. And then"—he
bent over past Mooney and leered
into Mr. Tutt's face—"and then be
damned to *you!*"
As the court officer marched
Mooney back to the pen a hand
pulled Mr. Tutt by the coat tails. He
turned and looked into the homely
face of the girl in the shawl.
"Oh, sir," she begged, "for God's
sake don't let them frame him! That
brute Delaney was a witness against
him on his first trial. He's Morrison's
man. They've made up their minds
to railroad him. Oh, sir! Save him!
He's a brave, good lad that never
harmed anyone. I know you're a big
lawyer and don't bother with the likes
of us, but"—she lowered her voice to
a whisper—"I've saved ninety dollars,
and it's yours if you get him off!"
Mr. Tutt patted her arm.
"All right! All right!" he said sooth-
ingly. "I'll do my best, but not for

your money! What's your name, my girl?"

"Annie Murphy."

"Do you know the man Paddy worked for before he was sent up?"

"Sure!"

"Go bring him here."

The girl hurried away and Mr. Tutt walked back to his seat.

"If I ever got that fellow to rights," he muttered, eying O'Brien as he swaggered at the rail, "may God have mercy on his soul!"

IV

In the good old mediæval days our Teutonic relatives had a jovial habit of strapping any particularly unruly serf beneath the belly of a wild horse and then hunting him to death with dogs. The serf in this pleasant game had very little chance, but at any rate he had a fair start, and the horse did not have a ball and chain attached to his leg. But in the coming course, in which the dogs of law would run down Paddy Mooney if they could, he was handicapped in two ways: first, he had a ball and chain on his leg in the shape of his prison record; and second, in addition to the hatred which O'Brien entertained for all defendants, and particularly for those who had served terms in prison, he was the object of the prosecutor's special malignity because he was to be defended by Mr. Tutt, who on more than one celebrated occasion had shown the braggart up for what he was. To his ancient grudge, fed fat by years of successful opposition upon the old lawyer's part, was now added the smart of present insult. His rage against Mooney for not being willing to plead guilty fanned his fury against Mr. Tutt, and his hatred of Mr. Tutt transformed his anger against Mooney

to poisonous serpents. To be in any way foiled made him a madman.

"Come here!" he growled at Delaney as he dragged him into the corridor. "Give me the goods on this fellow! I'll teach that sanctimonious old he-devil a lesson he won't forget in a hurry!"

The heart of Delaney leaped within him. That was the bally boy! He would have another conviction to add to his scroll of honor, and maybe the D. A. would write the Commissioner a letter of commendation, praising his services in sending up Mooney for another bit! Anyhow, Micky Morrison wouldn't forget it! Promotion dazzled him! He could have kissed O'Brien or licked his boots—which latter alternative most of us would have preferred.

"Listen here!" he said, fawning upon the prosecutor. "It's a cinch. I caught this guy and another gun—Mulligan—wit' a bag of goods. I gave ye the cannon I took off him already. Mulligan'll turn state's evidence for a suspended sentence. Everybody's here! You'll eat him alive!"

"All right! Tell Mulligan I'll use him; and bring him up into one of the jury rooms and go over his story with him. I don't want any slip-up now! I'm doing you a favor by trying this case myself."

"I know you are, Mr. O'Brien! I know you are!" declared Delaney in those tones of unctuous adoration that were as parmacety to the inward bruises of the Bloodhound's soul. " 'Tis the next district attorney you're going to be!"

"Then get busy! Get busy!" ordered O'Brien, stalking back toward the court-room.

The reader might well be pardoned were he incredulous of what O'Brien and Delaney purposed to do. Fortunately such prosecutors are rare; but

once in a generation—perhaps even more often—they arise; and against their villainy judges and lawyers are generally powerless, for their assassinations are hidden beneath the cloak of law and the pretense of public service. Little did the judge upon the bench wot of the proposed tragedy; had he done so he would have arisen and rent his official garments. But Mr. Tutt knew, and his heart turned faint within his old frock coat. O Justice, what crimes are sometimes committed in thy name!

v

The last disconsolate in the file of prisoners had pleaded not guilty and clumped back to the prison pen; the judge had listened to the manifold ingenious excuses urged upon him by talesmen reluctant to serve; the crowd in the court-room had thinned; it was twelve o'clock; the holocaust was about to begin.

The Bloodhound arose and strolled to the district attorney's table in front of the jury box.

"Have you any case to move, Mister District Attorney?" asked His Honor, and, at O'Brien's nod, added to the clerk, "Fill the box, Mr. Dougherty."

"Take your places, gentlemen," called the latter, drawing twelve names rapidly from the wheel. "People against Mooney! Patrick Mooney, you are indicted for burglary in the third degree, grand larceny in the first degree, assault in the first degree, receiving stolen goods and carrying concealed weapons. If you desire to challenge any talesman you may do so now!" One almost expected to hear him continue "Or forever after hold your peace!"

But Mr. Tutt did not wish to challenge anybody, and smiled so genially at the double row of miscellaneous citizens, and with such an air of gratification declared "The jury is more than satisfactory," that every man of them expanded his chest and lifted his chin a fraction of an inch, convinced that Mr. Tutt was a man of parts, and became his friend for life.

Then the Bloodhound summoned them to their duty of sending men to prison. The defendant, he told them, had been caught in possession of the proceeds of a burglary committed but a few moments before his arrest. He had a loaded pistol in his pocket, which he had sought to draw upon the officer, who luckily had reduced him to a timely submission. His fellow criminal would take the stand and testify against him. It was a cut-and-dried case, a routine affair; and they would have nothing to do but to convict. He called Delaney, whose immense blue bulk overflowed the witness chair; and the cop made good the prosecutor's opening in every particular. He described Mooney's attempted flight, his effort to pull his gun and how he had frustrated it by felling him with his night-stick. He then identified the gun which O'Brien produced from his pocket.

Cross-examine!

Mr. Tutt asked but two questions:

"Do you know Micky Morrison?"

"I do."

"Do you belong to the same club?"

"I do!" defiantly.

"That is all!" And the old lawyer waved him from the stand.

Then Mulligan was brought up from the pen and put in the chair, and swore that everything that Delaney had said was gospel. He admitted that he was a professional burglar, but allowed that on occasions a burglar could tell the truth, and that this was

one of them; and he supplemented the cop's story by describing in the most graphic detail how Mooney and he had planned and perpetrated the burglary of the cigar store; but, his imagination being limited and his general intelligence even more so, he made a sorry exhibition of himself under Mr. Tutt's good-natured yet searching cross-examination. Indeed, he soon became so involved in contradictions as to Mooney's part in the affair that no man in his senses would have convicted a dog of the larceny of a bone upon his testimony. One piece of evidence, however, remained unshaken—Delaney's testimony that he had taken a loaded pistol from Mooney's pocket; and Delaney had not been in any way discredited under cross-examination. Quickly O'Brien shifted his position. As a strategist he had no equal.

"If Your Honor please," he said, "I do not feel that the jury should be permitted to convict the defendant of burglary or larceny on this character of testimony. The co-defendant Mulligan is an ex-convict, besides being confessedly guilty in this case, and his statements should not be received without stronger corroboration. I shall therefore ask Your Honor to withdraw from the consideration of the jury all the counts in the indictment except that for carrying concealed weapons."

He spoke as if with an earnest hope for salvation—and the jury viewed him with approbation. The fox! He knew that Mooney could not meet the charge without taking the stand and admitting that he had been in prison, although had all the counts been left in the indictment the jury might well have been led to render a general verdict of acquittal, owing to the obvious unreliability of Mulligan's testimony.

"The People rest," said O'Brien. The jury turned to the defense. "Take the stand, Mr. Mooney," directed Mr. Tutt, while the Bloodhound licked his lips.

Paddy Mooney felt his way round behind the jury box and to the witness chair. He knew that he was innocent, but he knew that he was going to be pilloried on cross-examination and utterly discredited. He was an ex convict. That would be enough to send him up again. But unless he took the stand and denied that the weapon was his the jury would have no choice—would have to convict him. It was a slim chance but it was worth taking. No use giving up without a fight!

Doggedly under Mr. Tutt's lead he denied everything that had been testified to against him, including that he had, or ever had had, a revolver. Mulligan had joined him, he swore, unsolicited, and when Delaney had appeared he had made no attempt whatever to escape. Why should he have? He had done nothing.

"Your witness!" said Mr. Tutt with a bow toward the jury box.

The Bloodhound crept toward the witness chair with the stealth of a panther about to spring. At three feet he sprang!

"Mister Mooney, have you ever been convicted of a crime?"

"Yes," answered the defendant in a husky voice.

"Of what crime?"

"Assault."

"Ah! And you say you are a peaceable sort of person?"

"Yes."

"When did you get out of jail?"

"Last week."

The jury looked at one another. The poison had begun to work. But the dose might be too small. O'Brien intended to take no chances. As he

would have expressed it, he was going to "give him the gaff." He beckoned Delaney to the rail.

"What have you got on him?" he asked. "Give it to me quick."

"He's an old-timer," stammered the cop. "Gas House Gang. Cracked safes and done most everything."

O'Brien knew he was lying, but he had a right to take an officer's word for a thing like that.

"Go up to my office," he ordered Delaney, "and bring me down Jones' Professional Criminals of America."

The cop hesitated.

"He ain't in it!" he ventured.

"Did you hear what I said?" shouted O'Brien. "Go get it!"

While Delaney is waiting for the elevator to do his master's bidding let it be explained that when a criminal, or anybody else, for that matter, goes upon the witness stand to testify, he may be asked upon cross-examination by the opposing counsel any fact as to himself or his past which may tend to discredit him, for if he be a rascal and unworthy of credence the jury are entitled to know it so as to be guided by that knowledge in the performance of their holy office. Now there are only two limitations upon this sacred right of cross-examination as to credit—the discretion of the presiding judge and the fact that if the matter inquired about is not directly connected with the issue involved the lawyer asking the question is bound by the witness' answer and is not permitted to show in rebuttal that it is false.

Yet neither of these limitations amounts to anything, and the latter instead of being a handicap to a prosecutor really is an advantage; for often a lawyer asks a question from which the jury infers something which is not true and which the lawyer could not prove to be true if he were allowed

to try to do so in rebuttal. For example: If a reputable prosecuting attorney should ask a colored defendant, charged with stealing A's chickens on Friday, if it were not a fact that he had stolen B's chickens on Saturday and the colored defendant denied it, the jury would doubtless accept the interrogation of the prosecutor as based on fact and assume that the luckless negro had stolen chickens from both A and B. Yet if the prosecutor were at liberty to prove that the negro was lying when the latter denied that he had stolen B's poultry, he might find it exceedingly hard to do so. Thus the law's restriction, which is apparently an advantage to the witness, particularly if he be a defendant accused of a crime, in reality works against him; just as the right to take the stand in fact compels every defendant to do so or suffer the penalty of refusal in the form of the jury's natural assumption that he is afraid to do so because he is guilty. Of this great principle the Bloodhound now proposed to avail himself to the utter annihilation of Paddy Mooney and Mr. Tutt, both of whom he was resolved should plunge down into the abyss of discreditability.

For he knew that because he held a public office of large responsibility any question put by him to Mooney would be in the jury's eyes tantamount to an accusation; particularly after he had evinced such an apparent fair-mindedness by asking the judge to quash the burglary, receiving and larceny counts in the indictment.

The issue now hung in the balance. A police officer had sworn to finding a loaded pistol on the prisoner, and a self-confessed crook had corroborated him; the defendant had vehemently denied it, although the force of his denial had been somewhat tempered by his admission of having been pre-

viously convicted of assault. In view of the judge's admonition that the burden of proof would be on the prosecution to prove its case beyond a reasonable doubt, the jury might acquit. Something must be done. O'Brien did not hesitate. He would "smear" Mooney so that nobody would pay the slightest attention to his denials, however convincing under other circumstances they might have been. It would not be difficult. Any hint or suggestion that Mooney was a professional "gun" —the slightest innuendo to that effect, probably—would be enough; even if he didn't look it. For look it he certainly did not, as he sat motionless on the witness chair—more like a clay statue than a man, his chalky face set and his narrow shoulders foursquare to the world—an impotent yet defiant creature, like a wild animal driven into a hole or fettered to a stake. Only when his eyes over Mr. Tutt's shoulders met those of Annie Murphy did his stubborn expression soften. O'Brien caught the looks that passed between them and scowled. That sort of thing always had a bad effect on the jury. He must "can" it somehow. He strolled back to his place and faced Mooney again.

"You come from the Gas House district, don't you?" he asked.

"No," replied Mooney.

"Ever hear of the Gas House Gang?"

"Yes, but I'm not one of them."

"Oh, you're not, eh? I didn't ask you that. Why did you hurry so to slip that in?"

"I object!" interposed Mr. Tutt. "Such a suggestion is improper and prejudicial."

Judge Watkins, who despised technicalities, waved him aside.

"I will permit the question. The witness volunteered a statement. He may be examined upon it."

Mr. Tutt subsided.

"Because," retorted Mooney, "you were trying to make the jury think I was."

"Maybe you're right!" countered the Bloodhound with a grin at the jury box. "Now, how many times have you been convicted of crime in other States?"

"Never!" cried Mooney. "And you can't prove it either."

"Well, maybe I can't prove it," admitted O'Brien easily, "but," he added insinuatingly, "I can inquire how many times you have committed burglaries—say, in New Jersey?"

Mooney's jaws trembled and he grasped the arms of his chair so tight that his hands went white. He turned indignantly to the judge.

"Your Honor," he protested, "has this man got the right——"

"Answer the question!" admonished His Honor. "This is proper cross-examination."

"Well?" sneered O'Brien.

"I never committed any burglary!"

"No burglaries! What kind of crimes, then, have you committed?"

"I never committed any crimes!"

Mooney thrust forward in his seat toward his torturer and clinched his jaws. It was all nuts for O'Brien.

"Oh!" he laughed. "You didn't, eh? I thought you were just out of Sing Sing!"

"But I hadn't committed any crime."

"So you were innocent that time? Just as you claim to be now!"

"Delaney railroaded me for Micky Morrison!"

The Bloodhound reddened with anger.

"Strike that out!" ordered Judge Watkins. "Don't volunteer. Answer only the questions put to you. Were you innocent that time?"

"Yes—I was!" declared Mooney

with such obvious sincerity that O'Brien wished he had not asked the question. So far he had not scored heavily, although his adversary was getting groggy. At that instant Delaney re-entered the room and approached the rail with a large book in his hand. "S-st!" he whispered to O'Brien, handing over the book. "Ast him if last December he didn't smash Sugar Grady's nose down on Hudson Street wit' a blackjack; an', say, ast him if he wasn't one o' the bunch 'at beat up Inspector Boyle with brass knuckles over behind the engine-house."

The Bloodhound's eyes gleamed. Real stuff! He put the questions to Mooney, receiving with an indulgent grimace the latter's emphatic denials, and the jury, who had seen his conference with the police officer, made sure that a desperate thug was seated before them, while Mr. Tutt, a satiric smile playing about his withered lips, vowed vengeance deep and dire upon the unscrupulous O'Brien.

But the Bloodhound, frenzied at the scent of human gore, was now resolved to rend Mooney limb from limb. With all the gleeful malice of a Spanish inquisitor about to tear out his victim's beating heart with a pair of incandescent pincers, this charming understudy of Satan sauntered nonchalantly up to the witness and, holding the Professional Criminals of America so that the jury could plainly read the title, opened the book and running his finger down a page as if to mark the place—and looking up from time to time as he apparently read what he there had found—put to the hapless being in the moral death chair before him, as if solemnly declaring the accompanying accusation to be true, the following question:

"Did you not, on September 6, 1917, in company with Red Burke, alias the Roach; Tony Savelli, otherwise known as Tony the Greaser; and Dynamite Tom Meeghan, crack the safe of the American Railway Express at Rahway, New Jersey, and get away with six thousand dollars?"

There was no doubt about O'Brien's having caught the jury now. Just as John Hancock signed his name to the Declaration of Independence so large that no one need use spectacles to read it, so Paddy Mooney screamed his outraged denial so loud that even the dead might well have heard him.

"It's a lie!" he yelled, jumping up and shaking his fist at O'Brien. "I never knew any such people. And I never was in Rahway."

"So you say!" the Bloodhound taunted him. "But don't you know that both the Roach and the Greaser testified at their trials that you were there?"

"Wait a moment!" interpolated Judge Watkins. "Do not answer until your counsel has time to object. Mr. Tutt, do you object to the question? If you do I will exclude it."

But Mr. Tutt gravely shook his head.

"I prefer to have him answer it," he said.

"I know nothing about it at all!" protested Mooney. Once more he turned to the bench. "Your Honor," he cried, "he's framin' me! I—"

Judge Watkins banged his gavel.

"You will have your chance to explain on the redirect," he remarked coldly, for he, too, was now convinced that the witness was a desperate criminal.

"That is all!" declared O'Brien, as with an air of triumph he threw the book ostentatiously on the table in front of the jury box. The defendant was cooked. That question about Red Burke had done the trick, driven the last nail into the lid of his coffin. He sank gloatingly into his chair. He had

'em on the run. The jury could convict without leaving the box. There was nothing left for old Tutt to do but try to extract additional denials from his already discredited client. But the old lawyer made no such move. Instead he remarked:

"Mr. Mooney, you were asked whether you had not been previously convicted of assault, and you replied in the affirmative. I now ask you whom you were charged with assaulting?"

"Micky Morrison."

"Who arrested you for the alleged offense?"

"Officer Delaney."

"You mean the same officer who has just sworn that he found a pistol in your pocket?"

"Yes, sir."

Mr. Tutt drew in his lips. "That is all!" said he, without further attempt to rehabilitate his client. Then as Mooney left the stand Mr. Tutt addressed Judge Watkins:

"If Your Honor please, I had intended calling a character witness—a former employer—in behalf of the defendant, but what has transpired would seem to make any such testimony immaterial." He hesitated for an instant, and to O'Brien came the sudden thought that the old lawyer might be going to throw up the sponge and plead his client guilty after all. But to his astonishment he heard Mr. Tutt say: "There is one thing, however, to which I invite the court's attention. The prosecutor has produced a loaded pistol here which he claims was found in my client's possession. It is the basis of the charge against him. Yet the district attorney for some reason best known to himself has not offered it in evidence. Unless this is done, in view of the fact that the pistol has been exhibited to the jury, I shall ask for a dismissal."

O'Brien rose languidly to his feet. "The merest oversight, Your Honor. Here is the pistol. I offer it in evidence."

"I object," said Mr. Tutt—"unless it appears on the record from whose custody it is produced, how it got there, and that it is in the same condition as when received."

"Mr. Tutt is technically correct," nodded His Honor.

The Bloodhound's lips curled. "I got it from Officer Delaney this morning, and have had it in my pocket all the time. It is exactly as I received it. Does that satisfy you?"

"Not unless you so testify upon the stand," answered the old lawyer, looking fixedly at O'Brien, who experienced a curiously sickening sensation.

"If Mr. Tutt insists you will have to be sworn," ruled His Honor. "But it is a rather unusual demand for any lawyer to make under the circumstances."

"This is a rather unusual case," retorted Mr. Tutt, unperturbed.

O'Brien shifted his feet uneasily. He did not like the idea of facing Mr. Tutt from the witness chair—not in the least! Still—there was no help for it. With the pistol in his hand he ascended the stand, took the oath and without sitting down repeated in a rather shaky voice what he had just said.

"Have you any cross-examination?" asked Judge Watkins.

"I have," replied Mr. Tutt amid a sudden silence. What could the old codger be up to?

"You are one of the public prosecutors of this county?" he asked quietly.

"I am," shot back the Bloodhound.

"And you are sworn to uphold the law?"

"Yes."

"To prosecute those of whose guilt

you are satisfied through the introduction of legal evidence in a legal manner?"

"Of course." O'Brien's uneasiness was growing. But Mr. Tutt's next question momentarily allayed his anxiety while arousing his irritation.

"Where were you born?"

"New York City.".

Judge Watkins frowned at the questioner. This procedure was not at all according to Hoyle.

"Gas House section?"

One of the jury sniggered. His Honor raised his hand in gentle admonition.

"Is this relevant, Mr. Tutt? I do not wish to criticise, but your question seems rather trivial."

Mr. Tutt bowed.

"This is cross-examination," he replied. "However, I will withdraw it. Do you know one Micky Morrison, Mr. O'Brien?"

"Yes," scowled the Bloodhound.

"How much did you pay him for your appointment as assistant district attorney?"

O'Brien turned first red, then white. Judge Watkins brought down his gavel.

"That will do!" he remarked. "The jury will disregard the question!"

"If Your Honor please," replied Mr. Tutt quietly, "I have as much right to attack this witness' credibility as he had to attack that of my client. I press the question in another form:

"Did you not pay six thousand dollars to Michael McGurk to be delivered to Micky Morrison in consideration for his securing your appointment as assistant district attorney?"

"I did not!" shouted O'Brien. "And you know it! Your Honor, are you going to permit me to be insulted in this way?"

But a puzzled if not actually bewildered look had settled upon the learned justice's countenance. To coin a distinctly new phrase there was "a far-away look" in his gray eyes.

"Do you know Red Burke, alias the Roach; Tony Savelli, otherwise known as the Greaser; and Dynamite Tom Meeghan?"

"Mr. Tutt," expostulated Judge Watkins, "you may have a technical right to test the witness' credibility, but the matter is within my discretion and——"

"That is the precise question he asked my client," replied Mr. Tutt coolly. "What is sauce for the goose should be sauce for the gander."

"He may answer your question if you press it," acquiesced His Honor. "But there must be a limit to this sort of thing."

"Only a few more questions, Your Honor. Mr. O'Brien, have you ever been convicted of crime?"

"No!" valiantly answered the prosecutor, now gray as a ghost, for he saw his doom advancing upon him.

"Have you ever committed one?" O'Brien choked.

"I won't force you to answer that!" threw in Mr. Tutt gallantly.

"Have you any basis for that question?" demanded His Honor sharply.

Mr. Tutt smiled first at the jury and then at Judge Watkins.

"Your Honor," he replied in his most engaging manner, "you and I perhaps belong to a generation which has old-fashioned ideas of honor. I admit that I have had no basis for any of the questions which I have just asked the witness. Honor demands that I should do so; yet, in a sense, honor demanded that I should ask them, although I might later have to disown their sincerity. But, sir"—and his old voice rose high and vibrant—"but, sir, I do not abandon my attack upon this witness' credibility. I have

but one more question to ask of him, and upon his answer I stake my client's liberty. Let this witness but answer any way he may see fit—yes or no, I care not which—give any reply at all that may be officially recorded here, and not hereafter be disputed or denied by him—and these twelve men may return a verdict against my client."

Something in the old lawyer's tone drew the jury as one man toward the front of the box. Judge Watkins was gazing intently at Mr. Tutt. The faces in the court-room surged up and down like ocean waves beneath O'Brien's smarting eyes. He was gaffed himself. "Sir!" thundered Mr. Tutt, pointing an accusing finger at the miserable apology for a man now cowering upon the stand. "Sir! *When you took this book in your hand*"—he lifted Jones' Professional Criminals from where it lay upon the table—"*and pretended to read from its pages, were you reading something that was printed there or not? YES—OR NO?*"

In the silence all could distinctly hear the ticking of the clock upon the rear wall of the court-room. "Tick-tock! Tick-tock! Tick-tock! Yes—no! Yes—no! Yes—no!" it went.

O'Brien squirmed, looked down at the rocking floor, and turned faint. "Tick-tock! Tick-tock!" alternated the clock. "Yes—no! Yes—no!" answered O'Brien's pulse.

Everything was going black and white, and great pulpy gray spiders seemed grabbing at him from the circumambient air. If he put the thing through and answered "Yes"—insisted that he had been reading from the book, that old gray wolf down there would put the book in evidence and prove him a perjurer, send him up! A band of sweat oozed from beneath his red skullcap of hair. Yet if he answered "No"—admitted that he had made the whole thing up—that there was not a word in the book about Mooney at all—it would be nearly as bad!

In his agony he almost clutched the flimsy legal straw of refusing to answer on the ground that his reply might tend to degrade or incriminate him! But this would leave him in an even worse position. No, he must answer!

"Tick-tock! Yes—no! Tick-tock! Yes—no! Which—what!"

He moistened his parched lips and swallowed twice. He coughed—for time; and fumbled for his handkerchief. After all, he had done nothing that was not strictly legal. He had not charged that Mooney was a professional crook; he had only asked him the question. That didn't commit him to anything! You could ask what you chose and you were bound by the witness' answer. A gleam like sunrise flashed across his seething brain. Ah, that would save him, perhaps! Old Tutt would be bound by his answer. And then he saw himself tricked again! Yes, Tutt might be bound in the case at bar—although his muddy mind wasn't quite sure whether he would be or not—but he himself would be forever bound by the written record. He could never get rid of the millstone that his yes or no—no matter which he uttered—would hang about his neck! Old Tutt, like the Old Man of the Sea, would forever be upon his back!

"No," he muttered at last in a woolly voice, so low and thick as to be hardly audible. "I was not—reading from the book."

He bowed his head as if awaiting the headsman's stroke. A hiss—a score of hisses—writhed through the air toward him from the benches. Captain Phelan made no attempt to stop them.

"You mean——" began Judge Watkins incredulously. Then with a look of disgust he turned his back upon O'Brien.

"Ye snake!" This time the tense sibilant was that of a woman.

Mr. Tutt gazed at the jury. The Lord had delivered his enemy into his hands.

"Now, gentlemen," he said with a deprecating smile, "you may convict my client if you will."

There was a moment's puzzled silence, broken by the foreman.

"The hell we will!" he suddenly exploded. "The fellow we want to convict is O'Brien!"

And in the flurry of involuntary applause which followed, the ancient Dougherty was heard to murmur:

"Hearken unto your verdict as it stands recorded. You say the defendant is not guilty—and so say ye all!"

WHAT THE OLD MAN DOES
IS ALWAYS RIGHT

HANS CHRISTIAN ANDERSEN

I will tell you the story which was told to me when I was a little boy. Every time I thought of the story, it seemed to me to become more and more charming; for it is with stories as it is with many people—they become better as they grow older.

I take it for granted that you have been in the country, and seen a very old farmhouse with a thatched roof, and mosses and small plants growing wild upon the thatch. There is a stork's nest on the summit of the gable; for we can't do without the stork. The walls of the house are sloping, and the windows are low, and only one of the latter is made so that it will open. The baking-oven sticks out of the wall like a little fat body. The elder-tree hangs over the paling, and beneath its branches, at the foot of the paling, is a pool of water in which a few ducks are disporting themselves. There is a yard dog too, who barks at all comers.

Just such a farmhouse stood out in the country; and in this house dwelt an old couple—a peasant and his wife. Small as was their property, there was one article among it that they could do without—a horse, which made a living out of the grass it found by the side of the high-road. The old peasant rode into the town on this horse; and often his neighbours borrowed it of him, and rendered the old couple some service in return for the loan of it. But they thought it would be best if they sold the horse, or exchanged it for something that might be more useful to them. But what might this *something* be?

"You'll know that best, old man," said the wife. "It is fair-day to-day, so ride into town, and get rid of the horse for money, or make a good exchange: whichever you do will be right to me. Ride off to the fair."

And she fastened his neckerchief for him, for she could do that better than he could; and she tied it in a double bow, for she could do that very prettily. Then she brushed his hat round and round with the palm of her hand, and gave him a kiss. So he rode away upon the horse that was to be sold or to be bartered for something else. Yes, the old man knew what he was about.

The sun shone hotly down, and not a cloud was to be seen in the sky. The road was very dusty, for many people who were all bound for the fair were driving, or riding, or walking upon it. There was no shelter anywhere from the sunbeams.

Among the rest, a man was trudging along, and driving a cow to the

fair. The cow was as beautiful a creature as any cow can be.

"She gives good milk, I'm sure," said the peasant. "That would be a very good exchange—the cow for the horse.

"Hallo, you there with the cow!" he said; "I tell you what—I fancy a horse costs more than a cow, but I don't care for that; a cow would be more useful to me. If you like, we'll exchange."

"To be sure I will," said the man; and they exchanged accordingly.

So that was settled, and the peasant might have turned back, for he had done the business he came to do; but as he had once made up his mind to go to the fair, he determined to proceed, merely to have a look at it; and so he went on to the town with his cow.

Leading the animal, he strode sturdily on; and after a short time he overtook a man who was driving a sheep. It was a good fat sheep, with a fine fleece on its back.

"I should like to have that fellow," said our peasant to himself. "He would find plenty of grass by our palings, and in the winter we could keep him in the room with us. Perhaps it would be more practical to have a sheep instead of a cow. Shall we exchange?"

The man with the sheep was quite ready, and the bargain was struck. So our peasant went on in the high-road with his sheep.

Soon he overtook another man, who came into the road from a field, carrying a great goose under his arm.

"That's a heavy thing you have there. It has plenty of feathers and plenty of fat, and would look well

tied to a string, and paddling in the water at our place. That would be something for my old woman. She could make all kinds of profit out of it. How often she has said, 'If we only had a goose!' Now, perhaps, she can have one; and, if possible, it shall be hers. Shall we exchange? I'll give you my sheep for your goose, and thank you into the bargain."

The other man had not the least objection; and accordingly they exchanged, and our peasant became the proprietor of the goose.

By this time he was very near the town. The crowd on the high-road became greater and greater; there was quite a crush of men and cattle. They walked in the road, and close by the palings; and at the barrier they even walked into the toll-man's potato-field, where his own foul was strutting about with a string to its leg, lest it should take fright at the crowd, and stray away, and so be lost. This fowl had short tail-feathers, and winked with both its eyes, and looked very cunning. "Cluck, cluck!" said the fowl. What it thought when it said this I cannot tell you; but directly our good man saw it, he thought, "That's the finest fowl I've ever seen in my life! Why, it's finer than our parson's brood hen. On my word, I should like to have that fowl. A fowl can always find a grain or two, and can almost keep itself. I think it would be a good exchange if I could get that for my goose.

"Shall we exchange?" he asked the toll-taker.

"Exchange!" repeated the man; "well, that would not be a bad thing."

And so they exchanged; the toll-taker at the barrier kept the goose, and the peasant carried away the fowl.

Now he had done a good deal of business on his way to the fair, and he was hot and tired. He wanted something to eat, and a glass of brandy to drink; and soon he was in front of the inn. He was just about to step in, when the ostler came out, so they met at the door. The ostler was carrying a sack.

"What have you in that sack?" asked the peasant.

"Rotten apples," answered the ostler; "a whole sackful of them—enough to feed the pigs with."

"Why, that's terrible waste! I should like to take them to my old woman at home. Last year the old tree by the turf-hole only bore a single apple, and we kept it in the cupboard till it was quite rotten and spoiled. 'It was always property,' my old woman said; but here she could see a quantity of property—a whole sackful. Yes, I shall be glad to show them to her."

"What will you give me for the sackful?" asked the ostler.

"What will I give? I will give my fowl in exchange."

And he gave the fowl accordingly, and received the apples, which he carried into the guest-room. He leaned the sack carefully by the stove, and then went to the table. But the stove was hot: he had not thought of that. Many guests were present—horse-dealers, ox-herds, and two Englishmen—and the two Englishmen were so rich that their pockets bulged out with gold coins, and almost burst; and they could bet too, as you shall hear.

Hiss-s-s! hiss-s-s! What was that by the stove? The apples were beginning to roast!

"What is that?"

"Why, do you know——" said our peasant.

And he told the whole story of the horse that he had changed for a cow, and all the rest of it, down to the apples.

"Well, your old woman will give it you well when you get home!" said

one of the two Englishmen. "There will be a disturbance."

"What?—give me what?" said the peasant. "She will kiss me, and say, 'What the old man does is always right.'"

"Shall we wager?" said the Englishman. "We'll wager coined gold by the ton—a hundred pounds to the hundredweight!"

"A bushel will be enough," replied the peasant. "I can only set the bushel of apples against it; and I'll throw myself and my old woman into the bargain—and I fancy that's piling up the measure."

"Done—taken!"

And the bet was made. The host's carriage came up, and the Englishmen got in, and the peasant got in; away they went, and soon they stopped before the peasant's farm.

"Good evening, old woman."

"Good evening, old man."

"I've made the exchange."

"Yes, you understand what you're about," said the woman.

And she embraced him, and paid no attention to the stranger guests, nor did she notice the sack.

"I got a cow in exchange for the horse," said he.

"Heaven be thanked!" said she. "What glorious milk we shall now have, and butter and cheese on the table! That was a most capital exchange!"

"Yes, but I changed the cow for a sheep."

"Ah, that's better still!" cried the wife. "You always think of everything: we have just pasture enough for a sheep. Ewe's-milk and cheese, and woollen jackets and stockings! The cow cannot give those, and her hairs will only come off. How you think of everything!"

"But I changed away the sheep for a goose."

"Then this year we shall really have roast goose to eat, my dear old man. You are always thinking of something to give me pleasure. How charming that is! We can let the goose walk about with a string to her leg, and she'll grow fatter still before we roast her."

"But I gave away the goose for a fowl," said the man.

"A fowl? That *was* a good exchange!" replied the woman. "The fowl will lay eggs and hatch them, and we shall have chickens: we shall have a whole poultry-yard! Oh, that's just what I was wishing for."

"Yes, but I exchanged the fowl for a sack of shrivelled apples."

"What!—I must positively kiss you for that," exclaimed the wife. "My dear, good husband! Now I'll tell you something. Do you know, you had hardly left me this morning before I began thinking how I could give you something very nice this evening. I thought it should be pancakes with savoury herbs. I had eggs, and bacon too; but I wanted herbs. So I went over to the schoolmaster's—they have herbs there, I know—but the schoolmistress is a mean woman, though she looks so sweet. I begged her to lend me a handful of herbs. 'Lend!' she answered me; 'nothing at all grows in our garden, not even a shrivelled apple. I could not even lend you a shrivelled apple, my dear woman.' But now I can lend her ten, or a whole sackful. That I'm very glad of; that makes me laugh!" And with that she gave him a sounding kiss.

"I like that!" exclaimed both the Englishmen together. "Always going downhill, and always merry; that's worth the money."

So they paid a hundredweight of gold to the peasant, who was not scolded, but kissed.

Yes, it always pays, when the wife

sees and always asserts that her husband knows best, and that whatever he does is right.

You see, that is my story. I heard it when I was a child; and now you have heard it too, and know that "What the old man does is always right."

A Novel

THE SEA OF GRASS

CONRAD RICHTER

THE SEA OF GRASS

CONRAD RICHTER

PART I

LUTIE

That lusty pioneer blood is tamed now, broken and gelded like the wild horse and the frontier settlement. And I think that I shall never see it flowing through human veins again as it did in my Uncle Jim Brewton riding a lathered horse across his shaggy range or standing in his massive ranch house, bare of furniture as a garret, and holding together his empire of grass and cattle by the fire in his eyes.

His rude empire is dead and quartered today like a steer on the meatblock, but I still lie in bed at night and see it tossing, pitching, leaping in the golden sunlight of more than fifty years ago, sweeping up to his very door, stretching a hundred and twenty miles north and south along the river, and rolling as far into the sunset as stock could roam—a ranch larger than Massachusetts with Connecticut thrown in, his fabulous herds of Texas cattle sprinkled like grains of cinnamon across the horizons, his name a legend even then, his brand familiar as the A B C's in every packing-house, and his word the law, not dead sentences in a book, but a moving finger writing on a cottonwood tree where all who rode could very plainly read.

I can see his bedroom, just a bunk in the corner, with a fancy horsehair bridle and ropes on the wall, and a brown buckskin partly cut away in strips for whang leather. And I can see his huge parlor, without rugs or furniture, piled to the pine rafters with white sacks of flour and burlapped hills of sugar and green coffee, and wooden buttes of boxed tobacco, dried fruits, and canned tomatoes, just the provisions for his hundred hands and everyone else who passed that way, rancher or cowboy, settler or prospector, Mexican, Indian, or outlaw, all welcome at his table.

But what moves across my eye unforgettably is his spring roundup when six or seven wagons working back from the Arizona line reached the headquarters range with a vast, almost mythical herd the like of which will never be seen in this country again. Farther than the eye could strain through the dust, the grass was colored with milling cattle, while bulls rode and fought, and cows and calves bawled, and countless horns clacked, and sixty or seventy of us kept saddling fresh mounts and galloping here and there in a stirring, day-long excitement.

The free wild life we lived on that shaggy prairie was to me the life of the gods. And that there should be anyone who would not love it as we

did, who should even hate it passionately and secretly, and yet the memory of whose delicate presence in that violent land still stirs me with emotion after fifty years, had not occurred to me then. But I was only a boy whose face had never known a razor, in a pair of California britches turned up to let my boots into the stirrups, that early fall day I rode with re bellious young back to Salt Fork to be shipped off to Missouri to school before my uncle would fetch back to the ranch the scarcest article in the territory, a woman, the one we had never seen, who was coming all the way from St. Louis to marry him.

At the edge of town I scowled at an encampment of settlers' tents and wagons, the largest I remembered. They seemed to be waiting for something. Then I rode up to the hotel and heard someone say that the telegraph line was open after having been cut again by Indians in the Raton. "I'm going to let it to you, Hal, to see the Colonel gets this," the red-faced station agent told me mysteriously.

He handed me a sheet of unfolded gray paper, the writing in pencil and dated at St. Louis nearly a week before. It was, I think, the first telegram I had ever seen and for a moment I had the impression that the paper itself had come in some up-to-date manner over the telegraph wire and that the execrable writing was that of this woman who had signed it Lutie and who said with love that she was not stopping off in Denver as she had planned but would arrive in Salt Fork on a morning I knew was tomorrow.

I had not seen my uncle for more than two weeks, and with the telegram unpleasant as a perfumed handkerchief in my pocket, I rode down to the shipping corrals, half expecting to see his herd of fall beef steers come

sweeping down off the sand hills into town like the Rio Grande running bankful after the summer rains, washing across the tracks, flooding the stock-pens and overflowing along the river-bank from where, until shipped, they would fill the town night and day with their bawling.

But no Cross B steers were there and neither was my uncle, and I went to the dim adobe courtroom where they were outrageously trying two of our hands for shooting at and running off a nester. I couldn't get any nearer than the door. But from there I could hear the oratorical voice of the young district attorney, lately from the East and close to the President, bitterly assailing the high-handed methods on my uncle's vast range and promising new justice for emigrants in all his district from the Rio Grande to the Arizona line.

When the trial adjourned until morning, I pushed myself between groups of soberly talking men to Henry McCurtin, my uncle's lawyer, a ponderous man, who read the telegram over his great drooping dun mustaches.

"I haven't seen the Colonel since the trial opened," he rumbled. "I reckon, son, you better meet this woman tomorrow yourself."

For a long time I lay awake that night in the cavernous Bridal Chamber of the Exchange House, the corner room always reserved for my uncle when he came to town, feeling my hate for this woman who was banishing me to Missouri, and thinking that I had never known the town quite so swarming with men, the livery stable and wagon yards so choked with horses, or the night so deafening with the clatter of pianos and scream of fiddles pouring from open dance-hall windows; with the steady undertone of clinking glasses

from half a score of saloons; and men and sporting women talking, laughing, and yelling boisterous songs that paused only for the sudden rap of the six-shooter.

But through it all I could hear, like the wild, unceasing heartbeat of this frontier town, the sound of marching boots on the wooden sidewalk, pounding the planks from bar to bar. And I knew that not all these men, drawn from a hundred and two hundred remote miles, had come to ship beef. It was the trial, this new young district attorney from the East, challenging the power of my uncle and other big cattlemen, that had drawn them. And sitting up in that enormous bed I could see through the long window the distant white tents and sheeted wagons of the emigrants' camp glinting like the wet and treacherous quicksands of the Puerco.

When I awoke in the morning, I found to my regret that I had slept through another shooting. On the way to the depot I saw the dead man's oxen still hitched to his wagon, ten or twelve of them lying down patiently in the yoke, chewing their cud, while the stranger who had done it swung a slow pendulum on the railroad's wooden water-tower, his boots already pulled off by some low wretch and the water dripping over him, his head to one side and one leg curiously longer than the other as if he were trying to reach the ground.

He was cut down by the sheriff under the indignant direction of the new district attorney and laid temporarily under a wagon sheet in the freight house. But as soon as the officers had disappeared into the courthouse, some of the dead teamster's friends dragged him out again just as I faintly heard a bell ringing and hand-brakes screeching from every open platform. I stayed to watch them take a rope from somebody's saddle and pull him up again. And when I turned, the train from St. Louis was long in, with its short coaches coated with the dust of the Great Plains.

Up until now I expected that at the last moment my uncle would surely appear. But he wasn't there, and I cast about harshly in my mind what I should say to this woman and how I might recognize her. In the territory my uncle attended strictly to business, riding the range as hard as any of his hands. But in Kansas City, where he went regularly to sell his cattle, people said that he swung a wide loop and once when a prominent commission man he much disliked had solicited him too far for his business, even inviting him to a very elite party, my uncle had forever silenced him by coming in great style with a notorious and lavishly dressed sporting woman on his arm.

And now I looked for a woman bold and painted like Ready Money Kate from St. Louis, whom I had often seen sailing up and down the wooden sidewalks of Salt Fork in vivid silks with parasol to match and, when she crossed the dusty street, with plenty of red and white striped stocking showing.

All I saw was a lady standing by the car steps and behind her a respectful, bearded brakeman holding a pair of valises. Her face was hidden behind a heavy brown veil, but there was something unforgettable in the slender way she stood there, in a suit of unmistakable quality and tailoring, gloves and a plumed hat, a fragile feminine figure, alone and unmet, stared at by blanketed Indians, Mongol-like Mexicans, and shaggy white men with cartridge belts and with spur rowels coarse as cart-wheels, and over their heads on the water-tank the dead man still swinging.

A loafer in a buckskin shirt with all the beading long since lost said something and pointed to me, and I saw her move toward me. She did not speak until she was so close I could smell the fragrance of violets about her and could see the liquid of her eyes through the veil. Then she lifted it from her face, and although I was only a boy, I felt that quickening emotion she was always to arouse in me until the last time I should see her.

"So this is Hal?" she said softly, and kissed me, and I stood there young and rigid with my face burning in front of everyone. But if she saw it, she gave no sign. With the dead man slowly turning in front of her, she went on chatting to me in slightly incoherent but charming fashion, saying the gayest of things, that required little or none of my tongue-tied answers, all the while her delicate forehead shutting out the water-tank and that ring of staring loafers as completely as if she stood alone with me in my uncle's ranch house. And I realized that here was a finer-fibered creature than any my long black hair and rope-calloused hands had known.

When I stammered that her telegram had come only last evening and that I hadn't been able to deliver it to my uncle as yet, she took my arm with alive intimacy.

"We'll find him together, Hal," she said confidently.

"He'll come to the hotel, if you'll wait there," I told her.

"The bags can go to the hotel, but not I, Hal," she answered. "I've been shut up in a train for days and days. I want to walk. Miles and miles, until we find him."

Very stiffly and thinking these St. Louis ladies a little mad, I guided her through the deep dust strewn with horns and bones and the forelegs of sheep, between wagon hubs and saddle-pony heels, until we were up on the wooden sidewalk, where I took care to steer her away from the direction of the courthouse. But I couldn't avoid the wagon of the dead freighter, with boys climbing a wheel to stare at what we both could plainly see, a long figure lying on his back, with his red beard still sticking up defiantly from under the blue bandanna across his face. But Lutie Cameron's chatting never stopped. Only her soft live arm tightened in mine like a doeskin band.

I had the pride common in the territory that going about on foot was the mark of a hoeman and close to disgrace. And I was glad when the boardwalk came to an end. But Lutie Cameron had pinned her veil back now; her delicate face was thrown up and there was no stopping her. On and on we went past a few scattered Mexican houses and up the sloping sand hills, where she exclaimed over the common yerba de vibora still in blossom and pinned a yellow spray of it gayly across her coat.

But when we reached the top of the escarpment and, suddenly like coming on the ocean unaware, there in front of us stretched the vast, brown, empty plain, dipping and pitching endlessly like a parched sea, she stopped as if she had run into barbed wire. I tried to point out a remote, nearly indistinguishable cloud shadow that marked the general location of the distant ranch house, but she didn't seem to hear me, chatting almost breathlessly about a traveling acquaintance on the Pullman palace car on her way to join her husband at Fort Ewing, all the while striking out for the white village of tents and covered wagons of the emigrants' camp near by, where life was busily going on.

She waved brightly to a score or

more of children tumbling, rolling, and shouting over the ground, and bowed charmingly to tired-looking women in sunbonnets who had been sewing and knitting on a circle of wagon seats and rockers set on the grass and who stood up now to receive her as some great lady who had deigned to visit their humble abode.

When they told her they had come all the way from her own Missouri and hoped to settle far out on this very plain, something came into her eyes that I hadn't seen there before. She sparkled to grandmothers in knitted caps and wrinkled as Indians, swung a gurgling baby high in the air, and ran and shouted with the children who had clustered around her. And she climbed up into one of the wagons fitted up as a cabin with stovepipe pushing out of the canvas, where, as I stood stiff and disapproving, I could hear her complimenting the delighted owners on what she found.

"If you see Colonel Brewton," she said gayly before she left, "tell him we've been looking for him everywhere."

I was conscious of a shadow instantly falling over the camp. Even the children seemed to freeze at the sound of my uncle's name.

"I reckon you'll find him at court today, ma'am," a gaunt Missourian answered after a moment.

Lutie Cameron said nothing until we were a quarter-mile away.

"Why did they look at us so queerly, Hal? And why didn't you tell me we might find him at court?"

"We couldn't get in anyhow," I answered sullenly.

And when we reached the square, I could see at the courthouse a little crowd of men packed half-way across the boardwalk to the hitching-rack. I would have gone on to the Exchange House, but she stopped and lifted her head in that gesture I already knew so well, a slight feminine figure against the rude backs of a score of men.

"May we pass, please?" She spoke clearly, and to my surprise that gentle lady's voice of hers turned rough men about and tumbled off their hats as if a bullet had whipped them. A narrow but unmistakable aisle opened in front of us, and presently I found myself inside, with Blackjack Kerns, a rustler and outlaw, rising like a jack-in-the-box to give the lady his seat, and others on the bench moving over to make a few inches of room for me.

2

The Salt Fork County court was stuffed and smelly as a stock corral at shipping time, a dingy adobe room with earthen floor and small Mexican windows darkened by men sitting on the deep ledges so that it seemed as if we had entered a kind of rude twilight.

"Is he here, Hal?" Lutie Cameron whispered to me through her veil.

But even before my eyes grew accustomed to the dimness, I knew by the atmosphere that my uncle wasn't there.

"The jury's comin' in," a cowhand from the Three V's muttered behind me.

I saw now that the jury box of worn and whittled pine benches was empty. Then I heard a stir at the doorway behind us and presently I thought I could feel a wave of restrained excitement rising in the rear of the room and passing from bench to bench until beyond the railing I saw our two accused cowhands twist in their seats and Henry McCurtin turn like a mountain suddenly come to life.

I felt my arm brushed by Lutie Cameron's gloved fingers. "What is it, Hal?" she whispered.

Then I saw by her veiled eyes that she glimpsed something and, turning my head, I saw it, too, moving erect and towering down the crowded aisle along the wall, a familiar, proud, almost insolent figure in a long gray broadcloth coat with tails and bulging on the side toward us with what I knew was a holster capped with ivory handles, his coal-black eyebrows and mustache white with alkali dust, and in the abrupt quiet of the room the fall of his boot-heels like the shots of a pistol.

Since that day I have been in many a courtroom, but never any so quickly transformed from a dingy room to one kindled and illuminated by the lightning-flash of one man's vitality and power, so that today I can still see it as in the strongest sunshine, the dusty colors of the American flag on the whitewashed wall over the judge's pine bench, and beneath his parted black robe the gold links of his watch-chain, heavy enough for carriage traces, on the court rail a pair of buckled spurs swinging, and that fearless, moving figure of my uncle like some rude territorial czar.

Then I saw that those pitchfork eyes which missed nothing had found us. Deliberately, with scarcely a change in him, he was crossing to our aisle, the men on the bench he chose to pass by scattering for the moment like sheep in front of him. And presently he stood there beside us with bared head and a kind of mellowed dignity, pressing Lutie Cameron's hand, asking her health and welfare in quiet solicitude, his great lusty face gently warmed like the sunlight on a weathered cliff.

Saying he would join us later, he straightened, his black glance swept

those close by who had been listening, and he moved majestically on, passing inside the privileged railing where Henry McCurtin stood up in massive welcome and the two accused cowhands grinned and the sheriff hastily brought him the bailiff's chair, while the district clerk with a pen riding one ear stared respectfully and Judge White, peering as always with a glum and imperturbable face over his pine bench, broke into a friendly smile and his head bobbed in ceremonious greeting.

Only one man inside of the railing showed him no deference, and I watched Brice Chamberlain, the young district attorney appointed by the President, standing there tall and impressive, his plain sack coat buttoned close to his white collar, his brows frowning formidably, and his thick blond hair sweeping back in a kind of masterful and handsome disapproval.

"What's the case about, Hal?" Lutie Cameron whispered. "And who is the scowling gentleman?"

I didn't answer. The faded blue door beyond the railing had opened and men were starting to drift through, in single file, slouching Americans in sagging unbuttoned vests and slightly pompous Mexicans in leather chalecos, one after the other pulling off his hat as he entered, boots shuffling on the adobe floor.

Behind me a voice whispered loudly that for any other man except Jim Brewton the jury would have stayed out with their verdict until they had had their dinner on the county. Then I heard leathery Eli Jones, the jury foreman, answering Judge White's questions.

"We find," he drawled, "that Andy Boggs was shot at and run off the place he wanted to file on, by unknown parties."

I saw the strict face of the judge redden as if over some impropriety. "That's no verdict!" he reminded sharply. "The two defendants—"

"Oh, hell, they're not guilty," Eli waved.

I wanted to give the Apache warwhoop while behind me a row of cowhands stamped their boots and jingled their spurs until Judge White pounded his pine bench in anger. Then he demanded the formal written verdict of the grinning jury foreman and adjourned court.

"Is that the verdict you wanted, Hal?" Lutie Cameron asked eagerly, but I saw that her eyes were not on me or our freed cowhands; rather on the tall young district attorney, who had winced as if thrown by a horse.

Another moment and she had urged me up from our bench. With her arm in mine, she swept up the aisle, chatting with animation at every step, and through the railing, where she stopped beside my uncle, slipping her free arm delicately through his, just as I saw Brice Chamberlain get himself in hand and stiffly congratulate Henry McCurtin.

Then the defeated young district attorney turned to my uncle.

"May I ask you a few questions that I had no opportunity for during the trial, Colonel Brewton?"

His manner was courteous, but there was a faintly challenging ring in his voice and a blue fire in his eyes that kindled the silent attention of those of us standing inside of the railing. He went on without waiting for assent:

"Is it true, Colonel Brewton, that your range runs a hundred miles or more north and south, and west nearly to the Arizona line?"

My uncle merely inclined his head.

"Is it true," Chamberlain went on, his voice suddenly rising, "that of this vast country you control, you actually own only a few scattered waterholes that have been filed on either in your name or those of your men? And that by far the greater part still belongs to the government?"

"Legally, yes," my uncle conceded.

"Is it true, then," Chamberlain concluded, his voice gathering force and indignation, "that this million or more of acres still belonging to the government is the same land that Andrew Boggs, who only wanted a mere hundred and sixty acres for a homestead, was run off from and severely wounded by unknown parties?"

"No," my uncle said quietly but with great firmness and power. "He was not run off because he wanted to settle those hundred and sixty acres but because of what he wanted to do with the land."

So intent had I been on the sparks beginning to fly between the flint and steel of these two men that I had almost forgotten where we were. Now I heard a strong murmur of approval and, looking around, I saw a press of cowhands and cattlemen against the railing.

Brice Chamberlain did not glance around. But something seemed to pass behind his brightly burning blue eyes. His manner changed. An appeal came into his face and voice, and standing there bent persuasively toward my uncle, even I for a moment thought him modest and almost likable.

"Let's forget about this case, Colonel Brewton. Andrew Boggs was only a single man and the court has disposed of him. Waiting at the edge of Salt Fork to see how this trial comes out are other settlers. Not single men, but with families, from babes at the breast to grandmothers. They have given up their homes in the East, driven their wagons more than a thousand miles across the plains, and left their dead

from the Mississippi to the Rio Grande —all with the one purpose of finding homes for themselves in this great territory." His voice grew eloquent with pleading. "Now that you have won your case, Colonel Brewton, and can afford to show your sympathy and charity, I want to ask in the names of these families if you won't let them settle undisturbed on a few acres out of the million or more of government land on your range?"

I saw Lutie Cameron's eyes, soft under her veil, glance expectantly at my uncle. But he didn't see her. He had thrown up his head like an unruly lead steer smelling wolves or water.

"Chamberlain," he said, "I have sympathy for the pioneer settler who came out here and risked his life and family among the Indians. And I hope I have a little charity for the nester who waited until the country was safe and peaceable before he filed a homestead on someone else's range who fought for it. But—" and his voice began to ring in the small hushed courtroom, "when that nester picks country like my big vega, that's more than seven thousand feet above the sea, when he wants to plow it up to support his family where there isn't enough rain for crops to grow, where he only kills the grass that will grow, where he starves for water and feeds his family by killing my beef and becomes a man without respect to himself and a miserable menace to the territory, then I have neither sympathy nor charity!"

His eyes now were pitch-black, proud, insolent, his great face written with power and almost dissolute ruthlessness. "And I want to say," he finished, "that if I know the temper of the citizens who ran off that worthless nester, Boggs, they'll keep running off every granger who tries to destroy their range!"

For nearly a minute more the two men faced each other, one older, rugged, utterly fearless; the other young and white with emotion.

"They warned me," Brice Chamberlain said in a low burning voice, "not to bring action against you or your men. They told me there was no justice here, that you dominated the country and would never share your land with your less fortunate fellow men."

He turned on his heel and left, but all of us knew this was not the end. I looked at Lutie Cameron. She still hung on my uncle's arm, delicate, silent, rigid, her eyes on the stunned little group of listening Missourians in the patched blue and striped jumpers of farmers huddled there in the courtroom. And when she and my uncle went out to the hotel for dinner, I saw her take the spray of bright yellow blossoms she had pinned so gayly across her coat and throw it away.

With my hat hot and uncomfortable in my hand, I waited as long as I dared that afternoon outside the ladies' parlor of the Exchange House. When I pushed in the door, I saw my uncle standing with dignity in front of the tall window. Beside him stood Lutie Cameron, her head thrown firmly up, her brown veil raised, her plumes at a high and gallant angle, making an unforgettable picture in that dark, cavernous room with a single shaft of sunshine pouring over her, while Judge White in a long black coat with broad silken lapels kept sternly clearing his throat and compressing his lips as he read the unfamiliar marriage service.

Her cheeks were dusted as if with flour when she turned, but nothing else betrayed her as Dr. Reid, who, I think, must have denied himself liquor all afternoon for the occasion, bowed like the Virginian he was, over

her hand, and wished her happiness. And Henry McCurtin, in fresh linen unsullied by a single tobacco stain, asked her jovially through his dun mustaches how she had managed to rope such a shy war-horse.

She and my uncle took me to the depot, and the last thing I saw of Lutie Brewton, she was standing with one arm outstretched waving her handkerchief gayly after me, a gesture I coldly declined to answer. But late that night when the train was puffing through the dark New Mexican hills, I kept thinking about her in that walled island of ranch house on my lost sea of grass.

3

I have hated places in my life, but never any like that academy in Lexington where the woman who had waved me good-by so gayly had imprisoned me, with its brick walls and stone banisters still patched where grape-shot and Minié balls had torn through, with a winter of cold such as I had never known in the territory, with the sun not coming out for weeks at a time and a road of dirt and ashes across the mile-wide Missouri frozen into curious yellow ice.

And when spring came and the eaves dripped a steady tattoo and strange birds cheeped in the wet trees around the school, the ice went out of the Missouri with a roar. And I went, too, between two suns, as my uncle used to say of any man who disappeared. And late that afternoon I was in Kansas City, trying to keep my chin up and my back stiff and not to betray how bewildered I was in this cold young city with wagons and carriages clattering in every direction on the stone paving and no one paying

me more attention than if I were a burro dozing in the dusty streets of Old Town in Salt Fork. The thought of those quiet, dusty streets sleeping in the yellow sun made me more homesick for the territory than I have ever been in my life except for a half-hour later when I reached the stock-yards and smelled cattle again and saw the familiar colors of longhorns and listened to Nicholas Masters of the Masters Packing Company, the heavy flesh of his face quivering like a kind of purple jelly as he coughed and shook a fat finger at me and sputtered that if he helped me run home, my uncle would never sell him another trainload of steers.

But when I told him it had been the woman my uncle had married and whom I hated that had clapped me into this prison of a school, he stared at me thoughtfully as a companion in distress. And when I left, I had a pass and some money and had given a sacred promise never to let this woman know who it was had befriended me.

All the way out to the ranch on a Salt Fork horse from Dagget's livery stable, with the range already greening up in the sloughs, with Canada geese rising from the ponds and cutting the sky like joined Apache lances, with calves kicking and bucking in the spring sunshine and horses rubbing off winter hair, I felt the bitterness grow in me for the woman who would have kept me from all this. And I planned coldly how I would treat her and what curtness of speech she should hear from me.

Riding up Nester Draw so she should not see me coming, I cut across the rise and up to the rear of the ranch house, where a strange Chinaman cook eyed me suspiciously from the kitchen as I entered by the back door. I scowled to see that there were

strange pine settees covered with Navajo blankets in the wide hall. And glancing into the open door of the huge storeroom, I saw with dull anger that the familiar mountains of flour and coffee had vanished and the buttes of dried fruits gone, so that I hardly knew the room with a Brussels carpet on the floor and heavy dark red hangings at the windows and tufted horsehair chairs and sofa around the walls and a square piano with legs curved and lid polished as elegantly and offensively as the piano at school.

It all had an inexpressibly depressing effect on me, as if the old ranch house I had known and loved was gone. And I stood there lonely, bitter, and stiffening as a slender form appeared from the big front bedroom in the dim hall. Oh, she looked a bit thinner and paler, but her dark hair even here on these remote plains was done up in the latest St. Louis fashion; a spray of pink loco weed had been pinned freshly across her basque and she still moved with undiminished sparkle and aliveness.

Then she recognized me.

"Hal!" she almost screamed.

Her intense young arms hugged me as if she had seen no one for weeks. And with her delicate fragrance of violets about me like some sweet drug, I felt the hate go out of me as the ice had gone out of the Missouri at Lexington only a week or two before.

Another moment and she was holding me at arm's length, delightedly looking me over from head to foot, squeezing my hand and laughingly exclaiming what a manly boy I was on the way to becoming, and chattering that she had not had a visitor since day before yesterday and what a wonderful winter she had spent here on the ranch in this Western climate with blue sky and almost eternal sun-

and that my uncle was looking
distinguished than ever, and had
een the trees she had coaxed the
ands to plant for summer shade; de-
grading work, my uncle had called
it, that men who rode a horse would
never do.

But with nearly every word I ob-
served in her dark eyes the feverish
brilliance of the first day I had seen
her. And the following year when I
came home a little older and taller,
it still haunted her eyes although the
parlor hummed with company. And
I soon found out that scarcely a day
was intended to pass without midday
dinner guests or overnight guests or
guests to stay the week. And most
of them crocheted or embroidered,
laughed or sang, played charades or
whist, and were agreeable to almost
anything except to ride out and visit
the roundup, which Lutie Brewton
kept finding charming excuses to miss.

There were, I remember, the sport-
ing English owners of the Bar 44
and the dancing officers from Fort
Ewing, the lively Falconers and im-
portant Netherwoods, whose name
Lutie Brewton loved to trill over her
tongue, the guests from Santa Fe and
Albuquerque, and Judge White and
Brice Chamberlain on their respective
rounds of the district court.

But if I expected my uncle to re-
sent any of their coming, I was mis-
taken. He rode his range no less hard
than before, and it must have seemed
to him as it did to me a kind of miracle
to step from dark night into a lighted
house, from a hard saddle to a cush-
ioned chair, to come from the cold,
shaggy plain into warm curtained
rooms with Lutie Brewton bare-armed
in a silken gown and white candles
burning around her as in a cathedral,
with silver sparkling and stainless
cloth shining and a mellow atmos-

phere of company talking and laugh-
ing around his table.

My uncle would bow with proud
courtesy to everyone. But I heard him
talk very little, preferring to sit there
with a faint desert glow warming his
weathered face, his insolent eyes sof-
tening a little as he watched or lis-
tened to his wife. No matter who
came or how large the dinner, Lutie
Brewton was the tireless pure flame
burning in the center of it, her face
flatteringly raised to listen, her talk a
highly seasoned language of its own,
her headlong treble laughter leading
into general bursts of merriment, and
her ringed fingers skimming over the
white keys of the piano, with the soft
light from the tall marble, brass, and
china lamp golden on her dark hair.

She never stopped, not even for a
moment. And when I watched her so
alive on the black horsehair sofa, mak-
ing ecstatic gestures with her white
hands to the gentleman on either side
of her, I had the curious feeling that
she never slept, but, stimulated by
congenial friends, could go on bub-
bling night and day.

Certainly she never stopped when
she went to town with her fast team
of bays to spend the night at the
Netherwoods' or the Holdernesses',
who were kin of Brice Chamberlain.
Once or twice I drove her, and the
moment we passed out through the
dense wall of cottonwoods and tama-
risks, she chatted incessantly, her sen-
sitive face turned away from the wide
sea of grass as if it were the plague, so
that I swore she never saw the road
runner racing with the carriage wheel
or the antelope moving among the
cattle. And I thought that at last I
had begun to understand the reason
for her wall of cottonwoods and tama-
risks, which had not been planted for
summer shade at all.

"She'll settle down once she has ba-

bies," I heard Mrs. Netherwood say fondly to Judge White the day of the Holman wedding, when she wore diamond dust in her hair.

4

The babies came soon afterwards. One after the other I found them in the big front bedroom of the ranch house when I came home from school; the first, a fat gurgling girl with dark eyes and scarcely any hair to start with; the second, an unsmiling boy with the blackest of hair and eyes; and the third, a boy whose eyes were an unexpected bright blue, with hair so white and soft it turned and ruffled like a feather in my breath.

Yet neither I nor anyone else could see a change in Lutie Brewton. With her first baby in the cradle, I felt that out of respect I should call her Aunt Lutie, but she turned on me quickly.

"Don't you dare call me that, Hal!" she said and her eyes were black and flashing. "I shall never be old enough to be Auntie to anyone."

Black Hetty, who took care of the babies, showed the broad white of her teeth. But after the second child Lutie Brewton was still the same slender figure, alive, intense, her delicate white skin without a wrinkle. And with the third baby scarcely in his cradle, she danced eight out of ten square dances and waltzes with Brice Chamberlain as her partner in the huge English hall of the Bar 44.

He was at my uncle's ranch house now all too often to suit me, driving out as a rule with his dashing cousin, the young blond Mrs. Holderness, whether my uncle was home or not. The administration at Washington had long since changed and with it his and Judge White's appointments.

And Brice Chamberlain had opened a law office on the dusty Salt Fork plaza next door to Gidding's dance hall, where he specialized in the settling of titles to the huge land grants for profit and filing of homestead entries as a passion.

My uncle paid him little attention, while he treated my uncle with unfailing politeness. But more than once when the latter wasn't looking, I caught Brice Chamberlain's blue eyes measuring him and seeming to say: "You're of the past generation now. Your time is soon over. We will run the world from now on, not you." And to Lutie he openly and eloquently boasted: "Civilization is moving west fast. It will be here soon. And when it comes, the fertile plains around this ranch house will be dotted with farms and schoolhouses."

I paid him no more attention than my uncle. But once when I coldly carried him an invitation to dinner, I saw his desk piled high with semi-transparent blueprint maps of township and correction lines and with stacks of letters from scores of land-hungry Easterners he had circularized, a sight that gave me an angry, disturbed feeling.

I was in college at St. Louis when the Washington administration changed again. Almost as I was leaving for home I read with satisfaction in the Salt Fork paper, printed in both English and Spanish, that Brice Chamberlain was closing up his office, turning all his legal matters over to Lawyer Archie Meade and going to establish residence in Denver, where he had been promised the appointment of United States district attorney. And two weeks later when I found him still in Salt Fork, I scowled at his figure crossing the dusty plaza with that impressive long-legged stride, immaculately dressed as

always with high-buttoned Eastern suit under an imposing silver-gray Western hat.

I turned to see Henry McCurtin, a little heavier and slower, his drooping dun mustaches a little grayer, standing there ponderously watching him from his inscrutable, deeply buried eyes.

"You glad as I am he's going?" I asked when we had shaken hands.

"I'm not so sure, Hal, not so sure. The town is full of rumors," he rumbled. Then, as if he had said too much, he turned massively away.

For the first time I became sensitive to things unsaid, that the waves of sand hills rolling toward the town held a stormy and faintly ominous look. And when I glanced back, I saw that the landlocked harbor of the square was taut and white with the crowded canvas of settlers' wagons from a dozen Eastern ports. And now I remembered all the small emigrant trains I had glimpsed from my train window across Kansas and through the Raton wherever the wagon trail lay in sight of the tracks.

And when I reached the ranch next day, I thought that I had never seen Lutie Brewton more brilliantly alive and restless, her cheeks flushed, her eyes feverish, almost dazzling. All afternoon her tongue poured out a stream of gay excitement, one minute warm and frank and intimate as a sister, the next coaxing and teasing, while my small cousins burrowed under my chair and climbed on my shoulders and wore my new silver watch and chain.

As a rule Lutie Brewton treated her children like some gracious lady who had consented to be their godmother. But tonight to my mild surprise she told Black Hetty she would put them to bed herself. And with me standing in the doorway silent at the picture

they made, she poked grave, tender fun at little Jimmy's skinny freckled legs and arms, and called Sarah Beth's panty waist a corset, which embarrassed her, and frowned with mock seriousness at the transparent white skin of Brock, whom, she declared, God had intended to be a girl. And all the while her facile white hands helped them to slip off their garments and into their long muslin nightgowns which covered their toes as they knelt on the brown sheepskin.

But when we were back again in the parlor, I saw her shudder, and I stared at her until she turned on me like a white tigress.

"Why must you look at me like that, Hal? Am I older? Am I sallow? What do you see? Have I pouches under my eyes?"

I lied to her that I had seen nothing, telling her the truth that she looked scarcely older than the day I had met her at the South Fork depot, and in a moment she had changed back to the sparkling person I knew. But during the night I thought I heard someone moving about the great front bedroom, and when I awoke as the sun heaved up red above the plain, the one who hadn't slept was still walking.

Except for a few minutes at breakfast and noonday dinner, I did not see her all day. I had planned to ride out to the roundup as was my custom, but something in her eyes withheld me. All afternoon I could hear her moving about mysteriously in her room. About six o'clock I was lying on my back on the slippery horsehair sofa, staring up at the heavy pine ceiling, when I heard the swish of skirts through the hall. And when I turned my head, she was standing there.

"You are almost a man now, Hal," she told me. "You've been to St. Louis

and Kansas City, and you know the way of the world. And I think you'll understand when I tell you I'm going away."

Looking up from where I lay, the light in her eyes seemed almost blinding. She went on a little breathlessly: "Run away, perhaps, is what you'd call it, Hal. What people will call it. I'm running off. Leaving your uncle for always. I'm going tomorrow morning, and I shan't be back."

I sat up stupefied. I had heard of occasional women deserting their husbands, but for Lutie Brewton to leave my uncle and her position in this luxurious ranch house seemed unthinkable. I remembered he was still out at the roundup, which on our range lasted from spring to summer, and she must have read my thoughts in my eyes.

"Oh, I'm not running off behind his back, Hal," she said to me. "I told him nearly a month ago. When the first emigrant wagons came to Salt Fork. I told him I couldn't stand it another year. Not running them off again and perhaps killing them as they did that poor nester from Louisiana who shot at them last year. He was white trash, but he had a wife and six or seven children. Now, as far as I am concerned, it's all settled— all but the tearing out of a few roots and tendrils."

"But Jimmy and Brock and Sarah Beth?" I stammered.

The first white hardness came into her face.

"I went over it and over it with him, Hal! A thousand times, I think. You know your uncle. He thought he could hold me by holding the children. But nothing can stop me. My lawyer says I can't take them along. But I can fight for them after I'm away. Once we're settled. No jury, Hal, not even Mexicans, can keep

three children from their mother."

Something between the lines of what she said troubled me.

"You're going away with somebody?" I heard myself saying coldly.

Unexpected warm color crept up into her faintly wilted cheeks, freshening them like petals, and almost at once she was like a flower rooted again in rich wet earth with that unaccountable power we call life flowing through her.

"If I never knew it before, Hal, I'd know now you had the same blood as your uncle. You ask the same questions. But I shan't tell you any more than I shall him. He's coming now. Don't go, Hal!" she begged quickly as I stiffened and rose. Her slender fingers gripped my arm. "You'll break the ice between us. And don't look so frightened for me, you poor boy!" Something shining and irrevocable came into her face. "I'm not dying and being stuffed into a coffin. I'm going where there's life, Hal. I'm going to balls and theaters and shaded streets and up-to-date stores and where every day people drive in the parks!"

I could hear hoofbeats now. Turning, I saw through the deep windows my uncle riding toward the ranch house, sitting erect as always in his saddle, his right arm held stiffly down against his side with his thumb at the cantle edge as was his custom, unchanged from army days. Presently there was the sound of his boots and spurs through the hall, and he was in the room. But, contrary to what I feared, I had never seen him more quiet.

Lutie Brewton held up her face to be kissed as always and chatted brightly to him of some of the incidents I had told her of college, while my uncle shook my hand and inquired if I had seen Nicholas Masters as he had written me. There was a

curious absence of time and hurry, as if utterly nothing had happened or was expected to happen. Only when I glanced closely to see if Lutie had really told me the truth did I feel the fine filaments of strain in the air like those unseen currents that are said to lift the hair of a wolf before an August thunderclap.

"Supper's on the table, Miz Brewton," stoically called Jeff Calder, the old chuck-wagon cook who had long since followed the Chinaman in the ranch-house kitchen.

I would have given a great deal that night to have avoided the dining-room and the massive silver. My uncle ate gravely while Lutie Brewton single-handed with almost desperate gayety kept conversation alive. But every moment I saw that she curbed her eyes from the windows.

The children had had their supper early tonight as was their custom, and now, with Black Hetty standing by, they were all astride the bare back of Old Cherry, scarcely taller than a pony. Jimmy sat in front; Sarah Beth, who was six or seven, behind him; and Brock to the rear, each holding to a share of the bridle reins. A strip of gunnysack as a blinder had been tied over the gentle old barefoot mare's eyes, and she stood motionless until Jimmy yelled and pulled it off, when she came to life and bobbed up and down until one happily shrieking youngster after the other was deposited on the grass.

I could not look at them myself tonight, and under my breath I muttered that as soon as it was dark I should saddle one of the night horses and ride to the camp at Cottonwood Springs, where I would stay till it was over. Then just before Lutie Brewton rose, she gave me one of her indecipherable glances.

"If I don't see you any more to-night, Hal," she asked, "could you drive me to Salt Fork in the morning?"

My uncle had been sitting quietly on his chair, waiting for her signal to rise, the deferent courtesy he always had for her mellowing his face. Now his head was flung up in the gesture of a challenged wild stallion while his dark eyes flamed with sudden will and power.

"Hal will take your trunk in the buckboard," he told her proudly. "I'll drive you to the train myself."

"Thank you, Colonel Brewton," she said.

But I saw in an instant as she rose that an unusual pallor had swept her face. And when a few moments later I passed the length of the hall to the gallery, I saw her standing rigid in the huge front bedroom with her back toward a pair of ivory handles holstered in a heavy belt darkened by years of sweat and hanging on a high, brass harness hook out of reach of the children.

5

For a long time I lay awake that night in the bunk that had once been my uncle's, listening at intervals to the faint bawling of a calf for its mother in some dim, starlit cañada. And when I fell asleep I dreamed that something vaguely beautiful had gone out of this massive ranch house like the kernel of life out of a prairie seed, and all that remained was the brown shell of adobe walls staring from its empty sockets. And everywhere about the house in my dream, the sand was endlessly blowing, burying the print of the coyote and lizard, rattling in the vibora weed, drifting close to the ground like barren snow so that the whole earth seemed to be

moving, a restless gray ghost of itself trying to find those full, lusty prairie breasts, fertile as a woman and flowing with milk and wild honey, that used to be.

At the first sound of morning I was up pulling on my clothes in the darkness and drinking coffee in the kitchen to escape the breakfast-table, and lending a hand in the starlight to the hitching of the teams. And when I came back to the long dark hall, I glimpsed in a candle-lighted room, framed like a picture by the heavy doorway, Lutie Brewton, suited, hatted, and one hand gloved, sitting with three sleepy youngsters in their nightgowns about her. And I heard her promising in that clear, delightful, fun-loving voice she always used to children, that she would see them all sooner than soon and would have a double present for each one that Black Hetty should say had been a little lady or gentleman.

Old Jeff helped me carry out her trunk to the sagging buckboard. And soon Lutie Brewton came, a slender, almost jaunty figure in the dim, blue-black light, answering the children's good-by before my uncle helped her up into the top buggy. Before the horses started, she answered again. And from somewhere down beyond the spring I heard her voice a last time, high and clear above the thud of hoofs and rattle of spokes, like some incredibly sweet and lingering bell.

Old Jeff had waited by one of the buckboard wheels, never saying a word, but I could hear him draw hard and furiously on his pipe until the sounds of the buggy grew faint on the night air. Still saying nothing, he moved grimly into the house while I climbed into the rig and my horses without urging followed those that had gone before.

To the newcomer in our Southwestern land it seems that the days are very much alike, the same blue sky and unchanging sunshine and endless heat waves rising from the plain. But after he is here a year he learns to distinguish nuances in the weather he would never have noticed under a more violent sky; that one day may be clear enough, and yet some time during the night, without benefit of rain or cloud, a mysterious desert influence sweeps the heavens. And the following morning there is air clearer by half than yesterday, as if freshly rinsed by storm and rain.

It was such a morning that I hauled Lutie Brewton's trunk through the crystal air to Salt Fork, with horses and buckboard moving at first under the swinging lamp of the morning planet, and then through a green, velvet twilight that was half-way between stars and sun, and finally in the early purple light that poured over the plain like wine, until it seemed that with every breath I could taste it, and even the stolid cattle feeding beside the trail seemed to lift their heads to stare at it. And when the sun shook the earth finally clear, I saw a wave of antelope flowing inquisitively toward the buggy far ahead, a wave rusty as with kelp, rising and falling over the grassy swells and eventually turning in alarm, so that a thousand white rumps, whirled suddenly into view, were the breaking of that wide prairie wave on some unseen reef of this tossing upland sea.

Most of the way across the vegas I could have reached out my hand and touched the fragrant rows of bee balm starting to bloom on either side of the trail. But all I could smell was the perfume of violets rising from Lutie Brewton's trunk. And all I could see now was a faint, distant column of black smoke hanging in the sky,

little more than a smudge in that illimitable air, yet already it threw a shadow over buckboard and trail.

The sun was a branding iron on the back of my neck when we came at last to the edge of the sand hills and I saw the cottonwoods standing already cool in shadow in the river valley below. My spent horses plowed the floury dust of the long street. And the red-faced station agent himself came bustling out to oversee the careful lifting of Lutie Brewton's trunk to the steel-protected baggage truck slatted like a buckboard and trundled like a barrow.

Not until then did I look up and see with relief that everything about the station was normal and everyday, the groups of passengers through the open door of the waiting-room, the loafers playing mumbletypeg on the plank platform, and out near the tracks a circle of friends surrounding Lutie Brewton, laughing and chattering as always, wishing her a pleasant visit to St. Louis and promising gay times when she returned. I could smell the calm unhurried redolence of ties lately simmering in the sun, could hear down in their whitewashed shipping pens the monotonous baas of a flock of lambs. And nearer, the white dust floated from a car of flour being unloaded in sacks to a dusty wagon.

Then I glimpsed Lawyers Henry McCurtin and Archie Meade talking together in low, grave tones beyond the baggage barrow, and was slowly conscious that all was not quite what it seemed. And when I glanced around again, I was aware that the loafers kept peering up stealthily from under their brows, and a group of passengers whispered from the waiting-room doorway.

And now I was sure that all those happy friends were frantically playing a part and that they really had no more belief that Lutie Brewton was going to St. Louis than I had. And when I stumbled by as if I noticed nothing, I saw that for all her gay animation, her high lace collar was a pale branch whipsawing in the pounding stream of blood at her throat and that the veins on one of my uncle's hands stood out like long-suppressed whipcords of blue lightning.

I couldn't have gone now if I had wished. I could see the grim bulge in my uncle's coat of gray broadcloth and an untamed violence, like a prairie fire rimmed with black smoke, flaring in his dark eyes. Several loafers had risen to their feet licking their lips. Following their eyes, I glimpsed up the street the unmistakable tall figure of Brice Chamberlain in a new brown suit coming out of the Exchange House and pausing for a moment on the high stone steps, a Mexican behind him with a pair of gripsacks. Then both approaching figures were blotted out by the gray clot of rounded emigrant canvas.

PART II

THE COLONEL

6

There are pictures nearly dead in my memory now that I never thought I should forget: the curl of a yellow sand wave in the black malpais; the bend of grama grass in the June wind; and the glitter of mocking desert snow on the burning alkali flat. But that scene at Salt Fork in the shadow of the sand hills of nearly fifty years ago is still alive and moving in front of my eyes, and I can't wipe it away.

I can see the small red depot and the round gibbet of the railroad water-tower rimmed with the stubs of

old posse ropes. Somewhere along the Rio Grande I can hear the whistle of the eastbound train that was to take Lutie Brewton forever away with the voice of lambs from the shipping pens in her ears, almost human voices that might have been those of little Jimmy and Brock and Sarah Beth calling to her over nearly fifty miles of plain. And I can feel the long-controlled but now violently overflowing passion of my uncle standing there with his gun belt buckled under his long-tailed, gray broadcloth coat, while the man Lutie Brewton had refused to name, but whom we all knew, was coming toward us only a few hundred yards away, somewhere just behind that cloud of emigrant canvas.

I noticed that men were standing on the flat roof of the Baca hide and wool warehouse and that the teamster had finished loading his flat delivery wagon with a high pyramid of flour, but made no effort to drive it away. Above the bullet-punctured fence around the Kingman Mercantile Company store I could see a row of heads belonging to commission-house clerks all turned toward the square. And presently I became aware that young Lawyer Archie Meade had left the side of the troubled Henry McCurtin as if he couldn't bear to see what might happen to his approaching friend.

The train was whistling now by the small river ranchos and finally through the cottonwood bosque where of a summer afternoon the town boys played Jesse James. Some of the silent crowd, I saw, tried not to look up the street, but it was plain that everyone was standing there in a kind of strained expectancy, waiting for Chamberlain's creamy Western hat and brown-checked Eastern suit to appear.

Only Lutie Brewton refused to be still, throwing herself into saying good-by to her friends with an animated gayety that was almost incoherence, laughing to this one and chattering to that, hugging Myra Netherwood and dabbing quick kisses on Cora Holderness's cheeks, while her hands fluttered and flew and drew back like a pair of white falcons on the leash.

Some of the ladies were crying, although when Lutie Brewton turned to say good-by to me, I stood deaf and stony to hide everything I felt. "Thank you for bringing my trunk," she said brightly, but when I was kissed, with the scent of violets swimming about me, she whispered in my long hair: "Say nice things about me to my babies till I send for them, Hal!"

And now without a sign as yet of Brice Chamberlain, the train was in, with black smoke drifting from the bulging smoke-stack, and with women passengers staring curiously at Lutie Brewton as their full skirts rustled to the train. My uncle himself carried her valises into the palace car, where I could see him standing by her seat as she gracefully chatted and laughed at her open window to her friends outside on the raised plank platform, her modulated voice clear and charming as if nothing had happened or could happen and she might be only taking a flying trip to Santa Fe.

Even after the conductor, who had waited respectfully for my uncle to alight, gave the signal for the train to start, and when she and everybody else knew that the man who was to be United States district attorney in Colorado had not appeared from that tangle of emigrant canvas to join her, Lutie Brewton sat there alone and gallant as I had ever seen her, leaning

from the window to wave gayly and throw kisses to us all.

"Good-by! Good-by!" For a moment the air was filled with eager cries. Then she was gone. And suddenly the platform was silent and most curiously empty, and everyone stood there looking after the train that was already just a retreating door with a narrow window on either side and a streak of dark smoke drifting above it.

Only my uncle refused to look at it. With his head up and his dark eyes a warning to all he met, he walked toward the hotel, a lone, powerful figure to whom no one at the moment dared to speak.

7

As soon as he was gone, the crowd stirred and moved about like a pack of small dogs that had been cowed by the presence of a mastiff. Several men I knew edged to the side of my uncle's lawyer.

"They say Brice Chamberlain's up with Archie Meade in his office now, Mr. McCurtin," one of them said. "What do you reckon Chamberlain'll do now—take the train tomorrow?"

Henry McCurtin's eyes were pits of gray granite in the mountainous bulk of his cheeks.

"Whatever Brice Chamberlain intends to do, he certainly would not inform us, gentlemen." He bowed, and moved stolidly up the street.

And so did I, as well as I was able, knowing no more than Henry McCurtin. Contrary to my expectations, we stayed in town all next day and my uncle drew a thousand dollars in cash from John Kingman, who did a general banking business in his store. And when the time came for the next eastbound train, my uncle was on the plank platform again, with a tensely eager collection of human beings scattered for two hundred yards about the depot, trying to be casual and inconspicuous, clustered about wagons and leaning on saddle horses and board fences tacked with signs of sheep dip, liniment, and tobacco. One and all, friends or enemies, my uncle ignored them, pacing implacably up and down, a bulge still under one of the tails of his coat, his great head thrown up like the breech of a twentypounder, his pitch-black eyes from time to time throwing a fearless look up the street.

Henry McCurtin told me afterwards he believed my uncle had merely planned to take the train with Brice Chamberlain and stay with him until he made sure of his man. But Chamberlain did not appear that day or the next. No one saw either him or his gripsacks pass on the street, yet common knowledge had it he was staying with his kin, the John Holdernesses, from whose house a veritable stream of telegrams, it was said, had begun to pour to Washington.

For Lutie Brewton's sake I felt a kind of shame for him, holing up like a fox or coyote here in Salt Fork where everybody knew it. Even Archie Meade seemed embarrassed by his part in the affair, crossing the square as if in a hurry to shut himself out of sight in Brice Chamberlain's old office across the alley from the Courthouse Saloon. And my uncle bore a look of perpetual contempt on his rude face.

The fourth day he disdained to go to the depot, and several evenings later he broke his silence to me as we sat at supper in the hotel eatingroom under the mounted heads of antelope and the long twisted horns of steers that supported rifles belonging to the diners.

"You can drive your buckboard back to the ranch in the morning, Hal," he said, I thought, a little wearily.

All week I had slept on the red sofa in the cavernous Bridal Chamber, still my uncle's room when he came to town. I remember that when I went to bed that night it was still ▨▨▨▨ ▨▨▨ ▨▨ ▨▨▨▨▨ ▨ ▨▨▨▨▨ ▨▨▨ ▨▨▨▨▨ over the pointed back of the sofa, carved with scrolls and curlicues. And when I awoke I thought a bunch of cowhands from some remote ranch had arrived in town for a rowdy night at the dance halls.

Then I was conscious of an unaccustomed light in the darkened room and, slipping over to the long window, I saw a procession from the emigrant camps winding around the plaza, all men, some on horseback, some on foot, in patched hickory shirts and linsey-woolsey shirts and faded blue and striped and gray denim jumpers. A few carried long cap and ball rifles, but most of them held up hoes and pitchforks and American flags and two or three crude flares that threw waves of sultry light over their unshaven faces, the faces of tenant farmers from Kansas, of hunters from Arkansas, of Missouri backwoodsmen and Louisiana steamboaters and cotton choppers from East Texas and artisans and tradesmen whose living had been unsatisfactory in half a dozen Mississippi and Ohio River states.

I watched them pass, then pulled on my boots and clothes and ran down under the swinging red oil lamp on the hotel stairs. When I reached the street, it was empty, but I could see the nesters massed in front of the Holderness house, that stood with proud head and shoulders above all the squat adobe buildings of Salt Fork, the leaping flares lighting up the impressively mortared bricks, the yellow woodwork and round-eyed cupola on the roof.

As I stood in the shadows of the livery stable, a hoarse roar of enthusiasm rose from the emigrants, and I saw the familiar tall figure of Brice Chamberlain on the Holderness front porch, showing himself at last. A bit pale even at this distance in the flares, but ▨▨▨▨▨▨▨ ▨▨▨ ▨▨▨▨ ▨▨▨▨▨▨▨▨ ▨▨ ▨ long coat, his blond hair brushed vigorously back from his forehead, he advanced to the ornately runged railing.

What he said at first I do not know, for he spoke in a low tone. Then his voice rang down the street, and I think it could have been heard in the square.

"This much I dare tell you," he challenged, and I imagined I could see the blue fire in his eyes, "that the President is my friend. And he won't stand by in Washington while ruthless forces in this backwood territory oppose and oppress you. That I can promise you as surely as I can that the President of the United States today appointed me judge of your district court. And I have no fear but that he will see to it that the Senate confirms my appointment."

A thunder of approval with shouts of "Judge Chamberlain!" swelled and echoed in the dusty street. But I scarcely heard it, standing there stiff and incredulous, aware that something unexpected and tragic had happened, something that Lutie Brewton with all her quick mind, that saw into everything like a slender golden sword, had not foreseen.

And neither had I until now when everything stepped into its proper place like Dagget's livery horses into their own stalls. And I could see that Brice Chamberlain, lawyer that he was, had moved to clear himself from my uncle's silent threat against the unnamed man going away with Lutie

Brewton, and by the same stroke was vindicating himself in the eyes of certain Salt Fork people who would say now that the new judge had never intended to take the train to Denver at all.

All the way back to the hotel, I felt my anger rising against Chamberlain and wondered what Lutie Brewton would do now. And when I entered the room I was uncomfortable to find my uncle there, his shirt already off, the black growth curling on his chest like hair from a buggy cushion. He paid me no attention until he had worked off his boots and made himself ready for bed. Then he pinned me to the floor with his eyes that still mirrored a reflection of the emigrants' wild flares, and lifted a long leather wallet from the inside pocket of his removed gray coat with tails.

"Put this under your pillow," he said. "You're going to Denver tomorrow. I want you to find Lutie and give it to her. She'll need it."

"Yes, sir," I stammered, aware now that he knew of Chamberlain's change of appointment and thinking I would give almost anything rather than find Lutie Brewton in her humiliation. And yet somewhere in my blood I felt an inexpressible eagerness that I was to see her again.

I wanted to tell him what Brice Chamberlain had promised the nesters, but I didn't dare. Towering there in his long white night-shirt, his untamed black eyes and fierce dark hair and mustache, he reminded me of one of the uncontrollable Bedouin chiefs of whom I had read at school. Then he laid himself down on the huge Bridal Chamber bed, and even after I had undressed and blown out the light I could feel him there, powerful and motionless on his back, his eyes open, staring at the ceiling.

But some time during the night I heard him tossing and muttering. And once his voice came out thick and strong, like one of his roundup orders bawled above the din of cattle and men, although what he said tonight was sinister and utterly incomprehensible.

"Drink your saddle galls, nesters!" it sounded like. "You've got to plow deeper than that to find him."

8

The brilliant sunshine lay like a golden shawl over the rich mountain city that morning my train set me down for the first time in my life in young Denver. The names of strange railroads incited me from the sides of locomotives at the depot. As I passed up Seventeenth Street, a babel of voices from the doors of clothing stores, auction houses, and pawnbroker shops coaxed and flattered me with "sir" and "young gentleman." There was something in the streets I walked that morning, in the costly dress of the ladies in passing carriages, in the very air that swept down from the mountains, something lavish, dashing and sparkling like Lutie Brewton herself, and I thought I began to understand a little of her fever for this prodigal place that was growing by leaps and bounds.

Even in the business house of my uncle's friend, George Twitchell, the lavish touch was there. I felt I was walking on a silver floor as you did in the Silver Dollar Saloon, although the Twitchell establishment was only a hardware house, the largest west of St. Louis, with men from half a dozen states and territories joking and telling stories as they bought everything from six-shooters to mining machinery. And when George Twitchell

took me home to noon-day dinner in a fabulous brick mansion behind a tall ornamental fence where a wild Canada goose with one clipped wing swam endlessly around in a fountain, I knew that my uncle, who had said nothing of Lutie Brewton coming back, was aware that a thousand dollars would not let her stay in Denver forever.

That afternoon with the wallet in my pocket, with my hair freshly cut by a Denver barber, my boots shined, and an impressive card supplied and inscribed: "Mr. Harry Brewton" in George Twitchell's blue Spencerian flourishes, I stiffened my young back and pushed myself toward the new Brown Palace Hotel.

A lively bevy of ladies rustled out as I came in. They were hatted and gloved, in silks and satins, with bows and puffs, and laces and flounces, chatting gayly to each other like a group of brilliantly plumaged birds at one of my uncle's ponds on the Cross B. They left the scent of violets and other flowers floating behind them, and if I had doubted it before, I was sure I should find Lutie Brewton here now.

An elegant clerk with a small, trimmed beard, a long tailed coat and immaculate stand-up collar took my card in his fingers.

"Mrs. Colonel Brewton?" he repeated. "Oh, yes, Mrs. Lutie Cameron Brewton." His face lighted and at once he was treating me with respect. I knew now that he had surely seen her and talked to her, and for the moment it was almost as if she were already there in front of me, stepping lightly down the red-carpeted stairs, a lady no one need be ashamed of here, crying: "Hal!" in her clear, modulated voice and throwing her sensitive arms about me.

Then I became aware that his face had clouded and he was speaking to me with genuine regret.

"We all wished Mrs. Brewton might have stayed with us longer."

I stood there stiffly, aware that something beautiful was slipping out of my grasp. The clerk's hands, white as a lady's, were turning the leaves of a leather-bound ledger.

"Mrs. Brewton was here until day before yesterday," he said. "I think she received a letter or telegram. I remember she was very gay, but I had the distinct impression she had been disturbed. She paid her bill and left the hotel and gave us no address. I am very sorry."

When I stepped out into the street, the sun had vanished behind a cloud and the golden air of the city had fled. And all week while I called at the other hotels and boarding-houses, and while I watched from the mule cars for a delicate face and slender figure, and hung for whole afternoons along Broadway scanning the smart procession of ladies in carriages and fancy carts and rubber-tired runabouts, I never saw it again, although George Twitchell took me by night to the better restaurants, to the Tabor Grand Theater and to a quiet brick house that upstairs turned into a great room of which I remember Soapy Smith in his black ministerial garb and ladies and gentlemen gambling at a score of tables, scarcely noticing huge paintings on the wall that made me blush to my ears.

And when the week was done, all I had for my pains was an endless picture gallery of faces that kept passing me in my sleep, peering and staring at me, ladies' faces, homely and beautiful, soft and hard, sad and glittering. But none of them had that rare something that was Lutie Brewton.

Monday morning I took my uncle's

wallet from one of the tall iron safes in the hardware house.

"She's probably gone home," George Twitchell cheered me. "Where else could she go? You'll find her sitting on the ranch-house porch when you ride up."

He was a hearty man, tall and raw-boned, with an air that begat confidence. But when I reached Salt Fork and saw the old town with its dusty streets and plank sidewalks asleep in the yellow sun, I knew they had not been trod the last few days by the slender, alive foot of Lutie Brewton.

On the sugary counter of his mercantile company John Kingman counted the money, his lips moving through his heavy beard in time with his fingers. Once his eyes strayed to the store porch behind me. And when I had passed through the wide-open front doors of the Dagget livery sta-

ble, Frank Dagget's did the same. Then I understood.

"Hullo, Hal," he greeted. "See the elephant and hear the owl hoot up in Denver?" And when I nodded briefly, "Shorty Bowen took your buckboard. He said you could hire a buggy if you needed one."

"I don't need any," I said stiffly, knowing what he meant.

The liveryman looked indefinably disappointed.

"Shorty had to pack a couple cases of cartridges out to the ranch," he mentioned.

I felt my ears sharpen, but Frank Dagget's face held no more expression than one of his buggy curtains, neither then nor when he cinched up a horse for me while I forced open its mouth for the bit, a hard unwilling mouth that still dripped with the yellowish green of livery oats.

As I rode out the straggling street Lutie Brewton had walked with me that day now so long ago, Brice Chamberlain drove by me in a hired buggy and an impressive black frock coat like Judge White used to wear. He had always gone out of his way to cultivate my friendship, but today he greeted me with cool and scant ceremony, while I scowled at him in turn and wondered where he had been out here in a direction that led almost nowhere except to the remote ranches.

Then as my pony reached the top of the sand hills, I saw it, a cloud of emigrant canvas rolling where the escarpment fell away to the river, one united tent and covered-wagon city with horses and mules, oxen and milk cows grazing for miles on the mesa.

As the trail took me gradually closer, I grew aware of the unmistakable activity and excitement in the encampment; the sound of hammers on camp anvils and wagon wheels; the movement of nesters in and out of the canvas like ants; the men and women repacking scores of wagons, and voices calling exultantly to each other, while out on the mesa men and boys on horseback were herding the animals toward camp.

It was clear to me now where Brice Chamberlain had been. And if I hadn't guessed it then, I would have known it when I reached the ranch house that evening and found the bunkhouse almost an arsenal of six-shooters and Winchesters while out on the ground around the supper fire sprawled more Cross B hands than I had ever seen together at one time, tin plates of steak and biscuits in their laps, tin cups of black coffee in their hands, and a look in their eyes I well knew.

9

I was glad for all the dark war clouds as an excuse to put off reporting to my uncle about Lutie. But in the end I knew that all the time he stood there in the dim hall listening to what I had to say about the nesters and questioning me about their camp and numbers, there was only one person who walked in his mind.

"You didn't see her?" he demanded at last.

I stammered what had happened in Denver. He made no comment. But when Black Hetty came in from the children's room to light a lamp, I saw that his great arrogant face was lined and his eyes held orange flames that I know now were hatred for the man who had failed Lutie Brewton. And the following day when one of our riders brought word that the nesters had left their camp near the river and already, as if it were a fiesta, were swarming in wagons and on horseback over the eastern part of our fertile big prairie, the violence poured into his face like a living flood that would tear out any dam in the country, and from the dark clouds of his eyes I could see that torrents of anger were still falling.

"Is Judge Chamberlain with the nesters?" he growled deep in his throat.

"I think it was him in a livery buggy," the cowhand stammered.

"Go out and tell the boys to saddle up," my uncle ordered.

I knew what that meant. And when the hand had gone, my uncle must have seen it in my face, for he fixed his fearful gaze on me.

"Remember, boy," he said, "there are times in your life you've got to be hard. No man respects you for be-ing soft to him today and letting him ruin you and himself tomorrow. You're going to see things before sundown that aren't nice to look at and you better not come along if a college education's made a woman out of you."

"I can be plenty hard to a nester," I told him.

Adamant in his gray broadcloth coat with its tightly fitting shoulders and tails long spread by the saddle; his long, wrinkled boots, far different from the showy footgear of the modern West and unblacked since Lutie Brewton had gone away, he started for the corrals and the big buckskin I knew he would ride today.

Then we passed through the green wall of cottonwoods and misty spraying tamarisks that Lutie Brewton had had planted, I saw the hands at the corrals and bunkhouse watching three horsemen riding over the rise, the sun sparkling like quicksilver on them and their saddle rigging. And when they rode closer, I could make out blue uniforms and polished saber hilts, slouch hats with gold insignia, and the straight-laced backs of officers from Fort Ewing.

My uncle had thrown up his head with that lordly challenge of a wild stallion, and now he waited there in a kind of rude and insolent magnificence until the rider of the bald-faced horse in the lead turned into Major Wilberforce, a soldier of dignity and fierce red mustaches.

He drew off a gauntlet glove and reached down from the saddle to shake hands.

"We're camping by the spring on your big vega, Colonel," he greeted. "We've got a troop of sixty-five men, and the Captain and I couldn't resist riding over to have dinner with you."

What he said was perfectly smooth and friendly, but I could see that our

hands had stiffened and were watching my uncle, who stood there now with utter dignity, although his mustache seemed to bristle and his eyes were pitchforks. After what seemed to me an extremely long time, he inclined his head.

"Won't you gentlemen come in? Have your orderly feed your horses." With powerfully controlled steps and speech, he led the way back to the gallery of the ranch house.

All afternoon I watched the Major and the Captain perspire in their efforts to bring back the friendship of old times as they sat there facing their waiting host, drinking whisky on the tufted horsehair parlor chairs, telling stories of the service, with the children thumping and shouting at play somewhere in the big house, and dinner and supper in the familiar diningroom. No one mentioned Lutie Brewton's name, and yet it was plainly a mockery with her away and the nesters swarming like sheep over our big vega.

At the sound of their horses led to the gallery that evening, the officers rose with relief to ride back to camp. My uncle stood up.

"May I inquire, Major, who ordered the troops to my big prairie?"

The officer looked grave under his red mustaches.

"By order of the President, Colonel," he said in a low voice.

"The President," my uncle went on with pitiless irony, "wants you and your troops to stay for some time?"

"Until further orders, Colonel." The Major cleared his throat and looked up. "I hope we shall still be friends."

My uncle did not reply. He stood there with lips tight and eyes pitchblack with contempt for the man who had pulled strings for others to fight his battles for him. I could feel the bitterness working in him like the hot desert winds sweeping the cedars of the rocky canyons of Ladron. In the end the blue veins in his neck and hands gradually relaxed, and I knew the fury of the storm had for the time abated, that he would never send his men to fight against his country's troops, but would relentlessly put himself through the humiliation of sending them back to their respective camps in the morning.

"Good night, gentlemen," he said harshly when they left. "You can keep the nesters from being blown away, but God Himself can't the prairie!"

Long after they had gone, I watched him in the bright June moonlight that was almost like day, standing motionless on the gallery facing the big vega. And that night as I lay in my sleepless bunk staring into the white haze that entered my deep window, I fancied that in the milky mist I could see the prairie as I had seen it all my life and would never see it again, with the grass in summer sweeping my stirruped thighs and prairie chicken scuttling ahead of my pony; with the ponds in fall black and noisy with waterfowl, and my uncle's seventy thousand head of cattle rolling in fat; with the tracks of endless game in the winter snow and thousands of tons of wild hay cured and stored on the stem; and when the sloughs of the home range greened up in the spring, with the scent of warming wet earth and swag after swag catching the emerald fire, with horses shedding and snorting and grunting as they rolled, and everywhere the friendly indescribable solitude of that lost sea of grass.

10

It struck me as strange to see the sun come up as usual over the eastern plain next morning. And at breakfast

I asked my uncle if I could ride west with the Red Lake hands to look for my missing B B mare. He raked me with his coal-black eyes, and I think he knew why I didn't want to stay, but he said nothing, and by the time we reached our Red Lake camp the summer rains were sweeping down from La Ceja.

All night the water dripped from the camp-house roof with a steady clop until my ears seemed to fill with the sound, and suddenly I knew that I hadn't got away from it at all, and what I heard in my brain was the clop, clop, clop of the cloven hoofs of oxen, of wheels slopping in the sloughs, of the gutturals of men and shrill voices of women, of crying babies and crates of cackling barnyard fowl, of the baas of sheep and goats and all the rest of the despised chat-

tels of nesters scattering like a victorious army over our range.

When at last I rode reluctantly back to headquarters, I could see them squatting in likely places on our big vega, digging holes for their dugouts like prairie dogs in the ground, or plastering with mud a frame of cedar poles from Ladron, stringing barbed wire where our cattle and horses and the antelope had always grazed free, or yelling at their teams of mules and steers as they tore up the virgin sod with a breaking plow.

Hot and almost trembling with anger, I came through the wide hall of the ranch house at late dusk and halted, a little ashamed of myself, in the sitting-room doorway. Still the same rude, unconquerable figure, my uncle sat with his great proud face over his tan leather account books as

THE SEA OF GRASS

183

if there wasn't a nester within fifty miles, although I knew that from the near-by window he could have seen through the cottonwoods a half-dozen lights beginning to quiver across the dark prairie.

Sitting there that evening and other evenings between the heavy walls of the old ranch house, with my uncle's stool now scratching arrogantly on his two-weeks-old Kansas paper rattling in lusty gusts in his hands, with my young cousins stretched on the floor cutting out paper horses and cattle from old magazines, and all around us the familiar curtains, furniture, and carpet by lamplight, the feeling kept creeping over me that Lutie Brewton was somehow still here. And once when a faint scent of violets seemed to rise in the room from one of her despoiled magazines, I could almost swear that her slender figure was there in the shadows behind me, alive, delicate, and sparkling, waiting before calling out in that high clear fun-loving voice she always used to children.

A few days later Black Hetty whispered to me portentously:

"Heah dem wagons a-rollin' by, Mistah Hal? Miz Brewton come back mighty soon now. It ain't lonesome round heah no mo'. No, sah. You wait and see if Hetty doan know."

It was true, I told myself half bitterly, that we weren't a peacefully remote ranch house any more, forty or fifty miles from the nearest neighbor. From the bunkhouse doorway you could see fences and plowed furrows, and smoke rising from mud chimneys. Nearly every day nesters in spring wagons or road wagons rattled by to town or to visit other nesters. And nester children began to ride up on the backs of old horses to borrow matches or sour-dough leaven for biscuits or baking soda for a cow with the colic.

They avoided the ranch house as they would a pestilence, going straight to the bunkhouse. I saw little Jimmy and Sarah Beth stand stiffly under the cottonwoods watching them, but the tow-haired Brock ran right up and tried to get them to stay and play. It made me think of the time Lutie Brewton had run and shouted with the emigrant children, although those nester youngsters today were like another race, mute, staring, defiant, and yet scared. As soon as they climbed back on their horse from a wagon wheel, they rode hurriedly away. But I knew that Lutie Brewton would have coaxed them to stay and talk and smile with a glass of lemonade and a piece of democrat cake.

Once they were there as my uncle happened to come riding in, and they huddled together as if they had seen an ogre who would forbid what Will Lubbock, the bunkhouse cook, had just given them. But if my uncle saw them, there was no sign of it. In his eyes lately when he came riding up to the ranch house was a look as if he faintly expected someone. Tomorrow, always tomorrow, I told myself, we would glance up and there she would be in one of Frank Dagget's livery buggies as if she had just been to town. Dagget himself would be looking pleased and proud for the Colonel. My uncle's face would be grave, and he would inquire with unfailing courtesy of her health and not a word about where she had been or the skunk who had failed her. And every day the headquarters hands would listen to her high clear voice when she called the children.

But July passed and August passed, and the night before I went back east to college, my uncle called me into the big front bedroom. I hoped that he would order me to see the nun, Mercedes, at the convent in St

Louis to ask if she knew where Lutie Brewton was. But he did not mention Lutie's name. Once he glanced at her glove still lying untouched like a delicate part of her, feminine, sensitive, and crushed, on a shelf. And deep in his eyes I saw red coals like the implacable Indian pueblo fires that are never allowed to go out. And the rest of the evening I could feel him far back in his mind stirring the charred embers and laying fresh logs on the blaze.

And when I lay down that night in my bunk I knew my uncle's inner convictions that wherever she was, the sensitive white hand of Lutie Brewton felt humiliated, dishonored, and crushed like its glove on the shelf, and that she would never come back and show herself to the ranch house and town that had idolized her—not even for her children.

II

For three long years, part of them in medical school, I didn't see the massive ranch house, not a grain of sand or blade of grass from the Cross B. I remember the weather as unseasonably dry those years at St. Louis, with the Mississippi gaunt as a trail-driven steer. But the Salt Fork weekly told in glowing italics of the heavy snows that fell west of Kansas and the unusual spring rains that soaked the ranges of the territory until they spouted like the rock of Moses with springs. And in every issue there began to be more news of the nesters—emigrants, settlers, homesteaders, and agriculturists, it called them—and less of the cattlemen, until a thousand miles away my thumbs would bite through the paper in anger.

More settlers were landing in Salt Fork by steam and wagon train. The settlers were crowding the Las Cruces land office. The settlers were plowing up the rich brown prairie loam. The settlers were harrowing and planting corn. From the sand hills above Salt Fork the townspeople could see the velvety green patches of the settlers' winter wheat and rye. Judge Chamberlain said as the rains continued that God was clearly on the side of the settlers. The settlers' wheat stood golden in the sun. The heavy heads of the settlers' rye knocked off men's hats. And the settlers' corn could swallow up a horse and rider.

Not that anyone would have known the existence of a settler on the Cross B range from my uncle's letters. Brief as always, the handwriting was still spirited, erect and unquenchable as I had ever seen it, with the final letter of every word sweeping up like a lusty whiplash, and every proper name underlined, not for emphasis, but from an overflow of will and power.

But all those months he wrote me firmly that grass was good and beef high, that my B B mare had a pinto colt, that the hands and children sent me their best and he remained my uncle, Jas. B. I knew from other sources that his favorite saddle horse, Pompey, had thrown and tangled himself in nester barbed wire until he had to be shot; that in sheltered cañadas his cowhands were digging up the telltale buried horns and Cross B hides of butchered beeves; and that a score of nesters were suing him in Judge Chamberlain's court for the destruction by his cattle of their crops and gardens.

I expected the trial to be over before I came home. But in July when I stepped from the train, Salt Fork was like a nesters' holiday with grain wagons choking the square, and the sidewalks crowded with men often thick through the body as their gunny-

sacks of freshly thrashed wheat and rye, and most of them distinct from cowmen as a draft horse from a saddle pony. And everywhere in the stores the merchants were truckling to the nester women with the smiles and jokes I had thought they reserved for their cattleman friends.

Standing on the steps of the old Exchange House, I could scarcely be-lieve that this was the square for which only a few years ago I would grow desperately homesick. And when I looked for my uncle in Judge Chamberlain's new brick courthouse where Clancy's dance hall used to stand, it did not seem like the Salt Fork county court at all, with no buckled spurs swinging on the railing, with a floor of sawed pine, with pews for seats and all these stolid spectators standing up as in church while the tall figure of Brice Chamberlain swept up to the bar with his bright blond hair waving against the impressive black of his gown. Even the Henry McCurtin I knew had vanished. With sagging cheeks and sunken eyes, he defended my uncle's case like a man who had had his first stroke of paralysis and was calmly resigned to the second.

But it was when my uncle came in and the only notice these sluggish-faced men showed for that proud figure as he towered down the aisle were a few sullen looks and a derisive muttering among themselves that I felt the end had nearly come.

I tried not to listen to the court routine that followed, except when Judge Chamberlain, as if he were re-buking a Mexican cow-thief, reviewed the nester evidence against my uncle to the nester jurors and charged them, as it sounded to me, that they must find my uncle liable and fix the dam-ages. I was remembering a day twelve or fourteen years before when only the whisper that the owner of the

Cross B was at the courthouse door had been enough to stir the crowd's emotion. And when he had moved majestically down the aisle and through the railing with as much right as Judge White himself, the whole courtroom had been charged with his presence. And I realized that those golden wild horses of other days had slipped more safely out of my uncle's rope than he knew, and would never be caught again.

First to go had been Lutie Brewton, then the sea of grass. And now these people who had waited till the West was safe and the pioneering done, were barking and snapping around my uncle's legs like a pack of dogs. They had him fairly surrounded, were rais-ing their paws on him here and tear-ing out a piece of him there. But after I had watched him seat himself again in the old, fearless, unconquerable way, without so much as a glance at the nesters beside him, I knew that although he had lost his case they didn't have him down.

From where I sat I could see only the back of his head like some dark, shaggy Jove. And yet I was sure that the red coals of his eyes had fastened themselves on Brice Chamberlain, who might not realize it, but still had a debt to pay. Times might have changed, but my uncle never would change, never would forget till he died.

I remember that when I stepped out on the street I found that the two boys had come along to town with their father. When Brock saw me, he pulled off Jimmy's hat, waved it, ran up the plank sidewalk until he was about to be caught, and sailed the hat toward a nester wagon loaded with towsacks of wheat. For a moment the hat hung against the sky. Then it missed the wagon and fell into the deep mud. Little did I think this night that the

placid blue sky I saw was already re-
turning to its old mysterious cycle,
that this was the last deep mud and
one of the last wagonloads of wheat
that would be seen in Salt Fork for
what the Navajos north of Red Lake
called a land of snows.

12

At the time I thought it only the
way the cards happened to fall. But
when I look back on it now, it seems
immutable and fixed as a chapter out
of Genesis or Exodus, with the nesters
safe on their Promised Land; with my
uncle pushed back with his cattle on
a thousand hills; with Brice Chamber-
lain in the seat of the mighty; and
all the time the red eye of God watch-
ing from the burning bush, not to see
that what was to come would be hu-
mane and sweet and according to prog-
ress, but that it should be cruel and
just and true according to the book of
destiny which blinds a man from prop-
erly reading it until those who would
dictate it are dead and fifty or a thou-
sand years have passed.

When the news reached me that
the weather west of Kansas and Indian
Territory had changed, it was as if the
God few of us medical students be-
lieved in was in His heaven after all,
and my eyes must have burned with
a deep exultation in the dark halls of
my school and hospital. The nester
women were praying for rain. The
nester men were hauling water from
my uncle's ponds and windmills. The
more responsible nesters were packing
up to journey farther west and north,
some to join the Mormons. And Judge
Chamberlain had made a Fourth of
July oration that it was the greatest
drouth in the history of the territory.
But a letter signed "Cattleman" to the
paper said it was no drouth at all,

just normal old-fashioned New Mexi-
can weather, and pointed to the native
wild grasses that had not been plowed
under. With a desperate skill born of
long experience in this dry land, they
had caught the diminished rains and
rushed into growth and seed while
the nesters' corn and wheat scarcely
sprouted in the ground.

On my way home through Missouri
and eastern Kansas the following
spring, a veil of gray mist hugged the
car windows. But once the train had
climbed the high plateaus, the win-
dows were clear, the skies a dull blue,
and the plains toasted brown with sod.
And when we came close to Salt Fork
I had a glimpse from the train of puffs
of dust moving over the prairie that
were nesters plowing and harrowing a
dry land.

I hadn't seen my uncle since I
left, and I felt he would be almost in-
solent with triumph to be vindicated at
last. Then I stepped off the train at the
familiar red depot and he was there
with his buggy to meet me himself,
and I wasn't sure of his feelings at all.
With his great face plowed and har-
rowed, his mustache turning gray, but
his eyes still pitch-black as I had ever
seen them, he drove me home over
what had once been his fertile range
and was now a waste of barbed wire
and bare ground and squalid gates to
open and close, with a few of the
dugouts empty and already falling in,
and the song of an occasional mocking
bird or meadow lark a mockery in the
dead and dying young fruit trees. And
I can still see him sitting in his buggy,
silent and deaf, while a nester in an
unwashed undershirt tried to sell him
his barren, proven-up fields.

It was long after dark when we
reached home. The earthen ranch
house stood deep in the shadows of its
cottonwoods and tamarisks like a for-
gotten fortress decaying in its ancient

bosque. Sarah Beth was east at convent school, the boys asleep in bed, and I saw where, during my uncle's absence in town, the spring winds had deposited miniature dunes of sand and nester field dust along the wall boards as if no walls were there.

And that evening as we sat at the great hulking supper-table, bare of cloth and candles, with only the smoky light from a brass lamp trickling over us; and afterwards as I wandered through the rude hall and silent parlor with boys' quirts and ropes, spurs, bridles, and saddles scattered over the floor, and boys' rough fingerprints and boot-marks on the dusty lid of the piano; and again next morning when I heard the two boys fighting and tumbling like young savages over the parlor floor and then riding off hard on their ponies, it seemed strange to think that there had ever been a gentle lady in the house.

"She's gone and nobody but my uncle remembers her any more," I told myself, getting up from the bunk where she had once nursed me with the whitest and lightest of hands.

But when I rode out to the remote Cross B camps in the cedar-dotted hills where the nesters had not yet penetrated, and when I talked to some of her old friends in town, I found that they were still talking of the beautiful wife of Colonel Brewton.

Several thought they knew where she was. Young Mrs. Bob Kingman said she had seen Lutie Brewton's face, as young and beautiful as ever, in a nun's wimple on the streets of New Orleans. The gentlemanly wagon boss of the Bar 44, who had won a prize with her as his partner at whist, had seen someone he believed was Mrs. Brewton in a stunning black lace gown and diamonds gambling for high stakes in Tombstone. She was painted and powdered

like a dance-hall woman, but he had absolutely remembered the feverish gestures with which she played. And John McCandless, agent for the Mescalero Apaches, had gone to Washington on Indian bureau business and seen a lady he knew but couldn't place, in an open carriage on Pennsylvania Avenue, by the side of a foreign ambassador or someone with ribbons on his coat. She had flushed when stared at and turned her head, and not until they were by did he realize it had been Mrs. Brewton.

Myra Netherwood thought Lutie must be dead. But the story I clung to was told by Superintendent Bedford of the railroad, who had been at the famous Silver Ball given with full orchestra and waxed floor under a waterproof canopy at the bottom of a Colorado silver mine. During the evening a fall of rock in a near-by stope had frightened the dancers off the floor, all but a guest with another name, who was the image of Mrs. Brewton. For several minutes while the rocks continued to fall, she had kept on gayly dancing with her partner, encouraging the orchestra and laughing to her partner as if nothing had happened, until most of the guests were over their scare and back on the floor. Somehow I felt that had been the real Lutie Brewton, and the peculiar emotion I had always felt at the sight of her had welled up in me indescribably at the story.

But later I found that there was something else they were saying about her, although they did not say it to me. And I was to learn that nothing was too romantic and fantastic to speculate about Lutie Brewton.

All I noticed at first was that they took a great interest in young Brock when he came with me to town, laughing at his quick replies and provoking him to others. And all the

while the ladies admired his feathery blond hair and treated him to slices of layer cake, and while the men bribed him to strut up and down the Kingman store porch like certain well-known characters of town, I could see them exchange veiled glances and knowing nods. And yet for a medical student I was thick in the skull as a nester and thought nothing of it until in August when we had all driven to town to meet Sarah Beth, who was coming home alone by train from convent school in the morning.

The square swarmed as usual with nester wagons and all their nondescript conveyances, as if having a poor crop year meant nothing to them. My uncle's old friend Dr. Reid, as one professional man to another, invited me into the White Elephant Saloon, and I found several nesters drinking next year's wheat, appropriating the front of the long walnut bar. A little group of cattlemen and cowhands kept themselves distinct at the other end, and while I shook hands with several of them, the doctor gravely waited for me. His face and manner were courteous and serene, but I knew his hand was twitching to wrap itself around a dark bottle, a long white hand marked with veins that as a small boy I was sure must flow with purple wine.

The screen had been moved back from the open door, and across the street I could see young Brock and Jimmy facing each other on the Holderness porch steps as if they had had one of their usual differences and the men around them were tactfully stirring them up to fight. The two boys made a picture I can see now against the rough splintery background of the store, with colored tin signs tacked on the step rises and against the red wall—Jimmy, slim and dark, like a small, stiff image of his father, fists tightly clenched—and Brock leaning forward recklessly to hit him on the nose, his hat pushed back where it hung by its throat latch, his hair a kind of white gold in the afternoon sun.

Then it happened. A bushy, round-headed nubbin of a nester in a hickory shirt ridged like corduroy moved to the doorway.

"I'm a-bettin' on the Chamberlain young 'un," he called.

For a split fraction of a second as his meaning broke over me, I saw Lutie Brewton clear and beautiful as I had ever seen her in the life. And when the nester turned and grinned toward a sand-box, it was almost as if he had spat in her face. I was aware of the grave silence of the cowmen and of a curious wild hate sweeping over me like prairie fire. I had thought myself a medical student soon to go out in the world and save human lives. Now I found that the thin veneer of Eastern schools had cracked and I was only a savage young Brewton from an untamed sea of grass, moving through the little gate where customers' rifles and pistols stood or lay in their accustomed places on the back bar. I was aware of the cowmen backing out of range and of the bar-keeper ducking. And then I almost wanted to kill Dr. Reid, too, one of whose white hands had with surprising force suddenly thrown up my barrel so that oil from a brass hanging lamp started to pour on the walnut bar.

At the sound of the shot, men from the square began to wedge their heads into the saloon doorway until they were brushed aside like flies and my uncle stood there, sniffing the smell of black powder like an old war horse, his black eyes sweeping the room until they halted on me standing at the end of the bar with my unsuccessful six-shooter in my hand.

"What's going on, Hal?" he demanded.

I did not dare look at him now, only stood there rigid with my lips closed tight. He waited what seemed a half-hour.

"What was said in here, Walt?" he asked a huge uncomfortable cattleman with open vest and silver watch-chain tangled across it

The sweat poured from the cattleman's forehead, but he only shook his head. Something came into my uncle's great face. For some little time more he stood there unruly and aroused, dominating the long dim room like old times. Then, following the direction of a half-dozen glances, he turned his head and I saw that Jimmy and Brock had squirmed through the jammed doorway and were now standing there in the barroom with their black and white contrasting heads.

Just whom my uncle looked at the long minute he kept his head turned, I do not know, but I found it was Brock's eager young face and bright blue eyes I was staring at. In that short time I think there passed through my mind everything I had ever seen him do and heard him say, one minute mean and irrepressible, and the next charming and winning as Lutie Brewton herself so that you forgave everything. I remembered his taking to the nesters like his mother and how painstakingly impartial my uncle treated both boys, one like the other, always buying two when he bought one, and dividing equally the lash of his quirt although I felt that Brock usually deserved the most of it. And I wondered if this unnamable thing could have been the source of the deep-seated enmity between the two brothers ever since they had been old enough to walk, or what in God's name it was. When my uncle finally turned, I saw that something unutterable and terrible had come into his face.

"If any dog has something more to say, now is the time to say it!" he challenged them all, a wild violence fairly leaping from his dark eyes.

There was no sound in the long saloon but a chip someone dropped at a poker-table, the jingle of a horse shaking his harness at a hitching-rack, and the slow drip of oil on the bar like a clock ticking off the last minutes of the one who would speak. Then with almost a grimace of pain, my uncle nodded at me, and with the boys ahead of me, and my uncle to the rear, we pushed out into the square.

PART III

BROCK

13

It was the boy Brock I couldn't get off my mind the next few winters as a student assistant of a high-tempered French surgeon who operated at St. Mary's and the Alexian Brothers' hospitals. And I can't smell chloroform today without some of those old doubts and questionings rising up in front of me like ghosts. All the baffling memories I had of the boy kept turning over in my mind. Young Brock playing he was a priest and singing mass in his high soprano to a herd of grazing longhorns. And young Brock playing posse with the nester children and hanging the outlaw, which was a stray dog, to a nester gate-post. Young Brock leading the half-starved nester youngsters over to the ranch house for sour-dough biscuits and vinegar pies. And young Brock sharpening the rowels of his spur with a blacksmith's file. Young Brock's white hands galloping gracefully through *Black Jack*

Davey and *The Gypsy Maid* on the keys of Lutie Brewton's square piano. And the same white hands keeping a tomato-can rolling at fifty feet with the thirty-caliber, rim-fire five-shooter my uncle let him carry because it was hard to get the odd-sized cartridges.

It was Brock loving to talk. And Brock loving to ride. And Brock trading forty-five cartridges from his father's stores two to one for thirty rimfire. It was Brock shrewd as a judge and reckless as a Brewton and charming and magnificent as his vanished mother as he swindled his and Jimmy's tutor out of their lessons for the afternoon. And all the time his feathery blond hair kept blowing this way and that in my mind.

Peaceably as if he had been a bishop going to his reward, old Dr. Reid back in Salt Fork made ready to depart his life and his well-thumbed books of Robert Ingersoll in his room at the Exchange House, where the older guests would no longer hear his bedside glass and whisky bottle striking the hours of the night. And my uncle telegraphed for me to come home and take the practice.

When I walked up the sandy boardwalk from the train to the hotel, I found the old doctor in a coma. I tried to make him as comfortable as I could, but there was little I could do for him. Even the bottle had been drained of its comfort, and he knew neither me nor my uncle, who, when I came in, had been sitting there for several hours quietly smoking, as the two old friends had often sat in health with only an occasional word between them.

"The thoughts of the señor doctor viejo are not any more on this world," the Mexican woman who had been taking care of him told me.

Once Brock burst eagerly into the room, startling me as some blond Lutie Brewton in boots and spurs, shaking my hand now like a grown man, showing the gold piece he had won at monte, and paying no attention to the bed and its burned-out ember of a man who had brought him into the world. But while the boy stood there laughing and talking, fetching into the sickroom an air like a fresh wind blowing from out of the past, I saw a vestige of life and consciousness struggle into one of the old physician's eyes as if deep down in a well a man with a candle was trying to see and recognize the man at the windlass.

And after Brock had gone whistling down the hall, his boot-heels softened by the red carpet, his spurs jingling a purposefully manipulated tune, the old doctor tried slowly to sit up in bed.

"When did Mrs. Brewton come back?" he asked, staring at me, and I did not dare to look at my uncle, whose puffs on his cigar, I was aware, had suddenly ceased.

"I haven't seen her, doctor," I said in a low voice.

The light went out of his eye like the flame of a candle blown upon and he sank back, his long white hand with its veins of purple wine relaxing on the coverlet. But long after he was silent, the emotion I had always felt at a meeting with Lutie Brewton kept flooding and stirring me at the unexpected sound of her name.

We buried him a week or two later in one of those inexpressibly lonely and barren Southwestern graveyards, so different from the green graves he had known as a boy in his native Virginia. But the mourners, standing there with their hats off as men did forty years ago, did not see that. They were covertly watching the picture of Brock, taller than I, his blond feathery hair faintly yellow, standing only a few feet away from Judge Chamber-

lain, now a bit portly and distinguished-looking in a long black coat, a shiny high hat in his hand, his yellow hair faintly touched at the temples with silver, but still sweeping back over his head in a kind of masterful distinction.

And from then on, everything I remember of my uncle and Brock is timastered with iodoform and carbolic acid of the old doctor's office that became my own, with its green student lamp shining on the white shelves of drug jars and bottles, on the old leather operating-couch strewn with surgical instruments, and on the skeleton that ever since I could remember had stood in a corner.

Before I was back in Salt Fork a year, I found that Brock was already becoming almost as well known a figure in Salt Fork as Ingram Carter, the gambler, whose full-length portrait in oil hung in the White Elephant Saloon. It was blond, gentlemanly Brock Brewton, a favorite with all the dark-haired dance-hall women in Madame Nana's Sala de Baile, and the same Brock Brewton never losing caste but sedately dealing whist and euchre from the best horsehair furniture in town. It was Brock Brewton playing the *Blue Danube* waltz on Myra Netherwood's grand piano, and Brock Brewton driving up and down the town streets with his Choctaw-blooded nester girl beside him on the seat of his red-wheeled open buggy.

And it was Brock Brewton buying out a showcase of candy for the nester children standing around like orphans in the Kingman Mercantile Company store, and the same Brock Brewton shooting Mrs. Olson's three white ducks almost out of her hand while she fed them as he galloped by.

I can still see him in a long-legged brown suit that reminded me of the one Brice Chamberlain had once worn, taking his mother's friend Myra Netherwood devoutly to Mass. And I can see him in the same suit, his hat pushed back recklessly and his yellow hair curling, calling for a hundred or two hundred dollars' worth of chips at the White Elephant or Dutch Charley's.

He didn't pay for his chips like ordinary people. He was a Brewton, and if he called for a thousand dollars in gold, they would have tried to give it to him, the bartender marking it down as usual in his jawbone book. And when the Colonel came to town, he would have asked for his bill and there on the wet bar written out a check drawn on the Kingman Mercantile Company.

Brock and all his conflicting ways, together with my uncle's affection for and indulgence toward him, were one of the most puzzling things I had ever tried to solve. Perhaps it was that I refused to see Lutie Brewton as the others did, that to me she was still a young boy's beautiful lady. And it was summer with the bee balm in blossom again along the trail in the cañadas when fate tried to make me see it their way.

I had been called to a prairie dugout where a nester woman had tried to kill herself. She was very low and I couldn't leave her with her small baby fifty miles from a doctor. And several afternoons later when it was all over, I felt that I was no physician at all, only a tired and defeated ranch boy, and that I wanted nothing so much as to spend a night again among the old familiar things under my uncle's roof.

I was glad I had come. It was dusk when I approached the old ranch house and found light gleaming from a dozen windows, as I had often seen it in the past. And when I stepped into the bare old hall, I had the

strange feeling that a lady was there. For a moment the incredible notion came to me that Lutie Brewton had returned. Then Sarah Beth in a girlish white dress with red sash and cuffs sprang out of the massive dining-room doorway and cried a welcome to me and said that she had finished school forever and come through Salt Fork the very morning I left.

They laid a place for me at the table. The white dinner candles and their shades which I had not seen since Lutie Brewton left, the great mass of pink bee balm in the center of the huge old table, and all around me the familiar heavy silver on snowy damask affected me strongly. And all through the meal I observed that my uncle sat very quietly on his chair, the faint desert glow warming his weather-beaten face as I had not seen it for many a year, his pitch-black eyes softening a little as they rested on Sarah Beth. But far back in his eyes I had the impression that it was someone else with dark hair and slender bare arms he saw sitting here with other guests around a gayer and younger table.

We were in the parlor, Sarah Beth had opened the old piano and played some of her convent pieces, and my uncle said he wished Brock were home from town to hear them, when Jimmy was called outside. With the room very still, Sarah Beth's hands strayed into a waltz the name of which I do not know but which her mother's white hands had often played on the same black and yellow keyboard when the room was filled with guests from Fort Ewing to Santa Fe. I saw my uncle hold his cigar motionless in his hand, and for a minute or two with that old melody in the room it was almost as if the plague of nesters had never swarmed and that any minute Black Hetty might appear at the door-

way with the three small children to give their mother good-night.

The feeling was so strong that I glanced up at the doorway, and found Jimmy standing there. I thought for the moment he was listening, then I was conscious of the tautening tendons in his tanned young face. And before Sarah Beth had finished, he moved rigidly to where his father sat quiet and proud on the big horsehair armchair.

"I just heard," he said in a low voice, "that Brock shot Dutch Charley in town."

Sarah Beth went on playing without hearing and my uncle, who still seemed to be in Lutie Brewton's waltz, sat staring at the boy as if the latter had told him that several Cross B cows were bogged down in Red Lake and his loose and bitter lower lip was considering whether or not to send hands at this hour to pull them out.

"Brock shot who?" he repeated, lowering his great head like a powerful bull trying to protect himself from a deep wound already administered.

Guessing that something was wrong, Sarah Beth stopped playing. Somewhere on the trail we could hear a galloping horse. Then Jimmy's low answer came clear enough in the huge room.

"Dutch Charley. He claimed that black-haired woman that deals monte for him was in with Brock and favoring him. He said every time Brock came to the table, the house lost money. They had an argument. Charley went for his gun, but Brock got him before he could shoot."

Sarah Beth gave a little cry, but my uncle had hold of himself now and was sitting up slowly with his old iron will and power. Only the faint gray showed through his deeply lined face.

"Is Charley dead?" he asked after a little.

"I don't know," Jimmy said. "They locked Brock up."

I knew that must have hit my uncle, but he was sitting there like some rude czar in gray broadcloth and linen, his great unruly face written with the ruthless, almost dissolute pride I remembered, and there was no change in it as Jimmy gave him, bit after bit, what the hands had told him. Only when the boy mentioned the name of Judge Chamberlain did my uncle show emotion, throwing up his head with the old untamed lustiness while his shaggy gray hair bristled.

"What did Chamberlain have to do with it?" he demanded.

By the whiteness of the boy's knuckles I knew that he guessed more than I had supposed. He tried to evade it, but his father's violent eyes were pinning him to the floor and he struggled against them uselessly.

"Judge Chamberlain is the one who got Brock out," he said in a barely audible tone. "He said it was because Brock was so young and he wanted to make a private investigation in the circumstances. If Brock behaves himself, he said the case might not come up at the next term of court. But Brock's got to report to Judge Chamberlain as often as he says."

For a headlong, incredible moment it was as if I had seen the long arm and white hand of Brice Chamberlain, like that of a groomed and masterful colossus, reaching across all Salt Fork county in front of the nesters and the livery-stable loafers, in front of the town ladies, the ranchers' wives and the dance-hall women, to pin a final ugly red brand on the gay, slender figure of Lutie Brewton.

I had seen my uncle angry many times, but never when his blood ran black in his veins as it did now. His face was like a dark storm from which the lightning was constantly hurling.

Even across the room I could feel, as physically as I can waves of heat, the rising torrent of flame that, once aroused in him, burned like a prairie conflagration that no man could put out or stand up in front of, but must be let to run its own wild and volcanic course.

Then I saw that he had risen to his feet and was moving toward the door, and I don't think he knew any longer that we were in the room, but all of us knew where he was going. We watched him stop and pick up his old sweated gun belt where it hung from the post of a pine settee in the hall. And at the sight of it, Sarah Beth rose quickly from her stool and moved as far across the room as the painted china parlor lamp on its tall ornamental brass and marble stand.

"Don't go tonight, papa!" she begged him. "Let Hal and Jimmy go in tomorrow."

He stood there bleak and unhearing, strapping the double buckles of the belt before he turned and swept the three of us with his violently smoldering eyes that told us how far we could go and no farther, and that he was still lord of his family, including Brock.

But he did not go. He stood there for a little in the wide hall as if listening. Presently we heard a familiar footstep on the gallery and Brock, his yellow hair curling like a child's, came swinging past him and into the room as fresh and gallant and unscathed as I had ever seen him.

He must have guessed from all our faces that we knew, and it only made him more charming and desperately gayer, throwing himself into lively banter at Sarah Beth as if she wasn't standing there with white cheeks in front of him, ready to burst into tears on his shoulder; chiding her for not waking him up where he slept in the

hotel most of the day when she passed through town; laughing and chattering and grimacing; teasing her about Tom Milledeaux's love letters which the nuns rigorously read; and penitently coaxing her to play a duet with him at the piano, where he pulled up a horsehair chair and sat with one arm around her waist while the other ran a brilliant accompaniment on the lower part of the keyboard.

And I thought that no one in the territory, and perhaps no one anywhere but Lutie Brewton herself, could have come in at a moment like this and so disarmed us and held off my uncle until I saw him take again his horsehair armchair, where he sat waiting for the festivities to be over, the eyes in his great intractable face watching Brock with painful and unutterable affection.

At last Sarah Beth went to bed, and my uncle sat looking at the boy.

"I was just starting to town to talk to you, Brock," he began. "Is it true you shot Dutch Charley?"

The boy's face intangibly changed, and he stood there watching my uncle through narrowed eyes.

"I had to shoot him or he'd have shot me."

"Is it true," the older man went on with dogged patience, "that the woman who deals monte for Dutch Charley was favoring you and you knew it?"

"All women like me," Brock said. "Like everybody liked—" His lips closed, but he kept his cool, veiled, almost derisive eyes on my uncle.

The slow color rose in the latter's rude leathery cheeks.

"I don't mind the shooting so much," he said with difficulty. "Boys will fight, and I wouldn't think much of you if you couldn't defend yourself. I told you I'd pay your gambling debts so long as you played fair and square.

But I've always told you that cheating was the lowest form of animal life. Now you've cheated, and no matter what anybody else says, I want you to go through trial on your own feet until you clear yourself or take your punishment."

The boy was staring at him with a sudden curious, impersonal hatred.

"No father," he said defiantly, "would send his boy to prison when the judge got him out of it. Besides, I have a job. That's why I'm out here tonight. I'm going to be a counter jumper for George Holderness and Company."

At the sound of the name of Brice Chamberlain's uncle and all it implied, my uncle sat up and the veins swelled in his throat and hands until even the boy was afraid of him and backed across the room. But his eyes were burning in his white face with a restless and brilliant fever, and when he saw he wasn't going to be touched, he began to pace up and down the room.

"You can't keep me out on a ranch!" he was crying. "I'm eighteen. I wasn't cut out for ranching. I've got to be where there's excitement and people. I've got to be where there's stores and lights and music and things going on. Sooner than stay out here in this Godforsaken place, I'd rather be stuffed in a coffin—"

I did not hear any more. There was something fatalistic in the scene and words, as if I had been here before. My uncle and Jimmy seemed to be gone and I was on the same horsehair sofa seeing Lutie Brewton pacing up and down this very Brussels carpet, her eyes burning with a brilliant fever, her lips speaking almost the identical words.

When I looked at my uncle, his face was white and he was breathing heavily as if he had seen a ghost.

"All right, Brock," he brought out thickly. How much it cost him, I could only guess. "I stood in the way of somebody else years ago and I've always been sorry. I won't stand in yours."

Flashing a look of triumph at the dark silent face of his brother standing there, Brock went quickly out of the room. Long after he had gone my uncle sat in his chair staring out of the window. The window was dark and he could see nothing outside, I knew, but I could see him in the pane and I never realized before how utterly furrowed his face was, like a worn-out field, the face of an old man at last. And the rest of him there on the tufted horsehair chair was the once powerful frame of a man in whom some inward drouth had dried up the last few water-holes of life and power.

Only his eyes were the same, burning black and unspeakably bitter in their charred sockets. After a while he rose unsteadily, paying no attention to Jimmy and me standing helplessly by. Then brushing aside Jimmy's proffered help and planting his boots slowly but relentlessly in front of him, he went on without speaking to his lonely and barren bedroom.

14

There was a huge cottonwood that used to stand off the plaza in one of Salt Fork's crooked Mexican streets. Its bark was rougher than any tree I knew and its branches gnarled. It had seen Navajo and Apache raids and the long ox trains crawling on the Chihuahua trail. But it still stood there green and cool, sheltering a lowly adobe house beneath it and all who passed under its branches or pulled chairs into its broad shade.

Of late the nesters had been tying their bony horses to it, and the horses had chewed off half its bark. The lightning had struck it, and the woman of the house and her young son had tried to cut it down. And when of a morning I crossed the plaza to my office, I found myself glancing to see if the old tree had weathered last night's storm.

Back in my mind, I think, it was really not the tree I looked to see if it were still standing there with its roots in the territory and its head in the sky, but an old man who wasn't there at all, who had also known the Navajo and Apache raids and the long ox trains crawling on the Chihuahua trail and now knew the winds that in my profession usually blow in the night.

One evening just before the fall term of court came around, Dutch Charley died of his gunshot wounds in his rooms over the saloon, and some time during the night, Brock left the dim lights of Salt Fork and an empty money-box of Holderness and Company behind him. I had not seen my uncle since the evening after the shooting. It had not been pleasant to think of him coming to town where everyone would see for himself how deeply he had been stricken. And now it was my conviction that he would not be in Salt Fork, if at all, for a long time to come.

But only a day or two later I met him walking across the plaza, slower, grayer, not much more than a shadow of his old powerful self, yet still painfully erect and implacable in his gray broadcloth tails as I had ever seen him. And the men looked sober when they saw him coming, and said with respect: "Gettin' dry, Colonel," and "Yes-sirree, Colonel," and looked after him thoughtfully when he had passed.

And when the news came that Brock had been seen in El Paso and

called himself Brock Chamberlain now, everybody said it was all over and that you could take one look at Jim Brewton and know he himself admitted it. Certainly I seldom heard him mention Brock's name again. But it wasn't over. Once at Sarah Beth's wedding I thought I saw those burned-out eyes deep in their sockets keep staring dully at the guests as if there were someone missing in that familiar ranch-house parlor, although exactly who was missing I could never be quite sure.

I believe now that every piece of news about Brock my uncle read in the Albuquerque and Denver papers was a secret Apache lance in his heart. His forehead was incommunicable as an old rawhide and branded like one with the mark of the band of his hat. And of what went on behind it he never spoke. All I know was that as months passed and the stories kept coming in about Brock raking eight thousand dollars from a Cripple Creek gambling table and Brock holding up a Mexican sheep herder with three pesos on his person; of Brock a deputy in White Oaks for a day and Brock that night hitching a peddler's cart behind his saddle and shooting up the town; of Brock riding south into Old Mexico ahead of the sheriff, Brock riding west with Cochran's Wild Bunch to hide in the Chiricahuas and Brock riding east alone to bring a jeweled necklace to his Choctaw-blooded nester girl in our next county, he wasn't real to me any more.

He was just a glittering idea, someone I had never seen or known, only a name whose exploits were printed in the Western papers from Omaha to Oregon, talked about over wet bars and dry trails, from horseback to horseback, in the harness-rooms of livery stables and around lonely cow-camp fires.

And when they came to me in my office to drive forty miles into the next county to dress the wounds of a deputy who could not be moved, I sent word to Jimmy to keep it from my uncle, although it was all fantastic and unreal to me. This Brock Chamberlain, wanted for a dozen things over Arizona Territory, now making fools of a county posse nearer home, holding off twenty or thirty men from an abandoned nester's shack until the sheriff had sent for Judge Chamberlain to come and talk the boy into giving up, could not be the Brock whose feathery white hair had blown with my breath in his cradle.

Then suddenly I knew I was mistaken. The morning train had come and gone, and I was refilling the small bottles of my medicine valise and picking up my surgical instruments when a step sounded in the outer office, and when I looked up, Lutie Brewton was standing there. Oh, her veil hung heavy and dark and I could not distinguish a feature beneath it, and she wore clothes I had never seen before, but there was something in the straining high angle of the plumes of her hat that rang in my ears like calomel.

"Hal!" she said to me in the voice I hadn't heard for fifteen years.

Even without eyes or ears I would have known her. She hugged me in that silent integral part of speech of several generations ago which told things the lips neither would nor could. The familiar scent of violets closed around me again like some delicate, faintly purple cloud. And I was back in a world ten thousand times larger than the brain that contained it, still a long-haired ranch boy, Lutie Brewton had never gone away, and my uncle still rode the range in his lusty prime.

She pinned back her veil, not with the eager gesture of youth I remem-

bered, but almost defensively, and I saw that with all her struggled erectness, her face, dead white against the lifted black plumes, had begun to show the first branding marks of her hated arch-enemy, age. As if she knew I had seen, she threw herself into holding me at arm's length, inspecting me with that critical yet flattering air, telling me almost feverishly how proud she was of me as a doctor, that any woman just to see me must throw herself in my care, and that as a physician's ears must be filled with the woes of his patients, she knew I should never ask her the weary question where she had been all these years.

And I found myself gazing at that brilliant, animated face and asking under my breath if it were true that a few minutes ago I had seen any signs of age. But all the time she plied me with questions about Jimmy and Sarah Beth and Sarah Beth's husband, whom she had never seen, I knew it was Brock that had brought her. And it was strange how I could feel him now for the first time in years, one of those three sleepy youngsters around her in their nightgowns in that early, candle-lit room so long ago, peering at their mother sitting there, almost jaunty; suited, hatted, and gloved; hearing that she was going on a journey but would see them all sooner than soon, with a double present for each one who had been a little lady or gentleman.

Out of the window I could see across the street men watching from the gallery of Gaylord's saddlery, and I knew that someone had recognized Lutie Brewton. Then there were quick steps in my outer office, and Myra Netherwood, tall and gray-haired, an excited look on her dignified face, was there.

"Doctor, they tell me—" she began.

"Lutie!" And they were in each other's arms.

Out in the plaza I heard the rattle of my phaeton's wheels from the livery stable.

"You comin', doc?" called the messenger from the next county.

I moved to finish packing my doctor bag.

"I've got to make a little call—on a sick man," I told Lutie with my back turned. "I know you'll want to be with Mrs. Netherwood. I'll come over as soon as I get in."

I tried to put it as if it were only a near-by nester patient, but I knew when I turned, by the same pale branch whipsawing again in the stream of blood at her throat, that her sensitive mind had guessed where I was going. And all the long trail down into the South Prairie country, while the rancher who had ridden all night dozed beside me, I could see in the endless heat waves two unforgettable looks in Lutie Brewton's brilliant dark eyes. One of them was when she had seen on the wall the framed photograph of my uncle, an old man, a great frame without flesh, sitting in his buggy, holding the reins of his pair of sorrels. The other look she had given me when I left. It concerned nothing of this world, only a small boy in a long nightgown and tousled hair white in the candle-light of a world that had vanished like last year's snows.

15

It was Sunday morning when my horses' shoes splashed silently back again in the floury brown dust of Salt Fork streets. The wooden shutters were up on mercantile houses, the doors of business places closed, and that strange Sabbath stillness hung over

everything as if these whitewashed galleries and brown adobe walls had not heard only yesterday the untamed roar of dance hall and six-shooter or seen of an early morning the dregs of the wild night before swinging silently from tree and water-tower.

Even when I turned in my team at Dagget's livery stable, it was Sunday there among the peacefully munching horses in their stalls. But all the while I drew my straight razor above the wooden washstand in my room and while I made my way across the plaza with the Spanish bells from the thick-walled adobe church clanging in my ears, I dreaded meeting Lutie Brewton.

Then I knocked on the Nether-wood door, paneled and grained, with a kind of knob I seldom see any more, and Lutie Brewton opened it herself, slender and rigidly erect as I had ever remembered her. Only the plumed hat looked as if it were bearing down too hard on that fragile head and throat, and the eyes in the white face burned with a high fever.

"Don't tell me anything—yet, Hal!" she said. "Just take me to Mass. Myra can't go. And I don't want to be stared at alone."

My uncle and I seldom went to church. And I would have given a great deal to escape it this morning. I had never been out with Lutie Brewton before when the nearness of other people had not been the stimulus for the most animated conversation to her companion. But today the only emotion at their approach was the tightening of her arm in mine as it had that day so long ago when together we had passed the murdered teamster lying in the straw of his wagon with a bandanna over his face.

Once we were sitting in the dim church, with the candles mystically winking and the dull red of the sanctuary light glowing in the dark cave of the altar, it was as if she no longer knew I was there. The click of her beads was strangely like the click of six-shooters, and the sibilants of her lips like those of the wind draw-ing through rusty barbed wire and yerba de vibora. The whitewashed walls of the church kept passing away like mist, and instead of the altar, there in front of me was the barren South Prairie as I had driven through it the last several days, naked in the pitiless Southwestern sunlight, with discouraged nester families watching my phaeton from the doors of occu-pied dugouts and the doors of the empty houses half-fallen from their hinges. I saw plows rusting and gaunt horses standing motionless where there had once been grass. And the sand still drifted along the crazy pattern of abandoned fence-posts.

And at the end of the journey wounded men stupefied with whisky lay half-undressed under a leafless, sapless apple tree. A fresh mound of earth dried and cracked in the sun like a giant adobe brick. And I knew that around a rough circle of sand hills, hidden men with rifles watched the cañada where a deserted nester's shack stared sullenly from its empty windows.

Chamberlain had not yet arrived, and we had no idea then that he never expected to come, that even at this hour he was boarding a train for Santa Fe on some unnamed judicial business. And after the sun went down and a horse's hoofs sounded on the trail, we thought it was the judge or news of the judge at last, even when the sound told us there was no buggy. Then as it drew closer through the Western twilight that tonight hung almost red over the land, there was something familiar about the rider hunched on the saddle of a

weary, raw-boned roan with lathered shoulders.

"It's the old Colonel," someone muttered after a little.

The men stared at each other and back at the apparition. And now I could make out clearly enough the unmistakable figure of my uncle on his favorite, silver-horned saddle, a weary old man in a gray broadcloth coat too large for his shrunken girth and shoulders, unarmed, his coattails spreading behind the cantle, his trousers tucked into boots brown with dust. Who had told him about Brock I had no idea, but he had ridden a direct line across the country from the Cross B, over malpais and timbered ridges where no buggy trail ran. His roan was caked with mud far above the knees where he had plainly forded the treacherous Puerco, and the Navajo blanket protruding from the saddle was dark with sweat.

He halted beside us presently, his great head with its long gray mustaches forward on the soiled linen of his chest. His burned-out eyes seemed to peer at us from far back in his head where life had taken a final stand. And if there was a sign of recognition for any of us, I didn't see it, and for all the attention he showed me, I might have been a stranger instead of Brewton flesh and blood.

"Where's Brock?" was all he asked. The men stirred uncomfortably. One of them indicated the cañada. For several moments the old eyes peered at the deserted squalid shack, a symbol of all that he hated and that had brought him tragedy and pain. Then the gray wrinkled knees nudged his mount; his old fingers, no more than bone, veins, and skin, twitched the reins, and the tired roan started.

The sheriff caught the bridle.

"You can't go down there," he said. "Not till Judge Chamberlain comes."

For a little it seemed that my uncle didn't understand him, as if it took a long time for that name to penetrate some inner room of his being where the embers of life still glowed. Then he raised his shaggy head in a semblance of that old untamed gesture of a mossy-horned lead steer smelling water or water. I had never seen him lift it so slowly, but when the face came up, I saw with a feeling for which there are no words that somewhere in that old Indian-fighter frame still remained the breeding-place of the whirlwind and thunderbolt. Already the hate had begun to pour from his pitch-black eyes, and his face was written again with all those unforgettable black lines of insolent, almost dissolute, will and ruthlessness.

A dozen sheriffs could not have held him now, or said anything as we watched him, rigidly erect in the saddle, his right arm held stiffly down against his side with his thumb at the cantle edge as was his custom from army days, ride down alone into the cañada where a low deadly voice we could barely hear hailed him from the nester's shack, warning him he would never give himself up alive for trial, that the old man wasn't his father anyway, and that if he came any closer, he would drop both horse and rider in the trail.

No answer came from my uncle, and the only change in that lone, riding figure was that he seemed to tower in his stirrups so that two hundred yards away, with his back turned, I felt that time had leaped back twenty years, that the clumps of rattlesnake weed melting into each other on the horizon were solid green range, and I might almost see a wave of antelope, rusty as with kelp, rising

and falling over my uncle's sea of grass.

He had been in the shack only a few minutes when he was outside ordering me in his old-time thunder to come. When I got there, an unshaven man sat propped up against the wall with rifle and pistol on the floor beside him, mocking and grimacing at me, his yellow hair curling like a child's. And all the time my hand wanted to shake as I tried in the dim light from the doorway to stop the bleeding from a wound in his lung, and while my uncle stood there with tortured stolidity, Brock lay on the dirty floor, paying no attention to my command to be quiet, jibing and mimicking me, calling me a horse doctor, begging tobacco and smoking cigarettes, bantering about Jimmy and Tom Milledeaux and coaxing me to say nice things about him to Sarah Beth, so that no one, not even the sheriff, standing silent and listening some feet beyond the door, could help being won over to him now.

And in the firelight that evening, when he couldn't talk any more and there was no sound but the yapping of the coyotes, I thought I saw his sardonic blue eyes pointing to something behind me. The shack had been systematically riddled with lead by the posse until it was almost a sieve. Only one conspicuous place on the four walls remained untouched by bullets, and I found now that he was derisively drawing my attention to what hung pasted by unknown hands to the center of this spot, a faded, Christmas newspaper print of Christ in the manger, with the well-known words: "Peace on Earth, Good Will toward Men."

The ringing of a bell somewhere and the rising and dipping of the congregation brought the whitewashed walls of the church back again with

Lutie Brewton beside me. And when I looked about I was aware now that most of the people around us must have already heard of what had happened on the South Prairie. Their stares at Lutie Brewton carried a questioning as if they were not so sure but that yesterday they had wronged her. Her sensitive mind seemed to feel and respond to their new respect, and when the services were over, I thought she seemed to be again that clear pure flame burning from something far more precious than tallow.

When she went out she lifted her veil and smiled gently to the little Mexican girls admiring her as they kept dipping their knees at aisle and door, and spoke, as she had in the old days, to a sightless, black-shawled Mexican, now an old woman known as La Ciega. The latter, I am sure, had never understood one of Lutie Brewton's sparkling English sentences, although a look had always come into her blind, wrinkled face as if she had talked to someone who had seen the Blessed Virgin.

But today at the sound of that charming, unmistakable voice she had not heard for fifteen years, La Ciega let go of her rebozo and reached out to the speaker, and her hands were tight lumps of brown copper against Lutie Brewton's white slender ones. "Ay de mi, señora!" she began, and poured out a stream of Spanish from one woman to another.

Lutie stood there delicately responsive and sympathetic, glancing questioningly to me. But when, without translating any of it, I tried to urge her quietly on, she turned attentively to a Mexican youth who rolled barrels and pulled square nails in John Kingman's warehouse.

"What does the blind woman say?"

"She say," the boy said, arching his back with pride to be speaking to

Mrs. Brewton in front of everybody, "She say she have a boy too who is kill by a bullet. She said thank to God her boy and your boy don't suffer any more."

"Yes," Lutie Brewton said, drawing in her breath. "Yes, thank her for me."

She was erect again and very white as she took my arm and went in, steadily glooming the multicolored stream of churchgoers still flowing and eddying out of the ancient thick-walled church.

"Now I am ready to go to the ranch, Hal," she said. "Will you have someone from Dagget's livery drive me?"

"I wouldn't go until the funeral, Lutie?" I begged her in a low voice. The plumes of her hat were suddenly and rigidly higher.

"May I go right away this morning, Hal, please!" she asked, and I found that her clearly modulated voice impelled me toward the livery stable as effectively as twenty years ago it had turned rough men about and whipped off their hats until the aisle had opened for us into the crowded Salt Fork county courthouse.

A hundred times since she had gone away I had pictured Lutie Brewton coming back to the Cross B. And in my thoughts I was always there, feeling that extraordinary, quickening emotion just the sight of her had always called up in me. But today the old ranch house was the last place on earth I wanted to go with Lutie Brewton. And all the way to the livery stable I could see my uncle's eyes; flaming, terrible eyes as I had seen them in the South Prairie country only yesterday.

Frank Dagget gave me a queer look when I asked him for a pair of fresh horses in my phaeton to drive to the Cross B. And I knew he had guessed

who was going with me, for he lifted his best black harness from the long pins, laid it on the back of his fastest team, and said that the boxing of one of the wheels of my old dusty phaeton was loose and he would give me today the fine green-seated buggy he had only last week unloaded from the railroad. And before he let me go, he combed again the manes and tails of his team and flecked the fine particles of dust from shiny black spokes, leather dash and whipstock.

"Is she well?" he asked, not looking at me.

"I think so," I said.

"It takes spunk to go to the old Colonel now," he said as I climbed into the buggy. "But then she always had it."

There are days in our Southwestern country that people call brassy but should be called steel. The sun beats down with a merciless white fire until the cloudless sky is scarcely blue but rather like the blade of a knife that for days has been ground to the stone. And all day it cuts open the breathing body of the prairie and lays its bones dead and bare in the pitiless glare before you.

It was such a morning I drove out of the wide front doors of the livery, and I felt for Lutie Brewton and how she would flinch. But I had no need to. Although Myra Netherwood in a silk wrapper gave me an anguished glance, Lutie Brewton came out of her room delicate and fragile but up and never to be turned back now, showing me the valises to carry to the buggy as if she had been away from the ranch no more than to come to town and would find everything on her return as she had left it a few days before. She gave little sign that the townspeople watched her as we drove away, and once we had reached the prairie, she kept her face turned

from all the nester sores and scars, talking in a low incessant voice, as if she could not halt if she wished. But although I listened for any touch here or there that would reveal the pattern of her hidden years, I knew no more afterwards than before which of the stories of those who said they had seen her was the true one.

Only at dusk when, after pushing the team, we saw the ranch buildings and trees swimming ahead of us like an oasis in a purple desert, was she silent. And she didn't speak again until we had driven through the wall of cottonwoods and tamarisks she herself had had planted and had stopped by the dark familiar walls of the ranch house, dimly lighted by a lantern slung from a hook on the wide front gallery.

I learned that my uncle had not yet returned from the South Prairie, from where he was expected an hour or two ahead of the wagon. But under the candles that Lutie Brewton went about lighting, the whole house was grimly eloquent with his presence; his implacable, sweated gun belt hanging from its accustomed corner of the pine settee in the hall; his wrinkled, unyielding boots standing along the wall in the big front bedroom where Lutie directed me to set down her valises; the inflexible shape of his pipes lying about; and the fierce spartan barrenness of everything.

I wished to God that Jimmy might come in from somewhere in the cedar country, where, they told me, they had sent a rider with the news. As the evening went on, there was no sign of him. But after an hour the older headquarters hands who had known Mrs. Brewton moved in a body from the bunkhouse to greet her and pay their respects, lining up on the front gallery and pushing the foreman first, all grave and embarrassed, ceremoniously shaven and in clean shirts, holding their hats in their hands, scraping the high heels of their boots, feeling tremendously sorry for her about Brock and all that had happened before and all that might happen when the old Colonel came home, but the farthermost notion from their minds that of expressing a word of it.

Soberly each one spoke as he shook hands.

"Nice day, Miz Brewton."

"You have a nice trip from town, Miz Brewton?"

"Find the road pretty fair, Miz Brewton?"

And after that they said little enough, just stood around respectfully until such a time should elapse that it would be fitting for them to go. What few remarks they managed to make they chose with extreme care, avoiding anything that might assume that Brock had ever lived or died or that she had gone away. And all the while Lutie Brewton, her face very pale against her dark hair, tried to make them less uncomfortable, cross-stitching and embroidering their simplest subjects, picking up in her white fingers the most ordinary sentiment spoken with sawdust and awkwardness, and breathing upon it till it grew golden and exciting and important so that the others looked with surprise at the original speaker for having uttered it.

And when the time they waited for had elapsed, it was as hard for them to go as it had been to come. Once or twice I thought a cowhand near the door lifted his head to listen. Then even without ears I would have known by the way they stiffened and their features flattened into leather that a step had sounded on the front gallery. And when I looked up, my uncle was towering in the doorway, a picture struck violently on my brain

so that today he still seems to be standing there, an untamed shape in the shadows, charged with turbulent will and power, his deep eyes burning with orange flames at what they glimpsed in the wide hallway.

When I glanced back, the cowhands were solemnly taking their leave, mumbling: "Good night, Miz Brewton," going as they came, in single shuffling file, until at last Lutie Brewton stood there alone, a slight, almost frail, feminine figure, rooted against the approaching storm.

My uncle came forward slowly, still a kind of rude king in his tailed gray broadcloth, and when he was under the lights I could see that the forked veins stood out in his neck as he bowed over her hand, asking with unfailing courtesy about her health. But his furrowed face was a mask and his voice granite, and I knew that while all the others in Salt Fork county might tactfully shy from the subject where she had been all these years and what she had been doing, my uncle now would not for a moment avoid it.

And I think Lutie Brewton knew it, too, and resolved in her mind that she would never be cross-examined and compelled to explain as if she were a child, and it only made her eyes more brilliant and tilted back her fragile head piled with its black hair at a gallant, almost defiant angle, while she threw herself not into her old gayety but a grave and desperate incoherence, asking about his welfare, and where was Jimmy, and telling him that Myra had shown her Jimmy's and Sarah Beth's photographs, and mustn't he be terribly tired from his long ride, and couldn't she get something for him to eat and drink? And when my uncle's eyes grew darker with dammed-back questions, she spoke the faster, and her face became very thin and intense ivory, faintly streaked and stained as if by the blood of the creature that had borne it.

Until at last I couldn't bear it any longer and, while my uncle's eyes flared at me, I leaped to my feet and begged her to make us some coffee or rouse the cook to build a fire. Certainly I expected her to seize the chance to leave the room, but she only stood there with her face higher and cut finer, and an indecipherable look in her feverish eyes, till I was the one who escaped, bolting to the bunkhouse, where I found the hands up far beyond their bedtime, smoking, talking in low tones, waiting for the wagon.

When an hour or two later I went stiffly back across the front gallery, some chemical change had taken place in those ancient walls. The air of the massive old ranch house hung with the elusive scent of violets high on the peaceful fumes of cigar smoke. In the wide hall the brightly colored Navajo rugs had been laid again over the pine settees. A great white cloth hung low from the heavy dining-table set with four places for tomorrow's breakfast. And the parlor I could see was swept and dusted in readiness for the coming visitor who had not been home for many a day. There were fresh doilies on the marble-top tables and clean tidies on the chair backs. The piano still stood closed, but the tall ornamental brass floor-lamp had been lighted, and the blue, entwined flowers bloomed again on the hand-painted china shade.

Then my uncle, who had been sitting quietly on a horsehair armchair, raised his head in that undying gesture of a wild stallion, his half-smoked cigar held suddenly motionless in his hand. Through the door to the front bedroom I saw Lutie Brewton

stand perfectly still while she clutched folded clean sheets in her bare white arms. After a moment, far away on the lonely trail under the Southwestern stars I could hear the tolling rumble of the approaching wagon.

There is little more to tell except that the last time I was back the stone my uncle raised was still standing near the broken walls of the old ranch house.

"Brock Brewton, son of James B. and Lutie C. Brewton," it is carved in unequivocal letters that all who ride may read.

I remember very well the first time I saw it. In Salt Fork, people were still divided about Brock and where Mrs. Brewton had been. I was aware that Lutie Brewton herself would never reveal the truth to any of them, perhaps never to me. This particular day she and Sarah Beth, who was home for a month, had driven in the Colonel's pole buggy to the Bar 44. My uncle was sitting on the ranchhouse gallery from where he could see the stone. And from what he said to me while his eyes rested on it, his motives were clear to me at last as a + B brand.

"Have you noticed how young she still looks, Hal?" he asked, filling his chair again with that iron dignity and pride I remembered as a boy. "It was a hard thing for a lady to go through. But she's one in a thousand, Hal. No one else will ever be like her." And his deeply lined face warmed like the late afternoon sun touching and mellowing the rugged western slope of a shaggy old mountain.

THE SIRE DE MALÉTROIT'S DOOR

ROBERT LOUIS STEVENSON

Denis de Beaulieu was not yet two-and-twenty, but he counted himself a grown man, and a very accomplished cavalier into the bargain. Lads were early formed in that rough, warfaring epoch; and when one has been in a pitched battle and a dozen raids, has killed one's man in an honourable fashion, and knows a thing or two of strategy and mankind, a certain swagger in the gait is surely to be pardoned. He had put up his horse with due care, and supped with due deliberation; and then, in a very agreeable frame of mind, went out to pay a visit in the grey of the evening. It was not a very wise proceeding on the young man's part. He would have done better to remain beside the fire or go decently to bed. For the town was full of the troops of Burgundy and England under a mixed command; and though Denis was there on safe-conduct, his safe-conduct was like to serve him little on a chance encounter.

It was September, 1429; the weather had fallen sharp; a flighty piping wind, laden with showers, beat about the township; and the dead leaves ran riot along the streets. Here and there a window was already lighted up; and the noise of men-at-arms making merry over supper within, came forth in fits and was swallowed up and carried away by the wind. The night fell swiftly; the flag of England, fluttering on the spire-top, grew ever fainter and fainter against the flying clouds—a black speck like a swallow in the tumultuous, leaden chaos of the sky. As the night fell the wind rose, and began to hoot under archways and roar amid the tree-tops in the valley below the town.

Denis de Beaulieu walked fast and was soon knocking at his friend's door; but though he promised himself to stay only a little while and make an early return, his welcome was so pleasant, and he found so much to delay him, that it was already long past midnight before he said good-bye upon the threshold. The wind had fallen again in the meanwhile; the night was as black as the grave; not a star, nor a glimmer of moonshine, slipped through the canopy of cloud. Denis was ill-acquainted with the intricate lanes of Chateau Landon; even by daylight he had found some trouble in picking his way; and in this absolute darkness he soon lost it altogether. He was certain of one thing only—to keep mounting the hill; for his friend's house lay at the lower end, or tail, of Chateau Landon, while the inn was up at the head, under the great church spire. With this clue to go upon he stumbled and groped forward, now breathing more

freely in open places where there was a good slice of sky overhead, now feeling along the wall in stifling closeness. It is an eerie and mysterious position to be thus submerged in opaque blackness in an almost unknown town. The silence is terrifying in its possibilities. The touch of cold window bars to the exploring hand startles the man like the touch of a toad; the inequalities of the pavement shake his heart into his mouth; a piece of denser darkness threatens an ambuscade or a chasm in the pathway; and where the air is brighter, the houses put on strange and bewildering appearances, as if to lead him farther from his way. For Denis, who had to regain his inn without attracting notice, there was real danger as well as mere discomfort in the walk; and he went warily and boldly at once, and at every corner paused to make an observation.

He had been for some time threading a lane so narrow that he could touch a wall with either hand, when it began to open out and go sharply downward. Plainly this lay no longer in the direction of his inn; but the hope of a little more light tempted him forward to reconnoitre. The lane ended in a terrace with a bartizan wall, which gave an outlook between high houses, as out of an embrasure, into the valley lying dark and formless several hundred feet below. Denis looked down, and could discern a few tree-tops waving and a single speck of brightness where the river ran across a weir. The weather was clearing up, and the sky had lightened, so as to show the outline of the heavier clouds and the dark margin of the hills. By the uncertain glimmer, the house on his left hand should be a place of some pretensions; it was surmounted by several pinnacles and turret-tops; the round stern of a chapel, with a fringe of flying buttresses, projected boldly from the main block; and the door was sheltered under a deep porch carved with figures and overhung by two long gargoyles. The windows of the chapel gleamed through their intricate tracery with a light as of many tapers, and threw out the buttresses and the peaked roof in a more intense blackness against the sky. It was plainly the hotel of some great family of the neighbourhood; and as it reminded Denis of a town house of his own at Bourges, he stood for some time gazing up at it and mentally gauging the skill of the architects and the consideration of the two families.

There seemed to be no issue to the terrace but the lane by which he had reached it; he could only retrace his steps, but he had gained some notion of his whereabouts, and hoped by this means to hit the main thoroughfare and speedily regain the inn. He was reckoning without that chapter of accidents which was to make this night memorable above all others in his career; for he had not gone back above a hundred yards before he saw a light coming to meet him, and heard loud voices speaking together in the echoing narrows of the lane. It was a party of men-at-arms going the night round with torches. Denis assured himself that they had all been making free with the wine-bowl, and were in no mood to be particular about safe-conducts or the niceties of chivalrous war. It was as like as not that they would kill him like a dog and leave him where he fell. The situation was inspiriting but nervous. Their own torches would conceal him from sight, he reflected; and he hoped that they would drown the noise of his footsteps with their own empty voices. If he were but fleet and silent, he might evade their notice altogether.

Unfortunately, as he turned to beat

a retreat, his foot rolled upon a pebble; he fell against the wall with an ejaculation, and his sword rang loudly on the stones. Two or three voices demanded who went there—some in French, some in English; but Denis made no reply, and ran the faster down the lane. Once upon the terrace, he paused to look back. They still kept calling after him, and just then began to double the pace in pursuit, with a considerable clank of armour, and great tossing of the torch-light to and fro in the narrow jaws of the passage.

Denis cast a look around and darted into the porch. There he might escape observation, or—if that were too much to expect—was in a capital posture whether for parley or defence. So thinking, he drew his sword and tried to set his back against the door. To his surprise, it yielded behind his weight; and though he turned in a moment, continued to swing back on oiled and noiseless hinges, until it stood wide open on a black interior. When things fall out opportunely for the person concerned, he is not apt to be critical about the how or why, his own immediate personal convenience seeming a sufficient reason for the strangest oddities and revolutions in our sublunary things; and so Denis, without a moment's hesitation, stepped within and partly closed the door behind him to conceal his place of refuge. Nothing was further from his thoughts than to close it altogether; but for some inexplicable reason—perhaps by a spring or a weight—the ponderous mass of oak whipped itself out of his fingers and clanked to, with a formidable rumble and a noise like the falling of an automatic bar.

The round, at that very moment, debouched upon the terrace and proceeded to summon him with shouts and curses. He heard them ferreting in the dark corners; the stock of a lance even rattled along the outer surface of the door behind which he stood; but these gentlemen were in too high a humour to be long delayed, and soon made off down a corkscrew pathway which had escaped Denis' observation, and passed out of sight and hearing along the battlements of the town.

Denis breathed again. He gave them a few minutes' grace for fear of accidents, and then groped about for some means of opening the door and slipping forth again. The inner surface was quite smooth, not a handle, not a moulding, not a projection of any sort. He got his finger-nails round the edges and pulled, but the mass was immovable. He shook it, it was as firm as a rock. Denis de Beaulieu frowned and gave vent to a little noiseless whistle. What ailed the door? he wondered. Why was it open? How came it to shut so easily and so effectually after him? There was something obscure and underhand about all this, that was little to the young man's fancy. It looked like a snare; and yet who could suppose a snare in such a quiet by-street and in a house of so prosperous and even noble an exterior? And yet—snare or no snare, intentionally or unintentionally—here he was, prettily trapped; and for the life of him he could see no way out of it again. The darkness began to weigh upon him. He gave ear; all was silent without, but within and close by he seemed to catch a faint sighing, a faint sobbing rustle, a little stealthy creak—as though many persons were at his side, holding themselves quite still, and governing even their respiration with the extreme of slyness. The idea went to his vitals with a shock, and he faced about suddenly as if to defend his life. Then, for the first time, he became aware of

a light about the level of his eyes and at some distance in the interior of the house—a vertical thread of light, widening towards the bottom, such as might escape between two wings of arras over a doorway. To see anything was a relief to Denis; it was like a piece of solid ground to a man labouring in a morass; his mind seized upon it with avidity; and he stood staring at it and trying to piece together some logical conception of his surroundings. Plainly there was a flight of steps ascending from his own level to that of the illuminated doorway; and indeed he thought he could make out another thread of light, as fine as a needle and as faint as phosphorescence, which might very well be reflected along the polished wood of a handrail. Since he had begun to suspect that he was not alone, his heart had continued to beat with smothering violence, and an intolerable desire for action of any sort had possessed itself of his spirit. He was in deadly peril, he believed. What could be more natural than to mount the staircase, lift the curtain, and confront his difficulty at once? At least he would be dealing with something tangible; at least he would be no longer in the dark. He stepped slowly forward with outstretched hands, until his foot struck the bottom step; then he rapidly scaled the stairs, stood for a moment to compose his expression, lifted the arras and went in.

He found himself in a large apartment of polished stone. There were three doors; one on each of three sides; all similarly curtained with tapestry. The fourth side was occupied by two large windows and a great stone chimney-piece, carved with the arms of the Malétroits. Denis recognized the bearings, and was gratified to find himself in such good hands. The room was strongly illuminated;

but it contained little furniture except a heavy table and a chair or two, the hearth was innocent of fire, and the pavement was but sparsely strewn with rushes clearly many days old.

On a high chair beside the chimney, and directly facing Denis as he entered, sat a little old gentleman in a fur tippet. He sat with his legs crossed and his hands folded, and a cup of spiced wine stood by his elbow on a bracket on the wall. His countenance had a strongly masculine cast; not properly human, but such as we see in the bull, the goat, or the domestic boar, something equivocal and wheedling, something greedy, brutal, and dangerous. The upper lip was inordinately full, as though swollen by a blow or a toothache; and the smile, the peaked eyebrows, and the small, strong eyes were quaintly and almost comically evil in expression. Beautiful white hair hung straight all round his head, like a saint's, and fell in a single curl upon the tippet. His beard and moustache were the pink of venerable sweetness. Age, probably in consequence of inordinate precautions, had left no mark upon his hands; and the Malétroit hand was famous. It would be difficult to imagine anything at once so fleshy and so delicate in design; the tapered, sensual fingers were like those of one of Leonardo's women; the fork of the thumb made a dimpled protuberance when closed; the nails were perfectly shaped, and of a dead, surprising whiteness. It rendered his aspect tenfold more redoubtable, that a man with hands like these should keep them devoutly folded in his lap like a virgin martyr—that a man with so intense and startling an expression of face should sit patiently on his seat and contemplate people with an unwinking stare, like a god, or a god's statue. His quiescence seemed

ironical and treacherous, it fitted so poorly with his looks.

Such was Alain, Sire de Malétroit. Denis and he looked silently at each other for a second or two.

"Pray step in," said the Sire de Malétroit. "I have been expecting you all the evening."

He had not risen, but he accompanied his words with a smile and a slight but continuous inclination of the head. Partly from the smile, partly from the strange musical murmur with which the Sire prefaced his observation, Denis felt a strong shudder of disgust go through his marrow. And what with disgust and honest confusion of mind, he could scarcely get words together in reply.

"I fear," he said, "that this is a double accident. I am not the person you suppose me. It seems you were looking for a visit; but for my part, nothing was further from my thoughts —nothing could be more contrary to my wishes—than this intrusion."

"Well, well," replied the old gentleman indulgently, "here you are, which is the main point. Seat yourself, my friend, and put yourself entirely at your ease. We shall arrange our little affairs presently."

Denis perceived that the matter was still complicated with some misconception, and he hastened to continue his explanation.

"Your door . . ." he began.

"About my door?" asked the other, raising his peaked eyebrows. "A little piece of ingenuity." And he shrugged his shoulders. "A hospitable fancy! By your own account, you were not desirous of making my acquaintance. We old people look for such reluctance now and then; and when it touches our honours, we cast about until we find some way of overcoming it. You arrive uninvited, but believe me, very welcome."

"You persist in error, sir," said Denis. "There can be no question between you and me. I am a stranger in this countryside. My name is Denis, damoiseau de Beaulieu. If you see me in your house, it is only—"

"My found friend," interrupted the other, "you will permit me to have my own ideas on that subject. They probably differ from yours at the present moment," he added with a leer, "but time will show which of us is in the right."

Denis was convinced he had to do with a lunatic. He seated himself with a shrug, content to wait the upshot; and a pause ensued, during which he thought he could distinguish a hurried gabbling as of prayer from behind the arras immediately opposite him. Sometimes there seemed to be but one person engaged, sometimes two; and the vehemence of the voice, low as it was, seemed to indicate either great haste or an agony of spirit. It occurred to him that this piece of tapestry covered the entrance to the chapel he had noticed from without.

The old gentleman meanwhile surveyed Denis from head to foot with a smile, and from time to time emitted little noises like a bird or a mouse, which seemed to indicate a high degree of satisfaction. This state of matters became rapidly insupportable; and Denis, to put an end to it, remarked politely that the wind had gone down.

The old gentleman fell into a fit of silent laughter, so prolonged and violent that he became quite red in the face. Denis got upon his feet at once, and put on his hat with a flourish.

"Sir," he said, "if you are in your wits, you have affronted me grossly. If you are out of them, I flatter myself I can find better employment for my brains than to talk with lunatics.

My conscience is clear; you have made a fool of me from the first moment; you have refused to hear my explanations; and now there is no power under God will make me stay here any longer; and if I cannot make my way out in a more decent fashion, I will hack your door in pieces with my sword."

The Sire de Malétroit raised his right hand and wagged it at Denis with the fore and little fingers extended.

"My dear nephew," he said, "sit down."

"Nephew!" retorted Denis, "you lie in your throat"; and he snapped his fingers in his face.

"Sit down, you rogue!" cried the old gentleman, in a sudden, harsh voice, like the barking of a dog. "Do you fancy," he went on, "that when I had made my little contrivance for the door I had stopped short with that? If you prefer to be bound hand and foot till your bones ache, rise and try to go away. If you choose to remain a free young buck, agreeably conversing with an old gentleman—why, sit where you are in peace, and God be with you."

"Do you mean I am a prisoner?" demanded Denis.

"I state the facts," replied the other. "I would rather leave the conclusion to yourself."

Denis sat down again. Externally he managed to keep pretty calm; but within, he was now boiling with anger, now chilled with apprehension. He no longer felt convinced that he was dealing with a madman. And if the old gentleman was sane, what, in God's name, had he to look for? What absurd or tragical adventure had befallen him? What countenance was he to assume?

While he was thus unpleasantly reflecting, the arras that overhung the chapel door was raised, and a tall priest in his robes came forth and, giving a long, keen stare at Denis, said something in an undertone to Sire de Malétroit.

"She is in a better frame of spirit?" asked the latter.

"She is more resigned, messire," replied the priest.

"Now the Lord help her, she is hard to please!" sneered the old gentleman. "A likely stripling—not ill-born—and of her own choosing, too? Why, what more would the jade have?"

"The situation is not usual for a young damsel," said the other, "and somewhat trying to her blushes."

"She should have thought of that before she began the dance. It was none of my choosing, God knows that: but since she is in it, by our Lady, she shall carry it to the end." And then addressing Denis, "Monsieur de Beaulieu," he asked, "may I present you to my niece? She has been waiting your arrival, I may say, with even greater impatience than myself."

Denis had resigned himself with a good grace—all he desired was to know the worst of it as speedily as possible; so he rose at once, and bowed in acquiescence. The Sire de Malétroit followed his example and limped, with the assistance of the chaplain's arm, towards the chapel door. The priest pulled aside the arras, and all three entered. The building had considerable architectural pretensions. A light groining sprang from six stout columns, and hung down in two rich pendants from the centre of the vault. The place terminated behind the altar in a round end, embossed and honeycombed with a superfluity of ornament in relief, and pierced by many little windows shaped like stars, trefoils, or wheels. These windows were imperfectly glazed, so that the night air circulated freely in the chapel. The

tapers, of which there must have been half a hundred burning on the altar, were unmercifully blown about; and the light went through many different phases of brilliancy and semi-eclipse. On the steps in front of the altar knelt a young girl richly attired as a bride. A chill settled over Denis as he observed her costume; he fought with desperate energy against the conclusion that was being thrust upon his mind; it could not—it should not—be as he feared.

"Blanche," said the Sire, in his most flute-like tones, "I have brought a friend to see you, my little girl; turn around and give him your pretty hand. It is good to be devout; but it is necessary to be polite, my niece."

The girl rose to her feet and turned towards the new comer. She moved all of a piece; and shame and exhaustion were expressed in every line of her fresh young body; and she held her head down and kept her eyes upon the pavement, as she came slowly forward. In the course of her advance, her eyes fell upon Denis de Beaulieu's feet—feet of which he was justly vain, be it remarked, and wore in the most elegant accoutrement even while traveling. She paused—started, as if his yellow boots had conveyed some shocking meaning—and glanced suddenly up into the wearer's countenance. Their eyes met; shame gave place to horror and terror in her looks; the blood left her lips; with a piercing scream she covered her face with her hands and sank upon the chapel floor.

"That is not the man!" she cried. "My uncle, that is not the man!"

The Sire de Malétroit chirped agreeably. "Of course not," he said; "I expected as much. It was so unfortunate you could not remember his name."

"Indeed," she cried, "indeed, I have never seen this person till this moment —I have never so much as set eyes upon him—I never wish to see him again. Sir," she said, turning to Denis, "if you are a gentleman, you will bear me out. Have I ever seen you—have you ever seen me—before this accursed hour?"

"To speak for myself, I have never had that pleasure," answered the young man. "This is the first time, messire, that I have met with your engaging niece."

The old gentleman shrugged his shoulders.

"I am distressed to hear it," he said. "But it is never too late to begin. I had little more acquaintance with my own late lady ere I married her; which proves," he added with a grimace, "that these impromptu marriages may often produce an excellent understanding in the long-run. As the bridegroom is to have a voice in the matter, I will give him two hours to make up for lost time before we proceed with the ceremony." And he turned towards the door, followed by the clergyman.

The girl was on her feet in a moment. "My uncle, you cannot be in earnest," she said. "I declare before God I will stab myself rather than be forced on that young man. The heart rises at it; God forbids such marriages; you dishonour your white hair. Oh, my uncle, pity me! There is not a woman in all the world but would prefer death to such a nuptial. Is it possible," she added, faltering—"is it possible that you do not believe me— that you still think this"—and she pointed at Denis with a tremor of anger and contempt—"that you still think *this* to be the man?"

"Frankly," said the old gentleman, pausing on the threshold, "I do. But let me explain to you once for all, Blanche de Malétroit, my way of

thinking about this affair. When you took it into your head to dishonour my family and the name that I have borne, in peace and war, for more than three-score years, you forfeited, not only the right to question my designs, but that of looking me in the face. If your father had been alive, he would have spat on you and turned you out of doors. His was the hand of iron. You may bless your God you have only to deal with the hand of velvet, mademoiselle. It was my duty to get you married without delay. Out of pure goodwill, I have tried to find your own gallant for you. And I believe I have succeeded. But before God and all the holy angels, Blanche de Malétroit, if I have not, I care not one jack-straw. So let me recommend you to be polite to our young friend; for upon my word, your next groom may be less appetising."

And with that he went out, with the chaplain at his heels; and the arras fell behind the pair.

The girl turned upon Denis with flashing eyes.

"And what, sir," she demanded, "may be the meaning of all this?"

"God knows," returned Denis gloomily. "I am a prisoner in this house, which seems full of mad people. More I know not; and nothing do I understand."

"And pray how came you here?" she asked.

He told her as briefly as he could. "For the rest," he added, "perhaps you will follow my example, and tell me the answer to all these riddles, and what, in God's name, is like to be the end of it."

She stood silent for a little, and he could see her lips tremble and her tearless eyes burn with a feverish lustre. Then she pressed her forehead in both hands.

"Alas, how my head aches!" she said

wearily—"to say nothing of my poor heart! But it is due to you to know my story, unmaidenly as it must seem. I am called Blanche de Malétroit; I have been without father or mother for—oh! for as long as I can recollect, and indeed I have been most unhappy all my life. Three months ago a young captain began to stand near me every day in church. I could see that I pleased him; I am much to blame, but I was so glad that any one should love me; and when he passed me a letter, I took it home with me and read it with great pleasure. Since that time he has written many. He was so anxious to speak with me, poor fellow! and kept asking me to leave the door open some evening that we might have two words upon the stair. For he knew how much my uncle trusted me." She gave something like a sob at that, and it was a moment before she could go on. "My uncle is a hard man, but he is very shrewd," she said at last. "He has performed many feats in war, and was a great person at court, and much trusted by Queen Isabeau in old days. How he came to suspect me I cannot tell; but it is hard to keep anything from his knowledge; and this morning, as we came from mass, he took my hand in his, forced it open, and read my little billet, walking by my side all the while. When he had finished, he gave it back to me with great politeness. It contained another request to have the door left open; and this has been the ruin of us all. My uncle kept me strictly in my room until evening, and then ordered me to dress myself as you see me—a hard mockery for a young girl, do you not think so? I suppose, when he could not prevail with me to tell him the young captain's name, he must have laid a trap for him: into which, alas! you have fallen in the anger of God. I looked for much confusion; for how

could I tell whether he was willing to take me for his wife on these sharp terms? He might have been trifling with me from the first; or I might have made myself too cheap in his eyes. But truly I had not looked for such a shameful punishment as this? I could not think that God would let a girl be so disgraced before a young man. And now I have told you all; and I can scarcely hope that you will not despise me."

Denis made her a respectful inclination.

"Madam," he said, "you have honoured me by your confidence. It remains for me to prove that I am not unworthy of the honour. Is Messire de Malétroit at hand?"

"I believe he is writing in the salle without," she answered.

"May I lead you thither, madam?" asked Denis, offering his hand with his most courtly bearing.

She accepted it; and the pair passed out of the chapel, Blanche in a very drooping and shamefaced condition, but Denis strutting and ruffling in the consciousness of a mission, and the boyish certainty of accomplishing it with honour.

The Sire de Malétroit rose to meet them with an ironical obeisance.

"Sir," said Denis, with the grandest possible air, "I believe I am to have some say in the matter of this marriage; and let me tell you at once, I will be no party to forcing the inclination of this young lady. Had it been freely offered to me, I should have been proud to accept her hand, for I perceive she is as good as she is beautiful; but as things are, I have now the honour, messire, of refusing."

Blanche looked at him with gratitude in her eyes; but the old gentleman only smiled and smiled, until his smile grew positively sickening to Denis.

"I am afraid," he said, "Monsieur de Beaulieu, that you do not perfectly understand the choice I have to offer you. Follow me, I beseech you, to this window." And he led the way to one of the large windows which stood open on the night. "You observe," he went on, "there is an iron ring in the upper masonry, and reeved through that, a very efficacious rope. Now, mark my words. If you should find your disinclination to my niece's person insurmountable, I shall have you hanged out of this window before sunrise. I shall only proceed to such an extremity with the greatest regret, you may believe me. For it is not at all your death that I desire, but my niece's establishment in life. At the same time, it must come to that if you prove obstinate. Your family, Monsieur de Beaulieu, is very well in its way; but if you sprang from Charlemagne, you should not refuse the hand of a Malétroit with impunity—not if she had been as common as the Paris road —not if she were as hideous as the gargoyle over my door. Neither my niece nor you, nor my own private feelings, move me at all in this matter. The honour of my house has been compromised; I believe you to be the guilty person; at least you are now in the secret; and you can hardly wonder if I request you to wipe out the stain. If you will not, your blood be on your own head! It will be no great satisfaction to me to have your interesting relics kicking their heels in the breeze below my windows; but half a loaf is better than no bread, and if I cannot cure the dishonour, I shall at least stop the scandal."

There was a pause.

"I believe there are other ways of settling such imbroglios among gentlemen," said Denis. "You wear a sword, and I hear you have used it with distinction."

The Sire de Malétroit made a signal to the chaplain, who crossed the room with long silent strides and raised the arras over the third of the three doors. It was only a moment before he let it fall again; but Denis had time to see a dusky passage full of armed men.

"When I was a little younger, I should have been delighted to honour you, Monsieur de Beaulieu," said Sire Alain; "but I am now too old. Faithful retainers are the sinews of age, and I must employ the strength I have. This is one of the hardest things to swallow as a man grows up in years; but with a little patience, even this becomes habitual. You and the lady seem to prefer the salle for what remains of your two hours; and as I have no desire to cross your preference, I shall resign it to your use with all the pleasure in the world. No haste!" he added, holding up his hand, as he saw a dangerous look come into Denis de Beaulieu's face. "If your mind revolts against hanging, it will be time enough two hours hence to throw yourself out of the window or upon the pikes of my retainers. Two hours of life are always two hours. A great many things may turn up in even as little a while as that. And besides, if I understand her appearance, my niece has still something to say to you. You will not disfigure your last hours by a want of politeness to a lady?"

Denis looked at Blanche, and she made him an imploring gesture.

It is likely that the old gentleman was hugely pleased at this symptom of an understanding; for he smiled on both, and added sweetly: "If you will give me your word of honour, Monsieur de Beaulieu, to await my return at the end of the two hours before attempting anything desperate, I shall withdraw my retainers, and let you speak in greater privacy with mademoiselle."

Denis again glanced at the girl, who seemed to beseech him to agree.

"I give you my word of honour," he said.

Messire de Malétroit bowed, and proceeded to limp about the apartment, clearing his throat the while with that odd musical chirp which had already grown so irritating in the ears of Denis de Beaulieu. He first possessed himself of some papers which lay upon the table; then he went to the mouth of the passage and appeared to give an order to the men behind the arras; and lastly he hobbled out through the door by which Denis had come in, turning upon the threshold to address a last smiling bow to the young couple, and followed by the chaplain with a hand-lamp.

No sooner were they alone than Blanche advanced towards Denis with her hands extended. Her face was flushed and excited, and her eyes shone with tears.

"You shall not die!" she cried, "you shall marry me after all."

"You seem to think, madam," replied Denis, "that I stand much in fear of death."

"Oh, no, no," she said, "I see you are no poltroon. It is for my own sake —I could not bear to have you slain for such a scruple."

"I am afraid," returned Denis, "that you underrate the difficulty, madam. What you may be too generous to refuse, I may be too proud to accept. In a moment of noble feeling towards me, you forget what you perhaps owe to others."

He had the decency to keep his eyes upon the floor as he said this, and after he had finished, so as not to spy upon her confusion. She stood silent for a moment, then walked suddenly away, and falling on her uncle's chair, fairly burst out sobbing. Denis was in the acme of embarrassment. He

looked round, as if to seek for inspiration, and seeing a stool, plumped down upon it for something to do. There he sat, playing with the guard of his rapier, and wishing himself dead a thousand times over, and buried in the nastiest kitchen-heap in France. His eyes wandered round the apartment but found nothing to arrest them. There were such wide spaces between the furniture, the light fell so badly and cheerlessly over all, the dark outside air looked in so coldly through the windows, that he thought he had never seen a church so vast, nor a tomb so melancholy. The regular sobs of Blanche de Malétroit measured out the time like the ticking of a clock. He read the device upon the shield over and over again, until his eyes became obscured; he stared into shadowy corners until he imagined they were swarming with horrible animals; and every now and again he awoke with a start, to remember that his last two hours were running and death was on the march.

Oftener and oftener, as the time went on, did his glance settle on the girl herself. Her face was bowed forward and covered with her hands, and she was shaken at intervals by the convulsive hiccups of grief. Even thus she was not an unpleasant object to dwell upon, so plump and yet so fine, with a warm brown skin, and the most beautiful hair, Denis thought, in the whole world of womankind. Her hands were like her uncle's; but they were more in place at the end of her young arms, and looked infinitely soft and caressing. He remembered how her blue eyes had shone upon him, full of anger, pity, and innocence. And the more he dwelt on her perfections, the uglier death looked, and the more deeply was he smitten with penitence at her continued tears. Now he felt that no man could have the courage to leave a world which contained so beautiful a creature; and now he would have given forty minutes of his last hour to have unsaid his cruel speech.

Suddenly a hoarse and ragged peal of cockcrow rose to their ears from the dark valley below the windows. And this shattering noise in the silence all around way like a light in a dark place, and shook them both out of their reflections.

"Alas, can I do nothing to help you?" she said, looking up.

"Madam," replied Denis, with a fine irrelevancy, "if I have said anything to wound you, believe me, it was for your own sake and not for mine."

She thanked him with a tearful look.

"I feel your position cruelly," he went on. "The world has been bitter hard on you. Your uncle is a disgrace to mankind. Believe me, madam, there is no young gentleman in all France but would be glad of my opportunity, to die in doing you a momentary service."

"I know already that you can be very brave and generous," she answered. "What I *want* to know is whether I can serve you now or afterwards," she added, with a quaver.

"Most certainly," he answered with a smile. "Let me sit beside you as if I were a friend, instead of a foolish intruder; try to forget how awkwardly we are placed to one another; make my last moments go pleasantly; and you will do me the chief service possible."

"You are very gallant," she added, with a yet deeper sadness . . . "very gallant . . . and it somehow pains me. But draw nearer, if you please, and if you find anything to say to me, you will at least make certain of a very friendly listener. Ah! Monsieur de Beaulieu, how can I look you in

the face?" And she fell to weeping again with a renewed effusion.

"Madam," said Denis, taking her hand in both of his, "reflect on the little time I have before me, and the great bitterness into which I am cast by the sight of your distress. Spare me, in my last moments, the spectacle of what I cannot cure even with the sacrifice of my life."

"I am very selfish," answered Blanche. "I will be braver, Monsieur de Beaulieu, for your sake. But think if I can do you no kindness in the future—if you have no friends to whom I could carry your adieux. Charge me as heavily as you can; every burden will lighten, by so little, the invaluable gratitude I owe you. Put it in my power to do something more for you than weep."

"My mother is married again, and has a young family to care for. My brother Guichard will inherit my fiefs; and if I am not in error, that will content him amply for my death. Life is a little vapour that passeth away, as we are told by those in holy orders. When a man is in a fair way and sees all life open in front of him, he seems to himself to make a very important figure in the world. His horse whinnies to him; the trumpets blow and the girls look out of windows as he rides into town before his company; he receives many assurances of trust and regard—sometimes by express in a letter—sometimes face to face, with persons of great consequence falling on his neck. It is not wonderful if his head is turned for a time. But once he is dead, were he as brave as Hercules or as wise as Solomon, he is soon forgotten. It is not ten years since my father fell, with many other knights around him, in a very fierce encounter, and I do not think that any one of them, nor so much as the name of the fight, is now remembered.

No, no, madam, the nearer you come to it, you see that death is a dark and dusty corner, where a man gets into his tomb and has the door shut after him till the judgment day. I have few friends just now, and once I am dead I shall have none."

"Ah, Monsieur de Beaulieu!" she exclaimed, "you forget Blanche de Malétroit."

"You have a sweet nature, madam, and you are pleased to estimate a little service far beyond its worth."

"It is not that," she answered. "You mistake me if you think I am so easily touched by my own concerns. I say so, because you are the noblest man I have ever met; because I recognise in you a spirit that would have made even a common person famous in the land."

"And yet here I die in a mouse-trap—with no more noise about it than my own speaking," answered he.

A look of pain crossed her face, and she was silent for a little while. Then a light came into her eyes, and with a smile she spoke again.

"I cannot have my champion think meanly of himself. Anyone who gives his life for another will be met in Paradise by all the heralds and angels of the Lord God. And you have no such cause to hang your head. For . . . Pray, do you think me beautiful?" she asked, with a deep flush.

"Indeed, madam, I do," he said.

"I am glad of that," she answered, heartily. "Do you think there are many men in France who have been asked in marriage by a beautiful maiden—with her own lips—and who have refused her to her face? I know you men would half despise such a triumph; but believe me, we women know more of what is precious in love. There is nothing that should set a person higher in his own esteem; and

we women would prize nothing more dearly."

"You are very good," he said; "but you cannot make me forget that I was asked in pity and not for love."

"I am not so sure of that," she replied, holding down her head. "Hear me to an end, Monsieur de Beaulieu. I know how you must despise me; I feel you are right to do so; I am too poor a creature to occupy one thought of your mind, although, alas! you must die for me this morning. But when I asked you to marry me, indeed, and indeed, it was because I respected and admired you, and loved you with my whole soul, from the very moment that you took my part against my uncle. If you had seen yourself, and how noble you looked, you would pity rather than despise me. And now," she went on, hurriedly checking him with her hand, "although I have laid aside all reserve and told you so much, remember that I know your sentiments towards me already. I would not, believe me, being nobly born, weary you with importunities into consent. I too have a pride of my own: and I declare before the holy mother of God, if you should now go back from your word already given, I would no more marry you than I would marry my uncle's groom."

Denis smiled a little bitterly.

"It is a small love," he said, "that shies at a little pride."

She made no answer, although she probably had her own thought.

"Come hither to the window," he said, with a sigh. "Here is the dawn."

And indeed the dawn was already beginning. The hollow of the sky was full of essential daylight, colourless and clean; and the valley underneath

was flooded with a grey reflection. A few thin vapors clung in the coves of the forest or lay along the winding course of the river. The scene disengaged a surprising effect of stillness, which was hardly interrupted when the cocks began once more to crow among the steadings. Perhaps the same fellow who had made so horrid a clangour in the darkness not half an hour before, now sent up the merriest cheer to greet the coming day. A little wind went bustling and eddying among the tree-tops underneath the windows. And still the daylight kept flooding insensibly out of the east, which was soon to grow incandescent and cast up that red-hot cannonball, the rising sun.

Denis looked out over all this with a bit of a shiver. He had taken her hand and retained it in his almost unconsciously.

"Has the day begun already?" she said; and then, illogically enough: "the night has been so long! Alas! what shall we say to my uncle when he returns?"

"What you will," said Denis, and he pressed her fingers in his.

She was silent.

"Blanche," he said, with a swift, uncertain, passionate utterance, "you have seen whether I fear death. You must know well enough that I would as gladly leap out of the window into the empty air as to lay a finger on you without your free and full consent. But if you care for me at all do not let me lose my life in a misapprehension; for I love you better than the whole world; and though I will die for you blithely, it would be like all the joys of Paradise to live on and spend my life in your service."

As he stopped speaking, a bell began to ring loudly in the interior of the house, and a clatter of armour in the corridor showed that the retainers were returning to their post, and the two hours were at an end.

"After all that you have heard?" she whispered, leaning towards him with her lips and eyes.

"I have heard nothing," he replied.

"The captain's name was Florimond de Champdivers," she said in his ear.

"I did not hear it," he answered, taking her supple body in his arms and covering her wet face with kisses.

A melodious chirping was audible behind, followed by a beautiful chuckle, and the voice of Messire de Malétroit wished his new nephew a good morning.

THE NECKLACE

GUY DE MAUPASSANT

She was one of those pretty, charming young ladies, born, as if through an error of destiny, into a family of clerks. She had no dowry, no hopes, no means of becoming known, appreciated, loved and married by a man either rich or distinguished; and she allowed herself to marry a petty clerk in the office of the Board of Education.

She was simple, not being able to adorn herself, but she was unhappy, as one out of her class; for women belong to no caste, no race, their grace, their beauty and their charm serving them in the place of birth and family. Their inborn finesse, their instinctive elegance, their suppleness of wit, are their only aristocracy, making some daughters of the people the equal of great ladies.

She suffered incessantly, feeling herself born for all delicacies and luxuries. She suffered from the poverty of her apartment, the shabby walls, the worn chairs and the faded stuffs. All these things, which another woman of her station would not have noticed, tortured and angered her. The sight of the little Breton, who made this humble home, awoke in her sad regrets and desperate dreams. She thought of quiet antechambers with their oriental hangings lighted by high bronze torches and of the two great footmen in short trousers who sleep in the large armchairs, made sleepy by the heavy air from the heating apparatus. She thought of large drawing rooms hung in old silks, of graceful pieces of furniture carrying bric-a-brac of inestimable value and of the little perfumed coquettish apartments made for five o'clock chats with most intimate friends, men known and sought after, whose attention all women envied and desired.

When she seated herself for dinner before the round table, where the tablecloth had been used three days, opposite her husband who uncovered the tureen with a delighted air, saying: "Oh! the good potpie! I know nothing better than that," she would think of the elegant dinners, of the shining silver, of the tapestries peopling the walls with ancient personages and rare birds in the midst of fairy forests; she thought of the exquisite food scrved on marvelous dishes, of the whispered gallantries, listened to with the smile of the Sphinx while eating the rose-colored flesh of the trout or a chicken's wing.

She had neither frocks nor jewels, nothing. And she loved only those things. She felt that she was made for them. She had such a desire to please, to be sought after, to be clever and courted.

She had a rich friend, a schoolmate at the convent, whom she did not

like to visit; she suffered so much when she returned. And she wept for whole days from chagrin, from regret, from despair and disappointment.

One evening her husband returned, elated, bearing in his hand a large envelope.

"Here," he said, "here is something for you."

She quickly tore open the wrapper and drew out a printed card on which were inscribed these words:

The Minister of Public Instruction and Madame George Ramponneau ask the honor of M. and Mme Loisel's company Monday evening, January 18, at the Minister's residence.

Instead of being delighted, as her husband had hoped, she threw the invitation spitefully upon the table, murmuring:

"What do you suppose I want with that?"

"But, my dearie, I thought it would make you happy. You never go out, and this is an occasion, and a fine one! I had a great deal of trouble to get it. Everybody wishes one, and it is very select; not many are given to employees. You will see the whole official world there."

She looked at him with an irritated eye and declared impatiently:

"What do you suppose I have to wear to such a thing as that?"

He had not thought of that; he stammered:

"Why, the dress you wear when we go to the theater. It seems very pretty to me."

He was silent, stupefied, in dismay, at the sight of his wife weeping. Two great tears fell slowly from the corners of her eyes toward the corners of her mouth; he stammered:

"What is the matter? What is the matter?"

By a violent effort she had controlled her vexation and responded in a calm voice, wiping her moist cheeks:

"Nothing. Only I have no dress and consequently I cannot go to this affair. Give your card to some colleague whose wife is better fitted out than I."

He was grieved but answered:

"Let us see, Matilda. How much would a suitable costume cost, something that would serve for other occasions, something very simple?"

She reflected for some seconds, making estimates and thinking of a sum that she could ask for without bringing with it an immediate refusal and a frightened exclamation from the economical clerk.

Finally she said in a hesitating voice:

"I cannot tell exactly, but it seems to me that four hundred francs ought to cover it."

He turned a little pale, for he had saved just this sum to buy a gun that he might be able to join some hunting parties the next summer, on the plains at Nanterre, with some friends who went to shoot larks up there on Sunday. Nevertheless, he answered:

"Very well. I will give you four hundred francs. But try to have a pretty dress."

The day of the ball approached, and Mme Loisel seemed sad, disturbed, anxious. Nevertheless, her dress was nearly ready. Her husband said to her one evening:

"What is the matter with you? You have acted strangely for two or three days."

And she responded: "I am vexed not to have a jewel, not one stone, nothing to adorn myself with. I shall have such a poverty-laden look. I would prefer not to go to this party."

He replied: "You can wear some

natural flowers. At this season they look very chic. For ten francs you can have two or three magnificent roses."

She was not convinced. "No," she replied, "there is nothing more humiliating than to have a shabby air in the midst of rich women."

Then her husband cried out: "How stupid we are! Go and find your friend Madame Forestier and ask her to lend you her jewels. You are well enough acquainted with her to do this."

She uttered a cry of joy. "It is true!" she said. "I had not thought of that."

The next day she took herself to her friend's house and related her story of distress. Mme Forestier went to her closet with the glass doors, took out a large jewel case, brought it, opened it and said: "Choose, my dear."

She saw at first some bracelets, then a collar of pearls, then a Venetian cross of gold and jewels and of admirable workmanship. She tried the jewels before the glass, hesitated, but could neither decide to take them nor leave them. Then she asked:

"Have you nothing more?"

"Why, yes. Look for yourself. I do not know what will please you."

Suddenly she discovered in a black satin box a superb necklace of diamonds, and her heart beat fast with an immoderate desire. Her hands trembled as she took them up. She placed them about her throat, against her dress, and remained in ecstasy before them. Then she asked in a hesitating voice full of anxiety:

"Could you lend me this? Only this?"

"Why, yes, certainly."

She fell upon the neck of her friend, embraced her with passion, then went away with her treasure.

The day of the ball arrived. Mme

Loisel was a great success. She was the prettiest of all, elegant, gracious, smiling and full of joy. All the men noticed her, asked her name and wanted to be presented. All the members of the Cabinet wished to waltz with her. The minister of education paid her some attention.

She danced with enthusiasm, with passion, intoxicated with pleasure, thinking of nothing, in the triumph of her beauty, in the glory of her success, in a kind of cloud of happiness that came of all this homage and all this admiration, of all these awakened desires and this victory so complete and sweet to the heart of woman.

She went home toward four o'clock in the morning. Her husband had been half asleep in one of the little salons since midnight, with three other gentlemen whose wives were enjoying themselves very much.

He threw around her shoulders the wraps they had carried for the coming home, modest garments of everyday wear, whose poverty clashed with the elegance of the ball costume. She felt this and wished to hurry away in order not to be noticed by the other women who were wrapping themselves in rich furs.

Loisel detained her. "Wait," said he. "You will catch cold out there. I am going to call a cab."

But she would not listen and descended the steps rapidly. When they were in the street they found no carriage, and they began to seek for one, hailing the coachmen whom they saw at a distance.

They walked along toward the Seine, hopeless and shivering. Finally they found on the dock one of those old nocturnal coupés that one sees in Paris after nightfall, as if they were ashamed of their misery by day.

It took them as far as their door in Martyr Street, and they went wearily up to their apartment. It was all over for her. And on his part he remembered that he would have to be at the office by ten o'clock.

She removed the wraps from her shoulders before the glass for a final view of herself in her glory. Suddenly she uttered a cry. Her necklace was not around her neck.

Her husband, already half undressed, asked: "What is the matter?"

She turned toward him excitedly:

"I have—I have—I no longer have Madame Forestier's necklace."

He arose in dismay: "What! How is that? It is not possible."

And they looked in the folds of the dress, in the folds of the mantle, in the pockets, everywhere. They could not find it.

He asked: "You are sure you still had it when we left the house?"

"Yes, I felt it in the vestibule as we came out."

"But if you had lost it in the street we should have heard it fall. It must be in the cab."

"Yes. It is probable. Did you take the number?"

"No. And you, did you notice what it was?"

"No."

They looked at each other, utterly cast down. Finally Loisel dressed himself again.

"I am going," said he, "over the track where we went on foot, to see if I can find it."

And he went. She remained in her evening gown, not having the force to go to bed, stretched upon a chair, without ambition or thoughts.

Toward seven o'clock her husband returned. He had found nothing.

He went to the police and to the cab offices and put an advertisement in the newspapers, offering a reward; he did everything that afforded them a suspicion of hope.

She waited all day in a state of bewilderment before this frightful disaster. Loisel returned at evening, with his face harrowed and pale, and had discovered nothing.

"It will be necessary," said he, "to write to your friend that you have broken the clasp of the necklace and that you will have it repaired. That will give us time to turn around."

She wrote as he dictated.

At the end of a week they had lost all hope. And Loisel, older by five years, declared:

"We must take measures to replace this jewel."

The next day they took the box which had inclosed it to the jeweler whose name was on the inside. He consulted his books.

"It is not I, madame," said he, "who sold this necklace; I only furnished the casket."

Then they went from jeweler to jeweler, seeking a necklace like the other one, consulting their memories, and ill, both of them, with chagrin and anxiety.

In a shop of the Palais-Royal they found a chaplet of diamonds which

seemed to them exactly like the one they had lost. It was valued at forty thousand francs. They could get it for thirty-six thousand.

They begged the jeweler not to sell it for three days. And they made an arrangement by which they might return it for thirty-four thousand francs if they found the other one before the end of February.

Loisel possessed eighteen thousand francs which his father had left him. He borrowed the rest.

He borrowed it, asking for a thousand francs of one, five hundred of another, five louis of this one and three louis of that one. He gave notes, made ruinous promises, took money of usurers and the whole race of lenders. He compromised his whole existence, in fact, risked his signature without even knowing whether he could make it good or not, and, harassed by anxiety for the future, by the black misery which surrounded him and by the prospect of all physical privations and moral torture, he went to get the new necklace, depositing on the merchant's counter thirty-six thousand francs.

When Mme Loisel took back the jewels to Mme Forestier the latter said to her in a frigid tone:

"You should have returned them to me sooner, for I might have needed them."

She did open the jewel box as her friend feared she would. If she should perceive the substitution what would she think? What should she say? Would she take her for a robber?

Mme Loisel now knew the horrible life of necessity. She did her part, however, completely, heroically. It was necessary to pay this frightful debt. She would pay it. They sent away the maid; they changed their lodgings; they rented some rooms under a mansard roof.

She learned the heavy cares of a household, the odious work of a kitchen. She washed the dishes, using her rosy nails upon the greasy pots and the bottoms of the stewpans. She washed the soiled linen, the chemises and dishcloths, which she hung on the line to dry; she took down the refuse to the street each morning and brought up the water, stopping at each landing to breathe. And, clothed like a woman of the people, she went to the grocer's, the butcher's and the fruiterer's with her basket on her arm, shopping, haggling to the last sou her miserable money.

Every month it was necessary to renew some notes, thus obtaining time, and to pay others.

The husband worked evenings, putting the books of some merchants in order, and nights he often did copying at five sous a page.

And this life lasted for ten years.

At the end of ten years they had restored all, all, with interest of the usurer, and accumulated interest, besides.

Mme Loisel seemed old now. She had become a strong, hard woman, the crude woman of the poor household. Her hair badly dressed, her skirts awry, her hands red, she spoke in a loud tone and washed the floors in large pails of water. But sometimes, when her husband was at the office, she would seat herself before the window and think of that evening party of former times, of that ball where she was so beautiful and so flattered.

How would it have been if she had not lost that necklace? Who knows? Who knows? How singular is life and how full of changes! How small a thing will ruin or save one!

One Sunday, as she was taking a

walk in the Champs Elysées to rid herself of the cares of the week, she suddenly perceived a woman walking with a child. It was Mme Forestier, still young, still pretty, still attractive. Mme Loisel was affected. Should she speak to her? Yes, certainly. And now that she had paid, she would tell her all. Why not?

She approached her. "Good morning, Jeanne."

Her friend did not recognize her and was astonished to be so familiarly addressed by this common personage. She stammered:

"But, madame—I do not know— You must be mistaken."

"No, I am Matilda Loisel."

Her friend uttered a cry of astonishment: "Oh! my poor Matilda! How you have changed."

"Yes, I have had some hard days since I saw you, and some miserable ones—and all because of you."

"Because of me? How is that?"

"You recall the diamond necklace that you loaned me to wear to the minister's ball?"

"Yes, very well."

"Well, I lost it."

"How is that, since you returned it to me?"

"I returned another to you exactly like it. And it has taken us ten years to pay for it. You can understand that it was not easy for us who have nothing. But it is finished, and I am decently content."

Mme Forestier stopped short. She said:

"You say that you bought a diamond necklace to replace mine?"

"Yes. You did not perceive it then? They were just alike."

And she smiled with a proud and simple joy. Mme Forestier was touched and took both her hands as she replied:

"Oh, my poor Matilda! Mine were false. They were not worth over five hundred francs!"

BY THE WATERS OF BABYLON

STEPHEN VINCENT BENÉT

The north and the west and the south are good hunting ground, but it is forbidden to go east. It is forbidden to go to any of the Dead Places except to search for metal and then he who touches the metal must be a priest or the son of a priest. Afterwards, both the man and the metal must be purified. These are the rules and the laws; they are well made. It is forbidden to cross the great river and look upon the place that was the Place of the Gods—this is most strictly forbidden. We do not even say its name though we know its name. It is there that spirits live, and demons— it is there that there are the ashes of the Great Burning. These things are forbidden—they have been forbidden since the beginning of time.

My father is a priest; I am the son of a priest. I have been in the Dead Places near us, with my father—at first, I was afraid. When my father went into the house to search for the metal, I stood by the door and my heart felt small and weak. It was a dead man's house, a spirit house. It did not have the smell of man, though there were old bones in a corner. But it is not fitting that a priest's son should show fear. I looked at the bones in the shadow and kept my voice still.

Then my father came out with the metal—a good, strong piece. He looked at me with both eyes but I had not run away. He gave me the metal to hold—I took it and did not die. So he knew that I was truly his son and would be a priest in my time. That was when I was very young— nevertheless my brothers would not have done it, though they are good hunters. After that, they gave me the good piece of meat and the warm corner by the fire. My father watched over me—he was glad that I should be a priest. But when I boasted or wept without a reason, he punished me more strictly than my brothers. That was right.

After a time, I myself was allowed to go into the dead houses and search for metal. So I learned the ways of those houses—and if I saw bones, I was no longer afraid. The bones are light and old—sometimes they will fall into dust if you touch them. But that is a great sin.

I was taught the chants and the spells—I was taught how to stop the running of blood from a wound and many secrets. A priest must know many secrets—that was what my father said. If the hunters think we do all things by chants and spells, they may believe so—it does not hurt

From *Selected Works of Stephen Vincent Benét*. Rinehart & Company. Copyright 1937, by Stephen Vincent Benét.

them. I was taught how to read in the old books and how to make the old writings—that was hard and took a long time. My knowledge made me happy—it was like a fire in my heart. Most of all, I liked to hear of the Old Days and the stories of the gods. I asked myself many questions that I could not answer, but it was good to ask them. At night, I would lie awake and listen to the wind—it seemed to me that it was the voice of the gods as they flew through the air.

We are not ignorant like the Forest People—our women spin wool on the wheel, our priests wear a white robe. We do not eat grubs from the tree, we have not forgotten the old writings, although they are hard to understand. Nevertheless, my knowledge and my lack of knowledge burned in me—I wished to know more. When I was a man at last, I came to my father and said, "It is time for me to go on my journey. Give me your leave."

He looked at me for a long time, stroking his beard, then he said at last, "Yes. It is time." That night, in the house of the priesthood, I asked for and received purification. My body hurt but my spirit was a cool stone. It was my father himself who questioned me about my dreams.

He bade me look into the smoke of the fire and see—I saw and told what I saw. It was what I have always seen—a river, and, beyond it, a great Dead Place and in it the gods walking. I have always thought about that. His eyes were stern when I told him—he was no longer my father but a priest. He said, "This is a strong dream."

"It is mine," I said, while the smoke waved and my head felt light. They were singing the Star song in the outer chamber and it was like the buzzing of bees in my head.

He asked me how the gods were dressed and I told him how they were dressed. We know how they were dressed from the book, but I saw them as if they were before me. When I had finished, he threw the sticks three times and studied them as they fell. "This is a very strong dream," he said. "It may eat you up."

"I am not afraid," I said and looked at him with both eyes. My voice sounded thin in my ears but that was because of the smoke.

He touched me on the breast and the forehead. He gave me the bow and the three arrows.

"Take them," he said. "It is forbidden to travel east. It is forbidden to cross the river. It is forbidden to go to the Place of the Gods. All these things are forbidden."

"All these things are forbidden," I said, but it was my voice that spoke and not my spirit. He looked at me again.

"My son," he said. "Once I had young dreams. If your dreams do not eat you up, you may be a great priest. If they eat you, you are still my son. Now go on your journey."

I went fasting, as is the law. My body hurt but not my heart. When the dawn came, I was out of sight of the village. I prayed and purified myself, waiting for a sign. The sign was an eagle. It flew east.

Sometimes signs are sent by bad spirits. I waited again on the flat rock, fasting, taking no food. I was very still—I could feel the sky above me and the earth beneath. I waited till the sun was beginning to sink. Then three deer passed in the valley, going east—they did not wind me or see me. There was a white fawn with them— a very great sign.

I followed them, at a distance, waiting for what would happen. My heart was troubled about going east, yet I knew that I must go. My head hummed with my fasting—I did not

even see the panther spring upon the white fawn. But, before I knew it, the bow was in my hand. I shouted and the panther lifted his head from the fawn. It is not easy to kill a panther with one arrow but the arrow went through his eye and into his brain. He died as he tried to spring— he rolled over, tearing at the ground. Then I knew I was meant to go east —I knew that was my journey. When the night came, I made my fire and roasted meat.

It is eight suns' journey to the east and a man passes by many Dead Places. The Forest People are afraid of them but I am not. Once I made my fire on the edge of a Dead Place at night and, next morning, in the dead house, I found a good knife, little rusted. That was small to what came afterward but it made my heart feel big. Always when I looked for game, it was in front of my arrow, and twice I passed hunting parties of the Forest People without their knowing. So I knew my magic was strong and my journey clean, in spite of the law.

Toward the setting of the eighth sun, I came to the banks of the great river. It was half-a-day's journey after I had left the god-road—we do not use the god-roads now for they are falling apart into great blocks of stone, and the forest is safer going. A long way off, I had seen the water through trees but the trees were thick. At last, I came out upon an open place at the top of a cliff. There was the great river below, like a giant in the sun. It is very long, very wide. It could eat all the streams we know and still be thirsty. Its name is Ou-dis-sun, the Sacred, the Long. No man of my tribe had seen it, not even my father, the priest. It was magic and I prayed.

Then I raised my eyes and looked south. It was there, the Place of the Gods.

How can I tell what it was like— you do not know. It was there, in the red light, and they were too big to be houses. It was there with the red light upon it, mighty and ruined. I knew that in another moment the gods would see me. I covered my eyes with my hands and crept back into the forest.

Surely, that was enough to do, and live. Surely it was enough to spend the night upon the cliff. The Forest People themselves do not come near. Yet, all through the night, I knew that I should have to cross the river and walk in the Place of the Gods, although the gods ate me up. My magic did not help me at all and yet there was a fire in my bowels, a fire in my mind. When the sun rose, I thought, "My journey has been clean. Now I will go home from my journey." But, even as I thought so, I knew I could not. If I went to the Place of the Gods, I would surely die, but, if I did not go, I could never be at peace with my spirit again. It is better to lose one's life than one's spirit, if one is a priest and the son of a priest.

Nevertheless, as I made the raft, the tears ran out of my eyes. The Forest People could have killed me without fight, if they had come upon me then, but they did not come. When the raft was made, I said the sayings for the dead and painted myself for death. My heart was cold as a frog and my knees like water, but the burning in my mind would not let me have peace. As I pushed the raft from the shore, I began my death song—I had the right. It was a fine song.

"I am John, son of John," I sang. "My people are the Hill People. They are the men.

I go into the Dead Places but I am not slain.

I take the metal from the Dead Places but I am not blasted.

I travel upon the god-roads and am not afraid. E-yah! I have killed the panther, I have killed the fawn!

E-yah! I have come to the great river. No man has come there before. It is forbidden to go east, but I have gone, forbidden to go on the great river, but I am there.

Open your hearts, you spirits, and hear my song.

Now I go to the Place of the Gods, I shall not return.

My body is painted for death and my limbs weak, but my heart is big as I go to the Place of the Gods!"

All the same, when I came to the Place of the Gods, I was afraid, afraid. The current of the great river is very strong—it gripped my raft with its hands. That was magic, for the river itself is wide and calm. I could feel evil spirits about me, in the bright morning; I could feel their breath on my neck as I was swept down the stream. Never have I been so much alone—I tried to think of my knowledge, but it was a squirrel's heap of winter nuts. There was no strength in my knowledge any more and I felt small and naked as a new-hatched bird—alone upon the great river, the servant of the gods.

Yet, after awhile, my eyes were opened and I saw. I saw both banks of the river—I saw that once there had been god-roads across it, though now they were broken and fallen like broken vines. Very great they were, and wonderful and broken—broken in the time of the Great Burning when the fire fell out of the sky. And always the current took me nearer to the Place of the Gods, and the huge ruins rose before my eyes.

I do not know the customs of rivers—we are the People of the Hills. I tried to guide my raft with the pole but it spun around. I thought the river meant to take me past the Place of the Gods and out into the Bitter Water of the legends. I grew angry then—my heart felt strong. I said aloud, "I am a priest and the son of a priest!" The gods heard me—they showed me how to paddle with the pole on one side of the raft. The current changed itself—I drew near to the Place of the Gods.

When I was very near, my raft struck and turned over. I can swim in our lakes—I swam to the shore. There was a great spike of rusted metal sticking out into the river—I hauled myself up upon it and sat there, panting. I had saved my bow and two arrows and the knife I found in the Dead Place but that was all. My raft went whirling downstream toward the Bitter Water. I looked after it, and thought if it had trod me under, at least I would be safely dead. Nevertheless, when I had dried my bow-string and re-strung it, I walked forward to the Place of the Gods.

It felt like ground underfoot; it did not burn me. It is not true what some of the tales say, that the ground there burns forever, for I have been there. Here and there were the marks and stains of the Great Burning, on the ruins, that is true. But they were old marks and old stains. It is not true either, what some of our priests say, that it is an island covered with fogs and enchantments. It is not. It is a great Dead Place—greater than any Dead Place we know. Everywhere in it there are god-roads, though most are cracked and broken. Everywhere there are the ruins of the high towers of the gods.

How shall I tell what I saw? I went carefully, my strung bow in my hand, my skin ready for danger. There should have been the wailings of spirits and the shrieks of demons, but there were not. It was very silent and sunny where I had landed—the wind and the rain and the birds that drop seeds had done their work—the grass grew in the cracks of the broken stone. It is a fair island—no wonder the gods built there. If I had come there, a god, I also would have built.

How shall I tell what I saw? The towers are not all broken—here and there one still stands, like a great tree in a forest, and the birds nest high. But the towers themselves look blind, for the gods are gone. I saw a fish-hawk, catching fish in the river. I saw a little dance of white butterflies over a great heap of broken stones and columns. I went there and looked about me—there was a carved stone with cut-letters, broken in half. I can read letters but I could not understand these. They said UBTREAS. There was also the shattered image of a man or a god. It had been made of white stone and he wore his hair tied back like a woman's. His name was ASHING, as I read on the cracked half of a stone. I thought it wise to pray to ASHING, though I do not know that god.

How shall I tell what I saw? There was no smell of man left, on stone or metal. Nor were there many trees in that wilderness of stone. There are many pigeons, nesting and dropping in the towers—the gods must have loved them, or, perhaps, they used them for sacrifices. There are wild cats that roam the god-roads, green-eyed, unafraid of man. At night they wail like demons but they are

not demons. The wild dogs are more dangerous, for they hunt in a pack, but them I did not meet till later. Everywhere there are the carved stones, carved with magical numbers or words. I went North—I did not try to hide myself. When a god or a demon saw me, then I would die, but meanwhile I was no longer afraid. My hunger for knowledge burned in me—there was so much that I could not understand. After awhile, I knew that my belly was hungry. I could have hunted for my meat, but I did not hunt. It is known that the gods did not hunt as we do—they got their food from enchanted boxes and jars. Sometimes these are still found in the Dead Places—once, when I was a child and foolish, I opened such a jar and tasted it and found the food sweet. But my father found out and punished me for it strictly, for, often, that food is death. Now, though, I had long gone past what was forbidden, and I entered the likeliest towers, looking for the food of the gods.

I found it at last in the ruins of a great temple in the mid-city. A mighty temple it must have been, for the roof was painted like the sky at night with its stars—that much I could see, though the colors were faint and dim. It went down into great caves and tunnels—perhaps they kept their slaves there. But when I started to climb down, I heard the squeaking of rats, so I did not go—rats are unclean, and there must have been many tribes of them, from the squeaking. But near there, I found food, in the heart of a ruin, behind a door that still opened. I ate only the fruits from the jars—they had a very sweet taste. There was drink, too, in bottles of glass—the drink of the gods was strong and made my head swim. After I had

eaten and drunk, I slept on the top of a stone, my bow at my side.

When I woke, the sun was low. Looking down from where I lay, I saw a dog sitting on his haunches. His tongue was hanging out of his mouth; he looked as if he were laughing. He was a big dog, with a grey-brown coat, as big as a wolf. I sprang up and shouted at him but he did not move—he just sat there as if he were laughing. I did not like that. When I reached for a stone to throw, he moved swiftly out of the way of the stone. He was not afraid of me; he looked at me as if I were meat. No doubt I could have killed him with an arrow, but I did not know if there were others. Moreover, night was falling.

I looked about me—not far away there was a great, broken god-road, leading North. The towers were high enough, but not so high, and while many of the dead-houses were wrecked, there were some that stood. I went toward this god-road, keeping to heights of the ruins, while the dog followed. When I had reached the god-road, I saw that there were others behind him. If I had slept later, they would have come upon me asleep and torn out my throat. As it was, they were sure enough of me; they did not hurry. When I went into the dead-house, they kept watch at the entrance—doubtless they thought they would have a fine hunt. But a dog cannot open a door and I knew, from the books, that the gods did not like to live on the ground but on high.

I had just found a door I could open when the dogs decided to rush. Ha! They were surprised when I shut the door in their faces—it was a good door, of strong metal. I could hear their foolish baying beyond it but I did not stop to answer them. I was in darkness—I found stairs and climbed. There were many stairs, turning

around till my head was dizzy. At the top was another door—I found the knob and opened it. I was in a long small chamber—on one side of it was a bronze door that could not be opened, for it had no handle. Perhaps there was a magic word to open it but I did not have the word. I turned to the door in the opposite side of the wall. The lock of it was broken and I opened it and went in.

Within, there was a place of great riches. The god who lived there must have been a powerful god. The first room was a small ante-room—I waited there for some time, telling the spirits of the place that I came in peace and not as a robber. When it seemed to me that they had had time to hear me, I went on. Ah, what riches! Few, even, of the windows had been broken—it was all as it had been. The great windows that looked over the city had not been broken at all though they were dusty and streaked with many years. There were coverings on the floors, the colors not greatly faded, and the chairs were soft and deep. There were pictures upon the walls, very strange, very wonderful—I remember one of a bunch of flowers in a jar—if you came close to it, you could see nothing but bits of color, but if you stood away from it, the flowers might have been picked yesterday. It made my heart feel strange to look at this picture—and to look at the figure of a bird, in some hard clay, on a table and see it so like our birds. Everywhere there were books and writings, many in tongues that I could not read. The god who lived there must have been a wise god and full of knowledge. I felt I had right there, as I sought knowledge also.

Nevertheless, it was strange. There was a washing-place but no water—perhaps the gods washed in air. There was a cooking-place but no wood, and though there was a machine to cook food, there was no place to put fire in it. Nor were there candles or lamps—there were things that looked like lamps but they had neither oil nor wick. All these things were magic, but I touched them and lived—the magic had gone out of them. Let me tell one thing to show. In the washing-place, a thing said "Hot" but it was not hot to the touch—another thing said "Cold" but it was not cold. This must have been a strong magic but the magic was gone. I do not understand—they had ways—I wish that I knew.

It was close and dry and dusty in their house of the gods. I have said the magic was gone but that is not true—it had gone from the magic things but it had not gone from the place. I felt the spirits about me, weighing upon me. Nor had I ever slept in a Dead Place before—and yet, tonight, I must sleep there. When I thought of it, my tongue felt dry in my throat, in spite of my wish for knowledge. Almost I would have gone down again and faced the dogs, but I did not.

I had not gone through all the rooms when the darkness fell. When it fell, I went back to the big room looking over the city and made fire. There was a place to make fire in a box with wood in it, though I do not think they cooked there. I wrapped myself in a floor-covering and slept in front of the fire—I was very tired.

Now I tell what is very strong magic. I woke in the midst of the night. When I woke, the fire had gone out and I was cold. It seemed to me that all around me there were whisperings and voices. I closed my eyes to shut them out. Some will say that I slept again, but I do not think that I slept. I could feel the spirits

drawing my spirit out of my body as a fish is drawn on a line.

Why should I lie about it? I am a priest and the son of a priest. If there are spirits, as they say, in the small Dead Places near us, what spirits must there not be in that great Place of the Gods? And would not they wish to speak? After such long years? I know that I felt myself drawn as a fish is drawn on a line. I had stepped out of my body—I could see my body asleep in front of the cold fire, but it was not I. I was drawn to look out upon the city of the gods.

It should have been dark, for it was night, but it was not dark. Everywhere there were lights—lines of light—circles and blurs of light—ten thousand torches would not have been the same. The sky itself was alight—you could barely see the stars for the glow in the sky. I thought to myself "This is strong magic" and trembled. There was a roaring in my ears like the rushing of rivers. Then my eyes grew used to the light and my ears to the sound. I knew that I was seeing the city as it had been when the gods were alive.

That was a sight indeed—yes, that was a sight: I could not have seen it in the body—my body would have died. Everywhere went the gods, on foot and in chariots—there were gods beyond number and counting and their chariots blocked the streets. They had turned night to day for their pleasure—they did not sleep with the sun. The noise of their coming and going was the noise of many waters. It was magic what they could do—it was magic what they did.

I looked out of another window—the great vines of their bridges were mended and the god-roads went East and West. Restless, restless, were the gods and always in motion! They burrowed tunnels under rivers—they flew in the air. With unbelievable tools they did giant works—no part of the earth was safe from them, for, if they wished for a thing, they summoned it from the other side of the world. And always, as they labored and rested, as they feasted and made love, there was a drum in their ears—the pulse of the giant city, beating and beating like a man's heart.

Were they happy? What is happiness to the gods? They were great, they were mighty, they were wonderful and terrible. As I looked upon them and their magic, I felt like a child—but a little more, it seemed to me, and they would pull down the moon from the sky. I saw them with wisdom beyond wisdom and knowledge beyond knowledge. And yet not all they did was well done—even I could see that—and yet their wisdom could not but grow until all was peace.

Then I saw their fate come upon them and that was terrible past speech. It came upon them as they walked the streets of their city. I have been in the fights with the Forest People—I have seen men die. But this was not like that. When gods war with gods, they use weapons we do not know. It was fire falling out of the sky and a mist that poisoned. It was the time of the Great Burning and the Destruction. They ran about like ants in the streets of their city—poor gods, poor gods! Then the towers began to fall. A few escaped—yes, a few. The legends tell it. But, even after the city had become a Dead Place, for many years the poison was still in the ground. I saw it happen, I saw the last of them die. It was darkness over the broken city and I wept.

All this, I saw. I saw it as I have told it, though not in the body. When I woke in the morning, I was hungry,

but I did not think first of my hunger for my heart was perplexed and confused. I knew the reason for the Dead Places but I did not see why it had happened. It seemed to me it should not have happened, with all the magic they had. I went through the house looking for an answer. There was so much in the house I could not understand—and yet I am a priest and the son of a priest. It was like being on one side of the great river, at night, with no light to show the way.

Then I saw the dead god. He was sitting in his chair, by the window, in a room I had not entered before and, for the first moment, I thought that he was alive. Then I saw the skin on the back of his hand—it was like dry leather. The room was shut, hot and dry—no doubt that had kept him as he was. At first I was afraid to approach him—then the fear left me. He was sitting looking out over the city—he was dressed in the clothes of the gods. His age was neither young nor old—I could not tell his age. But there was wisdom in his face and great sadness. You could see that he would have not run away. He had sat at his window, watching his city die—then he himself had died. But it is better to lose one's life than one's spirit—and you could see from the face that his spirit had not been lost. I knew, that, if I touched him, he would fall into dust—and yet, there was something unconquered in the face.

That is all of my story, for then I knew he was a man—I knew then that they had been men, neither gods nor demons. It is a great knowledge, hard to tell and believe. They were men—they went a dark road, but they were men. I had no fear after that—I had no fear going home, though twice I fought off the dogs and once I

was hunted for two days by the Forest People. When I saw my father again, I prayed and was purified. He touched my lips and my breast, he said, "You went away a boy. You come back a man and a priest." I said, "Father, they were men! I have been in the Place of the Gods and seen it! Now slay me, if it is the law—but still I know they were men."

He looked at me out of both eyes. He said, "The law is not always the same shape—you have done what you have done. I could not have done it in my time, but you come after me. Tell!"

I told and he listened. After that, I wished to tell all the people but he showed me otherwise. He said, "Truth is a hard deer to hunt. If you eat too much truth at once, you may die of the truth. It was not idly that our fathers forbade the Dead Places." He was right—it is better the truth should come little by little. I have learned that, being a priest. Perhaps, in the old days, they ate knowledge too fast.

Nevertheless, we make a beginning. It is not for the metal alone we go to the Dead Places now—there are the books and the writings. They are hard to learn. And the magic tools are broken—but we can look at them and wonder. At least, we make a beginning. And, when I am chief priest we shall go beyond the great river. We shall go to the Place of the Gods— the place new-york—not one man but a company. We shall look for the images of the gods and find the god ASHING and the others—the gods Licoln and Biltmore and Moses. But they were men who built the city, not gods or demons. They were men. I remember the dead man's face. They were men who were here before us. We must build again.

A. V. LAIDER

MAX BEERBOHM

I unpacked my things and went down to await luncheon.

It was good to be here again in this little old sleepy hostel by the sea. Hostel I say, though it spelt itself without an s and even placed a circumflex above the o. It made no other pretension. It was very cosy indeed.

I had been here just a year before, in mid-February, after an attack of influenza. And now I had returned, after an attack of influenza. Nothing was changed. It had been raining when I left, and the waiter—there was but a single, a very old waiter—had told me it was only a shower. That waiter was still here, not a day older. And the shower had not ceased.

Steadfastly it fell on to the sands, steadfastly into the iron-grey sea. I stood looking out at it from the windows of the hall, admiring it very much. There seemed to be little else to do. What little there was I did. I mastered the contents of a blue handbill which, pinned to the wall just beneath the framed engraving of Queen Victoria's Coronation, gave token of a concert that was to be held—or rather, was to have been held some weeks ago—in the Town Hall, for the benefit of the Life-Boat Fund. I looked at the barometer, tapped it, was not the wiser. I glanced at a pamphlet about Our Dying Industries (a theme on which Mr. Joseph Chamberlain was at that time trying to alarm us). I wandered to the letter-board.

These letter-boards always fascinate me. Usually some two or three of the envelopes stuck into the cross-garterings have a certain newness and freshness. They seem sure they will yet be claimed. Why not? Why *shouldn't* John Doe, Esq., or Mrs. Richard Roe, turn up at any moment? I do not know. I can only say that nothing in the world seems to me more unlikely. Thus it is that these young bright envelopes touch my heart even more than do their dusty and sallow seniors. Sour resignation is less touching than impatience for what will not be, than the eagerness that has to wane and wither. Soured beyond measure these old envelopes are. They are not nearly so nice as they should be to the young ones. They lose no chance of sneering and discouraging. Such dialogues as this are only too frequent:

A Very Young Envelope. Something in me whispers that he will come to-day!

A Very Old Envelope. He? Well, that's good! Ha, ha, ha! Why didn't he come last week, when *you* came?

What reason have you for supposing he'll ever come *now?* It isn't as if he were a frequenter of the place. He's never been here. His name is utterly unknown here. You don't suppose he's coming on the chance of finding *you?* A V. Y. E. It may seem silly, but—something in me whispers——
A V. O. E. Something in *you?* One has only to look at you to see there's nothing in you but a note scribbled to him by a cousin. Look at *me!* There are three sheets, closely written, in *me.* The lady to whom I am addressed——
A V. Y. E. Yes, sir, yes; you told me all about her yesterday.
A V. O. E. And I shall do so to-day and to-morrow and every day and all day long. That young lady was a widow. She stayed here many times. She was delicate, and the air suited her. She was poor, and the tariff was just within her means. She was lonely, and had need of love. I have in me for her a passionate avowal and strictly honourable proposal, written to her, after many rough copies, by a gentleman who had made her acquaintance under this very roof. He was rich, he was charming, he was in the prime of life. He had asked if he might write to her. She had flutteringly granted his request. He posted me to her the day after his return to London. I looked forward to being torn open by her. I was very sure she would wear me and my contents next to her bosom. She was gone. She had left no address. She never returned. . . This I tell you, and shall continue to tell you, not because I want any of your callow sympathy,—no, *thank* you!—but that you may judge how much less than slight are the chances that you yourself——
But my reader has overheard these dialogues as often as I. He wants to know what was odd about this par-ticular letter-board before which I was standing. At first glance I saw nothing odd about it. But presently I distinguished a handwriting that was vaguely familiar. It was mine. I stared, I wondered. There is always a slight shock in seeing an envelope of one's own after it has gone through the post. It looks as if it had gone through so much. But this was the first time I had ever seen an envelope of mine eating its heart out in bondage on a letter-board. This was outrageous. This was hardly to be believed. Sheer kindness had impelled me to write to 'A. V. Laider, Esq.', and this was the result! I hadn't minded receiving no answer. Only now, indeed, did I remember that I hadn't received one. In multitudinous London the memory of A. V. Laider and his trouble had soon passed from my mind. But—well, what a lesson not to go out of one's way to write to casual acquaintances!
My envelope seemed not to recognise me as its writer. Its gaze was the more piteous for being blank. Even so had I once been gazed at by a dog that I had lost and, after many days, found in the Battersea Home. 'I don't know who you are, but whoever you are, claim me, take me out of this!' That was my dog's appeal. This was the appeal of my envelope.
I raised my hand to the letter-board, meaning to effect a swift and lawless rescue, but paused at sound of a footstep behind me. The old waiter had come to tell me that my luncheon was ready. I followed him out of the hall, not, however, without a bright glance across my shoulder to reassure the little captive that I should come back.
I had the sharp appetite of the convalescent, and this the sea-air had whetted already to a finer edge. In touch with a dozen oysters, and with

stout, I soon shed away the unreasoning anger I had felt against A. V. Laider. I became merely sorry for him that he had not received a letter which might perhaps have comforted him. In touch with cutlets, I felt how sorely he had needed comfort. And anon, by the big bright fireside of that small dark smoking-room where, a year ago, on the last evening of my stay here, he and I had at length spoken to each other, I reviewed in detail the tragic experience he had told me; and I fairly revelled in reminiscent sympathy with him. . . .

A. V. LAIDER—I had looked him up in the visitors' book on the night of his arrival. I myself had arrived the day before, and had been rather sorry there was no one else staying here. A convalescent by the sea likes to have some one to observe, to wonder about, at meal-time. I was glad when, on my second evening, I found seated at the table opposite to mine another guest. I was the gladder because he was just the right kind of guest. He was enigmatic. By this I mean that he did not look soldierly nor financial nor artistic nor anything definite at all. He offered a clean slate for speculation. And thank heaven! he evidently wasn't going to spoil the fun by engaging me in conversation later on. A decently unsociable man, anxious to be left alone.

The heartiness of his appetite, in contrast with his extreme fragility of aspect and limpness of demeanour, assured me that he, too, had just had influenza. I liked him for that. Now and again our eyes met and were instantly parted. We managed, as a rule, to observe each other indirectly. I was sure it was not merely because he had been ill that he looked interesting. Nor did it seem to me that a spiritual melancholy, though I imagined him sad at the best of times, was his sole asset. I conjectured that he was clever. I thought he might also be imaginative. At first glance I had mistrusted him. A shock of white hair, combined with a young face and dark eyebrows, does somehow make a man look like a charlatan. But it is foolish to be guided by an accident of colour. I had soon rejected my first impression of my fellow-diner. I found him very sympathetic.

Anywhere but in England it would be impossible for two solitary men, howsoever much reduced by influenza, to spend five or six days in the same hostel and not exchange a single word. That is one of the charms of England. Had Laider and I been born and bred in any other land we should have become acquainted before the end of our first evening in the small smoking-room, and have found ourselves irrevocably committed to go on talking to each other throughout the rest of our visit. We might, it is true, have happened to like each other more than any one we had ever met. This off-chance may have occurred to us both. But it counted for nothing as against the certain surrender of quietude and liberty. We slightly bowed to each other as we entered or left the dining-room or smoking-room, and as we met on the widespread sands or in the shop that had a small and faded circulating library. That was all. Our mutual aloofness was a positive bond between us.

Had he been much older than I, the responsibility for our silence would of course have been his alone. But he was not, I judged, more than five or six years ahead of me, and thus I might without impropriety have taken it on myself to perform that hard and perilous feat which English people call, with a shiver, 'breaking the ice.' He had reason, therefore, to be as

grateful to me as I to him. Each of us, not the less frankly because silently, recognised his obligation to the other. And when, on the last evening of my stay, the ice actually was broken no ill-will rose between us: neither of us was to blame.

It was a Sunday evening. I had been out for a long last walk and had come in very late to dinner. Laider left his table almost immediately after I sat down to mine. When I entered the smoking-room I found him reading a weekly review which I had bought the day before. It was a crisis. He could not silently offer, nor could I have silently accepted, sixpence. It was a crisis. We faced it like men. He made, by word of mouth, a graceful apology. Verbally, not by signs, I besought him to go on reading. But this, of course, was a vain counsel of perfection. The social code forced us to talk now. We obeyed it like men. To reassure him that our position was not so desperate as it might seem, I took the earliest opportunity to mention that I was going away early next morning. In the tone of his 'Oh, are you?' he tried bravely to imply that he was sorry, even now, to hear that. In a way, perhaps, he really was sorry. We had got on so well together, he and I. Nothing could efface the memory of that. Nay, we seemed to be hitting it off even now. Influenza was not our sole theme. We passed from that to the aforesaid weekly review, and to a correspondence that was raging therein on Faith and Reason.

This correspondence had now reached its fourth and penultimate stage—its Australian stage. It is hard to see why these correspondences spring up; one only knows that they do spring up, suddenly, like street crowds. There comes, it would seem, a moment when the whole English-speaking race is unconsciously bursting to have its say about some one thing—the split infinitive, or the habits of migratory birds, or faith and reason, or what-not. Whatever weekly review happens at such a moment to contain a reference, however remote, to the theme in question reaps the storm. Gusts of letters blow in from all corners of the British Isles. These are presently reinforced by Canada in full blast. A few weeks later the Anglo-Indians weigh in. In due course we have the help of our Australian cousins. By that time, however, we of the Mother Country have got our second wind, and so determined are we to make the most of it that at last even the Editor suddenly loses patience and says 'This correspondence must now cease.—Ed.' and wonders why on earth he ever allowed anything so tedious and idiotic to begin.

I pointed out to Laider one of the Australian letters that had especially pleased me in the current issue. It was from 'A Melbourne Man,' and was of the abrupt kind which declares that 'all your correspondents have been groping in the dark' and then settles the whole matter in one short sharp flash. The flash in this instance was 'Reason is faith, faith reason—that is all we know on earth and all we need to know.' The writer then inclosed his card and was, etc., 'A Melbourne Man.' I said to Laider how very restful it was, after influenza, to read anything that meant nothing whatsoever. Laider was inclined to take the letter more seriously than I, and to be mildly metaphysical. I said that for me faith and reason were two separate things, and (as I am no good at metaphysics, however mild) I offered a definite example, to coax the talk on to ground where I should be safer. 'Palmistry, for example,' I said. 'Deep down in my heart I believe in palmistry.'

Laider turned in his chair. 'You believe in palmistry?'

I hesitated. 'Yes, somehow I do. Why? I haven't the slightest notion. I can give myself all sorts of reasons for laughing it to scorn. My common sense utterly rejects it. Of course the shape of the hand means something— is more or less an index of character. But the idea that my past and future are neatly mapped out on my palms——' I shrugged my shoulders.

'You don't like that idea?' asked Laider in his gentle, rather academic voice.

'I only say it's a grotesque idea.'

'Yet you do believe in it?'

'I've a grotesque belief in it, yes.'

'Are you sure your reason for calling this idea "grotesque" isn't merely that you dislike it?'

'Well,' I said, with the thrilling hope that he was a companion in absurdity, 'doesn't it seem grotesque to you?'

'It seems strange.'

'You believe in it?'

'Oh, absolutely.'

'Hurrah!'

He smiled at my pleasure, and I, at the risk of re-entanglement in metaphysics, claimed him as standing shoulder to shoulder with me against 'A Melbourne Man.' This claim he gently disputed. 'You may think me very prosaic,' he said, 'but I can't believe without evidence.'

'Well, I'm equally prosaic and equally at a disadvantage: I can't take my own belief as evidence, and I've no other evidence to go on.'

He asked me if I had ever made a study of palmistry. I said I had read one of Desbarolles' books years ago, and one of Heron-Allen's. But, he asked, had I tried to test them by the lines on my own hands or on the hands of my friends? I confessed that my actual practice in palmistry had

been of a merely passive kind—the prompt extension of my palm to any one who would be so good as to 'read' it and truckle for a few minutes to my egoism. (I hoped Laider might do this.)

'Then I almost wonder,' he said, with his sad smile, 'that you haven't lost your belief, after all the nonsense you must have heard. There are so many young girls who go in for palmistry. I am sure all the five foolish virgins were "awfully keen on it" and used to say "You can be led, but not driven," and "You are likely to have a serious illness between the ages of forty and forty-five," and "You are by nature rather lazy, but can be very energetic by fits and starts." And most of the professionals, I'm told, are as silly as the young girls.'

For the honour of the profession, I named three practitioners whom I had found really good at reading character. He asked whether any of them had been right about past events. I confessed that, as a matter of fact, all three of them had been right in the main. This seemed to amuse him. He asked whether any of them had predicted anything which had since come true. I confessed that all three had predicted that I should do several things which I had since done rather unexpectedly. He asked if I didn't accept this as at any rate a scrap of evidence. I said I could only regard it as a fluke—a rather remarkable fluke.

The superiority of his sad smile was beginning to get on my nerves. I wanted him to see that he was as absurd as I. 'Suppose,' I said, 'suppose for sake of argument that you and I are nothing but helpless automata created to do just this and that, and to have just that and this done to us. Suppose, in fact, we *haven't* any free will whatsoever. Is it likely or conceivable that the Power that fashioned

us would take the trouble to jot down in cipher on our hands just what was in store for us?'

Laider did not answer this question, he did but annoyingly ask me another. 'You believe in free will?'

'Yes, of course. I'll be hanged if I'm an automaton.'

'And you believe in free will just as in palmistry—without any reason?'

'Oh, no. Everything points to our having free will.'

'Everything? What, for instance?'

This rather cornered me. I dodged out, as lightly as I could, by saying 'I suppose *you* would say it was written in my hand that I should be a believer in free will.'

'Ah, I've no doubt it is.'

I held out my palms. But, to my great disappointment, he looked quickly away from them. He had ceased to smile. There was agitation in his voice as he explained that he never looked at people's hands now. 'Never now—never again.' He shook his head as though to beat off some memory.

I was much embarrassed by my indiscretion. I hastened to tide over the awkward moment by saying that if I could read hands I wouldn't, for fear of the awful things I might see there.

'Awful things, yes,' he whispered, nodding at the fire.

'Not,' I said in self-defence, 'that there's anything very awful, so far as I know, to be read in *my* hands.'

He turned his gaze from the fire to me. 'You aren't a murderer, for example?'

'Oh, no,' I replied, with a nervous laugh.

'I am.'

This was a more than awkward, it was a painful, moment for me; and I am afraid I must have started or winced, for he instantly begged my pardon. 'I don't know,' he exclaimed, 'why I said it. I'm usually a very reticent man. But sometimes—' He pressed his brow. 'What you must think of me!'

I begged him to dismiss the matter from his mind.

'It's very good of you to say that; but—I've placed myself as well as you in a false position. I ask you to believe that I'm not the sort of man who is "wanted" or ever was "wanted" by the police. I should be bowed out of any police-station at which I gave myself up. I'm not a murderer in any bald sense of the word. No.'

My face must have perceptibly brightened, for 'Ah,' he said, 'don't imagine I'm not a murderer at all. Morally, I am.' He looked at the clock. I pointed out that the night was young. He assured me that his story was not a long one. I assured him that I hoped it was. He said I was very kind. I denied this. He warned me that what he had to tell might rather tend to stiffen my unwilling faith in palmistry, and to shake my opposite and cherished faith in free will. I said 'Never mind.' He stretched his hands pensively toward the fire. I settled myself back in my chair.

'My hands,' he said, staring at the backs of them, 'are the hands of a very weak man. I dare say you know enough of palmistry to see that for yourself. You notice the slightness of the thumbs and of the two "little" fingers. They are the hands of a weak and over-sensitive man—a man without confidence, a man who would certainly waver in an emergency. Rather Hamlet-ish hands,' he mused. 'And I'm like Hamlet in other respects, too: I'm no fool, and I've rather a noble disposition, and I'm unlucky. But Hamlet was luckier than I in one thing: he was a murderer by accident, whereas the murders that I committed

one day fourteen years ago—for I must tell you it wasn't one murder, but many murders that I committed—were all of them due to the wretched inherent weakness of my own wretched self.

'I was twenty-six—no, twenty-seven years old, and rather a nondescript person, as I am now. I was supposed to have been called to the Bar. In fact, I believe I *had* been called to the Bar. I hadn't listened to the call. I never intended to practise, and I never did practise. I only wanted an excuse in the eyes of the world for existing. I suppose the nearest I have ever come to practising is now at this moment: I am defending a murderer. My father had left me well enough provided with money. I was able to go my own desultory way, riding my hobbies where I would. I had a good stableful of hobbies. Palmistry was one of them. I was rather ashamed of this one. It seemed to me absurd, as it seems to you. Like you, though, I believed in it. Unlike you, I had done more than merely read a book or so about it. I had read innumerable books about it. I had taken casts of all my friends' hands. I had tested and tested again the points at which Desbarolles dissented from the gypsies, and—well, enough that I had gone into it all rather thoroughly, and was as sound a palmist as a man may be without giving his whole life to palmistry.

'One of the first things I had seen in my own hand, as soon as I had learned to read it, was that at about the age of twenty-six I should have a narrow escape from death—from a violent death. There was a clean break in the life-line, and a square joining it—the protective square, you know. The markings were precisely the same in both hands. It was to be the narrowest escape possible. And I wasn't going to escape without injury, either.

That is what bothered me. There was a faint line connecting the break in the life-line with a star on the line of health. Against that star was another square. I was to recover from the injury, whatever it might be. Still, I didn't exactly look forward to it. Soon after I had reached the age of twenty-five, I began to feel uncomfortable. The thing might be going to happen at any moment. In palmistry, you know, it is impossible to pin an event down hard and fast to one year. This particular event was to be when I was *about* twenty-six; it mightn't be till I was twenty-seven; it might be while I was only twenty-five.

'And I used to tell myself that it mightn't be at all. My reason rebelled against the whole notion of palmistry, just as yours does. I despised my faith in the thing, just as you despise yours. I used to try not to be so ridiculously careful as I was whenever I crossed a street. I lived in London at that time. Motor-cars had not yet come in, but—what hours, all told, I must have spent standing on curbs, very circumspect, very lamentable! It was a pity, I suppose, that I had no definite occupation—something to take me out of myself. I was one of the victims of private means. There came a time when I drove in four-wheelers rather than in hansoms, and was doubtful of four-wheelers. Oh, I assure you, I was very lamentable indeed.

'If a railway-journey could be avoided, I avoided it. My uncle had a place in Hampshire. I was very fond of him and of his wife. Theirs was the only house I ever went to stay in now. I was there for a week in November, not long after my twenty-seventh birthday. There were other people staying there, and at the end of the week we all travelled back to London together. There were six of us in the carriage: Colonel Elbourn

and his wife and their daughter, a girl of seventeen; and another married couple, the Blakes. I had been at Winchester with Blake, but had hardly seen him since that time. He was in the Indian Civil, and was home on leave. He was sailing for India next week. His wife was to remain in England for some months, and then join him out there. They had been married five years. She was now just twenty-four years old. He told me that this was her age.

'The Elbourns I had never met before. They were charming people. We had all been very happy together. The only trouble had been that on the last night, at dinner, my uncle asked me if I still went in for "the gypsy business," as he always called it; and of course the three ladies were immensely excited, and implored me to "do" their hands. I told them it was all nonsense, I said I had forgotten all I once knew, I made various excuses; and the matter dropped. It was quite true that I

had given up reading hands. I avoided anything that might remind me of what was in my own hands. And so, next morning, it was a great bore to me when, soon after the train started, Mrs. Elbourn said it would be "too cruel" of me if I refused to do their hands now. Her daughter and Mrs. Blake also said it would be "brutal"; and they were all taking off their gloves, and—well, of course I had to give in.

'I went to work methodically on Mrs. Elbourn's hands, in the usual way, you know, first sketching the character from the backs of them; and there was the usual hush, broken by the usual little noises—grunts of assent from the husband, cooings of recognition from the daughter. Presently I asked to see the palms, and from them I filled in the details of Mrs. Elbourn's character before going on to the events in her life. But while I talked I was calculating how old Mrs. Elbourn might be. In my first glance

at her palms I had seen that she could not have been less than twenty-five when she married. The daughter was seventeen. Suppose the daughter had been born a year later—how old would the mother be? Forty-three, yes. Not less than that, poor woman!' Laider looked at me. 'Why "poor woman," you wonder? Well, in that glance I had seen within things about her marriage-line. I had seen a very complete break in the lines of life and of fate. I had seen violent death there. At what age? Not later, not possibly *later*, than forty-three. While I talked to her about the things that had happened in her girlhood, the back of my brain was hard at work on those marks of catastrophe. I was horribly wondering that she was still alive. It was impossible that between her and that catastrophe there could be more than a few short months. And all the time I was talking; and I suppose I acquitted myself well, for I remember that when I ceased I had a sort of ovation from the Elbourns.

'It was a relief to turn to another pair of hands. Mrs. Blake was an amusing young creature, and her hands were very characteristic, and prettily odd in form. I allowed myself to be rather whimsical about her nature, and, having begun in that vein, I went on in it—somehow—even after she had turned her palms. In those palms were reduplicated the signs I had seen in Mrs. Elbourn's. It was as though they had been copied neatly out. The only difference was in the placing of them; and it was this difference that was the most horrible point. The fatal age in Mrs. Blake's hands was—not past, no, for here *she* was. But she might have died when she was twenty-one. Twenty-three seemed to be the utmost span. She was twenty-four, you know.

'I have said that I am a weak man. And you will have good proof of

that directly. Yet I showed a certain amount of strength that day—yes, even on that day which has humiliated and saddened the rest of my life. Neither my face nor my voice betrayed me when in the palms of Dorothy Elbourn I was again confronted with those same signs. She was all for knowing the future, poor child! I believe I told her all manner of things that were to be. And she had no future—none, none in *this* world—except——

'And then, while I talked, there came to me suddenly a suspicion. I wondered it hadn't come before. You guess what it was? It made me feel very cold and strange. I went on talking. But, also, I went on—quite separately—thinking. The suspicion wasn't a certainty. This mother and daughter were always together. What was to befall the one might anywhere—anywhere—befall the other. But a like fate, in an equally near future, was in store for that other lady. The coincidence was curious, very. Here we all were together—here, they and I— I who was narrowly to escape, so soon now, what they, so soon now, were to suffer. Oh, there was an inference to be drawn. Not a *sure* inference, I told myself. And always I was talking, talking, and the train was swinging and swaying noisily along—to what? It was a fast train. Our carriage was near the engine. I was talking loudly. Full well I had known what I should see in the Colonel's hands. I told myself I had not known. I told myself that even now the thing I dreaded was not sure to be. Don't think I was dreading it for myself. I wasn't so "lamentable" as all that—now. It was only of them that I thought—only for them. I hurried over the Colonel's character and career; I was perfunctory. It was Blake's hands that I wanted. *They* were the hands that mattered. If *they* had the marks—— Remember, Blake

was to start for India in the coming week, his wife was to remain in England. They would be apart. Therefore——

'And the marks were there. And I did nothing—nothing but hold forth on the subtleties of Blake's character. There was a thing for me to do. I wanted to do it. I wanted to spring to the window and pull the communication-cord. Quite a simple thing to do. Nothing easier than to stop a train. You just give a sharp pull, and the train slows down, comes to a standstill. And the Guard appears at your window. You explain to the Guard.

'Nothing easier than to tell him there is going to be a collision. Nothing easier than to insist that you and your friends and every other passenger in the train must get out at once. . . There *are* easier things than this? Things that need less courage than this? Some of *them* I could have done, I daresay. This thing I was going to do. Oh, I was determined that I would do it—directly.

'I had said all I had to say about Blake's hands. I had brought my entertainment to an end. I had been thanked and complimented all round. I was quite at liberty. I was going to do what I had to do. I was determined, yes.

'We were near the outskirts of London. The air was grey, thickening; and Dorothy Elbourn had said, "Oh, this horrible old London! I suppose there's the same old fog!" And presently I heard her father saying something about "prevention" and "a short act of Parliament" and "anthracite." And I sat and listened and agreed and——'

Laider closed his eyes. He passed his hand slowly through the air.

'I had a racking headache. And when I said so, I was told not to talk. I was in bed, and the nurses were always telling me not to talk. I was in a hospital. I knew that. But I didn't know why I was there. One day I thought I should like to know why, and so I asked. I was feeling much better now. They told me, by degrees, that I had had concussion of the brain. I had been brought there unconscious, and had remained unconscious for forty-eight hours. I had been in an accident—a railway accident. This seemed to me odd. I had arrived quite safely at my uncle's place, and I had no memory of any journey since that. In cases of concussion, you know, it's not uncommon for the patient to forget all that happened just before the accident; there may be a blank of several hours. So it was in my case. One day my uncle was allowed to come and see me. And somehow, suddenly, at sight of him, the blank was filled in. I remembered, in a flash, everything. I was quite calm, though. Or I made myself seem so, for I wanted to know how the collision had happened. My uncle told me that the engine-driver had failed to see a signal because of the fog, and our train had crashed into a goods-train. I didn't ask him about the people who were with me. You see, there was no need to ask. Very gently my uncle began to tell me, but —I had begun to talk strangely, I suppose. I remember the frightened look of my uncle's face, and the nurse scolding him in whispers.

'After that, all a blur. It seems that I became very ill indeed, wasn't expected to live. However, I live.'

There was a long silence. Laider did not look at me, nor I at him. The fire was burning low, and he watched it.

At length he spoke. 'You despise me. Naturally. I despise myself.'

'No, I don't despise you; but——'

'You blame me.' I did not meet his gaze. 'You blame me,' he repeated.

'Yes.'

'And there, if I may say so, you are a little unjust. It isn't my fault that I was born weak.'

'But a man may conquer weakness.'

'Yes, if he is endowed with the strength for that.'

His fatalism drew from me a gesture of disgust. 'Do you really mean,' I asked, 'that because you didn't pull that cord, you *couldn't* have pulled it?'

'Yes.'

'And it's written in your hands that you couldn't?'

He looked at the palms of his hands. 'They are the hands of a very weak man,' he said.

'A man so weak that he cannot believe in the possibility of free will for himself or for any one?'

'They are the hands of an intelligent man, who can weigh evidence and see things as they are.'

'But answer me: Was it fore-ordained that you should not pull that cord?'

'It was fore-ordained.'

'And was it actually marked in your hands that you were not going to pull it?'

'Ah, well, you see, it is rather the things one *is* going to do that are actually marked. The things one *isn't* going to do,—the innumerable negative things,—how could one expect *them* to be marked?'

'But the consequences of what one leaves undone may be positive?'

'Horribly positive,' he winced. 'My hand is the hand of a man who has suffered a great deal in later life.'

'And was it the hand of a man *destined* to suffer?'

'Oh, yes. I thought I told you that.'

There was a pause.

'Well,' I said, with awkward sympathy, 'I suppose all hands are the hands of people destined to suffer.'

'Not of people destined to suffer so much as *I* have suffered—as I still suffer.'

The insistence of his self-pity chilled me, and I harked back to a question he had not straightly answered. 'Tell me: Was it marked in your hands that you were not going to pull that cord?'

Again he looked at his hands, and then, having pressed them for a moment to his face, 'It was marked very clearly,' he answered, 'in *their* hands.'

Two or three days after this colloquy there had occurred to me in London an idea—an ingenious and comfortable doubt. How was Laider to be sure that his brain, recovering from concussion, had *remembered* what happened in the course of that railway-journey? How was he to know that his brain hadn't simply, in its abeyance, *invented* all this for him? It might be that he had never seen those signs in those hands. Assuredly, here was a bright loop-hole. I had forthwith written to Laider, pointing it out.

This was the letter which now, at my second visit, I had found miserably pent on the letter-board. I remembered my promise to rescue it. I arose from the retaining fireside, stretched my arms, yawned, and went forth to fulfil my Christian purpose. There was no one in the hall. The 'shower' had at length ceased. The sun had positively come out, and the front door had been thrown open in its honour. Everything along the sea-front was beautifully gleaming, drying, shimmering. But I was not to be diverted from my errand. I went to the letter-board. And—my letter was not there! Resourceful and plucky little thing—it had escaped! I did hope it would not be captured and brought back. Perhaps the alarm had already been raised by the tolling of that great bell

which warns the inhabitants for miles around that a letter has broken loose from the letter-board. I had a vision of my envelope skimming wildly along the coast-line, pursued by the old but active waiter and a breathless pack of local worthies. I saw it out-distancing them all, dodging past coast-guards, doubling on its tracks, leaping breakwaters, unluckily injuring itself, losing speed, and at last, in a splendour of desperation, taking to the open sea. But suddenly I had another idea. Perhaps Laider had returned?

He had. I espied afar on the sands a form that was recognisably, by the listless droop of it, his. I was glad and sorry—rather glad, because he completed the scene of last year; and very sorry, because this time we should be at each other's mercy: no restful silence and liberty, for either of us, this time. Perhaps he had been told I was here, and had gone out to avoid me while he yet could. Oh weak, weak! Why palter? I put on my hat and coat, and marched out to meet him.

'Influenza, of course?' we asked simultaneously.

There is a limit to the time which one man may spend in talking to another about his own influenza; and presently, as we paced the sands, I felt that Laider had passed this limit. I wondered that he didn't break off and thank me now for my letter. He must have read it. He ought to have thanked me for it at once. It was a very good letter, a remarkable letter. But surely he wasn't waiting to answer it by post? His silence about it gave me the absurd sense of having taken a liberty, confound him! He was evidently ill at ease while he talked. But it wasn't for me to help him out of his difficulty, whatever that might be. It was for him to remove the strain imposed on myself.

Abruptly, after a long pause, he did

now manage to say, 'It was—very good of you to—to write me that letter.' He told me he had only just got it, and he drifted away into otiose explanations of this fact. I thought he might at least say it was a remarkable letter; and you can imagine my annoyance when he said, after another interval, 'I was very much touched indeed.' I had wished to be convincing, not touching. I can't bear to be called touching.

'Don't you,' I asked, 'think it *is* quite possible that your brain invented all those memories of what—what happened before that accident?'

He drew a sharp sigh. 'You make me feel very guilty.'

'That's exactly what I tried to make you *not* feel!'

'I know, yes. That's why I feel so guilty.'

We had paused in our walk. He stood nervously prodding the hard wet sand with his walking-stick. 'In a way,' he said, 'your theory was quite right. But—it didn't go far enough. It's not only possible, it's a fact, that I didn't see those signs in those hands. I never examined those hands. They weren't there. *I* wasn't there. I haven't an uncle in Hampshire, even. I never had.'

I, too, prodded the sand. 'Well,' I said at length, 'I do feel rather a fool.'

'I've no right even to beg your pardon, but——'

'Oh, I'm not vexed. Only—I rather wish you hadn't told me this.'

'I wish I hadn't had to. It was your kindness, you see, that forced me. By trying to take an imaginary load off my conscience, you laid a very real one on it.'

'I'm sorry. But you, of your own free will, you know, exposed your conscience to me last year. I don't yet quite understand why you did that.'

'No, of course not. I don't deserve that you should. But I think you will.

May I explain? I'm afraid I've talked a great deal already about my influenza, and I shan't be able to keep it out of my explanation. Well, my weakest point—I told you this last year, but it happens to be perfectly true that my weakest point—is my will. Influenza, as you know, fastens unerringly on one's weakest point. It doesn't attempt to undermine my imagination. That would be a forlorn hope. I have, alas! a very strong imagination. At ordinary times my imagination allows itself to be governed by my will. My will keeps it in check by constant nagging. But when my will isn't strong enough even to nag, then my imagination stampedes. I become even as a little child. I tell myself the most preposterous fables, and —the trouble is—I can't help telling them to my friends. Until I've thoroughly shaken off influenza, I'm not fit company for any one. I perfectly realise this, and I have the good sense to go right away till I'm quite well again. I come here usually. It seems absurd, but I must confess I was sorry last year when we fell into conversation. I knew I should very soon be letting myself go, or rather, very soon be swept away. Perhaps I ought to have warned you; but—I'm a rather shy man. And then you mentioned the subject of palmistry. You said you believed in it. I wondered at that. I had once read Desbarolles' book about it, but I am bound to say I thought the whole thing very great nonsense indeed.'

'Then,' I gasped, 'it isn't even true that you believe in palmistry?'

'Oh, no. But I wasn't able to tell you that. You had begun by saying that you believed in palmistry, and then you proceeded to scoff at it. While you scoffed I saw myself as a man with a terribly good reason for not scoffing; and in a flash I saw the terribly good reason; I had the whole story—at least I had the broad outlines of it—clear before me.'

'You hadn't ever thought of it before?' He shook his head. My eyes beamed. 'The whole thing was a sheer improvisation?'

'Yes,' said Laider, humbly, 'I am as bad as all that. I don't say that all the details of the story I told you that evening were filled in at the very instant of its conception. I was filling them in while we talked about palmistry in general, and while I was waiting for the moment when the story would come in most effectively. And I've no doubt I added some extra touches in the course of the actual telling. Don't imagine that I took the slightest pleasure in deceiving you. It's only my will, not my conscience, that is weakened after influenza. I simply can't help telling what I've made up, and telling it to the best of my ability. But I'm thoroughly ashamed all the time.'

'Not of your ability, surely?'

'Yes, of that, too,' he said with his sad smile. 'I always feel that I'm not doing justice to my idea.'

'You are too stern a critic, believe me.'

'It is very kind of you to say that. You are very kind altogether. Had I known that you were so essentially a man of the world—in the best sense of that term—I shouldn't have so much dreaded seeing you just now and having to confess to you. But I'm not going to take advantage of your urbanity and your easygoing ways. I hope that some day we may meet somewhere when I haven't had influenza and am a not wholly undesirable acquaintance. As it is, I refuse to let you associate with me. I am an older man than you, and so I may without impertinence warn you against having anything to do with me.'

I deprecated this advice, of course; but, for a man of weakened will, he showed great firmness. 'You,' he said, 'in your heart of hearts don't want to have to walk and talk continually with a person who might at any moment try to bamboozle you with some ridiculous tale. And I, for my part, don't want to degrade myself by trying to bamboozle any one—especially one whom I have taught to see through me. Let the two talks we have had be as though they had not been. Let us bow to each other, as last year, but let that be all. Let us follow in all things the precedent of last year.'

With a smile that was almost gay he turned on his heel, and moved away with a step that was almost brisk. I was a little disconcerted. But I was also more than a little glad. The restfulness of silence, the charm of liberty—these things were not, after all, forfeit. My heart thanked Laider for that; and throughout the week I loyally seconded him in the system he had laid down for us. All was as it had been last year. We did not smile to each other, we merely bowed, when we entered or left the dining-room or smoking-room, and when we met on the widespread sands or in that shop which had a small and faded, but circulating, library.

Once or twice in the course of the week it did occur to me that perhaps Laider had told the simple truth at our first interview and an ingenious lie at our second. I frowned at this possibility. The idea of any one wishing to be quit of me was most distasteful. However, I was to find reassurance. On the last evening of my stay, I suggested, in the small smoking-room, that he and I should, as sticklers for precedent, converse. We did so, very pleasantly. And after a while I happened to say that I had seen this afternoon a great number of sea-gulls flying close to the shore.

'Sea-gulls?' said Laider, turning in his chair.

'Yes. And I don't think I had ever realised how extraordinarily beautiful they are when their wings catch the light.'

'Beautiful?' Laider threw a quick glance at me and away from me. 'You think them beautiful?'

'Surely.'

'Well, perhaps they are, yes; I suppose they are. But—I don't like seeing them. They always remind me of something—rather an awful thing— that once happened to me.'

It was a very awful thing indeed.

THE PILLAR OF FIRE

PERCIVAL WILDE

I

"Bill," Tony inquired suddenly, "do you believe in mind reading?"

It was Bill's twenty-fifth birthday, and Tony, nobly resolving to help him celebrate it, had invited him—urged him—plagued him to spend a week with him enjoying the many attractions offered by one of Tony's clubs. Bill had held out manfully—some sixth sense had warned him that a week in the company of his restless friend would be anything but a vacation—but even granite will wear away under the drip of water, and after the forty-seventh invitation Bill had capitulated. "I want it understood, however," he bargained, "that if I go with you this time you won't ask me again for a whole year."

Tony stiffened. "Don't you expect to enjoy it?"

"Why, of course——"

"You know I'll do everything in the world to give you a good time——"

"I'm a farmer," Bill had explained hastily. "My idea of a good time is different from yours."

Tony had grunted, and Bill, reluctant to offend his friend, had hastily packed a suitcase. But once installed in the privacy of a stateroom on the train, Tony had welcomed the opportunity to ask questions. Now an inquiring youngster of six can propound riddles which even a wise man cannot answer, and Tony, being five and one-half times that age, was as many times as inquisitive—and even more persistent.

For six years Bill Parmelee had followed the hazardous calling of a professional cardsharp. He had reformed; had done much to atone for his past by unmasking those of his former colleagues who still insisted upon preying on too-trustful acquaintances; and while the train speeded southward along the Atlantic coast he did even more by attempting valorously to answer the deluge of questions hurled at him by his insatiably curious friend.

For some deep, mysterious reason, unexplained and unexplainable, anything that has to do with the subject of dishonest gambling is fascinatingly interesting to the average man. Tony showed himself no exception. Methodically, proceeding in orderly fashion from year to year, from month to month, even from day to day, he pumped his informant dry of every detail having to do with his much-checkered career.

Bill had nothing to conceal and

From *Rogues in Clover*, by Percival Wilde, reprinted by permission of Mr. Roger Wilde.

met him in a spirit of complete frankness. He told how he had run away from home at the age of eighteen; how he had been introduced to the methods employed to make games of chance less chancy; how he had gradually become so familiar with those methods that he had qualified as a master of them. He unlocked the door of his reminiscences, and dwelt upon its high lights—and its shadows; its triumphs—and its reverses; its brief periods of prosperity—and its long periods of adversity; and Tony Claghorn, like Oliver Twist, demanded more and more.

Time and again Bill leaped desperately for the end of his story, attempted to terminate his autobiography by explaining, in a few words, how and why he had finally turned a new leaf, become a farmer, and forsworn the devious ways of his youth. But Tony, enjoying himself hugely, would not permit this, and kept his friend busy describing and annotating the earlier episodes which he found so interesting.

Anything—even an autobiography—must come to an end, and at quarter-past four in the afternoon Tony had asked and Bill had answered the final question. And then, while Bill, gazing out of the window, was mentally comparing a herd of Guernseys with his own sleek Jerseys, Tony opened a subject whose discussion might well prove interminable.

"Bill," he repeated, "do you believe in mind reading?"

Bill sighed. "Well, do you believe in it?" he countered wearily.

Tony settled himself in a judicial attitude. "Yes and no," he admitted.

"Meaning?"

"I'm a broad-minded man and I'm always open to conviction."

"And have you ever been convicted—I mean, convinced?" inquired Bill.

Tony nodded gravely. "Yes," he admitted.

Bill nodded with equal gravity. "Then there's nothing more to be said," he declared. The rhythmic click of the wheels was lulling him; he half-closed his eyes.

But Tony had barely begun. "Bill," he commanded, "get your mind on this."

"I can talk just as well in my sleep."

"Not to me," declared Tony emphatically. "We were discussing mind reading," he recalled, somewhat superfluously, "and I was about to tell you that I had seen examples of it."

"Such as?"

"Well," said Tony reflectively, "there was a chap I met some years ago who could do a very wonderful trick with three cards. He'd show you the faces before he started—one of them was a king——"

Bill interrupted. "And then he'd shuffle them clumsily, and bet you couldn't locate it."

"Yes."

"You'd win the first time, and the second time, but the third time, if the bet was big enough, you'd lose. You'd think that was impossible, because you'd noticed that the king was dog-eared. You knew the back of the card as well as you knew the face. Only when you put your money on it, you'd find that the dog-ear had gotten straightened out, and that another card—not the king—had become dog-eared at the same time. Is that correct?"

"Yes."

"And you called that mind reading? Tony, I'm ashamed of you!"

"He knew what was in my mind, didn't he?" persisted the clubman. "He knew I noticed the dog-ear. If that wasn't mind reading, what is it?"

"It was nothing but relying on an old, old maxim," retorted Bill.

"What maxim?" demanded Tony somewhat angrily.

Bill gazed innocently out of the window. "Tony, old fellow, it's a maxim to the effect that there's one born every minute."

"A sucker?"

"That word will do as well as any other."

Tony snorted. "Perhaps you'll say the same thing about the Marleys."

"Who are they?"

"Haven't you heard of them? The woman sits on the stage, blindfolded, and the man goes out into the audience——"

"And then the woman reads out what you've written on a piece of paper——"

"Yes."

"Or tells you the number engraved in your watch; or the initials on your ring; or the name of the maker of your hat——"

"Yes. Now that's mind reading, isn't it?"

Bill smiled wearily. "Tony, some time when we've got a few hours to spare I'll teach you how to do that with me. It might come in handy some time."

"You mean," gasped Tony, "that you know how it's done?"

Bill nodded. "I was taught by a tramp whom I met in a freight car. He had played the vaudeville houses with his partner. Then he took to drink, and got his signals mixed one night. That finished him. You see, when the sheriff's wife wrote on a bit of paper 'Whom does my husband love?' something went wrong, and the blindfolded lady answered, 'A beautiful young woman with blue eyes and golden hair.'"

"What of that?" queried Tony.

"Not much," said Bill, "only the sheriff's wife was so far from beautiful that she had no delusions on the subject—and she wasn't young—and, barring streaks of grey in her hair, she was a decided brunette. And she'd been having her suspicions about that husband of hers for a long time! The show stopped right there and the mind reader hopped on the first train leaving that town. He knew that the sheriff would be after him if he lingered."

"If he had been a mind reader," commented Tony, "a real mind reader, he would have foreseen trouble."

Bill laughed. "He foresaw trouble without the least difficulty, and he wasn't a mind reader! It didn't take a mind reader to do that—it needed nothing but plain common sense." Again he closed his eyes. "And now for a snooze," he murmured.

"What happened to the mind reader?" insisted Tony.

"Oh, he stuck to his trade and became prosperous again. We landed in St. Louis together. We were broke, both of us. He fixed that in short order. He'd walk into a saloon. He'd start talking about cards. He'd start talking about mind reading. Then he'd get into an argument with the best-dressed man in the place, and he'd invite him to pick any card out of a deck, call me on the telephone, and hear me tell him what card he held in his hand."

"It can't be done!" ejaculated Tony.

"There were lots of fellows who thought that way. In fact, they'd bet real money that it couldn't be done. My partner never went near the telephone, mind you. He'd say, "Call such and such a number, and ask for Mr. Parmelee."

"And you would name the card?"

"Every time."

"By George," admitted Tony, "that's wonderful!"

"Quite so," drawled Bill. "My partner visited eight or ten places a night. We started off with small bets: we

had to, because we began with only five dollars between us. But we split up over a thousand when we decided that it was time for us to make tracks."

"There was no reason that you should not have stayed there indefinitely."

"Oh, yes, there was! You see, the men who lost their bets might have found out that——"

"What could they have found out?"

Bill grinned reminiscently. "They might have found out that I had fifty-two different names! They'd call the same number every time—it was a public telephone in a cigar store—but once my partner would tell them to ask for 'Mr. Parmelee,' and once for 'Mr. Henderson,' and once for 'Mr. Bancroft,' and sometimes for 'Mr. Conroy,' or 'Mr. Hanford.' Of course I'd be standing right next to the 'phone all the time."

Tony corrugated his brows. "What's the big idea?"

"Don't you see it yet?" laughed Bill. "Each name indicated a different card. 'Parmelee' was the jack of spades—that was my partner's idea of humour; 'Henderson' was the queen of hearts; 'Hanford' was the queen of spades. Nothing could have been simpler: the first letter of the name told me the denomination of the card; the first vowel told me the suit. We had memorised a code—that was all."

"Whew!" whistled Tony.

"We couldn't work it more than once on the same crowd. That was the only objection to the scheme," confessed Bill, "but in a good-sized town we wouldn't do badly—not at all."

He turned to his bewildered friend, who was gazing at him with open mouth. "Tony," he declared, "any time you hear of a mind reading exhibition more wonderful than that,

you let me know where it is—I want to see it."

"I'll remember that," Tony promised. And he was so impressed that he allowed Bill to go to sleep without a protest, not to be wakened until they reached their destination.

II

When a man belongs to one club, he is likely to belong to another; and when he belongs to two, a third is nearly as inevitable as death and taxes. Tony belonged to the Windsor and to the Himalaya—had joined the first because it was the thing to do, and had joined the second in reaction against the oppressive respectability of the first.

The Windsor was rich, dignified, and exclusive; the Himalaya was rich, undignified, and the reverse of exclusive. By dividing his time between the two Tony convinced himself that he was neither too respectable nor too disreputable, neither a prig nor a sporting man, and ambled along on a middle course which impressed him as being just right. A spree at the Himalaya was atoned for by a staid evening at the Windsor; and after sojourning a while in the highly moral atmosphere of the latter organisation, a visit to the former would bring Tony back to the less exalted plane upon which he felt that he belonged. Membership in the Windsor alone would have branded Tony a snob; membership in the Himalaya alone would have marked him out as a rounder; membership in both qualified him far more congenially as a man about town, a true democrat equally at home in every society.

Yet a third club was necessary to the complete happiness of Tony and of other young men similarly situated,

with the result that a select group of them, taking into consideration the frequent vacations which a lifetime of doing nothing demanded, founded that justly celebrated organisation, the Riggs Island Association.

There were rumours that the association had been formed because Huntley Thornton, who had owned Riggs Island, a scrubby patch of sand off the South Carolina coast, had been anxious to sell it, and being in the real-estate business had painted its attractions to his friends in such glowing colours that he had been enabled to get out at a profit. This, however, was mere hearsay, and was never substantiated. Certain it was that Huntley Thornton had been a prime mover in bringing the Riggs Island Association into existence, and that his friends, oversupplied with money, and enraptured at the thought of an island paradise whither they might retreat to recuperate whenever so minded, had rallied loyally to his support.

To them it mattered nothing that the property consisted only of a few barren acres, a clump of discouraged scrub pines, and a billion gnats. The architect's drawings, prepared under Huntley Thornton's personal direction, featured a golf course, half a dozen tennis courts, a stone club-house, and a magnificent beach, and made no mention at all of the already existing features. Thornton's friends gazed upon the handsomely-framed water colours, admired the details, commended the general plan, and dug deep into their pockets for the funds which presently transformed a dream into a reality. In the process the original subscribers nobly paid assessment after assessment, but, as Chet Moulton said, "After we've spent a fortune on the clubhouse we can't shy at the cost of a breakwater. Hang it all, if we do, the clubhouse will be washed into the Atlantic Ocean!" The breakwater had been merely one of the costly necessities which Huntley Thornton's architect had not thought it necessary to mention. There were others—many, many others.

When the clubhouse was finished, when the tennis courts had been rolled to a glass-like smoothness, and the golf course had been completed, Thornton's friends journeyed down in groups, strolled over the property, admired the perfection of its appointments, and decided that it would do. Tony Claghorn trod experimentally on the tennis courts, hazarded the opinion that they would be fast—and never played. Chet Moulton cast an appraising eye upon the golf links, opined that par on the first hole should be four and not five—and never teed up a ball. Steve Forrester inspected the billiard tables, cast a languid glance at the rows of gleaming cues—but did not remove his coat to click off a few caroms. By tacit agreement the older men—those over thirty—left all forms of exercise to their juniors.

But it was on the beach, a spotless white strip protected by the costly breakwater, that all members met. It was Chet Moulton who first donned a bathing-suit, stuck an experimental toe into the water, and declared that the Atlantic Ocean, as sampled at Riggs Island, met with his approval. It was neither too cold nor too warm; there was neither too much nor too little current—this he discovered upon venturing in farther; and there was just enough tingle in the waves to make Chet—aged thirty-four—feel, as he himself expressed it, twenty years younger.

It was Steve Forrester, however, who discovered that the beach, gently sloping, firm, and warm to sit upon, was quite as suitable for games of

chance as for more strenuous pursuits. "Think of it, boys," he exclaimed, "I'll go home tanned like a bronze statue, and if anybody asks me where I got it, I'll mention I got sunburned playing poker!"

The conception tickled Steve's risibilities mightily. To don a bathing-suit immediately upon rising; to proceed to the beach after breakfast; to remain there, with occasional inter-missions for meals, a stack of chips at one hand, and a long, cold drink at the other, from morning till night!—the programme was most attractive. His fellow members voted for it en-thusiastically, and the demand for lo-tions to be applied to smarting shoul-ders was heavy for a few days. But after that the participants in the game became well hardened, and at nearly any hour a group of young men, tanned to a chrome-leather hue, might have been discovered squatting on the sand, listening to the plash of the waves, and debating mentally whether to raise or to call.

The tennis courts were often de-serted, the golf links neglected; but the beach was patronised so inces-santly that one could not walk across it, Chet Moulton complained, with-out stubbing a toe on a poker chip. "What are the wild waves saying?" inquired Chet. "Are they saying, 'Splash'? Not on your life. They're whispering 'Ante up!'"

In games, as everywhere else, there is the struggle for existence, and the survival of the fittest. At the Riggs Island Association, beach poker, as it was quickly called, drove everything else to the wall. They all played—all except Huntley Thornton, who made up for his non-participation in the games by acting as a lone spectator at them. Attired in immaculate flannels, jaunty in a Panama hat, with a ciga-rette, in a six-inch amber holder, dec-

orating his smiling countenance all day long, Thornton wandered from group to group, congratulating the winners, sympathising with the losers, and sooner or later squatting down to give his undivided attention to the play in the steepest game.

Repeatedly urged to take a hand, he had as often declined. "It may seem funny to you," he admitted, with a smile, "but I've never sat in a poker game in my life."

"No time to learn like the present."

"I promised my old mother," said Thornton, "that I would never gam-ble. I have yet to break that promise. I kept it in college. I kept it after college. I intend to keep it now."

Chet Moulton, who had just seen the most lucrative pot of the hour pass to an opponent, grinned ruefully. "Huntley," he declared, "I wish my mother had exacted a promise like that from me. It would have saved me a lot of money." Chet's sentiments were sincere. He had shown unlimited faith in a full hand, jacks up. He had backed it magnificently, only to see it lose dismally to a quartet of five-spots held by Don Felton. "If I had made a promise like that," mourned Chet, "and if I had kept it, I might have been a bloated capitalist to-day. Who knows?"

"And if I had made such a prom-ise," said Felton, carefully stacking his winnings, "I wouldn't be taking in this pot now."

"Never too late to start," suggested Chet. "You might give it back."

"I might—and then again, I might not," murmured Felton. He glanced at his cards, grinned at the discon-solate Chet, and tossed a chip into the centre of the little patch of sand about which they were sitting. "I'll open for the limit," he challenged.

It was into this atmosphere that

Tony Claghorn brought his friend, Bill Parmelee, for a complete rest.

III

"Your coming will be something of a sensation," predicted Tony, as he led the way to the launch which was to take them from the mainland to the island.

"How so?"

"You're a very well-known man, Bill. Everybody else knows it, even if you don't. I dare say that there's not a member of the club who hasn't heard of you."

"And you expect me to enjoy my vacation?"

"Why not?"

The ex-gambler shook his head. "I was never a great hand at advertising," he declared. "I'd prefer it—I'd prefer it greatly if not a soul knew me. Look here," he demanded suddenly, "have you told anybody I'm coming?"

"No," said Tony reluctantly, "I was saving that for a surprise."

"Well, suppose you save it a little longer."

"What do you mean?"

"Introduce me as your friend Brown—Bill Brown—that's a nice inoffensive name. Let me forget business—my peculiar kind of business—for a few days."

Tony's face fell. "I was rather set on introducing you to the boys. You see, I've told them so much about you."

Bill laughed. "Look here, old man," he inquired, "for whose pleasure did you get up this vacation? Theirs—or mine?"

"Yours, of course."

"Then remember my name is Bill Brown."

It hurt to do it, but it was under that name that Tony presented his friend to Huntley Thornton—and to Chet Moulton—and to Steve Forrester—and to the twenty or thirty other congenial spirits sojourning at the club. When, in conformity with established custom, the new arrivals donned bathing-suits, and were promptly drafted into games of beach poker, Tony nearly burst in the effort to keep his secret buried in his bosom, Felton, indeed, had asked Bill if he played, and Tony, beginning indignantly, "Does he play!" had been reminded to keep silence by a violent dig in his unprotected ribs.

To his distress, his friend was separated from him. As a newcomer, Felton, who invariably played in the steepest game, invited Bill to sit in. Tony, being a regular, found himself seated some twenty feet away—and nearly broke his neck in an attempt to observe what was happening to Bill. From time to time voices reached his ear; from time to time he observed Huntley Thornton, the lone spectator, intently watching the game in which he never took part; from time to time the players in his own game invited him to pay a little attention to it. But it was not until darkness had put an end to the afternoon's play that Tony received any authentic news from the front.

He led his friend out of earshot of the others. "How much did you win?" he inquired eagerly.

"I lost," said Bill.

"W-what?" stammered Tony. "You —you lost?"

"I lost. I lost heavily."

To Tony it seemed impossible that such a thing should ever occur to his friend. Then an improbable explanation flashed into his mind. "I understand, Bill," he guessed, "you were afraid of making them suspicious. You lost on purpose."

Bill laughed. "Why should I lose on purpose?" he countered. "In any event, why should I let them get into me for more than five hundred dollars? And what on earth should they be suspicious of? No; I didn't lose on purpose. I'm not a philanthropist. I tried my darnedest to win. And I didn't win because another fellow played a better game than I did. That happens sometimes, you know."

Tony choked. "But—but it's impossible!" he sputtered.

"Thanks for the compliment," smiled Bill.

"It's impossible," Tony insisted, "and I know it's impossible because I've played with every man in this club. There's not one of them that's in a class with you."

"How about Felton?"

"Don Felton?"

"The big fellow with the sandy hair."

"Was he the big winner?" gasped Tony.

"The big winner and the only winner."

Tony swallowed hard. "I played with him in New York, at the Himalaya, only a month ago, and I cleaned him out."

It was Bill's turn to swallow. "You —you cleaned him out?" he stammered.

"Without the least difficulty," asseverated Tony. His brain was whirling. "Lord knows I'm no crack," he pursued, "I play a tolerable game—a good average game—and I've played with enough really good players to know just where I get off. I'm not an expert——"

"And Felton?"

Tony threw up his hands. "Felton's game is to mine as my game is to yours. A month ago he wasn't even near my class."

"Yet to-day he played better poker than I did. He outguessed me from beginning to end. If he called, his cards were just a shade better than mine. And every time I had a really good hand he didn't even raise. He'd drop."

"He must have improved," said Tony idiotically.

"I'll say so," declared Bill. "If the man I played with to-day wasn't in your class a month ago——"

"He must have improved lots."

The eyes of the two men met. Yet it was Tony who voiced the thought that both were probably thinking. "There are many cheating devices," he murmured, "but which of them could be used by a man sitting on a sandy beach, in blazing sunlight, dressed in a one-piece bathing-suit?"

"None that I know of," said Bill.

IV

Tony returned to the attack at the first opportunity and that meant immediately after supper. With great self-control he had refrained from alluding to the subject for ninety consecutive minutes.

"The cards might have been marked," he suggested.

"They weren't."

"Are you sure?"

"I gathered up three or four after our talk, Tony. I have them in my pocket this minute. They're not marked—and I've gone over them with a glass."

"Felton might have resorted to sleight of hand."

"Not with me watching," said the ex-gambler emphatically. "It's gotten to be unconscious with me, I suppose, but I always watch the deal carefully."

"Then how did he do it?"

Bill's blue eyes twinkled. "Maybe he studied some good book on poker."

"Be serious, Bill."

"All right, I'll be serious," Bill promised. "On my word of honour, old fellow, I don't know how he did it. But I mean to find out."

It was Tony's turn to smile. "Nice, pleasant way of spending a vacation, isn't it? This is how you get away from cards for a change."

Bill grinned. "If I learn something new I won't complain."

"And in the meantime the problem is how can a man cheat, without marked cards, without sleight of hand, and dressed in a bathing-suit."

"That's all," assented Bill.

It is to be feared that Tony's night was far from peaceful. He tossed from side to side, a prey to weird speculations, racking his brains in an effort to discover some solution to the mystery. Dawn found him advanced not a step. In desperation he appealed to his friend.

"Bill, to-day when you play, let me watch."

"What for?"

"I might see something you don't."

Parmelee shook his head emphatically. "Tony, old fellow, you'd spoil it all. Felton's playing me for a sucker. It's an unusual part for me, and I'm enjoying it. But he'd stop like a shot if he thought I suspected. No, Tony, you can help me most by going about your own business and leaving me strictly alone."

Tony refused to be put off. "Look here," he insisted, "if you won't let me watch, you won't mind if I pass the word to Huntley Thornton?"

"What good would that do?"

"Huntley would keep his weather-eye open. Huntley always looks on."

It spoke volumes for Bill's self-control that he replied civilly. "He knows

nothing about cards. He told me so himself."

"Even so——"

"Tony, with what you know about me, are you really advising me to go to an amateur for assistance?"

"I don't know why not," ventured Tony.

"If you don't, then I do," said Bill decisively. "When I need a guardian, old man, I'll let you know. But for the time being I'll struggle on without help. And if you breathe a word to a soul I'll brain you!"

That threat kept Claghorn silent during the morning, but it did not prevent him from sidling up to Bill at noon to inquire, "How did it go?"

"Great!"

"You won?"

"I lost six hundred more."

"And you call that great?" gasped Tony.

"I call that most satisfactory," Bill declared. "For the first time I'm beginning to get my bearings."

Despite Tony's urgent questions he declined to add another word and left his friend in a condition bordering on collapse. Not once, but a dozen times, had Tony been an eye-witness of Bill's expertness at the profession which had been forced upon him: the profession of unmasking sharpers. Yet the memory of his repeated triumphs was less potent than the realisation that for once Bill was facing an extraordinary situation, and had, so far, met nothing but defeat.

Pride goeth before a fall; and Tony's pride in his idol departed on wings. Twenty-four hours earlier he would unhesitatingly have wagered his last cent that no problem connected with the devious arts of dishonest gambling was too difficult for the man who had solved so many. The events of the immediate past had shattered his faith to such an extent

that he had seriously offered his own help. That declined, he had offered, with equal seriousness, to ask Huntley Thornton—whose ignorance of cards was well known—to take Bill—whose knowledge of the subject was profound—under his wing.

The utter insanity of his proposals never occurred to Tony. Uppermost in his mind was the thought that his friend was in trouble, and that any straw was necessarily a promising straw.

During the afternoon Tony played so carelessly that for the first time in several sessions he found himself a winner. Had he stopped to analyse his own game he might have made the instructive discovery that it was undoubtedly at its best when his mind was not on it. But Tony was far too much concerned with graver matters to indulge in any such reflections. Being a winner, he retired from the game after an hour, and nonchalantly strolled towards the group which included Bill. At a distance of fifteen feet he was greeted with a look so fearful that he beat a hasty retreat.

Somewhat offended, he strode manfully into the water, and splashed around for an unconscionable period, a prey to disturbing meditations. How, he asked himself repeatedly, could a man cheat—attired only in a bathing-suit? The answer was perfectly clear: it could not be done, and Tony was reluctantly forced to the conclusion that his friend's game had deteriorated.

This decision was confirmed when at the end of the afternoon's play he made his way to Bill's side and hissed, "Well?"

The ex-gambler smiled cryptically.

"Well?" repeated Tony.

"Very well," said Bill.

Tony might have pursued his investigations further had he not, at that

moment, discerned Huntley Thornton, immaculate as always, stealthily endeavouring to attract his attention from the other end of the beach.

V

"Claghorn," began Thornton, "you don't mind if I ask you a few questions?"

"Not at all."

"Not even if they're rather personal questions about a friend of yours?"

"Why, what do you mean?"

Thornton wasted no time in beating around the bush. "Claghorn, I want to find out something about your guest, Mr. William Brown. Who is he? What is he? What do you know about him?"

Utterly astounded, Tony sparred for time. "Why do you ask?"

"Because he's a card-cheat," said Thornton flatly.

Tony gasped. "W-what did you say?" he sputtered.

"He's a card-cheat," Thornton repeated dispassionately. "How he does it, what methods he uses, I don't know. But the fact remains, nevertheless. I don't pretend to be an authority on cards. Quite the contrary, I am rather less than a novice; so I can't say how it's possible for a man—dressed in a bathing-suit—to cheat—"

The familiar words echoed in Tony's ears. "Possible?" he interrupted. "Why, it isn't possible."

"That's what I would have said in advance; but after what he did to poor Don Felton——"

"What he did?" Tony interrupted again. "Why, he lost five hundred to him yesterday."

"Yes."

"He lost six hundred more this morning."

"Quite so."

"And this afternoon I suppose he lost seven hundred."

"I'm sorry to say he didn't, Claghorn," said Thornton coldly. "This afternoon he got Don to raise the stakes, and he picked him clean."

"What?" gasped Tony. "He won?"

"He began by winning back the eleven hundred he had lost," said Thornton. "Then he won as much more from Don. Then he suggested raising the limit—which Don did, very foolishly—and it took your friend Brown less than an hour more to separate Don from every cent he had in the world."

Something in Tony urged him to cheer; to execute a dance of triumph; to shout his satisfaction aloud. But, for once, soberer second thought was with him, and he only murmured, "Isn't that too bad?"

"It's much too bad, Claghorn; it's very much too bad!"

"Tst! Tst!" clucked Tony.

"Don isn't a rich man——"

"No."

"The loss of the money means a lot to him."

"Of course it does."

"If he had lost it fairly and squarely——"

"What makes you think he didn't?" Tony interrupted.

"Impossible!" Thornton snapped. "This morning your friend Brown—so Felton said—played like a beginner. This afternoon he was infallible. Now, a man doesn't improve that much in an hour or two."

Familiar words! Familiar words! Inwardly Tony exulted, but he remarked shrewdly, "It was all right, you mean, so long as Brown played like a beginner, but it was all wrong the moment he began to play like an expert."

"That's not what I mean," said Thornton, "and you know it isn't."

"Well, what do you mean?"

"I mean this," and in the gathering darkness Tony could see his fists clench, "there's something wrong—something very wrong, indeed—somewhere. I want to find out what it is."

Tony smiled happily. "Why do you come to me?" he asked innocently.

"Because, like everybody else, I've heard of this Parmelee friend of yours, this man who makes it a business to expose cheats. I've heard how he showed up Graham in Palm Beach; and I've heard how he showed up others in New York. Now, if you will be so kind, I'd like you to wire Parmelee, and ask him to come here at once, at my expense, to investigate this man Brown."

Describing the episode afterwards Tony said: "I don't know how I stopped myself from breaking out into laughter. The idea was rich: asking Bill Parmelee to investigate himself! I was thankful that it was dark, and that Thornton couldn't see my face. Never in my life did I have a harder time keeping it straight!"

Thornton repeated his request: "I want you to wire for Parmelee. He's the man for the job. I want him to watch Brown play; to play with him himself if he wants to. And then I want him to expose him."

It was at this point that a familiar figure approached through the darkness, and Bill Parmelee—alias Brown—fully dressed, joined the speakers. "I couldn't help overhearing what you just said, Mr. Thornton," he declared. "I'm a great hand at coming right down to brass tacks. Let's have it out."

To say that Thornton was angry would be an under-statement. He was furious; beside himself with rage; and he began to speak in a tone which trembled with passion. Tony, listening, wondered why Thornton should take Felton's troubles so greatly to heart; and he wondered still more why Parmelee, sitting near him in the darkness, allowed the vitriolic blast to continue unchecked. Thornton was nothing if not specific: he did not hesitate to call names; to couple them with unpleasant adjectives; to express his opinions in the most elaborately insulting language.

To the torrent of invective, Bill answered not a word. It was only when Thornton ran out of breath, and stopped temporarily that Bill asked calmly, "Mr. Thornton, have you a cigarette?"

Utterly taken aback Thornton offered his case. Bill reached for it in the darkness, and found it.

"Have you a match?" Bill asked.

Tony had never seen his friend smoke. To his boundless astonishment, Bill now lighted a cigarette, inhaled a breath or two, and turned to his enemy.

"Go ahead, Mr. Thornton," he invited.

What followed according to Tony beggared description. Thornton, curiously confused, launched again into his invective. That it did not disturb Bill greatly was evidenced by the intermittent glimmer from his cigarette in the darkness. And then, in the middle of a word, Thornton stopped—stopped dead.

For a minute—two minutes—while Tony marvelled—there was absolute silence. Then, in curiously different voice, Thornton said, "I understand, Mr. Parmelee."

"Mr. Parmelee!" Tony felt his hair rising on end. By what process had Thornton discovered his identity? But he was speaking again.

"I beg your pardon, Mr. Claghorn," faltered Thornton. "I'm sorry I made such a scene." He paused—paused for another unearthly wait while the cigarette twinkled. "In the morning, Mr.

Parmelee; yes, I'll leave in the morning. Felton will go, too. I will answer for him. We are grateful, Mr. Parmelee, both of us." Again an unearthly pause, while Tony clenched his fists and wondered what supernatural forces were at work. Then, in a broken voice, Thornton was speaking: "Do you insist, Mr. Parmelee?" Utterly crushed, he turned to Tony. "Mr. Claghorn, at Mr. Parmelee's request, I tell you that Felton cheated —and that I was his accomplice. Is that enough, Mr. Parmelee? . . . Thank you. . . . Good night."

Through the darkness came the sound of Thornton's retreating footsteps. Then, in a glowing arc, Bill's cigarette flew through the air, to fall with a gentle hiss into the ocean.

Again Tony felt his hair rising. He had been in the presence of something strangely mysterious, something so uncanny that it partook of the miraculous. He stretched out a trembling hand and seized his friend's knee. "Bill," he begged, "for Heaven's sake, what was it?"

Came the familiar laugh, and then, for the first time in many minutes, the sound of Bill's voice. "It was mind reading," he said.

VI

It was not until they were again seated in the train, nearly a week later, that Bill consented to answer Tony's innumerable questions. Prior to that time he had maintained a stony silence. Even when Huntley Thornton and Don Felton had suddenly decided to go fishing in southern Florida, and had departed, bag and baggage, before daybreak, Bill had had no comment to offer.

"Surely you could have told me then," Tony protested.

"Why? You would never have been satisfied until you had told it to every man in the club."

"And why not?"

"You would have shown them up."

"They should have been shown up."

"I wonder!" said Bill. "They were amateurs—nothing but amateurs—and it's so much easier to ruin reputations than to make them. If I had spoken, I would have branded those two men for the rest of their lives. As it is, they've gone off together where they can think things over, and they may decide that honesty isn't such a bad policy after all."

"Humph!" snorted Tony.

"In the bottom of your heart, old fellow, you agree with me. I've shown up a good many men—but they've deserved it. These two were in a class by themselves. They'd made a mistake. I've given them a chance to let it be forgotten. If they go wrong again— well, it won't be on my conscience." He smiled. "Is that so, Tony?"

"I guess so," Tony admitted. "In fact, I'll agree with anything if you tell me just what happened. To me, it's all as clear as mud."

Bill laughed. "It began in a funny way. When I lost to Felton on that first afternoon, I had no suspicion that anything was wrong. He played as if he knew every card in my hand. Well, that's what I'd expect of a really fine player. I thought Felton was one.

"Then you told me what you knew about him: that he wasn't even in your class, and I tried to put two and two together. Generally two and two make four—but this time they didn't, and it wasn't until the next morning that I began to suspect what was going on. It was really the simplest thing in the world when I once put my mind on it. The cards weren't marked; Felton wasn't doing any legerdemain —he wasn't nearly clever enough for

that—yet he played as if he knew just what I held. There could be only one answer: he did actually know, and that meant that somebody was telling him.

"When you play indoors, your cards are dealt on to a table; you gather them together; you raise the pips just enough to read them, and you leave them right on the table. At any rate, that's what you do if you're a professional gambler—and I'm a professional. But playing on the sand you can't do that because it would take acrobatics. Instead, you take up your cards—and unless you hold them mighty close, a man sitting behind you can read them.

"That's where Thornton came in. I'm not a stingy player, and the moment I started betting liberally, Thornton plunked himself down where he could watch. Then he signalled my holdings to his partner."

"How did he do it?"

"It cost me six hundred dollars to find out. Naturally I couldn't face him. I watched him out of the corner of my eye: that was all I dared. Even then, it took me an hour to discover his system—it was so beautifully simple that you would never notice it if you weren't looking for it."

"Well? Well?" said Tony impatiently.

"Did you ever see Thornton without a cigarette in his mouth?" Bill inquired.

Tony could not control his vexation. "Bill," he pleaded, "I'm not a bit interested in Thornton's personal habits. And I'm very much interested in his method of signalling."

"You won't see a thing when it's right under your nose—or under his nose, I should say," laughed Bill. "That was how he did it. His cigarette, man! His cigarette!"

"What about it?"

"Well, it smoked, didn't it? It could produce short puffs, and it could produce long puffs—and it could produce any required alternation of them, couldn't it?"

"You mean——?" gasped Tony.

"I mean Thornton's cigarette was sending perfectly good Morse. And I thanked my lucky stars that telegraphy was one of the things I picked up in my six years on the road. Of course Thornton abbreviated: he didn't have to spell out, 'He's holding two pairs, kings up,' when it took no particular genius to condense that into three letters, and he didn't have to telegraph, 'Mr. Brown has just filled a straight, jack high,' when he could say the same thing in two letters. In fact, he didn't have to use Morse—a prearranged code would have answered just as well—and it would have given me no more trouble."

"How on earth could you beat such a team?"

"By playing straight poker," said Bill. "In the afternoon, instead of sitting up, I lay down, held my cards so that I could barely see them myself, and played the great American game just as well as I knew how. One of the peculiarities of beach poker," commented Bill, "is that you can play it lying on your stomach. I did—and for twenty-four hours afterwards I had a crick in the neck to show for it.

"I won back the eleven hundred I had lost in short order; and then Felton made the mistake of losing his temper. He had whipped me so easily that morning—and the day before—that he couldn't quite reconcile himself to the sudden change in the state of affairs. He got angry, and when I suggested raising the limit, he got angrier, but he didn't decline." Bill sighed reminiscently. "It was quick work after that, and towards the end I had Thornton telegraphing, 'Stop!

Stop! Stop!' That was all he could telegraph, and it only made his partner more furious than ever." He chuckled. "I enjoyed that game: 'pon my word, I did!"

"And then?" said Tony.

"What do you mean?"

"How do you explain what you did to Thornton? I never saw anything more wonderful in my life. He started in to abuse you—to call you every name he could think of—and you stopped him, you crushed him, you made him confess without saying a word. And then you insisted it was mind reading!"

Bill laughed. "Tony, old fellow, my artistic temperament is to blame. I hadn't thought of it until I walked back to the beach, but it suddenly struck me what a masterly touch it would be to pay Thornton out in his own coin—to tell him what I had to say with one of his own cigarettes!"

"You mean—you telegraphed?"

"I did."

"With puffs of smoke?"

"Not in the dark, old fellow. I remembered the Good Book: the 'pillar of cloud' and the 'pillar of fire'; I said what I had to say with the burning tip of my cigarette, and believe me, I didn't mince matters!"

He smiled as Tony gazed at him open-mouthed. "I am not ordinarily a profane man," said Bill, "but if you had been able to read what I said to Thornton, even you would have blushed. I'll bet he did."

He paused to witness Tony shaking in the throes of Homeric laughter. "There's something about it," Tony gasped, between explosions, "something about—the idea—of swearing—profanely—with the end—of a cigarette—that strikes me—as being awfully—awfully funny!" For an instant he mastered himself. Then he was off again. "To think—to think—that he asked me to send for Bill Parmelee—to investigate Bill Parmelee!"

"It would have been awkward, wouldn't it?" Bill admitted. He grinned as his friend went into spasm after spasm of uncontrollable laughter.

But the final question came later. "Bill," asked Tony, long after, "did those fellows—Thornton and Felton—actually think you cheated?"

Bill chuckled. "They did, Tony, and that's the chief reason why I forgave them. I didn't cheat. Of course I didn't cheat. But they thought I did. They were sure I did. They were such awful dubs, such hopeless amateurs, that they didn't recognise really good play when they saw it."

"Tony, old man," Bill concluded, "in my long career I've had compliments—many compliments. But to be accused of cheating because my game is so good: I'll never ask for a finer one than that!"

THE STRANGE WILL

from the novel *The Man with the Broken Ear*

EDMOND ABOUT

About ten o'clock in the evening, Mlle. Virginie Sambucco said it was time to think of going home: the ladies lived with monastic regularity. Leon protested; but Clementine obeyed, though not without pouting a little. Already the parlor door was open, and the old lady had taken her hood in the hall, when the engineer, suddenly struck with an idea, exclaimed:

"You surely won't go without helping me to open my trunks! I demand it of you as a favor, my good Mademoiselle Sambucco!"

The respectable lady paused: custom urged her to go; kindness inclined her to stay; an atom of curiosity swayed the balance.

"I'm so glad!" cried Clementine, replacing her aunt's hood on the rack.

Mme. Renault did not yet know where they had put Leon's baggage. Gothon came to say that everything had been thrown pell-mell into the sorcerer's den, to remain there until Monsieur should point out what he wanted taken to his own room. The whole company, armed with lamps and candles, betook themselves to a vast room on the ground floor, where furnaces, retorts, philosophical instruments, boxes, trunks, clothes bags, hat boxes and the famous steam-engine,

formed a confused and entertaining spectacle. The light played about this interior, as it appears to in certain pictures of the Dutch school. It glanced upon the great yellow cylinders of the electric machine, struck upon the long glass bottles, rebounded from two silver reflectors, and rested, in passing, upon a magnificent Fortin barometer. The Renaults and their friends, grouped in the midst of the boxes—some sitting, some standing, one holding a lamp, another a candle—detracted nothing from the picturesqueness of the scene.

Leon, with a bunch of little keys, opened the boxes one after another. Clementine was seated opposite him on a great oblong box, and watched him with all her eyes, more from affection than curiosity. They began by setting to one side two enormous square boxes which contained nothing but mineralogical specimens. After this they passed in review the riches of all kinds which the engineer had crowded among his linen and clothing.

A pleasant odor of Russia leather, tea from the caravans, Levant tobacco, and attar of roses soon permeated the laboratory. Leon brought forth a little at a time, as is the custom of all rich travellers who, on leaving home, left

a family and good stock of friends behind. He exhibited, in turn, fabrics of the Asiatic looms, narghiles of embossed silver from Persia, boxes of tea, sherbets flavored with rose, precious extracts, golden webs from Tarjok, antique armor, a service of frosted silver of Toula make, jewelry mounted in the Russian style, Caucasian bracelets, necklaces of milky amber, and a leather sack full of turquoises such as they sell at the fair of Nijni Novgorod. Each object passed from hand to hand amid questions, explanations, and interjections of all kinds. All the friends present received the gifts intended for them. There was a concert of polite refusals, friendly urgings, and 'thank-yous' in all sorts of voices. It is unnecessary to say that much the greater share fell to the lot of Clementine; but she did not wait to be urged to accept them, for, in the existing state of affairs, all these pretty things would be but as a part of the wedding gifts —not going out of the family.

Leon had brought his father an exceedingly handsome dressing gown of a cloth embroidered with gold, some antiquarian books found in Moscow, a pretty picture by Greuze, which had been stuck out of the way, by the luckiest of accidents, in a mean shop at Gastinitvor; two magnificent specimens of rock-crystal, and a cane that had belonged to Humboldt. "You see," said he to M. Renault, on handing him this historic staff, "that the postscript of your last letter did not fall overboard."

The old professor received the present with visible emotion.

"I will never use it," said he to his son. "The Napoleon of science has held it in his hand: what would one think if an old sergeant like me should permit himself to carry it in his walks in the woods? And the collections? Were you not able to buy anything

from them? Did they sell very high?"

"They were not sold," answered Leon. "All were placed in the National Museum at Berlin. But in my eagerness to satisfy you, I made a thief of myself in a strange way. The very day of my arrival, I told your wish to a guide who was showing me the place. He told me that a friend of his, a little Jew broker by the name of Ritter, wanted to sell a very fine anatomical specimen that had belonged to the estate. I ran to the Jew's, examined the mummy, for such it was, and, without any haggling, paid the price he asked. But the next day, a friend of Humboldt, Professor Hirtz, told me the history of this shred of a man, which had been lying around the shop for more than ten years, and never belonged to Humboldt at all."

* * *

Leon took his bunch of keys and opened a long oak box. The lid being raised, they saw a great leaden casket which enclosed a magnificent walnut box carefully polished on the outside, and lined on the inside with white silk, and padded. The others brought their lamps and candles near, and the colonel of the 23d of the line appeared as if he were in a chapel illuminated for his lying in state.

One would have said that the man was asleep. The perfect preservation of the body attested the paternal care of the murderer. It was truly a remarkable preparation, and would have borne comparison with the finest European mummies described by Vicq d'Azyr in 1779, and by the younger Puymaurin in 1787.

The part best preserved, as is always the case, was the face. All the features had maintained a proud and manly expression. If any old friend of the colonel had been present at

the opening of the third box, he would have recognized him at first sight.

Undoubtedly the point of the nose was a little sharper, the nostrils less expanded and thinner, and the bridge a little more marked than in the year 1813. The eyelids were thinned, the lips pinched, the corners of the mouth drawn down, the cheek bones too prominent, and the neck visibly shrunken, which exaggerated the prominence of the chin and larynx. But the eyelids were closed without contraction, and the sockets much less hollow than one could have expected; the mouth was not at all distorted like the mouth of a corpse; the skin was slightly wrinkled but had not changed color; it had only become a little more transparent, showing, after a fashion, the color of the tendons, the fat and the muscles, wherever it rested directly upon them. It also had a rosy tint which is not ordinarily seen in embalmed corpses. Doctor Martout explained this anomaly by saying that if the colonel had actually been dried alive, the globules of the blood were not decomposed, but simply collected

in the capillary vessels of the skin and subjacent tissues where they still preserved their proper color, and could be seen more easily than otherwise, on account of the semi-transparency of the skin.

The uniform had become much too large, as may be readily understood; though it did not seem, at a casual glance, that the members had become deformed. The hands were dry and angular, but the nails, although a little bent inward toward the root, had preserved all their freshness. The only very noticeable change was the excessive depression of the abdominal walls, which seemed crowded downward toward the posterior side; at the right, a slight elevation indicated the place of the liver. A tap of the finger on the various parts of the body, produced a sound like that from dry leather. While Leon was pointing out these details to his audience and doing the honors of his mummy he awkwardly broke off the lower part of the right ear, and a little piece of the colonel remained in his hand.

The Will

On this 20th day of January, 1824, being worn down by a cruel malady and feeling the approach of the time when my person shall be absorbed in the Great All;

I have written with my own hand this testament which is the expression of my last will.

I appoint as executor my nephew Nicholas Meiser, a wealthy brewer in the city of Dantzic.

I bequeath my books, papers and scientific collections of all kinds, except item 3712, to my very estimable and learned friend, Herr Von Humboldt.

I bequeath all the rest of my effects, real and personal, valued at 100,000 Prussian thalers or 375,000 francs, to Colonel Pierre Victor Fougas, at present desiccated, but living, and entered in my catalogue opposite No. 3712 (Zoology).

I trust that he will accept this feeble compensation for the ordeals he has undergone in my laboratory, and the service he has rendered to science.

Finally, in order that my nephew Nicholas Meiser may exactly understand the duties I leave him to perform, I have resolved to inscribe here a detailed account of the desiccation of Colonel Fougas, my sole heir.

It was on the 11th of November in that unhappy year 1813, that my relations with this brave young man began. I had long since quitted Dantzic, where the noise of cannon and the danger from bombs had rendered all labor impossible, and retired with my instruments and books under the protection of the Allied Armies in the fortified town of Liebenfeld. The French garrisons of Dantzic, Stettin, Custrin, Glogau, Hamburg and sev

eral other German towns could not communicate with each other or with their native land; meanwhile General Rapp was obstinately defending himself against the English fleet and the Russian army. Colonel Fougas was taken by a detachment of the Barclay de Tolly corps, as he was trying to pass the Vistula on the ice, on the way to Dantzic. They brought him prisoner to Liebenfeld on the 11th of November, just at my supper time, and Sergeant Garok, who commanded in the village, forced me to be present at the examination and act as interpreter.

The open countenance, manly voice, proud firmness and fine carriage of the unfortunate young man won my heart. He had made the sacrifice of his life. His only regret, he said, was having stranded so near port, after passing through four armies; and being unable to carry out the Emperor's orders. He appeared animated by that French fanaticism which has done so much harm to our beloved Germany. Nevertheless I could not help defending him; and I translated his words less as an interpreter than as an advocate. Unhappily, they found upon him a letter from Napoleon to General Rapp, of which I preserved a copy:

"Abandon Dantzic, break the blockade, unite with the garrisons of Stettin, Custrin and Glogau, march along the Elbe, arrange with St. Cyr and Davoust to concentrate the forces scattered at Dresden, Forgau, Wittenberg, Magdeburg and Hamburg; roll up an army like a snow ball; cross Westphalia, which is open, and come to defend the line of the Rhine with an army of 170,000 Frenchmen which you will have saved!

"NAPOLEON."

This letter was sent to the head-

quarters of the Russian army, whilst a half-dozen illiterate soldiers, drunk with joy and bad brandy, condemned the brave colonel of the 23d of the line to the death of a spy and a traitor. The execution was fixed for the next day, the 12th, and M. Pierre Victor Fougas, after having thanked and embraced me with the most touching sensibility, (He is a husband and a father.) was shut up in the little battlemented tower of Liebenfeld, where the wind whistles terribly through all the loopholes.

The night of the 11th and 12th of November was one of the severest of that terrible winter. My self-registering thermometer, which hung outside my window with a southeast exposure, marked nineteen degrees below zero, centigrade. I went early in the morning to bid the colonel a last farewell, and met Sergeant Garok, who said to me in bad German:

"We won't have to kill the Frantzouski, he is frozen to death."

I ran to the prison. The colonel was lying on his back, rigid. But I found after a few minutes' examination, that the rigidity of the body was not that of death. The joints, though they had not their ordinary suppleness, could be bent and extended without any great effort. The limbs, the face, and the chest gave my hands a sensation of cold, but very different from that which I had often experienced from contact with corpses.

Knowing that he had passed several nights without sleep, and endured extraordinary fatigues, I did not doubt that he had fallen into that profound and lethargic sleep which is superinduced by intense cold, and which if too far prolonged slackens respiration and circulation to a point where the most delicate physiological tests are necessary to discover the continuance of life. The pulse was insensible; at least my fingers, benumbed with cold, could not feel it. My hardness of hearing (I was then in my sixty-ninth year) prevented my determining by auscultation whether the beats of the heart still aroused those feeble though prolonged vibrations which the ear continues to hear some time after the hand fails to detect them.

The colonel had reached that point of torpor produced by cold, where to revive a man without causing him to die, requires numerous and delicate attentions. Some hours after, congelation would supervene, and with it, impossibility of restoration to life.

I was in the greatest perplexity. On the one hand I knew that he was dying on my hands by congelation; on the other, I could not, by myself, bestow upon him the attentions that were indispensable. If I were to administer stimulants without having him, at the same time, rubbed on the trunk and limbs by three or four vigorous assistants, I would revive him only to see him die. I had still before my eyes the spectacle of that lovely young girl asphyxiated in a fire, whom I succeeded in reviving by placing burning coals under the clavicles, but who could only call her mother, and died almost immediately, in spite of the administration of internal stimulants and electricity for inducing contractions of the diaphragm and heart.

And even if I should succeed in bringing him back to health and strength, was not he condemned by court-martial? Did not humanity forbid my rousing him from this repose akin to death, to deliver him to the horrors of execution?

I must confess that in the presence of this organism where life was suspended, my ideas on reanimation took, as it were, fresh hold upon me. I had so often desiccated and revived beings quite elevated in the animal scale, that

I did not doubt the success of the operation, even on a man. By myself alone I could not revive and save the colonel; but I had in my laboratory, all the instruments necessary to desiccate him without assistance.

To sum up, three alternatives offered themselves to me. I. To leave the colonel in the crenellated tower, where he would have died the same day of congelation. II. To revive him by stimulants, at the risk of killing him. And for what? To give him up, in case of success, to inevitable execution. III. To desiccate him in my laboratory with the quasi certainty of resuscitating him after the restoration of peace. All friends of humanity will doubtless comprehend that I could not hesitate long.

I had Sergeant Garok called, and I begged him to sell me the body of the colonel. It was not the first time that I had bought a corpse for dissection, so my request excited no suspicion. The bargain concluded, I gave him four bottles of kirsch-wasser, and soon two Russian soldiers brought me Colonel Fougas on a stretcher.

As soon as I was alone with him, I pricked one of his fingers: pressure forced out a drop of blood. To place it under a microscope between two plates of glass was the work of a minute. Oh, joy! The fibrin was not coagulated. The red globules appeared cleanly circular, flattened, biconcave, and without notches, indentations or spheroidal swellings. The white globules changed their shape, taking at intervals the spherical form, and varying their shapes again by delicate expansions. I was not deceived then, it was a torpid man that I had under my eyes, and not a dead one!

I placed him on a pair of scales. He weighed one hundred and forty pounds, clothing included. I did not care to undress him, for I had noticed that animals desiccated directly in contact with the air, died oftener than those which remained covered with moss and other soft materials, during the ordeal of desiccation.

My great air-pump, with its immense platform, its enormous oval wrought-iron receiver, which a rope running on a pulley firmly fixed in the ceiling easily raised and lowered by means of a windlass—all these thousand and one contrivances which I had so laboriously prepared in spite of the railleries of those who envied me, and which I felt desolate at seeing unemployed, were going to find their use! Unexpected circumstances had arisen at last to procure me such a subject for experiment, as I had in vain endeavored to procure, while I was attempting to reduce to torpidity dogs, rabbits, sheep and other mammals by the aid of freezing mixtures. Long ago, without doubt, would these results have been attained if I had been aided by those who surrounded me, instead of being made the butt of their railleries; if our authorities had sustained me with their influence instead of treating me as a subversive spirit.

I shut myself up tête-à-tête with the colonel, and took care that even old Getchen, my housekeeper, now deceased, should not trouble me during my work. I had substituted for the wearisome lever of the old fashioned air-pumps, a wheel arranged with an eccentric which transformed the circular movement of the axis into the rectilinear movement required by the pistons: the wheel, the eccentric, the connecting rod, and the joints of the apparatus all worked admirably, and enabled me to do everything by myself. The cold did not impede the play of the machine, and the lubricating oil was not gummed: I had refined it myself by a new process founded on

the then recent discoveries of the French *savant* M. Chevreul.

Having extended the body on the platform of the air-pump, lowered the receiver and luted the rim, I undertook to submit it gradually to the influence of a dry vacuum and cold. Capsules filled with chloride of calcium were placed around the colonel to absorb the water which should evaporate from the body, and to promote the desiccation.

I certainly found myself in the best possible situation for subjecting the human body to a process of gradual desiccation without sudden interruption of the functions, or disorganization of the tissues or fluids. Seldom had my experiments on rotifers and tardigrades been surrounded with equal chances of success, yet they had always succeeded. But the particular nature of the subject and the special scruples imposed upon my conscience, obliged me to employ a certain number of new conditions, which I had long since, in other connections, foreseen the expediency of. I had taken the pains to arrange an opening at each end of my oval receiver, and fit into it a heavy glass, which enabled me to follow with my eye the effects of the vacuum on the colonel. I was entirely prevented from shutting the windows of my laboratory, from fear that a too elevated temperature might put an end to the lethargy of the subject, or induce some change in the fluids. If a thaw had come on, all would have been over with my experiment. But the thermometer kept for several days between six and eight degrees below zero, and I was very happy in seeing the lethargic sleep continue, without having to fear congelation of the tissues.

I commenced to produce the vacuum with extreme slowness, for fear that the gases distributed through the blood, becoming free on account of the difference of their tension from that of rarified air, might escape in the vessels and so bring on immediate death. Moreover, I watched, every moment, the effects of the vacuum on the intestinal gases, for by expanding inside in proportion as the pressure of the air diminished outside of the body, they could have caused serious disorders. The tissues might not have been entirely ruptured by them, but an internal lesion would have been enough to occasion death in a few hours after reanimation. One observes this quite frequently in animals carelessly desiccated.

Several times, too rapid a protrusion of the abdomen put me on my guard against the danger which I feared, and I was obliged to let in a little air under the receiver. At last, the cessation of all phenomena of this kind satisfied me that the gases had disappeared by exosmose or had been expelled by the spontaneous contraction of the viscera. It was not until the end of the first day that I could give up these minute precautions, and carry the vacuum a little further.

The next day, the 13th, I pushed the vacuum to a point where the barometer fell to five millimetres. As no change had taken place in the position of the body or limbs, I was sure that no convulsion had been produced. The colonel had been desiccated, had become immobile, had lost the power of performing the functions of life, without death having supervened, and without the possibility of returning to activity having departed. His life was suspended, not extinguished.

Each time that a surplus of watery vapor caused the barometer to ascend, I pumped. On the 14th, the door of my laboratory was literally broken in by the Russian General, Count Trollohub, who had been sent from head-

quarters. This distinguished officer had run in all haste to prevent the execution of the colonel and to conduct him into the presence of the Commander in Chief. I loyally confessed to him what I had done under the inspiration of my conscience; I showed him the body through one of the bull's-eyes of the air-pump; I told him that I was happy to have preserved a man who could furnish useful information to the liberators of my country; and I offered to resuscitate him at my own expense if they would promise me to respect his life and liberty. The General, Count Trollohub, unquestionably a distinguished man, but one of an exclusively military education, thought that I was not speaking seriously. He went out slamming the door in my face, and treating me like an old fool.

I set myself to pumping again, and kept the vacuum at a pressure of from three to five millimetres for the space of three months. I knew by experience that animals can revive after being submitted to a dry vacuum and cold for eighty days.

On the 12th of February 1814, having observed that for a month no modification had taken place in the shrinking of the flesh, I resolved to submit the colonel to another series of operations, in order to insure more perfect preservation by complete desiccation. I let the air re-enter by the stop-cock arranged for the purpose, and, after raising the receiver, proceeded at once to my experiment.

The body did not weigh more than forty-six pounds; I had then reduced it nearly to a third of its original weight. It should be borne in mind that the clothing had not lost as much water as the other parts. Now the human body contains nearly four-fifths of its own weight of water, as is proved by a desiccation thoroughly made in a chemical drying furnace.

I accordingly placed the colonel on a tray, and, after sliding it into my great furnace, gradually raised the temperature to 75 degrees, centigrade. I did not dare to go beyond this heat, from fear of altering the albumen and rendering it insoluble, and also of taking away from the tissues the capacity of reabsorbing the water necessary to a return to their functions.

I had taken care to arrange a convenient apparatus so that the furnace was constantly traversed by a current of dry air. This air was dried in traversing a series of jars filled with sulphuric acid, quick-lime and chloride of calcium.

After a week passed in the furnace, the general appearance of the body had not changed, but its weight was reduced to forty pounds, clothing included. Eight days more brought no new decrease of weight. From this, I concluded that the desiccation was sufficient. I knew very well that corpses mummified in church vaults for a century or more, end by weighing no more than a half-score of pounds, but they do not become so light without a material alteration in their tissues.

On the 27th of February, I myself placed the colonel in the boxes which I had had made for his occupancy. Since that time, that is to say during a space of nine years and eleven months, we have never been separated. I carried him with me to Dantzic. He stays in my house. I have never placed him, according to his number, in my zoological collection; he remains by himself, in the chamber of honor. I do not grant any one the pleasure of re-using his chloride of calcium. I will take care of you till my dying day, Oh Colonel Fougas, dear and unfortunate friend! But I shall not have the joy of witnessing your resurrection. I

shall not share the delightful emotions of the warrior returning to life. Your lachrymal glands, inert to-day, but some day to be reanimated, will not pour upon the bosom of your old bene-factor, the sweet dew of recognition. For you will not recover your life until a day when mine will have long since departed! Perhaps you will be aston-ished that I, loving you as I do, should have so long delayed to draw you out of this profound slumber. Who knows but that some bitter reproach may come to taint the tenderness of the first offices of gratitude that you will perform over my tomb! Yes! I have prolonged, without any benefit to you, an experiment of general interest to others. I ought to have remained faith-ful to my first intention, and restored your life, immediately after the signa-ture of peace. But what! Was it well to send you back to France when the sun of your father-land was obscured by our soldiers and allies? I have spared you that spectacle—one so grievous to such a soul as yours. With-out doubt you would have had, in March, 1815, the consolation of again seeing that fatal man to whom you had consecrated your devotion; but are you entirely sure that you would not have been swallowed up with his fortune, in the shipwreck of Water-loo?

For five or six years past, it has not been your welfare nor even the welfare of science, that prevented me from reanimating you, it has been. . . . Forgive me, Colonel, it has been a cowardly attachment to life. The disorder from which I am suffer-ing, and which will soon carry me off, is an aneurism of the heart; violent emotions are interdicted to me. If I were myself to undertake the grand operation whose process I have traced in a memorandum annexed to this in-strument, I would, without any doubt,

succumb before finishing it; my death would be an untoward accident which might trouble my assistants and cause your resuscitation to fail.

Rest content! You will not have long to wait, and, moreover, what do you lose by waiting? You do not grow old, you are always twenty-four years of age; your children are growing up, you will be almost their contemporary when you come to life again. You came to Liebenfeld poor, you are now in my house poor, and my will makes you rich. That you may be happy also, is my dearest wish.

I direct that, the day after my death, my nephew, Nicholas Meiser, shall call together, by letter, the ten physicians most illustrious in the king-dom of Prussia, that he shall read to them my will and the annexed memo-randum, and that he shall cause them to proceed without delay, in my own laboratory, to the resuscitation of Colo-nel Fougas. The expenses of travel, maintenance, etc., etc., shall be de-ducted from the assets of my estate. The sum of two thousand thalers shall be devoted to the publication of the glorious results of the experiment, in German, French and Latin. A copy of this pamphlet shall be sent to each of the learned societies then existing in Europe.

In the entirely unexpected event of the efforts of science being unable to reanimate the colonel, all my effects shall revert to Nicholas Meiser, my sole surviving relative.

JOHN MEISER, M. D.

* * *

Doctor Hirtz of Berlin, who had copied this will himself, apologized very politely for not having sent it sooner. Business had obliged him to travel away from the Capital. In pass-ing through Dantzic, he had given himself the pleasure of visiting Herr

Nicholas Meiser, the former brewer, now a very wealthy land-owner and heavy holder of stocks, sixty-six years of age. This old man very well remembered the death and will of his uncle, the *savant;* but he did not speak of them without a certain reluctance. Moreover, he said that immediately after the decease of John Meiser, he had called together ten physicians of Dantzic around the mummy of the colonel; he also showed a unanimous statement of these gentlemen, affirming that a man desiccated in a furnace cannot in any way or by any means return to life. This certificate, drawn up by the professional competitors and enemies of the deceased, made no mention of the paper annexed to the will. Nicholas Meiser swore by all the gods (but not without visibly coloring) that this document concerning the methods to be pursued in resuscitating the colonel, had never been known by himself or his wife. When interrogated regarding the reasons which could have brought him to part with a trust as precious as the body of M. Fougas, he said that he had kept it in his house fifteen years with every imaginable respect and care, but that at the end of that time, becoming beset with visions and being awakened almost every night by the colonel's ghost coming and pulling at his feet, he concluded to sell it for twenty crowns to a Berlin amateur. Since he had been rid of this dismal neighbor, he had slept a great deal better, but not entirely well yet; for it had been impossible for him to forget the apparition of the colonel.

The Fulfillment

M. Nibor and his colleagues, who had been summoned to Paris, after the usual compliments, requested to see the subject. They had no time to lose, as the experiment could hardly last less than three days. Leon hastened to conduct them to the laboratory and to open the three boxes containing the colonel.

They found that the patient presented quite a favorable appearance. M. Nibor took off his clothes, which tore like tinder from having been too much dried in Father Meiser's furnace. The body, when naked, was pronounced entirely free from blemish and in a perfectly healthy condition. No one would yet have guaranteed success, but every one was full of hope.

After this preliminary examination, M. Renault put his laboratory at the service of his guests. He offered them all that he possessed, with a munificence which was not entirely free from vanity. In case the employment of electricity should appear necessary, he had a powerful battery of Leyden jars and forty of Bunsen's elements, which were entirely new. M. Nibor thanked him smilingly.

"Save your riches," said he. "With a bath-tub and caldron of boiling water, we will have everything we need. The colonel needs nothing but humidity. The thing is to give him the quantity of water necessary to the play of the organs. If you have a small room where one can introduce a jet of vapor, we will be more than content."

M. Audret, the architect, had very wisely built a little bath-room near the laboratory, which was convenient and well lighted. The celebrated steam engine was not far off, and its boiler had not, up to this time, answered any other purpose than that of warming the baths of M. and Mme. Renault.

The colonel was carried into this room, with all the care necessitated

by his fragility. It was not intended to break his second ear in the hurry of moving. Leon ran to light the fire under the boiler, and M. Nibor created him Fireman, on the field of battle.

Soon a jet of tepid vapor streamed into the bath-room, creating around the colonel a humid atmosphere which was elevated by degrees, and without any sudden increase, to the temperature of the human body. These conditions of heat and humidity were maintained with the greatest care for twenty-four hours. No one in the house went to sleep. The members of the Parisian Committee encamped in the laboratory. Leon kept up the fire; M. Nibor, M. Renault and M. Martout took turns in watching the thermometer. Madame Renault was making tea and coffee, and punch too. Gothon, who had taken communion in the morning, kept praying to God, in the corner of her kitchen, that this impious miracle might not succeed. A certain excitement already prevailed throughout the town, but one did not know whether it should be attributed to the *fête* of the 15th, or the famous undertaking of the seven wise men of Paris.

By two o'clock on the 16th, encouraging results were obtained. The skin and muscles had recovered nearly all their suppleness, but the joints were still hard to bend. The collapsed condition of the walls of the abdomen and the interval between the ribs, still indicated that the viscera were far from having reabsorbed the quantity of water which they had previously lost with Herr Meiser. A bath was prepared and kept at a temperature of thirty-seven degrees and a half. They left the colonel in it two hours and a half, taking care to frequently pass over his head a fine sponge soaked with water.

M. Nibor removed him from the bath as soon as the skin, which was filled out sooner than the other tissues, began to assume a whitish tinge and wrinkle slightly. They kept him until the evening of the 16th in this humid room, where they arranged an apparatus which, from time to time, occasioned a fine rain of a temperature of thirty-seven and a half degrees. A new bath was given in the evening. During the night, the body was enveloped in flannel, but kept constantly in the same steaming atmosphere.

On the morning of the 17th, after a third bath of an hour and a half, the general characteristics of the figure and the proportions of the body presented their natural aspect: one would have called it a sleeping man. Five or six curious persons were admitted to see it, among others the colonel of the 23d. In the presence of these witnesses, M. Nibor moved successively all the joints, and demonstrated that they had recovered their flexibility. He gently kneaded the limbs, trunk and abdomen. He partly opened the lips, and separated the jaws, which were quite firmly closed, and saw that the tongue had returned to its ordinary size and consistency. He also partly opened the eyelids: the eye-balls were firm and bright.

"Gentlemen," said the philosopher, "these are indications which do not deceive; I prophesy success. In a few hours you shall witness the first manifestations of life."

"But," interrupted one of the bystanders, "why not immediately?"

"Because the *conjunctivæ* are still a little paler than they ought to be. But the little veins traversing the whites of the eyes have already assumed a very encouraging appearance. The blood is almost entirely restored. What is the blood? Red globules floating in serum, or a sort of whey. The

serum in poor Fougas was dried up in his veins; the water which we have gradually introduced by a slow endosmose has saturated the albumen and fibrin of the serum, which is returned to the liquid state. The red globules which desiccation had agglutinated, had become motionless like ships stranded in shoal water. Now behold them afloat again; they thicken, swell, round out their edges, detach themselves from each other and prepare to circulate in their proper channels at the first impulse which shall be given them by the contractions of the heart."

"It remains to see," said M. Renault, "whether the heart will put itself in motion. In a living man, the heart moves under the impulse of the brain, transmitted by the nerves. The brain acts under the impulse of the heart, transmitted by the arteries. The whole forms a perfectly exact circle, without which there is no well-being. And when neither heart nor brain acts, as in the colonel's case, I don't see which of the two can set the other in motion. You remember the scene in the 'Ecole des femmes,' where Arnolphe knocks at his door? The valet and the maid, Alain and Georgette, are both in the house. 'Georgette!' cries Alain. —'Well?' replies Georgette.—'Open the door down there!'—'Go yourself! Go yourself!'—'Gracious me! I shan't go!'—'I shan't go either!'—'Open it right away!'—'Open it yourself!' And nobody opens it. I am inclined to think, Monsieur, that we are attending a performance of this comedy. The house is the body of the colonel; Arnolphe, who wants to get in, is the Vital Principle. The heart and brain act the parts of Alain and Georgette. 'Open the door!' says one.—'Open it yourself!' says the other. And the Vital Principle waits outside."

"Monsieur," replied Doctor Nibor smiling, "you forget the ending of the scene. Arnolphe gets angry, and cries out: 'Whichever of you two doesn't open the door, shan't have anything to eat for four days!' And forthwith Alain hurries himself, Georgette runs and the door is opened. Now bear in mind that I speak in this way only in order to conform to your own course of reasoning, for the term 'Vital Principle' is at variance with the actual assertions of science. Life will manifest itself as soon as the brain, or the heart, or any one of the organs which have the capacity of working spontaneously, shall have absorbed the quantity of water it needs. Organized matter has inherent properties which manifest themselves without the assistance of any foreign principle, whenever they are surrounded by certain conditions. Why do not M. Fougas' muscles contract yet? Why does not the tissue of the brain enter into action? Because they have not yet the amount of moisture necessary to them. In the fountain of life there is lacking, perhaps, a pint of water. But I shall be in no hurry to refill it: I am too much afraid of breaking it. Before giving this gallant fellow a final bath, it will be necessary to knead all his organs again, to subject his abdomen to regular compressions, in order that the serous membranes of the stomach, chest and heart may be perfectly disagglutinated and capable of slipping on each other. You are aware that the slightest tear in these parts, or the least resistance, would be enough to kill our subject at the moment of his revival."

While speaking, he united example to precept and kept kneading the trunk of the colonel. As the spectators had too nearly filled the bath-room, making it almost impossible to move, M. Nibor begged them to move into

the laboratory. But the laboratory became so full that it was necessary to leave it for the parlor: the Committee of the Biological Society, had scarcely a corner of the table on which to draw up their account of the proceedings. The parlor even was crowded with people, the dining room too, and so out to the court yard of the house. Friends, strangers, people not at all known to the family, elbowed each other and waited in silence. But the silence of a crowd is not much less noisy than the rolling of the sea. Fat Doctor Martout, apparently overwhelmed with responsibility, showed himself from time to time, and surged through the waves of curious people like a galleon laden with news. Every one of his words circulated from mouth to mouth, and spread even through the street, where several groups of soldiers and citizens were making a stir, in more senses than one. Never had the little "Rue de la Faisanderie" seen such a crowd.

* * *

About one o'clock, M. Nibor caused a new and prolonged bath to be given the colonel, on coming out of which, the body was subjected to a kneading harder and more complete than before.

"Now," said the Doctor, "we can carry M. Fougas into the laboratory, in order to give his resuscitation all the publicity desirable. But it will be well to dress him, and his uniform is in tatters."

"I think," answered good M. Renault, "that the colonel is about my size; so I can lend him some of my clothes. Heaven grant that he may use them! But, between us, I don't hope for it."

Gothon brought in, grumbling, all that was necessary to dress an entirely naked man. But her bad humor did not hold out before the beauty of the colonel:

"Poor gentleman!" she exclaimed, "he is young, fresh and fair as a little chicken. If he doesn't revive, it will be a great pity!"

There were about forty people in the laboratory when Fougas was carried thither. M. Nibor, assisted by M. Martout, placed him on a sofa, and begged a few moments of attentive silence. During these proceedings, Mme. Renault sent to inquire if she could come in. She was admitted.

"Madame and gentlemen," said Dr. Nibor, "life will manifest itself in a few minutes. It is possible that the muscles will act first, and that their action may be convulsive, on account of not yet being regulated by the influence of the nervous system. I ought to apprise you of this fact, in order that you may not be frightened if such a thing transpires. Madame, being a mother, ought to be less astonished at it than any one else; she has experienced, at the fourth month of pregnancy, the effect of those irregular movements which will, possibly, soon be presented to us on a larger scale. I am quite hopeful, however, that the first spontaneous contractions will take place in the fibres of the heart. Such is the case in the embryo, where the rhythmic movements of the heart, precede the nervous functions."

He again began making systematic compressions of the lower part of the chest, rubbing the skin with his hands, half opening the eyelids, examining the pulse, and auscultating the region of the heart.

The attention of the spectators was diverted an instant by a hubbub outside. A battalion of the 23d was passing, with music at the head, through the Rue de la Faisanderie. While the

Sax-horns were shaking the windows, a sudden flush mantled on the cheeks of the colonel. His eyes, which had stood half open, lit up with a brighter sparkle. At the same instant, Doctor Nibor, who had his ear applied to the chest, cried:

"I hear the beatings of the heart!"

Scarcely had he spoken, when the chest rose with a violent inspiration, the limbs contracted, the body straight-ened up, and out came a cry: *"Vive l'Empereur."*

EDITORS' NOTE: But the man thus brought back to life met nothing but disappointment. The money willed to him had increased to many millions but Herr Meiser showed no tendency to disgorge. The army would not take him back. He died after a little less than thirty-nine days of his new life.

THE HAND AT THE WINDOW

from the novel *Wuthering Heights*

EMILY BRONTË

While leading the way upstairs, she recommended that I should hide the candle, and not make a noise; for her master had an odd notion about the chamber she would put me in, and never let anybody lodge there willingly. I asked the reason. She did not know, she answered: she had only lived there a year or two; and they had so many queer goings on, she could not begin to be curious.

Too stupefied to be curious myself, I fastened the door and glanced round for the bed. The whole furniture consisted of a chair, a clothes-press, and a large oak case, with squares cut out near the top resembling coach windows. Having approached this structure I looked inside, and perceived it to be a singular sort of old-fashioned couch, very conveniently designed to obviate the necessity for every member of the family having a room to himself. In fact, it formed a little closet, and the ledge of a window, which it enclosed, served as a table. I slid back the panelled sides, got in with my light, pulled them together again, and felt secure against the vigilance of Heathcliff, and every one else.

The ledge, where I placed my candle, had a few mildewed books piled up in one corner; and it was covered with writing scratched on the paint.

This writing, however, was nothing but a name repeated in all kinds of characters, large and small—*Catherine Earnshaw*, here and there varied to *Catherine Heathcliff*, and then again to *Catherine Linton*.

In vapid listlessness I leant my head against the window, and continued spelling over Catherine Earnshaw—Heathcliff—Linton, till my eyes closed; but they had not rested five minutes when a glare of white letters started from the dark as vivid as spectres—the air swarmed with Catherines; and rousing myself to dispel the obtrusive name, I discovered my candle wick reclining on one of the antique volumes, and perfuming the place with an odour of roasted calf-skin. I snuffed it out, and, very ill at ease under the influence of cold and lingering nausea, sat up and spread open the injured tome on my knee. It was a Testament, in lean type, and smelling dreadfully musty: a fly-leaf bore the inscription—"Catherine Earnshaw, her book," and a date some quarter of a century back. I shut it, and took up another, and another, till I had examined all. Catherine's library was select, and its state of dilapidation proved it to have been well used; though not altogether for a legitimate purpose: scarcely one chapter had es-

caped a pen-and-ink commentary—at least, the appearance of one—covering every morsel of blank that the printer had left. Some were detached sentences; other parts took the form of a regular diary, scrawled in an unformed childish hand. At the top of an extra page (quite a treasure, probably, when first lighted on) I was greatly amused to behold an excellent caricature of my friend Joseph,—rudely, yet powerfully sketched. An immediate interest kindled within me for the unknown Catherine, and I began forthwith to decipher her faded hieroglyphics.

* * *

I began to nod drowsily over the dim page: my eye wandered from manuscript to print. I saw a red ornamented title—"Seventy Times Seven, and the First of the Seventy-First. A Pious Discourse delivered by the Reverend Jabes Branderham, in the Chapel of Gimmerdon Sough." And while I was, half consciously, worrying my brain to guess what Jabes Branderham would make of his subject, I sank back in bed, and fell asleep. Alas, for the effects of bad tea and bad temper! what else could it be that made me pass such a terrible night? I don't remember another that I can at all compare with it since I was capable of suffering.

I began to dream, almost before I ceased to be sensible of my locality. I thought it was morning; and I had set out on my way home, with Joseph for a guide. The snow lay yards deep in our road; and, as we floundered on, my companion wearied me with constant reproaches that I had not brought a pilgrim's staff: telling me that I could never get into the house without one, and boastfully flourishing a heavy-headed cudgel, which I understood to be so denominated.

For a moment I considered it absurd that I should need such a weapon to gain admittance into my own residence. Then a new idea flashed across me. I was not going there: we were journeying to hear the famous Jabes Branderham preach from the text— "Seventy Times Seven"; and either Joseph, the preacher, or I had committed the "First of the Seventy-First, and were to be publicly exposed and excommunicated.

We came to the chapel. I have passed it really in my walks, twice or thrice; it lies in a hollow, between two hills: an elevated hollow, near a swamp, whose peaty moisture is said to answer all the purposes of embalming on the few corpses deposited there. The roof has been kept whole hitherto; but as the clergyman's stipend is only twenty pounds per annum, and a house with two rooms, threatening speedily to determine into one, no clergyman will undertake the duties of pastor: especially as it is currently reported that his flock would rather let him starve than increase the living by one penny from their own pockets. However, in my dream, Jabes had a full and attentive congregation; and he preached—good God! what a sermon: divided into *four hundred and ninety* parts, each fully equal to an ordinary address from the pulpit, and each discussing a separate sin!

* * *

Presently the whole chapel resounded with rappings and counter-rappings: every man's hand was against his neighbour; and Branderham, unwilling to remain idle, poured forth his zeal in a shower of loud taps on the boards of the pulpit, which responded so smartly that, at last, to my unspeakable relief, they woke me. And what was it that had

suggested the tremendous tumult? What had played Jabes's part in the row? Merely, the branch of a fir-tree that touched my lattice, as the blast wailed by, and rattled its dry cones against the panes! I listened doubtingly an instant; detected the disturber, then turned and dozed, and dreamt again: if possible, still more disagreeably than before.

This time, I remembered I was lying in the oak closet, and I heard distinctly the gusty wind, and the driving of the snow; I heard, also, the fir-bough repeat its teasing sound, and ascribed it to the right cause: but it annoyed me so much, that I resolved to silence it, if possible; and, I thought, I rose and endeavoured to unhasp the casement. The hook was soldered into the staple: a circumstance observed by me when awake, but forgotten. "I must stop it, nevertheless!" I muttered, knocking my knuckles through the glass, and stretching an arm out to seize the importunate branch; instead of which, my fingers closed on the fingers of a little, ice-cold hand! The intense horror of nightmare came over me: I tried to draw back my arm, but the hand clung to it, and a most melancholy voice sobbed, "Let me in—let me in!" "Who are you?" I asked, struggling, meanwhile, to disengage myself. "Catherine Linton," it replied, shiveringly (why did I think of Linton? I had read Earnshaw twenty times for Linton); "I'm come home: I'd lost my way on the moor!" As it spoke, I discerned, obscurely, a child's face looking through the window. Terror made me cruel; and, finding it useless to attempt shaking the creature off, I pulled its wrist on to the broken pane, and rubbed it to and fro till the blood ran down and soaked the bedclothes: still it wailed, "Let me in!" and maintained its tenacious gripe, almost maddening me with fear. "How can I?" I said at length. "Let me go, if you want me to let you in!" The fingers relaxed, I snatched mine through the hole, hurriedly piled the books up in a pyramid against it, and stopped my ears to exclude the lamentable prayer. I seemed to keep them closed above a quarter of an hour; yet, the instant I listened again, there was the doleful cry moaning on! "Begone!" I shouted, "I'll never let you in, not if you beg for twenty years." "It is twenty years," mourned the voice: "twenty years. I've been a waif for twenty years!" Thereat began a feeble scratching outside, and the pile of books moved as if thrust forward. I tried to jump up; but could not stir a limb; and so yelled aloud, in a frenzy of fright. To my confusion, I discovered the yell was not ideal: hasty footsteps approached my chamber door; somebody pushed it open, with a vigorous hand, and a light glimmered through the squares at the top of the bed. I sat shuddering yet, and wiping the perspiration from my forehead: the intruder appeared to hesitate, and muttered to himself. At last, he said in a half-whisper, plainly not expecting an answer, "Is anyone here?" I considered it best to confess my presence; for I knew Heathcliff's accents, and feared he might search further, if I kept quiet. With this intention, I turned and opened the panels. I shall not soon forget the effect my action produced.

Heathcliff stood near the entrance, in his shirt and trousers: with a candle dripping over his fingers, and his face as white as the wall behind him. The first creak of the oak startled him like an electric shock! the light leaped from his hold to a distance of some feet, and his agitation was so extreme, that he could hardly pick it up.

"It is only your guest, sir," I called out, desirous to spare him the humiliation of exposing his cowardice further. "I had the misfortune to scream in my sleep, owing to a frightful nightmare. I'm sorry I disturbed you."

"Oh, God confound you, Mr. Lockwood! I wish you were at the——" commenced my host, setting the candle on a chair, because he found it impossible to hold it steady. "And who showed you up into this room?" he continued, crushing his nails into his palms, and grinding his teeth to subdue the maxillary convulsions. "Who was it? I've a good mind to turn them out of the house this moment!"

"It was your servant, Zillah," I replied, flinging myself on to the floor, and rapidly resuming my garments. "I should not care if you did, Mr. Heathcliff; she richly deserves it. I suppose that she wanted to get another proof that the place was haunted, at my expense. Well, it is—swarming with ghosts and goblins! You have reason in shutting it up, I assure you. No one will thank you for a doze in such a den!"

"What do you mean?" asked Heathcliff, "and what are you doing? Lie down and finish out the night, since you *are* here; but, for Heaven's sake! don't repeat that horrid noise; nothing could excuse it, unless you were having your throat cut!"

"If the little fiend had got in at the window, she probably would have strangled me!" I returned. "I'm not going to endure the persecutions of your hospitable ancestors again. Was not the Reverend Jabes Branderham akin to you on the mother's side? And that minx, Catherine Linton, or Earnshaw, or however she was called —she must have been a changeling— wicked little soul! She told me she had been walking the earth those twenty years: a just punishment for her mortal transgressions, I've no doubt!"

Scarcely were these words uttered, when I recollected the association of Heathcliff's with Catherine's name in the book, which had completely slipped from my memory, till thus awakened. I blushed at my inconsideration; but, without showing further consciousness of the offence, I hastened to add—"The truth is, sir, I

passed the first part of the night in"
—Here I stopped afresh—I was about
to say "perusing those old volumes,"
then it would have revealed my
knowledge of their written, as well
as their printed contents: so, correct-
ing myself, I went on, "in spelling
over the name scratched on that
window-ledge. A monotonous occupa-
tion, calculated to set me asleep, like
counting, or"——

"What *can* you mean by talking in
this way to *me?*" thundered Heath-
cliff with savage vehemence. "How—
how *dare* you, under my roof?—God!
he's mad to speak so!" And he struck
his forehead with rage.

I did not know whether to resent
this language or pursue my explana-
tion; but he seemed so powerfully
affected that I took pity and proceeded
with my dreams; affirming I had
never heard the appellation of "Cath-
erine Linton" before, but reading it
often over produced an impression
which personified itself when I had
no longer my imagination under con-
trol. Heathcliff gradually fell back
into the shelter of the bed, as I spoke;
finally sitting down almost concealed
behind it. I guessed, however, by his
irregular and intercepted breathing,
that he struggled to vanquish an excess
of violent emotion. Not liking to
show him that I had heard the con-
flict, I continued my toilette rather
noisily, looked at my watch, and
soliloquised on the length of the
night: "Not three o'clock yet! I could
have taken oath it had been six. Time
stagnates here: we must surely have
retired to rest at eight!"

"Always at nine in winter, and rise
at four," said my host, suppressing a

groan: and, as I fancied by the mo-
tion of his arm's shadow, dashing a
tear from his eyes. "Mr. Lockwood,"
he added, "you may go into my room:
you'll only be in the way, coming
downstairs so early; and your childish
outcry has sent sleep to the devil for
me."

"And for me, too," I replied. "I'll
walk in the yard till daylight, and
then I'll be off; and you need not
dread a repetition of my intrusion.
I'm now quite cured of seeking pleas-
ure in society, be it country or town.
A sensible man ought to find suffi-
cient company in himself."

"Delightful company!" muttered
Heathcliff. "Take the candle, and go
where you please. I shall join you
directly. Keep out of the yard, though,
the dogs are unchained; and the
house—Juno mounts sentinel there,
and—nay, you can only ramble about
the steps and passages. But, away
with you! I'll come in two minutes!"

I obeyed, so far as to quit the
chamber; when, ignorant where the
narrow lobbies led, I stood still, and
was witness, involuntarily, to a piece
of superstition on the part of my land-
lord, which belied, oddly, his apparent
sense. He got on to the bed, and
wrenched open the lattice, bursting,
as he pulled at it, into an uncon-
trollable passion of tears. "Come in!
come in!" he sobbed. "Cathy, do come.
Oh do—*once* more! Oh! my heart's
darling; hear me *this* time, Catherine,
at last!" The spectre showed a spectre's
ordinary caprice: it gave no sign of
being; but the snow and wind whirled
wildly through, even reaching my
station, and blowing out the light.

A Novel

"NATIONAL VELVET"

ENID BAGNOLD

"NATIONAL VELVET"

ENID BAGNOLD

Chapter One

Unearthly humps of land curved into the darkening sky like the backs of browsing pigs, like the rumps of elephants. At night when the stars rose over them they looked like a starlit herd of divine pigs. The villagers called them Hullocks.

The valleys were full of soft and windblown vegetation. The sea rolled at the foot of all as though God had brought his herd down to water.

The Hullocks were blackening as Velvet cantered down the chalk road to the village. She ran on her own slender legs, making horse-noises and chirrups and occasionally striking her thigh with a switch, holding at the same time something very small before her as she ran. The light on the chalk road was the last thing to gleam and die. The flints slipped and flashed under her feet. Her cotton dress and her cottony hair blew out, and her lips were parted for breath in a sweet metallic smile. She had the look of a sapling-Dante as she ran through the darkness downhill.

At the entrance to the village the sea was pounding up the sewer with a spring gale behind it. She passed to the third cottage, stopped at the door, opened it, let a gush of light on to the pavement, closed it and carried her tender object inside.

Edwina, Malvolia and Meredith sat in their father's, Mr. Brown's, sitting-room just before supper time. It was dark outside and hot inside, and outside in the darkness the Hullocks went up in great hoops above the village. There was an oil stove in the corner of the sitting-room and lesson books on the table. The ceiling was low and sagged. An Albert lamp with a green glass shade lit the table. There was no electric light. Donald, the boy of four, was asleep upstairs.

Edwina, Malvolia and Meredith were all exactly alike, like golden greyhounds. Their golden hair was sleek, their fine faces like antelopes, their shoulders still and steady like Zulu women carrying water, and their bodies beneath the shoulders rippled when they moved. They were seventeen, sixteen, and fifteen. Velvet was fourteen. Velvet had short pale hair, large, protruding teeth, a sweet smile and a mouthful of metal.

Mr. Brown was swilling down the

slaughter-house, as Mi Taylor was away for the day. The sound of the hose swished at the wooden partition which separated the slaughter-house from the sitting-room.

"He went beautifully!" said Velvet, and laying down a tiny paper horse on the table she wrenched at the gold band that bound her teeth back and laid it beside the horse.

"Father'll be in in a minute," said Edwina warningly.

"It's going in again directly I hear a sound," said Velvet and sitting down she swept the plate into her lap.

"Look at him," she said lovingly, taking up the paper horse. "I must unsaddle him and rub him down." The heads were bent on the lesson books again and Velvet took a tiny bridle of cotton threads from the horse. Then going to a shell-box on the sideboard she brought it to the table.

"It's just supper," said Mally. "You'll have to clear."

Velvet opened the box and took out a stable rubber two inches square, a portion of her handkerchief, hemmed round. Laying the little horse flat on the table she rubbed him with delicacy in circular motions, after having taken a paper saddle from his back.

The horse was a racer cut from the *Bystander*. He stood three inches high and had a raking neck and a keen, veined face. By dint of much rubbing the paper had given off a kind of coat, and now as Velvet rubbed there came a suède-like sheen on the horse's paper body. He was dark, most carefully cut out, and pasted upon cardboard. The bridle was made by the fingers of a fairy, noseband, chinstrap and all, in black cotton.

"He has a high action," said Velvet. "A lovely show canter, but a difficult trot. I didn't jump him to-day as he needs to settle down."

In the shell-box other horses lay.

"There's a marvellous picture of mares on the back of the *Times* to-day, but you can't cut a single one clear. They're all mixed up with the foals."

"I saw it," said Velvet. "I called at the Post Office. But it was no good."

"I called in too," said Mally. "They said in the Post Office that one of us looking at the *Times* was enough. We'd better take turns."

"Yes," said Velvet. "You can't think how lovely it was galloping up there. It was nearly dark. He never put a foot wrong. Somehow you can trust a horse like that."

"It's blood that counts," said Mally darkly.

"I haven't got the racing saddle cut right," went on Velvet. "I wish I could find a picture of one. I ride short when I ride this horse and with this saddle the knees come right off on to his shoulder."

"You need kneeflaps," said Edwina.

"I suppose there's not time," said Velvet, "to take the chestnut down for a stand in the pond? His hocks are still puffy."

"It's not you to lay to-night," said Mally. "You've got ten minutes. Don't let father see. . . . Mind your plate! It's fallen!"

Velvet dived under the table, picked it up, and examined it anxiously. Opening her mouth she worked it painfully in with both hands.

"S'bent a bit," she gasped. "It's a hell plate . . ."

"It's no good. Don't go on! Get on down to the pond."

Velvet packed the racer in the shell-box and carefully abstracted a smaller horse, a coloured picture of a polo pony cut from the *Tatler*. Putting the box away she slipped through the door with the chestnut and was gone.

A door at the other end of the sitting-room opened and Mrs. Brown

came in. She stood and looked at the daughters for a moment—an enormous woman who had once swum the Channel. Now she had become muscle-bound.

Towering over the Albert lamp she threw her shadow across the books and up the wall.

She said: "Lay supper." And went out.

"Meredith," said Edwina mechanically without looking up. Meredith got up and began to collect the books. When all the books were gone the two sisters sat tilting their chairs back so that Meredith could get the white cloth over the edge of the table past their knees. When this was done all their chairs came forward again. Kneeling by the Victorian sideboard Meredith pulled out plates, bread-knife, platter, sugar, knives and forks and salts and peppers.

The street door opened and Velvet stood on the mat. She had her shoes in her hand and her bare ankles were green with slime. Mrs. Brown who had come in glanced at her and took a duster from the sideboard. "Wipe them up," she said and threw the duster on to the mat. Velvet mopped her slimy ankles, whispering to Mally, pointing with her finger towards the door—"Stars like Christmas trees. Terrible stuff in the pond. Spawn. I stood five minutes."

"We ought to get some," said Mally. "I'll get a bottle after supper."

"Any spawn," said Mrs. Brown without looking up, "goes on a tin tray."

"Yes, mother."

"Larder," said Mrs. Brown.

Velvet put her shoes in the corner and the horse in the shell-box and disappeared. The others sat in silence till she came back with the tray.

Cold ham, jam, butter were placed on the table, and a dish of radishes.

Mr. Brown came in by the slaughter-house door, gum boots drawn to his thighs, his sleeves rolled up, his hands wet from the hose. He passed through the room on his way to wash for supper. Velvet and the three golden greyhounds sat on in brooding silence. A smell of liver and bacon stole in from the kitchen.

The two doors, that on the street and that on the kitchen, opened suddenly together. Out of the black hole of the street came Mi Taylor, brushed up for supper. Mrs. Brown came in from the kitchen carrying the liver and bacon.

The room filled with smells. Mr. Brown came in putting on his coat. Everyone sat down, Mi last of all, pulling up his chair gingerly.

"Well . . ." said Mr. Brown, and helped the liver round.

Meredith went out and fetched in the jugs of coffee and milk.

"Bin over to Worthing?" said Mr. Brown.

"I have," said Mi.

"Got that freezing-machine catalogue for me?"

"Shops shut again."

"Good God!" said Mr. Brown, exasperated. "Don't you ever learn the shut-shop day in Worthing? Whadyer do then?"

"Had three teeth out. Dentist was all there was open."

"Oh, Mi, where?" said Velvet.

Mi opened his jaw and pointed to a bloody wound.

"Oughter eat pap for it," said Mr. Brown. "It's pulpy."

"S'got to learn to harden," said Mi.

"Donald asleep?" said Mally.

"This hour gone," said Mrs. Brown.

They ate, sleek girls' heads bent under the lamp, Mr. Brown and Mrs. Brown square and full and steady, Mi silent and dexterous with his red hair boiling up in curls on his skull.

Jacob went grinning round the table from sister to sister.

"Nobody feeds him," ordered Mi under his breath.

His red hair boiled up on his skull fiercer than ever at Jacob's presumption.

The yard spaniels remained in the street on the doorstep through meals. They lay and leant against the front door, grouped on the step, so that the door creaked and groaned under their pressed bodies. When the door was opened from the inside they fell in. When this happened Mi sent them out again with a roar.

Jacob had been allowed in all his life. His fox terrier body, growing stout in middle age, still vibrated to a look. His lips curled and he grinned at the blink of a human eyelash. His tail ached with wagging, and even his hips waggled as he moved. But under cover of these virtues he was watchful for his benefit, watchful for human weakness, affected, a ready liar, disobedient, boastful, a sucker-up, and had a lifelong battle with Mi. Mi adored him, but seldom said a kind word to him. Jacob adored Mi, and there was no one whom he would not sooner deceive. At meals Jacob wriggled and grinned from sister to sister, making a circle round Mi, whose leg was scooping for him.

Just outside the slaughter-house was a black barking dog on the end of a string. This dog had a name but no character. It barked without ceasing day and night. Nobody heard it. The Browns slept and lived and ate beside its barking. The spaniels never opened their mouths. They pressed against doors and knee and furniture. They lived for love and never got it. They were herded indiscriminately together and none knew their characteristics but Mi. The sisters felt for

them what they felt for the fowls in the fowlyard. Mi fed them.

But Jacob's weaknesses and affectations and dubious sincerities were thrust upon everyone's notice. When Velvet came in at the front door, and pressing back the leaning spaniels, closed it, Jacob would rise, wriggle his hips at her, bow and grin.

"How exquisite, how condescending, how flattering!" said he, bowing lower and lower, with his front legs slid out on the floor and his back legs stiff. But if asked to go for a walk not a step would he come outside unless he had business of his own with the ashbin, or wanted to taunt the chained and raging dog with the spine of a herring dragged in the dust.

The chained dog chiefly barked. But sometimes he stopped rending the unheeding air and lay silent. Then he would whirl out on his chain like a fury and fall flat, half choked. And Jacob would stand without flinching, banking on the strength of the chain, and think, "You poor one-thoughted fool . . ."

The Browns loved Jacob as they loved each other, deeply, from the back of the soul, with intolerance in daily life.

As the girls ate a private dream floated in Velvet's mind. . . . It was a little horse, slender and perfect, rising divinely at a jump, forefeet tucked up neatly, intelligence and delight in its eager eye, and on its back, glued lightly and easily to the saddle . . . she, Velvet . . . Gymkhana Velvet. As she took the visionary jump in dream her living hand stole to her mouth. She pulled out the torturing plate and hid it in her lap. Mi's eyes were on her in a flash, he who never missed anything.

"Be windy for the Fair Thursday," said Mrs. Brown.

"It's coming in wild from the south-west," said Mr. Brown.

"Always does when it comes in at all," said Mrs. Brown. "Three-day gale."

All the trees in the dark village outside attested this. They were blown like fans set on one side. The rooks shuffled and slept in them, waving up and down among the breaking twigs. The village street was white with rook-droppings.

"Put that in again, Velvet," commanded Mrs. Brown.

"She got it out again?" asked Mr. Brown, looking up sharply.

"It aches me an' aches when I eat," said Velvet.

"Ache or no, argue or no, that plate cost me four pound ten an' it's solid gold an' it goes in," said Mr. Brown. "I'm not going to have a child like a rabbit if I can help it. You girls have got your faces for your fortunes and none other. I've told you often enough."

The three golden greyhounds sat up straighter than ever and Velvet fumbled with her teeth.

"It's got hooked up."

"Unhook it, then," said Mr. Brown. He sat back, satisfied, commanding and comfortable, and pulled the radishes towards him. Then he passed the dish around.

"Take a radish, Velvet."

"Couldn't bite a radish!"

"Go without then," said Mr. Brown happily, and leant back to light his pipe.

All the Browns tilted their chairs. Nobody ever told them it would hurt the carpet. They ate, ruminated, and tilted. Only Mrs. Brown sat solid and silent. She did not talk much, but managed the till down at the shop in the street. She knew all about courage and endurance, to the last ounce of strength, from the first swallow of

overcome timidity. She valued and appraised each daughter, she knew what each daughter could do. She was glad too that her daughters were not boys because she could not understand the courage of men, but only the courage of women. Mr. Brown was with dignity the head of the family. But Mrs. Brown was the standard of the family. When Velvet had fallen off the pier at the age of six her mother went in thirty feet after her, sixteen stone, royal-blue afternoon dress. A straight dive, like the dive of an ageing mammoth. The reporter from the *West Worthing News* came to make a story of it and said to Edwina, "Your mother swum the Channel, didn't she?" Edwina nodded towards her mother. "Better ask *her.*" "What's past's past, young man," said Mrs. Brown heavily and shut her mouth and her door.

Mi Taylor's father had trained Mrs. Brown for her swim, trained her when she had been a great girl of nineteen, neckless, clumsy, and incredibly enduring. Mi himself had been a fly-weight boxer, killed his man, because the wretched creature was in status lymphaticus, got exonerated and yet somehow disqualified, tramped the country, held horses, cleaned stables and drifted nearer and nearer to the racing world, till he knew all about it except the feel of a horse's back. Arriving somehow in the ebb of Lewes races he had been taken on by Mr. Brown for the slaughter-house, for running errands, and lately even for negotiating for stock.

Mrs. Brown stared at him when he came with a look of strange pleasure in her hooded eyes. Mi Taylor, the son of Father Taylor! He knew all about her, Taylor did. The only one who ever did. He knew what she was made of. He'd had the last ounce out of her. He and the doctor at her five

confinements, those men knew. Nobody else, ever. Mi was his son. Mi was welcome. He could stay. Henceforth he ate with the family and lodged in the extra loose-box. And Araminty Brown, embedded in fat, her keen, hooded eyes hardly lifting the rolls above them, cooked admirably, ran the accounts, watched the shop, looked after the till, spoke seldom, interfered hardly ever, sighed sometimes (because it would have taken a war on her home soil, the birth of a colony, or a great cataclysm to have dug from her what she was born for), moved about the house, brought up her four taut daughters under her heavy eye, and thought of death occasionally with a kind of sardonic shrug. Nobody could have said exactly whether she had a dull brain or no. Ed and Mally and Meredith behaved themselves at the wink of one of her heavy eyes. Velvet would have laid down her stringy life for her.

"Yer ma," said Mi, " 'sworth a bellyful. Pity she weighs what she does."

"Why?" said Mally.

"Binds her up," said Mi. And it was not constipation he was thinking of.

"Mi," said Mally to her mother, "thinks you ought to be riding in Lewes races."

Mrs. Brown made a noise in her nose.

"What?" said Mally.

"That's all right," said Mrs. Brown.

"You can never tell what mother's thinking," said Mally to Velvet.

"She doesn't think where we do," said Velvet. "She thinks at the back."

In the sitting-room at the close of supper Mrs. Brown stretched out an arm and turned the Albert lamp lower.

"Box," said Mr. Brown, indicating the sideboard. Edwina rose and brought him his small cigar.

The shadows whirled.

"Monday," said Mrs. Brown.

"Driving night," said Velvet.

"What I was thinking," said Mrs. Brown. "Get on off!"

"First?" said Velvet.

"First," said Mrs. Brown.

Velvet hunched her shoulder-blades and sniffed. Was driving worth it? She never could make up her mind. Out of bed it didn't seem so, but in bed it was worth while.

"Hush!" she said suddenly and held up her hand. "Cough . . ." she said, and went to the slaughter-house door.

"Gone to rub Miss Ada's chest," said Mi, grinning.

In the sitting-room the books for homework came out again.

"Gotta see a boy," murmured Mi as he went out into the street.

Velvet lit the hurricane lamp standing in the corner of the empty slaughter-house and passed through to the shed where the old pony lived.

Miss Ada was an old pink roan gone grey with age, her ears permanently back, a look of irritation about her creased nostrils, backbone sagging, horny growths on her legs.

"Hullo," said Velvet and opened the door. Miss Ada moved definitely round and turned her backside on Velvet.

Velvet put her hand on the quarters and the skin twitched irritably.

"You never do anything about being decent!" said Velvet. "Have you got a cough?"

Miss Ada bent her head suddenly and rubbed the itch off her right nostril on to her leg, and as she did it she flashed a robust, contemptuous look at Velvet. "Is there sugar?" said the look, "or no sugar? I want no subtleties, no sentimentalities. I don't care about your state of heart, your wretched conscience-prickings, your ambitious desires. Is there sugar or no

sugar? State your reasons for coming to see me and leave me to brood."

Velvet produced a piece of sugar and the pony bent her head round with a look of insolence, as though she still suspected the sugar to be an imitation lump. She took it with her lips, but she pressed her old teeth for a minute on the child's palm, and at this trick, as old as Velvet's childhood, Velvet thrust her arms over the sagging backbone and buried her face among the knobbles of the spine. The pony munched her lump stolidly, flirting her head up and down as though she were fishing for extra grains high up among her teeth.

"If we had another pony," said Velvet, "nobody would love you less. But we can't go on like this, it's awful. The gymkhanas all coming and nothing to ride. And you hate all that. It puts you in your worst mood."

The door opened and Mally came in.

"Has she got a cough?"

"She hasn't coughed since I've been here," said Velvet.

"Get over, you awful old thing!" said Mally, "and let me pass."

"Don't, Mally . . ."

"The only way is to be as horrid to her as she is to us."

"I've left the lamp down there. Hang it up somewhere. I can't reach the hook."

Mally hung the lamp carefully out of way of the straw. The two sat up on the manger together. The pony, utterly disgusted, drew her ears back almost flat with her head, hung out her twitching underlip and faced round at an angle from them, her tail tucked sourly in.

"Look at her!" said Mally. "My God, what a mount!"

Velvet took out her plate and wrapped it in her handkerchief.

"Don't you leave it here," said Mally. "It won't help us any. It was your plate-fiddling that went wrong at supper."

Mally got up on to the manger's rim, reached to a ledge of wood below the window and took down two sticks of dark gold paper.

"Crunchie?" said Velvet, her face lighting.

"I got them this morning."

"On tick still?"

"Yes. She was cross but I swore we'd pay by Saturday."

In the gold paper was a chocolate stick. Beneath the chocolate was a sort of honeycomb, crisp and friable, something between biscuit and burnt sugar. Fry's chocolate crunchie. Not one of the sisters ate any other kind of sweet that year. It was their year's choice. The year before it had been Carmel Crispies.

"We must pay her. She's a wispy woman. She's pappy."

"Aren't you queer about people. Always cutting 'em down to the bone."

"I don't like people," said Velvet, "except us and mother and Mi. I like only horses."

"Pity you weren't a boy."

"I should a bin a poor thin boy. With muscles just on one arm. From meat chopping."

"As it is," said Mally, "we're all going into tills. Into cages. To count out money."

"I'm not," said Velvet, examining her crunchie. "Do you like the end best or the middle?"

"I like the ones that don't seem cooked. Sticky in the middle."

"I wish I had a proper coat with checks," said Velvet.

"You? Why, Edwina's never had one."

"Edwina isn't me. I'm not going to be a jersey-jumping child in a gymkhana any more."

"I don't know how we're going to

do anything in the gymkhanas at all. Miss Ada's turning sourer and sourer on us. She'll end by refusing to go into the ring."

Miss Ada, seduced by the smell of the chocolate, turned slowly towards them, approaching by fractions.

"It's all right, Mally, I'll give her a bit of mine," said Velvet. "You bought 'em."

"It doesn't matter who bought 'em," said Mally. "We're all owing together. . . . She can have a crumb of mine too. Don't blow so, you idiot! She's sneezed her crumb off my hand!" Miss Ada stooped her head and began a vain search for one chocolate crumb in two inches of dingy straw.

The stable door opened and Mi put his head in.

"Meredith in here?"

"No . . . Whad'you want'er for?"

"*Canary Breeder's Annual's* come. Come on last post."

"Don' know where she is," said Malvolia. "She won't be fit to live with for weeks."

"Mi . . . Mi . . . Mi!" called a voice from the dark.

"In here. He's got your *Canary Breeder.*"

"Mother said so! Oh. . . . I'll come in. Give it to me!"

Meredith took the book from Mi. "You've taken off the wrapper," she said disappointedly; "I like to take it off myself," and leant back against Miss Ada, unconscious of the pony's body.

"'Nother time you can fetch your own *Annual*," said Mi.

"Bet you don't remember next year," said Mally.

"Listen to this! Listen to this! It's what I always thought!" said Meredith. "Listen to Mr. Lukie. He says (J. Lukie, Esquire, it's signed) he says, 'Cod liver oil should be given to mating birds. My own birds did magnifi-

cently on Poon's Finchmixture Cod-liver . . .' " Miss Ada removed her support sharply and Meredith sat violently on the straw. "Blast!" she said, without looking round at the pony, opened the *Annual* and searched again for the page.

"Yes, but his birds were already mating," said Mally. "You keep wanting to give them the cod liver oil to make them mate. It doesn't make them mate. Lukie doesn't say it does!"

"I don't see why . . ." said Meredith, still hunting for the page. "You've got to be lively to mate. Vital or something. Cod liver oil gives vitality. I read it . . . it's here . . . 'gives vitality to the mating bird.' "

"Miss Ada'll step on your hand if you leave it there," said Velvet.

Meredith got slowly up, reading as she rose. "It doesn't say whether it's the cock bird or the hen. Which do you think it is, Mi?"

"Cock before, hen after," said Mi.

"There you are!" said Meredith. "I *wish* mother'd let me order it."

"You got it all over the sofa last time."

"But I've got a fountain pen filler now. I've trained the cock on drops of water. He's as good as gold. The hen makes a fuss. I could do her in the yard."

"Bed," said Edwina from the darkness outside.

They filed out without a word, Meredith reading to the last by the flare of the hurricane lamp. The spring gale had gone. The spring sky was indefinite and still, with a star in it. There was a new moon.

"Are you coming, Velvet?"

"You can't leave Miss Ada with nothing when we've used her stable. I'll be a second." She opened the corn bin and Miss Ada dropped ten years off her looks. She plunged her nose on

the two hands that cupped the corn and ducked her head to sniff out the droppings before they sank too far in the straw. Velvet, alone, saw the new moon. She bowed three times, glanced round to see that no one saw, then standing in the shadow of the stable door she put her hands like thin white arrows together and prayed to the moon—"Oh, God, give me horses, give me horses! Let me be the best rider in England!"

Chapter Two

The next morning Meredith had to take some suet and a shin of beef over to Pendean. School was at nine. It was the last day of term. She rose at six. Mi called her on his way downstairs. He heated the coffee left over from last night and gave her three sardines between two pieces of bread. Then Meredith went out to saddle Miss Ada.

Miss Ada had a crupper to her saddle, partly because the hills were so steep and partly because she had no shoulders. Meredith forgot the crupper and left it dangling. She put the girths on twisted, put the *Canary Breeder* in the basket with the suet, and started off. Miss Ada tapped smartly up the village street on the tarmac. The flints on the church shone like looking-glass. Meredith trotted east into the rising sun. Her toes were warm and the sardines and the bread and coffee digested comfortingly. Over the Hullocks and down into the valleys, sun and shadow, cup and saucer, through the tarred gate, the wired gate, the broken gate, and finally into the Pendean valley and to the house. She gave in the beef and the suet, would have stopped to talk to Lucy the farm daughter (only Lucy had a temperature), started on the home journey, crupper still dangling, and Miss Ada restive now from the sore of the twisted girth.

"We'll go the Dead-Horse-Patch way," said Meredith suddenly, aloud; and then disliked the sound of the spoken words in the lonely landscape. One of Miss Ada's ears came forward. They were above the village now, though still two miles away. There were two ways down to the sea level. One by the two steep fields and the chalk road whence she had come up, the other by two more steep fields, two gates, a broken reaping machine, a cabbage field, to a haystack—and a place where a horse had once dropped dead.

For thirteen years Miss Ada had said that place was haunted. She had told Mr. Brown so plainly when Velvet was crawling. And he had never insisted with her, but let her come down the way she had planned for herself by the chalk road. Now to Meredith's mind came the desire to take Miss Ada the way she had never been taken by Edwina, Malvolia, Velvet or herself.

Even before the division of the ways the intention became communicated to the pony. A hardening took place, a clenching of spirit. A weight came into Miss Ada's head. She hung it provocatively upon her bit. Meredith sat uneasily and watchfully in her saddle.

Miss Ada's way was to the left. Meredith's was to the right. Miss Ada had two methods of getting her way. Either she didn't cede at all, or when Meredith pulled she ceded too fast and whipped round. This method she chose and the saddle slipped over on the too-slack girths. Meredith fell off.

Miss Ada with a look of sudden youth flicked her heels, cantered to the wire fence, stooped her head and cropped. The basket with the *Canary Breeder* had fallen too and Meredith, getting up, picked up her *Annual,* glanced at Miss Ada and after a minute sat down in the sun to read. She was now faced with a walk home. Nobody ever caught Miss Ada once she was loose. She would go home her own way and at her own time.

Meredith read comfortably what Mr. Lukie had to say, then closed her book and trudged off.

"You'll look an idiot!" she said partingly to Miss Ada. "Coming home with your saddle all upside down." The whites of Miss Ada's eyes glinted as she cropped. Meredith went down towards the Dead-Horse-Patch. When she was out of sight Miss Ada moved off by the way she had intended to go.

Meredith ran down over a steep field that lay in shadow with its back to the rising sun, then up the opposite slope with the sun shining on her back. Over the rise she saw a rider in the distance nearing the haystack that stood at the edge of the cabbage field, the haystack where the legendary horse had laid down and died. The rider coming towards her, she could not see at first whether he was walking or trotting. . . . Then came a flick of movement and he was off. The horse as usual had shied at the Dead-Horse-Patch.

When Meredith reached him he was on his feet dusting himself down, a tripper-rider, a great lad with loose flannel trousers and bicycle clips. The horse, like Miss Ada, was cropping feverishly as though it had never seen grass before.

"You got Mr. Belton's Bumble Bee," said Meredith.

"What's the matter with him? Seen a ghost?" said the young man.

"Yes, he did," said Meredith.

"Eh? How? You had a fall too?" eyeing the green-grass stain on her hip.

Meredith looked round to see if Miss Ada was in sight.

"Bin sliding," she said.

"Can we catch the horse?" said the tripper.

"Maybe," said Meredith, "but I shouldn't think so. I got to be in time for school."

"Jumped his whole length sideways," said the tripper.

"They always do, here," said Meredith, edging gently towards the horse.

"Why here?"

"There's a ghost in the ground. A horse ghost. Steams up mornings and evenings. Specially early when there's a dew drying off." Her hand was within a foot of the reins, extended soothingly. The young man saw her intention and ran round the other side. The horse, startled, removed itself another length away.

"You mucked it," said Meredith. "I must get on."

Miss Ada got home first. Velvet was putting saltpetre on her girth-gall as she stood in the sunlight on the street by the front door. The saddle was pitched up on the railings. The front door was open and Mr. Brown, bareheaded, was enjoying his after breakfast pipe.

"My girl," he said when he saw Meredith, "yer fifteen, annt you?"

Meredith nodded and stood still before him.

"Seven years you've saddled that pony and put her bits of leather on her, and to this day you onny hang 'em round her like blind cords. She's got a sore'll take a week to heal."

Miss Ada looked at Meredith with smug reproach.

"If it was canaries . . ." muttered Velvet, dabbing with a rag.

Meredith glowered at Velvet as she passed her to go in for her school books.

Inside the sitting-room Mi was telling Donald to get on with his porridge. It was cold porridge, turned out of a cup. There was a hole in the top and treacle was poured inside. Donald was laying a sap from the side in to the centre.

"You aren't eating what you cut out," said Mi, cleaning a rat-trap with emery paper and the rust covering the cloth in showers.

"I am," said Donald. But he wasn't.

"Donald done yet?" called Mrs. Brown. "I'm washing the plates."

"He's fiddling," said Mi.

Mrs. Brown came to the door. "You get down and bring that porridge in here," she said as she rubbed a plate.

The sweetness of Donald's face remained unchanged. He watched the treacle ran out down the sap. "I dooon't . . ." he drawled.

Mrs. Brown gave no second chances. It was her strength.

She took Donald in one great arm and the plate of porridge in the other and removed him. The sweetness of his face was still unchanged.

"He'll never eat that," said Meredith. "You're sitting on my atlas."

Mi pulled it out from beneath him. "He never eats anything he's fiddled with," said Mi, "because it's turned into something else in his mind. Hark to them hammering . . ."

"You'd never think, to look at the Green, that there'd be a Fair in twenty-four hours. Just a lot of old sticks and men hitting them in."

"It'll be ready. You won't be though."

"I'm just going. Last day. Holidays to-morrow."

"All four hanging round the house all day. Life'll be a joke."

"This bit a millet, Mi," said Meredith, dragging a length out of the sideboard drawer. "Stick it in for the male, Mi, *please*. . . ."

"Them birds . . ." Meredith blocked the light in the doorway and was gone.

. . . .

"Blast and blast and hell . . ." said Mi softly. He had caught his finger in the rat-trap.

"Hell," said Donald softly in the doorway. His silver hair hung in a lock over his forehead. His eyes were film-eyes and blue, with film-lashes. His platinum-blond, Hollywood head was set on a green jersey. His bottom was bare and his pants hung down unbuttoned.

"You've got off your pot!" said Mi threateningly. "Get on back." Donald disappeared again into the inner room, his behinds gleaming like the white polish of two peeled and hard-boiled eggs.

Edwina went in to Worthing for a piano lesson. Mally, Meredith and Velvet waded through a last day of grammar and map reading behind the walls of the village school. The children's voices droned behind the windows and the hammering on the Village Green increased. At break the children watched the hammers from the corner of the asphalt yard. The greasy pole was up, the cokernut shies were up, there was a frail porch with "Welcome" written on it.

Marks for the term were read out, and prizes given. Malvolia got *Hiawatha*.

At home it was steak and kidney pudding for dinner and Mr. Brown poured in the boiling water through a hole in the suet. Velvet kept her plate in and swallowed whole. The

kidneys went down like stones. Mr. Brown finished his *Meat Fancier* as he ate. Donald ate his meat well and said gently some six or seven times, "Is it castle puddings?" Nobody knew. His question was not insistent but soft. Sometimes he said it through his meat.

"Yer spitting, Donald," said Mi.

"I *said*," said Donald, dreamily.

Mrs. Brown looked at him. "It is," she said.

"You never used to tell *us!*" said Velvet.

"Times," said Mrs. Brown, "I don't do what I always did."

Malvolia cleared the plates. Mrs. Brown fetched in a city of castle puddings and a jam-pot full of heated jam. She served Donald, the baby, first. Two castle puddings and a dab of jam on the plate. He looked at his two puddings and began to examine them. He drooped his Hollywood head like a smiling angel.

"Fiddling again," said Mi ominously. "You wanted 'em too much."

"Yore putting it into his head," said Mally.

Edwina walked in and put down her music roll and her hat. She pulled a chair up.

"Your bit's there," said Mrs. Brown, "on the sideboard."

"Guvner an' me we wash," said Mi into his plate. "Funny how men wash for girls an' girls don' wash for men."

"Anybody knows boys are dirtier than girls," said Mally.

"Meybe. But grown men wash freer than women." Edwina sat down, ignoring criticism.

"Get on, get on," said Mrs. Brown to Donald.

"I am gettin' on," said Donald, and opened his mouth to show that it was full.

"Bin turning round and round," said Mi. "Give a swaller."

"Can't swaller," said Donald, "'tisn't slidy."

"Isn't he lovely!" said Velvet, coming out of a dream quite suddenly and looking as though she had seen him for the first time. "Shall I teach you to ride, Donald?"

"You've put him off proper," said Mrs. Brown.

Donald opened his eyes and struggled with his mouth. Then he leant over his plate and spat out the revolving mass. "Yes," he said, when he was empty, "yes, when? Now?"

Mrs. Brown rose slowly, took her own empty plate away to the sideboard, moved calmly and without anger round to Donald.

"You'll finish alone," she said, and gathered him up. Donald and his plate sailed into the back kitchen.

"Well, really, Velvet," said Edwina.

"He doesn't care," said Velvet. "Wouldn't he be lovely in the under six?"

"On Miss Ada?" said Mally.

"She's too wide really."

"You want a little narrow thing like Lucy's Rowanberry."

"Lucy never can find anyone small enough to ride Rowanberry anyway."

"Could we start him, father?" said Velvet.

"Eh?" said Mr. Brown, struggling to leave his page.

"Teach Donald. So's he could be ready for the under six?"

"Under what?" said Mr. Brown. "The under what?"

"Gymkhana," said Velvet. "The class for children under six. Six years."

"Ask your mother," said Mr. Brown, and returned to his page.

"Then that's that," said Velvet, rising happily. "Can I get down?"

There was no answer.

"F'whatayave received thank God,"

said Velvet to no one in particular, and disappeared into the kitchen.

"Did you give 'em that millet?" said Meredith suddenly.

"Forgot," said Mi.

"F'whatayave received thank God," said Meredith with a dark look at him, and shot from the room. Mr. Brown pushed back his chair.

"You girls said your grace?" he said, getting up.

"F'whatayave received thank God," said Edwina. And the meal was finished.

.

The candle in the scarlet-painted candlestick was burnt low and had a shroud. The bottle-candle was high and gave a good light.

Spring and evening sky showed between undrawn cotton curtains.

Mrs. Brown sat on a stout mahogany chair before her dressing table, and Velvet knelt behind her, unhooking her dress from neck to waist at the back. The dress was dark blue rep, built firm. It was like unhooking the strain on a shrunk sofa-covering. Hook after hook Velvet travelled down till at last she reached far below the waist. Then Mrs. Brown stood up and the dark blue dress dropped to the floor, leaving her in a princess petticoat like a great cotton lily. The strings of this, untied at neck and waist by Velvet, disclosed her in bust-bodice, stays and dark-blue cloth knickers.

"The iodine's in the wall cupboard," said mother.

Velvet went to the wall cupboard and extracted the iodine from an army of bottles and jars.

"'N' the cotton wool," said mother.

Velvet, behind her, undid the strings of the bust-bodice. Got down to bedrock, she knelt and examined the wound.

"Mus' take your stays off, mother."

Mrs. Brown rose and drew breath. Working from the bottom up she unhooked the metal fencework within which she lived, and sat down again. "Star out," she said, staring through the wind. The star was like a slip of silver tinfoil plumb between the hang of the curtains.

"M'm," said Velvet, and she glanced at the star over her mother's shoulder. "Metal's worked right through the top of the stays and cut you," said Velvet.

"Ought to get whalebone," said Mrs. Brown, sniffing at her own economy.

"Yes," said Velvet, "you ought. S'made a nasty place." She dabbed the iodine on the abrasion caused by the jutting shaft of the stays. "Hurt?"

"Stings," said Mrs. Brown. The star winked and stuttered.

"Stick on a band-aid piece," said Mrs. Brown.

"Thur's a tin'n the cupboard."

Velvet stuck the plaster on to the wide hard back.

Mrs. Brown glared at the star.

"Pray to God y'don't get fat, child," she said.

Velvet sat back on her heels aghast.

"You can't be," said Mrs. Brown, "what you don't look."

"You can, you can!" said Velvet. "You are, mother!"

"Maybe," said Mrs. Brown. . . . "But you gotter dig. You gotter know. You gotter believe."

Velvet put her thin arms on her mother's shoulders and kissed her on the enemy fat. She winced at a sign of regret or weakness in the belovèd mountain.

"There's nothing, nothing you can't do, mother. You've got us all beat. Mi thinks you're Godalmighty. N'we all do."

Mrs. Brown smiled in the glass.

"Chut, child! Don't mount up in a torment. M'not grumbling. M'out of condition, but it came on me. I'm only saying . . . you poor, thin hairpin . . . KEEP thin! There's no song an' dance . . ." Mrs. Brown was bolting herself back into the fence. She stood upright.

"S'awful to grow up," said Velvet.

"I dope," said Mrs. Brown.

"Why isn't it?"

"Things come suitable to the time," said Mrs. Brown.

The thin slip, the quivering twig looked back at her mother.

"Lot o' nonsense," said Mrs. Brown, "talked about growing up." She stepped into her princess petticoat and drew it up. "Tie me," she said. The candle in the red candlestick drowned itself in fat and went out. "Childbirth," said the voice, gruff and soothing, talking to the star and to the child (and the child knelt at the strings of the petticoat), "an' being in love. An' death. You can't know 'em till you come to 'em. No use guessing and dreading. You kin call it pain. . . . But what's pain? Depends on who you are an' how you take it. Tie that bottom string looser. Don't you dread nothing, Velvet."

"But you're so mighty. Like a tree," said Velvet.

"Shivery to be your age. You don't know nothin'. Later on you get coated over." (Silence, and the hypnotic night.) "S'a good thing to be coated over. You don't change nothin' underneath."

"All the same it's awful to grow up," said Velvet. "All this changing and changing, an' got to be ready for something. I don't ever want children. Only horses."

"Who can tell?" said Mrs. Brown.

"I've got Me," said Velvet, putting her thin hand across her breast. "I can't ever be anything else but Me."

"You're all safe," said Mrs. Brown carelessly, stooping with grunts to pull up her dress. "You got both of us, you *an'* me. Say your prayers now an' get along."

"Not yet, not yet."

"Say your prayers, I say. Down on your knees an' say your prayers. You go plunging off this time o' night, don't you? Cutting into your bed all of a daze an' a worry. Say your prayers, I say!"

Velvet went on her knees in the middle of the floor. Mrs. Brown sat down, the dress in wreaths around her, and took a knife to her nails.

"Ah . . . v'Farver . . . ch . . . art'n'eaven," mumbled the voice from the floor. The blue in the window had gone and the star had companions.

". . . power n'a GloryamEN. Mother . . ."

"Yes."

"You're all right, aren't you?"

"M'as good as living forever. Get on off to bed. N'I'm not comin' to say good-night. Father is."

Velvet kissed her. "Come an' say good-night . . ."

"No, I'm not. Hook me up before you go." Velvet nicked up the great line of steely hooks to the top.

"Now go." Velvet went.

"Child gets all alight at night," said Mrs. Brown to herself.

Velvet's head came back round the door.

"Good-night, mother—where you going?"

"Down the village."

"What for?"

"Will you GO!"

Mrs. Brown went down the village with the key of the empty shop in her pocket. She had accounts to finish. The Hullocks rose above her in hoops into the sky. The stars floated in the olive glaze of the weedy pond. The

boys and girls were hushed, black and still, against the doorways. Edwina stood like a statue at the cobbler's doorway as her mother passed, but her mother knew her.

"Growing," muttered Mrs. Brown as she went on. "Poor lass has to hide it."

The beautiful boy beside Edwina breathed again. He was golden-haired, and trying for the police. He felt he had no real chance for Mr. Brown's Edwina, and he had no idea he was her first, her breath-taking first man.

"What'll Velvet . . . ?" murmured Mrs. Brown, looking a moment at the sky, and seeing Velvet's bony, fairy face. "What'll men say about my Velvet?"

The sound of hoofs striking on metalled road came out of the darkness, and down the street, all alone, galloped a horse. Bodies shot out of the doorways and shouts sprang from shadows. Something black and white and furious raced down the street. Mrs. Brown stopped and stepped off the pavement. With a striking of hoofs, sparks flying on the flints, a piebald horse, naked of leather, wild and alone, slid almost to his haunches and stood stock-still, shaking and panting. He lowered his head.

"A suitor for Velvet!"

A suitor for Velvet. The horse glared at Mrs. Brown. It had strange eyes, a white wall eye and one of darkest blue. The light from the corner street lamp swam in its eyeballs. It trembled and glared; then at Mrs. Brown's slowly extended hand, shook its neck with a shudder, half reared and, turning, galloped off up the street towards the Hullocks.

"That perishin' piebald from Ede's," exclaimed a voice.

"That you, Mr. Croom?"

"Give me a turn," said Mr. Croom.

"That's the third time this week that creature's got loose. Ede says he'll raffle him for the Fair. Wouldn't be a bad idea. Wonderful what you get for those raffles."

While Malvolia and Meredith were undressing Velvet was driving her big toes with long pieces of tape. She lay on her back in bed, her knees bent, talking in a monotonous voice like a sleepwalker.

"Careful through the gate now. Mind now. Get on, Satin!" and she gave the side of her thigh a switch with a light twig she held in her hand. The long tapes ran through her fingers which she held on her stomach, and both her knees pranced up and down,—a restive pair of well-matched chestnuts in the shooting wagonette. With another switch and a spring forward the knees rose slightly in the air, were drawn back firmly by the reins, reined in, and stood still before the porch of the old castle. . . .

The door opened and Mr. Brown surveyed the spectacle of his youngest daughter, bare to the waist, her nightgown fallen on her chest, the bed-clothes peeled to the floor, her eyes bright and her toes chained to her hands by tapes. Mally was cleaning her teeth in her drawers. Meredith was covering the bird cages.

"Mother says it's time," he said, removing his pipe. "Ah . . . yer daft, Velvet."

"I'm only allowed on Mondays. I've two minutes more."

"Where'd you get it from I want to know? D'you other girls go driving nights a week?"

"I used to," said Malley. "Now I'm bigger mother says I'll break the bed."

"Where's the baize off the cages gone to?"

"Velvet's used it under Miss Ada's

saddle. That time she got a sore back."

"What's that you got on them?"

"It's Edwina's knickers she had for the party. They got burnt, drying."

"Shame burnin' your good knickers. Canaries wake early with that thin stuff. Thought I heard 'em yesterday morning. Where's Edwina?"

"Be up in a minute. Just gone down tho ntroot a cocond."

"There . . . I've finished!" said Velvet, fishing for the bedclothes from her bed. "The chestnuts hardly needed a rubdown. They were cool. I've left the roan cob for to-night. He can stay out to grass."

"Daft as a sparrow," said Mr. Brown at random. "I doubt if a girl ought to be what you are." Stooping, with his pipe in his mouth, he flung the bedclothes up on top of her, blew out the candle and made for the door.

"I'm not in bed!" said Mally.

"Then you ought to be," said Mr. Brown. "Say your prayers." And disappeared.

Velvet heard the cruelty and wild abandon of the iron feet and shuddered and sat up, excited. It was too late to move. The horse was gone. Gone into the sea? Was it a horse? The bed clung round her like protecting arms.

"Did you hear it?" (from the bed beside her).

In three beds three bodies were upright. Edwina's bed was empty. Then, after the pause, the iron feet plunged back again, and too late all three were at the window. The door opened and the curtains blew.

"Edwina!"

"Yes. Hush." Edwina was panting. She had flown up the street and up the stairs.

"Father put the light out?"

"Yes. What horse . . ."

"Did he say 'bout me not being here?"

"I daresay he thought you'd gone with mother. What horse . . ."

"Piebald. Ede's piebald. Let me . . ."

"Didn't know Ede had a piebald. How d'you know what . . . ?"

"Be quiet. Get back. I'm getting into bed."

"Aren't you going to wash?"

"No."

"TEETH?" said Mally, impressed.

"NO."

"You bin with Teddy," said Mally with satisfaction, getting back to bed.

"You shut up," said Edwina. "Won't tell you about the horse."

"Thur's nothin' to tell. Piebald horse. Farmer Ede's. Teddy's told you that."

"Huh, an' near ran into mother!" snarled Edwina, naked, pulling her dressing gown over the clothes tumbled on the chair.

"Mother? What's it done to mother?" said Velvet sharply.

"Mother was in the street," said Edwina in a wasp's voice, pulling on her pyjamas.

"Touched her? Knocked her?" said Velvet, flashing out of bed.

"Keep your hair on," said Edwina.

"Bitch!" sobbed Velvet and flew out of the door and down the stairs.

"Now you bitched yourself!" said Mally calmly. "Now they'll know you bin out with Teddy. You know well mother's not hurt."

"Of course she isn't hurt. Should I be here!" hissed Edwina.

"Stringing Velvet off like a catapult! First, you go off with boys. Second, you upset Velvet. Third, you'll be found out. Fourth, Velvet'll be sick all night. Sense, haven't you?"

"Be . . . quiet . . ." said Edwina, in bed, in a dull strangled voice.

"Meredith . . . Merry . . . Get her back . . ."

"What did the horse do to mother, 'Dwina?"

"Sorta bowed to her. Slid to a full stop and hung its head and really sorta bowed to her. An' it reared and dashed back up the street home again. Get Velvet, Merry."

Father was sitting looking at nothing in the living-room. He was just tipping his chair and swaying.

"Father!" said Velvet, scared, in the doorway, "is mother all right?"

"Fine," said father without moving. He turned his eyes slowly.

In the shadow behind the sideboard sat Mi mending Jacob's collar.

"There's bin a horse down the street . . ." said Velvet uncertainly.

"Gallopin'," assented father round the stem of his pipe.

There was a pause.

"I dreamt it hit mother," mumbled Velvet.

"You did?"

"Yes. But it *was* a horse. That wasn't the dream."

"I just come up the street," said Mi. "Yore ma's sitting with the blinds up, in the shop, totting up."

"I'll go back," said Velvet. "It was a dream." She turned and saw Meredith's face come round the doorway from the dark stairs.

"I had a dream, Meredith," she said. "I'm coming back."

Mi put the collar down and crossing to Velvet bent down and felt her ankles. "Cold as railings," he said. "I'll getchu a brick. Keep your stomach steady." He disappeared into the kitchen and Velvet turned back to the stairs. Suddenly, at the stairhead something caught her jumping heart. She was back in the room again at her father's side, by his tipping, swaying chair.

"You all right, too, father?" she whispered. He put his arm around her and pulled her on his lap. "You get them teeth straight!" he said to her, and rocked her meditatively while his pipe smoked up through her cotton hair.

Chapter Three

The back window on the yard was blocked with cactus pots. In front of the window stood the fern-table with two big ferns in brass holders.

The street window had pots of blue and red and pied cineraria standing along its shelf, looking like a Union Jack. The eastern light of the morning burst through the cactus greenery on Mally laying the table with a darned and yellowing cloth. She clattered the crockery on from the sideboard, and the girls' voices called from the larder and kitchen.

"Mice bin at the bottom. . . . It's all run out!"

"Mice where?"

"Porridge packet. They've made a hole."

"Don't cut the rim off the toast, 'Dwina. I like 'em with the binding."

Mi looked in with a packet in his hand. "Whur's Velvet?"

"Vel V E T!"

"Coming down now."

"Mi's got your pumice."

"Mi?" said Velvet, coming through the attic stair door. "Oh, thank you, Mi."

"Do it now," said Mi.

"Clean my plate before breakfast!" said Velvet, outraged.

"Yer pa's sure to ask."

"I do it AFTER breakfast! What's the good a-doing it before!"

"Acids of the night," said Mi and disappeared.

"Acids of what?"

"Get on an' do it," said Mally.

"You'd think that plate was jewelry!" said Velvet and went into the scullery.

"Cost more than your mother's engagement ring," said Mr. Brown, passing through to the slaughter-house.

"She grumbling again?"

"Gone to clean it," said Mally.

"Kedgeree!"

Mother brought in the soup basin of kedgeree. Donald stumped near her skirts. Edwina and Velvet came in and, sitting down, began to eat.

"I bin sick in the night," said Donald.

"You haven't," said Mrs. Brown. "Get on your chair."

"Why haven't I?" demanded Donald.

"Don't let him start whying!" said Mally.

"Why haven't I, I say?" demanded Donald. "Tell me why, I say?"

"Get on to your chair and don't let's hear any more about it," said Mrs. Brown.

"Why haven't I, I say?" Donald held on. "You changed my sheets. The new ones was cold."

"I changed your sheets for other reasons," said Mrs. Brown. "Now get on."

"The new ones was horrible," muttered Donald, subsiding. "Is it kedgeree?"

"Did you wash your neck, Velvet?"

"Yes, mother."

"Before your frock or after your frock?"

"After."

"Then don't. Your frock's soaking. Where's Meredith?"

"Canary's loose."

Mr. Brown opened the door again and came in.

Donald brightened. "I was sick in the night, daddy."

"Donald!"

"I was sick all over . . ."

Mrs. Brown removed Donald and the kedgeree to the kitchen.

"Lie. He wet his bed," said Mally.

"Oh," said Mr. Brown and helped himself to kedgeree. "I heard your mother moving about. Why don't she leave him wet. He won't hurt. He's no more than damp."

"Bad for his habits," said Mrs. Brown, returning. She sat down and drew the marmalade towards her.

"I've caught her!" Meredith came in glowing.

"Take your kedgeree into the kitchen and let Donald tell you how sick he's been," said Velvet.

"You'll do no such thing," said Mrs. Brown. "That child gets on one idea like a railway track. It's you and your stomach, Velvet, that puts him onto it."

"Can't help my stomach," said Velvet. " 'Dgive anything in the world to change it."

"You'll grow out of it."

"Sixteen, you said."

"Sixteen, I said."

"Why sixteen?"

"You eat," said Mrs. Brown.

"Can I come back now?" Donald appeared in the doorway, holding his plate unsteadily in his fists.

"Yes, if you've finished."

"I've finished."

"All?"

"All except the bones. Jacob's eaten them."

"Oh . . ." Velvet flew up and left the room. "Mi!" she called into the yard from the kitchen. "Jacob's eaten fishbones!"

Donald lifted his plate to the side-

board and the spoon flew over his head to the floor.

"That child say he finished?" demanded Mr. Brown.

"I finished," said Donald.

"It's all on his plate still," said Mr. Brown, and went on reading his paper.

"Velvet!" called Mally. "It's a do, Velvet! Come back. Jacob hasn't got a bone."

Velvet appeared in the doorway.

"Donald," said Mrs. Brown, turning full on him, "have you told me a story?"

"It *was* a story," said Donald gravely.

"Do you know what a story is?"

"No," said Donald.

Mrs. Brown removed him to her bedroom.

"Piebald's gone down the street again," said Mi, putting his hair in at the door and disappearing. The four sisters rose and streamed from the room. Mr. Brown, glancing up once and half turning round, went on with his paper. Mrs. Brown returned.

"Donald sorry?" said Mr. Brown.

"He's thinking," said Mrs. Brown. "He isn't sure. Girls gone?"

"That piebald of Ede's got loose again," said Mr. Brown. There was peace and silence.

The tiny windowpane between the cineraria was filled with black and white and the piebald went back up the street at a hard gallop. After his metal feet the street rustled with running shoes.

"That animal'll knock down a pram one of these days," observed Mr. Brown. "Seems to make for the sea."

"Curious horse," said Mrs. Brown. "Climbs out in the night when the moon's up."

"Don't he jump?" said Mr. Brown.

"Jumps a house," said Mrs. Brown.

"Sort of rodeo, so they say. . . . Yes, Donald? What is it?"

"I'm sorry," called Donald in muffled tones through the door.

Mrs. Brown opened the door.

"I'm sorry I was sick in the night," said Donald.

"Child'll make a lawyer," said Mr. Brown.

Meredith returned to the room.

"He went right through the poles they're hammering up for the Fair," she said. "Then down to the Post Office, an' slid about and up the chalk road back on to the Hullocks again. Mr. Ede was just going by 'n his cart. Cursed."

"He'll get into trouble if that horse hurts someone," said father. "Mi done his breakfast?"

"Had it early. He's got given a glass tongue. Ate it in his room."

"Well, tell'm I want'm at twelve for six sheep." Mr. Brown passed away through the slaughter-house door. Mi came in from the street.

"Six sheep at twelve, father says."

"M'm. Piebald jumped a five bar gate with a wire on the top. Sailed over."

"Who says so?"

"Fellow."

"Is it broke?"

"The gate?"

"No. The piebald."

"Ede says it's as quiet as a lamb. Just can't bear to be shut up. Bit mad."

Mi blew his nose carefully, polished it, replaced his handkerchief and went for the yard door.

"You got a bit a time?" said Meredith.

"Get on an' do your canaries. Gotter sweep my room."

"Done my canaries. I'll come an' sweep yours."

Mi sniffed and went off. Meredith

caught up a broom which stood beside the wall.

"You put that down," said Mi, who knew she had taken it without turning his head. "S'yer ma's own." The broom was meekly put back. Meredith followed him.

Mi's room was outside, next to Miss Ada. It was an old loose box that had fallen into disrepair. He took great pride in it and kept it spotless. Just within the door, which was propped open for freshness with a garden rake, was a large hole in the floor filled with rotting wood. The wood round the edges of the hole gave way like toast and Mi had marked a white ring round the hole and written in paint "Step further than this." He took his own broom and began to sweep.

"S'got no hairs on it," said Meredith, standing about and in the way.

No answer. Mi did not like criticism. He swept the dust of the room vigorously into a heap, then propelled it with his brush over a portion of the painted line and into the hole in the floor. Picking up an old milk bottle by the neck he rammed the dust horizontally under the floor boards.

"Now whadjer want?" he said.

"Hammer'n nails," said Meredith.

"Go out of the room then. Thurs no call fer you to see where I keep things."

Meredith went outside into the sunny yard and stood with her back to the wall on the far side of the door. Honourably she looked away and straight before her. Mi went to his bed and abstracted a hammer and tobacco box of nails from under his mattress.

"How big?" he called.

Meredith measured her thumb joint. "Inch an' a half."

"Whafor?"

"Hang my Roller cage."

"Find a joist then. It's rubble and such in between." Mi came to the doorway with the hammer and nails.

"D'you think . . . ?" began Meredith.

"No," said Mi shortly. "You get into yer own hot water fer puttin' yer own nails in the house. Yer pa's down the village."

"I know," said Meredith. "T'why I'm hurrying."

She disappeared with the hammer and nails, and Mi took down his shaving mirror and polished it with his handkerchief. He replaced a drawing pin or two on the corners of his series of "Grand National winners" pinned round the walls, and set the kettle on to his Primus that he might scald out his milk bottle.

Velvet and Mally appeared in the yard and hung about.

"Where's Merry?"

"Hammering," said Mi.

Silence fell and the kettle hummed. Mally and Velvet looked with envy from the yard into the loose-box-bedroom.

"Wish I had a room of my own," said Velvet. "So I could hang up pictures."

Mi came to the door, and holding the milk bottle over the hole in the floor poured the scalding water into it.

"I've earned it," said Mi when the last drop was in.

"Why?"

"Full-grown," he said, and sucked the gap in his teeth. He looked at them, long and straight. They looked back.

"They're puttin' that piebald up to raffle," he said at last, and yawned deceptively.

"Raffle!" said Velvet. "Raffle!" A pause. Then—"Anybody might get it?"

"Anybody with a shilling."

"Cost on'y a shilling? You got a shilling, Mally?"

"Nothing at all."

"Nor I've got nothing . . ."

"Oh, a shilling's easy got."

"But we ought to have five. Donald ought to have a chance."

"You'll never get five!"

"That's whur yer wrong," said Mi. "I'll give you five. You kin pay me back in yer time. I got a tip from a perisher."

"Oh, Mi darling! What perisher?"

"Togged-up perisher that was swanky and windy and couldn't sit his horse in his best suit."

"What'd you do?"

"Fellow hired Belton's May Day and went out galloping. Top boots, spurs and checks, an' a bowler with a string on it."

"Where were you?"

"Just walkin'."

"Oh, Mi! You were sitting behind the haystack with the ghost!"

"Had to sit somewhere."

"Tell us . . ."

"I saw May Day go out. Galloped out. Perisher'd never heard of walkin' or trottin'. Half the sky was dancin' up an' down under 'is bottom, so I legged up the other way an' come to the haystack."

Pause.

". . . an' he galloped round," egged Velvet.

"I see him coming down towards the haystack, May Day blowy and sweaty an' the ghost waiting for them as jolly as a daisy."

"Oh . . . Mi . . . YOU . . . SAW it."

"IT? No, s'not my kind. It's a horse ghost. Perisher was red in the face an' lumbering along. Toes pointin' down and not even clutching with his calves. Not clutchin' with anything. Heaving like a sack. Stock all out of place under his ear, having

a high old seven and sixpence worth. . . . Whoop . . . went May Day when the ghost made a pass at her. Sprung right across the road an' the perisher fell *on* the ghost, far's I c'd see. Serve it right, too. Real vicious horse that must've been that got killed there. To have a ghost like that. Why, you can't miss making a bit in that place. Every hiring fellow that comes down from London spins off at that haystack. You on'y got to sit behind it and pick up the bits."

"They don't all tip you though."

"Most do. This one give me five. Here you are!"

Mi pulled two half crowns out of his pocket and handed them to Velvet in trust for them all.

"Thank you awfully, Mi. I'll give it you back. Swear." And she hooked both middle fingers over her index fingers and held them up.

"Witches' stuff!" said Mi contemptuously. "Keep yer word and don't crack yer fingers. And see this, Velvet, I'm a fool to do it. That piebald's as big a perisher's the fellow that tipped me the five. 'M going up to look at him this afternoon and likely I'll be sorry when I see his murdering white eye."

"Can we come too, can we come too?"

"You got yer muslins to iron."

"MUSLINS!" said Velvet, outraged.

"Yer ma's just wrung 'em out of the suds. I seen 'em. For the Fair."

"I'm not going to wear MUSLIN," said Velvet with a voice of iron.

"You'll wear what yer told," said Mi placidly. "I'll slip up after dinner. Nearer one. I got them sheep at twelve. Sounds I won't get any dinner. See Donald . . ."

Donald was beautifully dressed in a fresh striped blouse and grey pants the length of a coat cuff. The insides

of both ankles were fastened up with sticking plaster and his silver hair had just left the prongs of a damp comb. The brown of his arms was a mixture of coffee and silk.

"Whur's the stinkin' ants?" said Donald.

"What's that?"

"A stinkin' ant jus' stung me."

"Where'd it sting you?"

"On my thumb," said Donald clearly, and held up his thumb.

There was no mark of any kind on the pink thumb.

"Say 'stinging,'" said Malley. "Ants don't sting. It was a wasp."

"Go on," said Mi. "Don't be s'old-fashioned. He'll say 'stinkin' ant' till he says 'stinging wasp' . . . and it'll all come natural."

Mally looked down her nose at Donald. "You're soft, Mi," she said. "You bin and killed something, Donald."

"It wanted to be dead," said Donald. "A very little ant."

"Throwing the blame on the ant!" said Mally. "I thought as much!"

Donald made a pass with his foot. "Thur's another one," he said. "They all want to be dead."

"Nice excuse!" said Velvet. "Stop it, Donald!"

"Every one of those ants," said Mally, taking a deep breath and blowing out her cheeks, "has got an aunt an' an uncle an' little brothers an' . . ."

"This one hadn't," said Donald, and ran away.

"S'awful to be so pretty," said Velvet, looking after him. "He's like an actress."

"Actress my boot," said Mally. "He's a common murderer."

"Likes to see things stop," said Mi. "Anybody's the same. You better go iron them muslins. Sooner you get them ironed sooner you see the piebald."

"Be in towels yet," said Velvet. "Mine was too short last summer. It'll look like a ham frill this."

"Got to get on," said Mi. "Frittering my morning away . . ." and disappeared.

"He won't go an' see that piebald without us?" said Velvet.

"What about the blasted muslins?" said Mally.

"Better go."

"Here's Meredith! What's the matter, Merry?"

"Went down the street," said Meredith. "Looking at the rooks' nests. Dropped a splodge. A rook dropped a splodge . . ." She was wiping her eye furiously with her dress. "Gummy," she said. "S'gummy stuff . . ."

"Get in under the tap," said Velvet. "It's lime. P'raps it's quicklime."

Meredith ran blindly into the scullery holding her eye. The lime ran off at the touch of water.

On the scullery ledge was a board with four objects on it like babies in long clothes, old bath towels, used for keeping the best washing evenly damp. Mally cautiously undid the first.

"It's them," she said, as though she had smelt a drain.

"What?" said Meredith.

"Muslin, ducky, for the Fair. Our muslins."

"Muslin!" said Meredith, stiff with offence.

"Muslin," said Mrs. Brown from behind with a soft and heavy certainty. "An' your white woolly pull-overs on top. You'll be warm an' you'll be pretty. Get on upstairs and look over your stockings for holes."

"STOCKINGS! We're not going to wear STOCKINGS!"

Mrs. Brown sat down on the scullery chair.

"We'll get it all over," she said. "I'll run through it. You'll wear your long black Christmas stockings, WITH suspenders, fastened to them calico belts I bought you for the Christmas dance. You'll wear white petticoats that go with . . ."

"PETTICOATS!"

"Petticoats. That belongs to the dresses. (Or should.) You'll wear your muslins, an' your pullovers, an' your black lace shoes . . ."

"SHOES!"

"If you get a shock over everything, Velvet, you'll be ill an' you won't go at all. When you have muslins you have black shoes an' when you have black shoes you have stockings, or your heels rub . . ." (Edwina came through the street door.) ". . . an' you'll iron your muslins . . ."

"MUSLINS!" said Edwina in exactly the same tone as the others.

"We've been through all that," said Malvolia. "Black shoes, black stockings, petticoats, suspenders, belts, pullovers. . . . P'raps you'd like to sit down an' rest, 'Dwina? Go on, mother. We're to iron our muslins when?"

"Father's at the bottom of this . . ." muttered Edwina.

Mrs. Brown reached for a longclothes baby and unrolled it. "Damp yet," she said, trying it to her cheek. "Soaking. They'll stay damp till the evening in the shade. You can iron them after tea. Go on and look over the stockings."

Edwina, Malvolia, Meredith and Velvet passed through the little black door on to the stairs.

The canaries were singing and shouting in the breeding cages and the new wooden cage, recently put up by Meredith, hung insecurely and crooked from the nail she had borrowed.

"You got it up," said Velvet.

"It's all soft stuff in that wall," said Meredith.

"Nail's going to come out," said Mally—and they pulled out the drawers to look over the stockings.

Edwina held up her calico petticoat and measured it against her willowy figure. "Dressed up in muslin!" she muttered.

"But I thought you liked dressing up," said Mally. Edwina made no reply.

"Not dressed up enough is your trouble," said Mally.

"It's time I had . . ." murmured Edwina, preoccupied and searching in a drawer . . . "something . . . more . . ." and she found what she was looking for.

"I'll wear it over the muslin," she said, holding up a tennis skirt of white flannel. "It's a bit yellow. I've got a blue leather belt somewhere."

"You'll make us look like a lot of dressed-up babies," said Mally, half enviously. "And mother won't let you."

"I'll slip it on last thing," said Edwina. "Mother doesn't really care. It's father. The top'll look like quite a nice muslin shirt. I wish I could cut off the bottom."

"Well, that's your trouble," said Mally. "My goodness, I wouldn't dare."

"Where's it kept?" said Velvet.

"I had it in this bottom drawer," said Edwina. Velvet turned and stared at her. After a pause she cleared her mind. "I mean the piebald," she amended.

"Oh, I meant to tell you!" said Edwina. "They're going to raffle it tomorrow . . ."

"We know," said Mally. "Mi said so. And he's given us five shillings to

have a ticket each. Even Donald."

"*Lent* us," said Velvet.

"I meant lent us. Where do we get the tickets?"

"They've got books at the Post Office. Books of tickets."

"Let's go down and choose early ones."

Edwina stuffed her skirt back in the drawer. The stockings lay in tight black balls on the bed.

"Come on, Meredith . . ."

"You go. I'll come in a minute."

Edwina, Mally and Velvet clattered down the stairs and left Meredith stooping beside a cage.

Velvet put her head back in at the door.

"Shall I get yours or will you get your own?"

Meredith answered without looking round. "The female's ill."

"Which is it?" said Velvet, coming nearer.

"Africa," said Meredith in a low voice.

Africa had been a male until she had been discovered to be a female. Now she lay in the palm of Meredith's hand, cloaking her eye with a little sagging hood.

"Is it the heat?" said Velvet, awed.

"I don't know," said Merry. "Get me the brandy. It's on the bottom shelf in the sideboard. In father's flask."

While Velvet went for the brandy Meredith reached for her fountain pen filler, her left hand groping in a drawer, her eyes steady on the faint yellow bird.

"Draw the blind," she said to Velvet who had returned. Velvet drew the blind behind the roaring cages and all song dropped like a flag when the wind has failed. There was a sickroom silence and anxiety.

"How much?" asked Velvet.

"One drop."

But Africa died. She died in the palm of Merry's hand without a sound or a sigh or a movement. She seemed to miss a little breath and go smaller, and Velvet, startled, glanced round, as though a whiff of life had drifted out of Africa.

"I can't hold her now she's dead," said Merry, her teeth chattering. "Take her off my hand."

"Tip her off," said Velvet, wincing too.

"Go on. Take her! I'll scream."

Velvet took her and laid her with distaste on the bedtable by Merry's bed.

"Horrible," said Merry. "It's a corpse. Poor little Africa. She's gone away."

"I truthfully," said Velvet in a low voice, "thought I saw her go."

"How?"

"When she went small. Just something."

"What?"

"Air."

"That was her spirit," said Merry suddenly, looking at her intently. Velvet and Meredith stared at Africa.

"I should like her just not to be here," said Merry savagely. "I should like her to be all buried and finished."

"Perhaps Mi will."

"No, he won't. He'll say, 'Bury your own bird.'"

"Mother will," said Velvet.

"Will she?"

"Yes, come on. Leave it there." Velvet flipped up the blind again and all the canaries cantered straight into open song. "Go on down to the Post Office an' I'll be down in a second."

"Who's got the shilling?"

"Mally has," said Velvet. "They'll be waiting for you. Don't get my ticket for me!"

"No—" Merry ran down the street.

"Mother," said Velvet, opening the scullery door. "Africa's died."

Mrs. Brown turned. "Merry know?" "Yes, she died in her hand. Just now."

"Where's Merry?"

"Gone down to the Post Office. But she can't touch Africa. She hates her dead. Could you bury her, do you think? She's on the table by Merry's bed."

"I'll see to her," said Mrs. Brown. "Bring her down."

"I can't touch her either," said Velvet. "She's . . ."

Mrs. Brown looked at her.

"You know when a thing's dead . . ." said Velvet uselessly. Then after a pause she went slowly upstairs and brought down the dead bird in her hand. Mrs. Brown reached up to a shelf for a little cardboard box. She put Africa inside and shut the lid. Velvet raced down to the Post Office.

In the sultry midday, with the Hullocks steaming above them, a little group of parcel-posters and stamp-buyers was jesting over the book-tickets. Edwina and her sisters stood in the shadow, their eyes grave and full of choosing. They were weighing the flashing, unequal importance of numbers.

The blacksmith was having his joke.

"Stand up, gentlemen," he shouted, "the horse is yours! Shilling a go for a mad piebald gelding. Or is it a stallion, Mr. Croom? Not clean gelded, eh? Thought as much. Mr. Ede done it on the cheap an' left a chip."

"Not a bad thing to have a horse for a shilling," suggested Mr. Croom. "You can always sell it for something."

"Not so easy done," said the blacksmith. "You got to feed it an' lodge it meanwhile."

"Ede says it'll ride quiet," said Mr. Croom. "He *says* it will. Anybody know?"

"I seen him ride it," said a voice.

"Went along quiet an' dull. He had a basket on his arm too. An' he opened a gate and let the basket fall. Never turned a hair."

"What's the matter with it that he wants to raffle it, then?"

"He can't tie it up an' he can't keep it in. Jumps any wall. Go sailing over the moon if you'd let it. Kink in its mind about being tied up or shut in. Ede's tired of catching it. Besides he's afraid it'll do a damage in the village. He bought it cheap in Lewes Market, but it's no good to him."

Some tickets were bought but there was no rush on them. Edwina walked out of the corner to the counter.

The raffle book was *one to two hundred*, got out in ink hurriedly by Mrs. Ede.

"He'll likely make his ten pound on him," said Mr. Croom. "That's more'n he paid for him at Lewes."

Solemnly the four girls lined against the counter and gazed at the book.

"I've thought of forty-seven," whispered Mally.

"But did you make yourself or did it come?"

"That's what I don't know."

"I've got ten . . . printed on my brain, large . . . in red letters," said Edwina.

Silence.

"It's like a visitation," persisted Edwina in a whisper.

Silence.

"But perhaps I'm meant to avoid it," she ended.

Each girl stretched her mind and tried to tremble to the finger of God.

"I'll have 119 please," said Velvet unexpectedly and firmly to the postmistress.

She paid her shilling, and the other three watched her, envious and dismayed.

"What did you . . ." began Mally.

"I don't want to talk about it," said Velvet, low, and walked out of the Post Office into the street.

The others followed her with tickets in their hands.

"We just took them anyhow," said Edwina, rather cross. "What's the good of thinking!"

"Have you got one for Donald?"

"Number One."

"Well, there we are anyway," said Mally. "Let's go an' pin them in the Bible. It's dinner time."

Meredith instantly thought of Africa. As they walked back towards the house Africa was like a yellow shade upon her mind. Where did she lie? Would she be visible again to the eye or was she packed up for ever? Mrs. Brown called to them from the door. "Wash your hands quick," she said, "it's hot dinner."

"I'll wash mine in the scullery," said Merry and fled through the sitting-room.

Velvet whispered to the others, "Africa's dead."

Mrs. Brown turned off the scullery tap that Merry might hear what she said. "Your little bird's buried," she said. "Cage is all cleaned an' I've put the cock in there. The greeny cock. But he's got no food or water yet. Run up an' see to him."

Merry turned with streaming eyes and kissed her. "I'll rearrange them," she choked, and went upstairs to the bedroom.

They sat down to dinner without Mr. Brown or Mi, and Mrs. Brown brought in the joint. Merry joined them, a little flushed, but peaceful.

A squawking and bleating came muffled through the wall.

"That's the last," said mother. "Father'll be in soon."

"Row those sheep make," said Mally.

Edwina got up to get the red jelly from the sideboard.

"We've taken five tickets, shilling tickets, for a raffle for the Fair to-morrow," said Velvet. "They're raffling that piebald."

"The piebald?" said Mrs. Brown. "Ede getting rid of it? Well, I'm not surprised."

"But what'll father . . ?"

"Time enough to worry when you get it," said Mrs. Brown. "Got that jelly, 'Dwina? It's there behind the pickles."

"Where's Donald?" said Velvet.

"Slep' on. But he ought to be woke now. You get him, Velvet."

Velvet got up and went out by the yard door. She pressed the spaniels back with her foot as they struggled and changed places, smelling the joint.

Jacob came wriggling and smiling round the wall. He was late in, having been down the village to the sea, watching the trippers unload from the charàbancs.

The whole day's heat was shimmering in the yard. The splendour of the heat stood upright like a tank of water. Dust moved in it and midges poured up and down. Immediately she faced the yard Velvet went into a vision. The bones and stones and boxes and dogs of the yard dropped away below her and she was mounted on a cliff beside the piebald, on the hip of a cliff overlooking the sea. The sea was pale and a ship swum up in a haze on the sky. The piebald stared like a lunatic at the cobbled wall which bound his field. Velvet choked as she stared with him, and saw the grasses wave at the foot of the cobbles. The wall gave way as they cleared it and sank together, the sea rushing up. A gull's wing zipped and she saw the indigo shadow, and with her knees

she felt the ribs spring in arcs from the horse's spine. His boundless heart rushed into hers. The soles of her feet cramped against the impending waters.

"I've woke," called Donald from the shade where he lay on a mattress in Miss Ada's unused cart—its shafts propped on an upright barrel. Velvet crossed the yard and opened the little door at the back of the cart. "Get up," she said, but the child only stared half-awake at the sky. She took him by his bare legs and pulled. His shirt left his pants and began to turn up over his arms.

"Can't walk. Carry me," he said. His teeth chattered. "I'm shivery," he said, and bumped his heavy head on to her thin chest as she struggled with him.

"That's only sleep," she said. "It's dinner time. You've slept too long."

Merry opened the sitting-room door. "Are you coming?" she called.

"I've slept too long," moaned Donald at the door, in Velvet's arms.

"Get down an' walk," said Mrs. Brown.

"Slept too long," he wailed self-pityingly.

"A little tap-water an' you'll feel better," said mother.

She took him and he wept a little and was carried away. He reappeared in a few minutes bright and silky. "I slept too long," he said in quite a different voice, engagingly, socially.

"Yes, we heard," said Mr. Brown who had come in. "Get up on your chair now. Here's your plate."

"The meat's sour," said Donald instantly, putting his nose to his meat.

"Poor lot those sheep," said Mr. Brown. "It's the drought. Bit ribby, weren't they, Mi."

"Dog bin racin' 'em," said Mi.

"It's sour," said Donald, giving his plate a push.

Mrs. Brown glanced over. "He's got capers put on his. Take them off, 'Dwina."

"It's you that's sour," said 'Dwina to him, getting up and stooping beside him. "Oh . . . Mother, he's spat at me!"

"Spit came out," said Donald, a little anxiously.

"Fractious," said Mr. Brown. "Sit down, 'Dwina, and get on both. I heard Ede's going to raffle that piebald animal that got loose."

There was no response. Everyone, thinking hard, ate silently.

"You oughter take a ticket, Velvet," said Mr. Brown genially.

"We've all . . . we've all taken tickets," said Velvet softly, unable to believe her ears. Mr. Brown's face changed. He had meant to make a joke.

"He'll be meat if you get him," he said after a pause, and not genially at all.

Velvet's face flushed faintly.

"Cabbage is stringy," said Donald, and created a diversion.

"He's possessed," said Mr. Brown vexedly. The condition of the sheep had annoyed him.

Edwina and Mally cleared the plates and brought in gooseberry fool. Velvet fetched the milk pudding from the oven. They started with fresh life on the fresh food.

"Want you s'afternoon, Mi," said Mr. Brown. The girls grew tense, and waited, spoons still.

"'Bout five," said Mr. Brown, and the breath of anxiety was let out again, and the spoons moved on.

The chairs were pushed in. "F'whatweave received . . . thank God!" they said as one voice and fled.

Chapter Four

The piebald cropped in just such a field, on just such a Hullock as Velvet had dreamed. There was the haze and the ship. Mi, Edwina, Malvolia, Meredith and Velvet stood in a row leaning against the cobbled wall. There was a long and watchful silence. The wild thyme smelt warm and looked pink. The sea lay below, not blue but dove-grey. The coping of the wall was hot and rough.

"Stands marvellous," said Mi at length.

Another long appreciative silence.

"See his bone . . ." said Mi.

Mi made a click with a gap in his teeth and turned to look at Velvet. "What's that number of yours?"

"119."

"Well, there!"

"What?"

"You ought to have a horse!"

The piebald looked up and saw them. Stared. Then cropped again.

"Seems quiet," said Edwina.

"Huh. No knowing. Think he's under fifteen hands?"

"Think he's more," said Velvet.

"See his white eye?"

They saw it. They saw everything. Their eyes, like birds' eyes, flickered over his startling patches of black and white. He was white in bold seas, and black in continents, marked in such a way that when he moved his white shoulders and his white quarters flashed, and his black body seemed to glide.

"Showy," said Mi.

Velvet climbed the wall into the field.

"He'll be off!" said Mally warningly.

Velvet went among the hot grasses towards him. She knew him. She had

already ridden him in her dream. He cropped, head towards her, but watched her coming. She walked steadily and straight and began to talk in low tones. He raised his head and looked at her as firmly as she looked at him. She paused. He walked several paces towards her with confidence. No quirk or tremor or snort of doubt.

"See that!" said Mi, hanging against the wall.

They saw Velvet pat him and run her hand slowly down his neck on to his shoulder.

"She'll be that upset now," said Mi, "if she don't get him."

Velvet moved away. The animal followed her, flashing and jaunty. He had a white mane, a long white tail, pink hooves, a sloping pastern, and he struck his feet out clean and hard as he walked.

"Isn't his neck thick?" said Edwina.

"Bit," said Mi. "Bin gelded late."

The piebald, whose desires were gone, had kept his pride. He walked after Velvet like a stocky prince. Thick-necked, muscular, short and proud. He left her a few paces from the wall, and stood looking, then turned and cropped quietly.

"Gotter be back," said Mi.

Velvet hung a moment longer by the wall, then all five in silence turned downhill. There was a wild snort behind them and the thunder of feet.

"He's off!" said Mi, turning sharp. "It's set him off!"

The piebald had his white tail raised and his head arched like a Persian drawing. He was galloping down the field towards the corner.

"Stop! Stand! He's never going over that!"

The ground had dropped away so sharply at the far corner that the original builder of the cobbled wall, to keep his coping straight, had heightened the wall itself. It was five feet two at the end of the field, with a fine downhill take-off. The horse sailed over like a dappled flying boat. It was a double spring. As he was high in the air he saw also to his hind feet and drew them up sharply.

". . . AND to spare," said Mi quietly, nodding his head. "A horse like that'd win the National."

"You don't mean it, Mi!"

"Gets his hocks under. Got heart. Grand take-off. Then when he's up in the air he gives a kind of second hitch an' his feet tuck up so he's on'y a body without legs. See him look before he took off? See his ears flitch forward and back again? You on'y got to sit on him."

"Oh, Mi, why don't you ride?"

". . . Got a nasty sort of look of Man-of-War too," pursued Mi, unheeding.

"Who was Man-of-War?"

"Man-eatin' stallion," said Mi.

"But a black and white horse like that doesn't look like anything to do with a race."

"Ever hear of the Tetrarch?"

"No."

"Looked like a rocking horse. Sorta dappled. Mr. Persse his trainer was. One mornin' he was sittin' eatin' his egg an' a stable lad rushed in an' screamed out, 'That coloured horse can beat anything!' an' rushed out again."

"And what did he win?"

"Didn't win anything so marvellous because they ran him as a two-year-old. But he sired twenty-seven thousand pounds!"

"How'd you know so much, Mi?"

"Used to read when I was up

there," Mi jerked his finger north, away from the sea.

"Why did the stable boy rush in?"

" 'Cause he won, didn't he, in the gallops in the morning."

"The piebald Tetrarch?"

"He wasn't piebald. Not even grey. He was coloured. Grey and roan and white. Mottled. They got him for a mascot. Just for a stable companion. And he brought them a fortune."

They walked down the slopes, wrapped in the eternal drama of the last being first.

"An' Mr. Persse," said Velvet, lifting her boy's face to the sky, "he rushed out?" She wanted to sit again over the breakfast table with Mr. Atty Persse. (The heavenly, escaping past—)

"He rushed out," said Mi, warming, "and he said: 'Where's that goddam boy? I'll wring his neck!' "

"Why?"

"He had a feel the boy was right."

"Well, and . . ."

"When you gotta good thing you keep it dark, don't you! Not shout all down the passages and right through the kitchen an' go back runnin' an' grinnin' like a fathead to the stables."

"Mustn't anybody know when you think you're going to win a race?"

"Money passes," said Mi. "Fortunes. Thousands. Millions. It's like the City."

"Do they race a lot in the North?" asked Velvet.

A landscape glittered behind her voice. There were icicles in it and savage fields of ice, great storms boiling over a flat countryside striped with white rails—a chessboard underneath a storm. Horses were stretched forever at the gallop. Tiny men in silk were brave beyond bearing and sat on the horses like embryos with their knees in their mouths. The gorgeous names of horses were cried from

mouth to mouth and circulated in a steam of fame. Lottery, The Hermit, the great mare Sceptre; the glorious ancestress Pocahontas, whose blood ran down like Time into her flying children; Easter Hero, the Lamb, that pony stallion.

"Race?" said Mi. "*All* the time." And Velvet knew she was right.

"If I won that piebald," said Velvet, "I might ride him in the Grand National myself."

"Girls can't ride in that," said Mi contemptuously.

"Girls!" said Velvet, stopping still beside him so that they all drew up. "Who's to know I'm a girl?" She cupped her face in her two hands so that her straight hair was taken from it.

" 'Tisn't your hair," said Mi, and his eyes fell on her chest. "Flat's a pancake," he said. "You'd pass. There's a changing room though."

"What'd you undress for?"

"Change your day things for your silks."

"But you needn't undress to your skin. You could keep the same vest."

"It *could* happen . . ." said Mi. "It never has. You got to get your horse first."

There was a silence as they walked.

"There he goes!" said Mi. The piebald was galloping below them, making as usual for the village. "Heavy galloper. Plunges as he goes."

"He's lovely," breathed Velvet, simply. They started to run. Below them they could see a sweeper at the entrance to the village wave his broom at the horse.

The piebald leapt round him and galloped on. He disappeared between the first houses on the street. Soon he was out again, driven away by men and boys whom they could see standing by the sea wall, and headed up the curve of the Hullocks again, still galloping, his white mane and tail flying.

"Carthorse and Arab in that animal," said Mi, pausing to look. The piebald tired on the steep hill and slowed to a trot, then stood still. He looked over his shoulder at the village below him.

"He's homesick," said Velvet suddenly. "He wants people. He hates it up there on that high field. Would he let me get near him?"

"Never while he's loose like that, an' after he's galloped," said Mi. "Not worth the trouble. What about those muslins?"

"Come along," said Edwina. "We've got to get them done. Don't keep staring at him, Velvet. He'll never belong to any of us, and if he did the Lord knows what father'd say!"

After tea they did the muslins.

"Ironing's lovely," said Meredith. They had forgotten their antagonism to the frocks. The irons were hot and had polished shoes that slid over the steaming damp of the muslin surface. There were two irons and Meredith and Mally ironed while Velvet waited sitting by the cactus window. They used the supper table. The frail muslin hardened and blanched as the irons poked and slid, and Edwina made a racket in the room above looking for her blue leather belt. Father passed through the room in his gum boots. He had been hosing.

"They want a steak. Over at Kingsworthy. Got to be there before breakfast," he said.

"Before breakfast!"

"That's what I said," said father. The door shut.

"What sort of a cook wants a steak before breakfast?" said Mally, shooting the nose of her iron in among the front pleats.

"Man-eating cook," said Edwina, standing in the doorway with her belt over her wrist. "Sucks 'em raw before she lights the stove."

"It's Mr. Cellini's, Kingsworthy," said Velvet. "He's got that chestnut we saw at the Show last year."

"Don't fiddle with the cactus," said Edwina. "The leaves break off."

Velvet folded her hands in her lap. "Sir Pericles," said Velvet. "He was called Sir Pericles, that chestnut. Won the novice's jumping."

"I'll go with the steak," said Meredith. "I'd love to. I'll go just as early as I wake, I'll creep out and get Miss Ada. Mother could leave the steak on the table overnight."

"Why couldn't we take it this evening?"

"Then they think it's to-day's meat."

"But it will be, anyway!"

"Yes, but they think it's fresher if it comes to-morrow."

"There!" Mally took her muslin dress and held it up by the puff sleeves.

It was stiff and fresh with ironing and almost stood by itself.

"It's like a paper bag," said Velvet. "Seems a pity to wear it. D'you want to start, Edwina, or shall I start mine?"

"I'm only wearing the top of mine. I've cut it off."

"Gosh! You *have?* You've been an' cut it?"

All the three heads were raised towards Edwina as she took this step into the future. They contemplated her for a second, then accepted her. Velvet got up and began to unroll her frock and lay it out.

"Ay . . . Merry. Look out! What's that . . . it's blood!"

Meredith shot one hand to her face.

"It's my nose," she cried from under her hand.

"It's dropped on the muslin. Get me a rag!"

"Here's the ironing duster! Hold your head off the dresses! Lie down on the cold scullery floor. It's brick."

Donald appeared in the doorway from the street and watched Meredith as she ran into the scullery holding the duster to her face.

"She hurt herself?" he asked.

"Her nose is bleeding," said Velvet.

"I laugh when my nose bleeds," said Donald.

"Your nose hasn't ever bled," said Velvet briefly.

"I would laugh if it did," said Donald, and went.

"Merry marked her muslin?" said Mrs. Brown, coming in from the scullery.

"Great drop," said Mally.

"Put it under cold water," said Mrs. Brown. "Not a touch of soap an' no hot. It sets it. It's Africa's made her nose bleed."

"I'll go with the steak to-morrow then," said Velvet. "There's the Fair an' all. She better keep still."

"What steak's that?"

"Father said Mr. Cellini wanted a steak before breakfast."

"Funny time," said Mrs. Brown.

"I'd like to go anyway," said Velvet. "I might see the chestnut."

That night, before the Fair, they went to bed early.

"Africa!" said Meredith, wildly and suddenly in the middle of the night. And slept again.

Chapter Five

Velvet's dreams were blowing about the bed. They were made of cloud but had the shapes of horses. Sometimes she dreamt of bits as women dream of jewellery. Snaffles and straights and pelhams and twisted pelhams were hanging, jointed and still in the shadows of a stable, and above

them went up the straight, damp, oiled lines of leathers and cheek straps. The weight of a shining bit and the delicacy of the leathery above it was what she adored. Sometimes she walked down an endless cool alley in summer, by the side of the gutter in the old red brick floor. On her left and right were open stalls made of dark wood and the buttocks of the bay horses shone like mahogany all the way down. The horses turned their heads to look at her as she walked. They had black manes hanging like silk as the thick necks turned. These dreams blew and played round her bed in the night and the early hours of the morning.

She got up while the sisters were sleeping and all the room was full of book-muslin and canaries singing. "How they can sleep!" she said wonderingly when she became aware of the canaries singing so madly. All the sisters lay dreaming of horses. The room seemed full of the shapes of horses. There was almost a dream-smell of stables. As she dressed they were stirring, shifting and tossing in white heaps beneath their cotton bed-spreads. The canaries screamed in a long yellow scream, and grew madder. Then Velvet left the room and softly shut the door and passed down into the silence of the cupboard-stairway.

In her striped cotton dress with a cardigan over it she picked up the parcel of steak that had been left on the kitchen table and drank the glass of milk with a playing card on the top of it that Mrs. Brown had left her overnight. Then she got a half packet of milk chocolate from the string drawer, and went out to saddle Miss Ada.

In the brilliance of a very early summer morning they went off together, Miss Ada's stomach rumbling with hunger. Velvet fed her from a bag of oats she had brought with her up on the top of the hill. There were spiders' webs stretched everywhere across the gorse bushes.

Coming down over the rolling grass above Kingsworthy Velvet could see the feathery garden looking like tropics asleep down below. Old Mr. Cellini by a miracle grew palms and bananas and mimosa in his. Miss Ada went stabbing and sliding down the steep hillside, hating the descent, switching her tail with vexation.

Velvet tied Miss Ada to the fence, climbed it and crept through the spiny undergrowth into the foreign garden. There was not a sound. Not a gardener was about. The grass-like moss, spongy with dew so that each foot sank in and made a black print which filled with water. Then she looked up and saw that the old gentleman had been looking at her all the time.

He had on a squarish hat and never took his eyes off her. He was standing by a tree. Velvet's feet went down in the moss as she stood. His queer hat was wet, and there was dew on the shoulders of his ancient black frock-coat which buttoned up to the neck; he looked like someone who had been out all the night.

Raising one black-coated arm he rubbed his lips as though they were stiff, and she could see how frail he was, unsteady, wet.

"What have you come to do?" he said in a very low voice.

"Sir?"

He moved a step forwards and stumbled.

"Are you staying? Going up to the house?"

"The house."

"Stay here," he said in an urgent tone which broke.

Velvet dropped her own eyes to her parcel, for she knew he was looking

at her and how his eyeballs shone round his eyes.

"How did you come?" (at last). She looked up. There was something transparent about his trembling face.

"On our pony," she said. "I rode. She's tied to the fence. There's some meat here for the cook, to leave at the back door."

"Do you like ponies?" said the rusty voice.

"Oh . . . yes. We've only the one."

"Better see mine," said the old gentleman in a different tone.

He moved towards her, and as they walked he rested one hand on her shoulder. They walked till they came to the open lawns and passed below some fancy bushes.

He stopped. And Velvet stopped. ". . . if there was anything you wanted very much," he said, as though to himself.

Velvet said nothing. She did not think it was a question.

"I'm very much too old," said the old gentleman. "Too old. What did you say you'd brought?"

"Meat," said Velvet. "Rump."

"Meat," said the old gentleman. "I shan't want it. Let's see it."

Velvet pulled the dank parcel out of her bag.

"Throw it away," said the old gentleman, and threw it into a bush.

They walked on a few paces.

Something struck her on the hip as she walked. It was when his coat swung out. He looked down too, and unbuttoned his coat and slowly took it off. Without a word he hung it over his arm, and they walked on again, he in his black hat and black waistcoat and shirt-sleeves.

"Going to the stables," said he. "Why, are you fond of horses?"

There was something about him that made Velvet feel he was going to say good-bye to her. She fancied he was going to be carried up to Heaven like Elisha.

"Horses," he said. "Did you say you had horses?"

"Only an old pony, sir."

"All my life I've had horses. Stables full of them. You like 'em?"

"I've seen your chestnut," said Velvet. "Sir Pericles. I seen him jump."

"I wish he was yours, then," said the old gentleman, suddenly and heartily. "You said you rode?"

"We've on'y got Miss Ada. The pony. She's old."

"Huh!"

"Not so much old," said Velvet hurriedly. "She's obstinate."

He stopped again.

"Would you tell me what you want most in the world? . . . Would you tell me that?"

He was looking at her.

"Horses," she said, "sir."

"To ride on? To own for yourself?"

He was still looking at her, as though he expected more.

"I tell myself stories about horses," she went on, desperately fishing at her shy desires. "Then I can dream about them. Now I dream about them every night. I want to be a famous rider, I should like to carry dispatches. I should like to get a first at Olympia; I should like to ride in a great race; I should like to have so many horses that I could walk down between the two rows of loose boxes and ride what I chose. I would have them all under fifteen hands. I like chestnuts best, but bays are lovely too, but I don't like blacks."

She ran out the words and caught her breath and stopped.

At the other end of the golden bushes the gardener's lad passed in the lit, green gap between two rhododendron clumps with a bodge on his arm. The old gentleman called to him. Then he walked onwards across the

grass and Velvet and the gardener's boy followed after. They neared a low building of old brick with a square cobbled yard outside it. The three passed in under the arched doorway.

"Five," said the old gentleman. "These are my little horses. I like little ones too." He opened the gate of the first loose box and a slender chestnut turned slowly towards him. It had a fine, artistic head, like horses which snort in ancient battles in Greece.

"Shake hands, Sir Pericles," said the old gentleman, and the little chestnut bent its knee and lifted a slender foreleg a few inches from the ground. "But I've no sugar," said the old gentleman. "You must do your tricks for love to-day."

He closed the gate of the loose box. In the next box was a grey mare. "She was a polo pony," he said. "Belonged to my son." He still wore his hat, black waistcoat, and shirtsleeves. He looked at the gardener's boy. "I need not have bothered you," he said. "Of course the grooms are up." But the gardener's boy, not getting a direct order, followed them gently in the shadow of the stables.

The grey mare had the snowy grey coat of the brink of age. All the blue and dapple had gone out of her, and her eyes burnt black and kind in her white face. When she had sniffed the old gentleman she turned her back on him. She did not care for stable-talk.

In the next loose box was a small pony, slim and strong, like a miniature horse. He had a sour, suspicious pony face. There were two more loose boxes to come and after that a gap in the stables. Far down the corridor between the boxes Velvet could see where the big horses stood—hunters and carriage horses and cart horses.

The gardener's boy never stirred.

The old gentleman seemed suddenly tired and still.

He moved and pulled a piece of paper from the pocket of his waistcoat. "Get me a chair," he said very loud. But before the boy could move a groom came running swiftly with a stable chair.

The old gentleman sat down and wrote. Then he looked up.

"What's your name?" he said and looked at Velvet.

"Velvet Brown," said Velvet.

"Velvet Brown," he said and tapped his pencil on his blue cheek. Then wrote it down. "Sign at the bottom, boy," he said to the gardener's boy, and the boy knelt down and wrote his name carefully. "Now you sign too," he said to the groom.

The old gentleman rose and Velvet followed him out into the sunlight of the yard. "Take that paper," he said to her, "and you stay there," and he walked from her with his coat on his arm.

He blew himself to smithereens just round the corner. Velvet never went to look. The grooms came running.

The warm of the brick in the yard was all she had to hold on to. She sat on it and listened to the calls and exclamations. "Gone up to Heaven, Elisha," she thought, and looked up into the sky. She would like to have seen him rising, sweet and sound and happy.

In the paper in her hand she read that all of his five horses belonged to her.

Taking the paper, avoiding the running and the calling of the household, she crept back through the garden to Miss Ada. When she got home she could not say what had happened, but cried and trembled and was put to bed and slept for hours under the golden screams of the canaries. At four o'clock Mally burst in and cried:

"They've drawn! They've drawn! We've got the piebald!"

"Whose ticket?" said Velvet faintly.

"Yours, oh, yours. Are you ill?"

"Mr. Cellini's dead," whispered Velvet. "Just round the corner!"

Mally stood transfixed to the floor. "They're bringing the piebald home," she said, staring. She could not be bothered by the death of Mr. Cellini.

Hearing a sound she ran to the window.

"It's here, it's down at the very door!" she called.

"Get mother," said Velvet, who could not move because the room was swaying.

. . .

Velvet went to Mr. Cellini's funeral. As an heiress. She did not bury him in her heart till then. The nights before she had seen him only smashed, but living. Seen his face with its looks. Could a look be smashed? That night before the funeral, the horses in her dreams galloped downhill. By the head down, like rockets. But when she had been to his funeral and walked in her winter black tarpaulin mackintosh, among his relations, her eyes like sad lights in her head and her bony teeth, veiled in gold, like a war chief's trophy across her thin face, then she knew he was still and folded and she could turn to the horses.

Mr. Brown was quite agreeable to the horses. It was all in the local papers, and lovely pictures of the girls looking like three gazelles. And Velvet? Velvet looking like Dante when he was a little girl.

Mr. Brown saw it was good for trade. "You'll be wanting a field," he said.

"But they've been kept in," said Velvet.

"Keep them in you won't, my girl. And it's summer."

"But next winter?" said Velvet.

"Next winter'll take care of itself." There were six horses now.

The strange piebald won at the Fair had been put that night by Mi into the Tablet Gully. In this narrow valley there was a tablet to a dead man, but the name had gone. The tablet said he died gathering moss in the snow, overwhelmed in a snowstorm and fallen down a mountain.

In all the ninety miles of the Hullocks there was no moss; there was no snow; no mountains to fall down, but only the curving breasts of hillsides. Still the legend of the nameless man remained intact, and here the piebald grazed, flashing like black and ivory in the dapple of the valley. He was six miles from the village and he had not yet attempted to break loose. He could not see a chimney or a roof from where he cropped, or hear any sound but the sheep who filled his valley. The food was new to him, richer than in the high burnt-up fields above the village, and his attention was caught, and his nostalgia for the time assuaged.

Now that the excitement in the village had blown out Mr. Brown began, and well he might, to fuss about expense.

"A man who leaves a butcher's daughter five horses might leave her some money to keep them with," he said.

"Why do you suppose he left them to you, Velvet?" asked Mally for the hundredth time.

Velvet looked at the table and said, "It was a joke he made with himself at the last minute."

"Just leave her," said Mrs. Brown calmly. "Don't keep on asking, Malvolia."

. . .

It was the green summer dawn of

the day the horses were due to arrive. Velvet woke up and she could hear the birds' feet walking up and down on the roof.

"Swi—ipe!" said one canary in a very loud voice, and all the sisters woke.

At breakfast Velvet sat back in her chair, a little yellow.

"Chew your toast well," said Mrs. Brown, "and don't drink your milk. It'll lay loose."

"Is it eleven or half past that they're coming?" asked Edwina.

"Don't talk about it," said Mrs. Brown. "Leave the subject alone." Velvet faintly chewed.

At nine she had a strong drink of peppermint, and some whitish powder of her mother's choosing. Sitting close to the kitchen stove she slowly recovered. Every now and then the sisters looked in at the door at her anxiously.

"Shall I ever grow out of it, mother?" asked Velvet once.

"Yes," said Mrs. Brown, like a palmist, "when you're sixteen."

The room, crammed with furniture, was faintly green as the light struck through the cactus window. The cactus pots were arranged on glass shelves. They were well cared for, of different sorts, and six of them were in peculiar flower. The street door was shut, the yard door was open. On one side of the room the mahogany sideboard stretched from wall to wall, with its bottles of vinegar, old decanters, a set of green wineglasses, salts, peppers, A1 and Demon sauces, and in the middle the Sheffield dish cover, 30 inches long, that covered the joint on Sundays. The Albert lamp, used at night in winter, stood on a table by itself. The dinner table, round, covered with a Paisley cloth, filled the centre of the room. The window on the street was blocked with cineraria. Motes of blue from the flowers floated on the belly of the dish cover.

Velvet held the shell-box of paper horses in her hand, like something to which she was being disloyal.

All the girls had on striped cotton frocks too big for their thin bodies. Edwina and Malvolia had belted theirs in with leather belts bought in the village, but the dresses of Meredith and Velvet hung loose on them.

"Half the village outside in the street," said Mr. Brown complacently, coming in with his pipe out of the sunlight. "Seems to have got round."

"Not surprising," said Mrs. Brown, "with three reporters coming here."

"This family's cut out for the newspapers," said Mr. Brown, putting his arm on her vast shoulder. Mrs. Brown said nothing.

"Got your strong knickers on?" said Mrs. Brown presently.

"Yes," said Velvet.

"What's that for?" said Mr. Brown. "She's not going to ride this string of racers she's getting."

"They're hacks. Little hacks," said Velvet.

Mrs. Brown rose.

"See to Donald," she said. "He's frittering his time."

But at that moment, as they fidgeted, the door opened and Donald walked in, all buttoned up and shining and his brow as black as thunder.

"Who's buttoned you?" asked Mrs. Brown.

"Mi's buttoned me," said Donald savagely.

"Huh!" said Mrs. Brown.

They measured each other.

"You forgot me," said Donald.

Mrs. Brown said nothing. Donald strutted down the room and out into the yard.

"Seems upset," said Mr. Brown.

Mi came in.

"I'll thank you not to button him again," said Mrs. Brown.

"Any sign of the horses?" said Mr. Brown.

"Early yet," said Mi, "but the whole village is waiting on the Green."

"Most of 'em's outside," said Mr. Brown, motioning to the flower-window with his pipe. The flower-window was black with faces. "Ask Mr. Croom in."

Mi opened the door and spoke through the crack of it. Mr. Croom, the grocer, came in.

"Wonderful," said Mr. Croom, "Velvet gettin' them horses."

Mr. Brown got up and looked at his watch, which lay under a tumbler on the sideboard. "Getting on time," he said, and Velvet, sitting at the stove, felt suddenly light and warm.

"Whur's the little chap?" said Mr. Croom. "Donald?"

"I'm here," said Donald through the half-open yard door.

"I got silver an' gold for you," said Mr. Croom.

"More'n he deserves," said Mrs. Brown.

Donald came in brightly with his sweet smile.

"Silver an' gold," said Mr. Croom, holding out a net bag full of chocolate coins covered in silver and gold paper. "Foreign," he said, "Dutch stuff. But Donald won't care."

"Say thank you," said Mr. Brown.

"Thank you," said Donald, with his heart in his face. He took the bag and wandered away.

"Fine chap," said Mr. Croom.

"Cup of coffee, Mr. Croom?" said Mrs. Brown.

"If you're making any." Mr. Croom peered through the street window. "Quite a stir in the village."

"Yes," said Mr. Brown.

"'Strordinary thing," said Mr. Croom. "Like a tale."

"Yes," said Mr. Brown again. "Took to Velvet, I suppose."

"Ever seen him before, Velvet?" said Mr. Croom.

"Yes," said Velvet faintly. "Once. At the Lingdown Horse Show."

"Better leave her," said Mrs. Brown. "Turns her stomach."

"Well, well . . ." said Mr. Croom regretfully. "Yes."

Mr. Cellini swam across the ceiling, frailer than memory, like a cobweb.

Mr. Brown rose again and looked at his watch on the sideboard. "Should be here," he said.

"Where's your gold and silver bag?" said Velvet suddenly to Donald.

"I put it away," said Donald.

"Don't you want it?" said Mr. Croom, hurt.

"No," said Donald. "I might want it some day."

"What you got there instead?"

"It's my spit bottle," said Donald, holding up a medicine bottle on a string.

He walked a little further into the room and dangled the bottle, showing a little viscous fluid in the bottom.

"That's my spit," he said.

"He's collecting his spit," said Velvet.

Donald applied his mouth at the top and with difficulty dribbled a little more spit into the neck.

"D'you let him do those sort o' things?" said Mr. Brown to Mrs. Brown.

"Take it outside," said Mrs. Brown. "Here's your coffee, Mr. Croom."

Edwina, Malvolia and Meredith burst the street door open with the crowd behind their shoulders. "Over the hill! You can see them!" Meredith panted, and all three disappeared.

Mrs. Brown picked up Donald, his spit bottle swinging. "Put your cardi-

gan on," she said to Velvet. "Keep warm an' you'll be all right."

They all went out, the crowd following them, and turned up the chalk road.

"Where's Mi?" said Velvet suddenly.

"Got a half dozen sheep to fetch," said Mr. Brown. "Be here any minute."

"Poor Mi," said Velvet, and walked on, rapt with happiness.

Over the brow of the hill five horses moved down towards them.

"Ther's three grooms. My word, ther's three of them," said Mally, who had joined the procession. The grooms were walking the horses, two horses to a groom, then one alone at the back. As they reached the foot of the grass slope and stepped on to the flashing chalky road in the sun, the black crêpe could be seen on the arm of each walking groom. They were bowler-hatted, and round each bowler a band of crêpe was tied. The head groom, walking in front with the grey mare and Sir Pericles, had a rosy face and a fine black coat of good cloth. The others wore dark grey.

The horses were halted at the entrance to the village.

The head groom produced a slip of paper. "Miss Velvet Brown?" he asked. Mr. Brown stepped forward, Velvet close behind. Her thin face shone, smile alight, frock ballooned under cardigan, legs bare and scratched. "I'm Velvet," she said.

She walked up to Sir Pericles, transfigured, touched him gently on his neck, took the rein from the groom.

"We'll go down to the house," she said softly. "I'll lead this one home."

"Better let me," said the groom. Velvet stared at him, shook her head, and walked on leading the shining horse.

"Daft to-day," said Mr. Brown to the groom.

"Mind she don't let him go then," said the groom.

The procession went on, Velvet first with her horse, Mr. Brown at her elbow, the horses and the village people following. "Keep the boys back! Don't let them frighten the horses!" said the old head groom.

"Keep back there," said Mr. Groom mildly, and the boys ran and skipped. Edwina and Malvolia and Meredith went ahead, turning to look over their shoulders.

"Better stop!" called Edwina.

The procession drew up and halted as it reached the street. Half a dozen sheep had arrived unexpectedly from a farm for the slaughter-house, and Mi was striving to get the last three in. He ran about in his Sunday clothes, put on for the arrival of the horses. They could hear him cursing. The three sheep skipped, butted and ran. "Yer poor slut!" yelled Mi to the last one, bounding like a hare to keep it out of the main road. He turned it, and the last of the sheep went dingily behind the great wooden door. With the clatter of delicate feet on brick the horses moved on till they reached the sunny square before the cottage.

Donald was swinging his bottle before the door. He had not kept up with the procession.

"Keep that child in!" called Mr. Brown. But Donald swung his bottle gently, and Mrs. Brown did no more than lay a finger on his head.

The horses were drawn up facing the doorway and the second groom took over the bunch of leather reins. They ran like soft straps of silk over his fingers, narrow, polished, and flexible.

"Better take this into the house and read it over," suggested the head

groom to Mr. Brown, handing him a typewritten sheet.

Mr. Brown glanced at it and called to Velvet. Together they went in at the door and sat down at the little fern table inside. Mr. Brown pushed the ferns gently to one side and laid out the sheet.

"One chestnut gelding. 14 hands. Seven years old, *Sir Pericles*. 1 snaffle bit, bridle, noseband and standing martingale. 1 Ambrose saddle, leathers and stirrups. 1 pair webbing girths."

And underneath this Velvet wrote "Velvet Brown."

"One grey polo pony. Mare. 15 hands. Nine years old. *Mrs. James*. 1 straight pelham, etc. . . . martingale . . . soft saddle and sewn girths."

And underneath Velvet wrote "Velvet Brown."

"1 child's pony, chestnut. 12.2 hands. Gelding. *George*. Snaffle bit and double bit. Soft saddle and sewn girths, etc."

And Velvet wrote "Velvet Brown."

"1 cob pony, for hacking or cart. 13.3 hands, dark bay gelding. *Fancy*. 1 double bit, etc. . . . old leather saddle, and harness for cart."

"Velvet Brown."

"1 Dartmoor filly, two years old, unbroken. 11 hands. Halter only. *Angelina*."

"Velvet Brown."

When Velvet had written her name for the fifth time, carefully, in ink, and with her breath held tight, her father touched her arm, and they both returned to the sunlight of the street. Mr. Brown gave the paper to the head groom.

"What are you doing with them straight away?" said the groom.

"Turning them into a field of mine," said Mr. Brown.

The groom hesitated. "Warm weather, but they've none of 'em been out at night yet. Won't hurt the little filly."

"They'll have to be out now," said Mr. Brown, with a slight rise of voice, as though he were being dictated to.

"Will they eat sugar?" said Mally.

"All except the grey mare," said the groom. "She likes apple."

Mally brought sugar out of her cotton pocket. Meredith went for an apple.

"Shall you be selling them, sir?" said the groom a little hesitatingly to Mr. Brown.

"They're mine!" said Velvet suddenly.

"We've not decided anything," said Mr. Brown. Velvet's soul became several sizes too large for her, her mouth opened, and she struggled with speech. Mrs. Brown's hand fell on her shoulder, and her soul sank back to its bed.

"I suppose you are fixed up with a man?" said the head groom tentatively. "I have a place myself, but . . ." He made a gesture towards the other two grooms.

"I'm a butcher," said Mr. Brown firmly. "My girl goes and gets herself five horses. Five! We've seven all told, with that piebald. If she has to have horses she must look after 'em. We've fields in plenty, and there's oats in the shed, and I've four girls all of an age to look after horses. Beyond that I won't go. I'll have no fancy stables here. I'm a plain man and a butcher, and we've got to live."

"Eh, yes," said the little old, rosy-headed groom. "Shall we unsaddle them and turn them into the field for you?"

"Saddles'll have to go in the slaughter-house," said Mr. Brown. "Through with them sheep yet?" he said to Mi.

"Ain't begun," said Mi.

"Well then, you can put the saddles in the sun here on the wood rail, and lead 'em to the field in the bridles. Head collars they have on 'em. P'raps you'd better leave the bridles here."

The head groom went up to the girths of Sir Pericles, but Velvet's thin hand was on his arm. "I'm going to try them all first," she said.

Mr. Brown heard what she said, though he made no sign. He looked at Donald, then at his wife. She made no sign either.

"Fetch your gold sweets now!" said Mr. Brown heavily and with unreality to Donald, tweaking his chin, and retired from the whole scene towards the slaughter-house.

"Let's go round to the field," said Velvet, with confidence, to the groom.

"Wait a bit," said Mrs. Brown. "You'll have a little something first. Edwina, there's that bottle of port. Bring it out. And glasses. Mr. Croom, you'll join too, a drop won't do anybody any harm."

Edwina and Mally brought out the fern table, a tin one, the sacred table that was never moved.

Velvet as the heroine, Edwina as the eldest, the head groom as the guest, and Mrs. Brown as the hostess sat down at the table and sipped a sip from the thick glasses of port. The village stood round at a respectful distance, and Mally and Meredith walked among the horses. Sir Pericles drooped his neck and nuzzled by the head groom's pockets. The second grooms shared a glass between them. Then they all went up to the field to try the horses.

Velvet mounted Sir Pericles. She had ridden Miss Ada for eight years, hopped her over bits of brushwood and gorse bushes, and trotted her round at the local gymkhana. Once she had ridden a black pony belonging to the farmer at Pendean. She

had a natural seat, and her bony hands gathered up the reins in a tender way. But she had never yet felt reins that had a trained mouth at the end of them, and, as she cantered up the slope of the sunny field with the brow of the hill and the height of the sky in front of her, Sir Pericles taught her in three minutes what she had not known existed. Her scraggy, childish fingers obtained results at a pressure. The living canter bent to right or left at her touch. He handed her the glory of command.

When she slid to the ground by the side of the head groom she was speechless, and leant her forehead for a second on the horse's flank.

"You ride him a treat," said the groom. "You done a bit of riding."

"Never ridden anything but her old pony," said Mi, his hair rising in pride.

"The mare here's harder," said the groom. "Excitable, and kind of tough."

He shot Velvet's light body and cotton frock into this second saddle. Her sockless feet, leather-shod, nosed for the stirrups. The groom shortened the leathers till they would go no more, and then tied knots in them. Mrs. James, the mare, broke into a sweat at once. She flirted her ears wildly back and forwards, curved her grey neck, shook her bit, gave backward glances with her black eyes, like polished stones in her pale face.

"Mind! She don't start straight! She'll leap as she starts, and then she'll settle. She was Mr. Frank's polo pony an' she's not really nervous but she's keen."

There was scum on the mare's neck already, and the reins carved it off on to the leather as she shook her head. Mrs. Brown, holding Donald by the wall, watched quietly. Edwina, Mally and Merry sat on the gate.

"Hang on!" said the groom, and

let go. Mrs. James, with a tremendous leap, started up the field. Her nostrils were distended, her ears pricked with alarm. She thought she carried a ghost. She could not feel anything on her back, yet her mouth was held. Velvet, whose hand had slipped down to the bridge of the saddle at the first leap, settled more steadily and lifted her hand to the reins. Mrs. James snorted as she cantered, like a single-cylindered car. She was not difficult to ride once the first start had been weathered. They rounded the field together; then Velvet got up on the pony George. George threw her as soon as her cotton frock touched his back.

"Get up again," said the head groom and held the pony tighter.

"Walk him, walk him," said the groom warningly. "Trot before you canter or he'll buck!"

George stuck his head out in an ugly line, and Velvet tried gently to haul him in. The whites of his eyes gleamed and his nose curled. He snatched at the bit when he felt her pressure and stretched his neck impatiently. Velvet's lips could not tighten, there was too much gold; but her eyes shone. She twirled the ends of the long reins and caught him hard, first on one shoulder, then on the other.

"She'll be off!" said Edwina.

"Not she!" said Mi. "It's what he's asking for."

George curved his neck and flirted archly with his bit, then trotted smartly back to the gate. Velvet dismounted and turned to Fancy, the cob.

Fancy was no faster than Miss Ada, and somewhat her build. He trotted round the field sedately.

"That's the lot," said the groom. "The filly's not broke."

"I must try George again," said Velvet.

"You bin on the lot," said Mrs. Brown. "Come home now."

"But Merry and Mally . . ."

"The horses'll get all of a do," said the head groom, "if they get too many on 'em. Better let them graze now, and to-morrow they'll be more themselves."

The horses were turned loose and the saddlery carried back to the slaughter-house, where it was straddled over iron hook-brackets among the sheep's bodies.

The head groom stayed to midday dinner. The two others went down to the inn. It was Irish stew, with dumplings and onions. As the groom ate, he gave Velvet advice on how to catch the horses. His hat with the crêpe on it was laid on the sideboard.

"They haven't been out since last summer, and they're sure to be a bit wild at first. But you want to be up there, sitting on the wall, and just feeding them and coaxing them for a bit before you try to catch them. Mrs. James, she's wily. Sir Pericles'll do anything in the world you tell him. He knows a lot and what he knows is all pure goodness. Mrs. James is what you might call worldly wise. The pony's just pure cuss. He'll jump his own height if you can ever get him to believe in you. You can use a bit of stick on him. He's suspicious of kindness. But never touch Sir Pericles with anything. He'll break his heart and go sour. Fancy, she's no temperament. The little one, Angelina, wants playing with an' fondling, like you might fondle this dog here." Jacob grinned and bowed.

"Nice dog," added the groom. Jacob trembled with expectation. But the groom, pulling a piece of gristle out of his mouth, only laid it on the edge of his plate.

"You haven't asked about food, Velvet," said Edwina. But Velvet, who couldn't manage dumplings and onions, looked more ready to be carried to bed.

"Food now," said the groom. "But they're to be out to grass entirely? Well, well. . . . They'll just have to get accustomed to it. It's to be hoped they won't blow their bellies out the first day. But the grass is thin up there and that's a mercy. If they get colic you'll have to bring 'em in and sweat 'em and draught 'em. Whisky and rum together's the thing."

"Half and half?" said Mi abruptly.

The groom looked at him. "You'll be taking 'em on, I daresay?" he said hopefully.

"Mi won't waste his time," said Mr. Brown with authority. "The girls must learn what there is to learn."

"Leave it, leave it," said Mrs. Brown. "It'll settle itself."

"My plate makes me retch," whispered Velvet to her mother.

"Grumble, grumble, grumble," said Mr. Brown, who had heard.

"Ho! I gotta huge, *huge* caterpillar in my greens!" said Donald, holding it up.

"It's dead!" said Mally. Velvet put her face in her hands.

Mrs. Brown rose and took a plate off the sideboard.

"Put it there, Donald," she said firmly, "and not another word about it."

"Let me see it," said Merry, leaning forward. Mr. Brown looked up, frowning. "There's manners about caterpillars," he said sharply. "Put them aside and *say nothing*."

"It's done me!" said Velvet through her hands. "Can I go?"

"Yes, you can go," said her mother. Mr. Brown looked up again. "No good keeping her," said Mrs. Brown. "She'll vomit."

Chapter Six

"Donald yelling on the Green!" called Mrs. Brown from the scullery.

Mi, with a bridle on his knees, in the living room, rose and looked through the flower-window.

"Mally's got him up in front on Mrs. James," he said.

"S'e all right?"

"Can't see what's wrong with him. He's screaming awful."

"Mally," called Mrs. Brown, opening the front door. "Stop it. He's got a pin or something."

Mrs. James was cantering jerkily round and round the Green at what Mally believed to be a show canter. Donald, sitting on the edge of the saddle in front of Mally, had his arms over her arms and his bare legs

were sinking beneath her knees, preventing her grip. He was scarlet in the face, his mouth was open, and he was screaming. His head jerked madly up and down as Mrs. James bounded. With difficulty Mally pulled up.

"Can't get off," called Mally (for Donald was half underneath her), then slid off in a heap with the child in her arms. Mrs. James sprang away in fear and trotted into the yard. Donald, sobbing, began at once to search in the grass.

"Whatever's the matter, Donald?" said Mrs. Brown from the doorway.

"Lost my sixpence. My chocolate sixpence," screamed Donald, hysterically turning over every tuft.

"Good God, is that all?" said Mally, rubbing her knee. She got up and went after Mrs. James.

"Lost his sixpence," said Mrs. Brown to Mi, closing the door and returning to the scullery.

"Ain't lost his nerve," said Mi, polishing the bit.

"Lot o' work we get out o' you, Mi!" said the butcher, coming in from the shed. "Place slimy with sheep stomach! Get on cleaning, do. Bits and leathers and irons and horses . . ." He disappeared again.

Mi grinned, put the bit on the sideboard and followed him. The little living room was dark and empty. Jacob parted the fringe of the sofa-covering with his beaded nose and stole out, dragging his hind-quarters after him with a yawn. He glanced round, grinned too, and leaped upon the sofa, turned round once or twice, scraped primevally with his foot and lay down.

Mi stuck his head back through the slaughter-shed door.

"Ha!" he said, and sprang for the sofa. Jacob was underneath again in a flash of white.

.

When the horses had been with the Browns a month, life readjusted itself and everything was easier than had been thought.

The horses had lost flesh a little in the dry, sea-blown field, and were very slightly out of condition. Mi knew it, but did not speak of it to Velvet. Velvet frowned and put her fingers into small hollows on the haunches, but said nothing. On the whole it was as well, for, corned-up as the horses had been when they arrived, the four girls would have had much more difficulty with them.

In the mornings they rode them in the field, and Mi, when he could sneak away, constructed jumps out of old packing cases, branches and bean poles, carrying up his precious hammer and nails. In the late afternoons they cantered over the Hullocks high up above the sea, preferably just before sunset. Mi watched them go off with a queer look in his eye, a look old Dan had worn when he saw Araminty Brown strike out from the brim of the land. There are men who like to make something out of women.

Velvet and Edwina usually rode Sir Pericles or Mrs. James. Mally liked her battles with George, and Meredith who never knew sufficiently what she was doing, was safest and happiest on Fancy.

"What shall we do when the summer's over?" said Velvet one evening to Edwina, as they rode along a chalk track on a ridge. "We can't keep Sir Pericles and Mrs. James out."

"It'll be murder," said Edwina.

"Mother'll do something with father," said Velvet.

While they cantered in a stream Merry always formed the tail. She went with a loose rein and trusted God. Fancy plodded along and minded his path. Merry liked the air whistling round her forehead, and the shifting clouds reflected on the Hullocks. She watched for partridge and thought of her canaries. The arrival of the horses had not disturbed her at all. The partridges rose and went skimming away sideways and downhill like falling arrowheads. The rooks tossed about in the sky like a tipcart of black paper in a whirlwind. The larks hung invisible and the hawk hung visible. But Meredith, glancing at them, knowing them, was reminded only of Arabelle, of Mountain Jim, of Butter and Dreadnought Susan. She was not romantic about wild birds. She liked her power over her little yellow flight at home.

"When we bring out Donald, what'll we start him on?" began Velvet. (This was a favourite theme.) Donald was to ride, youngest, in the under-eight. He was to ride well, for the sake of their honour, but capital might also be made of his youth and his silver hair. He was to ride home up the village, carrying the silver cup he had won as best boy rider in the under-eight. But what on? That was the everlasting question.

"George is the narrowest."

"George would have him off in a second."

"Do you suppose . . ." began Meredith, but nobody listened to her. Mating was her mania. She was certainly going to talk about mating.

They walked their horses slowly down the chalk road leading to the village and reached the field.

"Who's got the key? Meredith, you had the key."

Meredith fumbled under her cotton frock. Not one of them had riding breeches.

"It was in my knicker pocket," she said, turning her brown knickers almost inside out.

"You've lost it!" they all said instantly. Edwina got down and, undoing a bit of wire, took the gate off its hinges and opened it from the wrong side.

"I've got it!" said Mally suddenly, fishing in her knickers.

They rode up to a little lean-to allotment-shed with a padlock where they kept the saddlery and the rubbers. The horses were rubbed down and turned loose, and, wiring up the gate's hinge, the girls sauntered back along the road to the village.

"Let's see that schedule again," said Mally.

Velvet drew it out of her pocket. They came to a stop and sat on a flint bridge over a stream. The setting sun picked out the flints like pieces of glass.

"'Novices jumping,'" said Velvet, pointing to an item many times underlined. The whole programme was ready to drop to pieces.

"*Children's* Novice jumping," corrected Edwina.

"Well, of course! Sir Pericles couldn't do anything else. It'll be three foot.

"Three foot six, Mi says."

"Are you sure?"

"Well, you know what he is. He never likes to be wrong."

"Find out how he found out, anyway."

"George can jump three foot six."

"Easy, if he wants to," said Mally.

"About money," said Velvet. "We ought to look at it that way. There's more to be won in the jumping than in potatoes or bending. But there's most to be won in the hurdle races. Most of all. Pounds."

"But we . . . You wouldn't do that?"

"I don't know," said Velvet. "It isn't so awful. It's only low hurdles and a hustle."

"Don't you remember the way some of them crashed last year?"

"There's no need to crash like that," said Velvet. "It's the men who crash, not the women."

"Why is that?"

"I think they must be wilder," said Velvet.

"They win more too," said Mally.

"Sometimes women win," said Velvet in her clear voice, lifting her boy's face just a little.

"Would they let you?"

"Oh, yes, in gymkhanas. It's the size of the horse that counts. It doesn't matter who rides. It's 'Open.' It doesn't say 'Adults.' See in this one? First prize £3."

"We'll just have to borrow our

entries, and pay them back out of prizes."

"But if we don't get any prizes?" Nobody answered.

"Who can we borrow from?"

"We haven't paid Mi yet for the tickets for the raffle. And there's sixpence owing on Mar's Bars and twopence on Crunchies."

"Those are only shillings!" said Velvet impatiently.

"We are going to win pounds. We must just borrow again."

"Couldn't we sell something?"

"We ought to sell Miss Ada," said Meredith.

There was a silence like the silence of wasps before attack.

"I wasn't thinking!" said Meredith hurriedly.

"I should think not!" said Mally.

"But there's something in it," said Edwina. "We've got too many horses. If we sold the piebald we'd have money to pay for all the other horses."

"If anybody ever sells the piebald," said Velvet slowly, "I might as well die."

"Well, it's borrow or sell," said Edwina. "Come along. We've got to feed them still."

The sky green, the sun almost gone, they returned, buckets of oats mixed with chaff carried between them. They pulled branches of reeds and switched the horses off as they tried to steal each other's buckets. George ate with the whites gleaming in the corners of his eyes, and, as he finished, his ears went back. Then with a rush he stormed another bucket, and the evening rang with the clatter of iron shoes, girls' curses, and zinc buckets overturned. Mrs. James ate steadily and could lash out if interrupted. Sir Pericles was nervous and would rather not eat at all than be hurried. Fancy threw his bucket over, mixed his oats with earth. Angelina got the leavings.

Unbroken, she was definitely out to grass and was only a crumb-picker, like a dog.

The stars came out as they watched the horses eat.

"Mrs. James, Mrs. James," said Velvet suddenly, with love. And the mare laid her ears back at such nonsense.

"Why do you love her?" asked Meredith.

"She is like mother," said Velvet.

"Oh. . . . How?"

"She is," said Velvet. "Aren't they wild and lovely in this field at night! Look how their eyes shine! Look at Angelina's! Got kitten's eyes."

"Come . . . up, Mrs. James!" said Mally, tugging.

"What's a matter?"

Mally had the mare's off-fore in her hands. "Shoe gone. I thought so. Now there'll be shoeing bills. Had you thought of that?"

"That's upkeep. Father'll pay," said Edwina.

"Yes, but pay and pay, and there'll come an end. There's nothing coming in on these horses," said Mally.

"At Pendean . . . at Pendean . . ." said Velvet, stammering and desperate all at once.

"You won't make a fortune anyway. And you may break your neck. Mother won't let you do it."

"If I get the entry money, I'll enter. She won't know till I'm down at the starting post."

"Come along," said Edwina, holding the gate.

The horses who had finished hurried after them. They were shut out at the gate and hung their heads over into the dark.

"Cat in the ditch!" said Mally as they walked. They all saw the two fiery points among the dark weeds.

"Shush!" said Edwina, jumping suddenly to the brink of the ditch. The eyes winked and blew out.

"Cats' eyes shine like thieves' lamps," said Velvet. "What's for supper?"

"I just bin wondering," said Meredith.

"It's the two lobsters father brought!" said Mally suddenly. "Mother said she'd do 'em hot . . ." They ran, buckets clanking.

The spaniels pressed against the door, yelped as Mally pushed them aside.

The living room smelt alive with hot lobster—a red, entrancing smell.

Edwina snatched a little parcel that had come by post from off the sideboard.

"What's that!" said Velvet and Mally instantly.

"Mine," said Edwina. She shot up the stairway to the bedroom.

All three streamed after her.

"I wish to God I had a room of my own!" panted Edwina, turning on them at bay from the dressing table, the parcel in her hand. "I shan't . . . I won't undo it."

"Hey!" called Mrs. Brown. "Father's come! Come on down. Never mind washing. It won't stand a minute."

In a few seconds they were all grouped round the table as keen as the dogs outside.

Mi appeared from nowhere.

The lobster was borne in on a vast dish, surrounded by a bank of rice. It was chopped up, thickened with flour, buttered, and boiled hot.

"Where's that sherry?" said father, diving for the cupboard. "There was a drop."

"You'll cool it down," objected Mrs. Brown.

"Poof!" said father. "Where's the damn thing? Here it is . . ." He got the bottle and poured half a glass over the lobsters. "Turn it over then."

Mrs. Brown took up a spoon and turned the steaming lobster in the sherry. The helpings were ladled out, a lot of rice and a fair share of lobster. They ate.

"God, it's good," said Mally.

"You don't need to keep on saying God," said Mr. Brown, with his mouth full. "Just be quiet."

"Poor Donald," said Velvet.

"Glooping like an angel," said Mi.

"Empty angel," said Mally. "No lobster inside him."

"Stir him up if he had!" said Mi. "My word . . ."

At the thought of Donald stirred up with lobster to worse excesses they fell still again and continued to eat.

"No dog eats shellfish," said Mr. Brown sideways to Jacob, who was bowing at him.

"How d'you know?" asked Mally.

"Kind o' law," said Mr. Brown. "My father always said it to his dogs."

"Give him a bit an' see."

"Can't spare any," said Mr. Brown. Jacob mooned under the table.

"Father, Mrs. James's lost a shoe," said Velvet.

The storm broke swiftly over the supper table.

"Oats an' shoes an' soon there'll be bits o' saddlery . . . nothing to show for it . . . nothing but pleasure and a lot o' girls being spoiled for school . . ." The storm blew in a wind of indignation and as it blew Velvet was conscious of her father's case. It was a good one. There was no benefit to him in the horses. The lovely creatures ate, and were sterile. They laboured not, and ate and ate, and lost their shoes. Velvet had no answers and no comfort to offer. And all her promises were child's promises and air until she could carry them out.

When supper was over and cleared, and father was standing in the street with his pipe, she pulled out the

gymkhana schedule from the dresser drawer, and bent her urgent face over the yellow paper.

Mechanically her hand went up to rock the gold binder and lay it in her lap.

"You *would* choose to-night!" said Edwina, giving her a shove with her elbow.

Velvet stared at her.

"Get your plate in," said Edwina. "You always do it when he's angry."

Velvet stared at her still. A gust of loyalty to her father shook her heart. Edwina had a way of talking. . . . She eyed Edwina sideways. Edwina was rough, and she looked as fine as wire. Something about the beauty of the antelope face caught Velvet's attention. Suddenly she wondered if Edwina would save her if she were drowning. Then studied the schedule again.

"Seven two-and-sixes," she said finally.

"Make it eight. That's a pound," said Mally. "Wherever d'you suppose we're going to get that from?"

"Let's look again and see if there's anything we can leave out," said Meredith.

"No point in doing that," said Velvet. "It's just as difficult to borrow seventeen and six as a pound."

"Queer idea," said Mally.

"Why queer?"

"Thinking saving doesn't matter."

"We got nothing," said Velvet. "We got nothing, have we?"

"Nothing."

"Then we might as well ask for what we want as ask for less."

"Who you going to ask?"

"Don't know," said Velvet. "I'll have to see. Let's work it through once more."

There was a rustle by the door and she put her plate in.

"Let's go to Miss Ada."

They filed out across the yard, and stood and sat by Miss Ada's manger. Miss Ada stood droopingly and sour. She had not seen much of them lately.

"Give her something to brighten her up," said Edwina. "She's looking a crime."

Velvet pulled up her frock.

"You've always got sugar in your knickers," said Mally. "How does mother let you have so much?"

"I buy it."

"*Buy* it?"

"I promised Mr. Croom I'd pay after the gymkhana." She fumbled. "Here's a bit."

Miss Ada took it in her exasperated manner, and turned her back on them.

" 'Children's Bending,' " read Velvet. "That's Mally. On George. 'Children's Potato Race.' Me on Mrs. James. 'Children (Novice) Jumping.' Me on Sir Pericles . . . and on the piebald."

"The piebald!" The three voices snapped in the stall like whip-cracks. "The piebald! But you've never ridden him."

"I shall have ridden him by then. Remember how he jumped the wall?"

"Yes, but . . ."

"I shall have ridden him. I'm going over to-morrow afternoon."

"We'll all go. To-morrow afternoon," said Meredith.

"I'll ride him quietly up and down the valley. We'll take Sir Pericles and change the saddles. His ought to fit the piebald. There's nothing wrong with the piebald, except that he hates being shut in square fields with walls. Or else he likes jumping walls. Where's the list?"

"There's the Threadneedle Race. That's me."

"Who'll thread your needle?"

"Mother."

"Then you'll have to tell her you're racing?"

"At the last minute. She'll do it. What is the fuss about racing? You've got to sit on and go round. It isn't even like a professional race, where they catch their legs in yours, if you're an amateur, an' throw you off."

"How d'you know?"

"I read about it in the Library."

"Where'd you get the penny?"

"On tick again," said Velvet wearily. "There's an old book there on the National."

"What National?"

"The Grand National," said Velvet, with an undertone in her voice like a girl in love.

"The next's a Wheelbarrow Race," said Mally, reading.

"We can't all do everything," said Velvet, "because of the money. We must choose. Anyway, we've worked it out. We've eight half crowns."

"Where?"

"I mean that's what we're going to borrow."

"When's the closing day for the entries?"

"Friday," said Velvet. "I must get the pound by then."

"Bed yer ma says," said Mi, putting his head in at the door of the stable.

In the dark, when the light was out, Mally remembered. "What was that parcel, 'Dwina?" she asked.

"Hell!" said Edwina, settling herself angrily further into the clothes. "Not a minute by myself. . . . *Never* by myself!" she whispered into her pillow, and the tears of growth and self-pity heated her eyes.

Very soon they were all asleep, and the dreams waved like palm leaves over the room.

Chapter Seven

The sun poured down on the beach. The Hullocks blazed, hot and grey with burnt grass in the late gymkhana summer. Horses were everywhere, creeping over the dun hills, silhouetted on the skyline like plumes, plunging down the skyline to the sea. Donald came in to midday dinner, shoeless, with painted toenails.

"What's he got on his feet?" said Mally, Velvet and Meredith all together, with gimlet eyes and sharp voices. Donald climbed on to his chair and placed his ten scarlet toes on the table.

"'Dwina did me," he said. He looked pleased.

"Where's 'Dwina."

"Up in your bedroom."

Down came Edwina, blowing on her last finger. She held up her two hands, ten drops of deep crimson madder at the tips.

"The parcel!" she said tauntingly and with triumph. "Wet still. Don't touch!"

There was a silence.

"Have you got stuff to get it off?" asked Velvet in a cold voice.

"I'm not going to get it off."

"It won't wear off . . ."

"It'll stay like that for three weeks."

"Gymkhana's Friday week."

"Well?"

"D'you think you're going," said Velvet, "to ride Mrs. James with those red nails?"

"Why not?"

"Men have played polo on Mrs. James," said Velvet, choking, "an' you . . ."

"Coming!" called Mrs. Brown from the kitchen, with the dish.

"Godamighty, look at the boy's

feet! Who's dolled 'm up?" said Mr. Brown from the street door.

"I got PAINTED feet," said Donald with satisfaction. "'Dwina done it."

Mr. Brown paused and looked at 'Dwina. He saw her nails and still he looked. She shuffled a little and took her seat at the table. Mrs. Brown came into the room with the dish of oxtail, glutinous, steaming, crusts of toast swimming.

Mr. Brown sat down and began to help the food. Mi slipped in and took his seat. Jacob caught the door on his shoulder and squeezed in, squirming, as it closed. Mally, Velvet, Merry, everyone was silent. When the food was all around Mr. Brown observed that Donald's toes were one thing. Then he paused. Velvet waited, almost in pity, for what was to fall upon 'Dwina.

But father was strange. He only said, "I'm not against yer fingers, Edwina. Looks kind of finished to me. Yer getting on too. Time you worried about your appearance. Donald's toes is just silly."

"What's he done to his toes?" said Mrs. Brown, eating.

Donald arranged them again upon the tablecloth. His mother looked at them and went on with her dinner.

"Looks like my garnets," she remarked. "An' can you count 'em, Donald?"

So it was left to Velvet to undo Edwina. She clinched her spirit and knit it up again. When dinner was over she waited for Edwina in the bedroom where she knew she would come to look again at her bottle of nail varnish.

From the height of the window, beyond the canary cages, the immortal Hullocks browsed, burnished and lit, at two in the afternoon. Bowed like silver barrels they were set in rows endwise to the sea. Like pigs, like sheep, like elephants, hayblonde with burnt grass. Velvet's mind stuttered like a small candle before the light and the height and the savage stillness of the middle afternoon. As she gazed her heart rolled slowly over, a wheel on which something is written. Edwina seemed to her small and distressed. The piebald horse, the light of her mind, walked slowly across her imagination. She leant upon a cage. Merry opened the door and saw her.

"Looking at my canaries?" she asked, warmed to her marrow, like a mother whose baby is patted.

"No," said Velvet, turning round. Then seeing Meredith's face—"I was at first, and then I looked outside at the Hullocks. We're going over to the piebald as soon's Mally's washed up."

"What are you going to do about 'Dwina's nails?" said Meredith, and came towards the cages.

"Nothing," said Velvet. "She can have her nails if she likes."

"And ride Mrs. James?"

"If she likes to," said Velvet. "It's a disgrace to us but she can."

"I thought you minded so."

Velvet said nothing. Then she poked her finger in at Mountain Jim. "Will he sit on it?"

"On mine he will!" said Meredith eagerly, and opened the cage door. Mountain Jim bowed and fluttered his wing tips. Then descended to her finger and twisted his layered neck and cocked his easy head.

"You like them better than the horses, don't you?" said Velvet wonderingly.

"Nobody else wants them," said Meredith. "And they're small. They're like a doll's house."

"Why, there's a new one!"

"Mi bought it for me," said Merry in a small, touched voice, "because of

Africa. This morning. That new mate got it for him."

"What mate?"

"The plumber's mate. The boy with the glass eye. The cat got it an' it's got no tail, but Mi says rub it with oil an' it'll grow. Hair oil he says. He's going to give me a teaspoonful of his."

"Does Mi use hair oil?"

"No, he doesn't use it, but he bought it."

"Merry," said Velvet, "nobody's thought what we're going to wear at the gymkhana."

"Our knickers."

"Yes," said Velvet, pondering. "Yes, our knickers. Every other child will have jodhpurs. I suppose they'll *let* us ride? In knickers?"

"Oh, I should think so," said Meredith, cleaning out the drinking pots with her finger. "Look at Butter bowing!"

Butter opened her wings and bowed from her perch.

"She can't make up her mind to go from perch to perch without doing that," said Meredith. "She laid another useless egg this morning. Just drops them about."

"Are you sure it's useless?"

"I put it in water an' it floated. It's sterile."

"Does Mi say—"

"That's what Mi says. Float 'em. No good if they float."

"Mi comin' with us to the piebald this afternoon?"

"It's such a long way to walk," said Merry. "If only he would ride."

"Nothin'll ever make him," said Velvet. "He won't even talk about it."

Donald came round the bedroom door with naked feet and painted toes. He carried a postcard in his hand. "You gotta postcard. From Aunt Em."

"For me?" said Velvet.

"Sfer Meredith."

Meredith took it. "She's at Brighton. Just her love . . ."

"Thurs a picture," said Donald. He looked at it. "What is it? It's a church."

"No, it's a palace," said Meredith, reading the printed inscription. "It's the Pavilion at Brighton. 'Where George the Fourth lived,' it says."

"Who's George a Fourth?" asked Donald.

"Was a king . . . lived in this palace."

"Whur's he now?"

"Oh, he's dead. Ages ago."

"Who died 'im?"

"Nobody died him. He just died."

"Well, whur's he now?"

"Well, dead, Donald. Like everybody. Everybody dies."

"Why?"

"Well, they do. You will an' I will an' old people do."

"Do what?"

"Die."

"Who died that king then? Who died him, I say?"

"Velvet," said Meredith, exasperated. "You tell him. I got to finish these canaries."

Velvet considered Donald with a mild expression. He was frowning. His lovely face was angry.

"Where's your spit bottle?" she asked.

"Ts'full," said Donald, his whole face lighting with radiance. "I'll get it, shall I?"

"Yes," said Velvet, "only hurry up."

"You didn't do much," said Merry.

"He didn't really want to know," said Velvet. "He just wanted to be angry. Bin smacked or something downstairs. He knows all about death. Look how he trod on those ants."

"Perhaps he didn't like a king being dead. A king's not like an ant. He's coming with his beastly bottle."

Donald fell on the top step and his bottle was smashed. It had been the

work of weeks. The stairs ran with spit and blood and tinkled with broken glass. The house was rent. Mr. Brown, Mrs. Brown, Mi and all the sisters picked him up.

Mally cut her knee kneeling on the glass. Edwina read to Donald, who had to have a stitch in the ball of his foot. Mrs. Brown kept Merry to help her with the washing.

In the end Velvet took Sir Pericles and rode alone to Tablet Gully.

In Tablet Gully the piebald cropped, moving from tuft to tuft in sun and shadow, and flashing as he moved. The bone of his shoulder, thrown up by his stooping neck, rippled under his sliding skin. His parti-coloured mane hung forward over his neck, and his long tail tipped the ground.

He swung round with the sun. His teeth tore evenly as he worked. Now his quarters could be seen, slightly pear-shaped and faulty, but strong. His hocks, too thick, but straight and clean, waded in the burnt grasses. He lifted a sloping pastern finished with a pink hoof, and bit a fly off his leg. The clouds reared overhead, the legendary gully with its dead man's tablet was heavy with steady sun and shielded from the wind.

Among the scabious flowers on the north slope sat Velvet, steady as a gorse bush, cross-legged, and watching the horse. She had tied Sir Pericles to a gate in the valley behind her. Sitting like a Buddha, dreaming of the horse, riding the horse in dreams. A piece of cake and a Mar's Bar beside her in a paper bag, and the insects hummed and the mauve August flowers hardly moved. Just to look at him her heart beat violently with ambition. Her strong and inexperienced imagination saw no barriers. She was capable of apprehending death and of conceiving fame—in her own way, not for herself but for her horse. For a shilling she had won this wild creature that did not know its strength. In this valley, tucked away, she had got glory. What she meant to do made her heart beat afresh. She looked steadily at the piebald as though she pitied him. Eating his grass, prince, with his kingdom waiting for him! Her hand stole out and pulled the Mar's Bar from its bag, and she sucked its heavy stump, made from milk chocolate, toffee and nuts.

All the Hullocks were creeping with dowdy animals at livery. But here in Tablet Gully moved on its clever legs this living horse. Pulling gently at a blister on her heel she rode him in her mind. She would dazzle the world with this spot of luck, she and the creature together, breathing like one body, trying even to death, till their hearts burst. She would place her horse where he belonged, in history. She clasped the Mar's Bar like a prophet's child, with both hands.

"Leaders have been cut from coaches to do it . . ." she whispered as she rose. "Even horses out of carts. Why not him?"

A halter made of rope lay behind her and picking it up she walked gently down the valley holding it behind her frock. The piebald stared at her, interested. He loved humanity, and had it not been for the exceptional grass in Tablet Gully would have been off to the village long before this.

Frankly he watched her come, nostrils slightly distended and both calm eyes upon her, the blue eye and that white eye where the pied colour streaked across his cheek. She paused beside him and slipped the halter over his head. He shook his neck to free it from flies and came with her willingly.

They reached Sir Pericles, who snorted at sight of them and danced

his hind-quarters, looking from side to side, catching his soft nose on the reins. How could his mistress walk so out of valleys leading horses? He was intrigued and excited, jealous, pleased to see her again. Velvet loosed and mounted him, and the piebald walked sedately at their sides, striking out his forefeet in his own peculiar gait.

They reached a field not far away, enclosed by a stone wall, and Velvet changed the saddle and bridle, tying Sir Pericles with the halter to the gate. She mounted the piebald, and walked and trotted him quietly in large circles. His mouth was a mixture of lead and rubber. He had no notion how to obey the bit but imagined that to turn his neck was all that was wanted. He would trot onwards with his neck turned to one side like a horse that has no face. Velvet had to rock him with her knees to get him out of his orbit, and even then it was no more than a bewildered stagger to one side. She set him into a canter. It was clumsy and gallant, and accomplished with snorts. He flung his powerful white head up into the air and nearly smashed his rider's precious plate. Sir Pericles watched. The flashing piebald snorted excitedly round the field. Above him sat the noble child, thin as famine, bony as a Roman, aquiline nose and domed white forehead, tufted loonily with her cotton hair. Velvet, with her great teeth and her parted lips, her eye sockets and the pale eyes in them, looked like a child model for a head of Death, an eager, bold, young Death. She was thinking of something far outside the field. She was thinking of horses, great horses, as she sat her horse.

Turning in a flash in the middle of the field she drove him on with her knees. They went at the wall together. Over the grasses, over the tufts and mounds, both knitted in excitement, the horse sprang to the surge of her heart as her eyes gazed between his ears at the blue top of the flint wall. She bent slightly and held him firm and steady, her hands buried in the flying mane firm on the stout muscles of his neck. She urged him no more, there was no need, but sat him still. He was a natural jumper. She did not attempt to dictate to him. They cleared the wall together, wildly, ludicrously high, with savage effort and glory, and twice the power and the force that was needed. Velvet felt his hind-quarters drop when they should have hitched. But there was so much space to spare that the piebald could afford it. Nevertheless it was an intemperate and outlandish jump.

She rode him back to his own valley and loosed him, then returned home alone on Sir Pericles, parading in dreams. As she approached the village she was outlined against the sunset, on the brow of a Hullock. Stirrups short, angled knee and leg etched on the side of the saddle; childish, skeleton hands waving with the ebb and flow of the horse's mouth on the reins; hands that seemed knotted and tied like a bunch of flowers with streamers going from them, swinging together, knuckle to knuckle, thumb to thumb, while she sat erect above them, her face held on the wand of her body. The straw hair floated and stared above the wide-open eyes.

Sir Pericles walked like Velvet sat. His soft mouth held the snaffle as a retriever carries a bird. Yet he arched his neck as though his bit were a bit of thorns, and his long, almond, Chinese eyes looked both backward and forward at once. He seemed to be watching from either end of the agate stuff that was his window, watching Velvet's leg, watching the horizon before him. The oxygen in the evening

air intoxicated him. In the eye of little Sir Pericles something soft and immortal shone.

Velvet had laid down the piebald and her ambitions and was thinking comfortably of the coming gymkhana. In her mind she rose at white-painted gates and fences. Her knees crisped with her thoughts in the saddle and she leant forward. Sir Pericles never altered his tossing walk. His head and tail, both like plumes, flirted, and he walked within her dream with a spot of gold upon his eyeball.

It was not the silver cup standing above the wind-blown tablecloth that Velvet saw—but the perfection of accomplishment, the silken co-operation between two actors, the horse and the human, the sense of the lifting of the horse-soul into the sphere of human obedience, human effort, and the offering to it of the taste of human applause. All this she had learnt already from the trained mouth and the kneeling will of Sir Pericles.

And as the dim sense of this understanding sighed up and down her body it entered too into Sir Pericles' nerves, and through his nerves to his comprehension. Velvet lived her round of jumps, lips parted, the sunset shining on her golden mouth. She rose and fell at the triple bar, the water-jump, the gate, the imitation wall. She heard the hands, palm on palm, threshing the noise of applause. Sir Pericles dreamt it too, a wild dream beyond his understanding, but to be recognised when the taste came again.

His hoofs came down sweetly on violets, grass and knitted thyme, clanking on a flint, breaking the crisp edge of a wheel rut. He took in everything, behind, before, and from the body astride him. Below, the chimneys were smoking up like poplars and a light was lit in the cobbler's shop.

They sidled together down the steep grassy banks towards the village.

"Velvet!" said Mally out of the darkness by the bottom gate.

"That you, Mally? Open the gate."

"Who's wired it up like this?" Mally wrenched at the twist of wire. She opened it and horse and child passed through. "The piebald's out again. Nobody knew you bin riding him but us. Came thunderin' down the street ten minutes ago."

"Where's he now? Father angry?"

"Went down to the sea as usual, an' slid about. Went crackin' up a side street. Father doesn't know. Better not let him. He's bin carrying on about the horses. It would be the limit if he found the piebald had started cracking down the street again."

"F'e broke a leg!" said Velvet in a voice of horror. "F'e did! Might. Easily."

"You can't go after him now. It's pitch. Thurs stars coming."

Sir Pericles gave a whinny. There came a sharp, near answer, and the piebald stalked out of the shadows, gleaming in the dusk.

"He's here!" Velvet's marvelling whisper, as she slipped off Sir Pericles and held out her hand. The piebald came nearer, breathing hard.

"Mount, mount!" said Mally. "Get on again! He'll follow. He won't think you want to catch him."

"What'll we do with him?" said Velvet as she scrambled back.

"I'll go an' get a halter and we'll try an' put him. . . . Put him in Miss Ada's box to-night and put her in the toolhouse!"

The piebald followed, threshing his head, snorting the pleasant village smells, till they reached the yard of the cottage. He drooped his neck for the halter like a horse born in the

kitchen. Soon Miss Ada stood among the spades and shovels.

"Poor old darling Ada," said Velvet, as she pushed the shovels to safety behind a wooden case. "Get half the bedding from the loose-box, Mally. The piebald won't miss it. He's never had any before. I'll get Ada some oats to make her happy."

"What'll father say . . . about the piebald being in?"

"He won't know. I'll take him back early in the morning."

"Bet he neighs in the night. We'll shut both doors. He might try and jump the bottom one. Let's give him . . . What'll we give him?"

"Just hay," said Velvet. "He's not accustomed to oats."

"D'you know . . ." said Mally suddenly, pausing with an armful of hay.

"What?"

"He'll be worse than ever after this. He'll be coming back every night to get a night's lodging and a supper! You never saw . . ."

"What?"

"The way he came down the village street, slipping and sliding and snorting and his eyes shining."

"He's like a prince!" said Velvet.

"Eh?"

"Just a thing I thought," said Velvet. "I pretend he's a prince."

At supper everyone ate with memories behind them. Edwina had been kissed by Teddy for the first time. Her nails had shocked and enchanted him. Merry had oiled the canary's stump, and was worrying about what she should call him. She had got a list of gods' names and a birthday list of girls'. It was so hard to know the sex of canaries.

Mally and Velvet were thinking of what they had got in the stable, the prince who might kick up a row in the night. Donald was asleep now, stitches in his foot, blood and spit

mingled in his dreams. He yelped from time to time in his sleep like a puppy.

"Whur's Jacob?" said Mr. Brown suddenly as he ate.

"After they bitches," said Mi, with resentment.

"Seem bad this August."

"Bitches? Terrible they are. Crown's got one an' Ede's got one. That Jacob he . . ." Words failed, and slightly redder than before Mi continued to eat.

As the door opened for the pudding's entry they heard the impatient hammer of a hoof on wood. Mr. Brown continued to munch his bread. Mi sat up and his eyes flickered upon Velvet's face.

"I'm not hungry any more. Can I get down, mother?" said Velvet.

"Say your grace," said Mr. Brown.

"F'whatayave receivedthankGod," said Velvet, pushing her chair in, and went out in the dark. At the corner of the yard and the road four apple trees were enclosed by a broken fence. They were laden with little sweet apples and the ground was littered with the wind-blowings. She gathered two handfuls and went to the stable with them.

Mi hung about the yard all the evening, whistling for Jacob and looking down the road. Once he opened the top portion of the loose-box and looked in, grinning.

"Gettin' on all right?" he enquired. Velvet was sitting on the manger.

"He's quiet while I'm here," said Velvet. "But I can't stay here all night. Where's father?"

"Gone down to finish the bills," said Mi. "I thought he better."

Later in the evening Mally swinging on the gate by the apple trees saw Jacob coming up the empty road.

"Bitches good?" she asked him,

flinging him a block of lichen off the gate post.

"Succulent," said Jacob, making a half circle round her.

"Go an' tell Mi about it!" said Mally.

Jacob went, bowing and grinning. Mi walloped him and gave him his supper.

Later in the night the house was quiet, the piebald quiet (for he had Velvet in her nightgown sitting on his manger), the moon rose steadily. At two o'clock the moon began to sink. Mi came to the stable door and looked over the top. He wore his sleeping clothes, several old sleeveless jerseys, and a pair of shorts.

"Get to bed now," he said. "I'll do a bit."

Velvet lowered off the manger. "Here's six quarters left," she said, pointing in the manger. "Give him a piece every time he seems restless."

"What is it?"

"Apples," said Velvet. "I bin feeding him bits all night."

"You'll make him loose," said Mi. "Where's the sacking pieces?"

"In the corner. An' ties. Ties off the hay bales."

At five the sea was running up with a gale behind it and pounding in the sewer. The day broke in flashes of light and the elms soughed in the wind. The piebald's tail and mane were flung about as Mi led him out into the yard, his hooves bound up in sacking. Velvet met them in the road.

"How'd you wake?" asked Mi.

"An't bin asleep," said Velvet. "I just heard the wind. Isn't he good!"

"Perisher," said Mi.

"Oh, no," said Velvet. "Oh, no. Wait while I get a bridle."

She returned with a snaffle-bridle belonging to Sir Pericles, one which they had brought in to clean the night before.

"Gimme a leg up, Mi," and he jumped her on to the warm, round back.

"Key of the field's behind the manger. Come up an' help me get Sir Pericles. I got to ride back on him."

Mi walked beside her up the road to the field in the gale.

"Blowing awful up there," he said, looking to the Hullocks.

"Seaweed's smelling like drains," said Velvet, looking at the wild and shining east.

" 'Tis drains," said Mi, sniffing. "Lota nonsense they talk about seaweed. You had anything to eat?"

"No, I forgot."

Mi grunted with disfavour. "Fer a sickly girl you give yerself something to do!" he said.

"An't sickly. M'wiry," said Velvet. "Shove the gate wider. I'll stub my knee!"

Sir Pericles trotted down gladly, tail flying.

"Halter's under the stone in the corner," said Velvet.

Mi picked it up. Sir Pericles came willingly enough. The two horses hustled clumsily through the gate.

"Good-bye," said Velvet and went off across the reedy ditch, riding the piebald and leading the chestnut.

"Why don't you ride the other?" shouted Mi, but his voice blew back into his mouth as he called into the gale coming off the sea.

He watched the horses go up the chalk road and break into a canter on the crest. His old mackintosh flapped on his bare legs and the wind tore at the roots of his red hair. "If she were a boy . . ." he said longingly to himself. With that light body and grand heart he would get her into a racing stable. He knew of many up North. He had friends here and there. She'd be a great jockey some day. Fancy wasting those hands and

that spirit and that lightweight on a girl. "No more'n a skeleton," he said. "An' never will be, likely. She'd ride like a piece of lightning. No more weight'n a piece of lightning." He thought of her mother . . . and of his old father. "Velvet an' her. A feather an' a mountain. But both the same."

Boom . . . went the sea on the cliffs. The savage blow came up the valley. Mi hated water. Brought up by the Channel trainer he had edged back inland as soon as he could. He couldn't stand the waves and the empty trough that sucked and soaked along the lip of the beaches. It turned his head, and he went up the village whenever he thought of the sea. "How she ever!" he thought, with his mind's eye fixed sharp on Mrs. Brown. Great, wallowing woman, half submerged, water pouring backwards and forwards over her shoulders, threshing across the water like a whale. A stormy dawn when she had landed. "Bet old Dan was pleased," he thought.

"Wasn't many swimming the Channel those days."

His mind went back to Velvet. He too, like her, was longing to place his dream in history. This child, Velvet, was good for something.

He turned back to his bed, shivering, Velvet in his thoughts.

And hungry, sick, delicate, blown so that she could hardly breathe, Velvet in the grip of horses and of the gale went on across the blunt and unprotected Hullocks. Great skies slipped out of the folds, unfurled, and stood a thousand miles above her. The sight battered against unseeing eyeballs, was drunk into the marrow of something older than her brain. Flags and pennons and beacons waved above the high land as she sat below, thinking in slow brown drops of thought, sure of her future, counting her plans, warm in expectation, glorious butcher's Velvet, eyes cast down upon the moving shoulders of mortal horses.

Chapter Eight

Mi raised thirty shillings for the gymkhana. He borrowed it from his girl for Velvet's sake. That is to say he treated love worse than he treated adventure.

"Your girl," said Velvet, frowning in thought. "Which girl? Didn't know you had a girl."

"Nor I had. Met her at the dance last night," said Mi. "Pleased as Punch, she was. Lent me the money too." So Mi behaved badly, and Velvet knew it. But neither she nor Mi cared when they set their minds firm.

On the day of the gymkhana, about mid-morning, it grew suddenly very hot and the rain came down in sheets. Inside the living room, polishing the bits, it was like the tropics. The girls' faces were wet. Rain came down outside on full leaves, making a rattle and a sopping sound. Everything dripped. The windows streamed. The glass was like glycerine.

"Oh, Lord," said Mally, "oh, dear, oh, damn!"

"We've only two mackintoshes. Velvet's has stuck to the wall in the hot cupboard. Won't it rain itself out?"

"The grass'll be slippery. What about their shoes being roughed?"

"We've no money," said Velvet, "for roughing."

"If Mi had a file . . ." said Mally.

"A file's no good. You want nails in."

"I'm sweating," said Edwina. "Can't we have a window open?"

She opened the yard window and the rain came crackling in over the cactus.

"Hot's a pit in here!" said Mi, coming in from the yard and taking off his dripping coat. "The yard's swimming. Everything's floating."

"Will they put it off?"

"The gymkhana? No, it'll be over soon. It's a waterspout. There's a great light coming up the way the wind's coming from. Your ma going to serve the dinner early?"

"Yes, at twelve," said Edwina. "We better clear now. Put the bridles and things in the bedroom. Better father doesn't see too much of it!"

"He knows, doesn't he?" said Meredith.

"Yes, he knows, but he doesn't want to think too much about it."

At dinner they had sardines instead of pudding. Mrs. Brown always served sardines for staying power. Dan had dropped them into her mouth from the boat as she crossed the Channel.

Donald considered his on his plate.

"I'll take your spines out, Donald," said Meredith.

"I eat my spines," said Donald.

"No, you don't, Donald. Not the big spine. The little bones but not the big one in the middle. Look how it comes out!"

"I eat my spines, I say," said Donald firmly with rising colour, and held her knife-hand by the wrist.

"But look . . . they come out lovely!" said Merry, fishing with the fork. The spine of the slit sardine dangled in the air and was laid on the edge of the plate. Quick as lightning Donald popped it into his mouth with his fingers and looked at her dangerously.

"I crunch up my spines, I like them," he said.

"Leave him alone," said mother.

"D'you eat your tails too?" said Merry vexedly.

"I eat my tails and my spines," said Donald, and the discussion was finished.

At one the rain stopped and the sun shone. The grass was smouldering with light. The gutters ran long after the rain had stopped.

.

"Keep up on the hog," said Velvet, as the horses moved along. "We don't want 'em splashed. Gutters are all boggy." They were well on the way to the gymkhana, held in the football field at Pendean.

"We look better in our mackintoshes!" called Mally. "I'm glad it rained."

"I'm steamy," said Edwina. "Merry, you can wear mine. You'll look better."

"I'm all right. I don't want it, thank you, Edwina."

But Edwina was struggling out of her mackintosh. "You'll look better. You're all untidy. . . . Put it on!"

"I don't want it!"

"You're a bully, 'Dwina," said Mally. "You jus' want to get rid of it an' not sweat."

They turned up a chalk road between a cutting and in a few minutes they could see below them the gathering of horse-vans in the corner of Pendean field, the secretary's flagged tent, white-painted jumps dotting the course, and a stream of horses and ponies drawing along the road below.

The soaking land was spread below them, and the flat road of the valley shone like a steel knife. Getting off their horses they led them down the chalk path between blackberry bushes, and in ten minutes of slithering descent they were at the gates of the gymkhana field.

"Competitors' passes," murmured Edwina and showed their pasteboard tickets.

They picked out a free tree in the field and established themselves.

"Here's someone's programme!" said Mally. "Squashed and lost. Sixpence saved!"

They crowded round to read it.

After endless waiting the band arrived. Then the local broadcaster rattled up, mounted on its ancient Ford, and settling into its position against the ropes, began to shout in bleak, mechanical tones . . . "Event Number One! Event Number One! Competitors in the Collecting Ring, please . . . PLEASE."

Instantly the field was galvanised. Children and ponies appeared from behind trees and hedges and tents. Mally mounted George and rode towards the ring.

In five minutes it was over and Mally was back again. George had had no idea of bending. Nor Mally either. They had broken three poles on the way up and were disqualified.

"We haven't practised!" said Mally, trying to carry it off.

But Velvet, busy saddling Mrs. James, made no reply.

"Here's Jacob!" said Edwina suddenly. Jacob sprang lightly against Mrs. James's flank and grinned. "Mi must be here."

"Event Number Two!" shouted the Voice, and Velvet mounted, and made for the Collecting Ring. Seeing Pendean Lucy waiting at the gate for the first heat, she thrust up beside her. The bar fell and Velvet, Lucy and three others, two boys and a fat little girl, were let out to the potato posts.

"You know what to do?" shouted the Starter, his flag under his arm. "Leave the posts on your right! Take the furthest potato first! . . ."

Velvet tried to take it in but the trembling of Mrs. James distracted her attention. Mrs. James had broken already into a sweat of hysteria that had turned her grey coat steel-blue.

They were lined up, the flag fell, and Mrs. James made a start of such violence that Velvet could not pull her up at the fifth post. Six strides were lost before they could turn. Lucy was cantering down the posts with her potato and Velvet heard the jingle of the bucket as the potato fell neatly into it. The heat was over, and Mrs. James, too big, too wild, too excited, too convinced that she was once again playing polo, was left three potatoes behind when the winner had drawn up beside the Starter. Pendean Lucy won the first heat. . . .

"Five shillings gone . . ." muttered Velvet with humiliation as she trotted slowly back to the tree. Mi was there standing beside Sir Pericles.

"Five shillings gone, Mi," said Velvet aloud to him.

"It's a gamble," said Mi. "Keep yer head. Afternoon's young."

"Jumping . . ." said Mally. "It's the jumping now. Which you jumping first?"

"Sir Pericles."

The blazing sun had dried up the burnt grass and the afternoon shone like a diamond as Velvet sat on Sir Pericles in the Collecting Ring. Mi wormed his way between the crowds against the rope. Lucy came on her roan pony, but the pony refused at the Gate. Twice and thrice times, and she trotted back disqualified. A schoolboy in a school cap quartered in purple and white, rode out. His almost tailless pony jumped a clear round. Jacob wriggled with excitement between Mi's legs.

"Number Sixteen!" called the Broadcaster.

Sixteen was Lucy's elder sister, a fat girl in a bright blue shirt.

"Blasted girl!" said Mi under his breath, as the blue shirt cleared the first and second jumps. His heart was in his mouth, but he spat whistlingly and joyfully between his teeth as the pony landed astride the wall, and scrambled over in a panic, heaving the wall upon its side.

It seemed they would call every number in the world except Velvet's.

"Break her nerve, waiting!" grumbled Mi. He could see her cotton hair bobbing as she sat.

A small girl came, with pigtails. A little shriek burst from her throat each time her chestnut pony rose at a jump. The plaits flew up and down, the pony jumped like a bird. A clear round.

"Hell!" said Mi. "Two clear rounds."

"Number Fifteen!"

Out came Velvet from the black gap between the crowds. Sir Pericles arched his neck, strained on his martingale, and his long eyes shone. He flirted his feet in his delicious doll's canter and came tittupping down over the grass. Velvet in her cotton frock stood slightly in the stirrups, holding him short,—then sat down and shortened her reins still more. Mi's stomach ran to soup.

"Got her stirrups in her armpits . . ." sighed Mi approvingly. "Little swell!"

There was nothing mean, nothing poor about Sir Pericles. He looked gay as he raced at the first jump.

"Too fast, too fast!" said Mi, praying with his soul.

The horse was over safely and had his eyes fastened on the next jump.

"Haul 'im in, haul 'im in!" begged Mi of the empty air. "He'll rocket along . . ." He saw Velvet's hands creep further up the reins, and her body straighten itself a little. The horse's pace decreased. It was the dou-ble jump, the In-and-Out. Sir Pericles went over it with his little hop,—one landing and one take-off. Mi saw Velvet glance behind,—but nothing fell. And the Gate. The Gate was twelve paces ahead.

He cleared the Gate with one of his best jumps, an arc in the air, with inches to spare.

"He'll do the wall," said Mi with relief.

He did the wall, but a lath fell at the stile. Half a fault. She was out of it then. Mi yawned with fatigue. He had held his breath. His lungs were dry. Jacob was gone from between his legs. He looked round.

"Bitches . . ." he murmured vaguely, then turned again to the ropes to wait for the piebald.

There were no more clear rounds till the piebald came, and when it came a murmur went up from the villagers who stood in the crowd.

"Jumping *that* animal!" said a voice.

"Why, that's the one she won at the raffle!"

The piebald strode flashing into the sun. He paused, stood still, and gazed round him. Velvet's knees held him steadily, and she sat behind his raised neck without urging him on.

"I don't expect anything . . ." she whispered. "Do what you can. Keep steady. You're all right."

"You next," said a man at the bar of the Collecting Ring. "You waiting for anything?"

"I'm going," said Velvet quietly. "He just wants to look round."

Mi saw them come down the grass, the piebald trotting with a sort of hesitation.

"He's in two minds whether he'll bolt," thought Mi.

"Showy horse . . ." said a spectator.

"Butcher's girl . . ." said another.

"The youngest. Got a seat, 'ant she?"

The piebald's best eye was towards

the crowd, his white eye to the centre of the field.

The trot broke hesitatingly into a canter, but the horse had no concentration in him. He looked childishly from side to side, hardly glancing at the jump ahead.

"He'll refuse," said Mally, who had arrived at Mi's side. But Mi made no answer.

Sir Pericles had jumped like a trained horse. The piebald's jumping was a joke. Arrived at the jump in another two paces, he appeared to be astonished, planted his forelegs for a second, looked down, trembled, then leapt the little bush and rail with all four legs stiff in the air together. Dropping his hind-quarters badly he came down on the rail and broke it in two.

"Two faults," said Mi.

"Only two for breaking that?"

"Hind feet. Only two."

Again the piebald trotted, flashing, his grass-fed belly rounded, and his shoulders working under the peculiar colour of his hide.

"Why don't she canter 'im?" said a voice.

Mi turned on the voice. "First time he's seen anything but his own grazing. It's a miracle if she gets him round."

"The In-and-Out'll finish him," said Mally under her breath.

The piebald jumped willingly into the In-and-Out, then paused, and remained inside.

A shout of laughter went up from the crowd.

"Oh . . . poor Velvet . . ." murmured Malvolia, agonized.

The piebald attempted to graze, as though he were in a sheep pen, and again the crowd laughed.

"She's handling him gentle," said Mi. "She's trying to keep him thinking he's a winner. She's backin' him, see. . . . I don't believe he's ever

backed a pace before." The piebald had backed two paces till his quarters lay against the first jump of the In-and-Out. With a light heart he responded to his rider, and with a spring he was out again and cantering on.

"Do they count that as a fault?"

"I don't know," said Mi. "Watch out . . . now. . . . It's the Gate."

The piebald broke the gate. He would have liked a stout, stone wall, but this flimsy thing that stood up before him puzzled him and he did his goat-jump. All four legs in the air at once and landed back upon the laths and broke them.

"That horse is breaking up the field," said a voice.

Mi glared. "He's knocked his hock," said Mi; "that'll learn him." For the piebald limped a pace or two. It "learnt" him. Unlettered as he was he had no thought of refusing. He saw the friendly wall ahead, and taking it to be enduring flint he went for it with a glare of interest, ears pricked and eyes bright. The wall was three foot six. He leapt five. For a second it seemed to the crowd as though the horse had nothing to do with the wall but was away up in the air. A little cheer went up and hands clapped in a burst.

"Don't she ride him!" said the voice. "It's that Velvet girl. The ugly one."

"What, that kid with the teeth?"

"That's who it is."

Mi knew that Mally's beauty stood beside him and he resented it. He half turned his shoulder on her. While Velvet sat the piebald he thought her the loveliest thing on earth. Like Dan, his father, he hardly saw the faces of women.

"Hullo, she's missed the stile!"

"Did he refuse?" asked Mi, keenly.

"I don't think she saw it," said Mally. "She simply rode on."

The judge waved his stick and

called to a Starter. Velvet cantered, glowing, radiant, to the exit gate. The man who held the exit spoke to her and pointed. Velvet looked behind her, paused, then shook her head.

"Not coming . . ." shouted the man to the Steward.

After a brief pause . . .

"The last Competitor," announced the Broadcaster, "did not complete the round."

"Why ever didn't she!" said Mally, as she and Mi left the rope to fight their way round to the tree. They scrambled out from the crowd and ran.

Velvet was standing looking at the piebald as though bemused. Merry, her face happy with pride, was holding the horses.

"Marvellous, Velvet, to get him round!" said Mally, coming up. "Why didn't you jump the last jump?"

Velvet turned and looked, and Mi could see how her face was shining. "I thought I'd better not," she said gently.

"Why?"

"He did the wall so beautifully I thought he'd better end on that."

In a flash Mi felt again what she was made of. That she could take a decision for her horse's good and throw away her own honours.

"It was the right thing to do," said Mi.

Edwina arrived. "What made you miss the stile?"

Velvet said nothing.

"People near me thought you'd funked it," said Edwina half indignantly. "You must have been asleep to go and miss it."

"She's no more asleep 'n my eye," said Mi. And Mi's little eye, like an angry sapphire, raked Edwina till she shuffled her shoulder and itched.

"It's you, Edwina, now!" said Mally, looking at the torn programme. "On Mrs. James. Bending."

"A lot of chance I have!" said Edwina. "Mrs. James'll break every pole."

"She gets rough and excited," said Velvet.

"But it's Adults!" said Merry. "They won't have nippy ponies. It'll be easier."

But the Adults were seated on the smallest ponies they could ride. They looked like giants on dogs. Every grownup was riding his sister's pony, and Mrs. James, galloping like a wild animal, nostrils blowing and eyes rolling, broke all the poles she could break. Edwina led her back without a word, disgusted and silent.

It began to rain. Merry put a sack round her shoulders and pulled out the *Canary Breeder's Annual*. Edwina left them and went towards the tent.

"She got any money?" said Mally, looking after her keenly.

"Can't have," said Velvet. "She was broke yesterday."

"P'raps she's got twopence for an Idris. Wish to God I had a crunchie," muttered Mally.

"Kandy Korner's got a stall here," said Merry, reading. "What's happening now?"

"It's the tea interval," said Velvet gloomily. They had won nothing. They had made not a penny. They owed Mi thirty bob.

The rain slid, tapping, through the branches, and swept in windy puffs across the field.

It made a prison for them, it pressed them into a corner of life, a corner of the heart. They were hung up. Velvet was hung up in life. Where was she? A butcher's daughter, without money, in debt, under suzerainty, an amateur at her first trial of skill, destined that night to a bed of disappointment among the sleeping canar-

ies. She did not think like that. But cared only that the piebald had jumped one jump as she had dreamt he might jump, with power, with crashing confidence. He was ignorant but he had no stage nerves. Of her own powers she had no thought.

Staring out into the lines of rain, lightly she lifted her hands and placed them together in front of her, as though she held the leathers. So acute was the sensation of the piebald beneath her that she turned with surprise to see him standing under the dripping branches. A look of simplicity and adoration passed into her face, like the look of the mother of a child who has won honours. She had for him a future.

The rain came down in long knitting needles. Backwards and forwards blew the needles, as the wind puffed. Wet horses, wet mackintoshes, wet dogs, wet flapping of tents, and then as the storm was rent a lovely flushing of light in the raindrops. Wind blew the sky into hollows and rents.

"That Violet that Mi met, she's at Kandy Korner," said Merry. "Serving with them for a week on appro."

"We can't borrow from her if she's only on appro. She'll get into trouble."

"Mi," said Velvet, looking round the tree, "you round there? Is it dryer there?"

"No."

"Your Violet's with Kandy Korner. Got a stall down here."

Silence. Displeasure.

"You couldn't touch her for another twopence."

"Not till I see daylight with that thirty bob."

Edwina had gone off with one of the mackintoshes. The saddles were heaped under the other. Merry, Mally and Velvet flattened themselves, shivering, against the tree-trunk.

"There's mother!" said Velvet suddenly.

Across the field, swaying like a ship at sea, came the red and yellow meat van.

"She's brought tea!" said Merry.

"She'll thread my needle!" said Velvet.

Mally ran out into the open and waved. The van nosed and swayed towards them.

"Father's driving! If he stops . . . He'll never let you race, Velvet!"

"Stop him buying the programme if you can! Here, tear ours . . . give him the wrong half! Then he won't buy another."

Velvet snatched up the programme and tore a little piece out with her thumb-nail. The van drew up under the tree. Mi opened the door and the giant bulk of Mrs. Brown descended backwards.

"We've done nothing, mother! Nothing at all!" said Mally.

"That's bad," said Mrs. Brown. "Here's your tea."

"I'm not stopping," said Mr. Brown, from the wheel. "There's a sugar box in the back. Pull it out for your mother to sit on. You're wet through, the lot of you. You ought to come home."

"Coats is soppy," said Mrs. Brown. "How's your vests?"

"Dry," said Velvet, edging away. "Dry's a bone."

"You stay for one more race or whatever you call it," said Mr. Brown, "an' then you'll take them hosses home. I'll be back to fetch mother."

"But we've PAID . . ." began Velvet in horror. The self-starter whirred and he was gone.

"Does he mean it, mother?"

"You're dripping," said Mrs. Brown, cutting up a Madeira cake. "Mi, come round here an' get some food."

The cake grew wet even as they ate it.

"What's the next?" said mother. "Gimme the list." She studied it for a moment.

"That's next, mother," said Velvet, pointing.

"Was your name in it?" asked Mrs. Brown, looking at the hole.

"Yes . . . it was. 'Tis."

There was a long pause and Mrs. Brown slowly stroked her chin. Mi looked down on her old felt hat in which a pool of rain was settling. Velvet ran one nail under the other and shot out a piece of earth.

"I'll thread your needle," said Mrs. Brown at last.

Velvet looked into the heavy eyes and smiled. The eyes blinked with the violence and worship of the glance.

The voice of the Broadcaster came roughly through the wind and rain.

"Event Number Five," said the Voice . . . "Competitors for Event Number Five . . . go to the Collecting Ring."

Sir Pericles was saddled in a moment, and Mrs. Brown rose to her feet.

"Where'd I stand?" she asked.

"Mi'll take you. Mi! It's right far up there."

Mrs. Brown walked like a great soldier up the field.

In Velvet's heat she was the only child. She rode out of the gate of the Collecting Ring with four others,— two livery-stable-men from Worthing, a grizzled woman with short hair and a hanging underlip, and a young man in checks on a hired horse with poverty streaks.

"I've plenty of chance," she thought. "I'm lighter than any of them." All the horses were dripping and began to steam with excitement.

"Be slippery at the corner there," said one of the livery-stable-men.

They reached the starting post, and the sodden Starter came down towards them.

The faces, shining in the rain, looked back at him. The young man in the check suit lay up on the inside against the rail. The woman with the hanging lip scowled at him and edged her horse nearer. Velvet came next, and on the outside the two stable-men. The flag was raised. Before it could fall the young man made a false start. While he was getting back into position the grizzled woman took his place.

"Don't shove!" said the young man, but the woman made no reply. Up went the flag again and the bounding of Velvet's heart swept Sir Pericles forward.

"Get back . . . that child!" shouted the Starter.

Velvet swung Sir Pericles back behind the line and brought him up. The flag fell again neatly as she got him square. She drove for the centre of the first hurdle. Out of the corner of her eye she saw the grizzled woman's horse run out. The young man in the checks she never saw again. Perhaps he never started. As she landed she saw a horse and man on the ground beside her. The heat was between Velvet and one livery-stable-man.

Sir Pericles, the little creature, brilliant and honest, never looked to right or left but stayed where Velvet drove him, straight at the middle of each hurdle. He fled along the grass, jumping as neatly as a cat, swung round the sharp, uphill corner towards the table where the sewers stood, Velvet kicking the stirrups free, neck and neck with the livery-man on a blue roan. The roan drew ahead. The sewers' table neared. Velvet flung her-

self off as they drew up; her feet ran in the air, then met the ground and ran beside the horse.

"What have you got off for?" said Mrs. Brown calmly, as she began to sew.

Velvet glanced with horror at her rival, leaning from his saddle while a tall girl sewed at his sleeve. "Oh . . ." she breathed. She had forgotten the instructions. She had had no need to dismount.

But Mrs. Brown's needle flashed in and out, while the blue roan fidgeted and danced, and the tall girl pivoted on her feet.

It was an easy win for Velvet. She was in the saddle, off, and had time to glance behind, before the roan had started. She heard his galloping feet behind her but he never caught her up and Sir Pericles went steadily down the grassy slope, jumping his hurdles with willing care.

A burst of clapping and cheers went up.

"Stay in the field!" said a Steward. "Wait for the other heats to be run." Velvet sat alone in the rain, in a cloud of steam from the excited horse. One by one the winners of the three heats joined her.

The first was a boy of about nineteen, with a crooked jaw. Steaming and shining and smiling he rode up to her on a brown horse with a hunter-build, long tail and mane.

"You did a good one!" he said to her.

"I'd only one to beat," she said, "and even then it was the button that did it."

"That's a beautiful little horse," said the boy. "He's *neat*."

They turned to watch the finish of the next heat.

They were joined by a fat little man in a bowler hat, a dark grey riding coat and soaking white breeches. He took off his bowler as he rode towards them and mopped his shining bald head. His horse was a grey.

"What a horse . . ." he said as he rode up. "I hired him. Couldn't hold him fer a minute. Just went slap round as though he'd got a feed at the winning post. I'll never pull it off a second time, not unless he chooses to! Lands on his head too, every time. Not a bit of shoulder."

"The saddle looks too big for him," said the boy. "It's right up his neck. But he's a grand goer."

"It's right up his neck, an' so'm I," said the little man, dismounting. "It's the way he jumps. Next round I'll be down and off and rolling out of your light! Here's the last! It's Flora Banks!"

"Who's she?" said the boy.

"Tough nut from Bognor," said the little man under his breath.

Flora Banks wore a yellow waistcoat, had a face like a wet apple and dripping grey hair. She rode astride on a bay horse that looked like a racer, lean and powerful and fully sixteen hands. Velvet's heart sank.

"My poor Flora," said the little man calmly, bringing out a match, "you've got an overreach. You're out of it!"

The Tough Nut was off her bay in a second, flung her cigarette into the grass and knelt and took the bleeding forefoot tenderly in her hands. The big bay hung his head like a disappointed child. He was out of it. She led him, limping, away.

"Makes us three," said the little man, mopping his head. "Two really. I can't last another round. You go it, little girl, an' get the fiver. Hi, they're calling us."

Down went the three horses to the starting post, reins slipping in cold fingers, rain whirling in puffs. Velvet's breath would not sink evenly on

the downward stroke. She shuddered as she breathed.

"Lay up against the rails, little girl," said the bowler hat. "I'm so fast you can't beat me whatever you do, but I'm coming off. Where's that Starter? Goin' to keep our hearts beating while he drinks his coffee? Hi, where's that Starter? The blighter's drinkin' coffee!"

The Starter burst out of a little tent wiping his mouth and ran through the raindrops that suddenly grew less. The miraculous sun broke all over the soaking field. The freshness was like a shout. Velvet shaded her eyes, for the start was into the west. Water, filled with light, shone down the grass. The flag was raised and fell.

The boy on the brown horse got a bad start. Velvet and the little man rose together at the first hurdle. Vel-

vet had the inside and the grey lay behind her. At the second hurdle she heard him breathe, then lost him. At the slight curve before the third hurdle he had drawn up on her inside, between her and the rail. She had lost her advantage.

Suddenly the boy on the brown appeared on her left. Both the grey and the brown drew ahead and Velvet strung out a near third. Like hounds over a wall they rose, one, two, three over the fourth hurdle and went sweeping round the uphill curve to the table.

Mrs. Brown stood like an oak tree. Velvet galloped and drew up in a stagger beside her, throwing the single rein loose on Sir Pericles' neck. She stooped and hung over him, kicking both feet free from the stirrups to steady him. Trembling, panting, his

sides heaving in and out he stood, his four feet still upon the ground, like a bush blown by a gale but rooted. Mrs. Brown's needle flashed.

Velvet was off, stirrups flying, down the grass hill, the blazing light no longer in her eyes, going east. First the grey, then the brown, were after her. At the fifth hurdle the grey passed her, but the brown never drew near. The grey was wound up to go. Its hind-quarters opened and shut like springs in front of her. She saw it rise at the sixth hurdle just ahead of her, and come down almost upon its head. It slowed. As she drew up she saw the little man was done, stretched up unnaturally on its neck. He took a year falling. She passed him while he was still at it—jumped the seventh and eighth hurdles and whispered to herself as the noise went up behind the ropes, "A fiver . . ." And the pie-bald's glistening future spread like a river before her, the gates of the world all open. She pulled up, flung herself off Sir Pericles and glanced down at his feet.

He was all right. And the Steward was examining her button . . . That was all right too! Here came the sisters . . . The little man in the bowler, unhurt, was leading his horse down the track. Mrs. Brown . . . Where was mother? Mi was by her side.

"Lead him off! Don't stand there! You look daft," said Mi lovingly, and his little blue eyes winked and shone. "Good girl, Velvet!" said Mr. Croom as she neared the exit. And hands patted her and voices called.

The ruthless voice of the Broad-caster was gathering competitors for the next event.

. . . .

"Thirty shillings is yours, Mi."

"You'll have to give me forty. I want ten to get me teeth out of pawn."

"You put them in again?"

"I had to. Hadn't nothing."

"How is it they're so valuable, Mi?"

"Mass o' gold. My old dad got 'em done. He said, 'You always got money on you if you got gold in your mouth.' I can raise ten shillings on them most towns."

"You whistle better without them."

"Yes, I do," said Mi. "Where's that Jacob?"

It was the evening, before supper. They had turned the horses into the field after a good meal, and the pie-bald in with them. He had shown no sign of kicking. He trotted happily about among the new companions, his tail raised in an arch and his nostrils blown out with excitement. Velvet leant on the gate and Mi stood beside her. The others had gone home be-fore them down the road, clinking the buckets.

"Sir Pericles was lovely," said Vel-vet for the twentieth time. Mi was tired of grunting assent. The reddest sun that ever sank after a wet day went down behind them and sent streams of light through rushes and branches. Mi shaded his eyes to look for Jacob, that thorn in his side.

"Was The Lamb really only four-teen-two?" asked Velvet casually.

"Some say fourteen-two. Some say fifteen."

"Smallest horse ever won the Na-tional, wasn't he?"

"Won it twice."

"You ever bin round there?"

"The course? Know every stick. Been on it hundreds a times."

"What's the highest jump?"

Mi gazed into the field. He stuck his chin towards the piebald. "He jumped as high as any to-day."

"I thought he did," said Velvet, low and happy.

There was a long silence. The fields rolled uphill. The hedge at the top

of the field was indigo. Sir Pericles was cropping, like a tawny shadow against it. The piebald, disturbed and excited, cantered the length of the hedge, neighing. Sir Pericles looked up, kicked gaily at the empty air, and cantered too. Mrs. James rolled an eye and laid her ears back.

Evenings, after triumphs, are full of slack and fluid ecstasy. The air swims with motes, visions dip into reach like mild birds willing to be caught. Things are heavenly difficult, but nothing is impossible. Here stood gazing into the field in the sunset the Inspirer, the Inspired and, within the field, the Medium.

Under his boil of red hair Mi's thoughts were chattering "Why not?"

And beside him Velvet looked, throbbing with belief, at her horse.

"Pity *you* don't ride," said Velvet at last.

"The rider's all right," said Mi mystically.

"What rider?"

"You."

A pause.

"There's jockeys from Belgium," said Mi, following the insane thread of thought, "no one's ever seen before. Who's to know?"

"You think he could do it?"

"The two of you could do it."

"Mi . . . oh, Mi . . ."

Pause.

"Who'd you write to? Fer entries."

"Weatherby's."

"Where are they?"

"Telephone book. London somewhere."

"Weatherby's."

There are evenings, full of oxygen and soft air, evenings after rain (and triumph) when mist curls out of the mind, when reason is asleep, stretched out on a low beach at the bottom of the heart, when something sings like a cock at dawn, a long-drawn, wild note.

Velvet and Mi dreamed a boldness bordering on madness.

The race was being run in stage light, under the lamps of the mind. The incandescent grass streamed before Velvet's eyes. There was an unearthly light around the horses, their rumps shone. The white of the painted rails was blue-white like ice. The grass snaked in green water under the horses' feet. There was a thunder rolling in the piebald like a drum. His heart, beating for the great day of his life.

"Weatherby's," said Velvet again. The word was a gateway to a great park. You could touch it, crisp, crested, full of carving . . . *Weatherby's*. Green grass, white rails, silk jackets. Through the arch of Weatherby's.

"Who's to know I'm a girl?" said Velvet, very, very far along the road. Mi was not far behind her.

"Just wants thinking out," he said. His belly felt hollow with the night air. "Supper, Velvet." Slowly they left the gate and walked towards the village.

. . . .

"Once I caught a dove," said Donald, sitting up to supper on the gymkhana night.

"Oh, no," said Mrs. Brown absently.

"I did," said Donald. "It was in . . . July. When you was in France."

"Never bin to France but once," said Mrs. Brown. And suddenly the soles of her feet tingled with the sting of Calais cobbles, slipping, slipping under her tired weight. Memories surged up. In the air to-night, this gymkhana night, when little Velvet had touched the tail of glory, there was something abroad.

"It was on the roof," said Donald. (Coming up out of the water in the early dawn after a gale . . .) "I put a ladder up. A man gave it to me. I caught it in my hand." Silence . . . "I EAT it," said Donald quietly, and looked round. "Poor dove," said Velvet kindly, as nobody said anything.

"It said I could eat it," said Donald. (The water had been kinder than the beach. She had been exposed in front of thousands, dripping, huge, shapeless, tired. She had been held up by her soaking legs and chaired to the hotel. The battle with the water had been pure and dark, but in the morning she began to wonder why she had done it. Dan had been pleased. It was for Dan that she had done it.

He had made a warfare between the water and her strength and courage. She had never thought of the crowds on the beach, the cameras, and newspapers. She had a sense of honour and chastity as sharp as a needle, and she had been outraged. Great burning virgin as close as an oyster and dark as the water at night. Stupid, fierce, honourable, strong and courageous. She and Dan could have opened a new world together, he directing, she enduring. She could have been a great mare whom a jockey rode to victory. Dimly behind the hooded eyes of the innocent and savage mother those aspirations washed.)

"It was that dove that made me sick . . ." said Donald.

"Shut up with that dove," said Mr. Brown, reading his paper.

Chapter Nine

After three days of gale the sea's surface lay in an oily, moulded condition, yellow as clay, folds thick as treacle and casting shadows. Gulls tipped in the dun valleys and rose on the crests. No water broke. The clouds tumbled and heaved, subsiding, and shadows like the shadows of creatures streaked the sea.

After imprisonment of wind and rain the washing flew in banners down the gardens. Velvet mouched about the village, basking, her clothes and face dappled with sun. Little boys carried tyres to the yellow sea and floated in them. The village stank of seaweed.

By the head of the shore stood a singing mendicant, mouth yapping aimlessly, a thread of aged sound coming from him.

Edwina walked lightly down the street with Teddy. Teddy carried his beach gramophone and Edwina's bathing dress. They waved to Velvet leaning on the cobbled wall and went down the gap to the beach. They did not want her and she did not want them, there was nothing sad about that.

There are pleasures earlier than love. A may tree, a cat's back will evoke them. Earlier than love, nearer heaven. As Velvet leant on the wall and heard the cries of Teddy's gramophone she would not have changed her bliss for theirs.

She turned and saw Meredith coming towards her and the two watched the gulls idly, side by side.

"I could eat," said Meredith, yawning.

"M'm," said Velvet. She held the money bags.

After she had given Mi the forty shillings she had put three pounds in the Post Office Savings Bank. But Mr. Brown, pleased with the performance

at the gymkhana, had given her five shillings. She had wanted to bank this too but there had been outcry among the sisters.

"Come on, Velvet," urged Meredith. Velvet pulled out two shillings, and laid them in a crack on the top of the wall. One of the shillings she put back again.

"We'll have one between us."

"Doughnuts?"

"We can't eat six doughnuts each."

"We'll have," said Merry, "one doughnut each, one candle-grease bun, one crunchie, one Mars . . ."

"I should be sick," said Velvet decidedly.

"Perhaps sixpence between us is enough. One doughnut each, and one crunchie."

"You go an' get them then. An' bring me back the sixpence."

Velvet lolled happily on the hot wall, just tickled and touched awake by the idea of approaching food. The juices in her mouth got ready. An aeroplane flew over her head, spewing advertisements in smoke. She turned on her back with her shoulders over the wall to read what it wrote.

"Buy Nougat Nobs" she read, written across the pale blue seat of God.

"Did you see the aeroplane?" said Merry suddenly beside her. "I got Nougat Nobs instead of crunchies."

"Well, you can have 'em," said Velvet. "It'll bust my blessed plate."

"Thanks," said Merry contentedly, not protesting.

Meredith somnolent, loved her food, lived in dreams, loved her canaries, was inaccurate, incurable, and never quarrelled.

Standing against the sunny wall she had soon over-eaten, and undid the ends of her hard leather belt. The screaming of the canaries never really ceased for Meredith. As she ate slowly her head was full of yellow wings.

Dreadnoughts and Rollers and Hartz Mountain and mating. Mating was her preoccupation. If you mated a Hartz Mountain to a Roller . . . or a Yorkshire Dreadnought—what about the green streaks on the wings? Would they be increased if Mountain Jim were mated to Arabella? She leant back against the wall to ease her stomach and dreamt on. A child, when it has over-eaten, does not get a clouded brain.

In her mind the mating always took place safe and sure and certain, and with instant results. She saw a long line of descendants almost simultaneously created. She felt the power of the Patriarch; looking down her family line, and rambling, slow and vague she told a story to herself. Her memory tracks were scored by the noise of their songs wherever she walked. Constantly she was eased by dreams and sensations of flight. Some day she would construct a real aviary, real trees inside the wire netting, and she herself would walk inside the bird house and call the birds off the branches on to her shoulders.

"Where's that sixpence?" said Velvet suddenly.

Meredith handed her fourpence.

"I got an extra two doughnuts," she said. "I was simply frightfully . . ."

"What?" said Velvet.

"Hungry," said Merry.

There was a long, sun-warmed, friendly silence.

"I wish I could eat like that," said Velvet with a sigh.

"You're nearly the youngest. You're weak," said Merry, fallacious tags of breeding in her mind. "You can breed a hen right out."

"Mother's not bred out. Just look at her!" said Velvet, irking. "And Donald's not weak!"

"I shouldn't think strength matters," said Merry, yawning. "It's guts."

"Mother says I'll get over being sick," said Velvet. How often had she had assurance from the calm and rocklike eyes. Above the paunchy cheeks eyes that held neither anxiety nor alarm. Mrs. Brown watched the growth of Velvet as God might watch a sapling's growth: without concern, with unheeding conviction. She would grow, she would cease to be sick. Like Merry, if Mrs. Brown had been asked what her hope and expectancy in life was for Velvet she in her wordless way would have answered "guts." It was what Dan Taylor had required of her, endlessly, all through the night. Against the tide too. Father must see to the fal-lals and the gold plates. She, Dan's Araminty, only wanted staying power.

"You weren't sick at the gymkhana," said Merry. "I forgot to expect you to be."

"I prayed an' prayed," said Velvet. "D'you think that's any good?"

"Not much. Because I always do it. But I don't dare leave it out."

Merry flicked a grain of flint down towards Edwina's head. It missed. Edwina stretched herself in the sun below the wall and put her arms behind her head.

"Don't," said Velvet. "She'll make a row. We're so comfy."

"Pity she's getting a sort of enemy," said Merry.

"It's because she's in love."

"But why . . ."

"It just turns you. Like drink."

In happy silence they watched the silver enemy below them, her ash hair pillowed on her coffee arms. Teddy looked at her like a gooby. She flung a word to him now and then, and the gramophone, pushed into a hollow in the cobbles, sang on. "It's lovely, that noise," said Velvet dreamily, and licked the last stub of crunchie.

There was a sound of hooves be-hind them and three horses came round the corner from the livery stables, setting out for the Hullocks.

Merry and Velvet swung round and leant, backs to the sea, on the wall to watch.

"What's the matter with people who can't ride?" said Merry.

"Dunno," said Velvet.

They watched the riders intently. "Nothing's right," said Velvet.

"Look as though they were kneeling," said Merry. "Their knees are forward and their feet are back . . ."

"You can see miles away on the Hullocks," said Velvet, half shutting her eyes. "They heave as the horse heaves. They have enormous legs, all loose."

"It must be awful," said Meredith, "to ride like that."

The horses disappeared and sun and sparrows took their place.

"Must be awful," said Velvet after a while, "to be a livery horse."

Merry slid her feet further into the sunny dust. It rose in a roll round the toes of her shoes and she said nothing.

"It's not what they're born for."

"What are they born for?"

"They're simply born," said Velvet rather suddenly, "to try to get to know what one person thinks. Their backs and their mouths are like ears and eyes. That's why those horses move like that and hang their heads down from the wither like a steep hill."

"What horses?"

"The livery ones. They've got broken hearts."

"How d'you know?"

"Oh," said Velvet, "I can see. It's like seeing the dead go by."

"You once said you'd go in a livery stable when you grew up."

"I could never go in a livery stable," said Velvet.

The sun shone and warmed her, and Velvet was in a state of abeyance,

of waiting. She was a pond which stood empty but was certain of the mysterious, condensing dew.

"I'm going home," said Velvet, after a pause.

"I'm waiting here," said Meredith. Velvet left Meredith and slouched up the street. She looked in the shoe shop with an urge of heart. "Butcher's Velvet," thought Mr. Ede, and crossed the street to speak to her.

"Piebald didn' do too bad at the Pendean," he said, stopping and looking at the shoes. He was hardly prepared for the beaming eyes that turned on him. "He's beautiful, Mr. Ede," said Velvet earnestly. "I hope you'll never feel bad you let him go."

"Rough animal," said Mr. Ede, embarrassed. "Bit mad p'r'aps. You done wonders to him. Wouldn't stay in any field of mine."

"He's settled down nicely," said Velvet. "He's a very boyish horse."

Mr. Ede passed this over as fanciful. He thought she looked queer too. Delicate and spiny. And all them teeth. In truth Velvet could look like a fairy wolf gone blond. She had this look as she turned back upon the shoes. Ede left her and Mi touched her on the shoulder.

"Looked up Weatherby's?"

" 'Tisn't in the telephone book."

"Just write 'Weatherby's. Racin' experts. London,' " said Mi. "Just ask for the rules of entry."

"What'll I say?"

But Mi was in a hurry. He didn't know.

Her mind began its letter across tan and silver heels, plaid bedroom slippers and sea-shoes of canvas. She moved homewards, carrying disjointed words like broken crockery in a napkin.

The spaniels were sitting, sunning, round the door, Wednesday's joint disturbing them already. The bitch laid her nose from time to time to the bottom door-line and drew long breaths and rolled her yellow eyes. The chained house dog flew out silently, choked on the end of his chain and fell back.

The sitting-room was empty, mother in the kitchen. Velvet pulled her lesson books from the dresser drawer and found a sheet of foreign writing paper that had laid in the grammar book for months. The ink bottle was on the cactus shelf, the pen beside it.

She sat down and wrote swiftly for fear of being disturbed:

"DEAR SIRS,

"I am an Owner of a Horse. Please could you send me the Rules of entering for the Grand National Race? "I am, Sirs, Your obedient Servant,

"V. BROWN."

There was a bit of blotting paper in the meat ledger, an envelope in the dresser drawer. In five minutes she was going back down the street with the letter and a penny for the stamp machine, the letter addressed according to Mi's advice.

She and Mi met at the midday joint. She whispered: "I've done it."

"Written it?"

"An' posted it."

He seemed surprised. She could not eat.

"I don't like cabbage," said Donald. He was not answered.

"I don't like it but I eat it," he said, looking at Velvet.

"You're a marvel," said Mally.

"Yes, I am a marvel," said Donald. "I don't like cabbage, I don't like food, but I eat it. Velvet doesn't."

This provocation blew over.

"Eat your food, Velvet," said Mr. Brown after a suitable interval. "That plate sitting softer?"

"Much," said Velvet. "But I'm not hungry."

"I'm not hungry either," said Donald, "but I eat my food. I eat it all up, even when I'm not hungry."

"I don't like to see a great slice of English leg left like that," said Mr. Brown. "If you can't eat it lift it back." The slice was returned to the dish. Velvet thought, as she chopped up her cabbage and hid it round her baked potato, that the box at the Post Office had just been cleared.

"You girls bin eating snacks?" said Mr. Brown, looking at Meredith's plate.

"I got gristle," said Merry hurriedly, pushing with her fork, and dividing plot from plot.

"Doughnuts," said Mrs. Brown placidly. "They look like it."

"Pay for 'em or put 'em down?"

"Pay for 'em!" said Merry indignantly.

"I'll have no putting down," said Mr. Brown. "Hand me that plate, Merry. You're behaving like a customer."

Meredith got up and carried her plate to him.

"That's not gristle, that's fat," said Mr. Brown. "You just carry that back and eat it up. If snacks in the mid-morning's going to spoil a leg for you you better have no more of 'em. Ten sheep coming at four, Mi."

"Right," said Mi.

"To be killed?" said Donald.

"Yes," said Mi.

"Why killed?" said Donald.

"To make meat for you."

"For me?"

"I said so."

"I want to see 'em be killed," said Donald.

"Well, you can't," said his father.

"Do they break an' fall down and die?"

No answer.

"Who dies them?"

"I do," said Mr. Brown. "And Mi."

Donald looked at his father without the slightest disfavour but with added respect.

"If there's a sheep's head for to-night give it me while it's warm, Mi," said Mrs. Brown. "You can't cook it so tender once it's chilled down."

Chapter Ten

When the answer from Weatherby's came it contained terrible difficulties. Velvet took it to Mi.

"Oh, God," said Mi when he looked at the blue entry form. "I oughta known. It brings it all back." Mi's wicked knowledge of the North came over him in floods. "There's this to be done . . . an' that . . . and this and that. . . . See if we can't get round it. You'll be disqualified in the end in any case, my girl. Might as well be disqualified all round. All you want is the chance to do it. I wonder if we're dotty."

"Who could you ask?"

"Ask!" said Mi. "Ask the church-wardens. You leave it to me. It's Lewes races to-morrow. I'll be over there and have a talk. You get on with the animal. Leave a lot to me. An' don't talk!"

"I never!"

Mi glanced at her a moment. He had been absorbed in his thought.

"No, you don't," he said. "But 'Dwina'd hand it on to Teddy, and Merry'd forget she wasn't to speak . . . An' it may never happen. You'd best just get on with the animal if you think such a crack of it."

"Don't you?"

Mi heaved a big breath, first in, then out of his lungs. "I think more of you," he said in the end.

"I'm nothing without him," said Velvet.

"Get on now," said Mi. "An' don't keep asking me how I'm getting on. What's more, there's another thing. You might have a shot at the Tindles jumps in the mushroom valley."

"They're all wired up."

"Yes; well, I'd unwire 'em. Take some pliers. They're a lazy lot over there now the horses are gone. There's no one in the valley before seven."

September passed and October came. Velvet by now had grown bolder. She no longer rose in the dawn to fetch the piebald to the mushroom valley but took him in the red-haired Autumn under cold afternoon moons of October on dew-drenched grass. The mushroom pickers cleaned the valley before dawn. No one came down from Tindles, the hill village of the Derby winner. The old man was old, old. His horses gone, his men lazy. He warmed his toes and looked at his Derby cup but kept indoors between the sideboard and the fire.

Velvet grew so bold she ceased to replace the barbed wire over the jumps. The great brushwork barriers stood up free and clean and twice a week the piebald leapt them from end to end of the field. Sometimes Mi came with a bamboo rod and caught him a flick on his belly or his hock as he flew over.

One day when his work was over he came in the evening with a spade and dug a pit before one of the jumps and dragged logs to lie at the lip of the pit to make The Pie take off earlier. He came back with Velvet in the morning early and she and the horse leapt the contraption. After which Mi filled it in again and threw sods on it.

"They'll think we've buried someone," said Velvet. "You do take a lot of trouble, Mi."

"Know what he's just jumped?" said Mi, straightening his back.

"What?"

"Jumped the third on the National. Third jump's a ditch an' fence. Same as this one. I wrote to a chap on the railway up there for the measurements."

"Railway?"

"Truckline. Runs on the raised embankment alongside the Course. You on'y got to run down and measure."

Now the piebald jumped as he had jumped the five-foot wall when they had first seen him, hitching his quarters up behind him and leaving inches to spare. Not a twig on the jumps moved except from the wind of his passage. Velvet lay on his neck like the shadow of an ape and breathed her faith into him.

One evening before supper, Mi and Velvet alone under the Albert lamp, Velvet read the accounts of races. The Cesarewitch. Prophecies about it beforehand.

". . . the conditions will be ideal for all except the mudlarkers," she read aloud. "What's that, Mi?"

"Dud talk o' mutts," said Mi.

" 'Munition started so slowly he was always tailed'?"

"The same," said Mi.

"And 'he galloped the opposition down in grand style.' "

"And the same," said Mi.

"Oh, no!" said Velvet. "I like that! It's what I'll do. I'll gallop the opposition down. It's grand."

"If you like," said Mi.

"I do," said Velvet.

Silence.

"We gotta call him something," said Mi.

"What? The piebald? Can't we call him The Pie?"

"If you like. It's a mutt name."

"I'll always call him The Pie.

But if he's got to have something grand . . ."

"We gotta choose the name and choose racing colours and send up and ask Weatherby's if they'll pass 'em. Sooner the better. They'll print 'em in the Calendar."

"I'll have black and pink," said Velvet.

"You'll look awful."

"Could we call him Unicorn?" said Velvet slowly.

"That's the sort," said Mi. "Longish. Historical."

"Is Unicorn historical?"

"Seems to me."

"He could just be Unicorn for the race?"

"Yes, he could. But he'll be put down Unicorn for ever in the history books."

"On'y if he wins, Mi . . ."

"Win or no, he goes down. Some of those books put every runner that ever ran. Starting with the 'Lottery' year, with Jem Mason up. That was eighteen thirty-nine. Seventeen starters."

"You know a heap."

"Any chap knows anything knows the first Grand National."

"Lamp's smoking, Mi."

Mi turned it down.

"An', Mi."

"M'm."

"I don't like Unicorn."

"Well, think of something else."

"I'll never like anything but The Piebald. It's his name. He's got to go in the books like that."

Mi looked up. The thin face opposite him had grief in it.

"They weren't all so grand," he said at last. "There was Jerry M. and Shady Girl. An' Old Joe won it in eighteen eighty-six. An' there was Hunter an' Seaman and Miss Lizzie, an' The Doctor, an' The Colonel . . . Why, there was The Colonel! He won

it twice. You call him The Piebald an' it won't hurt. It'll do fine."

Velvet gave him a look of love. "Thank you, Mi," she murmured.

"Here, take the papers," said Mi, "an' look at 'em."

"Gotta enter his sire and his dam," said Velvet, poring over the Rules.

"Well, that's that," said Mi, yawning.

"Whad'you mean, that's that?" said Velvet. "He's got a sire and a dam somewhere, hasn't he?"

"Orphan. Horse is an orphan. Here, hand me the Rules!"

Mi drew the lamp nearer and leant his face deeply upon the little page. " 'In entering' . . . m'm . . . m'm . . . 'he shall be described by stating a name.' . . . We gotta name. Settled. 'The age he will be at the time of the race.' . . . Blacksmith says he's six. Might be more. We'll put 'aged.' "

"That's a horrid word."

"It's fine. It means grown up. No more o' them silly years. We'll put 'aged.' "

"What's next?"

" 'The colour' . . . (they'll cough a bit when they read he's a piebald) 'and whether a horse, marc or gelding, and the Calendar or Stud-Book names of his sire and dam.' That's where they get us!"

"Oh, Mi . . ."

"Wait a bit! 'If the sire or dam has no name in the Calendar' . . . wait a minute, wait a minute . . . 'or if the pedigree of the sire or dam be unknown, such further particulars as to where, when, and from whom the horse was purchased or obtained must be given as will identify him.' That's us all right."

"What'll you put? You can't put about the shilling an' the raffle."

"Make 'em sit up."

"Too much. They'll sit up and see me!"

"You're right, yes. Pity though. Been a bit a fun. We'll put 'Bought from Thomas Ede, Farmer,' an' the date. Previous bought in Lewes Market. . . ."

"That reads odd."

"You aren't asked to state all the buys. We'll leave it at Ede."

"Anything else?"

"Not that I can see."

"S'sh! Here's the others!"

. . . .

Donald had out his jigsaws. He was doing a map of the world in big simple pieces. He could not get it started because two bits of the margin were missing. He begged and pleaded and nagged, "Will you help me? WILL you help me?"

Merry helped him most. Mally stuck in a piece or two. Edwina bent over him and played the mother till she got bored.

"There's India!" said Edwina, skipping from mother to teacher.

"All the pink bits, Donald, belong to England."

"What's England?"

"Us."

"There's a pink bit and there's . . . LOOK, Donald . . . there's a . . ."

"D'you know," said Donald, looking at her with his earnest charm, "in my black socks I've got HOLES!"

"Goo!" said Edwina, laughing suddenly. "An' you haven't any black socks either . . ." And looking up she saw Teddy's face under the light of the lamp outside. She was gone with the swoop of a moth through the door.

"Will you help me?" began Donald again, leaning towards Mally. Mally flicked a slice of wood towards him. "There's England and France in that bit."

"What's France?"

"Over the water," said Mally, chucking her thumb over her shoulder. "Over the sea."

"I seen France once," said Donald. "No!"

"I seen France once an' all the houses were slipping down in the water."

"Huh!" said Mi. "He doesn't know it's land. Thinks it's built on the Channel!"

"Bed, Donald," said Mrs. Brown in the doorway.

"I'm busy," said Donald. "We're all busy."

"Get on, Donald," urged Mi.

"Why do they have supper'n not me?" said Donald, feverishly searching for a piece of wood.

. . . .

Lewes races had long gone by. Mi had made his arrangements. He had met a friend here and a friend there and had a talk or two and borrowed a bit, had his week's wages in advance from Mr. Brown, and finally had paid a visit to Croydon. Edwina didn't notice, Merry didn't ask, and Mally, her nose twitching, didn't know enough to go upon, though sometimes she prodded like a person prodding with a stick in mud who thinks a treasure can be seen.

One day Mi came to Velvet after supper. He whistled her out of the living-room with a suck of his tooth and a cock of his eye. "Sign this," he said in Miss Ada's stall, the private sitting-room of their lives. Miss Ada ate her bedding undisturbed.

"What is it?" said Velvet.

"It's a Clearance," said Mi. "You put 'James Tasky' here."

He had his pen in his hand and a glass bottle of ink.

"Who's James Tasky?"

"He's you. He will be you in a post or two. Just ask me nothing. Sign what I say."

Velvet wrote at the bottom of the paper "James Tasky," balancing the paper on the lip of the manger. Mi produced three inches of blotting paper from his pocket.

"Now . . ." he said with satisfaction. "Now we post it . . . see? An' we get a licence . . . see? An' the real Mr. Tasky's not even in England. What a catch!"

"Where is he?"

"Being sick on the Baltic, I shouldn't wonder. He told me all about it. Horrible sea, the Baltic. Water's shallow and bumps on the bottom an' comes up again. How people can go in ships beats me."

"We gotta have the name in by the second Tuesday in January," said Velvet.

"Say that on the form?"

"Yes."

"Well, we'll have it in. We've put our backs in this now, and our shirts an' all. What d'you call it? About that horse? Putting it what?"

"Putting The Piebald in history," said Velvet. "I think of that whenever I feel giddy and it stops."

"Well, I'm putting you in history. See? Like my old Dan put Araminty Potter. It's a foreseen thing. Like God might a thought of. Believe in God, Velvet?"

"Yes and no," said Velvet. "Yes and no," and sighed.

"Shouldn't have asked," said Mi cheerfully. "Private. Come along now and get a stamp out of your mother for me. I'm done this week to a penny."

Christmas came and went. The Piebald's muscles grew tauter. One evening in the first days of January, Mr. Brown took Edwina and Mally and Meredith to the pictures. Velvet would have gone but she felt shivery after tea. When they had left the house Velvet and her mother and Mi sat alone. Mrs. Brown did a patience, Mi cut a piece of cork to fit a bottle, Velvet did nothing, the wind howled round them, the carpet rose against the door. The spaniels lay heaped in Miss Ada's stall.

"Bus'll be near blown over," said Mi. "They'll catch it going in."

Mrs. Brown laid out another card. Jacob shivered and recrossed his delicate forefeet.

Mi looked at Mrs. Brown as he cut his cork and knew the moment had come to include her. When he looked at her he saw a pillar of fire. He put aside the great dun-coloured coating, the enormous thighs, the shoulders which bore a pack of muscle like a yoke across them. He saw instead those mysterious qualities that made him say of any uncouth, unwieldy, unmanageable horse, "He's got heart." By heart he meant a heart that would stay.

"There's a horse," he said, feeling his way to break the silence, "over at Pendean would carry you."

"Never bin on a horse," said Mrs. Brown.

"Makes no odds," said Mi indifferently—but he would not let the silence close again.

"Should tell yer ma f'I were you, Velvet," he said in an odd voice. "Now's your minute."

Velvet looked up. Mrs. Brown laid out her cards unmoved.

Velvet watched her own feet. "Piebald's fit," she mumbled, "to run in the National."

Mrs. Brown ruminated, laid down her cards. Said:

"What about it?"

"Thought of runnin' it," said Velvet.

"You did?"

"M'm . . ."

"The Grand National with them jumps?"

"M'm. . . . Thirty jumps."

"Stiff," said Mrs. Brown.

Nobody spoke. Mi cut his cork. His fingers stuck and slipped. Velvet would never disobey her mother.

"What'll it cost?" said Mrs. Brown.

"A hundred pounds to enter. And money for a horse-box. An' me night's lodging. (I gotta see it.)"

"What do you win if you win?"

"Oh," said Velvet vaguely, "thousands and a cup. But it's not that, it's for the horse. Besides, if they find out they'll disqualify me. It's only for the horse."

"What makes you think it can win?"

"It can."

"Can it, Mi?"

"Shouldn't wonder."

"Well," said Mrs. Brown, and gathered up the cards into a neat pack. Her peasant's eye, half shrewd, half visionary, insected the idea, and the features of her big face not stirring she moved her head with elephantine majesty. Then she rose and going to the sideboard took out a key from a drawer. She left the room and was heard above walking in her own.

Velvet closed her eyes. Her feet were cold.

"My feet are cold, Mi."

"Keep still. Lie still."

Mrs. Brown came back with a box, her lips moving as though she were talking to herself. Unlocking the box on the table she counted out money, old-fashioned money, gold—gold sovereigns.

Mi leant forward. Velvet sat up. Mi knew what they were.

"Your prize? What you won?" said Mi, quiet.

"Kept it," said Mrs. Brown. "Thought I might. Thought I would."

"Look at it," said Mi. "Never seen such a thing since I was a lad."

Mrs. Brown's thick fingers built castles with the coins.

"There's a hundred. Twenty fer expenses." She looked straight at Velvet. "I gotta fancy, Velvet, that you pay your entry in this." She tapped the castles.

"Pay in the gold itself?" said Mi.

"It'll bring you luck," said Mrs. Brown.

"Weatherby's'll think it odd," said Mi.

"You got a thing you sign?" said Mrs. Brown.

"Yes," said Mi, and fumbled in his coat pocket.

Mrs. Brown took the blue form and read it.

"Not there," said Mi, "that's the Grand Military. Next page. Top o' page seventeen. 'Liverpool—continued,' it says."

Mrs. Brown read in silence.

"Queer," she said at last. "Queer thing. I had a feeling."

"What?" said Mi.

"An' see there," said Mrs. Brown, handing him the form and plunging her finger on it. "See what it says. 'Sov. Ten sov. each. Fifty sov. extra.' There's the wording clear. They can't go back on it. You use them sovereigns. I had a fancy they'd come in."

Velvet hung softly against her mother, putting her arms round her shoulders. Mrs. Brown took her suddenly on her lap. Mi was so affected he called Jacob into the yard. But before he went he hit his lips three times with his index finger at Velvet behind her mother's back. She stared at him vacantly and he shook his head and closed the door.

"Who'll tell father?" whispered Velvet.

"I'll tell your father," said Mrs. Brown, rocking her.

Of this discussion Velvet heard nothing. When the battle was over she was given no more than the result. But in the deep of the night forces were involved that stirred Araminty

Potter to love and to fury, and finally to love again. In meeting a hard, but as it turned out a brittle, opposition from her husband, Araminty rose like a sea monster from its home. After her years of silence she grunted with astonishing anger, and William, powerless and exasperated, stung like a gnat upon a knotted hide. That something which was obstinate and visionary and childish bound Mi and Velvet and her mother together, and in the night Araminty, in doing battle for their dreams, fought too for her own inarticulate honour.

The difference ran to its end, they were shaken profoundly, and slept in friendship at dawn. Mr. Brown rose next morning, spiritually bruised, feeling that he was going to be made ridiculous, but acquiescent.

The first effect of this discussion was that The Piebald stood in Miss Ada's stall and Miss Ada found herself once more among the tools (which she shared at night with the spaniels). Velvet took her gymkhana money out of the bank to buy oats, and what she could not buy her mother saved from the housekeeping.

The horse was walked endlessly uphill. There was not a steep hill-surface for miles around that Velvet had not sought out and ascended. The faulty, pear-shaped quarters of The Piebald swelled with muscle. Clipped out, he shone blacker and whiter than ever, his long tail and mane washed in the vinegar suds from Edwina's hair-rinsings, his pink albino hooves scrubbed with a nail brush and polished. He grew to look like a newly-painted rocking horse, freshly delivered.

. . . .

On the first Monday in January Mi took the whole entry money of a hundred pounds in gold sovereigns in a bag up to London. He went to Messrs. Weatherby in Cavendish Square, walked up the stone steps, pushed the doors, and stood at a wooden counter not unlike a bank. A tall man asked him offhandedly what he wanted.

"Entry. Fer the Gran' National," said Mi, pulling out the completed form, dumping the heavy bag on the counter, and pushing it towards the man.

"What's that?"

"Th'entry money," said Mi.

"Ten pounds. Have you brought it in silver?" said the man superciliously, touching the neck of the bag with his fingers.

"Ten? I've brought a hundred. In gold."

The man drew the bag towards him and opened it. He peered inside with astonishment. "What's this? Sovereigns?"

"A hundred sovereigns," said Mi.

The man looked at Mi consideringly. He indicated a stool. "Will you wait?" he said. He was away a moment, then returned with a companion whose air was even more exalted and critical.

"Do I understand," said the second man, "that you have brought a hundred sovereigns in pre-war gold to pay for an entry for the Grand National . . . Race?" He brought out the word "race" as though it were the crime which Mi had committed.

"Yes, sir," said Mi cheerfully and simply and shifted his feet and leant on the counter. "It's quite simple, sir. I thought you'd like it best jus' as it was. I didn't know where best to change it into paper an' as this is as good's a bank (the man's eyes lightened just a shade) I thought I'd bring it here."

"To what horse does this refer?"

"It's a piebald horse. Property of Miss V. Brown. She owns it. Her father's a butcher down . . . The ad-

dress is here." He smoothed out the form.

"Who is the trainer?"

"Privately trained, sir."

"Not by the owner?"

"Well, yes, by the owner. Yes, sir, trained by her since she's had it."

"How do you come to bring up this money?"

Mi paused a moment and sucked his tooth.

"It's a fancy of Miss Brown's mother, sir. She had the sovereigns tucked away for years. Kind of store, sir. She had a fancy it would bring the horse luck if she paid the entry money with the sovereigns."

"I'm afraid we can't do deals in gold. This is worth more than a hundred pounds."

"You mean I get some change back?"

"You would if we took it. But we can't have anything to do with the price of gold at the present rate. That is not our business."

"I don't think," said Mi slowly, "that Mrs. Brown wants any change. A hundred sovereigns is a hundred pounds to her. She's old-fashioned. She's set on paying the entry with this hundred pounds here in this bag, sir."

"There's another thing," said the man. "You don't need to pay a hundred now. It's ten sovereigns now, fifty sovereigns extra if left in after January 30th, with an additional forty sovereigns if left in after March 13th."

"Sovereigns," murmured Mi. "It says 'sovereigns,' and these are sovereigns."

"Well, that's the . . ." (the gentlemen looked acid), "the wording dating from the original . . . er . . . inception of this form."

"Clear enough," said Mi. "Sovereigns it says. I don't want to make

difficulties, sir, but I've brought you sovereigns, haven't I?"

"I think you had better wait," said the gentleman, and he and his companion disappeared. Mi sat on the stool again and eyed his bag. He read the antique sporting notices. There was a ginger and green notice, stiff with discoloured varnish, about paying for the weights in the weighing room. He frowned at it. He had never heard of such a thing. Then he saw that it was dated a hundred years ago.

After a long interval the gentleman returned, alone.

"The sovereigns will be accepted," he said curtly, "but there is no need to deposit more than ten as yet."

"I'd sooner leave the lot," said Mi obstinately.

"The reason for the division of the entry amounts," said the gentleman, disliking Mi more and more, "is in case the horse becomes by a later date unable to run."

"This horse'll run," said Mi.

"You cannot foresee," said the gentleman, "acts of God."

"M'm, I can," said Mi, "m'm, I can. You take the lot an' stack it for me. Safer here. I might get it lifted off me on the way home. You got a fine big place here. You got room for ninety sovereigns stacked away. You can give me a paper for it. They need me at the butcher's down there. 'Tisn't easy to keep making journeys. You'll need the lot before we're done."

Again the gentleman disappeared and a very exalted head was put round the lintel of an inner cubicle and two very shrewd and dwelling eyes inspected Mi.

Finally a receipt was handed to him, the bag and form taken from him and Mi was ready to depart.

"Who's your rider?" said the gentleman, almost sociably at last.

"Foreign chap," said Mi instantly. "Comin' over later."

"He'll have to get his Clearance, you know," said the gentleman, "from his own accredited Jockey Club."

"Yes, sir," said Mi quickly. "Yes, thank you, sir."

"What's his name? Do we know him?"

"Tasky. James Tasky."

"English?"

"Mother's English. Chap's half Russian."

"From which country then does he get his Clearance? There is racing of course still in Russia."

"Mr. Brown's working it all out," said Mi. "I'm just the hand down there. I know what I hear them say, that's about all."

"Well, good-day then. Just a minute. You'll notice on that receipt 'Received one hundred sovereigns in gold sovereigns, value to be decided by Coult's Bank when the final payment is due.' That means you get an amount returned. You'll explain that to the Owner, please."

"Right, sir. Good-day, sir."

Mi was out in the airy light of Cavendish Square and he ran his hand across his brow.

"Mother nearly bitched it with 'er whimsies," he said.

.

It was March. The days of March creeping gustily on like something that man couldn't hinder and God wouldn't hurry.

"What about me jacket?" said Velvet in her whisper, somewhat hoarse, again and again.

"*Leave* yer jacket!" said Mi testily. "I keep telling you. Leave me thinking of it."

"I can't sew, remember," said Velvet warningly.

"Think I don't know that! My sister's sewing it."

"Your SISTER! You gotta sister!" Velvet sat bolt upright.

"I gotta sister. I got two."

"You never told us!"

"I'm no family man," said Mi shortly.

"Your old Dan . . . your old father's dead?"

"He's dead!"

"You gotta mother?"

"Dead too. But where I sprung from an' what I left behind's my business."

"But your sister's my business. She's sewing my coat."

"And well she can do that for me," said Mi, reflecting. "I never asked her for a penny. I got her her job. Bin there years."

"Where?"

"Sews for a tailor at Newmarket. Does the tailored shirts. I sent her that top of yours yer ma said was past darning."

"The top of that cotton dress what mother used the bottom for knickers?"

"That's the one."

"Well, it was too small, anyway. I hope she makes it bigger. What about the stuff?"

"Black an' pink I told her. She's in the way of getting the stuff up there. She'll get the cap made, too."

"And the breeches and the boots?"

"You leave it to me up at Aintree. That'll sort itself up at Aintree. Overnight. The valets go round with spares in their cases."

"Valets?"

"Fellows that look after the jockeys. Press up their clothes an' do their boots. There's a gang of them go round the race meetings."

"Now," said Velvet at last, as low as low, "there's another thing."

"M'm?"

"Mother," said Velvet. And the spinning air seemed to stop round them in anxiety.

"It's a thing I'm thinking of too," said Mi. "Worries me."

"Yes," said Velvet. "D'you know, Mi?"

"What?"

"I couldn't do it f'I didn' tell her." The telling was done at the shop at night. Mi arranged it when Mrs. Brown was totting up. She spared the electric and totted by candlelight.

"You gotta pretend I'm not your child," said Velvet, long after bedtime. She dragged up her words as though the roots were deep.

"You was nineteen when you swum the Channel," said Velvet. "I'm fourteen but my chance's come early. You mustn't think I'm your child. I'm a girl with a Chance."

Her mother's throat clicked. She blazed into fire without moving an eyelash.

"Mi's in the street, waitin'," said Velvet. "It's him an' me." (She paused at the gasp her mother gave.)

"We're out on it together," went on Velvet, not knowing the terror that cooled her mother's fire. "We think . . . I think . . ." (coming up closer and speaking very low) "I kin *ride* the horse."

"Almighty God," said Mrs. Brown, mild and reverent. She was thanking Him that her child was her shining Velvet. Not all messed up with love. Not all messed up with love an' such. That Mi was to Velvet what Dan had been to her, that stuff grander and tougher than a lover. Now what was this suggestion that was like a wild dream?

"In the race, Velvet?"

Velvet described the machinery, Mi's plans, Mi's devices.

"If I'm found out then they'll send me home. Father'll be angry. Just as likely I won't be found out. Well, then, we'll do our best. The horse is great. He's like a Bible horse."

The interview was over, except the silence and the thinking.

"I don' want to speak to Mi about it," said Mrs. Brown at last. "Tell him not to speak to me about it. Not a word. It's a weight on me. It's a terrible . . . I can't be but your mother, Velvet. . . . To think Mi shoulda lent himself to this."

Then at the very end . . . "I'm all ashake. Let there be no whisperin' an' talkin'. I must put it from me an' pray to God."

Velvet left her. The candle guttered but the totting did not continue. Later the heavy woman walked home.

Chapter Eleven

March ran two-thirds of its days.

Mr. Larke, the chemist, called in to fetch his meat book. "I'm hair-washing," called Mrs. Brown from the scullery. Mr. Larke stood in the scullery door critically.

"Two drops a' camomile is what you ought to add," he said.

"Bleach 'em?"

"Bleach 'em."

"Bleached enough already."

"When I say 'bleach' I should say 'bring out the colour.' "

"Vinegar's what I use," said Mrs. Brown.

"So I can smell," said Mr. Larke.

"I got your last week's book made up," said Mrs. Brown, rinsing Edwina; "it's on the sideboard by the apples. Now Velvet. Edwina, you go and rub your head an' Mally'll give you a hand."

Edwina came staggering back into the living-room, her head and face blindly wrapped in the bath towel Mrs. Brown had popped over her. "My back aches," she grumbled. "I wish I could wash my own."

"Velvet!" called Mrs. Brown.

"I'm coming . . ."

When Velvet reached the scullery Mrs. Brown looked at her. "I won't risk it," she said. "Might make you squeamish, bending. I'll brush it through with a wet brush an' you can sit by the fire an' comb it."

"I'm taking the book then," called Mr. Larke loudly. "It's a great day for you all. Anxious. I'm not a racing man myself but we've all got our eyes on you, Velvet. There's a bit of money on you in the village."

"Thank you," said Velvet, through the brushing.

"Say it louder," said Mrs. Brown.

"Thank YOU," shouted Velvet.

"Right," said Mr. Larke. "Where you stopping?"

"Hotel," shouted Mrs. Brown. "She's doing it slipslap. (Why don't he go? Makes you testy all this popping in an' good-wishing.) . . ."

("There he goes," said Velvet. "I can feel the draught on my legs.")

"I'm dry!" shouted Edwina. "Can I go?"

"You can't be dry. Come here an' let me feel."

Edwina came in.

"Damp all roun' your glands," said Mrs. Brown, feeling. "You don't go down the street like that."

"Teddy's just . . ."

"Teddy kin wait."

"He can't."

"Anybody kin wait, Edwina," said Mrs. Brown, brushing hard, "for a pretty girl."

Edwina suddenly smiled all over her light-built face. She went back to the living-room.

"Isn't she getting grown-up," said Velvet.

"You're all on the edge of it."

"Not me."

"There you are!" said Mrs. Brown, laying down the brush. "You fluff up with a bit of water."

"It'll all be down again flat in an hour."

"Greasy scalp," said Mrs. Brown. "Get Meredith down for me. She's with the birds."

. . . .

It was the last evening before the start at dawn. Velvet and Mi were travelling to Aintree in the horse-box. The last evening meal. Donald was allowed to sit up. Taps came on the door as they ate and friendly voices called in. The whole village had of course long known that the piebald horse, won for a shilling, was going to be run in the Grand National. Velvet's Grand National. "Gran' National Velvet," Mr. Croom called out to her in the street. "Good morning, Gran' National Velvet!" and two boys outside the sweet-shop had clapped their hands. "Got any tips for the National?" called the postman.

"The Piebald!" said Velvet with her shy look.

"Yes, they're going up to Liverpool to-morrow," said Mrs. Brown at the door twenty times. "Mi an' Velvet are going in the horse-box." She filled the doorway with her body and behind her shadow Velvet sat. It was a soft March night between a pair of howling gales, a black, cold trough of peace, pierced with stars. Stars that above her mother's head as she stood in the open street doorway seemed like Christmas trees, slender, growing into the sky. The Albert lamp on Edwina's hair, her father's folded neck, her mother's majesty and silence, Donald's film face and dear,

disgusting habits, the sideboard, heavy, loaded, bottles of ink, dishcovers, salmon tins, apples, vinegar bottles, Merry's bird-absorbed face, Mally's loyal and sharp eyes, Mi's grin, Mi's slouch, Mi's way of coming through the door, Mi's shadow, the lying Jacob, the bitch-seeking, pleasure-loving, self-indulgent Jacob, agreeable dog, sensitive, agreeable dog . . . these things (not in words, but in the burning warmth of the present) swelled her leave-taking heart. She had a wordless premonition that this was an egg into which it was impossible to re-enter. When the shell had burst, it was burst for ever. She felt this only as a dog howls for packing, mournful and simple and going, going, gone.

Going, going, gone, full of stars and cacti, and yellow canaries screaming in the morning.

"What d'you want, Velvet?"

"I'm getting my shell-box."

In silence they watched her fetch her box and put it beside her plate.

Edwina laughed suddenly.

"Coo lummy, Velvet! Paper horses just before the Grand National!"

"Beastly pair o' words," muttered father. "Get 'em from Teddy . . ."

"H'm . . . Teddy uses better words 'an that!"

(Warm bickering of family life. Fathers and daughters. . . .)

"Can I see wot's inside that box?" said Donald.

Velvet's face lightened. Donald should look at them to-night. He had never set his fingers on them before.

"Have you finished, Donald? Come an' sit on my lap."

"I kin climb up. Don' you help me." He walked up the bars of her chair like a ladder and bumped himself down on to her lap from the arm.

She opened the lid and a little shell fell off.

"You've dropped a shell!" (burstingly).

"I must stick it back."

"Let me look!"

"Ssh, wait . . ." Velvet put her thin finger inside and hooked up a race-horse.

"Hullo! This is Grakle!" she said. "Who's been changing them round? Who's touched my box?"

"I did," said Merry in a small voice, "I did, Velvet. I'm sorry."

Velvet looked astonished. "I don't mind, Merry," she said. "I didn't think you ever cared about them."

"It was yesterday afternoon," said Merry. "The canaries were so alive. You can't do anything with them. I took your horses out to exercise. I just took out the National winners and jumped a bush behind Peg's Farm."

"Show me, show me," hammered Donald, leaning over the box and poking his fingers inside.

Velvet put her hand over his fingers. "(In a second, Donald . . .) But I'm glad, Merry. I'd love you to take them out. Which ones did you take?"

"Tipperary Tim an' Sergeant Murphy and Manifesto. Doesn't Manifesto look lovely with his ears forward and the shine on his shoulder? He's a right-facing one. Where'd you cut him from?"

But Velvet bent her head suddenly over Donald. She had cut him from a library book down at the schoolhouse.

"Now pull them out!" said Donald.

"All the National Winners are on top," said Velvet, groping. "The ponies are underneath. There's a tiny . . . there's a Shetland. . . . Here it is. Look, Donald! Isn't he fat and like a kitten!"

"I like real horses," said Donald, unmoved.

"Good, good boy," said Mally.

"Oh, there's my darling Chestnut Fourteen-Two!" said Velvet, half

mourning over them. "Oh, why haven't I looked at them for so long?"

"Can't do everything, Velvet," said her father, twisting his chair round so that he could read better under the lamp. "You got your things packed up?"

"They're ready," said mother, clearing away the last dish.

"I'm going to bed," said Mi. "We're off at five. Won't do her no good to sit up."

"She won't," said Mrs. Brown. "She'll go in half an hour."

"On top o' my food!" said Velvet indignantly.

"Food or no," said mother.

"Plate all right?" said father.

"Sitting fine," said Velvet, who knew this was a gesture of love.

"Let me see that Manifesto," said Mi, standing in the doorway. Velvet picked the horse out.

"Won twice," said Mi. "97 . . . an' '99."

"How'd you know all that, Mi?" said Mr. Brown from his lamp and paper.

"Dunno," said Mi. "There it is. What a shoulder . . . eh? What a horse . . . eh? Looks too clever to win."

"Shouldn't they be clever?" said Edwina.

"Jumpin' thirty jumps when they can stan' still . . . !" said Mi. "He did that Course eight times. Greatest National horse ever was. Why he won it twice."

"I can't understand you, Mi," said Edwina. "You just said he wasn't clever."

" 'Tisn't everything to be clever," said Mi, and disappeared to bed.

"How come Mi never to ride?" said Mr. Brown into his newspaper.

"Tell me some more," said Donald.

"I wish we could all go to Liverpool," said Mally.

"Cost too much," said Mr. Brown. "Yer mother plumpin' her prize-money on Velvet, that's one thing! We can't spend no more—just in the air."

"Bed for you, Donald," said mother.

"Tell me one more horse 'fore I go."

"There was once a horse called Moifaa," gabbled Velvet, looking at her mother.

Mrs. Brown nodded. "Just to-night. Just a quick one."

Donald swung round his eyes and hooked them upon Velvet's lips.

"Moifaa was sent from New Zealand in a ship."

"Where's that?"

Velvet pointed to the floor with her finger. "Same as Australia. Down there. Th'other side."

"M'm . . . m'm . . ." said Donald greedily, waiting.

"The horse was sent right round the world and the ship went down near Ireland."

"How d'you know?" said Mally, listening like Donald.

"Mi told me. An' the ship went down an' the horse swam to an island off the coast, and the island had salt grass an' there was nothing to eat an' the horse walked up an' down the seashore looking out to sea an' neighing."

"An' what?"

"Screaming for help."

"The horse did?"

"Yes. An' fishermen were fishing an' they rowed near an' saw him. A horse standing neighing on an island where there'd never bin a horse. Never bin a cow. Never bin anything. It gave 'em the creeps an' they went home."

"Did they leave him there?"

"Left him there all night with all that grass an' all of it salt an' all that water an' all of it salt, and him used to a good stable and lots of men.

He musta bin scared stiff. He was a great big ugly horse, seventeen hands high, an' I bet he was a brave horse."

"Did he die?" said Donald, his eyes blazing.

"No, he didn't die."

"Yes, he did. I KNOW he did."

"You can't know because he didn't. He was fetched by a steamer or something . . ."

"He DIED," said Donald with a blazing, inner look.

"He didn't, he didn't. He won the National."

"He died on that island," said Donald like a fanatic. "I was there."

"You weren't. What a story. You weren't born."

"I was born, I was born . . ."

"You were a star," said Edwina annoyingly.

"I wasn' a star. I was born an' I was there an' that horse died. He died on that salty place an' I saw 'im die and he lay down an' his eyes . . ."

"Hysterics," said Mrs. Brown calmly and whisked him up. "He's never any good when he's missed his hour." Donald went to bed weeping and was asleep in ten minutes.

"You didn't wash him, mother!" said Mally, scandalized, on her mother's return.

"Wants sleep, not washin'," said Mrs. Brown. "Now, Velvet!"

"Just after Donald? Not NOW?"

"This minute."

"I must put my shell-box away."

"Put it away."

"I'll put the race-horses in at the bottom."

In went Manifesto, Tipperary Tim, Sergeant Murphy, Ally Sloper, Why Not, and Shannon Lass,—five right-handers and one left. Then the Shetland, then the four ponies, and on the very top of all the prize among her findings (another theft from the Free Library book) the little grey stallion,

the Lamb (by Zouave—dam by Arthur).

"There they are," she said with a sigh, and shut the lid.

"Cheer up, Velvet," said Mr. Brown.

"Feels mixed up," said Mrs. Brown. "Get on, Velvet, don't hang about."

Slowly Velvet climbed the wooden stairs to bed. Her head seemed hardly to have touched the pillow when mother, dressed in her pink dressing gown, shook her in her bed. Dizzy, she rose, and, shivering, dressed, then swallowed the hot cocoa, and holding a piece of cold sausage in her fingers climbed into the lobby of the horse-box which had arrived in the dark before dawn. Her suitcase was stuffed in after her, Mi arrived, carrying another through the dark yard, a spaniel yelped from Miss Ada's tool shed, and the box was off, The Piebald already housed by Mi twenty minutes earlier.

"We're off, we're off!" whispered Velvet.

"Tscht!" said Mi. "You stow it till it gets light," and he settled himself on the straw to finish his night's sleep.

Endless journey in the horse-box till the South gave way to the North, bit by bit, and the day was broken by fresh packets of sandwiches.

"Don't we stop anywhere, Mi?" said Velvet as the hours crawled on.

But Mi was full of thought. There was a frown on his forehead and an edge to his tongue, and now and again he glanced at his large suitcase.

The horse-box driver, hired from Worthing, was a stranger, a glum fellow who seemed to have no interest in horses, the Grand National, the countryside, or the passengers he carried. His eye was glazed on the road ahead of him, and his mind was mesmerised by hours on the clock and miles to be covered, and the relation of those to each other.

Five miles outside Aintree they paused and broke the journey for a pot of tea. Mi glanced at Velvet and rose.

"You off?" said the driver, half asleep over his cup.

"Girl got an aunt here," said Mi gruffly. "Takin' her to her aunt."

The driver slipped his legs out and lay back deeply in his chair. His eyes closed.

It took Mi twenty minutes to get Velvet's hair chopped perfunctorily in the lobby of the horse-box. It was the back by the nape of the neck that took the time. He bent down and crushed the sweepings in among the straw with the horse.

"Whiter'n straw," he muttered. "Looks like stubble."

"Won't he come any minute?" said Velvet anxiously.

"Any minute," said Mi. "Can't be helped. Got nowhere else to do it. Pull up them trousers and give me yer skirt." The aged little skirt, the width of a schoolboy's pants, was stuffed into the suitcase.

"Where'd you get 'em all?"

"Don't talk. Hurry. Slip your arm in the braces, they're all ready."

A hard white collar, slightly soiled, and a spotted tie hung on a nail.

"Can you manage 'em?"

"Yes, I expect. Is there a stud?"

Mi took his own from his neck, and tied his handkerchief in its place.

"You manage 'em an' I'll go an' talk to him if he wakes."

"What'll I do when I'm finished?"

"Slope round the back an' wait about. When we've gone get some tea or ginger an' sit in there. Here's a shilling. I'll be back in a couple of hours, near. Then we'll take the tram into Liverpool an' go an' have a look at the Adelphi. Look sharp now."

The little man who emerged from the back of the horse-van was very much thrown together. As he walked he seemed to settle down; he turned up his coat collar to hide the badly-tied tie, and jammed his greasy hat more confidently over his brow.

Mi and the driver emerged, the engine started, the horse-box moved away.

The skies, which had held off, now lowered and broke. Rain fell and the little man stirred his cold tea endlessly, fencing the occasional questions from the landlady.

The landlady had no sort of doubt.

"It's a girl," she said to her husband in the kitchen.

"No business of ours," said her husband.

"None," she agreed.

The inn was empty, the rain thudded, the white-faced clock tocked on, no customer came in. When Mi pushed the door open and dropped down upon the mat Velvet woke with a jerk from a cold half-sleep.

They started up the road, Mi carrying the heavy suitcase, Velvet the small papier-mâché one she had brought. The trams began half a mile away, but by the time they reached them rain was entering their collars and wallowing in their shoes.

Climbing on to the hard seats they jolted off, huddling close together for warmth, the little sturdy man with the red hair and the lad with the greasy Homburg hat.

"What's the Adelphi?" said the lad, low.

"Toff's place," said the other. "Maybe it's too toff. I've forgot. There's the Stork too. We'll walk round and see."

"Be wet. Walking round."

"Couldn't be wetter."

"Funny, that chap driving off with my hair."

"Turn your head round this way

and let's look." Mi inspected the nape of the neck under the Homburg hat.

"I'll have to trim it better," he said, "s'choppy."

Chapter Twelve

Drenched with rain they stood at the portals of the Adelphi. Mi laid his hand on the little man's shoulder. "Mind the porter!" he said in a whisper. "Stand back here behind the concrete. I gone an' forgot. This place is too swell."

"Feet are sopped," said the little man.

"This rain's like ink. It's a bad start off. Stop a minute . . ."

"Ah," said the little man and looked hungrily through the revolving doors. "Coo lummy," he whispered, "aren't they gay in there! It's all looking-glass!"

They were on the arrival terrace of the Adelphi above the dripping Square, rustling with the noise of falling rain and overflowing pipes. The trams nosed by, the wet lamps flashed, "Ovaltine" went in and out, the grey buildings were polished with water.

"See the toffs go in," said Mi as the taxis drew up. "Gawd, ther's Lord Derby!"

"Where?"

"Crossing the hall, see? Why . . . he's got Tommy Weston with him."

"The big man?"

"No, his Lordship's the big one. Let's go to the Stork."

They trudged away in the rain, Mi carrying the bigger suitcase, which seemed to be melting at one corner.

"S'chap wantsa room," said Mi. "He's a foreign. Name Tasky. I'm not looking for one for myself. I'm lodged."

The Stork took them in.

Velvet stared at him.

They went up the stairs to a small room at the back.

"How'd you mean you're lodged?"

"Tsch! Talk quiet."

They reached number seven, went in, and Mi shut the door. It was a bare room with a small bed and a sixty-volt electric light.

"I don' need a room. See? I got to do some nosing round. There's chaps I'll see an' chaps I'll listen to. I might go round to th' Adelphi."

"The Adelphi!"

"Why not? Place is full o' chaps like me. Not on the top level. Round the pantries. You can see things if you cross the hall purposeful from time to time. Nobody asks. There's the telephone lobbies. Head lads doing a bit of telephoning. Michael Beary'll be chatting about I daresay."

"Who's he?"

"Dear God, Velvet!"

"Eh . . . I'll never get my feet warm," said Velvet, sighing.

"Get undressed an' I'll poke round an' get you a hot bottle."

"But . . . Me being a lad . . ."

"Yepp. Beat your feet with a brush, then. I'll do it."

"Rub 'em."

"Beat's better. Where's the brush?"

Velvet knelt down and undid her suitcase. "I didn't bring a brush," she said, desisting suddenly. "I thought my hair, now it's off . . ."

"I done it not so bad," said Mi with pride. "It's white skin where the hair used to hang. I'll snip it cleaner in the morning."

"Can't we get something? It's the one place that shows when I've got

that cap on. How much money you got left?"

"Precious little," said Mi. "Enough fer your room an' gettin' out there. You get into bed an' I'll come back in ten minutes."

Velvet lay shivering in bed, too tired to turn out the devouring light which blanched her under its beams. The bones of her forehead were sore when she pressed her head in her hands.

Mi returned. He carried a tiny glass full of a brilliant green liquid, placed it carefully on the mantelpiece and took out from under his coat a gin bottle which he had filled with boiling water.

"There goes one an' six," he said. "We gotta be careful."

Velvet opened her eyes.

"Got this in the yard at the back," said Mi, shoving the gin bottle under the bed-clothes and near her feet. "Filled it myself. That's peppermint drink on the mantelpiece. Alcohol. It'll keep till the morning. It's mint an' spirits. Now you go to sleep an' I'll look in some time in the night."

He went out and shut the door, leaving the light still on. Velvet slept fitfully beneath its glare, unaware of what was amiss. At three Mi looked in but she was still and he closed the door. At five he came in and found her awake. It was yet deep night, the light on and the windowpane black.

"Streaming outside," he said. He looked white and tired. Then, turning to the mantelpiece, "You've *drank that stuff!*"

"I thought I was going to die," said Velvet, sitting up and looking bright, "n'hour ago. The room was going round. I got up an' drank it off. S'marvellous. Have you got another one an' six case I feel worse?"

"I might have," said Mi, sitting

down on the one hard chair. "Don't you go taking to drink."

"Drink? Is it drink?"

"Told you it was spirits."

"Well, I forgot. I was bad. It's saved me. Just look at that black rain on the glass. They won't put the race off, will they?"

"The going'll be heavy as lead. Now see, Velvet. You ready to listen to a lot o' things?"

"Yes, Mi."

"Well an' ready? 'Cos I got a lot to say."

"Yes, Mi."

"Well, first here's a map of the Course. I got it from a chap. You oughta walked round with me this morning but it's so wet an' if I get you tired you'll be no use. Besides it's best you do without seeing what the other side o' Becher's is like."

"When did you see it?"

"When did I see it? Didn't I tell you I know it all up here like my thumb? One time I used to shift coal on trucks on the line alongside Becher's. You can't see much on the National, there's such a crowd, but the Liverpool Autumn Meeting in November you got all to yourself. You can stand up there an' see the ambulance come an' see the men standing there with ropes ready an' all."

"Ooh, Mi, ready for what?"

"Ready to lug the horses out of the drop."

"Ooh—Mi."

"Huh! It's not going to happen to you! You got The Piebald jumping under you. Don't you forget that. All I mean is don't be surprised when you ride at Becher's, an' don't think you've jumped over the lip of a quarry, 'cos it isn't a quarry and you'll stop dropping in the end an' if you're not surprised the horse won't be."

"Yes, Mi."

"Now. We'll take the jumps all

round. Same as if you were walking round, which you should be."

Mi pulled his chair up to Velvet's bed and flattened the thin paper map on her sheet.

"Plan of the Liverpool Racecourse," it said. "Distance of Grand National Course about four miles 856 yards."

"Now then," said Mi. "Just listen. You start . . . *here* at the corner. It says 'Paddock' just behind."

"Yes, Mi."

"(An' don' keep saying, 'Yes, Mi.') Don't fuss too much about your start. It's no odds getting off in a tear-away. What you got to do is to jump round and jump clean and go as fast as you can when you know what you're doing. But wait till you know what you're doing before you hurry. Mind you, he doesn't know nothing about racing. He won't be hard to hold. I know you got him under your thumb. Now. . . . First you cross a road. On tan. The tan'll fly up in your eye. Keep 'em shut across the road. Then the first fence. Plain fence. Then the next. Plain fence. You done just as big in the mushroom valley. There's nothing in them, but don't you despise 'em. Many's come down in the first two. There won't be much tailing there. You'll be all clustered up.

"Then comes a rail, ditch, and fence. I'm not saying it isn't an awful whopper for them as stands at the sides an' looks. It looks awful from the truckway. But it won't look so bad to you, you won't know it. You'll see a yellow-looking log lying low on the ground and you must take off in time before it. It's on the lip of the ditch. It's not the landing so much there as the take-off.

"Then there's two more thorn fences. Then there's Becher's.

"Now *there's no need to fall at Becher's.* No need at all. I watched it an' I know. If I was sitting below you

on the far side I wouldn't want to see the eyes popping out of your head as you came down. Just sit back. If you lie back you'll only be upright to the ground. Don't jerk his head whatever you do. It's a long way down but he'll land steady. Just keep as still as if you were a dummy, and put confidence into him."

"What's the drop, Mi?"

"I don' know but it looks twenty. On account of the ditch at the bottom. But you clear the ditch. That's nothing to do with you. You land on up-hill grass an' gallop on. Then there's a . . . (I can't read that one! It's printed on the black. It's a plain jump anyway.) Then there's the Canal Turn . . ."

"Mi, I can't remember it all!"

"Put yer mind to it. The Canal Turn's a teaser. You got to put yer mind to it. There's a chance of horses running out there. They got a screen up to stop it but they seem to want to run out to the left. There's the canal shinin' right ahead. Perhaps that's it. They don't want to swim.

"You want to make for the middle of the jump at the Canal Turn. Don't you go skidding in to the left and saving ground. If you get on the inside as they turn an' you've just landed, God help you. Even if you can't remember anything else remember to keep to the middle at the Canal Turn. You can't go wrong. There's the Canal shinin' just in front of you. A pack of seagulls'll rise most likely as you come up. They always do."

"Mi, I swear I can't remember any more."

"But I gotta tell you about Valentine's."

"I'm getting sick again. You're making me sick again."

"You're a nice one. Wish I'd got you a double!"

"That mint stuff?"

"M'm. Gotta get all this into you. Even if I drop the rest of the jumps I gotta tell you it's twice round the Course."

"Well, I know that! Is it too early to get the mint?"

"It's not six yet. It's dark. Gosh a'mighty look at the rain!" Mi walked to the window.

"Well, go on. But not about the jumps. Yes . . . tell me about the water jump."

"The water jump's pink," said Mi despondently.

"How d'you mean?"

"You got to say to yourself, 'It's pink. I gotta jump all of the pink.'"

"Why's it pink?"

"Everything else is grey," said Mi, dully. "The water's puddled on pink clay. It looks meaty. It's opposite the Grand Stand. The people'll be yelling."

"Go on, Mi! Tell me some more!" Velvet sat up straighter seeing that her supporter was flagging.

"M'murdering you, Velvet? V'I brought you up here to kill you . . . ?"

"No fear. No you aren't! You're tired. You're soppy! It's no more'n a day's hunting."

"Oh, yes, it is! An' you never done a day's hunting."

"Come on, Mi. Piebald an' me'll go round like crickets. Tell me some more."

"I wish yer mother was here, Velvet."

"She *is* here! She's inside me. Ain't you always telling me that if she hadn't swum the Channel I shouldn't be up here?"

"Tha's true. But you get so sick an' all. It's an awful drawback, this vomiting."

"I'll grow out of it."

"I'll get you some more mint when it's daylight."

"Where's the money coming from?"

"I got that much. On'y we gotta be careful. It don' matter f'we land at the end of the race without a bean but we gotta have enough to get there."

"How we going out?"

Mi looked at her. "Taxi," he said. "That's what I bin saving up for. Chap'll do it fer three and six."

"Gosh!" said Velvet.

"I gotta get you out there fresh . . . see?"

"Well then, come on then, tell me some more."

"Look here now, I talked to a lotta chaps. This is how it is. Them jumps in the valley you gather yer horse up, don't you?"

"Yes."

"Well, you can't go on doing that twice roun' the National. Or if you do you gotta do it like silk. 'Cos when a horse gets as done as that he can't stand being gathered up, not like you would at the beginning. You gotta haul him in. You remember that! You gotta haul him in s'though he . . . s'though he was a big fish that was on'y half hooked. When he gets on to the Racecourse . . ."

"At the beginning?"

"No . . . that's what they call the end. The Racecourse. It means getting on to the straight after the jumps. It's when you get off the National Course an' come galloping up on the Gold Cup Course just before the Grand Stand. They call it 'coming on to the Racecourse.'"

"Yes, Mi. Yes . . . well, I mean?"

"What was I saying? Oh, yes. When the horses get on to the second round, or a bit after (some don't do it till the second time Becher's), they begin to get their necks stickin' out so far you wouldn't know 'em. They can't jump like that. On the other

374 ENID BAGNOLD

hand if you pull 'em in with a jerk you throw 'em down. You want to haul. You want to take a pull an' a pull, s'gentle s'though you got 'em on a piece of silk an' it'll break. You gotta judge yourself how much you'll hustle after you've landed an' how soon before the next you'll take a little swig at the hauling."

Quite suddenly Mi dozed. Velvet sat and looked at him and tried to remember the order of the jumps. The map had fallen out of his hand on to the floor but she did not like to disturb him to reach for it. The rain slashed and dribbled on the whitening pane. The electric light flickered once or twice as though the power stations were swimming up into daylight and meeting the morning shift. Mi woke again with a start.

"Th' Adelphia's full o' chaps," he said at once, brightly. "They say 'Yellow Messenger's' your trouble. He's a bay. Seventeen hands. Yellow jacket, crimson sleeves. And the Yank horse too. 'Bluebottle.' I shouldn't bother though. Just go round s'though you was alone."

"You bin about all night?"

"Won't hurt this one night in the year. It's nearly six. I'm going to get you some breakfast. Everyone's about already."

"Shall I get up?"

"No, you stop there. You'll be warmer. No point taking you about till I've got to. I'm going to get some stuff somewhere to tan up your neck."

Mi left her with the map to study and went out. Velvet looked idly at the map but she seemed to learn nothing from it. The rain and the blackness and the night had beaten everything flat in her. "I wish Mi hadn't told me so much," she thought. "I like it to come to me while I'm doing it." And she pushed the map slightly to one side and shut her mind against

it. Mi came in with some coffee and slices of white bread and a square of butter.

"Mi," she said at once, "don't tell me a thing more. I want just to slide along till it's time thinking of nothing at all."

"Huh!" said Mi, putting the tray on the one chair. "Think a race like this is won by luck?"

"Everyone riding to-day," said Velvet, "knows more'n I do. I can't win that way."

"What's your way, then?"

"Jus' knowin' The Piebald can do it, an' tellin' him so," said Velvet, buttering her bread.

"Easy with that butter," said Mi. "Spread it thin. You've no stomach for grease. Here's the stuff for your neck. It's iodine. I borrowed it."

"Won't it smell that blood-smell?"

"It'll wear off. We'll put a drop of water to it so it won't look so yellow. Bend your head down, let's try."

Mi had mixed a drop or two in the tooth glass, and painted it on below the white cropped hair. "It's that queer hair of yours is the trouble," said Mi. "Look like an albino."

"What's that?"

"Soft chaps. Soft-shell chaps, like eggs."

"Gimme the cap an' le's look."

Mi dived into the suitcase and pulled out a black silk cap. Velvet drew it over her cropped hair and well over her eyes.

"It's not too bad," said Mi. "Not much hair shows. The brown of your neck's much better, but where'll I end it off?"

"Wash it round weaker an' weaker with water."

Mi did his best.

Slowly the morning drew into wet daylight.

"Now I'm going out to the horse,"

said Mi. "I got him locked in an' I got the key. I'll pay the bill here. Don't you move till twelve."

"All that time?"

"You'll give yourself away if you put your nose out. At twelve jus' walk down with the bag an' walk out an' pop into the taxi."

"What taxi?"

"He'll be waiting. He don' know nothing about you but he's a chap I used to know. He'll be here at twelve sharp waiting to pick you up. Ferret-faced chap but he's all right."

"Where'll I find you?"

"He'll bring you to where I want you, near the Course. I'll have your dinner waiting for you."

"Don' give me anything to eat, Mi. Not jus' before like that. I'll never stand it."

"Not a ham sandwich?" said Mi, arrested at the door.

"Oh, my God," said Velvet.

The morning drifted by. Velvet rose and became the little man. At twelve to the tick he walked sharply down the stairs carrying his suitcase. He had padded shoulders, a common suit, a dingy white shirt and pale blue tie, a brownish overcoat with a half belt and Mi's old Homburg hat spotted with oil.

The taxi was there, the little man nodded and stepped inside. Under his coat he had an empty heart. He was crushed by delay and the rain.

The taxi took him through the mean streets for twenty minutes. It seemed impossible that so great a race-course could lie buried in so mean a place. Suddenly there was a clearing on the right, and gates. Like the clearing and the gates of a cemetery lying in the surf of a metropolis. The taxi stopped and the little man leant out of the window. Mi walked towards him from the corner of a fence.

Chapter Thirteen

This was the North with its ever-lasting white railings. The stands were filling already. The Union Jack, Stars and Stripes, and Tricolour flew over the Grand Stand. The minor bookies under their stand-umbrellas had been in position since eleven. Their fantastic names were chalked on boards so that they looked like a fresh haul of fish in a market. "Special this Day! Bream . . . Ernie Bream . . . Alfy Haddock . . . Mossie Halibut . . . Duke Cod!" They were shouting and clattering and taking turns in gangs at the Snack Bar. Everything else was more or less awaiting the glory of the day. "Champagne Bar . . . Champagne only." This was empty. Inside the dining-room the white tables were spread and the knowing old waiters

hung like old flies swarming in door-ways.

The police had marched out in a dark stream an hour before and had taken up positions round the Course. There was a constable at every jump with a folded stretcher laid beside him, its rug within its folds. Each man had a red flag and a yellow flag with which to call his neighbour.

The Public was flowing in like a river.

The whole Course was blackening on the rim like a lake that has thrown up seaweed upon its banks. It had been black since daylight, but the sea-weed was deepening and deepening, the truckway was solid with life, the ten-shilling Stand at the Canal Turn was groaning, the Melling Road,

which crossed the Course, from being an ivory band across the green became an ebony. Great passenger aeroplanes hummed over the stands and made their descent. A foreign king and queen arrived in Lord Sefton's box.

Tattersalls was like a thawed ice-rink. Pools had long appeared over the Course. Thousands and thousands of people were wet, but not yet to the skin. And they hardly felt it.

The Changing Room for jockeys was warm and gay like a busy nursery. Jockeys' valets, with the air of slightly derelict family butlers, had been ironing in their shirt-sleeves since seven in the morning. Two large coal fires behind nursery wire-guards were burning briskly, and over the guards hung strips of colour. Gipsy silks were all across the long tables stretched down the middle, and the valets ironed and pressed and swore and grunted and cleaned soft boots and hunted for odds and ends in their enormous suitcases, the travelling houses of their livelihood. Down one side of the room hung little saddles, touching little saddles. Below them saddle cloths, numnahs, girths. Below them on the boot boxes countless little boots. Brown boots with black tops so soft you could hardly walk in them. Boots like gloves that are drawn on to a child's ankle, and filled out with a child's toes. Boots as touching as the saddles.

Outside in the Weighing Room the hooded scales had been uncloaked and the Clerk of the Scales was already at his desk. The Declaration Counter had its pens and inks and its stacks of empty forms waiting to be filled.

In the hospital room the nurse put a few more coals, delicately with her coal pincers, on to the bright fire.

While the second race was being run Mi signed "Michael Taylor" at the foot of his declaration card, and

paused a second higher up the card. "James Tasky" he wrote firmly. Then filled in the horse's name. He blotted the card and passed it into the box.

Then he went back to a little haunt of his.

. . . .

"Now . . ." he said, half an hour later, crooking his finger in the doorway, and the little man picked up his suitcase and followed him.

"I'll take that," said Mi huskily.

Mi hustled the little man in past the unsaddling enclosure to the holy stillness of the Weighing Room, and through the swing door into a corner of the Changing Room, pushing him down on a boot-box overshadowed by hanging garments.

"They're nak . . ." gasped the little man, sitting down.

"Tscht!" muttered Mi, standing over him.

The jockeys' valets bustled here and there, grumbled, stumbled, fell over boots. Two of their charges with hard red faces and snowy bodies were standing naked by the nursery fireguard. Mi looked grimly down at the little man.

"Keep yer eyes on yer knees," he muttered fiercely. And knelt to hold up the white breeches he had fished out of the suitcase.

"Who's your lady-friend?" said one of the naked midgets, turning round to warm his other buttock.

"Miss Tasky. From Russia," said Mi without a flicker.

"Speak English?" said the midget, turning again like a chicken on a spit.

"No use wasting any dope on him," said Mi. "Can't speak a bloody word. He's a Bolshie they've sent over. To pick the winnings!"

"You sim to be doing the lady-friend to the lady-friend all right?"

"Doin' what I'm paid for," said Mi.

"Times are ugly down South. I on'y jus' come up."

"Well, of all the muck-rakin' cheek," said the other naked midget, scratching his stomach . . . "that's that Tasky's riding that out-a-condition, pot-bellied whisky horse I saw brought in last night. Turnin' the Gran' National into a bloody circus!" and he cracked the end bone of his index finger like a pistol shot.

"Come on, Bibby, get dressed, do," begged an austere butler. "Going to ride the National in your pink skin?"

As Bibby turned away Tasky stood up gently, black, pink sleeves, black cap, white breeches, little black boots, brown tops. Mi pulled the saddle, saddle cloth and numnah, off the iron bracket. "Sit down an' wait," he said loudly as to a foreigner, pushed him back on the boot-box and stood over him.

Then, on the door opening, "They want you for the chair," he said.

"Thought he didn't understand English," said a voice.

"No reason why 'e shouldn't begin," said Mi. "CHAIR, I said," he yelled into Tasky's ear. "Come on!"

Outside in the Weighing Room all was quiet and regulated. "That's a toff," thought Mi, seeing a tall man get off the chair. He was obviously a gentleman rider, a "bumper."

"Weight?" said the Clerk of the Scales.

"Ten seven, near enough," said Mi. "He don't speak no English, sir. Russian."

Mi pushed the little man towards the scales. "Sit, can't you," he said in a hoarse whisper. "Double up!"

Tasky sat in the chair and nursed his saddle.

"Ten six and eleven," said the Clerk's assistant.

"Penny piece," said the Clerk quietly, and dropped a small piece of lead into the weight flap.

"An' a half," said the Clerk. In went another piece. The Clerk wrote carefully in his book.

"Get off," hissed Mi. Tasky never budged.

Mi gave him a pull. "Job, sir, this is," he said. "Seems more a nitwit than . . ." He bustled the little man out of the room, throwing his brown overcoat round his shoulders.

"Who's that?" said someone, opening the door of the Stewards' Room.

"The Russian, sir," said the Clerk of the Scales, looking up at the Clerk of the Course.

The heavy, streaming daylight broke on them. The worst for Mi was over, the worst for Velvet to come.

"Keep in the crowd," said Mi. "I got to go for the horse. Keep movin'. Don't come out into the open. Don't rush at the horse when you see me lead him out. I got to go roun' and roun'. Wait till you see the others walk in to the Paddock . . ."

"Paddock?"

"Rails. There. Walk straight up to near me and stand by the bushes in the middle. I'll lead him up to you. I'll jump you up."

"Jump me up?"

"Jump you. I gotta take yer knee an' jump you. Like the horse was too high fer you to get on. I'll take yer coat and I'll lead you out an' that's all I can do for you."

"You going now?" said Velvet, small, small in voice.

"I'm going. An' I got togs. You'll see. White leading rein an' all. Borrowed 'em off a head lad, friend o' mine."

Mi was gone and Velvet drifted through the crowd.

But suddenly Mi was back again. "Keep your eyes skinned an' keep

AWAY from everyone who'll talk!" he hissed, and was gone again.

The crowd buzzed round the Tote, and many looked curiously at Velvet's black cap and bony childish face. She was not unlike an apprentice lad.

The horses were parading in the Paddock. There came The Piebald. Velvet stared at him in shivering appreciation. He wore borrowed clothes with a knotted yellow rope bumping on his quarters. Mi led him with a white leading rein, wide like a tape. The number . . . 4 . . . was tied on Mi's left arm. As he came into the Paddock a buzz came from the crowd and here and there laughter. Round and round went the horses, and the rain down Velvet's neck.

Suddenly she saw the little men go in. Wide shoulders, gay caps and little feet. She walked forward, entered the Paddock, and went straight to the bushes. There was a pause. The horses circled. Every jockey went up to his Owner. She alone had no one. She stood firm and looked around her, conscious that this was her worst moment today.

Then up came Mi with The Piebald. She stripped her coat off and he held it on his arm, pulled the rugs off the horse on to his shoulder, stooped to her left leg and flung her up into the saddle. Almost at once the horses moved away, Mi walking beside her to the gate.

She was quite definite, quite easy. Now it was over, the creeping like a thief, the doubts, the waiting. No one would stop her now. The worst moments had come and gone, and there could be no doubt at all that now she and The Piebald were in together for the Grand National.

"There . . . I never told you," said Mi, low and hoarse, walking beside her. "Don't lie up on his neck! But it's too late now . . ."

"Ssh," said Velvet, looking straight ahead of her at something that seemed like a crane upon a raised embankment.

"I'll not 'ssh'!" said Mi, his heart bursting. "I'll say, 'Think of yer ma!' "

He snipped off the leading rein by its chromium hook and The Piebald swung through the gate.

"Gawd . . . a'might . . ." said Mi, struck short. "I never told her to ride down in front of the Stands before going to the post . . ."

But for Velvet it was only follow-my-leader. She went down easily with the other horses, turned, stood slightly in her saddle, and galloped back. Mi started running for the truckway. "I'll never make Becher's . . . not in this crowd. Not unless there's a muck-up at the post."

Just ahead of him, turning out from the stable-roadway, came the black motor ambulance, with the doctor sitting sideways in the back, looking at a paper. Behind the ambulance, from the same turning, crawled out a sinister, square-bottomed coffin, a knacker's cart, drawn by an enormous pigeon-chested shire-horse. Ahead of the ambulance, and blocking the way, went the horse ambulance, with its crane, drawn by two shire-horses in tandem. All made their way to Becher's. Another knacker's cart was trundling along far away by Valentine's, and yet another pushed its way in Melling Road.

"Black slugs . . ." said Mi, running, panting, pushing.

• • • •

At the post the twenty horses were swaying like the sea. Forward. . . . No good! Back again. Forward. . . . No good! Back again.

The line formed . . . and rebroke. Waves of the sea. Drawing a breath . . . breaking. Velvet fifth from the

rail, between a bay and a brown. The Starter had long finished his instructions. Nothing more was said aloud, but low oaths flew, the cursing and grumbling flashed like a storm. An eye glanced at her with a look of hate. The breaking of movement was too close to movement to be borne. It was like water clinging to the tilted rim of the glass, like the sound of the dreaded explosion after the great shell has fallen. The will to surge forward overlaid by something delicate and terrible and strong, human obedience at bursting-point, but not broken. Horses' eyes gleamed openly, men's eyes set like chips of steel. Rough man, checked in violence, barely master of himself, barely master of his horse. The Piebald ominously quiet, and nothing coming from him . . . up went the tape.

The green Course poured in a river before her as she lay forward, and with the plunge of movement sat in the stream.

.

"Black slugs . . ." said Mi, cursing under his breath, running, dodging, suffocated with the crowd. It was the one thing he had overlooked, that the crowd was too dense ever to allow him to reach Becher's in the time. Away up above him was the truck-line, his once-glorious free seat, separated from him by a fence. "God's liver . . ." he mumbled, his throat gone cold, and stumbled into an old fool in a mackintosh. "Are they off?" he yelled at the heavy crowd as he ran, but no one bothered with him.

He was cursed if he was heeded at all. He ran, gauging his position by the cranes on the embankment. Velvet coming over Becher's in a minute and he not there to see her. "They're off." All around him a sea of throats offered up the gasp.

He was opposite Becher's but could see nothing: the crowd thirty deep between him and the Course. All around fell the terrible silence of expectancy. Mi stood like a rock. If he could not see then he must use his ears, hear. Enclosed in the dense, silent, dripping pack he heard the thunder coming. It roared up on the wet turf like the single approach of a multiple-footed animal. There were stifled exclamations, grunts, thuds. Something in the air flashed and descended. The first over Becher's! A roar went up from the crowd, then silence. The things flashing in the air were indistinguishable. The tip of a cap exposed for the briefest of seconds. The race went by like an express train, and was gone. Could Velvet be alive in that?

Sweat ran off Mi's forehead and into his eyes. But it was not sweat that turned the air grey and blotted out the faces before him. The ground on all sides seemed to be smoking. An extraordinary mist like a low prairie fire was formed in the air. It had dwelt heavily all day behind the Canal, but the whole of the Course had remained clear till now. And now, before you could turn to look at your neighbour, his face was gone. The mist blew in shreds, drifted, left the crowd clear again but hid the whole of the Canal Corner, fences, stand and horses.

There was a struggle going on at Becher's; a horse had fallen and was being got out with ropes. Mi's legs turned to water and he asked his neighbour gruffly, "Who's fallen?" But the neighbour, straining to the tip of his toes, and glued to his glasses, was deaf as lead.

Suddenly Mi lashed round him in a frenzy. "Who's fallen, I say? Who's hurt!"

"Steady on," said a little man whom he had prodded in the stomach.

"Who's fallen?" said Mi desperately. "I gotta brother in this . . ."

"It's his brother!" said the crowd all around him. "Let him through."

Mi was pushed and pummelled to the front and remained embedded two from the front line. The horse that had fallen was a black horse, its neck unnaturally stretched by the ropes that were hauling it from the ditch.

There was a shout and a horse, not riderless, but ridden by a tugging, cursing man, came galloping back through the curling fumes of the mist, rolled its wild eye at the wrong side of Becher's and disappeared away out of the Course. An uproar began along the fringes of the crowd and rolled back to where Mi stood. Two more horses came back out of the mist, one riderless. The shades of others could be discerned in the fog. Curses rapped out from unseen mouths.

"What's happened at the Canal Turn? What's wrong down at the Turn?"

"The whole field!" shouted a man. The crowd took it up.

"The field's out. The whole field's come back. There's no race!" It was unearthly. Something a hundred yards down there in the fog had risen up and destroyed the greatest steeplechase in the world.

Nineteen horses had streamed down to the Canal Turn, and suddenly, there across the Course, at the boundary of the fog, four horses appeared beyond Valentine's, and among them, fourth, was The Piebald.

"Yer little lovely, yer little lovely," yelled Mi, wringing his hands and hitting his knees. "It's her, it's him, it's me brother!"

No one took any notice. The scene immediately before them occupied all the attention. Horses that had fallen galloped by riderless, stirrups flying

from their saddles, jockeys returned on foot, covered with mud, limping, holding their sides, some running slowly and miserably over the soggy course, trying to catch and sort the horses.

"It's 'Yellow Messenger,'" said a jockey savagely, who had just seized his horse. "Stuck on the fence down there and kicking hell." And he mounted.

"And wouldn't they jump over him?" called a girl shrilly.

"They didn't wanter hurt the pore thing, lady," said the jockey, grinning through his mud, and rode off.

"Whole lot piled up and refused," said a man who came up the line. "Get the Course clear now, quick!"

"They're coming again!" yelled Mi, watching the galloping four. "Get the Course clear! They'll be coming!"

They were out of his vision now, stuck down under Becher's high fence

as he was. Once past Becher's on the second round would he have time to extricate himself and get back to the post before they were home? He stood indecisively and a minute went by. The Course in front of him was clear. Horses and men had melted. The hush of anticipation began to fall. "They're on the tan again," said a single voice. Mi flashed to a decision. He could not afford the minutes to be at Becher's. He must get back for the finish and it would take him all his time. He backed and plunged and ducked, got cursed afresh. The thunder was coming again as he reached the road and turned to face the far-off Stands. This time he could see nothing at all, not even a cap in the air. "What's leading? What's leading?"

"Big brown. Tantibus, Tantibus. Tantibus leading."

"Where's The Piebald?"

"See that! Leonora coming up . . ."

They were deaf to his frantic questions. He could not wait, but ran. The mist was ahead of him again, driving in frills and wafting sedgily about. Could Velvet have survived Becher's twice? In any case no good wondering. He couldn't get at her to help her. If she fell he would find her more quickly at the hospital door than struggle through the crowd and be forbidden the now empty Course.

Then a yell. "There's one down!"

"It's the Yank mare!"

The horse ambulance was trundling back with Yellow Messenger from the Canal Turn. Mi leapt for a second on to the turning hub of the wheel, and saw in a flash, across the momentarily mist-clear Course, the pride of Baltimore in the mud underneath Valentine's. The Piebald was lying third. The wheel turned and he could see no more. Five fences from the finish; he would not allow himself to hope, but ran and ran. How far away the Stands in the gaps of the mist as he pushed, gasping, through the people. Would she fall now? What had he done, bringing her up here? But would she fall now? He ran and ran.

"They're coming on to the Racecourse . . . coming on to the Racecourse . . ."

"How many?"

"Rain, rain, can't see a thing."

"How many?"

Down sank the fog again, as a puff of wind blew and gathered it together. There was a steady roaring from the Stands, then silence, then a hub-bub. No one could see the telegraph.

Mi, running, gasped, "Who's won?"

But everyone was asking the same question. Men were running, pushing, running, just as he. He came up to the gates of Melling Road, crossed the road on the fringe of the tan, and suddenly, out of the mist, The Pie-

bald galloped riderless, lolloping unsteadily along, reins hanging, stirrups dangling. Mi burst through on to the Course, his heart wrung.

"Get back there!" shouted a policeman. "Loose horse!"

"Hullo, Old Pie there!" shouted Mi. The animal, soaked, panting, spent, staggered and slipped and drew up.

"What've you done with 'er?" said Mi, weeping, and bent down to lift the hoof back through the rein. "You let 'er down, Pie? What in God's sake?" He led the horse down the Course, running, his breath catching, his heart thumping, tears and rain on his face.

Two men came towards him out of the mist.

"You got him?" shouted one. "Good fer you. Gimme!"

"You want him?" said Mi, in a stupor, giving up the rein.

"Raised an objection. Want him for the enclosure. Chap come queer."

"Chap did? What chap?"

"This here's the winner! Where you bin all day, Percy?"

"Foggy," said Mi. "Very foggy. Oh, my God."

. . . .

Back in the fog a voice had spoken into a telephone. It had need only to say one word. All else had been written out beforehand. And in that very second in the offices of the Associated Press in New York men had taken off the message. "Urgent Associated New York Flash Piebald Wins." The one word the voice had said into the fog was "Piebald."

. . . .

Up went the red flag. The crowd buzzed. "What is it?" "Did he fall?"

"Must've hurt hisself jumping . . ."

"Fainted."

"Jus' dismounted, the silly b . . ."

Dismounted before reaching the unsaddling enclosure. Objection. Up went the red flag. There was tenseness along the line of private bookies, pandemonium in the bookies' stand under the umbrellas, tight knots gathered round the opening to the Weighing Room, behind which was the Stewards' Room. Glasses were levelled from everywhere upon the board. If a white flag went up the objection was over-ruled. If a green it was sustained. But the red remained unwaveringly.

"Taken him round to the hospital."

"Stretcher, was it?"

"Jus' gone through where all those people are . . ."

The doctor had got back from his tour of the Course in his ambulance. Two riders had already been brought in and the nurse had prepared them in readiness for his examination. Now the winner himself coming in on a stretcher. Busy thirty minutes ahead.

"Get him ready, Sister."

The winner lay unconscious wrapped in a horse blanket, his face mottled with the mud that had leapt up from flying hoofs.

"Looks sixteen," said the doctor curiously, and knelt to turn the gas a little lower under the forceps.

"Bin boiling for twenty minutes," said the Sister.

"Place full of steam," said the doctor. "Been watching . . . ?" and he passed to the end cubicle.

"No," said the Sister shortly to his back. She disliked the Grand National, and had waited behind the Stands to patch up the damage.

The constables with the stretcher placed the winner on the bed by the door, leaving him still wrapped in his blanket. They retired and closed the door. The Sister slipped a towel under the muddy head, and turning back the blanket started to undo the soaking jacket of black silk.

"Sister," roared the doctor from another cubicle. . . . "No, stay where you are! I've got it!"

"Could you come here a minute?"

said the Sister, at his side a few minutes later.

The doctor straightened his back. He had a touch of lumbago. "I'll be back, Jem," he said. "You're not much hurt. Cover up. Yes?"

"Just a minute . . . over here."

She whispered to him quietly. He slapped his rain-coated cheek and went to the bed by the door. "Put your screens round." She planted them. "Constable," he said, poking his head out of the door, "get one of the Stewards here, will you." (The roar of the crowd came in at the door.) "One of the Stewards! Quick's you can. Here, I'll let you in this side door. You can get through." The crowd seethed, seizing upon every sign.

.

Mi crouched by the door without daring to ask after his child. He heard the doctor call. He saw the Steward go in. "Anyway," he thought, "they've found out at once. They would. What's it matter if she's all right. She's won, the little beggar, the little beggar. Oh, my God."

.

The Sergeant of Police was by the Stables. "Message from up there," he said briefly to his Second. "Squad to go up to the hospital door. Row round the door. Something up with the winner."

The police marched up in a black snake. The people fell back. An ambulance came in from the Ormskirk Road and backed down the line of police. The red flag remained for a moment, then slowly the green flag mounted on the board. Objection sustained. A frightful clamour burst out in the Grand Stand.

In the Stewards' Room the glittering Manifesto looked down out of his frame and heard the low talk of this appalling desecration. A butcher's girl on a piebald horse had pounced up beside him into history.

"Got her off?" said one of the Stewards in a low voice.

"Just about. There was a bit of a rush for a second. She called out something as the stretcher was being shoved in. Called out she was all right . . . to somebody in the crowd. Good God, it's . . . I'm glad we got her off quick. The crowd's boiling with excitement."

"How'd it get out so quick?"

"I dunno. Swell row this'll be. It'll have to be referred back to Weatherby's." The Clerk of the Course came in. "Crowd's bubbling like kettles out there, Lord Henry. By Jove, it's the biggest ramp. How'd she pull it over!"

"Who's gone with her?"

"The doctor couldn't go. He's got two other men, one a baddish crash at Valentine's."

"Well, somebody ought to 'a' gone. Find out who's gone, will you?"

The Clerk of the Course disappeared.

"Tim's Chance wins, of course."

"Yes, that's been announced. There's no question. The objection is sustained definitely here on the Course, and the rest must be referred to London. There'll be a special of the N.H.C., I should think it might be a case for legal proceedings. Well . . ." (as the door opened) "did you find out who went with her?"

"A second doctor, Lord Henry. A young man who's here very often. Friend of Doctor Bodie's. And a constable."

"There should have been an official. Of course there should have been an official. What's the hospital?"

"Liverpool Central . . ."

"Isn't there a friend or relation with her?"

"Nobody."

"Well, she called out to somebody!"
"The somebody's hidden himself all right. Well for him! She's quite alone s'far as we can make out."
"D'she say anything?"
"Won't speak. Except that one shout she gave."

"If my daughter'd done it," said Lord Henry Vile, "I'd be . . ." He paused and stroked his lip with his finger.
"Pretty upset, I should think . . ."
"I wasn't going to say that," said Lord Henry. "No."

Chapter Fourteen

Almost as soon as the ambulance was off the ground little breezes began to blow hither and thither bearing the fact. Without the name. A girl had won the Grand National.

A girl had won the Grand National. By the look of the stretcher "a slip of a girl." By the memory of the crouching black and pink ant on The Piebald, again "a slip of a girl." The news began to crack like gunpowder trailed to percussion caps. At each percussion cap an explosion. At each explosion men flung, hurled about their business.

The U.P. man on the roof of the Grand Stand went on with his telephoning (at two pounds a minute). He had laid his field glasses down now and was talking feverishly. "Urgent bulletin," he said violently, "astounding rumours circulating track. Is winning jockey girl. We upchecking." And a little later, in his shorthand Chinese, "Stewards' decision. Quiz moved London."

As the ambulance turned into the Ormskirk Road the news had broken. It was flashing to London in waves of light, in waves of air. It was "breaking" on London. At first the smaller men flashed it, unscrupulous, out for speed at all costs. The graver men hung back. Verify, verify! It *couldn't* be. The serious sporting reporters, associated for a lifetime with the Turf, felt it couldn't be. Almost . . . it had better not be. Such frivolity, but, God

. . . what news! NEWS, sparkling, rainbow NEWS. London was disturbed, tickled, a few seconds before the graver men felt they could spring for it. Then they sprang. And the full blast swept down the lines and the airways. Like a whiff . . . the miraculous transmission of accurate, verified, imagination-shaking news. It could hardly be a scoop because before one could close the telephone box everyone knew it. But details . . . where was the girl? In a second, having delivered their blast on London, they turned like hounds after the girl. The ambulance was gone. Where? The Liverpool Central . . . Ah . . . The taxi rank was in the Ormskirk Road.

But once before the Liverpool Central had housed a Fame-Shaker. And the Resident Medical Officer was a grim fellow with yellow hair, blue eyes and set mouth. He had been through the war and he had been through that strange medical upbringing in a good Scottish hospital which gets into a man's bones and transmutes him for ever from common humanity. He was steady and wily and fine, and he could act as quick as news could flash. And for reasons of his own connected with his attitude and their attitude towards truth and scientific thought he had a cold impatience of the Press.

The murmurs surrounding Velvet came with her like raindrops on the

ambulance. She had not long been wheeled into the Women's Accident Ward, and the Sister-in-Charge had hardly propped screens round her bed, before the Resident Medical Officer had mopped up the rumours, his curiously flat ears very wide awake.

"Be down from Aintree," he thought, "in a jiffy."

He found, actually, that they were already drawing up at the gates. The Resident M.O. closed the ward doors and placed the constable who had come with the ambulance on duty.

The constable was not sure it was his right duty . . .

"Just a minute, Officer . . ." said the Resident M.O. swiftly, increasing the constable's rank and giving him a cold-water flash out of the blue eyes. "Not more than a second while we wheel her into a private ward. Can't have the Press in round the bed. I think you'll find that's why you were asked to whip out of Aintree. Right ahead, Sister. 'Nother blanket over her . . . (right over her) when you get her on the trolley."

Two white-coated men sped down the ward with a trolley.

"Over your face, girl, too, for a minute," said the Resident M.O., leaving the constable at the door and going down the ward to meet the trolley. "It's all right. Want to get you into another ward. Quiet."

A nurse sprang to push the double doors back onto their catches for the trolley to pass.

A Press Association man approached the M.O.

"Let the trolley pass," said the M.O. abruptly. "Stand back. Operation case."

The trolley passed swiftly out of view under the nose of bowler-hatted men who were arriving.

But the balloon of notoriety wasn't going to stay on the ground just because of the Principal M.O. The Press Bellows had now begun to blow and the balloon to lift.

Yet the little creature still lay snug like a kernel in the private ward of the Liverpool Central, with the door locked and a Sister giving her a blanket bath. Then in came tea on a tray, two meat sandwiches cut in triangles, a chocolate bun in a paper, a rice bun, a piece of plum cake and two slices of white bread and butter. Velvet snuggled down and began to wonder what next and what next and when the heavens were going to fall. And above all where was Mi?

Mi, rubbing down the piebald horse in the stables at Aintree, was bearing the brunt of everything. He was knee-deep in the Press, he was wanted in the Stewards' Room, he was wanted by everybody. Even the bookmakers would have liked to get at him.

"This horse won the National, ain't it? This horse 'as got to be rubbed down. I don't know a thing 'cept that I was hired to do over the horse. Hired at the last minute. Well . . . what? Well, if I'm wanted in the Stewards' Room I'll have to go. But this horse wants rubbin' and rubbin'. Who's going to do it for me?"

There were plenty of offers. There were even men who had a nodding knowledge of him.

"Why, Mi, you old tout . . . who's your lady friend? D'you mean to say you didn't know? What about the Changing Room? You pulled her breeches on, didn't you?"

"How was I to know? She got pants on, ha'n't she? A girl an' a boy they're that alike you gotter have the pants off to see? I on'y know she couldn't speak a word a' King's English, an' was s'flat's a pancake and as dumb's an oyster . . . Comin', sir . . . Rub him well . . . Give his back-line a

massage . . . under the saddle. Makes the blood flow . . . I'll be back in a minute. I got nothing to say to 'em. Stewards . . . My hat! . . . Comin', sir!"

In the Stewards' Room nothing could be got out of Mi. He was heavy-minded, obstinate and repetitive. Lord Henry Vile did not look as though he believed him, and finally it was decided to take his address and refer the inquest to London, at a special meeting of the National Hunt Committee. Mi gave his address as Post Restante, Lewes.

"Fishy sort of address," said Colonel "Ruby" Allbrow, looking at him straight.

"I can't hide, sir," said Mi, suddenly looking as straight back. "I'm known here to lots, an' I'm known there. The police'd lay their hands on me in a day 'f I was to monkey up."

"And the horse?"

"Horse goes back to the owner, sir. Horse-box is coming for it to-night."

"And not you?"

"Not me, sir."

"And the owner's address . . . We have the owner's address, Mr. Gray?"

"Yes, we have the address," said the official. "The owner must be behind it all, m'lord, if you'll excuse me interrupting."

"Yes . . . that'll be looked into. Letter must be sent and so on. Who's going down to the hospital?"

A spasm crossed Mi's face. He opened his mouth but said nothing. Velvet alone in that hospital. 'S sick as a cat. But there were doctors an' all that. It'd soon be in the papers how she was.

Velvet lay in the hospital refusing her name. She and Mi had no plan beyond the winning of the Grand National. How should they? They had bitten off a piece of dream together, and like winged children accomplished it. Beyond, all was an uncharted sea. They had not had one glance at life after the winning.

Still by instinct she refused her name. The heavens were going to fall. Father was going to know, the village was going to know, Edwina was going to say sarcastic things because Teddy didn't like all the fuss. There was going to be trouble for her and Mi, though pure white glory for The Piebald. And the longer she kept her name secret the slower the trouble would be in coming. She lay and smiled wanly, and shook her clipped white head.

Indeed she wasn't pressed enormously to tell. The M.O. didn't care a rap about her name, and the Sister-in-Charge of her simply washed her and fed her and choked back her curiosity because she too had had a cold-water flash from the blue eyes of the hospital's Despot. The young doctor who had brought Velvet down had disappeared, but he came back later accompanied by Dr. Bodie from Aintree and the Clerk of the Course himself.

The M.O. stared at them with his curious look and told them quietly that they must not stay more than five minutes with the patient. The Sister was present at the interview. The Clerk of the Course asked formally for Velvet's name and address. Dr. Bodie blustered a little when Velvet sighed and said shyly she couldn't give it. The young doctor said nothing. He was more than thrilled whichever way the situation turned. At the end of five minutes the M.O. came himself to say it was time.

"Shock," said the M.O. with a grudging apology in the corridor. "Very young."

After they had gone the M.O. came back. "Sorry, I must have your name for hospital purposes," he said, and

he pulled the silver pencil out of his note-book.

Velvet looked up with confidence into the ledger of that secure face, and said at once "Velvet Brown," and spelt the address clearly for him.

"Age?" he said.

"Fourteen. Nearly fifteen."

"There'll be a doctor up to go over you in a few minutes. Dr. Bodie tells me there's nothing broken."

"I didn't fall off," said Velvet. "I slid off. After the post. I couldn't feel my knees."

"Feel any pain anywhere?"

"No, thank you. I could have got up, only my legs . . ."

"All right. Right. Enjoyed your tea?"

And the M.O. went, like an iron ghost, and the door closed invisibly behind him.

At five-thirty she had a drink of bromide and chloral, and twenty minutes later the gates of the world closed down on her while the second batch of posters in London and Liverpool and all the great cities of England, France, Germany, Italy . . . fell slopily off the printing machines, were baled up, dispatched, and, drying, fluttered at street corners and receded on the backs of newspaper cars. "Drama of Winner of National this afternoon." "Unknown girl wins National." (This paper thought the fact so first-rate that there was no need to attract by mystery.)

"Extraordinary affair at Aintree."

"Piebald wins but disqualified. Rider found to be woman."

Ten minutes later more posters . . .

"Girl winner in Liverpool Central Hospital."

In the great cities of America the boys were calling "Extra!" and the Stop Press of all the papers shone in green, red, and blue ink. From France the *Intransigeant* and the *Paris Soir*

sent two men over in aeroplanes to Aintree. The Associated Press of America got an all-clear interview with the Clerk of the Course. In Shanghai the first 3.30 flash had just caught the last editions of the morning *North China Daily News*. Rome and Berlin did not trouble themselves profoundly. The thing grew and grew and grew, and turned over on itself, and heaped itself up. People walked in the streets not knowing that the air quivered with question marks. The common air, not seeing or tasting or breathing any different, was heavy with one idea, one burden, an incoming wave of query into England. This questioning air, sweeping through impediment in a silvery attack, poured round flesh, wood, and stone till it found the wireless masts and there, settling and transmuting itself into something more possible to human understanding, became the word of man.

There was a pause. The queries massed like birds and waited. "We must know more!" cried every foreign agency and every newspaper.

"You shall know more," soothed the deep voice of Reuter, sedate and cautious, before it ringed the world with its answer.

The reporters had been baffled at the Liverpool Central but Dr. Bodie was got at. Eager, in fact, to be got at.

He could not tell the rider's name but he described this and that, and after a while, the information having been looked over and binged up here and toned down there, and written almost all in most expensive plain language (that there should be no delay anywhere in decoding) Reuter sent round the world the following message . . . "61610 Lead all stop Girl has won and lost Grand National stop Most sensational incident in Aintree history occurred to-day when discovered winning jockey mounted Pie-

bald was young girl stop Since women jockeys unallowed compete National Piebald disqualified by stewards stop Girl fainted after passing post carried ambulance room on stretcher where sex discovered by doctor who states age between 14–16 years stop Faint due fatigue unserious injuries stop Girl who refused reveal identity rode under Russian jockey Taskys' name stop Stewards National Hunt Committee ordered fullest investigation stop For women to complete National course regarded as one most extraordinary feats in annals British racing stop Drama mystery associated this amazing affair whipped up excitement feverpitch countrywide stop Result race now reads . . ." (and the names of the first three horses were given).

As this message left London it flashed in a few seconds along the trunk lines that were being held open for it, through Egypt, to India, South Africa, Australia, and to Singapore and the Far East. From the arteries ran the veins. Men in Shanghai, Sydney, Capetown became disseminators almost at the same moment that they had been receivers. And in a steady spreading belt round the world ran the reply to the frantic queries.

In each country there was a Smaller Proper Machinery to receive it and its re-distribution was carried out in eddies from the main encircling belt. In each country the Smaller Proper Machinery distributed it to the newspapers, and newspapers set it up in print, printed it, issued it, sold it, and it was read by white, brown, yellow, red and black men who exclaimed in their tongues—"Whew!"

Heads of news agencies, heads of syndicates, heads of newspapers said in their various languages, "This is a Press Ballyhoo. Spread all out on this. This is front-page stuff."

"We gotta splurge," said a great man in New York. "Get the dope from that dame. She's swell!" And he cabled, "Ten thousand dollars for exclusive rights of personal story." A girl in London got into a fast car and drove rapidly down to the coast.

It was the great bellows of the Glory-Machine starting to blow. But it had not nearly got its wind up yet. The pink balloon of notoriety had hardly done more than shake loose its ropes and fill out. And the little creature whose name it bore lay very slight, very sheltered, under the deep and fumy blanket.

. . . .

"It's Velvet. Sure's fate it's Velvet," said Mr. Brown, standing in the street doorway. "Come in, gentlemen!"

"Mother! Hi! Come on in here!" he called. "Here's our Velvet gone . . . I feel hot in the stomach, gentlemen. She ain't hurt herself? (I gotta sit down.) She safe?"

Mrs. Brown filled the inner doorway.

"Mother," said Mr. Brown, looking white and shaken, "our Velvet gone an' won the Grand National. Ridden it herself . . ."

Certainly Mrs. Brown's eyes changed their colour in some way. They did not gleam. They were too high in their shallows for that, but a curious light seemed to shift in them.

"She's not one for words, sir," said Mr. Brown, taking out his handkerchief and wiping his hands. "(Fingers gone all sticky. Takes me that way.) I can't take it in what she done. Where is she, then?"

"She's in the Liverpool Central Hospital . . ." began one of the reporters.

"Why?" said Mrs. Brown like a pistol shot.

"Just fatigue, so we understand," said the reporter.

"They're from the newspapers, mother," said Mr. Brown.

"She slipped off her horse, Mrs. Brown," said the reporter. "Fainted after she had passed the winning post. No bones broken, no harm done. Is this the first you have heard of it?"

"Papers don't get here till seven," said Mr. Brown. "On the Tilling's bus." He looked at his watch. "It's a quarter of now."

"Then you have no doubt," said another reporter, "that the rider is also the owner, your daughter Velvet?"

"He don't even know," said Mrs. Brown suddenly. "Don't you tell him nothing, William. I know them."

"Why ever not?" said Mr. Brown. "She's got a bit of a down on newspaper gentlemen, sir," said he apologetically. "Haven't you, mother? She had a bit of a bad time with 'em once."

"Tell 'em what you like. You've begun," said Mrs. Brown, shutting the door. She crossed the room in majesty and went up to her room.

Mr. Brown gave a lengthy interview only interrupted by the gentlemen's desire to get away and to the telephone to catch the last edition of the evening papers.

The reporters were shown the paper horses in the shell-box.

One of them thought the shell-box touching, but did not say so.

"Fresh, fresh, fresh an' hot!" said another as they sped down the street.

"Old lady's bin in the news," said another. "Wonder how?"

"Bloody old cathedral!" said the first.

. . . .

In the morning at the Liverpool Central mother sat by Velvet's bed (mother, carrying her washing things in her old "Art" bag).

"I've come to take you home, dearie," she said.

Velvet, dazed with her sleep, still, and brilliantly happy, smiled through her dreams.

"Nice kettle of fish," said Mrs. Brown.

"Travelled up through the night," said mother. "You done well, Velvet."

This was the summit, and Velvet felt the beating of glory.

Before coming in mother had had a talk to the Resident Medical Officer and they discovered in their wordless way that they felt alike on certain subjects. It was found that Velvet could be taken out by the laundry entrance.

"She's ser little she could go in a laundry basket," said mother.

"No need for that," objected the M.O. who was against exaggeration.

And Velvet (and Mrs. Brown with her, for her bulk had not yet become as famous as it did a few days later) went in the laundry van, its rear backed up against the laundry entrance.

They reached the station in safety, for though the film of the Grand National had already been on the screens of thousands of cinema houses the night before, and the morning papers were alive with Mr. Brown's interview, there were no pictures as yet (Mr. Brown had not dared to ask for the one off Mrs. Brown's dressing-table), and the crouching black ant flashing by on the film bore no relation to the peaky young man walking beside the big woman to a third class carriage on the "Merseyside" as its engines got up steam.

"Better you kep' 'em on," Mrs. Brown had said in the van. "N'anyway I never thought to bring your others. Look the proper boy!"

The carriage was full, but no one's attention was caught. Velvet behaved

like the obscure child she thought herself to be.

They reached London, crossed it on the Underground, and took the local train.

A taxi stood in a dark corner of the station yard. As Velvet was pushed into its gloom by her mother she was caught by the eager hands of her sisters. "Velvet, Velvet . . . Oh, Velvet. . . . What you got on? Coo lummy, she's dressed like a boy!"

"Ssh!" said mother. "Don' talk so . . ." The taxi started off.

"Velvet, it's glorious! All the afternoon, ever since yesterday, everybody comin' to ask. We knew it was you las' night when the newspaper men came. All the papers got pictures of us in, but it's you they're waiting to get! American girl come in a car, an' the things she asked father said it made him hot to hear her. She said she gotta get your story."

"What story?" said Velvet.

"Don' talk ser much," said mother. "She don' know about all that yet."

. . . .

When the celebrated child returned home that night she was able to walk under the triumphal arch which the villagers had built with haste in the morning.

(And this arch and this street opening were the gateway to a village whose roofs and whose faces were the same but whose nature was changed to her. From now on she walked, fastened to that glory, whose teeth were sharp and held well, but whose wings were golden. She walked with an eagle on her back, observed by all.)

As the station taxi turned into the narrow lane of the village shouts and dangling lights brought it to a halt. There was a rope across the street, hung with lanterns, and by its light the glossy flutter of the leafy arch could be seen. Mr. Croom was at the taxi door, a bouquet of lit faces behind his shoulder, and Velvet was lifted out and walked under the arch and was carried home, rockily, on many shoulders. Mrs. Brown paid off the taxi, and strode with her face glum. She was reminded of Calais.

In the living-room at home there was not room for everybody, and the villagers hung in the doorway and shuffled in a tail in the street. The bottle of port came out but there was not much in it, and Mr. Brown sent Mally out for more. It was not long before Mrs. Brown bore Velvet, like a child of paper, to her bedroom. "You'll lay there," she said, "an' I'll bring you your supper."

Greatest wonder, it was Edwina who brought her a hot-water bottle, who stayed to talk in marvelling whispers, and listened with Velvet to the clamour down below. Mother brought the tray up, cold salt beef and chopped beetroot and a cup of cocoa. Velvet nibbled gently, changed feet on her hot-water bottle, watched the dark sky through the undrawn curtains.

"No one's to come up," said Mrs. Brown. And Velvet finished her supper and lay and waited for Mally and Merry, who came when the visitors had melted.

Mi turned up, having mysteriously come by a later train for nothing. Velvet slipped on her clothes again.

"You got up?" said Mrs. Brown as Velvet walked into the living-room.

"It's dark now. Pitch," said Velvet. "I mus' just go up the field an' fetch him in." She turned and took her shell-box of paper horses off the sideboard.

"They seen that, Velvet."

"Who did?"

"The newspaper men," said Mr. Brown. But Velvet did not seem to understand.

Mrs. Brown expanded her breast in an unusual and vigorous sigh.

"She won't pass no one now, though the whole village's bin hanging round the horse from what I hear. Better let her go. She won't pass no one ser late. Heigho . . . I bin a darn donkey once in my life an' it seems I bin it twice."

Velvet, dressed in her own clothes, went up the road between the ditches with Mally. The cats' eyes gleamed and shifted and went out. Nettles and cats' eyes and stars and stillness and not a soul about. The Piebald was flashing his colours under stars by the gate. The other horses hearing her step cantered down the slope whinnying. They greeted her with little jealous screams and lashings.

"D'you know what you've done?" said Velvet to The Piebald, but he shook his head suddenly as though a night gnat was on it.

"Wasa matter, Pie ole darling? Hasn' he gone in at the haunches terrible, Mally? Just in one day."

". . . An' what a day!" said Mally.

Velvet, her cheek on the top of the gate, Sir Pericles' breath blew her hair. "The worse was I got my mouth open an' couldn't shut it because the wind dried it. What was *your* worse, Pie ole darling?"

Velvet turned solemnly to Mally. "He'll be in every book, Mally. He'll be the horse of this year, that won it this year. Though they disqualify us they'll never dare to drop him out altogether. He won't be on the Aintree Roll of Honour . . ."

"What's that?"

"A brown board with gold letters. But he'll be in the books the writers write. The first piebald horse that ever won the National. By what I've heard about it they'll try to buy him, but I'll never sell him. SELL you, Piebald!"

"The poor others!" said Mally. "Do they mind?"

"No, no . . . Pericles! Little sweetie . . . Mrs. James! You're squealing, you jealous old woman. She's tried to kick George, Mally. Get away . . . there . . ."

"George deserves all he gets," said Mally. "He pokes his nose in everywhere and it's food he wants, not love. He and Mrs. James thought you'd come with a bucket."

"Come on, Piebald," called Velvet, searching for the old halter they kept behind the wall. But The Piebald was cropping the cool night grass away with a layer of dark air between them, as though horses that had won the Grand National were turned out to grass in the early spring every night. Unceremonious and incredibly enduring, he moved away.

"Come on," said Mally, "I should leave him. It's warm. He won't hurt. Mother said not to let you stay long. You're dead tired."

"I gotta see Donald before I sleep," said Velvet.

"Donald?"

"I thought about him the night I was going to ride. In that hotel bedroom. I was sick as anything . . ."

"Oh, poor Velvet! An' all alone!"

"No, Mi kep' comin' in an' out. I thought about if I was killed an' never saw Donald again. On'y for a flash, but I thought it."

"Funny thing to think. Why Donald?"

"It was funny. But I thought it anyway," said Velvet doggedly. "I mus' jus' see him when I go in."

They entered the house.

"Velvet wants to see Donald," said Mally, somewhat aggrieved.

"I wanter kiss him in his bed," said Velvet.

"She's overstrung," said Mrs.

Brown. "Go on up, he's dead asleep."

Donald lay flung out in an abandoned and charming attitude. His eyelashes were tender, bronze and shadowy; his hair a touch damp. The strangeness of his youth and exposed face, his battle for power by day and his abdication by night were something that Velvet had hardly expected. A gateway drew open within her and the misery and wild alarm of life rushed in.

"Velvet's crying over Donald!" said Mally aghast, running down to the living-room.

"Carry her to her bed, father," said Mrs. Brown calmly. "It's to be expected."

Chapter Fifteen

Next morning the Browns rose as usual. Edwina came down to take in the milk and the greeting of the milkman was a little long because it contained moderate congratulations. The milkman was a steady fellow.

From then on, however, nothing else was as usual. The crowd began to collect upon the Green in knots about nine, and by ten it was definitely clotted and pooling in the street. Mally, with her twitching nose, went out towards it early and scented radiations. The crowd, which was small and scattered at the time, definitely stirred as the front door opened, and something in the white faces and black eyes all looking one way made Mally shut the door again.

"I believe it's about Velvet," she said with a gasp into the scullery. "Ther's people outside."

"People?" said Mrs. Brown. "Someone want her?"

"Just people," said Mally. "Standing about."

Mrs. Brown went to look. She pulled the front blinds down over the cinerarias. So on a sunny morning at the end of March Velvet started her first day of glory as though someone had died in the house.

The crowd grew denser during the morning and none of the Browns put a nose out of doors. Mrs. Brown set the four girls at little jobs in their bedrooms and told them to keep the yard end by the canary cages. The crowd made a great deal of noise in the street as it drifted about, and the house seemed very small.

"Are you sure it is only about Velvet?" said Meredith. "It isn't a revolution?"

Mr. Brown finally decided that this wouldn't do and he must go down to his shop. He went out the back way and was not definitely recognised, except by the local man on the Worthing *Witness and Echo*. This man walked beside him and asked him questions as he went towards his shop. Mr. Brown was not at all unwilling. "She was always a one for horses," he said, and gave a lot of details.

"I kin do without me shopping," said Mrs. Brown in the gloom at home. "There's enough of that cold salt beef."

"Jolly!" said Edwina. "Winning the Grand National an' living with the blinds down an' eating cold salt beef. I don't know that Velvet's done us much of a turn."

The first gloomy morning of fame went by, blinds down, salt beef, and everyone immured in the house. In the one local paper which they took there was a lot about Velvet, but no one thought of sending out for all the other papers.

"The ink don't print up Velvet's face too good," said Mrs. Brown with distaste. It was only what she expected.

The picture was called "The Gate-Crasher at the Grand National."

"Dam' silly title," said Mally. "She didn't knock a thing."

Velvet was suffering from reaction and sat about limp. She did not bother about the newspaper except to glance at her picture. "I'd like to go out an' look at The Pie."

"You don't no one leave this house," said Mrs. Brown. They yawned and moped and grumbled.

"We'll have to go to an hotel if this goes on," said Edwina, who had once been to an hotel.

"That's what we'll do," said Mrs. Brown surprisingly, "if it don't blow over in a day or two. It's not but what I'm not proud of you, Velvet. But what's the good of you standing up for them gaping loonies to look at. They can't get no more out of you than they have done. You done your best up at Aintree and that ought to be enough. But what gets me is this gaping an' gaping an' handshaking an' behaving unfriendly an' curious as though you were a black savage they'd caught on the beach."

"Did they do it to you, mother, too? When you swum it?" Velvet jerked her head to the sea.

"They'd no modesty," said Mrs. Brown shortly, and said no more.

"Mother'd like to go out with a broom," said Meredith, after Mrs. Brown had left the room, "an' sweep 'em away."

"Mother's a one," said Mally, pulling a chair up for her feet.

But the middle-day post consoled Edwina and gave them all something to do. The door bell had been rung incessantly by the representatives of newspapers, but Mrs. Brown had the big bar-arm down and stuffed a duster in the bell. She knew the postman's knock, however, and he had had the sense to go round to the back.

There was an enormous box of chocolates for Velvet from an unknown admirer, and almost at the same moment a florist's man appeared groaning under a silver wicker basket loaded with pots of ferns and pink azaleas, and draped from head to foot in pink ribbon. This was from two of the Aldermen on the Worthing Corporation.

But in the post itself there was something incredible. Among seven letters for Velvet, six were love letters, and again among them two were proposals of marriage. Edwina and Mally read them aloud with yelps of delight.

But the seventh, addressed to Miss V. Brown in a clerkly hand, was a different affair. It was written on paper like cardboard, its heading was neat and in fine scrollwork, and it explained to her that the Stewards at Aintree, not being satisfied with explanations given on March 23rd, the matter was referred to the Stewards of the National Hunt Committee, and the enquiry into the running of The Piebald by an unqualified rider would be held at 15, Cavendish Square on the following Tuesday, at which meeting Miss V. Brown, Owner, was requested to appear.

"Trouble's got to come," said Mr. Brown, when he had heard the letter too. He had by degrees, and through the day, night, and morning, become a father who walked on air. "Trouble's got to come, Velvet, but nothing can take away what you done, my girl."

In the early afternoon the crowds grew denser.

"Brown family totally surrounded," read the headlines in the London papers. "Extra police drafted in." This

brought more crowds. Worthing made hurried arrangements for a special bus-line, that people might see the crowds and become part of them.

Mrs. Brown closed the door upon reporters. And closed her lips. And closed her eyes and thought. To her the house seemed threatened. Edwina, Mally, Meredith . . . even the canaries seemed threatened. And Velvet most of all. The warmth, the cosiness, the privacy of life were blown with draught. Her house had a side taken out of it and she could not close it four-square.

How long would it take to live it down? It was like a gale. It was like staying indoors in a gale. She let the spaniels into the living-room, as one calls in a yard animal in a dangerous hurricane.

"I gotta get some air," said Velvet feverishly at three o'clock, and stepped out of the back door to the orchard.

"Good day, Miss Velvet," said a slim lady instantly.

"Good day, Miss," said Velvet.

"I just wanted to ask you," said the lady—

"I've got a car here," said the lady. "Let's sit in it."

Velvet hesitated. It was not in her to refuse. She crossed to the lane, looking back at the cactus window.

The lady opened the door of the car and Velvet got in.

"Now," said the lady, settling down with Velvet beside her, "you're a great girl. Why, you're not as much as fourteen!"

"Fourteen," said Velvet shyly.

"Got any boy friends?"

"Oh . . . Mi. Mi Taylor."

"Who's he?"

"Dad's help. Father's help. In the slaughter-house."

Velvet was without defences. Her innocent and murmured sentences were like poppy seeds in a corn field.

The field went scarlet and smelt narcotic and bloomed. But mercifully this was in America, and Velvet never knew what was written and said.

They had not got far (but far enough) with the interview when Mrs. Brown intervened. She called from the back doorway and Velvet, breathing relief, sprang from the car and went to her. The lady followed. "One moment . . ." she said, crossing the road too.

"No!" said Mrs. Brown sharply, and sent Velvet in behind her bulk.

"Excuse me," began the lady, "it's for the American Press."

"In England we got rights," said Mrs. Brown, and shut the door in her face.

A big Daimler pushed its way up the street at three-thirty. Out of it got a little man with a big head and a garden of rich fur on his coat collar. He had a talk with Mr. Brown, whom by luck he saw going in at the street door. He sat in the living-room for half-an-hour and as he rose to go he was heard to say that he would send his Daimler for both of them.

"Both who?" said Mrs. Brown, coming in when he had gone.

"Gentleman from the pictures," said father. "An actor. Well, an actor-manager. Come from Elstree in Essex. Come all the way to ask if Velvet could go an' pose for them."

"She's going?"

"Says he's sending fer her tomorrow."

"Well," said Mrs. Brown, coming further into the room, "had she ought?"

Mr. Brown looked at her uneasily. "Hear that, Velvet?" he said to Velvet, who was sticking pictures of The Piebald into an album. "What do you feel about it yourself?"

"Think it might be fun," said Velvet carelessly.

"There y'are," said Mr. Brown irritably. "An' I don' see any harm. He wants the horse too. He's sending down a horse-box . . ."

"Wants the horse?" said Velvet, looking up.

"Says he's made for a film, that horse."

"Can't have the horse," said Velvet swiftly, and went on pasting.

"What's that?"

"Piebald on the films!" said Velvet with a light firmness that had never been there before. "He seems to forget."

"What's he forget?"

"That *that's* the horse that won the National."

"That's why he wants him, Velvet," said father with unaccustomed patience.

"*I'll* go," said Velvet, getting up. "It won't be half bad for us all to go and see me doing things on the curtain an' the band playing and us sitting looking. But The Piebald! He doesn't know, he wouldn't know. He's out there in that field steady and safe. He believes in me. I wouldn't let him in for a thing that he couldn't understand. He's not like a human. He doesn't know how to be funny, and he shan't learn!" And the tears of her unwonted defiance streamed down her face.

"Well!" said Mr. Brown.

"An' what's more," sobbed Velvet, "an' what's more . . ."

"Well?" said Mr. Brown.

"I've read about horses . . . horses that has won . . . an' they write about them n-nobly's though they were statues. How can you write about a horse nobly if it goes on the films!"

"But what'll they be writing about your horse more'n they have done?"

"Not in the papers," said Velvet, now fairly howling, "not in the p-papers. That's nothing. Mother—mother —mother l-lights the fire with that! In books! Big books. Roll-of-Honour books where they put down the winners an' call them the Immortal Manifesto."

"The Immortal what?" said Mr. Brown.

"Manifesto. 'N' how can they call him the Immortal Piebald if he goes on the . . ."

"More like call you the Immortal Velvet!" growled Mr. Brown, thoroughly taken aback.

"Me! That's nothing. I'm nothing. If you could see what he did for me. He burst himself for me. 'N' when I asked him he burst himself more. 'N' when I asked him again he—he— doubled it. He tried near to death, he did. I'd sooner have that horse happy than go to heaven!"

"Behave yourself, Velvet!" said Mrs. Brown sharply. "Get upstairs. Merry's in an awful mess. She's upset the canary cage, water an' sand 'n' all on your bed. Get on up and help her."

As the door shut—"That child's got something that you don't value, William! That child's more mine than all the rest."

"I valued you all right once, didn't I, Araminty?"

"You did, William. Or maybe was it the pop an' squeak roun' me?"

"Now, Araminty," said Mr. Brown, rising, "don't you go an' cut queer with me over this. I'm bound to say I don't know whether I'm on my head or my heels sometimes. It's like having a gunfire of bouquets thrown on you all at once n'you hardly know where it's coming from. It's like them sweepstakes that we all read break up the home, but we won't let all this to-do break up this home, will we?"

"You always was a nice chap," said

Mrs. Brown. "On'y I'm so buried under me fat I feel half ashamed to tell you so. Love don't seem dainty on a fat woman. Nothin's going to break up this home not even if you lose yer head, but it'll make it easier if you keep it. On'y leave that child to me. She's got more to come. You think the Grand National's the end of all things, but a child that can do that can do more when she's grown. On'y keep her level, keep her going quiet. We'll live this down presently an' you'll see."

After this, the longest speech Mrs. Brown had made for years, she went out into the yard to look for Donald.

She found, as she had hardly expected, that Donald was talking to a reporter.

There had been a pause. The reporter had not before tackled a mind which answered when it chose, on what lines it chose, or not at all.

Donald's interest in him was flickering, subterranean, critical. He was as usual torn by the suspicion that there might be something better to do.

"But she's a nice girl, your sister?" said the reporter desperately.

"She wasn't a nice girl larse . . . July," said Donald. "She didn' pull the plug after she'd sat down. Mother said she wasn't nice."

"Oh, well!" said the reporter almost gaily. "That's nothing! I've got a Gertrude that does that. She gets smacked for it."

"Older'n me?"

"Much older than you."

"I like pulling the plug but I'm not allowed to."

The reporter's note-book remained blank.

"Yes, but . . . all that's no good to me."

"Velvet tried to pull it," went on Donald. "She broke it. It wouldn't pull. Father said it was a trashy plug."

"Tell me something more about her."

"She doesn't wash her neck sometimes."

"Tell me something different," said the reporter. "When your sister, Velvet, was a little girl . . ."

"I wasn't here," said Donald quickly.

"No, of course," said the reporter. "You were . . ."

"I wasn't a star either," said Donald. "I was somewhere. Doing things. Where do you smack your Gertrude?"

"Tell me, like a nice little chap . . ." (contempt surged over Donald and his lashes half veiled his eyes) "what sort of things does your sister play with?"

"My sister Velvet?"

"Your sister Velvet."

Donald considered. The reporter waited.

"See where I cut my ankle?" said Donald, holding up his leg. "I arsed fer the iodine myself."

"Yes," said the reporter dully, "it looks a bad cut."

Donald, like Jacob, could do a thousand things at once. He could hear, feel, see, gauge, forecast, decide, act. He was a twinkling surface, giving off and taking in. He was an incredible telephone exchange run by motes and atoms and impulsions. He had heard Velvet crying, he knew it was nearly dinner time, he knew there was a broccoli stump blocking the water gutter, he knew at last that this fellow was as empty as a bladder, and his mind went white towards him and turned red and blue and yellow towards everything else.

"Velvet's bin crying," he remarked, practically to himself.

"Why's that?" said the reporter keenly.

"I gotta go," said Donald, seeing his mother coming, and walked away.

Chapter Sixteen

Velvet Brown, at a tender age and of a tender sex, won the Grand National. The mind of the public was at once stormed, irradiated and convulsed with a new surprise, fresh, keen, voracious. The fact crashed in the papers like a set of bells. The Mind of the public swung like bells too, pealing, pealing. As newspaper edition after edition came out the peals were set going in waves one after the other. The Mind could only swing and swing and ask to be pushed again. And the pushers flocked to push. The bell-ringers pealed and hauled. The music of news broke and poured over the land. Portions of the Mind began almost at once to rebel. There are people who prefer Wonder to arc through the sky, fall with its own curve, and cease on its fall. But the professional bell-pealers and wonder-mongers were not going to allow much of that. Bells must be handled again as their sound dies; Wonder must be propped up and carry on in a straight line through the sky; the gaping Mind which had come alive like a young chicken must be stuffed with details and choked with news.

The enormous and delicate and intricate machinery which hangs on the fringe of news was set going. Men hammered tin because piebald horses must prance on the heads of tiepins, women painted little mugs and tea-cups in Staffordshire, Velvet galloped across nearly a mile of white cardboard, stamped out in diamond-shapes and bent to hold a pound of chocolate creams. It was for the second impossible to be more notorious.

For a time Velvet and the sisters wandered in Arcady. They became princesses in Eden. People gave them sweets, adored their horses, took their photographs. What was so piquant in the papers was that in a row of beauties "it was the plain one that did it." This was somehow full of salt.

Only when the portraits of the paper horses, surreptitiously lent by Mr. Brown, appeared below a picture of the shell-box in a Sunday paper did Velvet say slowly, "Who gave them that?"

"What?"

"My shell-box."

But this blew over, and the shell-box was safe again on the sideboard, and Velvet hardly remembered that she had felt little scratches on her youth.

"Coo lummy . . ." began Edwina one day.

"You will please . . ." said Mr. Brown, "remember that you are now in the public eye."

"It's Velvet's public eye," said Edwina rather rudely. She was getting out of hand. But except for Edwina's rudeness, and that was always latent in the poor, upgrowing, beautiful child, and except for Mrs. Brown's not unusual silence, and for little plumes of unhelpful vanity in Mr. Brown, there was no real deterioration in the Brown household.

Mally and Meredith adored the fuss and the sweets and the visits from newspapers, and the marvel of the cinemas, and took delight in spotting "Velvet Novelties"; that piebald horse which now definitely galloped on the head of a tiepin at Woolworth's, and postcards with Velvet crouching in a black shirt tearing past a winning post.

"Let's collect them!" said Mally. And they began to make a collection.

When Velvet saw her face for the first time on the cinema she felt a

little strange. It was an enlargement face, done thin on the canvas in black and white. It seemed like her. She could not say it wasn't.

"I look like that," she thought. And took it for granted that she did.

The same face, transplanted on to postcards, became almost a code-sign. She could not have said what she felt but it was queer. However, she shook it off. "If you want something for your collection," said Edwina one day, "there's a brown silk in the window at Tinkler's called 'Velvet Brown.'"

"Tinkler's?"

"In Worthing."

"Is it expensive? Could we get a yard?"

"Ask them to give you a sample bit with the label pinned to it."

"Will they?"

"Get Velvet to ask them."

"Oh, yes, of course."

That was one of Velvet's very little burdens. The sisters always pushed her forward to ask for anything they wanted. Nobody refused Velvet anything. She became aware of this and grew delicate and obstinate.

When she went out she felt an insistent desire on the part of other people to get in touch with her. And once in touch it was quite literal—they touched her. They shook or held her hand, since the hand is not private but only the body.

They came with a rush, with eagerness, as though they could get virtue, as though they could draw meat and drink. And when the "touching" was over and the child's hand had been shaken they hovered a second with baffled hunger, and murmuring, "It was fine," retired. It crossed Velvet's mind occasionally to think they wanted something more of her.

Mally kept the "collection" with energy. It was in a box in the bed-

room and was beginning to look like a ragbag. There was a powder-puff called "The Velvet," in gold letters on printed voile, and a mechanical piebald horse that wound up and hopped across the floor. There was a cartoon in one of the evening papers of Velvet coming over Becher's sitting between the wings of Pegasus, and all the other horses looking scared. It was called "The Unseen Adversary." There were marvellous love letters from strangers, and boys at school, and workmen. One of the best began "Divine Equestrian"—but they all got very crumpled up and difficult to find.

. . . .

There may be wonder in money, but, dear God, there is money in wonder. And nothing is so cheap as a newspaper, where, when true news is truly breaking it starts up under the feet like a hare on the downs, and prince and poor man come in on the equal and swing along for their pennies while the news runs. And now the news was running hot and strong and pouring from it, as it ran, the true authentic scent. No basket hare this, let out and egged on to trot tamely by its keeper, and while Velvet lasted there was no need to bring carted news to the Meet.

While the day approached for the sitting of the National Hunt Committee, the whole world was made to believe it was waiting for details.

"Coo lummy . . ." said Velvet, late on Monday night. And Mr. Brown found this excusable.

"Can't eat you," said Mrs. Brown, and glanced at Mi. It was Mi they could eat, she felt.

"We'll get away an' up to London early," said Mi. "We don' want to be messed up with hand-shaking to-morrow."

Chapter Seventeen

In an upper room in 15, Cavendish Square, round a Board Table, the Board had assembled. It was a distinguished company, mainly of robust and kindly men. They had as their spokesman, Messrs. Weatherby's lawyer, Mr. Simkin, and as their Chairman, Lord Tunmarsh. The others were Colonel "Ruby" Allbrow, a man with an extraordinarily scarlet forehead, which turned his name into a better joke than it already was, Mits Schreiber, who had ridden in the National three times, Lord Henry Vile, Mr. Little (a descendant of Captain Joseph Lockhart Little), and Mr. Thomas, who was no descendant of "Mr. Thomas" (since the famous bearer rode under a pseudonym) but liked to think he was, Mr. Seckham, Mr. Coleman, Sir Harry Hall, and others. The Clerk, Cotton, was in attendance.

"Sickening, this Velvet uproar," said Mr. Little, as they met.

"I've read none of it," said the Chairman, taking his seat, "or as little as I could help. I'm in a position to judge the case on its merit. I only read *The Times.*"

"What about the evening papers?"

"The evening papers," said Lord Tunmarsh, "are for the servants' hall. Is the girl here?"

"She's downstairs, waiting."

"Very well, Mr. Simkin! Will you tell us our position? Is it a case for prosecution? Is it a case coming under our own laws, how we stand in fact?"

Mr. Simkin delivered a small oration on the laws of impersonation, standing as a black silhouette against the windows facing on Cavendish Square. He sat down. "It's beyond my imagination," he finished—"that is

why I find it so difficult to give you, gentlemen, a crisp ruling—it's beyond my imagination to suppose that a female should have done such a thing. Should have so deceived US."

"But a female *has* done it, you ass!" (muttered Mits Schreiber). "Very much done it."

Simkin rose and went to a row of yellow calf volumes on the shelf.

He took down one. Over clapped the pages, flying under his dusty thumb. His long upper lip closed over his teeth.

"Attempting to defraud," he muttered. He looked sharply over his shoulder. "It's understood that we judge the case entirely—" There was an irritable and suspicious note in his voice.

The Chairman looked up sharply. "You're not referring to the newspaper hurly-burly, I hope, are you, Mr. Simkin?"

"No, well, I hardly imagined, Mr. Chairman, no. And this is a case of— (if I'm not mistaken) of fraud. I have it here. 'Attempting to obtain money under' . . . 'Obtaining money under' . . . no, she hasn't 'obtained.' Attempting to obtain. That's it. Attempting to obtain. It's very clear." He looked up. "We can prosecute."

"Legal, is it?"

Lord Tunmarsh looked uncomfortable. "Let's see the girl first. She's waiting?"

"Downstairs."

"Let's see her," said Colonel "Ruby" Allbrow. "Have her up. After all it was a good show. A first class show she put up. What's her age?"

"Her age," broke in Mr. Simkin, looking at the Chairman, "is said to be fourteen. This I should say was a

romantic understatement on the part of the Press. Might I say, Mr. Chairman, before the . . . young woman . . . comes into the room that I think that it would be a pity if any note of admiration be acknowledged during the interview. If indeed any is felt."

The Chairman nodded. "I think, Mr. Simkin, you can leave that to me. No admiration can be felt for what is practically a criminal proceeding. Involving forgery very probably. We'll have to look into that question of the faked Clearance."

Mits Schreiber addressed the Chairman.

"But if she's fourteen, can we prosecute a child of fourteen? Who put her up to do it?"

"Apparently nobody."

"Impossible! Are we prepared as to what . . ."

"Have her up," said the Chairman. "We shall know better when we see her. I'm not prepared, any more than Mr. Simkin is, to take it from her that she is fourteen. We have been loaded with more or less inaccurate (I daresay) descriptions of this young woman morning after morning. I need hardly say that— Not that we've any of us read 'em all, but—"

"Every bally word, Mr. Chairman!" broke in Mits Schreiber. "I'm a Velvet fan."

Lord Tunmarsh did not smile.

"Well, keep it to yourself, Mits. This is a meeting of the National Hunt Committee, and for myself I feel that we have been extremely offended by a piece of vulgarity. Mr. Simkin feels the same on behalf of Messrs. Weatherby. Please ask her to come up."

"Call her up, Cotton."

Velvet was shown up to the Committee Room of the National Hunt Committee.

The dusty stairs were dark. The door opened. The room was light.

All the men sitting round the table rose. Lord Tunmarsh drew a chair out for her. Velvet sank, sat on the edge, folded her hands. Fourteen men saw a featherweight plain child in a red jersey, dark blue wool skirt, blue wool coat with brass buttons and childish brown shoes with stub toes. They drew a breath.

"Good afternoon," said Lord Tunmarsh at last. "You are Miss Velvet Brown?"

"Yes," Velvet nodded gently. (Oh, God, don't let me be sick . . .)

"I really . . ." said Lord Tunmarsh, after a pause, but stopped himself.

"Well, was it you all right riding that piebald? It was you, wasn't it, Miss Brown?" broke in Colonel "Ruby" Allbrow on the silence.

"Me."

"What put it into your head, girl, to do a frivolous thing like that?"

Velvet slowly spread out her thin hands and counted the fan of muscles. She breathed something about the horse.

"What's that?"

"I knew the horse could do it," she said again.

"But why you riding? What d'you want to ride him yourself? Why not get a professional?"

"He . . ."

"Yes?" said Lord Tunmarsh, leaning a little towards her.

"He goes very well for me."

There was a pause.

Like an explosion, "He DID do that!" from a red-faced gentleman in checks.

"I think we shall have," said Lord Tunmarsh, "to ask Mr. Simkin to explain to her . . . just what . . . what we feel about the matter."

Mr. Simkin rose with alacrity.

Rustled his papers. Blew out and drew down his upper lip.

Velvet looked up at him with her docile look. The fine bone round her white temple was blue with shadow, her newly-cropped pale hair hung close and uneven round her ears, she raised her head, and watched him with mild, intelligent eyes. Her lips parted slowly over the gold band and white teeth. Lord Tunmarsh whispered to his neighbour "hard to believe" and the neighbour whispered and shook his head.

Mr. Simkin read his clause from the yellow volume, under the heading, "Attempting to obtain money under false pretences."

"You being a female," said Mr. Simkin . . . "and not an accredited male rider . . . come under this heading. It was a . . . for the time being . . . successful deception. Upon . . . ah . . . US. Upon Messrs. Weatherby (and the Committee of the National Hunt). It was done to obtain a prize of . . ."

"No, no, it wasn't!" said Velvet.

"Eh . . . what . . . why not? You stood to get the prize?"

"Yes, sir. Yes, I did. But it wasn't done for that reason. It was done because . . ."

"And why was it done? We should like to know that?"

"Because," said Velvet, looking out of the window into the chimney pots of Cavendish Square, "the horse jumps lovely and I wanted him to be famous. I didn't think of the money when I planned it all."

"Ah, and now we come to that!" said Mr. Simkin. "You say you planned it all. That, Miss Brown, is hard to believe. You are, I understand, a child. You have obtained a false certificate from my . . . er . . . people. From US. From Messrs. Weatherby. You posted an Esthonian

Clearance to us and in exchange we forwarded to you the usual Licence. It was a monstrous imposture. How was it done?"

Velvet looked at him, her eyes full of light.

"There was so much to be done," she said at length.

"You mean that I am choosing only one of the grave impostures which you and your friends have . . . er . . . practised. It is precisely the name of those friends which we wish to have laid before us. This is . . . Miss Brown . . . a very SERIOUS OF-FENCE. A grave deceit has been prac-tised not on . . . upon US . . . but upon the Public. The money of the Public is in our trusteeship. We guarantee to the Public that this great and famous race . . . into which you have entered so lightly, so frivolously, so mockingly, is a race which is run in such a way that they can put their money on it . . . er . . . safely."

" 'Safely's' a bit strong, Simkin," said Lord Tunmarsh.

" 'Safely,' m'lord," said Simkin with obstinate pride. "Weatherby's prides themselves that they make racing safe up to the limits of the usual chances."

Lord Tunmarsh bit a piece of nail off his thumb. Mits Schreiber laughed.

"How old are you?" said Lord Tun-marsh suddenly.

"Fourteen, sir. Fifteen next month." This no longer seemed doubtful. Mr. Simkin resumed.

"Who has helped you in this?" he said startlingly to Velvet. "We want the names of your friends!"

"Mother knew. At the end," said Velvet.

"Your mother knew. That is im-portant. Your mother is Mrs. Brown."

"My mother was Araminty Potter. She swam the Channel once."

"Her mother was Araminty Potter!" said Sir Harry Hall, whistling.

"Swam the Channel breast-stroke twenty years ago. She downstairs?"

"No, sir."

"Your father's a . . ."

"Butcher, sir. A slaughterer-butcher."

"He knew?"

"No, he didn't know. Only after-wards. When I got my fall."

"So Araminty Potter married a butcher and got you?" said Sir Harry Hall. "And you've gone and swindled the almighty Weatherby's and won the Grand National . . ."

"Sir Harry," intervened Mr. Sim-kin, "I don't think this conduces to her understanding of the situation. Doesn't help. Doesn't help at all. If your father didn't know, Miss Brown (supposing this to be exact), and only your mother knew, then we must look for *other supporters*. I should like to begin with the Esthonian Clear-ance? How was that got? And who procured it?"

Velvet looked at them, halting. Gazed at them. The light filled her face and she seemed to rest and wait. It was not a question of deciding. She and Mi had decided already. Both had known that they would have to pay for The Piebald's fame. In Mi's case he was praying for Velvet's.

"Mi's downstairs," she said at length. "Mi will tell you. We knew he would have to."

"And Mi is . . . ?" said Mr. Sim-kin, still standing against the windows in silhouette.

"Mi is Mi Taylor. He helps my father in the slaughter-house," and even to her child's ears it seemed a rummy description of the glory of Mi.

"This Mi Taylor . . ." said Mr. Simkin, and stooped to whisper to his neighbour. The neighbour sent a paper round to the Chairman. Lord Tunmarsh nodded.

"Will you wait downstairs, Miss

Brown?" he said. "We should like to speak to Mr. Taylor."

Velvet disappeared and Mi was before them. His cap in his hand, his hair already rising from the damp comb he had run through it on the stairs (having spat on the comb).

"Mi Taylor," he said, nodding.

"Mi . . . ?" said Mr. Simkin, writing.

"Michael," corrected Mi.

"And you are Mr. Brown's assistant in the business?"

"I landed up there," said Mi, "to do anything. Clean the slaughter-house, buy sheep, help their ma, and so on. The boy's a handful."

"A boy?"

"Just a small one. No account yet."

"Well now, Taylor," said Mr. Simkin, clearing his throat, "I don't need to tell you that a frivolous and monstrous outrage has been committed. An impertinence and also, I imagine, a legally punishable fraud."

"Yes, sir."

"This fraud has ostensibly been committed by a child, the young lady we have just seen, Miss Velvet Brown. Obviously she could neither have planned it nor carried it through. Without help. Without the direction of another mind. What part did you play in all this, Taylor? We have got to know and we are going to know and I warn you to make no trouble over speaking the truth." Mr. Simkin sat down abruptly and gave the table a pencil tap. Everyone looked at Mi.

"I knew a boy," said Mi very simply, and he paused and sucked the hollow beside his tooth. "This boy knew a boy. . . . It was at Lewes races. Well, it was at Brighton races first and then I saw the other boy at Lewes races . . ."

"Their names?" said Mr. Simkin, writing.

"No," said Mi. "I ain't going to give you their names. You kin judge fer yourself when I've done. There was a whole trail o' boys. All talkin'. You know what they are, these races. Ain't got nothing to do. Lean up against each other an' jabber. More an' more kept coming in. No good to give you their names, I don't know 'em all. But the upshot was there was someone knew a fellow coming over that had a Clearance from Esthonia. Going to ride a horse that come by air and dropped dead at Croydon. Then he hadn't any horse, see? So I met him. 'Long of these fellows I'm telling you about. They didn't do anything but jabber, so it's no good giving you the names. All they did was to say they knew a fellow had a Clearance and didn't want his Clearance. I oiled up the fellow an' got his Clearance. Didn't want it so I got it. He didn't think any more about it. He's a half-Russian boy's bin riding out there for some Count. He's gone back now. Never thought no more about it. Then I just posted in the Clearance and got a Licence. See?"

"And this boy from Esthonia? Where is he now? He is, I suppose, the boy whose name is on the Licence? Tasky?"

"That's him. Where's he now? He's in Russia, s'far as I know. He got orders to cut off the hoof o' the dead horse an' take it back to the Count. Fer an inkstand, I daresay. They make them into stands. Told me he was going straight to Esthonia, and then on to Russia where the Count's got a winter job as a sort of a riding master with the Bolsheviks. Tasky and he, they go together most winters, so he said."

"Not much chance," whispered the Chairman to Colonel Allbrow, "of getting at Tasky. ('Less he ever comes again.) Looks to me as though the only culprit's here, in the room."

"So it seems to me, Taylor," said Mr. Simkin, "that the whole of this monstrous affair has been engineered by you and by you alone, if we are to believe you?"

Mi chuckled. Or the shade of a chuckle brushed him. He flicked it away and answered, "No."

"No, sir," he said. "There's Velvet. Velvet thought out the thing. It come to her. It come to her like the horse did, out of the sky."

"How did the horse come to her?" asked Captain Little, leaning forward.

"Why, she got it fer a shilling in a raffle in the village! There were yards about it in the *Express!*" said Mits.

Mr. Simkin frowned.

"Is that so, Taylor?" he said sharply.

"Yes, sir. You can go down to the village an' see. Anybody'd tell you. The horse belonged to Farmer Ede an' it made a filthy nuisance of itself, getting over walls and tearing down the village street. Nearly killed a child and nearly had a pushcart over twice. Ede couldn't do anything with it. He stuck it up for a raffle at the village fair in the summer. Didn't do badly: got nine pounds six shillings. Velvet took a ticket and won it. Then things went on an' on and she got moony about the horse, religious. She's a queer child. An' one day . . . when I see it jump a five foot wall by itself an' make away . . . I said . . . just kind of careless . . . just said . . ." (Mi waved his hand.) "'Make a Grand National jumper, that would!' Then Velvet never said anything but she never let up on that. She just went on."

"It seems not possible . . ." said Lord Tunmarsh. "I never heard such a tale!"

"It's no tale," said Mi earnestly. "It's just Velvet. I know what's in her blood because my old father . . ." He paused.

"Your father?" said Mr. Simkin drily. He did not like the eager, little-boy interest the Committee was taking in the tale.

"My father was old Dan Taylor," said Mi, "an' he was a Channel trainer. He trained Araminty (Velvet's mother) to swim the Channel. An' she swum it. Against the tide in a terrible dirty morning in a storm . . ."

"I remember!" said Sir Harry Hall. "It was a bigger thing than anything that's bin done since. It was done breast stroke. It seemed incredible."

"Well, then, that's her mother. It's in her blood. If you'd see her mother now you'd never believe it. Great old woman she is, all muscled up an' tight. An' silent. An' plucky's fire still. The father, he's not added nothing. It's the mare that's done it. An' Velvet, fer all she's such a sickly bit, she's like her. She'll sit on a horse like a shadow and breathe her soul into it. An' her hands. . . . She's got little hands like piano wires. I never seen such a creature on a horse."

"What are you by trade, Taylor? A professional rider?"

"I can't ride," said Mi slowly.

Sensation in the room.

"You can't ride, Taylor?" said the Chairman, after a pause.

"Never bin on a horse," said Mi, and it seemed to come home to him. He looked out of the window at the chimney pots.

"What's your history, then?"

"I couldn't swim," said Mi. "An' my old man carried on terrible. I went inland. I couldn't bear the sea. I wouldn't stick the sea down there at the coast now if it wasn't for Velvet. I went up North and I did this an' that. Got in with this lot an' got in with that lot. I was all round the racecourses and the livery stables. Doesn't take me much to live. I walked from here an' there an' landed up at Lewes

at the races an' did a job fer Mr. Brown—Velvet's father. He asked me to help fer a day with some sheep in the slaughter-house and then I saw that Mrs. Brown was my old man's Araminty. So I stayed."

"Well, gentlemen," said Mr. Simkin, looking more sour than ever, "we've heard the history of how it was done, and on the face of it, and *for the time being* it seems as though this deception *might* have been carried through in this way and by this one man. I say 'might.' We shall have to verify. It remains now of course to decide on our course of action. The man can be proceeded against legally, I should suppose, for attempting to obtain money under false pretences. There is no doubt in my mind that had this fall of the rider's not taken place and had the prize money of £7,560 (not to speak of a Cup worth two hundred pounds) been awarded, as it would have been if no objection had been lodged, then this man Taylor stood to gain, either the whole sum (the child being obviously under his influence) or in the case of the family being in the plan then no doubt the money would have been divided. It is not there . . ."

"Here!" said Mi. "What are you getting at!"

". . . it is not therefore . . ."

"I'm no thief!" said Mi. "The money'd 'a' bin Velvet's. She's the Owner, isn't she? I did no more'n believe in her an' talk to her an' get her the Clearance. She's the little wonder 'at's done it all. It would 'a' bin her money an' I'd 'a' seen that she kep' it. Her mother knew about it. She's no soft chicken. As for the money. . . . Why, we were so busy pulling it off we hadn't begun to think about what Velvet would do with the money. It was the horse she was thinking of. 'Putting the horse in history'

she called it. She'd got that out of somewhere an' she kept thinking it and saying it too, sometimes. She'd think it at her dinner and at her tea. You could see her, with her eyes shining and her stomach heaving too, pretty often. She's got a terrible stomach, and when she gets excited she's an awful vomiter. *Me* the money. What's the use of seven thousand pounds to me?"

"Seven thousand pounds, Taylor, is always useful."

"I shouldn't know what to do with it! What'd I do? I don't want to live any better'n I live. It suits me. I don't want to be cluttered up. I wouldn't know the first thing what to do with seven thousand pounds. It would give me the itch. Maybe I'd bury it."

"The whole story," intervened Lord Tunmarsh, "is so strange that I think we should like to discuss it alone. Will you wait downstairs, Taylor? There seems to be a commotion outside, Allbrow." The Chairman turned towards the window. "Is it a fire?"

Mr. Simkin looked outside into the Square.

"Crowds of people," he said. "Thick on the pavement."

The door was knocked upon and hurriedly opened. A clerk came swiftly in and looked enquiringly at Mr. Simkin. Mr. Simkin pointed to the Chairman. The clerk whispered.

"Good God!" said Lord Tunmarsh. "Open the window, Simkin."

Mr. Simkin struggled with the dusty catch. Mr. Seckham helped him and the ancient window flew up. A roar flooded in on the air. The Committee listened.

"They want the child," said the Chairman. "Taylor, go down and look after her. Bolt the doors, Simkin! Get down and see everything's shut. What's your back way out?"

"The bar's down across the street

door, m'lord," said the clerk. "But they're all up over the window sills. They seem to think Miss Brown is getting . . ."

"Getting what?"

"Two men, m'lord, shouted through the doorway as I was shutting it, 'You tick her off an' we'll cut your livers out!' m'lord."

"'Ticking her off,' they think! Well, so we are. Come on, young Mits! You get her out the back way!"

"The crowd's gone round there like water flowing, m'lord."

"I suppose there's a roof exit?" said the Chairman, looking at the ceiling. "These old massive roofs. . . . Where's your fire exit? Here she is!"

"I brought her up," said Mi. "Such a din and faces at the windows. You better up here, an't you, Velvet?"

"What do they want?" said Velvet, looking white.

"To save you from us," said the Chairman. "It looks to me as though you're going to get a Lindbergh-Amy-Johnson week. I suggest we suspend the Committee and that Captain Schreiber take the victim out over the roof. Here y'are, Mits! Take my card as Chairman."

"The police are coming," said Mr. Simkin, looking down. "Mounted police."

"Oh, let me look!" said Velvet.

She hung out of the window and the crowd caught sight of her. A roar went up.

"Now you've done it!" said the Chairman.

It took the police an hour to disperse the crowd. Meanwhile Mits Schreiber, Velvet, Mi and a clerk crossed the roofs of Cavendish Square and descended by J. Denvers' "Cotton House." They knocked at the glass window of the fire escape and were let in by a typist.

"Fire down the Square!" said the typist.

"Yes, we're from it," said Mits briefly. "Is this the way down?"

They went down into the street by the iron staircase and were met by the Manager of the Cotton Works at the bottom.

"Card," said Mits Schreiber. "Thank you very much. Thank that girl of yours for letting us through."

"Fire, m'lord?" said the Manager.

"Kind of fire," said Mits. "There's a taxi. Come on while the crowd's busy down there."

They left the clerk behind and bundled into a taxi. Velvet and Mits sat together and Mi on the strap seat.

"Where d'you want to go?" said Mits to Mi.

"Victoria Station, sir," said Mi. "But I'd like to take her to the pictures first."

"I shouldn't," said Mits Schreiber. "Not to-day. You'll be mobbed. They're still running the film of the National. But you'll be mobbed if you put your nose inside. The place is simply feverish to-day."

"Where to?" said the taxi-man again.

"Victoria Station," said Mits, "and drop me off at Brook Street." The taxi started. "I've got to get to Scotland to-night."

"What'll you all do to us?" said Velvet timidly.

"Drop the whole thing of course," said Mits absently. "But you won't get your money or your cup, you know."

"That bay'll get it," said Velvet. "He was a good bay."

"I'm not sure you won't be officially warned off, too. No Newmarket Plate for you now."

"Oh . . . THAT . . ." said Velvet.

"Yes, I forgot. It's not much after

winning the Grand National. What are you going to do now?"

"Oh, jes' go home," said Velvet. "I expect I'll go out an' have a look at the horse to-night."

"Look here . . ." said Mits Schreiber earnestly. "We're getting to Brook Street. I've bin all over the world with horses an' I want to say this. You try to keep life just the same for you from now on. The public's been after you, but they're flogged tired, and they'll drop it soon. There'll be a tale about our flight to-morrow in the Press, and that clerk Cotton'll go an' give away what he dare. You've been having a queer kind of hot air puffing round you. You've bin blown up like a pink pig in the air fit to burst, and maybe now they'll let you die away with a squeak like a pink pig does. Don't let me find you one day with a hard face an' a dirty bit of cigarette and nerves all gone to blazes, looking for this hot air again! It's bad stuff. Mi—what's yer name, look after her! Here I am. Stop, man, stop! Blast! he's over-shot the house. I bin some funny crowds an' I know! That child's bin written across the sky like somebody's pills. You see she gets over it! Good-bye, both of you. Off you go. Victoria Station, Brighton line."

"Oh, isn't he nice!" said Velvet. "So they're going to let us off! Aren't they sweet, Mi? I say, Mi, have you got money for the taxi?"

"No, I haven't," said Mi. "I got the tickets an' a shilling. I knew I hadn't."

"It's two and nine," said Velvet, leaning forward. "Here's the station, too."

The taxi drew up and Mi opened the door and got out. As Velvet stood in the door there was a soft fluttering noise, like veiled pistols being shot into blankets. Velvet was snapped and snapped again from every angle. The black hoods of the cameras were turned on her in a set circle. She saw hooded men kneeling, squatting, standing. Mi clutched Velvet by the arm and swung her towards the taxi-man. "I'm short," he said. "Ain't got it, Percy. Give you a shilling an' . . ."

"It's all right. I can lend it to you," said a nice-looking boy in a blue suit. ("Gentleman!" thought Mi.)

"Here y'are, taxi," said the boy. "Look here, Miss Brown, I've got a car here. I'll drive you . . . both . . . down to Brighton. Drive you home, see? Sports Bentley."

"You the Press?" said Mi shortly.

"You come in my car and see," said the boy. "I won't publish a thing you don't . . ."

"Come on, Velvet," said Mi. "Run for it!"

It was too late. They couldn't run in a heavy sea. The crowd pressed in from behind to see what was happening. "What'sa matter? Accident? No, that girl that won the National. They're photographing her. Where? What? National Velvet!"

"National Velvet!" shouted the crowd as Mi and Velvet pressed slowly forward.

"Won't you let me pass!" said Velvet in a small voice. She had her foot trodden on. Several shook her hands. Left hand, right hand. She lost her purse.

"No fun about this," muttered Mi. "This is awful."

"My purse has dropped. Now I've no ticket," she called to Mi.

"Leave it. Don't stoop down. You'll be trodden on," said Mi, getting his arm round her.

They surged past the fruit shop and the telephone boxes and a door opened in the great ticket office and a man swept them inside. Velvet dropped on to a chair panting.

Half an hour later the police got them into their train. An hour later the red Buicks were tearing up the Embankment from Carmelite Street . . . "National Velvet at Victoria Station."

"National Velvet had up before the Hunt Committee," "Great Crowds in Cavendish Square. Flight with Lord Tunmarsh over the roofs." (This was an error, owing to the card.)

The fever about her raged until the findings of the National Hunt Committee came out in the evening papers. *They had decided to drop the whole thing.*

Again the news machinery was set in motion. Cleared lines gulped that which sped along them. But by the morning the story was dead. The public had been overwhipped. It could stand no more. Dead news like dead love has no phoenix in its ashes.

.

"Velvet Brown," said the man in New York, whipping out his orders. "Cut her out. Old stuff. That Jane only rates a couple of sticks."

.

Chrysanthemums, roses in winter, glacéd sweets, love letters, interviews, satin pillow-dolls,—the house had flowed with gifts, Edwina, Mally and Merry had eaten themselves sick, but Velvet, who did not care for flowers, could not stomach many sweets, did not read the love letters, never played with dolls, remained with her real desires sharp and intact, the ascending spirit with which she was threaded unquenched by surfeit.

While the glory had sedged and seethed about her she had been aware that as she moved so had the public rippled. That she had been like a boat that made a wake, that waves on either side had clapped and sparkled.

But no one had learnt anything about her. No one had formed the slightest picture of her, and she had gathered an impression of isolation as she moved, was touched, hemmed in. Her thin face on the sheet of the cinema was not more strange than how portrait had been in the minds of those who had surrounded her. Her name, which had blazed in the sky, now hung there in a quiet corner with the letters unlit. The arch at the opening of the street first withered, then blew down. The village took her back. If people called her "National Velvet" it was in fun and affection, and like a dig in the ribs. It meant "What next, you little blighter! Get on with your growing."

Mrs. Brown found an old trunk for the chocolate boxes and the flower ribbons and Mally's collection. It was April. The gymkhana summer was all before them.

Thus Velvet was not fifteen when the thing left her and passed on, the alienating substance, the glory-wine. She was like a child who is offered wine too young and does not really drink. She put her lips to the goblet while thinking of other things. She got off. She glanced the most acute and heady danger and got off. The Press blew, the public stared, hands flew out like a million little fishes after bread. Velvet had shone, a wonder, a glory, a miracle child.

And now, finished with that puzzling mixture of insane intimacy and isolation which is notoriety, Velvet was able to get on quietly to her next adventures. For obviously she was a person to whom things happened, since in a year she had become an heiress, got a horse for a shilling, and won the Grand National.

Author's Note

With reference to Chapter Thirteen the race in this book is run earlier than 1931.

Before that date it was not necessary for a horse to have distinguished itself

"by being placed first, second, or third (by the Judge) in a steeplechase of three miles and upwards value 200 sovs. to the winner"—

and for all I can find in the Rules a zebra could have entered, provided he was the proper age.

. . . .

As regards the objection which was lodged after The Piebald passed the post, I don't think this objection would eventually have been sustained on the ground of "dismounting before reaching the unsaddling enclosure" alone. The fact of the rider's sex of course disqualified her. But the contention that the objection would immediately have been lodged is based upon Rule 144 of the National Hunt Rules.

"144. If a rider do not present himself to be weighed in, or dismount before reaching the place appointed for that purpose, or touch (except accidentally) any person or thing other than his own equipments before weighing in, his horse is disqualified, unless he can satisfy the Stewards that he was justified by extraordinary circumstances."